The author is now retired and living in \
life he has been a policeman, a publican _ years in
international trade. He now spends his ti ₅ and working in his
garden.

For my late wife, Patricia, in whose memory I find inspiration.

John Bromley

SONS OF THE EARTH

AUSTIN MACAULEY PUBLISHERS™

LONDON · CAMBRIDGE · NEW YORK · SHARJAH

A CIP catalogue record for this title is available from the British Library.

ISBN 9781398466029 (Paperback)
ISBN 9781398466036 (ePub e-book)

www.austinmacauley.com

First Published 2022
Austin Macauley Publishers Ltd®
1 Canada Square
1 Canary Wharf
London
E14 5AA

National army museum for access to its archives.

Chapter One

The dark clouds that had been gathering in the west since early morning now rolled out over the gently undulating countryside, and as the first drops of rain began to sting his face, Paul Pearson pulled the battered peak of his cap further down over his forehead.

As he leaned wearily against the gate, surveying, with sadness, the acres of pastureland that had represented the extent of his world for more than twenty years, he thought what a long, dreary winter it had been, one made worse by his mother's lingering illness. At that moment, he had no recollection of times that had been easy or fruitful, just the unhappy memories of the constant struggle to wrestle a decent living from the land, the same land that had claimed the life of his father all those years ago, and was now about to do the same to his mother, as she lay in her bed and close to death.

The first few drops of rain had passed unnoticed into a steady drizzle, but Paul was in no hurry to return to the house, taking an unnatural comfort in the chill elements that had plagued him for so much of his life. It was certainly a refreshing relief from the clinging funereal atmosphere of their small farmhouse. For several weeks, he had prayed that his mother would give up hanging defiantly onto a life that had deserted her long ago, but now, as her time drew near, he silently begged her forgiveness.

For some years, even before his mother became ill, Paul had known the land held no prospect of a prosperous future, and that he would not be prepared to forfeit his life, as his parents had done, in the pursuit of a false and elusive dream. Now, at the age of twenty-four, he felt no obligation towards his parents, or his two brothers, to carry on a tradition that would lead inevitably to poverty or an early grave. The death of his mother would finally break his last link to the land and give him the future that belonged to him alone. As the eldest of the three brothers, it was natural that the mantle of protector should fall to him, but while he felt some responsibility towards them, he knew it could never extend to a binding or lasting commitment. They were old enough now to fend for themselves.

He pushed open the gate to the meadow and was about to tramp across the wet grass, to distance himself from the depressing events unfolding back at the house when Matthew caught up with him.

Two years younger than Paul, Matthew was the reincarnation of his late father, inheriting his fair hair and pale blue, almost grey, piercing eyes. Although shorter in height than his older brother, he had developed a powerful build from his years of toil on the farm, and his face already bore the ruddy weather beaten, complexion of a seasoned farmer.

"Mrs Caldicot thinks you should come now," he said breathlessly, gripping the sodden sleeve of Paul's jacket. "She says it's nearly time, that you ought to be there."

Paul glared back at him with unwarranted harshness, the rain dripping from the peak of his cap and mingling with the tears that had begun to form in the corners of his eyes. "Time for what? The time for her to die?" He demanded angrily. "Hadn't you noticed, Matt, she's been dead for months, probably years, and that's what we've all got to look forward to if we carry on trying to scratch a living from this godforsaken place."

As Paul tried to walk away, Matthew swung him round, holding him firmly by the arms. "Our parents gave their lives for this farm, it's our birth right." He spat the words at Paul as the rain beat into his handsome, tormented features. "What gives you the right to think they failed, that they died for nothing? They'll only have failed if we let them."

"Don't you moralise with me, Matthew, not when you're the one who should be looking to his conscience." He shook himself free and, turning towards the house, he glared at his brother. "Don't worry, I'll be with her at the end, but only out of respect for her and not for the inheritance she's left us with."

Old Mrs Caldicot scowled at them as they entered the kitchen, their wet clothes dripping water over the bare stone floor. She wiped her hands on her apron. "Young John's upstairs with her," she muttered disparagingly. "I just hope you're not too late, that's all."

Without speaking, and stopping only to hang their jackets on the back of the door, they trudged sullenly up the worn, wooden staircase.

10

A thin cotton curtain drawn across the small window filtered what little light would usually have been allowed into the bedroom, giving it an added sombreness, and on the bed in the premature darkness lay the sad, frail being that was once Emily Pearson, blending perfectly into the bleak surroundings.

In a dim corner next to the bed, John sat on a stool clasping his mother's thin hand in his own, as if willing his life into hers. He glanced up as his brothers came into the room, sorrow etched into his young face.

"Mrs Caldicot says it could be any time," he whispered, choking back the tears he felt his brothers would regard as unmanly. "She opened her eyes just now, but I don't think she could see me. Do you think she's in any pain?"

Paul moved around the bed and placed a comforting hand on his brother's shoulder. "She's not feeling a thing, John, I promise you. And it's all right to cry, if you feel the need."

He sat down on the edge of the bed and studied his mother's pale, wasted face, framed in a tangled mass of greying hair. Seeing her like that, it was difficult to imagine how attractive she had once been, and now, still only in her mid-forties, she could so easily pass for a woman more than twenty years older. More than ever, it saddened him how futile her life appeared to have been, and yet, even close to death, her countenance displayed a calm dignity and he had no doubt at all that she would never have regretted one minute of her life. With certainty she would, given the choice, have settled for the life of devotion to her husband and her sons.

Her breathing was shallow and erratic, and several times her two sons were forced to lean close, to convince themselves she had not yet left them.

"Do you think she can hear us?" asked John, his voice muted in grief.

"I'm not sure, I don't think so," replied Paul, "but I'm sure she knows we are all here."

From the deep shadow of the far wall, Matthew shuffled forward, but he held back from the bed. "I just hope she doesn't know you plan to desert us as soon as she's gone. At least that way she'll die believing you to be the man our father was."

"Whatever I choose to do, she'll think none the worse of me, and I'm sure that goes for you two as well," Paul spoke calmly as he gently brushed the hair from his mother's face and stroked her sallow cheek with the back of his hand. "She'll expect nothing more from us than what we want for ourselves."

"And how do you know what she wanted of us? Did you ever take the trouble to ask her?" Matthew moved back into the shadows as though preferring to remain an anonymous spectator to his mother's final moments.

Paul threw a troubled glance at his youngest brother sitting next to him before turning on Matthew, now almost invisible in the deepening gloom. "I'm sure you know as well as any of us what our mother felt, but this is not the time to discuss it, and I pray that time will never come." He spoke the words softly, but the threatening undertone was clear enough. He waited in the expectation that his brother would retaliate and was relieved when Matthew remained silent.

A heavy tension hung in the bedroom and Paul hoped that John would be too preoccupied with their mother to notice. That preoccupation became clear when John suddenly cried out, "Paul, Matt, look, look!"

The suddenness of the outburst even bought Matthew out of the shadows, and as Paul looked down at his mother, he could see that her eyes were open and she was feverishly trying to raise her head off the pillow. Still holding on to her hand, John leapt to his feet while Paul leaned further forward to cradle her head in the crook of his arm.

As Matthew edged cautiously closer to the bed the woman's dull, sunken eyes seemed to flick from one face to the other as though assuring herself that all her sons were there. Once assured her pale, thin lips parted into a weak smile before moving to form words that would not come, the only thing passing her lips being wisps of stale, death tainted breath. Frustration was etched deep into the lines of her face as she desperately tried again, and this time there were a few whispered words.

"Don't be angry," she gasped into Paul's ear, each word causing her great distress. "Please forgive me."

Having uttered these final few words, her head fell heavily to one side, and with a last heavy gasp of apology, her life left her.

John felt her hand tighten on his and no amount of pride could stem the flood of tears that streamed down his cheeks. Paul pressed his face to hers and kissed her tenderly before sliding his arm out from under her head.

Only Matthew made no outward display of emotion, although it would be wrong to say he felt no grief at her passing, and after a few moments of quiet contemplation, he asked, "What did she say?"

Paul helped John release his hand from his mother's grip before spreading a sheet over her face. He then turned to face Matthew across the bed. "She asked us not to be angry, and to forgive her," he replied in a soft, trembling voice.

Leaning heavily on his brother, John continued to sob. "Why should we be angry? And what do we need to forgive in her? She was our mother, everything she ever did was for us, or for father when he was alive."

"Perhaps that's it," said Paul, placing a comforting arm around his young brother's shoulder. "Perhaps she thought we would be angry because she wasn't going to be around to care for us. Perhaps she wants to be forgiven for leaving us."

"Is that what you really think?" Matthew glowered at his brothers from the darker side of the room. He jabbed an accusing finger at John. "Or was that just for his benefit?" Clearly agitated, he paced the floor. "She knew you hated the farm, and that you'd leave given the first opportunity. She wasn't asking us not to be angry with her, but with each other."

Still supporting his young brother, Paul turned on Matthew, anger now merging with the sorrow. "Shut your mouth, Matt, this isn't the time. If you had no respect for her when she was alive, for God's sake, have some for her in death. I'll forgive her anything, but I've yet to forgive you."

"And why should I need forgiveness from you, or from anyone?" Whether or not his arrogant tone was to hide a festering guilt it was hard to say, but to someone who knew the truth it would be easy to assume.

"I'll not discuss it further with you, Matthew, not here and certainly not now." Paul took John's arm to lead him from the bedroom. "I think she deserves to be left in peace. Come John, we'll go down. Matthew can stay if he wishes."

In the kitchen Mrs Caldicot was tending a pot on the range when the pair came down. She looked at them through her small, narrow eyes and gave a knowing nod of her scarf-covered head. "It would have been a happy release." She heaved the pot off the range and carried it unsteadily across to the table. "I've made you some broth, and I'll be back in the morning to tidy her up before the undertaker comes. You'll be making all the arrangements, won't you, master Paul?"

Unprepared for the question, Paul gave a quick nod. He had given no thought to the funeral arrangements, but he was the eldest and the responsibility was his.

It was only after Mrs Caldicot had left that Matthew joined his two brothers in the kitchen, sullenly helping himself to some of the broth that the other two had already started. Nothing was said as they each came to terms with the loss in their separate ways, although Matthew's mood appeared darker and more brooding.

"We have to talk," he said, once they had all finished eating. "There are things that need to be discussed and I don't see that they should wait."

Paul had been staring into his empty bowl, but looked up, first at one brother and then the other. "I think anything that needs to be said should wait until after our mother is buried. It doesn't seem right for us to sit down here discussing the future, with her up there, not yet cold."

John nodded, his face streaked with tears. "Paul's right, things should stay as they are until after the funeral."

Matthew glared across the table at him, his pale eyes mocking his younger brother. "I should have known you'd agree with him. All your life you've hung on to the coat tails of your big brother, so why should things change now."

"That's not fair, Matt," protested John, bravely meeting his brother's stare. "I've got a mind of my own, and I just don't think we should be arguing, not at a time like this."

They were all edgy, but Paul was determined that their petty squabbles should not escalate into a full-blown argument. "It's not too much to ask, is it, Matt?" he said calmly. "The last thing our mother would have wanted is us rowing amongst ourselves."

"I just want to know where I stand," persisted Matthew defiantly. "This farm needs the three of us to run it, and if you're going to walk out to look for a better life somewhere else then we need to know."

John shot an anxious glance at Paul. "I didn't know you were leaving. You never said anything to me about that."

Paul gave him a benevolent smile. "A lot of things have gone on in this house that have never been spoken about, little brother, but that doesn't mean they never happened." He paused, looking hard at Matthew. "Nor does it mean they may never be spoken about." He took a deep breath, leaning back on his chair and clasping his hands behind his head. "Anyway, now that it's been mentioned, it's no secret that I've no ambition to stay a farmer all my life and end my days a broken man, like our father." He lowered his head out of respect. "Now, I've said all I'm going to say, at least until after our mother is in the ground."

"Well, that's fine with me, just as long as it's agreed that when you leave it's with nothing but your few miserable possessions. Me and John keep the farm."

14

To reinforce his point Matthew slammed his hand hard down on the table, making the bowls jump.

Paul smiled again, more sardonic this time. He was intent on putting an end to the conversation, but Matthew's belligerence was making it difficult. "I'm sorry, Matt, but aren't you being a bit presumptuous with John's future? After all, he is eighteen now and more than capable of making his own decisions. Why don't you ask him what he wants to do with his life?" He turned to look encouragingly at John.

Matthew laughed scornfully. "I don't need to ask him. The Pearsons have always been farmers, and just because you have some high and mighty ideas it doesn't mean he's going to follow you."

"But you've already said I have influence over his thinking, so perhaps you ought to ask him," said Paul, without trying to sound smug.

"I don't need to. Some things are beyond influence and he's got farming in his blood, just like me."

"Well, I think you should ask him anyway. Don't you, John?"

John fidgeted awkwardly on his chair, his head dropping to his chest as he played with his fingers.

Matthew glared over at him in disbelief and disgust as his young brother's silence betrayed the answer. "You spineless little bastard!" He lunged across the table, snatching at John's shirt. "Haven't you got the guts to make up your own mind?"

Paul threw himself between them, forcing them apart. "That's enough, Matt. It is his decision, and it's got nothing to do with me."

John looked shocked, as well as sheepish, and met Paul's apologetic gaze. "How did you know? I've never spoken of this to anyone, not even mother."

"You had no need to say anything, little brother. I've seen it in your face often enough, and I know it's never far from your thoughts."

"What the hell are you talking about?" demanded Matthew, thumping the table again.

Paul's expression encouraged his brother to speak. "Go on, John, tell him. It's not a crime to have ambition, not even in this family."

John turned nervously to face Matthew's threatening glare, but lowered his eyes as he spoke. "I want to join the army, the Northamptons. It's all I've ever wanted." Still avoiding Matthew's harsh gaze he slowly raised his eyes to the ceiling, tearfully remembering what had brought them to this. "I'm sorry, Matt, but I couldn't say anything, not while mother was still alive. She would probably have tried to stop me."

"Of course, she would have stopped you," snapped Matthew. "And if you think we're going to give you our blessing then you're sorely mistaken." He jerked his head at Paul. "I can't stop him from going, nor would I want to, but your place is here with me, running this farm."

Paul placed a restraining hand on his brother's arm. "I'm sorry, Matt, but John's duty is to himself now, as it is with all of us. If the army is what he wants then I'll not stand in his way, and neither will you."

"I won't need to," he sneered in reply, giving John a contemptuous look. "Haven't you noticed, he's still a boy. Just look at the snivelling little brat. The army won't take the likes of him."

John flushed with a mixture of anger and embarrassment. So that is what his brother really thought of him. He was the youngest and nothing could change that, but it had been some years since he considered himself a boy. Since his father had died, he had shouldered more than his fair share of the work on the farm, as much as his schooling would allow, and after that he had shared the full burden with his two brothers. It had been enough to convince him that, like Paul, farming was not in his blood.

Although not as tall as Paul or as broad shouldered as Matthew he was still powerfully built for his young age, good looking with thick, dark brown hair inherited from his mother and warm blue eyes that appeared to deepen in colour whenever he became excited or passionate on any subject. The elements had aged him a little beyond his eighteen years, but not enough to dull his boyish enthusiasm.

From somewhere he found the confidence to face up to his brother. "I'm no boy, Matt, and I am old enough for the army. They will take me you just wait and see."

"All right, you join the army and get yourself killed. See if I care." He jabbed a finger at Paul. "But the same applies to you as to him. You go and the farm becomes mine, you forfeit your right to any part of it."

Noisily Paul pushed back his chair and jumped up from the table. "I don't think so, Matt," he said quietly, walking slowly towards the bottom of the stairs.

As they sat in a tentative silence Matthew and John exchanged cautious glances, listening to their brother rummaging about in the bedroom they shared. A few minutes later Paul came back down carrying a small wooden box bound with metal straps which he placed on the table in front of them. Taking a key from the fob of his waistcoat he unlocked it and threw back the lid.

"When mother became ill, she entrusted this to my keeping, to be opened after her death. I intended waiting until after the funeral before opening it, but clearly Matt's not prepared to wait." He looked directly at his brother as he drew a yellowed paper from the box. "This is a copy of father's will." He carefully unfolded the paper and laid it on the table. "It clearly sets out what happens to the farm, and there's no mention of our losing our rights should we choose to leave. On his death the farm and everything belonging to it passed to mother and then equally to the three of us after she dies. The only condition it makes is that John's share is held in trust until he reaches his majority."

Matthew snatched the paper off the table, his eyes flicking frantically over the copperplate writing. "That can't be right," he cried. "How can I be expected to run this farm on my own when most of it still belongs to you two?"

"Don't you think you're being a bit naïve, Matt? That's not what father intended and you know it."

"Of course, that's not what he intended." Matthew slammed the will back down onto the table with a ferocity that made John start. "What he intended was that the three of us should carry on running the farm, that's what he would have expected, and so would mother. You go and you betray both of them."

The rage that was slowly building in Paul's expression was frightening to watch. "Don't you ever talk to me of betrayal, Matthew," he hissed, his voice hushed and menacing. "I could have killed you for what you did and no one would have thought ill of me. If I don't leave this place, I may kill you yet." His usually warm eyes burned fiercely. "We both know it could come to that, so my going should suit us both."

As the two brothers faced up to each other, both threatening violence, John got to his feet, ready to pull them apart." Stop this, the two of you," he pleaded, staring again towards the ceiling. "Have you forgotten, our mother's dead up there and the two of you are talking about killing each other." He searched the face of each one for an answer. "For God's sake, will one of you tell me what this is all about? It can't be just about the farm, and it can't be that bad either."

Paul raised his hands submissively as his rage slowly subsided and a sense of the occasion returned. "I promised myself I would never speak of it, and God forbid I ever will." He looked pointedly at Matthew. "But if I'm forced to I will, so don't ever make me, Matt."

Backing away Paul began pacing the kitchen floor as he brought his temper under control while the others watched him cautiously, wrestling with their own emotions. For John it was a side of his brother's character he had not seen before, and it frightened him. He knew that Matthew was capable of a violent temper, but Paul had always displayed a calmness of nature he admired, and whatever had provoked such an outburst was frightening to contemplate. The fact that it had so effectively silenced Matthew only added to the menace.

Every now and then as he paced the floor Paul would stop to raise his eyes to the ceiling in a silent apology to his dead mother until, eventually, he felt able to take his place at the table.

"Right," he said, indicating that the others should join him, "this has to be settled, so let us try doing it like brothers." He waited for them to sit, watching Matthew carefully as he grudgingly took his place on the opposite side of the table. "We have to look at the choices open to us, which, given mine and John's dislike of farming, leaves only a few."

"It leaves none," muttered Matthew in a more subdued tone. "I haven't the money to buy your shares, you know that, so the farm will have to be sold."

Paul sighed heavily. Despite their fierce confrontation a few moments before, he took no pleasure in this victory over his brother. He well knew what the farm meant to Matthew, a passion shared only with their father, and it pained him that it should end like this.

"If we get a good price you could buy yourself a smaller farm, something you could more easily manage on your own, with a little hired help," he said optimistically.

"And who would give us a good price, with you two so desperate to sell?" enquired Matthew with the resigned air of despair. "Besides, I don't want another farm, to start again. Not when I've spent all my years working this land."

"I'm sorry Matt, I wish there could be another way, but my mind is made up, as I'm sure is John's." He looked to his young brother for confirmation and John nodded an apology to Matthew. "Anyway, I think I know of someone who might be prepared to give us a good price."

The other two appeared puzzled until John asked cautiously, "Mr Haveringham?"

Paul allowed himself a guarded smile. "Sir Rufus Haveringham indeed. He certainly has the means."

Matthew's eyes narrowed. "And what makes you think he would be interested in buying our farm?" he demanded scornfully.

"Rufus Haveringham has been interested in buying our land ever since he bought Willson's farm. Our land sits in the middle of both his holdings, and since father died, he has made more than one approach to mother. He'll be interested well enough." He got up from the table. "Now, I'm off to Daventry to make the arrangements for the funeral." He glanced down at John. "Will you come with me, for the company?"

John glanced across at Matthew's brooding face and readily agreed.

"It will give Matt a chance to think about his future," went on Paul as he put on his coat and ushered John towards the door. While John got ready to leave Paul returned to the table and bent close to Matthew. "And make your peace with mother while we're gone," he whispered.

It was refreshing to get back out into the open air after the confrontational oppression inside the house. Together Paul and John pulled the gig from the old, crumbling stone barn at the edge of the yard before John went to fetch Sally, the nag, from the wooden shed that served as a stable. The old horse, which had been with them for as long as John could remember, looked as sad and careworn as the occasion demanded, standing impassively disinterested as the harness was slid over her head.

Thankfully it had now stopped raining, although the sky was still heavy with dark clouds hanging low over the rolling landscape. A damp chill hung in the air, and as Paul flicked the reins to stir Sally into life the pair hunched forward against the cold.

As the horse trotted along the lanes, drops of water dripped from the overhanging branches adding further discomfort to what could only be a miserable journey. With neither of them in any mood for conversation the time was likely to pass slowly, but after some time bumping along in silence it was John who at last felt the need to speak first.

He turned on the seat to face his brother. "How did you know I wanted to join the army?" he asked, when he really wanted to know what had caused such an argument back at the house. "I've never spoken of it to anyone."

Paul gave him the patronising smile of an older brother as he tried unsuccessfully to coax Sally into greater effort. "Do you remember that day, a few years back, when father took us all down to Northampton for the fair?"

John stared straight ahead, deep in thought, before nodding excitedly. "The Northamptons were parading in the next field!"

"We couldn't drag you away. You had no interest in the fair once they arrived, and there was no hiding the way your eyes lit up whenever the army came up in conversation. I remember the way you cried when father told you the story of the massacre at Isandhlwana, and the sheer pride you felt when you heard about the defence at Rourke's Drift. Mother noticed too. She used to smile and give me a sly wink, but she would never say anything."

"Do you think she would have minded, about my joining the army?" He asked the question as though the answer, and her blessing, was important to him.

Paul gave some thought to his reply. "Father would have done, I think. The farm was his life, and he assumed it would be ours too. I loved him dearly, but he had a very narrow view on life, not like mother. He was born to the farm, but she came from the town and was much more a realist than him. Although she wanted everything father wanted when he was alive, she knew that once he was gone it would be hard to hold on to his way of life. The world's changing, young John, and she would have wanted us to change with it, but more than anything she would have wanted us to be happy. And if that means leaving the farm then I'm sure she would have understood."

John was a sensitive soul and his face took of a worried expression. "I know what I want, but what about Matt, do you think he'll be all right? And what about you, Paul, what are you going to do? You've never spoken about what you want to do."

Paul gave a reassuring smile. "I don't think you need to worry yourself about Matt, he's well able to look after himself. If Mr Haveringham buys the farm, as I'm sure he will, I'm certain he'll keep him on. Whatever his faults, Matt's a good farmer." His face took on a wistful look. "As for me, young John, I know where my future lies, and it's not here. It's away in the colonies."

John threw him a shocked glance. "You mean Canada or Australia, somewhere like that?"

Paul shook his head. "South Africa, John, that's where fortunes are being made." He stared ahead into the distance, not at the road but much further towards the land where men were clawing riches from the ground, the land that had filled the headlines for much of his youth.

"But I've heard people talking, and seen the newspapers," said John, his voice tinged with alarm. "They say the miners aren't welcome there, that there could be war."

As touching as his brother's concern was Paul laughed and gave him a slap on the back, making light of the rumours that had been circulating for months.

"There'll be no trouble, not while we've got the best army in the world to look after our interests. Who knows, John, we may even meet up there one day."

John smiled back, but it merely disguised his continued concerns as he allowed his mind to wander, conjuring up the image of an emotional reunion in that far off land. But Paul had been right about his ambitions; ever since that day in Northampton when he had watched with envy the queue of young men waiting in line to receive the Queen's shilling from the recruiting sergeant. One day, he had thought, that will be me, and his one regret as he bobbed along on the narrow seat of the gig was that it had taken his mother's death for him to finally realise his dream. He tried to visualise her reaction when he returned home on his first leave, bursting with pride in his smart new uniform. Would she have hidden her true feeling, giving him a hug and telling him how handsome he looked? He would never know.

By the time they drove into the town they had both retreated once again into the silence of their own private thoughts.

For some time after his brothers had left Matthew sat alone in the kitchen sulking over his own uncertain future and trying to come to terms with the sudden and dramatic change in his circumstances. The life that a few hours earlier he would have considered inviolable was in danger of being snatched away, and at that moment he felt nothing but hatred towards his two brothers. He just wanted to forget what had happened in the past, a moment of insanity that had hung over him ever since, that Paul was now using against him to force him out of the farm he so dearly loved. His mother had forgiven him, he knew that, so why not Paul?

Eventually, either from remorse or love, he found himself being dragged against his will towards the stairs. The bedroom was quite dark now, full of pervading shadows that shrouded his mother's body far more effectively than the thin sheet. As he entered the room the impulse that had driven him that far now seemed to desert him and he clutched at the wall for support.

"I'm so sorry," he sobbed, looking down on the wasted body. "I never meant you harm, I swear. I loved you." Gradually his legs found the strength to carry him across the room and he dropped to his knees beside the bed. Clutching at the sheet with trembling hands he buried his head in the bed. "Please forgive me."

He was still there when his brothers returned that evening.

Chapter Two

If God chose the elements to match the occasion, then the day of Emily Pearson's funeral dawned perfectly, with the fine rain casting a dull, misty hue over the little churchyard where she was to be laid to rest next to her husband. The thick blanket of dark clouds hung low in the sky and showed no signs of breaking, to allow even the smallest glimmer of brightness to lessen the solemnity of the occasion. When the mourners filed from the fifteenth century church led by the young clergyman it was in an atmosphere of cold, damp sorrow, fully befitting the final months of her life.

The three brothers had been joined by only a few of the local population, none of whom could claim to be a close friend of Emily Pearson, she had precious few of those. Even old Mrs Caldicot, who had ministered to her during those last weeks, attended more from a sense of duty than from any real affection, and Mr Caldicot came simply because his wife had ordered him to. The boys' father, William Pearson, had been a dour, insular man with few interests beyond his farm, and had never encouraged his wife to pursue her own social activities. Coming from the town she never shared his passion for the land and had bowed to his will purely from a wife's sense of unbending duty.

As Paul scanned the faces of the mourners gathered around the grave, he could detect only a superficial sorrow and an impatience to shelter from the elements. It served to prove what he already knew, that his mother had led a largely friendless, yet unselfish, life. As the young clergyman rushed through an empty eulogy for a woman he hardly knew, the impatience grew with the intensity of the rain, and even before he had finished speaking many began drifting away with a few passing words of insincere condolences.

Paul thanked them politely while John continued to stare tearfully at the pine coffin lying six feet beneath his feet. Matthew simply glowered at the passing faces and said nothing until only the clergyman and two miserable looking gravediggers remained.

While Paul shook hands with the churchman, Matthew jerked his head in the direction of a lone figure standing at the fringe of the churchyard. "What's he doing here?" he muttered sullenly as the gravediggers began shovelling the sodden earth down onto the coffin. "No one invited him."

Paul glanced over before bending to gather up a handful of soil which he threw down into the hole. "He's as much right to be here as the rest of them. Maybe more, considering the circumstances."

"Like a damned vulture, waiting to pick over the bones of our farm even before our mother is in the ground."

"He's here to pay his respects, nothing more." Paul joined John in his silent vigil, watching the coffin slowly disappear beneath the shovelled soil. "Perhaps that's what you should be doing, Matt."

Not until the three of them finally turned away from the grave and begun trudging out of the churchyard did the man approach them. "I didn't want to intrude upon your grief," he said, nodding to the three brothers in turn. He looked up at the dark grey skies. "A bad day all round, I fear."

"Our thanks to you for taking the trouble to come, Mr Haveringham," said Paul generously, extending his hand.

"I'm grateful for the opportunity to pay my respects," he replied with a benevolent smile. "I've known your parents for a good many years, since before you were all born. They were good people. My one regret is that we were never really friends, not in the way neighbours should be."

"Perhaps that's because our father saw you for what you really were, not as a neighbour but someone who just wanted our farm," muttered Matthew acidly.

"For pity's sake, Matthew, watch your tongue," snapped Paul angrily. "I'm sorry, Mr Haveringham, he didn't mean ..."

Rufus Haveringham held up a gloved hand. "No need for apologies master Paul," he said, giving Matthew a patronising smile. "I understand what a difficult time this must be for the three of you. Anyway, I've intruded long enough, so I'll leave you to your grieving." He was about to turn away when he hesitated. "Remember, should you need my help at any time you only need to ask. You know where I am."

Paul thanked him, but before the man had gone more than a few yards he called after him. "I'm sorry, Mr Haveringham, but there is a matter we need to discuss with you. Would it be convenient to call on you in a few days?"

Despite the discomfort they were all suffering from the weather Rufus Haveringham beamed broadly. "Why, of course, my boy, it will be my pleasure." Then, as if struck by a monumental notion, he threw his arms up into the air, his waterproof cloak spraying rain in all directions. "I have a splendid idea. Why don't the three of you join me for dinner, I'm sure we have a great deal to talk about, and I find that fine food and good conversation make admirable table companions. Do you not think?" He directed that last remark at Matthew. "Shall we say two days from now, eight o'clock?"

As Paul watched him stride away to a waiting carriage Matthew grabbed him roughly by the arm. "You just can't wait to rid yourself of our home, can you?" he breathed through clenched teeth. "You made me feel ashamed, the way you grovelled to him, and with our mother barely in the ground. I just hope it gave you some satisfaction."

Paul shook his head despairingly as he clamped a hand firmly over his brother's. "No satisfaction at all, Matt, but it needed to be done and I think the sooner the better."

"Paul's right," said John, speaking for the first time since before the funeral service. "All this anger is tearing us apart, and I can't see an end to it until we all go our separate ways. The sooner we get it settled the sooner we can get on with our lives."

"Wise words from such a young head," teased Paul, ruffling his brother's hair through his soaked cap.

"And easy for you to say, seeing that the two of you are getting the better of the deal, and the lives you want." Matthew cast a brief look back at the grave before slowly walking away.

During the days following the funeral the three brothers worked the farm with an uneasy truce existing between them. For Paul and John there was little enthusiasm for the daily toil, and their only incentive was the knowledge that within a short time they would be leaving for the new life they both craved. Only Matthew threw himself into the work, leaving the house at first light and returning long after dusk had settled over the farm. The arrangement suited them all, preserving the tentative peace until they were ready to tread their separate paths.

At the end of the second day Paul and John finished their work and were chatting excitedly in the kitchen, speculating on what they would be eating and drinking that evening in the auspicious surroundings of Millwood House. Paul stripped off his shirt and began washing at the sink as John sat at the table awaiting his turn. Although nothing had been said they were both anxious that Matthew would wish to make the evening as difficult as possible, and that it may be preferable if he were not there. But it was his future as well, and he had as much right as them to have his say.

As he washed, Paul peered through the window at the deepening gloom outside. "I just hope he's not going to make us late," he said, drying himself on a threadbare towel.

"Perhaps it's better he didn't come," said John with a wry grin as he took his turn at the sink. "He'll only cause trouble with Mr Haveringham."

Paul gave his brother a playful flick with the towel, but was prevented from agreeing when the kitchen door was thrown open and Matthew stormed in.

"Come on, Matt, we don't want to appear rude by arriving late," Paul said with fake cheerfulness.

"There's still work to be done, we haven't lost the farm yet." He sat down at the table and glared at his two brothers. "Besides, I've no intention of arriving at all. If you think I'm sitting down at table with that man while you two give away our inheritance, then you don't know me. Anyway, I would probably choke on the food."

"Please yourself," Paul replied casually. He sat down opposite his brother, meeting his caustic gaze. "I just assumed you would want to be there, to make sure we don't sell you short. Remember, John and me want shot of this place so we'll be happy to accept whatever Mr Haveringham wants to offer, within reason. How can you guarantee we'll get the best price if you're not there?"

The contempt Matthew felt for his brother was exacerbated by his rising anger. Although Paul was making light of the situation, he was right, the only way to ensure an acceptable deal was to be there himself. "All right," he grunted reluctantly, "but don't expect me to be civil. You know that's the only reason I'm going, and I'll make that clear to him as well."

"I'm sure you will, Matt," said Paul with a resigned shake of his head, "but it may be well to remember that a little courtesy may be to our advantage. After all, he's under no obligation to buy the farm at any price, so some good manners could get us a better deal."

Matthew's response as he stripped off his shirt was a contemptuous snort. "He'll buy, there's no doubt about that. He's always wanted our land, you said so yourself, and mother's death won't have changed anything."

With the sky still covered in a blanket of dark clouds very little moonlight filtered through to light their way to Millwood House. Only by a thorough knowledge of the narrow lanes did John skilfully guide Sally and the gig through the night without mishap. He had always been good with horses; ever since he was old enough to sit astride one without support he had formed a bond with the animal that had never extended to his older brothers. Never missing any opportunity to ride Paul had thought it strange that his brother was intent on joining an infantry regiment.

They were all deep in their own thoughts when the two great stone pillars that marked the entrance to the Millwood Estate loomed out of the blackness and John had to rein in Sally to make the sharp turn.

Oil filled lanterns illuminated the entire length of the long, sweeping drive and John slowed Sally to a sedate walk along the gravelled surface until he drew to a halt in front of the magnificent house.

Three wide marble steps led up to the four columned portico covered entrance that sheltered visitors arriving at the tall, deeply panelled, oak double doors. The size of the house was impressive enough, but to those more accustomed to humbler surroundings its appearance must have presented an intimidating spectre. With its façade covered almost entirely in ivy it looked as though the house was attempting to disguise the fact that it was a structure born of man and not of nature.

Whatever thoughts ran through the brothers' minds as they stared up at the grandness of the house one thing was certain, that whatever happened that evening it was bound to change all their lives forever. For John the sheer proportions of the house were awe inspiring, but he felt drawn involuntarily towards it by the prospect that within its walls lay the means to achieve his boyhood ambition. This night would be the start of his new life, and whatever that brought with it.

Paul had been to the house before, accompanying his father on some farm business, but then they had entered through the back of the house, and not, as far as he was aware, at the express invitation of the owner. What the night held for him, apart from probably the finest meal he had ever eaten, or likely to eat, was a time for fruitful and positive negotiations with a gracious host. The only imponderable, as far as he was concerned, was when his personal adventure could begin.

Only for Matthew was there no deep feeling of excitement or expectation. To him the house appeared as offensive as its owner, and he could never be persuaded that the evening would end in anything other than disaster. That he may be the instrument of that disaster was yet to be determined. In any event, he could see no way that it would end to his advantage.

"I never thought I would ever be able to say this," he said bitterly, "but I feel pleased mother and father are dead. God alone knows what they would have made of us dressed up in our Sunday best just to satisfy the likes of him."

Paul rounded on him angrily. "We do the best we can for ourselves, Matthew, for our own dignity, not for him or anyone else." They climbed down off the gig as John handed the reins to a groom who had magically appeared from the side of the house. "We are here to do the best we can for all our futures, yours as well as ours, so I suggest you bite your tongue and accept that the farm will be sold, with or without any help from you."

Matthew made no reply. There was nothing he could say that would resolves matters in his favour, but his morose expression, as he followed his brothers up the steps, made it clear he would not give up without a fight.

A lion's head cast in bronze hung threateningly from the bell chain, daring visitors to announce their presence, and as Paul and John stood in front of the doors they exchanged tentative glances, their earlier exuberance having turned to nervous anticipation.

"For pity's sake," hissed Matthew scornfully, pushing past them. "We're here so we might as well get it over with."

As he pulled heavily on the chain, they could all hear the deep toll of the bell resonating from somewhere within, like an announcement of impending doom that made John take a step back. Before the ringing had subsided the echoing sound of footsteps could be heard from the other side of the door which was opened by a liveried footman who looked them up and down in a haughty, condescending manner. Despite their best clothes the three brothers were hardly the type of visitors the footman was familiar with, and after a moment's hesitation he reluctantly bowed his head and stood aside for them to enter.

The three of them stood in the entrance hall taking in its size and opulence. The ornate marble tiled floor led to a broad mahogany staircase that swept in a wide arch up to a galleried landing surrounded by an intricately carved balustrade. High above them an enormous crystal chandelier hung from the ceiling casting a kaleidoscope of coloured light in all directions. From either side of the hall a number of panelled doors led off to anonymous rooms that seemed to conceal the secrets of the house.

While Paul and John were both suitably impressed, Matthew remained obdurate, outwardly unmoved by his affluent surroundings, staring down at his feet as the footman waved them towards a door in a corner of the hall.

"Mr Haveringham asked that you wait for him in the library," he said in a cold, emotionless tone as he pushed open the door. "If you leave me with your coats and hats he will be with you presently." He looked disdainfully at the garments as he laid them across his arm as though they were likely to contaminate his uniform.

"Snotty-nosed bastard," commented Matthew as the door closed behind them. "Even the paid help think they're better than us."

"He's only doing his job, Matt," Paul tried to assure him, even though he was inclined to agree with his brother's opinion. "He probably treats all the guests the same."

As soon as they were alone John detached himself from his older brothers and became completely absorbed by the contents of the room. Three sides of the library were covered by bookshelves all filled to capacity with countless volumes, most leather bound, covering every possible subject and reading preference.

"Just look at all these books," he said excitedly, running his finger along the gold inlaid spines. "Do you think Mr Haveringham could have read them all?"

"Of course not, they're just for show, like everything else in this damned house," sneered Matthew, airing his contempt for their host. "They mean nothing to him, except to prove how much money he has."

"If they were mine, I would read them," remarked John, studying some of the titles.

"I'm sure you would, and be a better man for it, no doubt." The voice came from the open doorway. "As for me, I can't admit to having read more than a dozen or so of them." Rufus Haveringham was smiling directly at Matthew, making it clear he had heard the exchange between the two brothers. "But then I have no need to read all of them when I have the means to pay others for the information they contain."

The three of them had swung around to face their host and Haveringham came towards them, his hand extended. He smiled at them warmly, his round, open face, framed by thick mutton-chop whiskers, had the ruddy complexion of a man who spent much of his time in the open air and at odds with a cosseted existence. His clothes, though clearly of expensive cut, did not quite match the opulence of the house and were, perhaps, in due deference to his guests' humbler circumstances. He was of medium height with a slightly corpulent figure, and his age could be judged at anywhere in his fifties, although his bearing was erect and he looked at them in turn through brown eyes that betrayed a liveliness of mind.

"Is there nothing in this world you have wanted that could not be bought?" enquired Matthew bluntly as he reluctantly accepted the man's hand.

"Matthew, for pity's sake, won't you stop this. Remember where you are." Paul glared at his brother, clearly embarrassed.

Rufus Haveringham grinned and held up his hand. "No matter," he said graciously, "I admire someone prepared to speak his mind. It's a rare experience for a man in my position."

"I think you will find we are all prepared to speak our mind, Mr Haveringham, should we feel it necessary," commented Paul. Without encouraging his brother's rudeness, he wanted it made clear they were not there purely to be patronised.

"I'm sure you will Master Paul. Knowing your parents as I did, I should expect nothing less from you." He turned and gave a casual nod to a man servant who had silently appeared in the doorway. "It is usual to offer sherry before dinner, but as we are all men here," he gave John a dubious look, "I think whisky is more appropriate. Do we include your younger brother?"

Paul patted John proudly on the back as they watched the drinks being poured. "Our young brother here is set to join the army, so I believe that qualifies him as a man, don't you? Perhaps just a small one though."

As John nervously accepted a glass from the offered tray Haveringham regarded him closely. "Breaking with family tradition and joining the army, I must say that does surprise me," he exclaimed, before fixing the other two with an enquiring gaze. "I wonder what other surprises we can expect this evening."

"Well, as you mention it, there is another matter we did intend to discuss with you this evening," said Paul hesitantly. "But as you were kind enough to invite us here to dinner it seems impolite to mention it now. Perhaps after we have eaten?"

"What a very mature suggestion," Haveringham said heartily, "but then you are the man of the house now, and I can tell you, nothing matures a man like responsibility." He swallowed his drink in a single gulp and indicated his guests should do the same. "Now let us go and eat before impatience ruins my appetite." He laughed loudly as he led the way from the library.

The four place settings looked lost and pathetic arranged on the vastness of the large oak dining table which was more used to accommodating far greater numbers. In the open fireplace at the far end of the dining room a log fire crackled brightly, although it did little to lift the sad atmosphere of a room that had presumably known happier times.

As John sat down, he couldn't help focussing on the great array of silver cutlery laid out before him, trying to recall the advice Paul had given him the day before. Should he start from the inside or outside? He would have to be guided by the others' lead.

Matthew, on the other hand, was affected by no such inhibitions concerning social etiquette. There was no shame in his birth right, he was proud to be accepted for what he was, a farmer. The evening, and his host's generosity were both there to be used.

For Paul the evening was to be a rare insight into a life that was a world away from anything within his experience, and one with which he could happily become better acquainted. More than that it, convinced him, if indeed he was in need of convincing, that his decision to leave the farm was the right one if he was ever to achieve success, to better himself. Before the food arrived, however, he made a silent apology to his parents for what they may misinterpret as greed.

"Well, let us see what the wonderful Mrs Rafferty has prepared for us," said Haveringham, raising a glass as the first course arrived.

They were treated to a spicy mulligatawny soup, followed by a very palatable mutton served with vegetables, all from Haveringham's own estate. There was nothing overtly fancy or rich about the food, and when the last course arrived, they were treated to a selection of cheeses instead of the expected pudding. The conversation that accompanied each course had been as uncontroversial as the wine was congenial, although Matthew accepted one with relish while taking little part in the other. Whether it was to appease the truculent nature of one of his guests, or an honest statement of fact was unclear, but Haveringham was at pains to explain that it was not his habit to eat so lavishly when he dined alone, which he did most days. "In essence I am a simple man with simple pleasures," he said, draining the last of his wine. Then, as if in contradiction, he called for the port to be served. "It would be usual to take this in the drawing room, but I think we are all comfortable enough here." He took the decanter from his man, helped himself and passed it on. "It occurs to me," he said, sniffing at his port while looking pointedly at Matthew, "that I gave no answer to the question posed by our young friend here. It was quite unintentional and I apologise."

Matthew exchanged a cautious glance with his older brother, while John was rendered largely incapable of contributing anything further to the evening's proceedings.

"A question?" queried Matthew. "I don't recall asking you a question."

Haveringham nodded knowingly. "You most certainly did, and one deserving of an answer, since it implied you have a low opinion of me." He paused long enough to attract a response, but got none. "You asked me, if you remember? whether there was anything I wanted that could not be bought. Well, I can tell you, although there is no reason that I should, seeing that it is no one's business but my own, that there are at least two things I have passionately wished for that all the money in England could never buy." He paused again, staring wistfully into the distance. "The first is that I have not been blessed with a son and heir to whom I could pass on all this." He swept his arm flamboyantly around the room before his face took on a more solemn aspect. "The second was the health of my dear wife. She became ill many years ago, and even the skills of the most eminent doctors, and believe me she had those, could not save her life. She died not long before your own father." He took a deep breath to compose himself and then smiled briefly. "There is a third, but I fear this is neither the time nor place to mention it, if indeed such a time exists."

He leaned back in his chair to stare up at the ceiling as though reflecting on what he had just said, or possibly to consider that he had said too much.

"Would that third thing have anything to do with our farm?" demanded Matthew, unwilling to let the matter rest. "We know you spoke to our mother after our father died."

Rather than reacting angrily to the harsh intrusion into his private thoughts Haveringham slowly lowered his head and fixed the two older brothers with a penetrating stared, as John's head dropped forward onto his chest. "I spoke to your mother on a number of occasions, about many things," he said with a long, deep sigh. "I make no secret of the fact that your land was of interest to me, after all it does border my own and buying it would make good business sense." Again, he looked hard at the two of them. "But it was more than that, much more, and I'm not sure you would forgive my mentioning it, not at a time like this."

Matthew glanced angrily at Paul, expecting some reaction from his brother, before turning on his host. "Don't play games with us, Mr Haveringham, if this has anything to do with our farm then we have every right to hear of it."

Haveringham helped himself to another glass of port, breathing in its heady aroma before raising his eyes to the two brothers who stared back at him expectantly. "Very well, if you insist." He took a deep swallow of the port to set his nerves. "You well know that I did visit your mother on a number of occasions after your father died. To begin with it was as a concerned neighbour, both of us struggling with a recent loss. The subject of buying your land was raised, but she was loyal to your father's memory, and your inheritance. She had made him a pledge and I respected that. But I continued to visit because I took great comfort in her company, she was an intelligent, sensitive woman and had a knowledge of many things." He finished his port and dabbed his mouth delicately with a napkin, an anxious expression on his flushed face. "The truth is I grew very fond of her, although I have no idea if those feelings were ever reciprocated. I never dared ask, but if she had given me the least encouragement then I would not have hesitated to ask for her hand."

As Paul and Matthew stared at him in disbelief a look of relief spread across his face, as though he had been unburdened of a terrible secret.

"I had no idea," was all Paul was able to say after several moments of tense silence.

Without warning Matthew thumped the table with his fist, shaking John back into a temporary consciousness before he slumped forward again. "You would have married our mother just to get your hands on our farm?"

Haveringham shook his head vigorously, protesting his innocence at the accusation, but before he could reply Paul was on his feet, glaring at his brother across the table. "Enough of this, Matt. I'm sure Mr Haveringham had no such thing in mind."

Haveringham held up a placating hand. "Thank you," he said quietly to Paul, "but I have every sympathy with your brother's feelings. This news must have come as a shock to both of you." He pushed the decanter towards Matthew. "I'm sorry, I meant no offence to you, or your mother and her memory, but my feelings towards her were entirely genuine." He gave a resigned sigh. "Had she accepted then some of my wishes would have been fulfilled. Aside from the hand of a good woman it would have provided me with heirs to the estate."

Paul was stunned, and even Matthew appeared at a loss of something to say, although not for very long. "I don't believe you," he scoffed, helping himself to another drink. "If you had married our mother, we would have inherited all this?"

"That's quite a question," teased Haveringham, "but academic now, I fear. Had I married your mother then it is entirely possible that Master Paul, as the eldest, would have become my heir, but that would depend on him. I would rather sell than let everything I have fall into the hands of an unworthy beneficiary. Does that answer your question?"

Matthew was still trying to come to terms with what might have been when Paul spoke for both of them. "As you say, Mr Haveringham, it's all academic now. Whatever the future may have held for us is passed and we have to consider what we do now."

His host gave him a quizzical look. "Don't tell me you are thinking of leaving the land like your young brother here?" He waved his hand at John who was slumbering peacefully at the table.

"I've no desire to be a farmer and I don't think I ever did. It was just expected, but with both our parents gone I think my only obligation now is to myself." He glanced cautiously at Matthew who maintained a sullen silence. "Which brings us to the matter I mentioned a few days ago."

"Haveringham beamed broadly. "I rather thought it might. Let me guess, you wish me to buy your farm?"

"They do, I don't," intervened Matthew sourly, unable to stay out of it any longer.

"But it's been agreed," insisted Paul. "It doesn't suit all three of us, but it's been agreed."

"And what makes you think I will still be interested in buying, after all it has been some time since I made my offer?"

"Because it would be foolish not to," said Paul. "Our farm lies between your estate and Willson's Farm you bought a few years ago. Buying our land would tie the whole estate together. Besides, we have good pasture, better than Willson's."

"A sound argument, I agree. And how much do you expect me to pay for this land of yours?"

Paul hesitated, his heart was pounding heavily inside his chest at the prospect of concluding an immediate sale. He prayed that Matthew stayed silent. "I know what offer was made to our mother and I think that was a fair price. We would be happy to accept the seven thousand guineas."

Haveringham gave a chuckle and shook his head. "It would be foolish of me to make the same offer again, considering the circumstances."

"What circumstance?" snapped Matthew, unable to hold his tongue against his rising agitation. He glared sharply at his brother. "I warned you he couldn't be trusted."

Paul took up the challenge on behalf of his brother. "What had changed, and how much are you proposing?"

Their host drummed on the table with his fingers, a smug smile on his face. "There's a lot to life you've both yet to learn," he lectured. "When I wanted to buy it was worth seven thousand, but now you are the ones wishing to sell and that places a different complexion on the deal. Now my offer would be six thousand guineas."

"But we could sell the farm on the open market, and ask for the full price," protested Paul. "How would that benefit you?"

"You could try, but I doubt you would succeed. There are few people with money like that these days." He was trying hard not to sound condescending. "I suspect you need a quick sale, and that being the case my offer will stand for only a limited time."

"So much for the memory of our mother," sneered Matthew. "Is that all she really means to you, six thousand guineas? You couldn't buy her then so you're making us pay now."

"That's enough, Matt. Mr Haveringham has made his offer and given us his reasons. It's up to us now to decide if we accept or not."

"Well, I can tell you now, I don't accept, and I never will."

"In that case then," said Haveringham, getting up from the table, "I see no point in prolonging an evening that looks set to end on an acrimonious note." He looked down at John. "Besides, I think it is time our young friend here was in his bed."

"I'm sorry, sir," apologised Paul, shaking John by the shoulder to rouse him. "I think this is something we need to discuss further, amongst ourselves. As you can see, my young brother here is in no condition to make any decisions, not tonight"

While Paul and Matthew hauled John to his feet, Haveringham rang for their coats and for the gig to be brought to the front of the house.

"We will be in touch in a day or two with our decision," said Paul as they waited in the hall. "And I apologise again that the evening ended so abruptly."

"No need for any apology, Master Paul. The first real decision a man has to make in his life is the most important, and my offer will now stand for as long as it takes."

Chapter Three

The chill night air had done nothing to shake John from his inebriation. On the journey home he had to be supported between his two brothers to stop him from lurching out of the gig while it was left to Paul to negotiate Sally through the pitch-black lanes.

By the time they reached home John was slumped forward on the seat and had to be carried into the house where Matthew left him in Paul's care.

"So, you still think he's man enough to join the army?" he said callously. "He won't last long if he can't hold a few drinks."

Paul chose to ignore the remark, and after throwing his brother a look of contempt he struggled to get John up the stairs and into bed.

Matthew preferred to remain down in the kitchen, apparently less affected by the evening's indulgences than the other two. With Haveringham's words still vivid, and playing havoc with his thoughts, he was in no mood for sleep and sat brooding at the table, his head supported in his hands. The arrogance of the man to think he could buy his mother's affections! Yet what if she had married him, would he now be sitting in that cold, dreary kitchen facing an uncertain future? A vision of what might have been flashed through his mind again and again before lingering dreamlike to send him almost mad with remorse. While his brothers slept soundly above him he spent the night either pacing the floor or sat at the table drifting between regret and anger, until sleep finally overtook him.

It was not yet dawn when he lifted his head off the table and massaged some life into his face and neck. It took a moment or two to reconcile himself with his surroundings; the dream had been so real that the disappointment of finding himself in his own humble home almost overwhelmed him and a loud sob escaped from his dry lips.

Without bothering to change his clothes he threw open the kitchen door and went out to stand in the yard, breathing deeply at the fresh, chill morning air.

This had always been his favourite time of day; like his father he would rise early to take advantage of the dawn's special peace.

As he looked about him bleary eyed, at his inheritance, he began to wonder how much longer he would be able to enjoy the simple pleasure of surveying the land he could call his own. The thought of losing it, combined with the notion of what might have been, tormented him beyond measure and he clutched at his head, barely able to stifle a scream of sheer frustration.

It a state of blind confusion he began walking, with no apparent thought of where he was going, or of the work that would usually occupy his day. Nothing in his life now was as it should be, having been thrown into turmoil by the selfish ambitions of his two brothers, and the revelations of a man he barely knew. How he despised them all.

Beyond the yard, and the few farm buildings that surrounded it, the undulating pastureland spread out before him, providing good grazing for their herds of sheep and cattle that should, over the past years, have given them a reasonable living. But men like Haveringham, with their vast estates and intensive farming methods, had driven down the prices at market, giving small farmers little opportunity of showing a profit. As he trudged aimlessly across the damp grassland all these thoughts ran through his mind, adding to the rage that smouldered within him.

With his mind torn to distraction time and distance were lost to him, and without realising it the ground began to rise and he was climbing towards a wooded knoll which, since childhood, had been a place of solace and solitude, a special place. He had often come there over the years to be alone, dreaming of his future, a perfect life with a wife and children, strong sons who would share in his passion for the farm they would one day inherit.

Now, all those plans were set to be destroyed, and it was with a sense of overwhelming sorrow that he slumped down on the rotting trunk of a beech tree that had been brought down by lightening many years before. His head dropped heavily into his hands and he was finally able to release all his pent-up emotions in an uncontrollable flood of tears. But these were not tears of self-pity, he had no time for that, this was his way of freeing his mind to more rational thinking. When the sobbing was over, he slowly lifted his head, finding refreshment in the drops of dew that fell on him from the overhanging branches. With the rage and frustration gradually subsiding he was able to devote himself to the embryonic and audacious scheme that had struck him just as suddenly and dramatically as the lightening that had struck the tree.

Dawn was just creeping up on him from behind the knoll as he stood up with a determination that set him on a course back down the hill and across the fields, but not towards home. There was something he had to do immediately, while the idea was still fresh in his mind, and before his nerve deserted him.

It was a few hours later when Paul stirred and struggled bleary eyed and heavy headed down the stairs. John was still sleeping heavily and his brother felt no inclination to disturb him just yet. That Matthew's bed had not been slept in had escaped Paul's notice, although it would have aroused no suspicion. Matthew was a habitual early riser like his father, anxious to be about his business by first light.

Only when he reached the kitchen was Paul aware that old Mrs Caldicot was already there with a pot of stew she had prepared for their evening meal. As he peered into the pot and saw the thick layer of mutton fat floating on the surface his stomach lurched noisily and he feared he would vomit.

"I promised your mother, God rest her soul, that I wouldn't let you starve," she said in her high pitched, penetrating voice that pained his ears. "Heaven knows what she would think of you, in your bed to all hours."

"I'm sorry, Mrs Caldicot, I know it's a bit late," he replied contritely and, although it was none of her business, he purposely didn't mention that John was still asleep upstairs. "It's very good of you to look after us, but it's really not necessary, we are quite able to manage for ourselves."

She sniffed loudly. "Well, a promise is a promise. And this is how you look after yourselves, laying in your beds half the day?" She shuffled over to the stove carrying the pot. "Well, I've enough to do looking after an idle beggar of me own, so I'll leave you to it." She snorted again as she put on her coat. "I'll be back tomorrow for the pot."

Grateful to be left alone Paul leaned over the sink and pumped cold water onto his head, the initial shock turning to blissful relief as the throbbing began to subside. When he had dried himself and drunk several cups of water he sat down at the table, trying hard not to think of the glutinous stew a few feet away. He had eaten and drunk enough the previous evening to last him for more than a few days.

Slowly his thoughts turned away from the self-indulgence to the conversation they had had with Haveringham. Things had been said that had surprised, if not shocked, both him and his brother, and, like Matthew, he too was struggling to come to terms with what might have been a very different future for all of them. But that time had passed and there still remained the matter of their farm that needed to be settled. Although John could be spared some of the details, his young brother needed to be acquainted with Haveringham's offer before any final decision could be made.

Leaving John to sleep on, Paul went out into the yard. A watery sun was forcing its way through a thin covering of cloud, although there was still a chill in the morning air. He breathed deeply, the exhilarating freshness filling his lungs and bringing his whole body to life. He would need a clear head and sharp mind when he and Matthew met.

Although of no great size compared to the vast acreage of Millwood Estate, their farm was of sufficient size to render it difficult to cover easily on foot, so Paul strode resolutely over to the shed. Sally eyed him suspiciously as he entered. She had not yet forgiven them for dragging her out the previous night, and showed her yellow teeth and shied away when he offered up the bridle. They had couple of other horses, younger and more enthusiastic than Sally, but she suited his disposition and riding ability, and never anxious to break into a gallop at the merest encouragement.

With a contemptuous look over her shoulder Sally was spurred into a sedate walk out through the yard until she felt the soft pastureland beneath her hooves when she condescended to increase her pace into a gentle trot.

Matthew could have been anywhere on the farm, but rather than a haphazard search Paul set a course for the knoll. Apart from being Matthew's secret sanctuary it was also the highest point on their land. From the top of the hill Paul looked down on the rich green fields that surrounded him, on the small herds of sheep and cattle that grazed apparently oblivious to their uncertain future. The small river that formed the boundary between their farm and Haveringham's estate wound its way through the fields like a shimmering ribbon each time the sun broke through the clouds.

For Paul it was like he was looking down on the scene for both the first and last time, not taking it for granted as he would something that was a permanent part of his life. Now, with the prospect of leaving it all behind, he took in every detail with a sentimental eye. But even that sentimentality did not distract him from his purpose, and one detail became immediately conspicuous by its absence; there was no sign of Matthew.

Clambering back up into the saddle he patted the horse on her neck. "Where do you think he's got to, Sal? Let's head back home, he's bound to turn up there sooner or later."

As if in complete agreement Sally turned back down the hill, almost breaking into a canter in her impatience to return to the comfort of her shed.

With the sun rising from behind its expanse of red brick and ivy, Millwood House rose out of the early morning mist like a giant silhouette, larger and more imposing than it had appeared at night. Constantly adjusting his pace in order to arrive at a convenient hour Matthew had trudged across the fields and along the deserted lanes for more than an hour and now he stood at the end of the long, sweeping drive, questioning the reason that had brought him there. The determined excitement that had first gripped him up on the knoll and had slowly developed into a logical and tangible argument, now lost much of its substance in the shadow of the great building.

But for Matthew there was little to be lost; his brothers would surely vote to accept Haveringham's offer and the farm would be lost, so what was a small amount of humiliation set against an even smaller glimmer of hope. Perhaps the audacity of his proposal would be sufficient to impress a man who had, perhaps, accumulated much of his wealth under similar circumstances.

Taking a deep breath to steel his nerves he strode purposefully up the drive, the gravel crunching noisily beneath his boots, cutting through the stillness of the morning. As he stood before the oak doors, he snatched the cap from his head and ran his fingers through his blonde hair. Although still wearing his best suit, the trek from his farm had taken its toll on his appearance, with his boots covered in mud and the bottom of his trousers hanging damp and limp.

He stood, fidgeting anxiously with his cap, while the lion's head on the end of the bell chain taunted him, daring him to take hold. Finally, setting his teeth, he reached out and gave the brass sculpture a sharp jerk, then quickly stepped back away from the door.

It was some time before he heard any response from within and he fought an almost overpowering urge to run away. He was on the verge of succumbing when the sound of bolts being drawn made him stiffen and take a tighter grip on his cap.

Whether or not it was the same footman from the previous evening Matthew couldn't say as the man looked him up and down in the same condescending manner.

"Tradesmen around the back," snapped the servant, having completed his inspection of the visitor.

He was about to close the door when Matthew held out his hand to stop him. "I'm here to see Mr Haveringham," he said with as much authority as his nerves allowed. "On a matter of important business."

The footman continued to eye him suspiciously, but stopped short of closing the door completely. "Is he expecting you? What's your name?"

"Not exactly. It's Pearson, Matthew Pearson. I was here last evening, for dinner."

"I'll have to see. Wait here."

With the door closed on him and the sound of footsteps slowly retreating across the hall Matthew began pacing agitatedly beneath the tall portico, slapping his thigh with his cap while frantically rehearsing the words he had practiced on the way there.

By the time the door reopened he was no closer to settling on a convincing argument that would justify this uninvited intrusion. To his surprise the footman stood to one side and beckoned him to enter.

"The master is at breakfast. He will see you straight away in the breakfast room."

Matthew followed him through to the back of the house and was shown into a fairly small and uninspiring room that opened out into a glass covered conservatory overlooking the rear gardens. Matthew was struck by the pervading smell of damp vegetation shrouding the underlying aroma of smoked kippers.

Haveringham sat at a small, round table with his back to Matthew from where he could look through the conservatory and into the gardens. When the footman made the announcement, he merely raised a hand with a beckoning motion.

"I never thought to find you here at such an early hour," he said without turning to his visitor. "I fully expected that brother of yours to put up more of a fight against my offer."

As the footman left Matthew took a few steps forward. "I am that brother, Mr Haveringham, as you can see."

Haveringham glanced up from his breakfast, his round face displaying a mild surprise. "Well, strike me lad, so you are." He dabbed the corner of his mouth with a napkin. "I do apologise. My man simply announced you as Mr Pearson." He waved a hand to the chair opposite and waited for Matthew to sit down. "I simply assumed that if it wasn't all three of you then your older brother would come to speak on your behalf." He gestured towards a silver salver on a dresser by the wall. "Some breakfast? I have the kippers sent over fresh from Great Yarmouth."

Matthew nodded and got up to help himself. "I'm not here to speak for the other two," he said, manoeuvring two of the fish onto a plate. "They know nothing of this, I'm here on my own account."

"To insult me further?" Haveringham gave a curt laugh. "Well, at least you can do it in a civilised manner, over a good breakfast."

"And I'm not here to insult you either," replied Matthew, somewhat disarmed by the remark. "At least not intentionally."

"That's a relief, but now you intrigue me, Master Matthew." He beamed broadly as he spoke. "Perhaps we should just settle for polite conversation for now and leave any insults until after breakfast."

With a limited acquaintance with polite conversation Matthew preferred to finish his breakfast in silence, spending the time glancing around at his unfamiliar surroundings.

"A very pleasant room, don't you think?" enquired Haveringham, noticing Matthew's interest. "I usually eat here when I'm alone, which, unfortunately, is much of the time." He raised his eyes in a resigned fashion. "I expect that comes as something of a surprise to you, that I am a lonely man, but since the death of my dear wife that is very much the case." He gave a self-deprecating shake of his head. "Forgive me, a little self-pity, I'm afraid. You and your brothers have troubles enough of your own without listening to my woes." Matthew was about to assure him that was not the case when he went on. "I take it you are not here to accept my offer so perhaps it is time for the insults."

"I told you, Mr Haveringham, not insults." He pushed his plate away. "I should like to make you a proposal that would satisfy me and my brothers."

Haveringham raised his bushy eyebrows inquisitively. "Satisfy you and your brothers, eh? I notice you make no mention of satisfying me. I gave you my offer last night and it's up to the three of you to accept or reject it. I'm in no mind to negotiate."

"If you'll just hear me out, sir," persisted Matthew. "I think my proposal will suit us all."

"Then let's hear it, lad." He slapped the table impatiently. "I haven't all day."

Matthew hesitated, ensuring the words came out as he intended. There would be no room for error. "You offered our mother seven thousand guineas for our farm therefore you must have known it was worth as much. Now you say you will pay six thousand, but all I'm asking you to spend is only four."

Haveringham stared intently from across the table. "Get to the point, lad."

Knowing he had the other's attention Matthew sat forward on his chair. His heart was thumping against the wall of his chest and he felt breathless. "What I propose is that you pay my brothers four thousand guineas for their share of the farm and that you and I become partners."

Haveringham continued to stare, as though digesting the offer before he threw back his head and roared with laughter. "That's quite a proposal, lad," he said once he had recovered, "but I have no need of a partner. Why would I wish to share with you what I can so easily own outright?"

"Why pay six thousand guineas for that which you could have for four? Our land has water and good pasture, and you are in need of both, I believe." Matthew was not to be deterred.

"But why should I want to share it with you? I can see no logic in your proposal." There was still a note of interest in his voice, it was not the outright dismissal Matthew had feared.

"Even to a man of your means, Mr Haveringham, a saving of two thousand guineas must have some merit." He paused before continuing. What he was about to say would either sink or save his argument. "You made the point last night that you regretted having no son and heir," he began slowly, "therefore you rely entirely on paid labour to run your estate." He looked pointedly at his host. "How much trust can you put in a man who works purely for wages?"

A flash of anger crossed Haveringham's face before his expression relaxed and his mouth curled into a vague smile. "A cynical and naïve statement from someone who has neither employed nor been employed. I do indeed rely on paid labour, but understand this, I suffer neither fools nor cheats, and any of my workers, no matter what his position, stupid enough to think he can have the better of me leaves here a poorer and wiser man."

Matthew listened intently, but he was not to be defeated. Having come this far he was determined to press home his argument. "I'm sure you have a very loyal lot of workers," he began, trying hard not to sound patronising, "but you can never be entirely certain. I am a good farmer, anyone who knows me will say as much. In exchange for accepting my offer I will work for you, be your eyes and ears, report anything that requires your attention. In short, sir, I will be the son you never had, and in return you pay me a small wage and a rent for the use of my land."

Haveringham's expression was a strange mix of astonishment and indignation. "Don't you mean my land, lad? Pay a rent for land that has already cost me four thousand guineas?" He struck the table again, more violently this time. "It strikes me that you're no better than those you seek to protect me from. Perhaps we should end this meeting now before one of us says something we may regret."

He made to get up from the table, but Matthew reached across and clutched at his arm. "I'm sorry you took it that way, I meant no offence, but I'm not good with words." As Haveringham glared at him he quickly let go of the arm. "You do agree that I should be entitled to some recompense and the rent would be just that. The wages I leave up to you." He took a deep breath. "Looking to the future, perhaps you would give me the opportunity to take over the estate in the event of your death. That way at least you would be assured that everything you have worked for will pass into good hands."

For several seconds Haveringham appeared to be struck dumb, staring straight ahead, although not focusing on anything in particular. For Matthew the silence was agonising and interminable, not knowing what his host was thinking, while fearing the worst. He wanted to speak, to explain himself, to salvage the disaster he had created, but the words were lost to him.

Then, quite suddenly and unexpectedly Haveringham began to chuckle. It began as a gurgling in his throat before slowly developing into a full belly laugh which seemed to run out of control.

"Well, lad," he breathed when he was finally able to rein in his hilarity, "as you reminded me, I have no son and heir, but should I have then I would hope he was blessed with your audacity and ingenuity. It's a great shame your mother and me were never wed." His face took on a thoughtful, more serious expression. "You must have known when you came here this morning that there was little chance of my listening to such a proposal, let alone agreeing to such a thing. But you had the courage to persevere, and I admire you for that. From one with no business experience, it was certainly an imaginative notion, preposterous even."

Matthew stared blandly across at him with no understanding of whether he had been taken seriously, or simply ridiculed. Either way, sense dictated that he should say nothing.

"And what do your brothers have to say about all this?" asked Haveringham, still somewhat bemused.

"They don't know I'm here," he admitted cautiously. "But I can't see them having any objection to any deal that would give them their money. After all, that's all they want from this."

"A reasonable assumption, under the circumstance." Haveringham leaned back in his chair, his chin resting on his chest and his hands clasped together as if in prayer. Every now and then he would raise his eyes to study Matthew across the table. "You know, lad, I'll be damned if I'm not in danger of losing my faculties just for giving the idea one second of consideration, yet here I am doing just that."

Matthew's heart jumped and his pulse began to race. He hardly dared ask the question. "So, you accept my proposal?"

Haveringham held up his hand. "That's not what I said, lad, and it is certainly not what I meant." He pushed his chair back and got up from the table. "Come with me, I want to show you something."

Matthew followed him out into the conservatory where the smell of vegetation was almost overwhelming in the warm, damp air. He looked around at the vast array of strange and exotic plants that filled the room with their profuse foliage and colourful, pungent blooms. Yet, while he found them fascinating, his mind was still engaged on more important thoughts.

"Beautiful, aren't they," said Haveringham proudly, casting his hand around the conservatory. "Some of these specimens can be found nowhere else in England other than the hothouses of Kew Gardens. What do you think?"

"Yes, very beautiful, but …"

"They thrive here in an alien environment, in an artificial atmosphere." He looked hard at Matthew. "Could you do the same?"

The question had taken Matthew completely off guard and he found himself back on the defensive. "I'm sorry, sir, I don't think I understand."

"I'm sure you don't, lad." He turned to gaze out of the window. "These plants thrive here because we have created the right conditions for them to do so. If I agreed to your proposal, you would be leaving the safe, natural environment of your small farm, which is all you have ever known, and embarking on a life the complexities of which you have no comprehension. The difference between you and my plants is that I cannot, and would not, change the climate of my estate to suit you. You are the one who would have to adapt if you were to survive here. I doubt that is something you are capable of."

Matthew considered the question, and his reply very carefully, his whole future hinged on giving the right answer. He ran his hand over the fleshy leaves of one of the plants. "I'm not one of these plants, Mr Haveringham," he said after some consideration, "but I do have passion, and a mind of my own. I love farming, and even though it would be easier for me to take your money and go off to enjoy myself, I am prepared to do whatever is necessary to keep hold of my land. What greater incentive is there for someone like me than to try and make something of my life by doing what I love?"

Haveringham turned away from the window, a glint of admiration in his steely eyes. "An impressive answer, and you speak with some conviction. You certainly have farming in your blood. I can see that." His round face creased into a frown. "But is that enough to give loyalty to a man who only yesterday you were calling a cheat?"

Haveringham was toying with him, Matthew knew that, but this was no game for him, it was his life that was being played with, yet he held his temper in check. "I believe I expressed my feelings as I felt them at the time. I'm used to speaking my mind and I make no apologies for that. But I am prepared to be proved wrong, and at the same time prove my worth to you, and this estate."

"How, by my accepting your offer?" He smiled. "You almost have me believing you, lad."

Matthew returned the smile. "Is it necessary for us to like each other to be good partners? Perhaps a little distrust between us would keep us both on our toes."

Haveringham laughed loudly and clapped Matthew on the back. "You know, I think you would have made an admirable son."

With the suspense of not knowing even more unpalatable than receiving the wrong answer Matthew could no longer refrain from asking the question. "So, we have a deal then?"

Returning his gaze to the landscaped gardens that fell away from the back of the house to the rolling pastureland beyond, Haveringham's expression gave little away. "You ask a lot of me, lad, and offer very little in return. I have never had to share anything in my life, except with my dear wife, and she never asked as much of me as you are doing now." He turned back to face him. "But, although you ask for much, it is no more than I would have given my own son. Come back

47

in two days with your brothers and I will give you my answer, but do not assume it is the one you wish to hear." He returned his gaze to the gardens. The meeting was over.

John looked pale and delicate as he made his way unsteadily down the stairs, causing Paul to give him a mocking grin, having now fully recovered from his own fragile condition. It was now late in the morning, and after returning from his ride up to the coppice Paul had gone through the motions of carrying out a few chores around the yard before returning to the house to await his missing brother.

"Would you like some breakfast, little brother?" he asked as John sat down heavily at the table. "Although it is nearly afternoon."

John shook his head tentatively as he supported it between his hands. He looked up at his brother through bloodshot eyes. "Shouldn't you be working? Matt won't be too pleased if he comes back and finds us both just sitting here. How was he this morning?"

Paul raised his eyebrows and shrugged his shoulders. "I don't know, I haven't seen him. He was gone by the time I came down, and I haven't seen anything of him since."

"He's probably off sulking somewhere." John struggled to his feet and went over to the sink where he threw some water into his face. "What happened last night? I don't remember much after the meal was over. Did Mr Haveringham agree to buy the farm?"

"In a manner of speaking," replied Paul with a sigh. He went on to tell his brother of the offer and Matthew's response.

"Then we had best get to work," said John, drying his face on the towel. "He's not going to be in the best of moods as it is. No need to make things worse."

"He has no choice, not if the two of us both agree to accept the offer," said Paul determinedly. "I feel bad for him, but this is our life too and we have every right to do with it as we wish. If we don't do this now, we'll regret it for the rest of our lives, and come to despise him for it."

"I just wish it didn't have to be like this." His attention was drawn to the sound of footsteps out in the yard. "Here he comes now, still in his best clothes."

Paul joined his brother at the window. "Where the hell has he been dressed like that?"

There was an atmosphere of curious anticipation in the kitchen as the door opened and Matthew marched in. Instead of the expected black mood he appeared almost cheerful beneath the flushed breathlessness.

He smirked as he took in the cautious expressions on the faces of his two brothers. "What's the matter, been worried about me? Well, as you can see, there's no need, I'm quite well." He jerked his head at John. "A lot better than him by the looks of it."

"You were out early this morning," remarked Paul, trying to sound unconcerned. "I went looking for you, but it seems you didn't want to be found."

"Why, was there something you needed me for?" he asked sarcastically, peering into the pot of Mrs Caldicot's congealed stew. "That looks appetising."

"Don't be flippant, Matt, you know damn well we have to discuss Mr Haveringham's offer," said Paul angrily.

"Discuss it! I'm sure the two of you have already discussed it," he snapped back. "If you're waiting for me to agree then you'll have a long wait."

"We haven't even talked about it yet," said Paul defensively. "But yes, I am prepared to accept, providing John here is of the same mind." He looked to his young brother for agreement.

John shrugged negatively before nodding his head. "The money's not so important to me. I won't have much need of it in the army. But as we both have a mind to leave the farm, I just want this settled without any more fighting between us."

"Well, there you are then," said Matthew, looking directly at Paul. "You have your answer." He walked slowly towards the stairs before stopping and turning towards them, a smug expression of his face. "Enjoy your little victory, but before you start celebrating there's something you ought to know." He grinned. "You wondered where I went this morning, well, it was to see Haveringham and I made him a proposal of my own."

Paul exchanged an anxious glance with John. "A proposal! What kind of proposal?"

"Oh, don't worry, you'll still get your money. But I get something out of it as well." He watched their faces, savouring the moment. "You know what they say about the early bird."

Paul marched over and grabbed him by the arm. "You had no right making deals with him behind our backs. You said yourself he can't be trusted."

"He's agreed to nothing yet. We're to see him the day after tomorrow." He shook his arm free and started up the stairs. "Now I'm going to get changed. We still have a farm to run, for the next few days at least, but what happens after that is up to Haveringham."

The next two days passed slowly with an uneasy truce existing between the three of them. Matthew had said nothing more about his meeting with Haveringham, leaving the others to speculate on what had been said. While Matthew threw himself into the work with his customary enthusiasm Paul and John merely went through the motions, preoccupied as they were by their separate ambitions.

If the day of their mother's funeral had been suitably marked by the bleak weather, then the day appointed for the meeting with Haveringham dawned clear and bright. An omen of success? If that was Matthew's view then it was not something he cared to share with his brothers. He appeared sullen and agitated with the smug confidence of a few days earlier having dissipated somewhat. He was anxious to be on his way to Millwood House.

"Eleven o'clock you said," Paul pointed out as they sat down to breakfast. "We've plenty of time yet."

"I'm not hungry, I'll harness up the gig," responded Matthew, unable to settle. "We'd best not be late. We don't want to ruin our chances."

"Your chances, Matt," Paul reminded him as his brother got up to leave. "We've already made our decision."

During the whole journey to Millwood House, Matthew sat in brooding silence while the other two made idle conversation between themselves on subjects entirely unrelated to the forthcoming meeting. Other than the successful sale of the farm at the agreed price little else mattered to Paul and John, and Matthew's private arrangement would remain his own affair.

At the house they were shown straight through to the library. A fire had been lit and in front of it stood Haveringham and another gentleman. In contrast to their host's portly figure the other man was tall and thin, dressed in a black suit and with long black hair that framed a narrow, sour looking face. A large hook nose and small piercing eyes completed his appearance, giving him the look of an undertaker.

The two men were drawing on fat cigars and a halo of blue, aromatic smoke hung above their heads. Haveringham beckoned to the brothers as they were shown in.

"Gentlemen, do come in," he said in a tone that persuaded Matthew into an air of optimism. He waved his hand towards some wing backed chairs that had been arranged in an arc in front of a large leather topped deck. "Please sit." A stream of smoke followed him around the desk and he sat down in a deep black leather chair. He opened a box and held it out to them. "A cigar, gentlemen?"

In unison they all shook their heads. Paul and Matthew had both tried smoking, but gave up when the experience made them feel sick, and it was time now to keep a clear head. John had never tried and felt it wiser not to start.

"Well then," Haveringham continued, "let me introduce you to Mr Miles Fennymore, my very good friend and lawyer."

The man gave them a curt nod of acknowledgement, but made no further effort to ingratiate himself. He took up a position by the side of the desk from where he could address both his client and the three brothers.

From behind his desk Haveringham appeared a little bemused. "I have to say, gentlemen, that this is a most extraordinary occasion for me." He patted the top of his desk thoughtfully. "So much so I hardly know where to begin. Young Matthew here," he gestured for the benefit of his lawyer, "has presented me with something of a dilemma. He has made me an audacious, and some might say ill conceived, proposal that should have been dismissed out of hand, yet it amused me enough to discuss it with Mr Fennymore." He glanced up at the emotionless features beside him and got a dismissive response. "I have to say he was less than enthusiastic, but nevertheless I brought him here to clarify our various legal positions."

As he paused Paul got to his feet, feeling it proper to do so. "Before you go any further, Mr Haveringham, you have to know that my young brother and I know nothing of any private arrangements Matthew may have made with you." He glared down at his brother. "If there is any question of avoiding the sale of our farm then it would be as well to end the meeting now."

Haveringham held up a placating hand. "I believe, Master Paul, that provided you and your brother receive a fair price for your share of the farm Matthew can do as he wishes with his share?"

Paul looked questioningly at Matthew who sat with a self-satisfied grin. "To some extent yes, but since the death of our parents I feel a certain responsibility towards both my brothers and I wouldn't want to see them disadvantaged."

"Oh, don't worry, brother," retorted Matthew, "I'm not the one being disadvantaged."

"Let's not argue, gentlemen." Haveringham flapped a hand at the lawyer. "Why don't we let Mr Fennymore explain matters, after all that's what I pay him good money for."

Fennymore cleared his throat as he unfolded the sheaf of papers he had been clutching in his bony hand. With a sniff and a quick glance at his client he began. "Without wishing to exceed my legal authority I should like to say that, having looked after Mr Haveringham's affairs for a number years, I have certain reservations which I have expressed to my client here." He gave Haveringham another imploring glance, but the look he received in return persuaded him to continue. "I have here two quite separated contracts. The first is quite straightforward and confines itself purely to the sale of the property known as Hibberd's Farm, currently owned by," he studied the papers, "Paul, Matthew and John Pearson."

Paul and John exchanged cautionary glances while Matthew continued to grin contentedly.

In the same monotone voice the lawyer carried on. "A two thirds share of this afore mentioned property will be purchased by my client for the sum of four thousand guineas, the remaining third share to be retained by Matthew Pearson under the terms of a separate agreement. Am I correct so far, Rufus?"

Haveringham nodded impatiently. "Yes Miles, yes. Now do get on with it, man."

"Yes, of course." He refreshed his memory from the papers before continuing. "Now, the second agreement is rather more complex and deals exclusively with my client and Mr … er… Matthew Pearson. As already stated, the property known as Hibberd's Farm will now be jointly owned by these two parties in the proportion of two thirds and one third in favour of my client." He held up some of the papers. "I have here the various contracts to be signed by the relevant parties, but I'm sure my client will have no objection should you wish your own lawyer to peruse them first." Haveringham nodded his assent.

Matthew was on his feet, his eyes fixed questioningly on Haveringham. "But what about the rest of our agreement?"

Fennymore looked for instruction, but Haveringham preferred to answer for himself. "We have no agreement, yet," he said curtly. "What you mean surely is what about the rest of your demands. I did warn you not to expect too much." He nodded for the lawyer to continue.

"In return for the use of the whole of Hibberd's Farm, and for as yet unspecified duties to be agreed at a later date, my client will pay Matthew Pearson an annual remuneration of one hundred guineas."

Unable to conceal his admiration Paul clapped his brother on the back, shaking his head in disbelief. "It's a good deal you've got for yourself, Matt. Is this what you want?"

"It's just the beginning," he replied, his pale eyes reflecting a deeply buried ambition.

"If I might continue," interrupted the lawyer with undisguised annoyance. "In the unfortunate death of my client his holding in Hibberd's Farm will be offered back to Matthew Pearson at the original purchase price of four thousand guineas, such money going to the deceased estate. Should Mr Pearson be unable to meet this condition then the whole of the farm will be absorbed into my client's estate and Mr Pearson will receive a payment equivalent to his holding, two thousand guineas."

Fennymore had barely finished speaking when Matthew was on his feet again, his cap wrung tightly in his hands. "But what about the estate, what happens to that? I thought I would be given the chance to …"

"Don't be so naïve, lad," snapped Haveringham, thumping the desk top with his fist. "What happens to my estate is my affair and of no concern to you. Have you any idea how much all this is worth? More money than you could raise in two lifetimes on what I will be paying you. Just pray that I live to a ripe old age so that you can at least save enough to buy back your land. You'll be no worse off than you are now and, perhaps, a good deal wiser." He looked hard across his desk at all three brothers. "Now, you've all heard my various offers, so it's up to you to make up your minds whether you accept or not, but as far as I am concerned there is no need for any further discussion."

Paul looked at John who, after a moment of thought, nodded.

"As far as the two of us are concerned, Mr Haveringham, it's a good offer, under the circumstances, but our acceptance is conditional of Matthew doing the same. If he is happy to sign, so will we."

"I don't suppose I have much choice if I'm to stand any chance of keeping the farm. I suppose it's a fair enough deal," he said grudgingly, shaking the creases from his cap. "I wish you a long and healthy life, Mr Haveringham, but should you die tomorrow I will find some way to keep my farm."

Haveringham came around from behind the desk, smiling warmly, his hand extended to the brothers. "My farm now, lad, my farm now."

Chapter Four

In the weeks following that eventful meeting at Millwood House there had been much frantic activity as Paul and John began the necessary arrangements for their new and differing futures. Some men had been sent over from the estate to help Matthew, who appeared unconcerned by his brothers' imminent departure from his life. He had thrown himself into the work with a renewed vigour, leaving the house before dawn and only returning well after dusk.

"Take care, Matt," Paul had warned him one evening when he returned to the house close to exhaustion, "you'll end up as our father did. Don't forget, you have a partner now."

"It's just a piece of paper," he replied conceitedly. "This will always be my farm."

"A piece of paper and six thousand guineas. Just have a care, that's all I'm saying."

Paul had words of advice for his young brother too. A few days before John was due to report to the barracks in Northampton, and he prepared to leave for London to make arrangements for his voyage to South Africa, he took John to one side.

"I don't know what father would have said, but I'm sure mother would have been proud of you," he told him. "You've no need to worry about me or Matt, so just look after yourself and be the man I know you to be. There's enough danger in the profession you've chosen for yourself without attracting more. Choose your friends carefully and don't go looking for trouble, but if it finds you face up to it bravely, and however it turns out you'll always be the winner." He took John in his arms and pulled him to his breast. "And stay clear of women, especially those who loiter around the barrack gates on pay day."

With both of them close to tears John forced a smile, raising himself up to his full height. "I know how to look after myself well enough," he said with self-assured confidence. "It's you I'm worried about. There's talk of another war with the Boers."

Paul smiled back. "Just rumours, idle gossip to stop more like me from going out there. They want to keep all that gold and diamonds for themselves. I'm sure it won't come to anything."

With a few more tears and words of fatherly wisdom Paul said a final farewell to his young brother and set off for London to book his passage to Cape Town.

There was no such sorrow for Matthew at the departure of his brothers, he remained entirely sanguine as he watched each of them leave. For him life was complete without going anywhere beyond the borders of his beloved farm, and as long as Haveringham demanded nothing from him he was content to carry on as before. He was beginning to believe that the man had forgotten about him, but it took only a few more days for that notion to be proved wrong.

It was a little after dawn when a lad about John's age came trotting into the yard on a grey mare that looked too big for the rider to handle.

"What do you want?" Matthew asked curtly.

"Master wants you," was his equally curt reply. "I was sent to fetch you."

"Well, there's no need to wait," Matthew snapped impatiently. "I know the way up to the house. I'll be there presently."

"Not going to the house," returned the lad, showing little of the respect to which Matthew felt entitled. "Have to fetch you straight away, that's what he said."

Being summoned in such a way didn't sit well with Matthew, but he said nothing as he strode away to the shed.

Ignoring the disdainful look that Sally gave him he saddled the more spirited Roscoe, a black roan that was John's favourite.

They left the farm and took a track that was unfamiliar to Matthew. It threaded its way through the arable part of the estate some distance from Millwood House. It gave him some insight into the extent of Haveringham's holdings, but rather than causing him apprehension in what he had become involved it only served to further whet his ambitions.

After nearly an hour they stopped outside a large barn, brick built around an oak frame. The boy pointed to the doors at the end of the building.

"In there," he said, before pulling his horse's head around and galloping away.

So, this is to be my introduction to my new duties, thought Matthew. It was not what he had expected, but then he had no real conception of what to expect from a man like Haveringham. He climbed down, absently patted the horse on the neck before walking slowly towards the doors.

If he was expecting to find Haveringham alone inside he was to be disappointed. There were four of five men in the barn, and as he entered all eyes turned on him. He walked uncertainly over towards them while his benefactor detached himself from the group and came across to meet him with a look that appeared far from welcoming.

As he ignored Matthew's outstretched hand, Haveringham gestured to the others to carry on, and as they sullenly sauntered past him they kept the newcomer in their gaze.

"Well lad, the honeymoon's over," said Haveringham unceremoniously. "It's time to start earning the money I'm paying you."

"I didn't wish to trouble you, sir. I've been waiting for you to explain my duties," he replied contritely, sweeping his arm around the expanse of the barn. "I just never thought it would be here. If I've caused you any offence then I'm truly sorry."

Haveringham gave a snort. "You assumed it would be over brandy in the library, no doubt," he said with more than a touch of sarcasm. "You've set your sights high, my boy. Too high for your own good, I'm thinking. You see yourself as master one day, but I'm wondering if you have the stomach for such haughty ambitions."

"If it's hard work and responsibility you're meaning then you'll not find me wanting," said Matthew defensively. "You'll find me equal to any task you set me, more than any other man in your pay."

Haveringham smiled grimly. "And you'll be given every chance to prove it, believe me."

A commotion from outside the barn drew their attention, and when Haveringham marched over to the door Matthew followed. The men that had been in the barn a few moments earlier were there and had been joined by another, a tall, powerfully built man who stood passively in the centre of the group, his head dropping with shame at the sight of Haveringham.

"All set, sir," said one of the men who appeared to be in charge of the others. "He'll not be giving us any trouble."

"All right, Ned, bring him inside and let us be getting on with it. I'm sure we have all got things we would rather be doing." Haveringham led the way back into the barn while Matthew could only look on and wonder.

As the whole group moved to the back of the barn Matthew took an interest in the man called Ned. He had an air of authority about him that seemed natural, someone who commanded respect. He was also better dressed than the other men in a suit to brown treed, a belted jacket, and trousers that were bound below the knee in leather gaiters. Matthew judged his age to be approaching sixty years, although his eyes were lively and his movements brisk.

The group had stopped between two stout oak pillars that supported the roof trusses.

"Get your shirt off, Giddins," said Ned quietly, with a sympathetic tone to his voice. "We don't want to be spoiling that now, do we?"

As Giddins meekly did as he was told it became clear to Matthew that he had been summoned to the barn to witness a punishment, to view the harsher side of estate life. So, this is what Haveringham meant by having stomach for the work, he thought. Although the idea was not totally unpalatable to him, what he did find unnatural was the way in which the man seemed to be submitting to his punishment without so much as a struggle, or word of protest as his wrists were bound to the pillars.

When everything was set Haveringham came over to where Matthew was standing. "Giddins here is a stockman of mine, been with me ever since he was a lad. Isn't that right Giddins?"

"Sir."

"Would you say in all those years I've been a fair man?"

"I would that, sir, very fair," replied the poor wretch with absolute conviction.

"Yet despite that you saw fit to cheat me, did you not?"

"I did indeed, sir, and I'm truly sorry for it. Me little lad was taken bad see and we needed medicine. I didn't mean you no disrespect, sir, 'onest I didn't."

"I know that, Giddins, but we can't allow it to go unpunished now, can we? If I did, then less honourable men than you will think they can take advantage of my generous nature."

"Don't worry yerself about it, sir, I understands that."

While the conversation had been taking place the man Ned had produced a short handled leather whip from a canvas bag that was hanging from one of the

58

pillars. Matthew felt the hairs on the back of his neck prickle in anticipation as the thong cracked from a few practise flicks.

"I'll be getting on with it then, sir," said Ned with little outward emotion before turning to the unfortunate Giddins. "Will you have the cloth to bite on?"

Giddins shook his head while shuffling his feet to brace himself for the flogging. "I'll not be needing that. I'll not disgrace meself in front of the master."

Ned took a step back, measuring his reach. "Ten it is then, sir?"

Haveringham nodded. "It is, but not from you, Ned." He turned to Matthew with hard, penetrating eyes. "Our young friend here is keen to prove his worth, and I should be failing in my duty if I denied him that opportunity."

Even before the words had time to register Matthew felt the blood drain from his face, and he knew the others had seen it too. As Ned held out the whip to him, he shrank away, his legs struggling to support him. To be brought here under such circumstances was a necessary, yet unsavoury, part of his training, but to actually administer the flogging was something he was unprepared for.

"You can't ask me to do that," he shouted hoarsely. His mouth was dry and his hand trembled. "I don't even know what it is he's supposed to have done."

"It doesn't matter, it's enough for you to know that he's done it," said Haveringham coldly. "If you're not the man for this work then you're not the man I can make use of. Like I said, lad, the honeymoon is over."

Matthew could feel the other men watching him closely, judgementally, particularly Ned, and he knew immediately if he was to have any future at all in managing the estate then much would depend on his actions in the next few minutes. If he was to command any respect, refusing the order was not an option. Haveringham knew it too, and it was easy to see that he relished the dilemma of his young protégé. It had been a carefully contrived plan with one man's misfortune leading to the downfall of another, with enough witnesses to ensure that the matter would be well reported.

Ned's look was scornful as he waited for Matthew to take the whip. He knew something of an arrangement being made between his master and this young upstart, and there was no pretending it did not give him cause for concern. He had been manager on the estate for many years, and anything that was likely to affect his authority was bound to leave a sour taste.

"The lad has no heart for it, sir," he sneered, goading Matthew into taking the whip, while hoping he would refuse. "Shall I see to it?"

"I think you're right, Ned, we can't be wasting any more time here." Haveringham gave Matthew a look of contempt, tinged with disappointment. "Go back to your farm, lad, I've no further use of you here."

Struggling to conceal his humiliation Matthew fixed Ned with a cold stare. "Give me the whip, and stand out of my way." He walked around to face Giddins, who had remained impassive throughout the exchange. "I don't know you, or what you've done to deserve this, but I'm going to beat you for it anyway. I bear you no malice, believe me."

"Then best get to it young sir, there's other things I'd rather be doin' meself."

Matthew breathed deeply, but as he tried for a practice swing the strength in his right arm seemed to desert him. He breathed again, composing himself for the greatest trial of his life.

He braced himself and the first stroke was a half-hearted effort that caught Giddins on the lower back, his wide leather belt taking most of the punishment.

Haveringham shook head in dismay. "With a will, lad, with a will," he urged impatiently, "otherwise Giddins here won't know when you've started, nor when you've finished."

There was a ripple of sniggering amongst the other men, forcing Matthew to take a tighter grip of both the handle of the whip, and his emotions. The fine leather thong snaked out again in a sickening crack, catching Giddins across his exposed shoulder blade, making him wince with pain.

Two, thought Matthew, as a few beads of sweat broke out on his forehead and he felt the rush of adrenaline through his body.

The third drew a scarlet weal across the middle of the back and Matthew set his teeth before the fourth found the same mark. The poor man arched his back as the pain tore through his spine.

Matthew sucked in air and laid down a fifth with even greater vigour, taking a perverse satisfaction from the thin trickle of blood that broke through the skin. The sixth one now, and it was getting easier, he couldn't understand his previous reluctance. The seventh brought the first muted cry of pain from the victim and a small smile of pleasure from his tormentor.

The eighth and ninth drew a steadier flow of blood, and mumbled protests from some of the spectators who looked to Ned for support.

"He'll skin him, sir," intervened the manager. "He'll not be fit for work."

"Ease up, lad," ordered Haveringham, but not before Matthew brought the whip down a final time with even greater ferocity. "That's enough."

Two men were already freeing Giddins from his bonds and supporting him as he sunk to his knees. Matthew looked on through glazed eyes, detached from his surroundings, as if in a dream. His body was drenched in sweat and his right arm hung limply at his side as he let the whip drop to the floor. At that moment he appeared incapable of making any judgement on himself.

As Giddins was helped from the barn Haveringham took a coin from his pocket and pressed it into Ned's hand. "See to it that his wife gets that," he said quietly. "Tell her I wish her boy a speedy recovery."

When they were alone, he gave Matthew a long, hard look that conveyed little of what he felt. "Come with me up to the house, lad, there are things we need to talk about."

The reality of what he had done struck Matthew with a suddenness that brought him back to his senses, yet he had no feeling of shame or pity. Is that what Haveringham expected of him?

In the library of Millwood House Haveringham poured two glasses of whisky and offered one to Matthew. "It may not be what you are used to at this time of day, but I suggest you drink it." It was no polite invitation to a sociable drink, it was a firm order.

It wasn't what Matthew was used to at any time of day, but he accepted it gratefully. "Will he be all right, that man Giddins?" he asked after a few hasty gulps. "Was I too harsh with him?"

"Taste the Pierian spring, did you lad?" Haveringham asked caustically.

"What?"

"A little power, lad, like learning, can be a dangerous thing. You were given a little power this morning and you allowed it to take possession of you." He savoured his drink as he studied Matthew closely, seeking some sign of understanding. "It's not enough to have power," he went on, "you need to know how to use it and, more importantly, how to control it, or it will control you. In these things you have much to learn."

"But I was only doing your bidding," protested Matthew vociferously. "He deserved it, you said …"

"Yes, he did deserve it," interrupted Haveringham harshly, "and Giddins knew that. Why do you think he accepted his punishment without complaint?" He sipped his whisky reflectively. "No one should take any pleasure from punishing a man like Giddins."

"Then why do it, why beat him like that?" challenged Matthew defiantly. "If he's cheated you then why not let the law deal with him?"

Haveringham's response was to thump the top of the desk violently with his fist. "You impudent young whelp," he shouted, "how dare you question my actions when you know nothing of the reasons behind them." To calm himself he finished his drink in a single swallow. "Sit down," he breathed. "Sit down, damn you."

Unsure of what he had done Matthew meekly did as he was told. "I'm sorry."

Haveringham paced the room for a while until he felt able to continue. "If you learned anything from what happened this morning then the suffering you caused Giddins may have served some purpose." He poured himself another drink and perched on the edge of the desk facing Matthew. "Let me tell you what he did to deserve the beating you gave him. One of my herd got taken sick and died. As was his duty Giddins called in the knacker to take away the carcass and he pocketed the few shillings he got for it. I know on some farms that's a stockman's perk, but not here, and Giddins knows that. You heard the reason he needed the money and no one can blame him for thinking of his boy, but if I allowed it to go unpunished then every man working for me would see it as a weakness and take advantage." He took a long, thoughtful swallow. "You questioned why I didn't let the law deal with him. Well, what do you think would happen to him if I had? Like as not he would have received a fine he couldn't pay, so he would go to prison. Then he would lose his job and his wife and child would be forced out of the tied cottage they occupy. Would you have all that happen to him just for the sake of a few shillings? Ask Giddins what his choice would be."

"I see that, but I was only carrying out your orders," pleaded Matthew innocently. "It was either me or that man Ned. I can't see the difference."

"No, you can't, and that is what concerns me. It shows your ignorance. The difference was the state of Giddins' back when you had finished. For Ned Stiles it would have been a distasteful part of his duties, but it was plain to me that you were beginning to enjoy it. It's a great responsibility having power over other men, and how to use it." He drummed his fingers thoughtfully on the top of the desk. "I noticed something between you and Ned this morning that didn't sit right. I can understand that he may see you as a threat to his position. But what of you, why should you have a dislike of him?"

Matthew gave him a puzzled look. "But I don't know the man. Why should you say I dislike him?"

"Why indeed! But the signs were plain enough. You could learn a lot from Ned Stiles, that's why I expect the two of you to work together. He's not a young man anymore, and when the time comes, I shall need a good replacement for him." He took some pleasure in the questioning look that crossed Matthew's face, knowing the boy would have little enthusiasm for the arrangement. "I take it you have no objection?"

Matthew turned away, hoping to hide his disappointment. "If that is what you want. If I still need to prove myself I will, but I don't think there's as much Stiles can teach me about farming as you seem to think."

Haveringham let out a hoarse laugh. "You're an arrogant young man Matthew Pearson, and you'll not learn anything until you can accept how little you know. Have I not already said that for one so young you have an excellent understanding of farming, but that is not enough. If you have any aspirations to run this estate then you will need to learn a good deal more. You can beat a cow with a stick or twist the ring in a bull's nose to bend it to your will, but to lead men you need first to earn their respect. The men respect Ned Stiles. They may not necessarily like him, but they respect him because he is fair. Can you earn their respect? I have grave doubts, so prove me wrong."

"So that's what you want of me, to be like Stiles?" questioned Matthew.

"The only person on this estate more important than Stiles is myself. Is there any greater ambition for a young man like you than that?" He paused to consider his next statement. "I have another, more personal, reason for wishing you to do well, but I'll say nothing of that until I have the measure of you."

Matthew was intrigued, although he knew better than to press the matter further. "Perhaps I do have much to learn," he said humbly. "For so long it has just been me and my brothers, so I've little experience in the giving or taking of orders."

"Then learn to do both with equal humility and you'll have the makings of a good man and respected master." It was not intended as a patronising remark, just an honest belief that he would be proved right. He gave a wry smile. "The two men Ned sent over to help you will let him know if they have any complaints. I'll give you another day or two and then you'll be told what's needed of you."

It had been a morning of stark discovery for Matthew, and as he left the house, he realised there was much he had discovered about himself, but not enough about the man he was set to replace. What was certain in his mind, though, was a firm resolve to achieve what was expected of him in as little time as possible. For Ned Stiles, his days of usefulness were numbered.

Chapter Five

Paul hated London. It was his first visit and the noise and pervading smells assaulted his rural senses. When he tried to walk the pavements, he was jostled into shop doorways by a constant stream of mankind who, it seemed, all wished to go in the opposite direction than himself. And walking in the road was no better, risking his life amongst the frenetic flow of traffic. How so much humanity could share so little air confounded his understanding.

He was pleased that he had completed his business within a few days and was keen to escape the claustrophobic atmosphere of the metropolis. Unexpectedly he had been able to book passage on a vessel leaving at the end of the following week and had just ten days to make all his final arrangements. That all the years of dreaming and planning had finally become a reality struck home only when he tucked the ticket carefully into his jacket pocket and the booking clerk wished him safe passage. Now he stood on the platform of the railway station debating the sanity of his ambitions.

It was the rare and exciting experience of having money in his pocket that had driven him to buy a first-class ticket for the journey back to Northampton, and once he had settled into his seat he unfolded a copy of 'The Times' he had bought outside the station. News from South Africa dominated the headlines and should have served as a warning that he was mistaken in the logic of investing his fortune in that country. Instead, he gave a resigned sigh, it was too late now to change his arrangements and, besides, it was probably only scare mongering.

With a loud hiss of steam, the train jerked and began to rattle its way out of the station. It had not cleared the platform when the carriage door opened and he was joined by two other passengers. One was a girl whose age Paul guessed at close to twenty. She was of rare beauty, elegantly, though not extravagantly, dressed, and when she sat down opposite him, she gave the slightest nod of acknowledgement. Her complexion was pale, but not pallid, and the hair that hung in long ringlets from beneath her bonnet was of dark auburn that reflected the sunlight flickering through the carriage window.

Her companion was a woman of advancing years, a governess, thought Paul, as he peered surreptitiously at them over the top of his newspaper. The woman had the sour, pinched face of someone who had dedicated her life to the detriment of others, and when Paul's attention to the girl became too apparent, she gave him a look that would have turned milk.

He took some pleasure from the fact that the girl appeared neither offended nor discouraged by their discreet exchange of glances, and it emboldened him to enquire, "are you travelling to Northampton by any chance, or going on to Birmingham?"

Before the girl could even think of replying the woman fixed him with her cold, piercing eyes and spoke through thin lips that barely moved. "I believe that is entirely our affair."

The girl lowered her eyes demurely, although her pale pink lips curled into a sly smile that suggested a sense of humour. Apart from a few more guarded glances in her direction Paul made no further attempt to communicate with her and contented himself with the knowledge that, given his imminent departure from the country, there could be no possible future in the acquaintance.

When the train pulled into Northampton station the girl was quickly ushered away by her travelling companion to an awaiting carriage, while Paul was left to hitch a ride on a tanners cart back to Weedon Bec.

As the cart bumped and jolted its way along the road. his thoughts switched between expectations for his new life and the girl he had just met on the train, the one giving rise to apprehension the other to regret. But, by the time the cart drew to a halt outside the Farrier's Inn he had reconciled himself to the fact that he would never see her again and she would only ever be a passing fancy.

He stood outside the public house that had been familiar to him since long before he had been old enough to take his first drink. He had attended the village school with the landlord's daughter, Jenny, and at the tender age of fourteen she had been his first real sweetheart. During the summer months, when work on the farm permitted, she had visited him, and in the evenings he would walk her home while there was still sufficient light to see their way. In the lengthening shadows they would stop and he would steal a sly, childish kiss, the dusk concealing his embarrassment. He remembered her as being more precocious than himself. She often took the lead in the development of their young relationship. She had been the first to offer up her lips for a tender kiss, and, on that most memorable of occasions, the one who took his hand and placed it on her small, firm breast. Had she not been sent away to service in Birmingham soon after that there was no doubt in Paul's mind that she would have been the first to offer him her complete body. He had long pondered what that may have led to. Marriage and children would certainly have changed his present circumstances.

Paul pushed open the door to the bar and stepped inside the dim interior. There were a few customers sitting at the tables that were sparsely placed around the room and he felt eyes following him as he walked over to the counter. He gave them a nod of acknowledgement, but they simply stared back at him.

The landlord turned to face his new customer. "Hello lad, not seen you in here for a while." Jack Conners greeted him cheerily and held out his hand. "Sorry to hear about your ma, a good woman she was. Been kept busy, I expect. A pint, is it?"

"Thanks Mr Conners. It's been a bad time, but we've come through it well enough." He took a coin from his pocket but the landlord waved it away.

"Well, if there's anything I can do for you or your brothers."

Paul gave him a nod of gratitude as he savoured his ale. Even the sound of a chair being scraped across the bare wooden floor failed to distract him from the first long swallow. From a table in the corner of the bar a man sauntered over, and it was only after he stood directly behind him did Paul become aware of his presence.

"One of them Pearson boys, ain't yer?" The man was a little shorter than Paul, and wiry. He shook Paul by the shoulder. "Well, ain't yer?"

Casually Paul turned to face him, noticing the look of menace in his eyes. He recognised him as being one of Haveringham's men. "You know I am, so why ask?"

The man took a step back to look Paul up and down. "A bit dandified fer a farm boy, ain't yer? You taking 'averingham's money as well?"

Paul gave him a quizzical look. "I don't see that it's any of your business. I'm just here for a quiet drink." He turned away and picked up his glass.

Behind him the man snorted derisively. "Too 'igh an' mighty I suppose to talk to the likes o' me?" He grabbed hold of Paul's arm and pulled him round.

Paul glared angrily at him. "I don't know what it is you want, but if you've got something to say spit it out and let me get on with my pint. I'm in no mood for any games."

"Games is it?" he sneered back, turning to his two mates still sitting at the table. "'ear that. Only games was it, that took the skin from the back of poor Joe Giddins not a day since. 'e ain't laughing, and that's a fact."

Paul's eyes narrowed into a frown. "I've no idea what you're talking about. I've been in London for the past few days." He threw an enquiring look at Jack Conners who had been following the exchange closely.

"It seems your brother took the whip to one of Haveringham's men. A bit too handy by all accounts." He turned to the man and his mates. "You heard what he said, he wasn't even here. It's nothing to do with him."

"That don't mean nothin' to me. As I sees, it a Pearson's a Pearson." There were some murmured words of agreement from the two men at the table, although they showed little interest in making themselves further involved. A stubby, black nailed finger prodded Paul in the chest. "Let's see 'ow much of a man you are wiv someone what's not tied up."

Still holding his drink, Paul shoved him away with his free hand. "I've told you, it's got nothing to do with me, so leave me alone."

"Or what," sneered the man, standing his ground as he looked to his mates for support. "You goin' to give me a beating too?"

He lunged at Paul who deftly stepped to one side and threw the remainder of his beer into the man's face. Regaining his balance, the farm worker wiped his face with the back of his hand and lunged at Paul, fists clenched. The other two men were on their feet, but before they made another move a warning from the landlord stopped them.

"That's enough, gentlemen," said Jack Conners in a controlled voice that still carried some menace. In his hand he held a large wooden spoke from a cart wheel. "Now, Harry, if you and the lad have anything to settle I suggest you take it out the back."

Paul straightened his jacket and glared back at the man shaping up to him. "That's fine with me, Mr Conners, for I'll not be accused of something I know nothing about."

Harry eyed him closely, paying particular attention to the younger man's height and muscular build. He sniffed loudly. "He's now't but a lad, so I'll leave him be this time." He glanced back as he slouched over to his mates. "But next time."

Paul put the empty glass on the counter. "Sorry about that Mr Conners. Do you know what it was about?"

The landlord shook his head. "Not much. Seems something went on up at the estate that involved your brother. That's all I know."

"Well, I'm off up to the farm now, so I'll find out soon enough. I don't suppose you have a horse I could hire for a day or so?"

Jack Conners grinned. "There's just the old bay mare out the back in the stables. She's not up to much nowadays, but she's yours for as long as you need her. You'll find tack out there too." Before Paul could thank him, Jack leaned across the counter and caught him by the arm. "Our Jenny's back, you know. She's upstairs now with her mother. I'm betting she'd love to see you again. I could give her a shout."

Paul felt an involuntary fluttering in his stomach. Was there still something there after all those years? "I'd love to see her," he said with an embarrassed grin. "Would it be all right if I called back later, only there are things I must do first?"

"Of course, I'll tell her to expect you, shall I?"

With a promise to return and a cursory glance at the three men still sitting at the table Paul left the inn.

As he rode the old mare slowly towards the farm Paul's brain tried to cope with a confusion of thoughts. So much had happened in that single day that it was impossible to devote his attention to anything with real clarity. It had begun well enough with the booking of his passage, before he was reminded of the prospect of war with the Boers. Then there had been the mysterious girl on the train, followed by a near brawl that somehow involved Matthew, and finally to find out that his first real love was back in the village. All this when he was about to leave the country. What was he leaving behind? And what was he travelling into."

He tried to coax a little more speed from the horse, but, like Sally, she seemed content to amble along at a steady walk which did little to alleviate Paul's mounting impatience.

It was early evening by the time he rode into the yard at the back of his old house, and he was about to dismount when a young lad appeared from one of the sheds pushing a loaded wheelbarrow. He looked shocked when he saw Paul and dropped the wheelbarrow.

"I'm working here for Master Matthew," he stuttered nervously, clearly feeling obliged to explain himself.

Paul shrugged as he looked down on the lad. "It's all right, it's got nothing to do with me, not now. I'm just looking for my brother, do you know where I can find him?"

The lad scratched his chin thoughtfully before pointing indiscriminately into the distance. "Last I knew he was bringing cows up from bottom meadow. Might find him down there."

Paul thanked him and pulled on the reins. At first the horse refused to move, having just caught the scent of fresh hay in the wheelbarrow, and Paul had to dig in his heels to persuade it otherwise.

A few minutes later he caught sight of his brother as he and another man were herding the cows out of the meadow and into the narrow track that led to the milking shed. With no way of reaching Matthew until all the cows were in the shed Paul waited at the end of the track and, as the last one disappeared inside, he urged his horse forward. Matthew barely gave him a glance and was about to follow the cows when Paul called to him.

"Hold up there, Matt, I need to speak with you."

Matthew looked over his shoulder and could barely contain a smile. "A fine looking mount you've got yourself there. Is this how you begin that grand life of yours, on a nag like that?"

"It suits me well enough," replied Paul dismissively. "How does your new life suit you?"

"Well enough too, but I don't suppose you're bothered about me anymore."

Paul dismounted and walked the horse over to where his brother stood by the entrance to the milking shed. "Oh, but I am, Matt, especially when your new life involves me."

Matthew's disinterested expression gave way to a look of mild curiosity. "How could anything I do now affect you. You're rid of the farm now, and it's well rid of you."

"I thought that too until a few hours ago." He went on to explain to Matthew what had happened at the Farrier's Inn, but if he was expecting an explanation when he had finished, he was to be disappointed. "Have you nothing to say about it?" he was obliged to ask.

"I was doing Haveringham's bidding," was all he would say, with no hint of sadness or regret in his voice. "It's what's expected of you when you manage an estate like that."

"It's not so much what you did, Matt, it was the way you did it. Surely this isn't what Haveringham wants from you. I know you're an ambitious man, but I never thought you cruel."

Matthew's manner was unrelenting. "I know what I want, and I'll let nothing stop me from getting it. Maybe I was a bit too hard on the man, but he won't forget about it in a hurry, and neither will the others. They'll all know who there're dealing with when I'm in charge."

Paul shook his head despairingly. "Is this what you've become already, Matt? If it is then I don't know you anymore. I've always thought Haveringham to be a decent man who won't want someone like you working for him. He'll see through you long before he gives you that sort of power." Any hope he had of departing on good terms with his brother was receding, so he decided to say nothing more on the subject. "I leave for Cape Town next week and God knows when we'll see each other again, but I wish you well and hope you get everything you deserve."

With no outward show of emotion Matthew held out his hand. "I expect we'll both get what we deserve, but I think only one of us will get what we want. Perhaps when we do meet again, we'll understand each other a little better."

Paul took the hand and shook it warmly. They should have embraced, but that closeness had been pushed aside by recent events, perhaps never to return. "I will be back, brother, with or without my fortune, but either way I'll be richer from the experience."

As they parted Paul looked back over his shoulder hoping for a wave of goodbye, but Matthew had already disappeared into the shed. For him the moment had been forgotten.

Paul went back up to the house to collect the last of his scant possessions. He had hoped to spend his final days in England at the farm, but felt it unwise to jeopardise the fragile peace with his brother by staying there. Instead, he would return to the village which now offered the additional attraction of the renewed acquaintance with Jenny Conners.

After taking everything he needed from his old room, he went through to his mother's bedroom and took a long, nostalgic look around. It struck him how little remained of her existence, and all that was left were the memories. Two photographs sat on the dressing table, one of his parents and one of the three brothers, both taken in happier times. Paul removed them from their frames and slipped them inside his bag, knowing that Matthew wouldn't even notice they had gone. He patted the pillow on the bed, remembering vividly the day she had died and the futility of her life. Would she really forgive him and John for trying to make something of theirs?

As he wandered slowly through the house each of the rooms offered up their own memories, each one causing Paul to sigh deeply. Tears welled up from within him and he prayed that he was not deceiving himself into believing that the future will bring him more contentment than the past. With one last look around he finally closed the door on that episode of his life.

The bar at the Farrier's Inn was empty of customers when Paul entered and he looked around cautiously. He was anxious not to repeat the earlier confrontation, as much for the sake of the landlord as for himself. Having stabled the horse, he had come in through the back, taking Jack Conners by surprise. The landlord was further bemused by the sight of the large portmanteaux Paul was carrying.

He nodded towards the bag. "If I didn't know better, I would say you was off somewhere, lad," he said as his expression changed to one of mild concern. "Not before you see our Jenny, I hope. She got quite excited when I told her you were coming back to see her." He jerked his head up at the ceiling. "She's up there now prettying herself up, I shouldn't wonder.

"I'm looking forward to seeing her too. I just hope she's not too disappointed." He sat down on a stool and dropped the bag on the floor. "As for this, yes, I am off somewhere. Next week, in fact."

He pulled the stool closer to the counter and set about giving the landlord a potted account of everything that had happened since the death of his mother. In a way it was a relief to unburden himself to someone prepared to listen without making any judgements.

Jack Conners listened intently, his expression changing to match each unfolding event. "That's quite a story, lad, and I'm sorry to hear you're leaving." He poured Paul a beer. "I don't doubt Jenny's going to be a bit upset too when she finds out." He shook his head as he tried to imagine her disappointment.

"I was hoping I could stay here for a few days before I leave," said Paul nervously. "If you have a room, that is? Apart from the farm, I can't think of anywhere else I'd rather spend my last days in this country."

"You make it sound like you're never coming back," said Jack sternly, before his lips parted in a broad smile. "Of course, you should stay here. I know Jenny will be pleased."

72

Paul sipped pensively on his drink. "How is she, Mr Conners? I thought she would have been married by now."

Jack stroked the stubble on his chin and stared wistfully at nothing in particular. "Our Jenny, no. Oh, there was a lad a few years back. A soldier, he was, promised her everything and then went off somewhere or other and wasn't heard of again. She grieved for a while and then just got on with things. That's our Jenny." He reached across the counter and placed a fatherly hand on Paul's shoulder. "Saving herself for you, maybe."

"I'll thank you to keep such silly notions to yourself, father." The voice came from a gloomy corner behind the counter, near the bottom of the stairs. "And you. Paul Pearson, you're no better than that fool of a father of mine, sitting down here gossiping and supping ale while I'm waiting upstairs."

Jenny Conners emerged from the shadows and stood behind the counter in front of Paul, her hands planted firmly on her hips. She was still as pretty as he remembered her, older of course, but her face still radiated a youthful glow. Her long black hair, which she had obviously spent some time combing, hung loosely about her shoulders, and it was impossible not to notice that her body had developed into that of a woman, full breasted and curvaceous. Her full, red lips that had been pressed into an exaggerated pout slowly parted into an excited smile that brought back memories of those summer days, and, having lost none of her precociousness, she ran around from behind the counter and held out her arms to Paul.

"Hello Jenny love," was all he could think to say as she threw her arms around his neck. He held her by the waist and swung her around as natural as though they had never been parted. "Pretty as ever, I see."

For a while she was content to gaze into his eyes, absorbing all the memories of the time they had spent together. Then she noticed the bag at his feet and her expression darkened.

She looked from Paul to her father and back again, tapping the bag with her foot. "You're not leaving, not now we've only just met again?"

"Now Jenny, leave the lad alone," warned her father. "There'll be time enough to talk later, after Paul's settled into his room."

"You're staying here?" she asked, staring into Paul's face.

"Just for a few nights, and then I'll be off," replied Paul with a touch of regret. It would either be too long or not long enough.

"Off, where?"

"Jenny, I told you to leave the lad be," said her father, more harshly than necessary. "What he wants you to know he'll tell you in his own good time. Now, show him up to the spare room, and no more questions."

It was a wasted warning as she continued to interrogate him all the way up the narrow staircase and along the landing to his room. Paul fended off the barrage of questions with the promise that he would tell her everything when they could talk properly later, which seemed to satisfy her because, as soon as the door was closed, she kissed him full on the lips.

"It's so good to see you again, Paul," she said, pulling away. "I've thought about you so often, and now you're going away again."

"It wasn't me who went away the first time," Paul reminded her, putting his hands on her shoulders and holding her at arm's length. "And it wasn't me who nearly married a soldier."

It was her turn to show some regret. "I thought I was in love, but I know now I wasn't."

"Well, neither of us could know how things would turn out," said Paul, sensing the direction the conversation was taking. "Hadn't you better let your mother know I'm staying here? She might not approve."

"She will. I'll tell her you're having supper with us. She'll be so pleased."

Paul harboured some doubt about that. Although not openly hostile to their friendship she had never encouraged them as enthusiastically as her husband, telling Jenny they were too young and that it could only end in tears. Paul always suspected that Mary Conners was responsible for sending Jenny away. But as Jenny left the bedroom Paul could not help feeling it could yet end in tears.

The rabbit pie Mrs Conners placed on the table in front of Paul looked and smelt infinitely more appetising than the greasy concoctions that Mrs Caldicot had prepared for them, and the company more agreeable than Matthew's miserable face glaring at him from across the table. If Jenny's mother still nurtured any doubts concerning his friendship with her daughter, she kept them to herself during the meal, deftly steering the conversation to subjects that suited her.

As soon as the meal was over Jenny made it clear that she was anxious to be alone with Paul, and not wishing to cause offence he asked Mrs Conners for permission to take her daughter for a walk.

While Jenny went to fetch a shawl Jack Conners drew him to one side. "Don't let her talk you out of your dreams, lad," he said quietly. "If it's meant to be it will be."

Outside the inn, Jenny took his hand in hers, as she had done all those years before, and led him into the lane leading out of the village.

Paul felt her shiver. "We can go back if you're cold," he said protectively.

"No, I'm fine," she replied, clutching his arm and pulling him closer. "I've been cooped up inside all day, and it's all been a bit of a shock, seeing you again."

"Do I make you shiver?" he teased.

"Paul Pearson, what a question to ask a girl," she scolded with a wicked glint in her eyes. "But I am pleased to see you, really I am. Are you really going away again, and how long will you be gone?"

Paul felt reluctant, unable even, to give her an honest answer. He was enjoying their reunion, more than he could have imagined, and under different circumstances he was sure it was a relationship that would develop to its natural conclusion.

"I've no idea how long I shall be away," he said finally, sensing her growing impatience. "I'm booked on a ship sailing for South Africa next week." He went on to tell her, as sensitively as possible, of all his plans, and even in the thin moonlight he could see clearly the disappointment etched into her face. "If only I had known a few days ago that you were back," he said, trying to ease the pain.

"No, I'm just being selfish. Of course, you have to go." In the dark she smiled bravely. "After all, a few hours ago we were both thinking about other things."

"Like your soldier boy, perhaps?"

She stopped and punched him sharply on the arm. "My father has a big mouth, and I never give that man a thought. I'm sure I don't even remember his name. And what about you? I'll wager you've broken a heart or two while I was away."

Paul shook his head. "Since our father died, I've barely left the farm. And you well know the choice of suitable girls around here, none near as pretty as you. A dalliance here and there, nothing more than that."

With the village and the last of the houses left behind, the lane was plunged into a deeper darkness as the fields on either side were bordered with tall hedgerows. The conversation between the two of them turned to the poignant moments of their youth; the first touch in the classroom, and the first kiss. They giggled like children at their clumsy attempts at maturity, and for a few minutes at least all thoughts of another separation were forgotten. They stopped by a stile and she leaned close for warmth as a fresh breeze swept across the fields behind them.

Quite suddenly she took his hand and placed it on her breast beneath the shawl. "Do you remember this? Does it feel different now?"

For Paul it felt just as pleasurable and exciting as it had done the first time, and now, as then, his heart pounded furiously against the wall of his chest. Was this her way of reminding him what he would be missing if he left, a womanly attempt to persuade him to stay?

"I think we should go back now," he said against his will, taking her by the shoulders and looking into her big, dark eyes. "Tomorrow I'll leave for London. I think it's for the best."

In the darkness her face was a shadowy mask of sadness and resignation as she nodded forlornly. "Remember us like this, Paul," she said softly, "and come back to me, if you can. There'll be no other man for me, I promise you that."

He didn't want her to promise, although he felt the same way. In the few hours they had been reunited she had kindled within him all the feelings that had laid dormant for so many years.

They walked back in sorrowful silence and entered the inn by the back door, keen to avoid the knowing looks and speculative comments of any customers still in the bar.

In the cosy little parlour Mary Conners sat dozing with her needlework in her lap, and she sat up with a start as soon as the pair entered.

"Did you enjoy your walk?" she asked, disguising her concerns and the more pertinent questions she would have liked to ask.

Having been told of Paul's plans by her husband she was well aware of the consequences this brief reunion could have for her daughter, given her previous relationship with the soldier. Now she feared the same would happen again. She seemed almost relieved when Jenny told her Paul was leaving the next morning, and even invited the young couple to join her for a cup of chocolate before retiring.

Afterwards Jenny insisted on accompanying him as far as the bedroom door under the watchful eye of her mother.

"Tell your father I'll see him in the morning before I leave," said Paul, kissing her lightly on the cheek. "And perhaps I'll see you as well."

Paul lay in bed, hoping that sleep would relieve him of the tortuous problems that plagued his mind. For years he had dreamed of leaving the farm and setting out on a life of his own making instead of settling for one that had been mapped out for him. He had often tried to imagine what that day would be like, when he finally broke free of the shackles in which he had been bound, and to feel the exhilarating sense of liberty. Now that day had arrived, but as he lay in bed, he experienced none of the excitement that should have been his, there was just a torment that for hour after hour denied him peace of mind and sleep. When he should have been dreaming about Africa his waking thoughts were of his two brothers he was leaving behind, and the girl who had so suddenly and unexpectedly been thrust back into his life. Was he really ready to abandon all that for some idealistic notion of adventure and fortune?

He must have finally fallen asleep because he became aware of being woken, though by what he had no idea. As he struggled to reconcile himself with the unfamiliar surroundings it quickly became clear there was someone else in the room.

Paul shook the sleep from his eyes and sat up, staring hard into the blackness. "You shouldn't be here, go back to your room," he said in a hushed, trembling voice.

As his eyes became more accustomed to the dark, he could make out the shape of Jenny as she stood motionless at the foot of the bed. Had there been a little more light in the room he would have seen her reach up and untie the ribbon at the neck of her nightdress and the nimble fingers that undid the line of buttons before the garment slipped silently to the floor.

She appeared to glide as she came around the side of the bed. He felt her breath on his face as she stroked his cheek with the tips of her fingers, and when she slipped naked into the bed and he felt the soft warmth of her bare body he struggled to contain his feelings.

"Is this truly what you want?" he asked in a breathless whisper, turning to face her. "You know I have to go in the morning? I can't stay with you."

She placed a finger tenderly against his lips. "Be quiet, Paul Pearson. I left you once without saying goodbye, but this is going to be a proper farewell. And even if I never see you again, I want us both to treasure the memory of this night." She wrapped him in her arms and, unable to stop himself, he did the same.

Once some of the urgency had subsided, she raised his nightshirt and allowed him to roll over on top of her, and when he entered her, it felt completely natural for both of them, that it was always meant to happen.

"No regrets?" he breathed into her ear as he thrust against her.

"Only one, that you're not the first," she replied before kissing him forcefully on the lips. "But I promise, you will be the last."

It was a timeless experience, passionate and tender, urgent and unhurried, rising and falling until they were both completely spent and there was nothing more to give. But for the fear of being discovered by her parents they would have remained locked in that final embrace until morning.

As she left his bed, she extracted from him one more promise. "Be gone early in the morning. I've no more goodbyes left in me," she said, holding back the tears until she was in the solitude of her own room.

Paul kept the promise, and, in the morning, he rose soon after dawn before she was about. Only Jack Conners saw him leave, and embraced him as he would his own son.

"Take good care of yourself, lad," he said with genuine affection. "I know this is something you have to do, but I've a lass that's going to miss you and would want to see you back, and I wouldn't want to see her hurting again."

"If it's within my powers then you have my word."

With that, and a last look back at the inn, he left behind him the village and the last vestiges of his former life.

Chapter Six

Ned Stiles appeared to be no more pleased to greet Matthew in the stable yard at the back of Millwood House than the lad was to be there. Having been summoned early that morning, he had ridden Roscoe over at his own pace, clearly without the urgency required by his new mentor.

"Morning," Matthew said sullenly as he dismounted and handed the reins to a waiting stable lad.

"Been waiting for you more than an hour since," Stiles responded gruffly. "I don't like to be kept waiting."

Matthew shrugged his shoulders dismissively. The man meant nothing to him, although he did take the opportunity to study him more closely than he had the first time they had met. The top of his head was bald and surrounded by a heavy fringe of greying hair that descended down the sides of his face into thick mutton-chop whiskers. His face displayed a strength of character, weather beaten and leathery. Dark, bushy eyebrows hung over brown, penetrating eyes and a large hook nose gave him an owlish appearance.

"Master wants to see us up at the house," said Stiles bluntly as he turned and marched briskly towards the back of the house. Matthew followed as they went through a narrow doorway and along a passage that led past first a scullery and then the kitchen. "You'll use this way always in future, or at the side door. Never present yourself at the front."

Matthew made no reply, he simply wondered if those were Haveringham's instructions or whether Stiles had taken it upon himself to impose his own set of rules.

With no further words between them they went through to the now familiar surroundings of the library where Haveringham was sat behind his desk engrossed in an array of papers that were spread out before him. Without the offer of a seat the two stood before the desk like a pair of errant schoolboys, Stiles standing stiff and still while Matthew shuffled impatiently.

Eventually Haveringham looked up and studied them through narrow eyes. "Thank you for coming, gentlemen," he said, as though the choice had been theirs. For a few moments he drummed the top of his desk with his fingers as though considering how best to proceed. His attention settled on Ned Stiles. "You've served me well over the years, Ned," he began, ominously enough for the old man, "and I hope you'll continue to serve be for a good many more." He paused to await a reaction that failed to come. "However, I have to take into account your advancing years, we are neither of us getting any younger and the rigours of daily life take their toll. So, I take it you'll not think ill of me for looking to the future." He continued to look hard at Stiles who this time nodded compliantly, if not with enthusiasm. "You'll take this as no reflection on you, Ned, on your ability or your loyalty, both of which are beyond question, but I want you to give young Matthew here the full benefit of your knowledge and experience, everything he will need to manage this estate when you are no longer able to do so. You understand?"

Ned Stiles nodded while giving Matthew a glance of undisguised scorn. "If that's what you want, sir, then I'll do what I can for the boy." He placed particular emphasis on the last word.

If Haveringham noticed any sign of contempt in Ned's voice he chose to ignore it as he turned his attention to Matthew. "You and I have already discussed your position here at some length so you know what is expected of you," he said with the sternness of a school master. "From today you'll do exactly as Ned instructs, and you'll only question what you don't understand. You'll give him the respect he deserves, and in return you can expect the same." His eyes flashed towards Stiles who remained uncommitted. "Any disagreement between the pair of you will be resolved by me, and me alone." With that he returned his attention to the papers. The meeting was over.

As they walked back through the kitchen, Matthew appeared oblivious to the curious looks and giggling of the few servant girls who were working there, as they speculated on who the handsome young stranger might be. What he saw or heard he chose to ignore, while Haveringham's words were still vivid in his thoughts.

"We'll take a turn around the estate," Stiles announced caustically as they made their way back to the stables. "You'll need to know your way about. You won't always have me to wet nurse you."

Matthew's pale lips curled into a sardonic sneer. "Your worth to Mr Haveringham will last only for the short time it takes me to learn your job, so make the most of it while you can."

The dislike they had for each other had been immediate and looked set to endure, although it was unlikely that either of them could say what had provoked such an early animosity. Perhaps for Ned Stiles it was the threat to his employment by someone he saw as little more than a boy who needed putting in his place. But Matthew's motives were a little more obscure, unless he perceived the older man to be an unnecessary obstruction to his ambitions.

They mounted their horses and Matthew allowed Stiles to take the lead as they headed out of the stable yard and past the array of surrounding outbuildings. He had no wish to engage in conversation with his reluctant tutor and was content to remain a length or two behind.

Once they were clear of the buildings Stiles dug his heels into the flanks of his horse and it lurched forward into a cantor, leaving Matthew trailing behind.

They were following a deeply rutted track mainly used by wagons transporting fodder to the stables, a track more suited to slow moving traffic than the exercising of horses. Although not quite the equestrian of his younger brother, Matthew was still a competent rider and resolved straight away he would not be bettered by the older man this early in his education.

The track rose slightly and twisted away to the right, following the contour of a small, steep sided hill that obstructed their view to no more than fifty yards to their front. Matthew spurred Roscoe forward, keeping the horse to the comparatively even ground at the centre of the track, and began gaining on Stiles with each stride. At the top of the rise the ground levelled off for a short distance before falling away down the far side of the hill. With a little more encouragement, he managed to close the gap to just a short length.

Stiles looked back over his shoulder and Matthew thought he detected a taunting grin, an opinion reinforced when the gap suddenly widened as Stiles' horse leapt forward into a gallop. What was supposed to be an instructive tour of the estate was clearly turning into a race to establish a position of superiority. Although uncomfortable with the speed in that unfamiliar terrain Matthew had no choice but to set off in pursuit as they descended the hill towards the flat pastureland below, pushing his riding skills to the limit.

The narrowness of the track allowed no room for overtaking with any safety, but as they neared the bottom Matthew could see an opening through to the field immediately to their front. It was clear that Stiles was making for the gap, intent on continuing the race over the open ground, and Matthew smiled to himself as he placed his faith in Roscoe's speed and stamina.

Stiles was just ahead going through the opening, but instead of spurring his mount to greater effort he leant back in the saddle and pulled hard at the reins. The horse took off, easily clearing a wide drainage ditch that bordered the field. It all happened too quick and unexpectedly for Matthew to give Roscoe any such instructions and seeing the obstruction the horse dug in his forelegs and slewed frantically around to the left, sending its rider flying from the saddle and landing heavily into the thick, dark quagmire at the bottom of the ditch.

For a moment or two Matthew laid still, unsure if he had been injured, slowly recovering the breath that had been knocked from him. Gradually he scrambled unsteadily to his feet, scraping a thick covering of black, glutinous mud from his eyes. Tentatively he flexed his arms and back to convince himself that the only real damage done was to his clothes and pride before clambering up the slippery side of the ditch. Stiles was waiting for him, his face flushed with mocking success as Matthew glared back through his mask of mud. He had an almost overwhelming urge to drag his tormentor from the saddle and toss him into the same bath of mud, but an unexplained surge of self-restraint held him back. He was breathless with rage and Stiles would pay, that much was certain, but in his own time and in his own way.

Stiles wiped away a few tears of laughter. "Local knowledge, lad, that's what you've learned today. If you farm as well as you ride, then you've certainly still got a lot to learn." He looked Matthew up and down with open amusement. "Now you had better get yourself home to change, you're not going to make the right impression with the men looking like that."

With the only consolation being that there were no other witness to his humiliation, Matthew went to retrieve his horse, who appeared quite ambivalent to the state of his rider.

Still seething with vengeful thoughts Matthew swung uncomfortably into the saddle with the stinking, cloying mud weighing him down. No words could suitably describe the anger and hatred he felt for the man to whom he had been ordered to give respect, feeling now he owed no such obligation.

Anxious to avoid, as far as was possible, contact with any person on his journey home he took a long and circuitous route around the edge of the estate, bypassing by some distance Millwood House and any other place that might be occupied by estate workers. It was a good deal of time later that he finally reached the lane that passed by the front of the house, and the mud that covered his clothes and face had begun to dry into a cracked, putrid crust. He could only imagine the sight he would present to any unsuspecting soul that came upon him and prayed he would meet no one before he was able to leave the lane and cross the fields to his home.

He spurred Roscoe into a brisk canter to cover as much ground as quickly as possible and had reached a sharp bend in the lane that hid the pillared entrance to the drive of Millwood House. As he cleared the bend, he found himself in the path of a landau drawn by two black horses that was about to turn into the drive. Matthew barely had time to pull his horse over to the side of the lane, causing the liveried driver of the landau to curse him loudly before apologising to his two passengers.

The younger of the two women giggled loudly as she pointed at the mounted spectacle, but was quickly hushed by the sharp reprimand of her elderly companion. As the landau swung into the drive the girl looked back, still smiling visibly.

Matthew swore at the driver, his passengers, Ned Stiles and himself before galloping off across the fields and home. Being embarrassed twice in one day was something that would sit badly with him for a long, long time.

***

Rufus Haveringham threw out his arms in an effusive gesture of welcome as the girl came forward with hesitant embarrassment.

"Grace, my dear, dear girl." He held her by the hands, keeping her at arm's length as he studied her in great detail from head to toe. "But not a girl any longer, a beautiful young woman. I swear that, had I not been expecting you, I should never have recognised the girl I last saw all those years ago."

Self-consciously she lowered her eyes and spoke with a quiet reserve. "Hello Uncle Rufus, it's so good to see you again."

When they did finally embrace it was strained and tentative, suggesting they were both as nervous as the other and ill prepared for this long-anticipated moment, but the pleasure and admiration on Haveringham's face could not be denied.

Holding on to his niece's hand he turned to the older woman who had been silently viewing the reunion through small, disapproving eyes. "Miss Loxley, I cannot thank you enough for bringing Grace safely back from Europe," he said with genuine gratitude. "Naturally I would have gone myself, but the affairs of the estate keep me here. How was your journey?"

Miss Loxley pursed her thin lips and sniffed. "From Switzerland, tiring and uneventful. It was only when we were outside your very gates that we were almost run off the road by some imbecile on horseback."

"Oh, I don't think it was quite as bad as that," said Grace with undisguised amusement that was cut short by a reproachful look from the woman.

"I dread to think, Mr Haveringham, what sort of company your niece will be exposed to if what I witnessed was typical behaviour in this part of the country. I do believe she would be better placed to move in more suitable society if she were to reside in London under my care and protection."

Noticing the look of alarm that flashed across Grace's face Haveringham placed a reassuring arm around her slim waist. "You can rest assured, Miss Loxley, that young Grace will be no more exposed here to any threat to her morals or person than she was in Switzerland, or would be in London. Any man stupid enough to trifle with her will have me to deal with." He inclined his head and gave his niece a warm smile. "Now, my dear, I expect you would like to see your room and rest before dinner. Then we can have a proper chat."

She thanked him, kissing him lightly on the cheek before following a maid up the broad staircase, while a footman trailed behind carrying some of her luggage.

Miss Loxley waited until the girl had reached the top of the stairs before giving a disapproving snort. "I have to say, Mr Haveringham, that you appear to have a somewhat cavalier opinion on what is needed for your niece's future development. You seem to forget that she has spent the past four years in a very cloistered environment, the strictest of regimes. I believe she would greatly benefit from the same mature influence she had at the school, and as you have no wife to provide that influence, I think it would do her no harm if I stayed on here to make sure she has the very best start to her new life."

Incensed by the apparent arrogance of the woman, and in particular by the reference to his dead wife, Haveringham reacted angrily. "I think we can safely say, Miss Loxley that my niece has spent long enough under 'the strictest of regimes' and now requires the freedom to develop in her own way." He glared at her fiercely. "Now, you are welcome to stay the night and have dinner with us, but we will have no more talk concerning Grace's future."

She huffed loudly. "Under the circumstances I think I shall return to London immediately. If you'll have your man bring the carriage around."

From her bedroom window Grace watched with a sense of immense relief and delight as the groom helped the harridan into the landau, continuing to watch until it had disappeared around the sweep of the drive. Goodbye and good riddance, she mouthed silently.

As Grace unpacked her belongings it was impossible not to compare the relative opulence of her present surroundings with the Spartan dormitory of the ladies finishing school. She ran her fingers over the dark wood dressing table, picking up and admiring the array of gilded silver hand mirrors, hair brushes and perfume bottles. She reclined on the chaise that nestled against the foot of the bed before dancing around in the spacious room she could now call her own. Her mouth dropped open in sheer surprise when she opened the door to the large wardrobe and saw the half dozen dresses hanging there. As she took them down one at a time and held them up to her body in front of the long mirror, tears of gratitude rolled over her cheeks. The thoughtfulness of her uncle overwhelmed her, bringing an outpouring of affection for a man she hardly knew.

Before the death of her mother, Haveringham's younger sister, she had met her uncle on only a few occasions. Although nothing had ever been said on the subject, Grace had always suspected there had been something in her mother's past that had alienated her from that side of the family. Although she had never gone without, there had been few luxuries in her life, but she never thought to question her mother about the source of her income. Now she knew, her uncle had been their benefactor.

Grace's mother had died soon after she started school in Switzerland, the telegram with the sad news coming from her uncle, and when she came home for the funeral, he made it known that he was prepared to become her legal guardian. Never having known, or being told anything about her father, Rufus Haveringham was set to become the first man in her life and, as far as she knew, her only living relative. For some considerable time Grace had suspected it had been her uncle's suggestion, and money, that had sent her abroad, perhaps to protect her from a family scandal surrounding her birth.

Unaware of any conditions attached to his patronage she now looked on her uncle and his kindness with a feeling of warmth, and with a determination to repay his benevolence. She chose one of the dresses he had bought for her to wear at dinner that evening. It was in pale green satin and styled in the latest London fashion, and it fitted perfectly. After the restraints of the school, and Miss Loxley, that had kept her in plain cotton, unflattering dresses, it was a delight to be able to display her womanly charms to full effect, the colour of the dress complimenting her auburn hair. And when she glided down the stairs a few hours later she had metamorphosed from a girl with ribbons in her hair into a beautiful, confident young woman that had her uncle speechless with admiration.

As he took her hand at the bottom of the stairs there were tears of fatherly pride in his eyes, and when he spoke his voice trembled with emotion. "Your mother would weep for joy if she could see you, as I do now. She was a rare enough beauty in her youth, but I know she would forgive me for saying she couldn't hold a candle to you, my dear."

Grace fought to hold back her own feelings of joy and regret. "Uncle Rufus, I shall never be able to repay you for all the kindness you have shown me, except to promise that I will never do anything that would shame or hurt you."

He sniffed back the tears and beamed widely. "There is nothing you could do to make me feel less for you than I do at this moment." He let go of her hand and held out his arm for her to take. "You are now the lady of the house, and there is nothing that could make me prouder."

He escorted her through to the dining room where he had chosen to eat on this most special of occasions, and he took great pleasure in pulling out her chair and personally attending to her every comfort.

With everything that needed to be said it was strange that the soup course came, and went, in comparative silence, with only a few polite remarks passing between them. The questions Grace was anxious to ask seemed inappropriate so early in their new relationship, and it was clear her uncle was not about to introduce any subject that would prove remotely insensitive.

"How was the soup, my dear? All the vegetables were from my own gardens, you know."

She gave him an agreeable smile and nodded politely, but a burning curiosity overcame the polite reserve. "Uncle Rufus, there is something I need to ask you," she said timidly.

"You must make the acquaintance of my cook, Mrs Rafferty," he put in, ignoring her remark. "A most remarkable woman."

"Uncle Rufus." She was more forceful this time. "I want to ask you about my father. Do you know of him, and is he still alive?"

Haveringham pushed his empty bowl away. He leaned back in his chair, pursed his lips and clasped his hands in front of him. He knew the question would come one day. "Your mother never spoke of him?"

She shook her head.

"Then it's as well we do the same." He spoke quietly, but firmly. "It was agreed when you were born that you would know only your mother, and your father would have no place in your life."

"And was that my mother's wish too?" she asked, feeling her birth right had been unfairly denied her. "And my father, did he know of my existence?"

For a while he sat in silence, contemplating his reply. She had a right to the truth, but he had sworn to keep the secret. "Your mother left here before you were born and never returned. That was agreed. The father knew there was to be a child and that was all. There was no further contact between him and your mother."

"So, he must have been a local man, someone you knew?"

"I can tell you no more about him."

"But she was cut off from the family for all those years. What she did, was it such a terrible thing?" She looked hard at her uncle. "Was I such a terrible thing?"

"Grace, my dear, you must never think anything of the sort." Seeing how distressed she had become he got up from the table and went around to console her, putting an arm around her shoulders. "Please don't upset yourself like this. It was a long time ago, and knowing his name would serve no good purpose. Your mother accepted the arrangements that were made on her behalf, it was for the best. More than that I can't tell you."

"Can't uncle, or won't?"

He kissed her tenderly on the forehead before returning to his seat. "Can't or won't, it makes no difference, child." He gave her a kindly smile. "What's done is done and it's all in the past. The only thing important now is the future, your future, and your happiness."

It was pointless to continue, Grace concluded, at least until she and her uncle were better acquainted and she could use her womanly wiles to overcome his stubbornness. It was their first evening together and to spoil it with disagreeable conversation would only serve to sour their future relationship. Instead, as the meal and the evening progressed, the talk was of her experiences of school in Switzerland and his plans for the house and the estate, in which he wanted her to play some substantial part.

It had been a tentative start to their lives together, but by the end of the evening they had both secretly vowed to do nothing that would cause upset or unpleasantness to the other.

As Grace was preparing for the start of her new life at Millwood House, Matthew was equally determined to make some changes to his own.

By the time he had arrived home and stripped off his mud caked clothes there had been no lessening of his loathing for Ned Stiles. The vision of the man's jeering face still haunted him and stiffen his resolve to make him pay.

He dragged the battered tin bath in from the yard, a ritual usually reserved for Saturday nights, and immersed himself in the lukewarm water that was soon covered in a brown film. As he lay there he gazed around the kitchen, remembering how it had once been the comforting hub of the house, but since the death of his parents and departure of his brothers it echoed with a sorry emptiness which mingled with the accumulated mess of someone who cared little for what went on inside the house. Added to this was now a pile of foul tainted clothes that sat on the floor next to the sink and were likely to stay there until necessity forced him to wash them. With the start of his education now set to make more demands on his working day he had even less time, or inclination, for domestic chores.

Late in the afternoon he left the house with the intention of diluting his anger with a few pints of ale. He was not by habit a drinking man, preferring to follow his father's habit of taking a drink only at the end of the working week. But today he would make an exception, driven to that decision by the man who stood between him and his ambitions.

It would have been natural to make the relatively short journey to the Farrier's Inn, but after what Paul had told him he felt it prudent to stay clear of the place until all memories of that morning in the barn had faded. The prospect of two humiliating events in one day was something he was not prepared to risk. So, with Roscoe suitably chastised, he set a steady pace towards Daventry, cleaner, but still with a lingering resentment that would be harder to shift.

Lodged in the back of his mind was another reason for making the longer journey to the town, a thought that had occurred to him as he lay in the bath, and after two pints in an unsavoury public house and numerous enquiries he found himself in a narrow, cobbled street of small workers cottages. Years of neglect had relegated them to little more than hovels, with most of the inhabitants one small step away from the poor house. Unworthy of street lighting it was only the dim glow of candle light through the grimy windows and the fleeting glimpse of a watery moon that allowed any illumination into that miserable place.

From the deeper shadow of a doorway a pair of suspicious eyes followed Matthew's progress along the street as he looked for the house he had been directed to. Strangers usually meant trouble to those at the lowest end of the social scale, and, as Matthew passed by, a man stepped out behind him.

"What d'you want here?" he demanded gruffly. "What's yer business?"

Matthew turned to face him. "What's it to you?" As he made out the man's features in the gloom, he could see he was more scared than threatening. "I'm looking for a Mrs Budden. I was told she lived in this street."

"What d'you want her for?"

"That's my business, but I mean her no harm."

The man looked over Matthew's shoulder and nodded his head. "Second from the end. And see you don't."

The man continued to watch as Matthew carried on up the street and stopped outside the house. He gave the man a quick glance before lightly tapping on the door and stepping away. If the occupants of the houses were so scared of visitors it would do no good to appear intimidating, especially at that time of the evening.

After a few seconds there was a shuffling from inside and the door opened by no more than a few inches. Half of a frightened face peered out at him. "Who is it?" she asked timidly.

As he took a step forward, she backed away. "Mrs Budden? It's me, Matthew. Emily Pearson's son. Do you remember me?"

Cautiously she opened the door a little further, allowing the thin glow of a candle to spread out across the cobbled street. Without venturing out she stretched forward to get a better look. "My goodness!" she exclaimed with excited recognition. "If it isn't you as well. I'd not forget that face." She threw the door wide open and beckoned him in. "My word, this is a shock and no mistake."

Matthew stepped into the room, lit by two stubby pieces of candle that guttered in the sudden draught, causing dancing patterns on the bare walls. "I hope I didn't frighten you," he said, taking in the miserable surrounding as he took off his cap. "Calling at this hour, I mean."

"Gracious me, no!" she replied, pulling at her shabby dress and patting her hair. "Not that I get many visitors at this hour, and me in this state."

He gave her a look that he hoped would reassure her. "I know you must think it strange, me coming here like this, but I was in the town and I wanted to let you know that our mother had died."

She let out a little cry and threw her hands up to her face. "Gracious me, no!" she repeated. "And me not knowing. When did it happen?"

She sat down on one of the two rickety chairs that sat either side of a small table. Matthew took the other, pulling it closer to her. "No more than two months since. She had been ill for a while."

Mrs Budden lifted her head from her hands and looked hard into Matthew's face. "It was that farm as did it, like it did for your father. I told her it would, and it'll do the same for you."

Matthew made no reply. He couldn't agree, but it would do his cause no good to argue. Instead, he looked around the room and its pitiful furnishings. Apart from the table and chairs there was only a well-worn armchair and threadbare rug, and with no pictures on the walls it was clear this place served merely as somewhere to shelter. It was not a home.

"I'll be fine, Mrs Budden. There's no need to worry about me," he said self-consciously avoiding her gaze.

"Well, you take care, you and those brothers of yours or you'll all end up in the ground before your time," she warned with real concern. Then her expression changed as she became flustered and embarrassed. "Look at me, sitting here with a visitor and not even offering him a cup of tea. What must you think of me?"

"It's all right, Mrs Budden, I'm fine," he said, doubting that she even had the means to make him a cup of tea. He looked beyond her and into the dark interior of the tiny scullery, trying to imagine the frugal contents of her larder.

She caught him looking and nodded her head as though agreeing with his thoughts. "Not much to show for half a lifetime, is it?" she said in a resigned tone that suggested no sense of shame, just an acceptance of her life. "When my husband died, he left me with nothing but his debts. I didn't have three strong sons to look out for me."

"I'm sorry, I didn't mean ..." Matthew felt his face flush, fearing it had betrayed his thoughts. "I'm sure it must have been hard for you."

"It's been hard all right, but I've not yet stooped to begging, and God willing I never will," she said with pride, dabbing her eyes with the sleeve of her dress and patting her hair again. "Listen to me, going on like that. You didn't come here for me to go on about my problems. Tell me about those brothers of yours."

She listened intently as Matthew gave her a biased account of all that had happened since the death of his mother, an account that included words like deceit and betrayal. He told how Paul and John had deserted him at a time when he needed them most. She shook her head sympathetically at the appropriate times and when he had finished, she let out a long, sorrowful sigh.

"You poor boy," she said, her voice heavy with sadness, "how ever do you cope?"

But Matthew dismissed her concern with a wave of his hand. "Tell me, Mrs Budden, how did you meet my mother?"

A thin smile creased her unhappy face as her memory reached back to that distant part of her life. "Well, there's a story. It was when I did for those Haveringham's up at, what was it called, Mill something house."

"Millwood," prompted Matthew. "Millwood House."

"Bless you, yes, Millwood House, that was it. I was nothing but a girl back in those days and it was Christmas. Your mother and father had been invited up to the house to take sherry with the family. Traditional it was. My job was to hand around the drinks to the guests, but I trips on a rug and the drink got spilt down your mother's best frock. Got a right tongue lashing from the young master I did and no mistake. I think I would have got the sack there and then if it wasn't for Emily, your mother, saying it was all her fault. So kind she was and we went through to the kitchen to clean her up, with me so upset and her putting her arm around me." She sniffed back some tears. "We got on famously after that, stayed friends for years until I moved out here. After a while we stopped visiting."

"I can remember you coming to the house, when I was just a boy. Mother often spoke about you."

"I came a few times on my day off, but your father was a bit funny about her having company at the house, so we met up in the village more often as not." She reached across the table and patted Matthew on the arm. "We used to laugh a lot in those days, but there's precious little to laugh about now."

Matthew nodded solemnly in agreement, although his thoughts were focussed elsewhere. "When you worked up at the house did you ever know a man called Stiles?"

For a while she pondered the question before her face broke into a broad grin and she rolled her eyes. "Ned Stiles, don't tell me he's still around up there. The old devil, I could tell you a few tales about him and no mistake."

"Tales! What tales?" There was more than just a mild curiosity in his enquiry.

She rolled her eyes again and laughed. "Nothing that would be of any interest to you, young Matthew."

"Don't depend on that, Mrs Budden," he said, a little disappointed. He was keen to press the point, but felt it unwise to do so. If everything went according to his plan there would be plenty of opportunity to dredge up information about Ned Stiles. He let the moment pass and looked across at her intently. "Please don't think me impertinent, but do you have any employment, any means of income?"

Her eyes narrowed as she looked sideways at him. "Your mother and me might have been friends, but I don't see as how that gives you the right to ask me such a question, not a woman of my age." Her hand was still resting on his arm and she snatched it away. "I'll tell you this, though, as poor as I may be, I've never earned a penny by dishonest or immoral means, and I never would."

Matthew's face flushed. "I'm so sorry. I didn't mean … I never meant to imply."

She glared directly at him. "Then what a question to ask."

"It was not to offer offence, you have my word on that." It was his turn to reach out his hand to her. "I asked only because I'm in need of a housekeeper, Mrs Budden, someone to look after the house, and me." He paused to give her time to absorb the offer. "I couldn't pay much, but there would be enough to eat and, if you'll excuse my saying, more comfort than you have here. It would please me if you would at least consider it."

Unwittingly he was holding her hand and he felt it tense as she studied him closely. "You're a direct young man, Matthew Pearson, much like your father as I recall. You certainly have the look of him." She spoke as though it was not intended to flatter. "We barely know each other, yet here you are asking me to live under your roof."

Matthew smiled at her in an attempt to hide his embarrassment. "How much better should I know you? It's just a job I'm offering, nothing more than that. Besides, you remind me of my mother, so it would be as if she were looking after me."

She pulled her hand away sharply, her expression was severe. "Your mother and me were good friends and no mistake, but I would never presume to take her place, and you've no right to suggest such a thing."

Matthew appeared shocked by her reaction, what had intended to flatter had clearly offended. "I think it is you who presume too much, Mrs Budden. I am truly in need of a housekeeper and I thought it would please my mother if I were to be looked after by someone she once called her friend. It was nothing more than that." He gave her an impassioned look. "If you have other commitments that prevent you from accepting, I understand, but otherwise I think it is a good arrangement, for both of us."

She stared reflectively around the room before turning her eyes on Matthew. "It's right enough what you say," she admitted sadly. "This place has no happy memories I'd be leaving behind, and I would be a liar if I said I wasn't fed up with my own miserable company. I don't see what I have to lose."

He beamed delightedly. "It's settled then," he said, taking her hand and shaking it enthusiastically. "I'll come over and collect you on Saturday, if that's convenient?"

As he got up to leave, she did the same, following him to the door. "It must be a sad house with your parents and brothers all gone," she said, opening the door for him. "Perhaps we can make it happy again."

"Perhaps! I hope so." Without looking back, he disappeared into the night.

Chapter Seven

When Matthew arrived to collect her, Rose Budden's appearance was a little less careworn than it had been a few days before. Perhaps it was the prospect of a better, more purposeful, life ahead of her that had put some colour into her pallid cheeks, and the afternoon sunshine breathed some life into her dull hair. Her meagre possessions had been rolled into a bundle and tied with string, and after Matthew helped her up onto the gig there was not a single, nostalgic look back as they drove away.

The journey back to Hibberd's Farm was pleasant, certainly for Rose who seemed to relish the fresh air that swept her face. She breathed in the smell of blossom and freshly cut grass with the passion of someone who had spent years in confinement. Perhaps she had thought of her home as a prison, and her very existence as a life sentence. Now that she had been so unexpectedly released, she wanted to savour every moment to the utmost.

Once or twice, she noticed Matthew giving a sly glance in her direction and self-consciously she pulled the old woollen shawl up across her shoulders.

"I didn't always look like this," she said, as though reading what was in his mind, but with no hint of apology. "I used to be a bit of a looker in my day. Could have had the pick of the lads up at the big house."

Matthew flushed. "I'm sorry, I didn't mean to …"

She laughed, squeezing his arm reassuringly. "No need of apologies. I stopped looking in the mirror long ago, but I know I haven't worn too well over these past years."

"Well, you look fine enough to me," he lied. "Nothing that a few good meals and a change of clothes won't put to rights." He wanted to pursue her on the time she had spent at Millwood House but felt their relationship was too new and fragile to speak of matters that may be sensitive to her. For the time being he would content himself with flattery.

When they arrived at the farm, she looked about her, as though reliving times all those years before. She shivered visibly when Matthew pushed open the kitchen door and ushered her inside, like she had seen the ghost of Emily Pearson waiting to greet her.

She stared around the kitchen with a look of dismay. "It needs a woman's touch," she commented as she followed Matthew up to his mother's room. "I remember it being much brighter."

"It's just a place to eat and sleep," was his muttered response. "You can do whatever you think fit if it pleases you, and it doesn't cost me much time or money. The farm takes all of that."

Behind his back she smiled and nodded knowingly, remembering his father.

For the next few weeks everything went well, both for Matthew and his new housekeeper. He had been right about her appearance. In that short time her scrawny figure had filled out now that she was no longer forced to survive on a diet of thin soup and dwindling hope. Her body had more shape, with fuller breasts and pronounced hips that filled one of Emily Pearson's old dresses to full effect. Each evening she had taken to combing out her long, fair hair until it had lost its wild, lacklustre state and, when not tied back with a ribbon, cascaded over her shoulders. Fresh air, and her new life, had put some colour in her cheeks, and her once dull, hazel eyes now sparkled in the sunlight. It struck Matthew that perhaps she had not been exaggerating by claiming to be a beauty in her youth, and often he found himself watching her as she moved about the kitchen and he wondered what secrets she kept.

Most evenings, after work, they would go through to the parlour that had been little used since the death of his mother. There he would sit in the old wooden armchair that his father used to occupy, while she took her place on the settle beside the hearth. For an hour or so before bedtime they would talk. She asked him endless questions about his mother concerning the final years of her life and whether anything could have been done to prevent her death. Any inference that the farm contributed to that death was angrily dismissed by Matthew and the subject was changed. The main topic of his interest was the time she had spent up at Millwood House, which she was happy to talk about until he turned it inevitably to Ned Stiles, and any part he had played in her life. Then she would simply smile wistfully and stare into the distance. "He was a man and no mistake," she would say. "The things I could tell you about him."

Then she would say nothing more, and as the days passed a festering resentment started to grow within Matthew.

During the day he divided his time between his own farm and the estate, but nowhere did he feel free from Stiles' influence. It was as though the man was constantly looking over his shoulder, ready to criticise and mock his ability. How much of it was real or merely existing in Matthew's mind was impossible to separate, but he started to arrive home each evening in a state of growing agitation. What had begun as pleasant evenings in the parlour were gradually being tainted by his moroseness that Rose Budden soon came to recognise, but was reluctant to address. Nevertheless, she worried that the pressure of work was becoming too much for him and that he would end up as his parents did.

One evening when he was even more troubled than usual, she decided she could hold her tongue no longer. They were sitting down to supper and she watched as he picked sullenly at his food. "You'll fret yourself into an early grave if you carry on the way you are. I don't know what it is that troubles you, but you're far too young to be carrying such worries, it's not natural. Why, a lad of your age should be spending his evenings with a sweetheart, not sat at home like this night after night."

He pushed his plate away and glared at her across the table. "I pay you to look after the house, not to poke your nose into my affairs."

"And it's not in my general nature to interfere in such things, and I wouldn't be now if I didn't care what becomes of you." She took the plate away as he got up from the table and crossed to sit in his armchair. Against her better judgement she decided to follow. "As I understand it, I was brought here to look after you as well as this house, and your mother, God rest her soul, wouldn't thank me if I failed in that duty." She took a deep breath before adding, "just look at you sitting there, looking as old and as miserable as your father, and we know what happened to him."

The words had barely passed her lips when she knew it had been a mistake to mention his father in such terms. Matthew's pale eyes flashed with a burning anger as he leapt up from the chair and gripped her tightly by the wrists.

"No one speaks of my father like that, especially not you. If you weren't a woman, I'd give you a …" As the words died on his lips his twisted features convinced her it was no idle threat. "My father was a good man, an honest farmer and there's no shame in that."

Common sense dictated that she should not test his anger further and keep her mouth shut, especially while he had hold of her wrists. But there were things she had learned of his father that had to be said and there was no better time.

"An honest farmer right enough, but one who cared more for his precious farm than he did for his family," she said quietly, but with firm determination. "He used your mother like a breeding sow, and once she had borne him three sons he wanted nothing more to do with her. She never knew what proper love was, not from him."

Before she could say anything further, he released one of her wrists and brought the back of his free hand down hard across her cheek. "You lying bitch," he screamed at her, angry tears welling up in his eyes. "He loved my mother and you've no right to say otherwise."

She wrenched her other wrist free and rubbed her cheek. She was hurt, yet unrepentant. "You were too young to know. You saw only what you wanted to see, and believed what you wanted to believe." She knew what she was risking by continuing. "I'm not telling you this just to hurt you, or to turn you away from the memory of your father. But I saw how he made your mother's life a misery, and God forbid you should do the same with a wife of your own."

Matthew turned away from her, his rage spent as he listened to her words. His emotions were raw and he had no answer to her, none that he could swear to as the truth. He well knew of his father's failings, of his stubborn indifference to the needs of others, especially when they ran contrary to his own, and those of his beloved farm. How like him I must be, thought Matthew as he went quietly up to bed, leaving Rose Budden with her chores, and any misgivings she now had for accepting her employment.

Throughout the night Matthew brooded on all the negative aspects of his life, the constant humiliation by Ned Stiles, lack of recognition from Rufus Haveringham, and now the desecration of his father's memory by the hired help. Instead of giving thanks for the advantageous arrangement he had made to keep his farm. and what else that may lead to, he dwelled only on what he perceived as a conspiracy against him.

When morning finally came, he rose early and left the house before Rose was out of her bed.

***

Rufus Haveringham wandered around his conservatory picking dead leaves from his treasured plants. "They're getting far too much water," he muttered to himself. "I must speak to Jenkins about it."

"I'm sorry, uncle, what did you say?" Grace had been quietly watching him for a few minutes.

He turned in surprise, unaware of her presence. "What? Oh, nothing my dear. I was just talking to myself." He gave her a smile. "I do that quite a lot, you know."

Grace took off her hat and shook her hair free, making the ringlets dance around her shoulders. She had just returned from her morning ride and her face still displayed a ruddy glow from the exercise.

"It's because you've spent too long in your own company," she said sadly. "I know what it's like to feel lonely."

"You feel lonely here?" he enquired gravely, coming over to her. "I never realised. You never said."

She shook her head. "No, not here, uncle. But I know what it's like to lose someone." She sighed deeply. "I shouldn't have said anything, I'm just being a silly young girl."

He pressed her hand in his. "You're not at all silly, and you're certainly not a young girl." He tried not to sound patronising. "But there is something troubling you, I can see that."

"I'm fine, uncle, really I am." There was little conviction in her voice.

His round face creased into a sceptical frown. "I may not have too much experience in the ways of young ladies, but I know enough about people to recognise if they are telling me the truth or not." He gave her hand an encouraging squeeze. "There is something troubling you, but if you don't tell me what it is I've no way of putting it right."

She looked at his apologetically. "You've been so kind to me, Uncle Rufus, and I'm afraid if I tell you what it is you'll think me ungrateful."

"I shall think nothing of the sort," he retorted, "but I shall be offended if you feel you can't come to me with your problems." He paused for a second to consider. "Unless of course it's a problem you can only discuss with another woman."

She flushed and giggled with embarrassment. "No …! No, nothing like that …"

"Because if it is Mrs Rafferty will …"

"No uncle," she said firmly. "It's nothing of the kind." Her voice became hesitant. "Please don't think I'm complaining when I say I feel lonely." She led him towards a low couch at the end of the conservatory and sat him down. "When I was at school in Switzerland we were never allowed out, except with a chaperone, and then it was only to stuffy museums and art galleries. But at least I had friends, girls of my own age and we had lots of fun together. Since I've been back here the only occasion I go out is when I'm riding on the estate, and even then I'm on my own. I've tried to make friends with some of the maids and the girls in the kitchen but they all seem too scared to talk to me and call me Miss Grace."

Haveringham gave her a look of surprise. "Of course, they do, my dear!" He laughed at her naivety. "They know their place and it's right they should show you proper respect. If you become too friendly with them, they will only take advantage of you sooner or later."

"But you don't understand, uncle, I've no one of my own age I can talk to, and nothing to do except riding and reading." She rested her head on his shoulder and looked up into his attentive face. "Please don't be angry, it's just that I miss my friends and need to make new ones."

He drew away so that he could see her clearly. "You must forgive me, my dear, this is all so new to me. I've no experience of being a parent, and the needs of the young are a mystery to me." He laid a hand against her cheek. "I never realised, but even on an estate of this size it must be easy to feel like a prisoner when you've no agreeable company with whom to spend your time. The past weeks must have seemed like an eternity to you." He stroked his chin thoughtfully. "It's time for me to make amends. A trip to London, I think. We can buy you some new clothes, visit the theatre or ballet, whatever you wish, then dinner at the Ritz. And when we come home, I shall make arrangements to properly launch you into local society."

Her eyes lit up excitedly at the prospect before her expression changed to one of guilt. "Oh, Uncle Rufus! I didn't say those things to make you feel guilty and to spoil me even more than you have done already."

He placed a restraining finger against her lips. "Nonsense, it's an uncle's right to spoil his niece, and it's no more than I should have done without being prompted."

She threw her arms around his neck and embraced him warmly. That was reward enough for him.

On the stairs leading up from the kitchen into the main body of Millwood House, Matthew found his way blocked by Jenkins, who he now knew to be in charge of Haveringham's household staff, a butler in all but name. Like Stiles, Matthew viewed the man as a further impediment on the path to his rightful position.

"I need to see Mr Haveringham," Matthew demanded bluntly when Jenkins refused to move.

Jenkins had been too long in his job to be intimidated by someone like Matthew. "The master's busy, I'm not sure he can see you now."

He held his ground as Matthew tried to push past him. "Well, you won't know if you don't go and ask him."

With his height, and having the advantage of the stairs, Jenkins stared down on Matthew with an air of superiority. "Wait in the hall while I go and see."

Grace and her uncle were still locked in their embrace when Jenkins coughed discreetly to attract their attention. "I'm very sorry, sir, but that young Mr Pearson is here to see you. I told him you were busy but he was most persistent. I can send him away, if you wish."

Haveringham huffed loudly and rolled his eyes. "What now?" he said impatiently, as much to himself as to his man. He took a deep breath. "All right Jenkins, have him wait in the library. I'll be along presently." He turned to his niece. "I'm sorry, my dear, but this shouldn't take too long and then we can discuss our trip to London."

He watched her as she swept out of the conservatory, admiring her poise and sophistication and knowing that the money spent on her education had not been wasted. But now she was ready to complete her development in the company of her peers. How short sighted he had been.

Out in the hall Matthew paced the marble floor, going over in his mind everything he intended to say, but the more he rehearsed the more trite and complaining it sounded, and he was beginning to regret his decision to come. That was until he caught sight of the girl as she appeared to glide across the hall, the same girl he thought he had seen in the landau. She hardly gave him a glance as he stared after her, yet he convinced himself that she had flashed him the merest hint of a smile before she disappeared around the sweep of the stairs.

"The master will see you in the library," said Jenkins bitterly, shattering the magic of the moment.

Matthew continued his pacing in the library as Haveringham made the conscious decision to keep him waiting, but now it was the girl who occupied his thoughts, and not his perception of the injustice being metered out by Ned Stiles. He was about to change his mind and leave when Haveringham came into the room.

"And to what do I owe the pleasure of this visit," he said, his voice heavy with sarcasm. "If you are here simply to complain then I would rather you left now."

Matthew spun around to face him, his opening speech completely forgotten. "I'm, er … very sorry to have troubled you, sir," he stuttered.

"I shall be more troubled if you are here wasting my time, lad. There are more important things I need to be doing."

Matthew breathed deeply to compose himself. "That fact is, sir, I feel I am being treated unfairly, and you did say, if there were any problems, I was to bring them to you."

Haveringham gave a loud, contemptuous sniff. "Treated unfairly! By whom? I hope it's Ned Stiles you're referring to, because I've given you more of my time and patience than I've given to any man in my employ, and I should take it as a personal insult if you are here to accuse me of unfairness."

His stinging attack had left Matthew searching for a reply that wouldn't offend. "No, not at all," he muttered, wringing his cap in his hands. "But Mr Stiles is holding me back, not giving me the responsibilities I deserve. He doesn't want me to succeed because he feels threatened by me."

"And wouldn't you feel threatened if you were in his position?" he questioned harshly. "Ned Stiles is well aware of why I've given you this position, and he'll give you responsibility when he thinks you are ready for it, and not before. Those are my orders, not his. If you think by coming here and whining to me you will be treated any differently then you've made a serious misjudgement."

"And I'm to be lectured to in front of the men like a schoolboy, and have them laughing at me behind my back? Are those your orders?"

"Is that the truth of it, or just your fertile imagination?" He took his seat behind the desk and waved a hand at Matthew. "Sit down, lad, and listen to me carefully, because this is the last conversation we will have on this matter. You came to me with an unsolicited and, dare I say, outrageous proposal, seeking a way to hold on to that farm of yours. I found that commendable, and I even admired your nerve and ingenuity. Against my better judgement, and the advice of my lawyer, I accepted most of your proposal because it impressed me, and because of my regard for your parents." He drummed thoughtfully on the top of his desk. "I told you at the time, and I'll tell you again now, I saw in you the spirit of the son I never had, and believe me when I say that I want for you what I should have wanted for him. And, his treatment would have been no different than the very treatment that you are here to complain about now." He stared hard at Matthew. "So, you can well imagine how offended I feel right now."

Matthew felt his face burning, and his nerves smarting. "It was never intended as an insult to you," he said defensively. "I just needed to feel that I'm being given some respect by Mr Stiles, that's all."

Haveringham held up his hands impatiently. "In a few weeks you expect to know what it has taken Ned Stiles a lifetime to learn. Don't be in too much of a hurry to take on responsibilities you are not ready for because, rest assured, they will break you. He has my complete support and, after this little discussion, yours too, I should hope."

Matthew thought carefully about his reply, being in no doubt where he stood in the estimation of Rufus Haveringham. He forced a weak smile. "I can see that further complaining will be of no use, so I've little choice but to accept things as they are."

Haveringham leaned across the desk towards him. "We all have choices, lad. Yours is simple. You either accept what I say or terminate our agreement. Each is of little consequence to me."

Matthew felt a brief moment of panic sweep over him. Had he pushed too far? "Then you know what my choice has to be," he replied quickly. "I have too much to lose."

Haveringham gave him a sardonic grin. "Indeed, you do, lad, indeed you do. Now, if you'll excuse me, I have things to do as, I'm sure, do you."

Matthew nodded as he got to his feet. Having achieved nothing but the further wrath of his mentor he felt bitter and dejected as he walked slowly to the door. He was about to leave when Haveringham called after him.

"One more thing," he said in a more congenial tone. "I shall be giving a little house party in honour of someone very dear to me and, against my better judgement, I think I should like you to attend. Let us see how you behave in polite society, shall we. Part of your education, if you like."

Matthew turned back, his spirits raised. "The young lady I saw in the hall just now? Is she a relative of yours?"

Without replying, Haveringham dismissed him with a wave of the hand, leaving Matthew to ponder even further on what the future held for him.

Ned Stiles pulled out his pocket watch and flicked open the cover. He didn't like being kept waiting, especially by the likes of Matthew Pearson. The lad had shown little sign of relaxing his obstructive attitude to following instructions and Ned was rapidly reaching the conclusion that he never would. Now, after just a few weeks, he was reaching the end of his patience, yet he was equally determined to show his master that he was not about to be beaten. With a final check of the time, he dug his heels into the flanks of his horse and started off at an easy canter towards Hibberd's Farm.

The last time he had been at the farm was many years before, carrying a message from Haveringham to William Pearson. He remembered Matthew as an ill-mannered, objectionable child even then, and there had been nothing recently to move him from that opinion.

The first thing he noticed as he approached the farm house was a thin wisp of grey smoke curling up from the chimney in the still morning air. Although not in itself unusual, he did think it strange that the lad should light a fire when he expected to be away from the house all day. As he urged his horse forward his first thought was that Matthew had been taken ill. At least that would explain his lateness that morning.

He dismounted in the yard at the back of the house, some of his anger having subsided as a vision of Matthew lying sick in his bed pricked at Ned's conscience. But then he was struck by a sight that took a good deal more explaining than a wisp of smoke. On a line stretched across the yard, amongst the shirts and vests was a dress and a collection of female under garments. Perhaps he had been wrong in his assumption that Matthew lived alone. With his curiosity roused he rapped on the door.

After a few moments the door opened no more than an inch or two and a face peered nervously out at him. "What do you want?" asked the woman cautiously.

"I'm sorry, I was looking for Matthew Pearson," Stiles said, keeping his distance. "Is he at home?"

"He's not here. Been gone a few hours since." Rose opened the door a little further, encouraging Stiles to move closer.

"Would you know where I can find him?" he enquired softly, not wanting to alarm her any more than necessary.

She shook her head thoughtfully. "Out on the farm, I shouldn't wonder, or on the estate yonder, wherever his work takes him. More than that I couldn't say." She ventured out into the doorway and looked hard into his face. "I have a notion I should know you. It's been some years but the face is familiar. What's your name?"

He snatched his cap from his head and stared at her curiously. "It's Stiles, missus, Ned Stiles, but I'm afraid you have the better of me."

Rose threw open wide the door and stepped out into the yard. "Well, bless me, so it is!" she exclaimed excitedly, pulling at the neck of her dress and straightening her hair. "It's Rose Budden, Rose Chamberlain as was. I was no more than a slip of a girl back then of course, a maid up at the big house. It's not likely you'll remember me."

Stiles massaged his weathered forehead as he took in her features. "Not the name, but the face. Now that's one I'll not forget. Pretty as a picture you was then, and still are … I'm sorry … I'm speaking out of turn."

She put a hand to her mouth and giggled. "Still the same Ned Stiles, as I recall. None of us girls were safe from that silver tongue of yours, or those wandering hands."

He hid his embarrassment behind a broad smile. "Harmless fun and kitchen gossip, it was enough to get a man hanged in those days," he chortled. "If I gave any offence back then I apologise for it now. Seeing you like this certainly brings back some memories, I can tell you."

They stood silently looking at each other as a flood of fresh memories flowed through their minds. He had a reputation, and there had been rumours, but the households of big houses thrived on rumours that were soon forgotten, to be replaced by new ones. As far as Rose could recall he had done her neither insult nor injury, and the sight of him now had certainly raised her flagging spirits.

"I swear you've not changed a bit, Ned Stiles," she said, throwing back her long hair. "A bit older maybe, but still a caution." She stepped back into the open doorway. "Look at me, leaving you standing out here. Won't you come in?"

"I'd better not, but it's been a real tonic seeing you like this. You've worn the years well. Anyway, this is the last place I would have expected to see you. What are you doing here?"

Rose was about to explain how she had come to be at Hibberd's Farm when the pair were distracted by the sound of hooves on the flagstones of the yard. With his eyes fixed firmly on Stiles, Matthew slid from the saddle and strode over to the house.

"What are you doing here? I don't want you here unless I invite you, and that's not likely," he snapped, before rounding on Rose. "And what are you doing talking to him? I pay you to look after the house, not to stand around gossiping."

"I wouldn't need to be here if you had met me as we agreed," said Stiles in a calm, firm voice.

"Well, I don't want you here." Matthew jabbed a finger at Rose. "And I don't want you talking to him either."

"Now you listen to me, lad," said Stiles, raising his voice. "You can talk to me how you wish if it makes you feel like a man, but you'll keep a civil tongue in your head when you talk to this lady."

Matthew gave a scornful laugh. "Lady! I've already seen one lady this morning, and I think I know the difference."

Stiles rammed the cap back on his head and turned on Matthew, grabbing him violently by the lapels of his jacket. "Why, you young ..."

"No, Mr Stiles, please ..." Rose rushed forward and tugged at his arm until he released his grip. "Don't go getting yourself into any trouble, not on my account."

"It would be no trouble at all, believe me." Reluctantly Stiles pushed Matthew away. "He needs a lesson in manners and it would be my pleasure."

The suddenness and severity of the attack had shaken Matthew, but he quickly recovered and pushed Rose by the shoulder. "Get back in the house and on with what I pay you for. I'll speak to you later." He turned to Stiles who was still seething, his fists clenched. "Stay away from my house, and stay away from her. Your only concern is Haveringham's estate, and what goes on here is my affair. Now, get to your horse, we've work to do."

"You're forgetting something, lad, it's not just your farm any more now," said Stiles smugly. He gave Rose a knowing nod. "If he gives you any trouble, come and find me."

Anxiously Rose watched them ride off. As she closed the door, she wondered what had made Matthew so angry, and again questioned the wisdom of accepting the position he had offered her. Was his abusive behaviour the price she had to pay to save her from her previous existence? Was it worth the exchange of her pitiful hovel for a comfortable home? She concluded that perhaps it was, and that in future she would keep her opinions to herself, and pray that Matthew found some peace in his life.

Far from finding peace Matthew spent the rest of the day brooding on the events of the morning. First, he had received no assurances from Rufus Haveringham, having been fobbed off with lame platitudes. Then there was the girl. Who was she, and how could she affect his dreams of one day taking over the estate? And finally, the humiliation in front of his housekeeper. None of these things he had envisaged when he had bathed in the euphoria of saving his farm.

He was still brooding on all these things when he arrived home that evening. Rose had resolved to speak to him only when necessary, or until his mood had sufficiently lightened to make a civil conversation possible. She served his meal in silence and was relieved when he made no effort to talk to her as she went about her chores. She did, however, feel his eyes following her as she moved about the kitchen, making her feel uncomfortable and vulnerable.

After finishing his meal, he went through to the parlour to sit as usual in his father's chair and stare sullenly at the dying embers of the fire, and it was only when Rose had finished her work and was preparing to go up to bed that he finally spoke to her.

"I won't have that man in my house," he said vehemently, as though the thought had been festering in his mind all evening.

Rose's first inclination was to ignore the remark and go straight to bed, but if this was his attempt at a reconciliation it would be wrong of her to avoid the opportunity.

"It wasn't me who invited him," she replied softly. "He came here looking for you, not me."

"But you were encouraging him, that was plain enough." She now knew he was looking for an argument, not conciliation. "It seems to me you once had feelings for him. Perhaps you still do. Is that why you came to work here, to be nearer to him?"

"You talk such nonsense, Matthew Pearson. Aren't you the one who speaks of him all the time?" she retorted dismissively, trying to make light of the accusation. "Now, I'm off to bed, so I'll say goodnight to you and hope we'll speak no more of this."

Matthew made no reply, continuing to stare moodily into the fireplace as she went up the stairs. As he listened to the creaking of the floorboards above his head, he sat in brooding contemplation for a few more minutes before going up himself.

After undressing he lay on the bed, listening to Rose moving about in the next room just a few feet away. It reminded him of when his mother was alive, hearing clearly the rustling of cotton fabric as she removed her clothes. He could even identify the various garments and knew the very moment when she would be naked, absorbing the vision until it evaporated beneath the flannel nightdress. It was in that brief moment when he would grip himself hard and find relief as his brothers slept. How many nights had he laid there like that just listening, and fighting forlornly against his demons.

Now it was Rose Buddon in that same room, deliberately taunting him with her body, tormenting him with what she knew he couldn't see, her small, firm breasts and full rounded buttocks exposed to his lurid imagination. She knew he would be excited. It was her way of punishing him for treating her the way he had. But she had misjudged him, this was to be another night when he feared his demons would triumph.

Rose sat on the edge of the bed brushing out her long tresses, taking time with each stroke and picking the loose hairs from her nightdress. It was a routine she went through each night, and usually she thought of nothing more exciting than the routine of the following day. But this night she thought of Ned Stiles, and smiled to herself at the simple pleasure of just seeing him again. So lost was she in this small bout of nostalgia that when the door opened behind her it passed unnoticed. It was only the creaking floorboard that caused her to swivel around on the bed, and at the sight of Matthew she clutched at the open top of her nightdress.

"You've no right in her," she said in a calm, firm voice, taking little notice of his nakedness. "This may be your house, but this is my room and I've a right to my privacy."

"My house, my chattels," he replied coldly. She stood up to face him as he approached the bed. "You're a fine looking woman, Rose Budden, and I'll wager it's been some time since you've had the pleasure of a man."

"Is that what you're calling yourself, Matthew Pearson, a man? I've seen enough men in my time, and been bedded by a few too, so you've got nothing to offer me I've not had before, and certainly nothing I can't do without." She showed no sign of alarm, and her tone was unequivocal. As he came closer she stood and backed away a little. "Now, for the sake of your mother's memory, go back to your room and we'll say nothing more about this."

She was talking down to him, just as Stiles did. They were both the same. "Is that how you think of me, a stupid little boy?"

With no further means of retreat she looked him up and down through contemptuous eyes. "Oh, you've a man's body right enough, but you've not got the sense to know when you are wrong." Her expression softened to one of pity. "I can see the anger inside you, but you'll get no satisfaction taking it out on me, not like this."

"You think not?" he sneered, close enough now to grab hold of her arms and pulling her into him so that her breasts were hard against his chest. "You think we'll both not get some satisfaction from this?"

He kissed her crudely on the mouth and she neither responded nor turned away. When his hands began feverishly groping her through the thin material of the nightdress she stood still and impassive, tensing only when he forced his hand between her thighs. He gave a whimper of uncontrolled excitement as he tugged at the garment, lifting it up over her head and tossing it onto the floor. She had already made up her mind not to give him the satisfaction of a fight, knowing it would be far more painful if she tried to stop him taking her by force. He was too strong for her to resist for long, but she would make sure he knew of the contempt she felt and the pleasure she didn't.

His hands and his eyes covered her body in a frenzy of lustful activity until she allowed herself to be pushed onto the bed. Even when he spread her legs and made clumsy, frantic efforts to enter her she offered no resistance. He thrust at her, letting out anguished cries of pure frustration that turned to pitiful sobs as it became clear that impotence and Rose Budden were conspiring to rob him of the satisfaction and domination he craved.

Coldly she pushed him off her and got up from the bed. "Do you feel like a man now?" she asked scornfully, pulling on her nightdress. "Don't worry, I feel no bitterness towards you, just pity. You've learned a harsh lesson here tonight. If you're meant to have anything in this life it will come to you naturally. You'll never keep what you take by force. You've still got a lot of growing up in you yet before you've the right to call yourself a man." She went to the door and held it open. "Now, get out of my room and don't be pestering me ever again."

Without a single word of abuse or apology Matthew got up off the bed and with his head bowed he slunk out of the room. When he had gone, Rose took a chair and wedged it under the door handle. In the morning she would make her position clear, but for the remainder of the night she would sleep sound.

Chapter Eight

Although the sun shone brightly over Hibberd's Farm the following morning, it was black clouds of despondency that hung low over the horizons of Matthew's future. It was not from any feelings of guilt or remorse for his actions the previous night that darkened his mood, that moment had passed into obscurity, requiring no further consideration. But as he faced the new day he realised, with stark disappointment, that nothing had changed, that all the trials and tribulations that had so far plagued his life still existed.

When Rose came down Matthew had already left the house, but as she washed at the sink the bruising on her arms served to remind her that there was unfinished business between them. It would have been easy to pack up her belongings and return to her previous Spartan existence, but she felt the worst was over, that she now had the measure of her young master. After the humiliation he had suffered she was certain he would make no further attempt to prove his manhood. And now she had a further reason to remain. The renewed acquaintance with Ned Stiles had somehow bolstered her confidence, now she no longer felt friendless.

When Matthew returned home that evening, he made no attempt to speak to her, choosing to be his same sullen self that she had come to recognise as normal. He washed at the sink before sitting at the kitchen table while she put his meal in front of him, barely acknowledging her presence.

"If you're thinking your behaviour last night will drive me away, then I'm sorry to disappoint you. I have a place here and I'll stay until you tell me to leave," she said calmly, as a prelude to what she hoped would resolve their differences.

"And why would I do that," he replied, without looking up from his food. "You serve me well enough."

"That I do, as long as you remember I serve you down here, and not up there." She sat down opposite him, trying to elicit some rapport. "I bear you no malice

110

for what you tried to do, and if you had succeeded, I doubt it would have given you the satisfaction you were looking for. I'm well aware of the needs of men, and there's plenty as will provide it, at a price, but that won't be me." She looked hard at him. "Do we have an understanding?"

For a while he carried on eating as though her words had meant nothing to him, until he eventually raised his head a little and gave a brief nod.

Following that he would arrive home each evening with no apparent change in his mood, eat his meal in silence and sit in his father's chair staring into the fire until it was time for bed.

***

It was about a week later that he came home in the evening to find something that would finally lift the gloom that surrounded him. He was washing himself as usual before Rose pointed to an envelope she had earlier placed on the mantelpiece.

"That came for you," she said blandly, expecting that it could contain only bad news. "A lad from the big house brought it over."

As he dried himself, he glared from her to the letter before throwing the towel on the table and ambling over to the fireplace. He picked up the envelope and turned it over in his hands, studying the embossed crest on the back. On the front, in copperplate hand was his name; MATTHEW PEARSON ESQ. Carefully he opened the flap of the envelope and pulled out a gold edged card and read the words, not once but several times.

"Requests the company!" he exclaimed excitedly. "Rufus Haveringham Esq. requests the company." He looked at Rose jubilantly, waving the card in the air. "Let's see if your Mr Stiles gets one of these."

Rose chose to ignore the remark and continued to clear the plates until Matthew strode over and thrust the card in her face. "Well, what do you think of that, me being invited to a posh do up at the house?"

She turned her head away. "I don't think anything of it, but it clearly pleases you, so for that I should be grateful."

"There'll be a lot of important people there," he insisted on telling her, still brandishing the card. He read the wording again. "White tie, what does that mean?"

"It means you'll look out of place even dressed in your Sunday best," she replied smugly.

"I shall have to buy some new clothes. You worked up at the house, you must know about these things. You can come with me."

"I will not!" she exclaimed indignantly. "I'll do only what I'm paid to do, cooking and cleaning, nothing more than that. And if you think a new suit of clothes is going to turn you into a gentleman then you're in for a shock."

Matthew shrugged and turned away, smiling to himself. He had only asked for her help as a courtesy, he placed no value on her advice.

Rose Budden had allowed Matthew the privacy of the tin bath in the kitchen. Having made sure there was enough hot water she had shut herself in her room until he had finished his preparations for what he had told her would be the most important evening of his life.

Since receiving the invitation to what Rufus Haveringham would casually refer to as an informal gathering, Matthew's demeanour had changed significantly, although Rose could not say it was necessarily for the better. Instead of his usual sullenness and anger he had talked endlessly and arrogantly of how the evening would change his life, propelling him into the upper echelons of local society. The people he would meet would see him for his true worth, recognising him as the natural successor to the great estate. That was his belief.

But when he tapped on her bedroom door before leaving the house some of that ebullience had deserted him in favour of a little self-doubt.

"How do I look?" he asked when she finally opened the door.

She looked him up and down and grudgingly admitted to herself that in appearance he was every inch the gentleman. "If you're judged on how you look then I've no doubt you'll impress everyone that meets you. I just hope your manners match your clothes and you'll not disgrace yourself."

"Perhaps this is what I was born to," he replied arrogantly strutting around the floor outside her room. "Your friend Stiles will have to show me more respect after tonight."

A steady procession of carriages made their way up the sweeping drive of Millwood House, the liveried drivers and attendants delivering their cargo of local dignitaries and land owning gentry. A footman, positioned beneath the portico, stepped smartly forward to open the door as each carriage drew to a standstill, and the occupants were ushered inside to be announced by Jenkins.

No such formality was accorded Matthew as he pulled back on the reins and waited for a groom to take hold of the bridle. Small groups of drivers standing around idly chatting gave him a curious glance when the footman asked to see his invitation.

"You know damn well who I am," he snapped, ignoring the request as he marched up the steps. "I've as much right to be here as any of them."

To call it a ballroom may have been a small exaggeration when compared to some of the grander houses of the county. The Haveringhams had acquired their land and wealth by guile and hard work and not from an accident of birth, and although Millwood House was a fine testament to their achievements it was no match for some of the more ancient piles. The room was an attachment to the side of the house with a high, vaulted ceiling from which hung three large crystal chandeliers. It could be shut off from the rest of the house and had been so since the death of Haveringham's wife; there had been no occasion to celebrate since those halcyon days when such gatherings were a common, and popular, event.

Down each side of the ballroom was a line of columns from which were draped brightly coloured ribbons, with each column displaying a large bouquet of fresh flowers. At the far end of the room was a raise dais on which a string quartet played a selection from Handl and Brahms, although the music was generally drowned beneath the ebb and flow of conversation from the guests who had already arrived. And above the conversations rose the voice of Rufus Haveringham who sought to impress or flatter those around him as he flitted from one group to another.

As Jenkins announced him, in a less than enthusiastic tone, Matthew nervously scanned the room. He estimated that there were close to fifty guests, more people than he had been in close proximity to with since school. He suddenly felt lost and alone, until his host detached himself from the group he was talking to and strode over, his hand extended.

"Very pleased to see you here, my boy. You cut a very dashing figure, a credit to yourself." He gave a wry smile as he looked over his suit. "I hope the investment you made will be worth it."

Matthew thanked him and continued to peer cautiously around the room.

"Not many familiar faces here, I fear," said Haveringham, sensing Matthew's unease. He took him by the arm and led him into the room. "But if you want to make your mark in the society to which you aspire then this is where it begins." He swept the ballroom with his arm. "Most of these people have business in farming, so you should have no trouble engaging them in conversation. I shall make one or two introductions and then leave you to fend for yourself. This evening, I'm afraid, is for the benefit of someone far closer to my heart than you, I'm afraid."

He led Matthew towards one small group who appeared to be enjoying the music rather than the company of the other guests. The oldest member of the group, a tall man of advancing years stood with stiff, military bearing, his hands clasped firmly behind his back as he looked imperiously down on the other three. The woman, presumably his wife, appeared a few years younger with a pleasant face that twitched nervously. She played with her gloved fingers while pretending to appreciate the skill of the musicians. The girl had the looks and anxious traits of her mother, standing close by her side. No beauty, thought Matthew, but adequately compensated, no doubt, by her father's wealth. The young man appeared to be of similar age to Matthew, though taller with a lean build. He had inherited the prominent nose of his father which he looked down in a similarly imperious fashion.

"Roderick," gushed Haveringham as they approached. In unison the group turned to face their host. "Roderick, may I introduce Matthew Pearson." He placed a hand on the lad's shoulder. "Matthew, this is Sir Roderick Mortimer, his wife Lady Margaret, their son Giles and daughter Penelope." He smiled benignly as he eased Matthew into their midst. "The lad's a neighbour of mine, and now, I suppose, a protégé. But he's a stranger to these little gatherings of ours so we need to nurse him along until he finds his own feet. Perhaps I could leave him to make your better acquaintance."

Haveringham turned smartly away, leaving Matthew to give the Mortimers a weak smile and a brief nod of acknowledgement. He fidgeted uncomfortably as all the self-confident blustering of the past weeks deserted him in the company of those who clearly considered him their inferior. Even the timid Lady Margaret discovered a voice alongside him.

"Delighted to meet you," she said unconvincingly when the rest of her family failed to volunteer a greeting. She feigned a dignified thoughtfulness. "Pearson you say? Yes, I know the name. Your family farm, do they?"

"Yes. Well, at least, they did," he replied almost apologetically. "My parents are both dead. I run the farm now."

"Dead! How tragic. I'm so sorry to hear that," continued the woman with undisguised indifference while her husband made a great display of appearing bored.

As Matthew continued in the discomfort of his new clothes and the stiff collar that chafed his neck, Giles had indiscreetly been sizing up this new addition the society that had been his since birth. "And how much do you farm?" he enquired casually.

Matthew held his sneering gaze while he considered his reply. It would be easy to tell them the truth and endure their mockery, but he had already made up his mind that he wouldn't play their games. "More than enough for one person to manage."

Giles looked at Matthew down his long, narrow nose. "Then, no doubt, the other person has charge while you entertain us here." He turned to his father and got the approval he sought.

Matthew felt his anger rising and his fists clenched involuntarily. Then the thought struck him that perhaps this was another test contrived by Rufus Haveringham. He smiled smugly. "No, not at all. The other man is here, our host Mr Haveringham. We farm jointly."

Penelope squealed with delight and clapped her hands as she focussed her limited female charms on Matthew. "Oh, well done! You deserved that, Giles, I sometimes think you're too clever for your own good."

For her efforts she drew a severe look of rebuke from her father. "Quiet girl," he ordered.

She lowered her eyes, attracting Matthew's passing sympathy, but nothing more. He felt the conversation and his welcome had run its course and he wanted nothing more than to hide away in a quiet corner while he waited for the main event they had all been brought there to witness. He could see relief on three of the four faces as he humbly made his excuses and backed away from the group to seek refuge behind one of the decorated columns, after helping himself to a glass of champagne from the tray of a passing footman. Having given up any possibility of being included as an equal in this social gathering, he would content himself with remaining anonymous while he viewed the evening's proceedings. His only interest now was the identity of Haveringham's mysterious house guest, and the threat she may pose to his ambitions.

He watched intently as Haveringham played the accomplished host, something he had not practised for a number of years, passing with impeccable precision from one group of guests to the other while keeping the conversation seamless.

Matthew took particular notice of Giles Mortimer when he left his parents side to join three of four other pallid faced young men who had occupied a position in the centre of the ballroom, attracting unnecessary attention to themselves with their loud laughter and exaggerated posturing. Every so often their eyes would turn in Matthew's direction, when the laughter became even louder. Their behaviour only served to push Matthew further away from any regard he had for all the guests. He vowed he would never be the same as them in any way but wealth.

Just as Matthew was beginning to think that the evening was a waste of his time and money the laughter and conversation suddenly dropped to a low murmuring and Haveringham emerged from the throng and almost ran across the floor to the open doorway, his arms outstretched. Matthew followed the combined gaze of the guests until the object became apparent.

Framed in the doorway, and as still as a picture. stood the girl that he and all the other guests had come to meet. The gold silk dress, recently purchased in London, hung delicately from her pale, slender shoulders, the colour of the material perfectly complimenting her auburn hair that cascaded down in tight ringlets. Her complexion had the purity of a young girl yet she carried herself with the poise and confidence of a mature woman.

Unable to conceal his delight and pride, Haveringham offered her his arm and escorted her into the room. With a wave of his hand the musicians ceased their playing, and with a swish of silk the pair crossed the floor to the dais, accompanied by a ripple of muttered comments and admiring gasps. Haveringham beamed at them all, while the girl hid behind a façade of feminine coyness. As they mounted the dais and turned to face their guests a silence fell over the room, and even Matthew emerged from the sanctity of his corner for a better view.

"My dear friends and neighbours," began Haveringham after a short pause, allowing a tentative silence to descend over the room, "apart from the immense pleasure of your company, I have invited you here this evening to introduce you to someone who is very dear to my heart." He took Grace's hand and held it up causing her to blush slightly and give a little curtsey. "This beautiful young lady is my niece, Grace, the daughter of my sister and, until very recently, at school in Switzerland." Some murmured speculation regarding the girl's parentage ran through the audience. Unperturbed their host continued. "You can have no idea the pleasure it gives me to have her here with me, and I know you will all do what you can to welcome her into the bosom of our little community." He made a general sweeping gesture for the musicians to continue. "Now, please, enjoy the remainder of the evening."

As they stepped down from the dais some of the guests surged forward, most of them women, no doubt anxious to make a case for their unmarried sons. Whilst lacking the titles and aristocratic ancestry of many of his guests he had something many of them did not, business success and money. Hidden behind their superior posturing and fine clothes were a lot of impecunious parents who could see the advantage of a good marriage for their offspring. To his credit, Haveringham deftly fended off most of the offers thrust upon her, and dealt with any questions regarding her father with equal skill, simple saying he had died when she was very young, and leaving them to make whatever assumptions they wished.

Occasionally Grace appeared flustered by all the attention she was receiving, and as she extricated herself from one group another would close in to bombard her with more questions and offers. With so much interest in her past and her plans for the future she was beginning to regret complaining to her uncle of loneliness, and several times he was forced to intervene to prevent her from being completely overwhelmed.

All the while Matthew hung back, watching the proceedings from behind the garlanded columns. At least he now knew who she was, but it had brought him no closer to making her acquaintance, and he feared that in the present company he would never be given the opportunity to do so. After all, what could he offer her that they could not? So, he consoled himself with more champagne and self-pity.

As Grace moved around the ballroom she was pursued relentlessly by Giles Mortimer and his pack of simpering predators. They constantly snapped at her heels with their infantile humour and outrageous boasting, and as one got too close the others would jostle her for position. Having been schooled to be polite at all times she smiled back at them, feigning interest in what they had to say until it became increasingly clear that she was tiring of their vacuous company, giving Matthew the vague hope that she would eventually notice him.

Keeping a discreet yet protective eye on her, Haveringham too had recognised her predicament and moved in to rescue her, taking her gently by the arm and leading her away.

"Please excuse me, gentlemen," he said graciously, "but there's someone else I should like my niece to meet. I'm sure there will be plenty of opportunities to speak to her again."

"I do so hope not, uncle," she whispered with a wry smile. "I shall never complain again."

"Oh, I'm sure you will," he responded with a twinkle in his eye. "But that wasn't just an idle ploy to rescue you, there really is someone I should like you to meet, before he makes a nuisance of himself."

She gave him a mischievous grin. "He sounds interesting, uncle. I don't suppose he is rich and handsome as well?"

He gave his niece a cautionary look. "I suppose he is possibly one, and he certainly has ambitions to be the other, but don't allow yourself to be persuaded by either. Just let your feminine instincts get the measure of him first."

Matthew stiffened with anticipation as he watched them approach, hardly daring to believe his luck. Perhaps there was some justice in his life after all. His eyes followed her elegant progress across the floor, and as she met his gaze his stomach fluttered with a mild attack of panic before he quickly swallowed the last of his champagne.

Haveringham regarded his obvious discomfort with an amused expression. "You look to me, lad, as though you're not entirely enjoying the evening. Is the company not to your liking?"

Matthew shrugged his shoulders as his eyes remained firmly fixed on Grace. "It would be difficult to answer that without giving offence. Let's just say I preferred my own company to that of your friends, the Mortimers."

"Well, I hope you find the company of my niece a little more agreeable. Grace, this young man is Matthew Pearson. I've no doubt you'll find him ill-mannered and totally lacking in the social graces of my other guests, but he is, as you say, interesting."

She smiled demurely and held out her hand. With his courage bolstered by the drink he raised her hand to his lips, as he had seen others do that evening. "If I am everything your uncle accuses me of then it's because I've not yet been spoilt by wealth," he said pragmatically, looking deep into her searching green eyes. "But I make no apologies for my birth."

"You see, my dear," declared Haveringham jubilantly, "completely without tact."

"Perhaps, uncle, you mistake tact for honesty," she replied smiling, her hand still in Matthew's. "It's certainly a refreshing change from everything else I've listened to this evening."

"What an innocent young lady you are, my dear, to be more impressed by honesty than wealth," teased her uncle, easing her hand free. "Well, I shall leave the two of you to exchange moral views, but be warned, what he lacks in breeding he more than makes up for in guile."

As Haveringham left them, Matthew grew aware that many of the guests had been keeping a curious and disdainful eye on them, in particular Giles Mortimer and his coterie. It occurred to Matthew that to most of them he was still a stranger and it pleased him to believe there was some jealousy in their furtive glances.

For her part Grace appeared oblivious to the eyes, and opinions, of others and stared apologetically at Matthew. "I'm sorry, I'm sure my uncle meant no offence by the remarks he made about you, he's just so very protective of me."

"No offence taken," he assured her. "Your uncle and me understand each other. We both speak our minds."

"It's a shame more people aren't the same." She cast her eyes around the ballroom, at the fraudulent laughter and vacuous conversations. "It's strange how people can speak so much and say so little that has any real meaning."

Matthew sneered cynically as he joined with her to survey their opulent surroundings. "When you have the wealth they have truth has little meaning, they speak and the poor have to listen. That's just the way it is. But their wealth doesn't impress me. Most have done nothing to earn it, and have little idea how to use it."

Grace studied him hard. "What a bitter man you appear to be, Matthew Pearson. And what about my uncle, is that how you see him?"

Matthew grinned. It was the question he was expecting. "Your uncle knows well enough what I think of him, so, it would do me little good to try and flatter him in front of you. I also know that everything we speak about will go straight back to him and that he wouldn't believe it if I spoke well of him. Let's just say I think him a little devious."

"Why do you say that?"

Matthew remained thoughtful for a moment. "Well, for one thing, he led me to believe he had no living relatives, yet here you are. I don't understand why you were kept such a secret."

Grace shrugged her bare shoulders. "I wasn't aware that I was a secret until this evening, that so few people were aware of my existence. I can only assume it never occurred to him to speak of me, after all we were virtual strangers until I arrived here." An expression of boredom flickered across her face. "Anyway, I don't wish to talk about me any further, it's all I've done all evening." She cocked her head to one side. "Why don't you tell me about yourself instead, and your relationship with Uncle Rufus"

"Are you really that interested in me or just being polite like the rest of them?" He asked with unintentional brusqueness.

She seemed a little annoyed. "I think your honesty is becoming a little trying," she said curtly. "Are you always this suspicious with everyone?"

Matthew smiled defensively. "I'm sorry, but I'm not used to people taking any interest in me, at least not since my parents died. Perhaps it's because I have never had much to offer in return, and still haven't."

"In that case then you have no reason to object to my asking about you, seeing as I can't expect anything in return." Her eyes narrowed. "You interest me simply because you are not like my uncle's other guests. Despite your smart clothes you look out of place here. I suppose you and I are much the same, neither of us were born into this."

"But we're not the same," he responded vehemently. "You have the benefit of your uncle's money, all I have is his faith in me, and I don't know how long that will last. I think you have the best of the deal."

"And what sort of deal do you have with my uncle? He has told me nothing about you, and when I first saw you in this house, I wondered what business you had here. You dressed like one of the farm workers, but your manner told me otherwise, and the fact that you were invited here proves me right."

Matthew gave her a tantalising grin. "Perhaps it was just to meet you."

She shook her head. "No. All these people were invited here to meet me, and most of them will expect me to return the compliment and visit them, probably because they have a son seeking a suitable wife or a daughter looking for a companion. Bur what sort of invitation could I expect from you?" She smiled, pausing long enough to acknowledge an effete wave from Giles Mortimer and one or two of his friends as they edged closer to her. "Don't you think they are more the sort of young men my uncle would wish me to associate with in preference to someone like yourself. That's why you interest me, Matthew Pearson."

With his entourage crowded up behind him Giles Mortimer moved to Grace's side. "Is this person bothering you, Miss Haveringham?" He gave Matthew a sideways look of contempt. "Your uncle asked that we make his acquaintance, but it seems he is more interested in making yours than ours." To a round of sniggering from his friends he glared hard at Matthew. "Why don't you be a good chap and run along now. I'm sure there are others here who would better benefit from your charming company and eloquent conversation."

As more infantile giggling rippled through the little group Matthew felt his face flush and the anger churning in his stomach. He clenched his fists, barely able to hold himself in check. He stood inches from Giles, glaring hard into the leering face.

Grace caught hold of his arm. "Don't, Matthew," she said firmly, "not here, not in my uncle's house. Besides, I'm sure they are only teasing you. Just ignore them." She focussed her attention on Giles and smiled pleasantly. "Just teasing, isn't that right … I'm sorry, but I can't quite recall your name. Anyway, it's not important. Why don't the two of you shake hands like gentlemen?"

Matthew took a step back and grudgingly held out his hand, feeling that Grace had won him back a little ground. "I'm willing if he is," he said with all the sincerity he could muster. If this was another test he was determined not to fail.

Giles' mean mouth twisted into a sneer as he looked for support from his friends. "I would willingly shake the hand on any gentleman, but I would no more shake his hand than shoe my own horse." He acknowledged the chorus of laughter.

Clinging to a fragile self-control Matthew gritted his teeth as he sensed the pleading gaze from Grace. "It would surprise me if you could recognise the difference between the hand of a gentleman and the hoof of a horse," he replied disdainfully.

As the two men faced up to each other Grace stepped between them. "That's enough," she snapped harshly. "You are both behaving like children and I want an end to it now. My uncle arranged this evening for me to meet new friends, but from what I've seen so far he might just as well not have bothered, for I've seen no one yet I would wish to be friends with."

Matthew found some comfort in the fact that her remarks appeared to be directed more at Giles and his friends than himself, although he still smarted from the notion that she considered him childish.

"If I've caused offence to anyone then I apologise," he said with forced humility.

"It's your presence here that's offensive," whined Giles. "You've no business here, anyone can see that." He gave Grace a curt nod of the head. "My apologies too, Miss Haveringham, and I hope to meet with you again under more conducive circumstances." He bowed before turning away.

"Perhaps he was right," said Matthew when they had gone. "I don't belong here."

"That's nonsense. My uncle invited you so that gives you as much right to be here as any of them." Her green eyes scrutinised him sympathetically. "You shouldn't feel guilty about your background, you know. All this is new to me too."

"Oh, I don't feel guilty." He cast his hand around the ballroom. "Most of these have done nothing to earn what they have. At least, when I'm as rich as them I'll know it was by my own efforts, and not by some accident of birth."

"Uncle Rufus said you were ambitious." She peered at him through narrowed eyes. "So, tell me, how do you intend to become rich?"

Matthew met her gaze. "Perhaps by marrying you, then one day all this will be ours."

He looked so serious that for a moment she believed him and her expression was one of shocked indignation, until he suddenly burst out laughing. Realising that it was her being teased she joined in the laughter, attracting the unwelcome attention of those nearest them, including her uncle.

"You are a bad influence on me, Matthew Pearson," she said breathlessly as the laughter subsided. "I can see why my uncle warned me about you. Mind you, I have to admit that I find you a good deal more entertaining than most of those I've met this evening, so perhaps he did have a good reason for inviting you after all."

She had hardly finished speaking when her uncle appeared at her side. "I'm afraid you've monopolised her long enough," he said to Matthew. "She'll make precious few friends talking to you all evening. Come my dear."

Grace glanced back over her shoulder as she was led away, and Matthew could not avoid the conclusion that he had made something of an impression on her. Could he even dare to believe that something said in jest may possibly have some substance?

For the remainder of the evening Matthew stayed in the shelter of the columns, avoiding, as far as possible, any contact with the other guests, especially Giles Mortimer and his friends, but all the while observing Grace as she moved about the room making the polite conversation that was expected of her. Every now and then he caught her glancing in his direction when she would raise her eyes with bored resignation. He smiled back in amused sympathy.

He was relieved when the guests finally started to leave. Grace and her uncle positioned themselves by the doors to the ballroom from where they graciously thanked everyone for coming and offering their assurance that the compliment would be returned at the first opportunity.

Matthew hung back, hoping for a few more minutes with Grace, but he could see that Haveringham would not leave her side, so he joined the end of the throng leaving the room.

"It has been a pleasure meeting you, Mr Pearson," she said with the same reserve shat had been accorded all the other guests. "I've no doubt I shall be seeing more of you since you and Uncle Rufus are in business together."

"But that gives you no more liberty with my niece's affections than any other young man," pointed out Haveringham sharply as she offered Matthew her hand. "So have a care, lad, do nothing that would cause me upset, and you my displeasure."

"You have my assurance on that, sir." Matthew placed her hand to his lips. "Now, I'll say goodnight and look forward to seeing you again, soon."

He allowed himself a self-satisfied smile as he left the house. The evening had been an even greater success than he had dared hope, and for quite different reasons. He had no need for the patronage of the rich and influential, they meant nothing to him. No, the only object of his interest now was Grace, and how she could influence his future. A wave of smugness swept over him as he stood at the top of the steps breathing in the night air.

There was no sign of the footman to send for his gig and with a resigned shrug of his shoulders Matthew decided to fetch it himself. He needed to stretch his legs after standing around all evening.

The path to the stabling block led around the side of the house, falling away in a gentle slope that led through a thick shrubbery of rhododendrons, forsythia and bush roses that were heavy with early foliage. With the moon in its final quarter and no lights showing from that side of the house the pathway was in almost total darkness, and it was only familiarity that allowed him to make his way without stumbling and falling. Not far away an owl hooted followed by the swish of powerful wings. In the undergrowth something moved and scuttled away, probably disturbed by his footsteps. Then there was a louder, more pronounced rustling of leaves. Matthew stopped to listen. He was used to the night sounds of the countryside, he had been born to it, but he thought he heard something else, muffled voices amongst the shrubbery. He turned his ear towards the sound and assumed he had been mistaken. A fox or badger, perhaps.

He walked on a few more yards then stopped again, abruptly, when a figure stepped out onto the path in front of him.

Matthew peered into the gloom. "Who is it? What do you want?"

"Goodness me, not afraid of the dark are you, old chap?" came back the now familiar thin, whining voice of Giles Mortimer.

"Not of the dark, nor of you, old chap," sneered Matthew through gritted teeth. "What do you want, to fight me?"

Giles let out a short, hoarse laugh. "A fight! You mean brawl like common fellows. No, not at all, I'm not here to fight, old chap, just to teach you a lesson in manners."

Matthew knew that Giles would never attempt anything on his own, that his friends had to be close by, but the thought had hardly entered his head when there was a disturbance behind him and before he could react his arms were pinned behind his back. Violently he threw himself about, trying to free his arms, which he may well have achieved until another hand grabbed hold of his hair and jerked his head back. The pain in his scalp made his eyes water and he gave up the struggle to stare defiantly at the tormentor facing him.

Satisfied that Matthew was no longer a threat Giles stepped forward. "It's no use, old chap, you'll just have to take your medicine like a man." He swung a fist that caught Matthew on the side of the mouth.

Matthew smiled back bitterly, licking a small drop of blood from his lip. "Is that the best you can do?" He swung his foot at Giles, but it was a wild effort, easily avoided.

As Giles side stepped, he drove his fist viciously into Matthew's ribs, forcing the air from his lungs. Cursing loudly and gasping for breath he bent forward and a knee crunched into the side of his face and nose. Blood ran freely into his mouth as he looked up and glared at Giles through hate ridden, watery eyes.

"You can beat me as much as you like, but you won't get the better of me. I might not be a gentleman, but I'm twice the man you'll ever be."

"Oh, I don't want to get the better of you, farm boy, I'm already that. This is just to teach you your place. You should know you can't cross a purebred with a mongrel, it's simply not done. Perhaps you won't be such a ladies' man after tonight. Lift his head."

The unseen hand snatched at his hair, dragging his head back. Matthew managed to turn it enough to see Giles' flushed face and their eyes met the instant a fist slammed into his jaw, spinning his head sideways. His eyes glazed and despite the hands still holding his arms he slumped forward onto his knees. Giles took a step back and kicked him hard in the ribs, toppling him sideways onto the narrow path where he lay half conscious.

The voices above him seemed vague and distant, but Matthew was acutely aware of the foot that caught him just above the eye, splitting the skin and causing more blood to trickle down his face. After that his senses merged with the night and everything became black.

***

It was less than an hour after Matthew had left his farm for Millwood House that Rose Budden was suddenly disturbed by a sharp rap on the kitchen door. She had just settled herself in front of the parlour fire with a book, a rare treat for someone more used to spending most evenings shut in her room. Her life at Hibberd's Farm was proving to be only a little less lonely than when she lived alone, with Matthew's dubious company of no real comfort. The companionship she had looked forward to had turned into a hollow dream.

There had been so few callers at the house that any unexpected visitor, especially at that hour, caused her some alarm. Nervously she put down her book and went through to the kitchen, hoping the caller would go away. Then a second, louder rap brought a startled gasp to her lips.

"Who is it?" she called out timidly, pressing her ear to the door.

There was no reply so she called louder, her hand sliding the bolt shut. She could hear the shuffling of feet and then a muffled voice.

"It's me, Rose, Ned Stiles."

For a moment she was rooted to the spot, unable to decide on a reaction. Slowly she drew back the bolt and opened the door a few inches. A thin shaft of light spread out into the yard and Stiles stepped into it, a shadowy figure, his face hidden by a cap pulled low over his forehead and a scarf covering his mouth and nose.

Rose stared hard at him before fully opening the door and stepping back. "Gracious me, Ned Stiles!" she exclaimed, breathless with shock, "you near gave me a turn knocking on the door like that, and at this hour. And look at you, all done up like a footpad."

"I'm sorry, Rose, if I caused you a fright." He snatched the cap from his head and pulled down the scarf. "I thought it best if I wasn't recognised, you know how folk gossip. I swear I didn't mean you no upset."

"You think I'm bothered by a bit of gossip," she said indignantly, beckoning him inside. "No one knows me hereabouts, except you and Master Matthew, so a few wagging tongues won't do me no harm." She closed the door behind him. "But what brings you here? Young Matthew's up at the big house, some sort of a do."

He gave her an impish grin, his lively eyes twinkling deviously. "I know he's up there, I wouldn't have been here otherwise. It's you I've come to see." Deliberately he unbuttoned his coat and unwrapped the scarf from around his neck. "But will I be invited to stay?"

Rose appeared a little anxious as she nodded her reply. "You're always welcome enough as far as I'm concerned. But it's young Matthew, I don't know what time he's expected back. I wouldn't want any more trouble."

"Don't worry about him, he'll be gone a good while yet. I think there's a good deal more to interest him up there than down here." He patted her arm reassuringly. "I wouldn't do anything to put you at risk, Rose, you can be sure of that."

"Too much of a gentleman, are you?" she teased, relaxing a little and warming to his company. "But not too much of a gentleman to call on a woman on her own, at this time of night?"

Ned's face creased into a guilty frown. "You're right, I'm sorry. I shouldn't have come here uninvited. It was stupid and thoughtless of me."

She allowed him a moment of regret before breaking into a fit of girlish giggling. "You're a stupid man all right, Ned Stiles, but not for that reason, for taking me seriously." She held out her hand. "Give me your coat and I'll make us a pot of tea. Go and sit yourself down by the fire."

They exchanged small talk while she made the tea, and Ned settled into the chair that Matthew usually occupied. When Rose joined him, he was staring into the fire as though his mind were in some other place. She put down the tea and took her place on the old wooden settle.

She glanced across at him questioningly. "You look troubled, Ned, what is it?"

He turned to face her, shaking his head slowly. "I was just thinking how cosy this feels. I'm used to spending my evenings alone, so I'm not sure what sort of company I'll be."

"Hush yourself now," she scolded. "Do you know how many days and nights I spent alone before I came here? Even now I'm alone all day, and if you think young Matthew's any company when he comes home then you're sorely mistaken."

"And that's another reason I came here this evening," he said putting down his cup and leaning over to her. "I've been wanting to see you ever since that business when I was last here. I was worried about you."

Her lips parted in a thin smile. "That's very kind of you, Ned, but you've no need to worry on my account, I'm well able to look after myself."

Ned returned the smile. "I'm sure you are, Rose, but it wasn't just the worry that brought me here." His face reflected the glow from the fire as he put a hand into his trouser pocket. "Would you mind if I took a pipe?"

"Why, Ned Stiles, I would say you were a little bit bashful if I didn't know you better. That's not how I remember you all those years since." She nodded as he held up his pipe. "You can hide behind that if you like, but there's something else on your mind and I think I've a right to hear it."

His cheeks glowed with a deeper hue as he filled the pipe and stuck it in the corner of his mouth. He felt Rose's eyes on him as he struck a match and sucked deeply until the tobacco caught and he blew little puffs of blue smoke from the other side of his mouth.

"The truth is, Rose …" he began hesitantly, taking the pipe from his mouth. "The truth is I've been thinking of you quite a bit since I first saw you here." He took a few more sharp draws before continuing. "Maybe it was just that it brought back the memories from all those years ago when we were a bit more free and easy, I don't know. Anyway, I've been thinking about you all the same. We've both seen our fair share of life since then I don't doubt, but it strikes me that we've ended up pretty much the same, on our own."

As he paused to puff reflectively on his pipe, she leaned closer. "Did you never marry, Ned? The way you flirted with us girls back then it's hard to believe you didn't settle with someone." She sipped on her tea. "Was there anyone?"

He looked up at the smoke-stained ceiling. "There was someone once, but it didn't turn out right. She went away and we never saw each other again. After that it was just a bit of dallying here and there, nothing serious, and the years just passed me by." He gave her a wistful smile. "Time has a way of doing that, Rose, passing you by, I mean. But what about you?"

"Oh, I got married all right, but nothing special I can assure you. A waster he was. A drunk and a waster who promised me the earth and gave me nothing but plenty of beatings and left me a lot of debt. But even that was better than the loneliness I felt after he was gone. Loneliness is the worst thing." She put down her cup and joined him in staring into the fire. "You're right what you said, though, this is cosy, a real pleasure."

He turned his face to hers and took the pipe from his mouth. "I think that's the real reason I came here tonight, Rose." His lips trembled as he fought over the words. "You and me, we could spend all our evenings like this if we've a mind to. What do you think?"

Her eyes widened in astonishment. "I think young Matthew would have something to say about that," she retorted incredulously. "Have you forgotten the state he was in when you last came here? You said yourself you only came this evening because you knew he wouldn't be here. What on earth could you be thinking, saying something like that?"

Ned laid his pipe on the hearth to give her his full attention. "No, no, Rose, you misunderstand me!" There was an intensity in his voice she found almost frightening. "I'm asking that you leave here to come and live with me."

Rose turned away from him to stare open mouthed at the fire. Her mind was in turmoil as she tried to assemble his words into some sort of order. Slowly she looked around at him, breathing deeply to compose herself. "Ned Stiles, what are you saying? We barely know each other, yet here you are suggesting …! I don't know what it is you're suggesting."

He picked up his pipe again and chewed anxiously on the stem. "I'm sorry, Rose, I didn't mean …" He took out the pipe then just as quickly put it back again. "I just meant if you're not happy here you can come and stay with me. Housekeeper, companion, whatever you want. I enjoy your company and I believe you feel the same."

Rose got up from the settle and took her cup through to the kitchen. It was an unnecessary act, but she was still shaken by his suggestion and needed time to clear her head.

When she returned Ned was standing, his face a picture of regret. "I'm so sorry, Rose, that was stupid and thoughtless of me. I know the sort of man you live here with and I thought I could offer you something better, something you deserve."

She cocked her head to one side, her eyes narrowed and penetrating. "Are you sure it's me you are really concerned about, or are you wanting to score points over the lad? I know there's no love lost between the two of you and it strikes me I might just be a pawn in your little game."

He shook his head vigorously. "No, no, not at all," he protested in a firm voice. "I can't deny the lad and me aren't exactly on friendly terms, and for the life of me I don't know why, but I would never use you to get at him, it's not my way." He held out his hand to her. "Come, sit down and hear me out."

Still overwhelmed by her emotions she allowed him to keep hold of her hand as she sat down. "You've given me quite a turn, Ned, and no mistake, but say what you've got to say."

"I never came here with anything like this in mind, I just wanted to satisfy myself you were all right," he began nervously, giving her hand a gentle squeeze. "It was the cosiness of all this that got me thinking. You and me seemed right together, comfortable if you like. I know I'm not a young man anymore, and lost my looks some years since, but I would treat you right and expect nothing back in return, apart from the company." He paused to let her absorb his offer. "I don't expect you to give an answer now. You think on it, but I have to tell you that I feel a real affection for you, Rose and, who knows, you may come to feel something for me in time."

There was a genuine sincerity in both his face and voice that Rose found truly touching, and tempting. Instinctively she knew he would cause her no harm, that under his roof she would be treated with respect, with nothing to fear. It was only the suddenness of the offer that made her confused and indecisive.

"I'm flattered, Ned, truly I am. I can't tell you that I feel the same, but I can't say I never would. It's been a long time since I've had the proper company of a man, but it don't mean I'm ready to jump into bed with the first one who says he likes the look of me, if that's what you've got in mind."

He flushed with embarrassment and lowered his head. "You're a plain speaker Rose, right enough, so I'll pay you the compliment of doing the same." He sucked in a deep breath. "I won't say the thought of sharing a bed with you hasn't crossed my mind more than once since I first saw you here. You're a fine figure of a woman and any man would be a liar if he said he didn't feel the same, but I want you first as a friend and any more than that can come as it may." He was now holding both her hands and studying her intently. "Just tell me you'll think on it and give me an answer when you can."

"I promise I will think on it, Ned, and give you an answer. That's all I can say for now." She stood up, bringing him with her. "Now, I think you had better be going, I need to clear the house of pipe smoke before young Matthew gets home. We don't want no more trouble from him."

Ned nodded his agreement. "I can't pretend I wasn't hoping for a better answer than that, but I'll settle for a kiss before I go."

Rose smiled. "Still a caution, Ned Stiles, but you can have your kiss with pleasure." Their lips met and lingered for several seconds before parting. "Now go, I've got a lot of thinking to do."

Chapter Nine

Matthew slowly blinked his eyes open and was surprised to find it was daylight. He was even more surprised to be staring up at a finely plastered ceiling with a delicately designed cornice. He tried to lift his head from the soft down pillow to take in more of his strange surroundings, but a throbbing pain made him sink back down again. Instead, he had to content himself with flicking his good eye around the room, taking in the heavy burgundy-coloured drapes that let in only a few thin shafts of light through the windows. On one side of the bed was a large wing back chair, and on the other a small round table. The bed itself was larger than any he had seen and he felt lost in its vast expanse. He was covered by a white cotton sheet and quilted counterpane.

For Matthew there was no mystery about where he was, it could have only been one place. And there was nothing wrong with his memory; he could recall clearly the beating he had received at the hands of Giles Mortimer and his cowardly friends. The only thing he couldn't fathom was how he came to be in the room after being left lying on the footpath at the side of the house. He came to the conclusion that one of the grooms must have found him when he failed to collect the gig, but who had given permission to bring him into the house and put him to bed? Tentatively he peered beneath the sheets and was concerned to find his clothes had been removed and he was now dressed in a voluminous nightshirt.

He ran his fingers over his face. Someone had bandaged over his right eye which felt tender and swollen, and the burning in his nose when he breathed suggested it was broken. His jaw ached when he flexed his mouth, and his ribs felt sore, sending sharp pains shooting through his upper body whenever he moved.

With no idea of how long he had slept and so little light filtering into the room it was difficult to make any accurate assessment of the time of day. Against the wishes of his body, he forced himself into a sitting position, but before he could make any further effort to get out of bed he gave in to the waves of pain and lay back down. Frustrated by his incapacity Matthew thumped his fist into the mattress. Someone was going to pay for the injuries, and he knew exactly who.

He was distracted from his thoughts of revenge by the door quietly opening and the soft tread of footsteps across the floor.

"The master has sent me to see if you are awake and to enquire if there is anything you need." Jenkins stood at the foot of the bed, his monotone voice reflecting no degree of personal concern.

Matthew pulled the sheet up to his chin and glared at the man through his one good eye. "As you can see, I'm very much awake," he replied, the pain in his jaw making speech difficult. "You could get my clothes for me, I don't want to be seen by anyone dressed like this."

"If that's what you wish. I'll let Mr Haveringham know." Without another word he turned and left the room just as quietly as he entered.

Matthew allowed his head to sink back into the softness of the pillows and he closed his eyes to the throbbing pain. To ease his discomfort, he forced a vision of Grace to drift through his mind, and imagined her hands gently massaging his aching body. How long he enjoyed her sympathetic ministrations he had no idea, and the magic was only broken when he became aware of some distant and indistinct voices. He opened his eyes and at first saw nothing, assuming they had been part of the same dream, until a more familiar voice brought him starkly into the present.

"Awake, and keen to get up, that's what Jenkins said." The voice was unmistakeably Haveringham's. "He appears neither to me."

Matthew rolled his head on the pillow, but instead of Haveringham the first he saw was Grace by the side of the bed holding a silver tray.

"He's awake now, uncle," she said softly. "How are you feeling?"

"Bruised and battered, if looks are anything to go by," commented her uncle from the other side of the bed. "It's been a bad business, my boy, and you have my sincere apologies."

"Why? It's not your fault," said Matthew, his eye still firmly fixed on the girl.

"Because it happened in the shadow of my house and I feel a responsibility." He took a step closer to the bed. "I'm pretty sure you're not badly hurt, but I've sent for my doctor to have a look at you. He should be here shortly. Best be safe than sorry."

As Grace set down the tray on the bedside table Matthew thought he caught the feint scent of perfume that he recognised from the previous evening. "I'll be all right," he muttered stoically. "I've had a worse kicking from a calving heifer."

"No, uncle's right, we can't be too careful. You're to stay in bed until the doctor has seen you." She fussed with his pillows and he forced himself to sit up, taking pleasure when a concerned frown creased her face as he winced with pain. "There you are, you see, you can't possibly get out of bed in that condition."

"Well, I don't suppose we have to look far to know who is responsible for this," said Haveringham sternly. "I shall be speaking to Sir Roderick first thing in the morning and see to it that young Giles and his friends are brought to book. I won't have such behaviour, not on my property."

"Such a cowardly thing to do," added Grace. "It was him, wasn't it?"

It would have been proper and simple for Matthew to nod his head and the matter would have been settled, but even as she asked the question his mind was racing towards another conclusion. "No, it wasn't him, or his friends."

Grace and her uncle exchanged incredulous glances before concentrating their attention back on Matthew.

"What do you mean, not Giles Mortimer?" queried Haveringham dubiously. "Who else could it have been?"

Matthew's bruised face took on the sad expression of a reluctant witness. "I hardly like to say." He stared forlornly up at the ceiling. "It's not like you're going to believe me."

"Don't play games with me, lad. If you know who it is then I demand you tell me. If not Giles Mortimer, then who?"

Matthew let out an emphatic sigh. "It was Stiles, Ned Stiles" He pointed a finger towards his face. "It was him who did this to me."

"Ned Stiles, don't be ridiculous! It couldn't possibly have been him!" The words exploded from Haveringham's lips. "You must be mistaken, lad. Your memory has been affected by the beating. I refuse to believe that Ned would do something like this."

"I said you wouldn't believe me, but it was him right enough." He looked hard at Grace as he spoke. "There's nothing wrong with my memory."

"No, I won't have it," insisted Haveringham. "This is not his way. You're confused, lad, delirious probably. You don't know what you're saying."

"He sounds very positive to me, Uncle Rufus," said Grace, looking hard at Matthew. "You're absolutely sure it was him?"

"Of course, I'm sure. It was dark, but I know Stiles well enough to recognise him. I don't know who the others are, but there's plenty around here that will do his bidding and ask no questions."

"This is sheer madness," said Haveringham, still refusing to believe Matthew's version of events. "It's plain enough you and Ned don't get along, but he's not a vindictive man and would have no reason to behave in such an abominable way. I simply won't have it."

Matthew lay back against the headboard, his face contorted with the pain in his ribs. "Well, I expected nothing less," he said in a rasping voice that cried out for a sympathetic ear.

"Do we need to talk about this any further right now? He's told us who did it so there's nothing to be gained from more questioning." Grace straightened the bed covers. "Let's hope the doctor arrives soon and he can give you something for the pain."

Haveringham gave a loud snort of disagreement. "Well, I'm not convinced, not by a long shot. I'll speak to Stiles in the morning and get to the bottom of this, you see if I don't."

As Grace and her uncle prepared to leave the room, she gave Matthew a thin smile. "Don't worry, Uncle Rufus will sort it out, and in the meantime you're to rest, at least until after the doctor has seen you."

Outside, on the wide oak panelled landing she took hold of Haveringham's arm. "What is it, uncle, why won't you believe him? Surely he's got no reason to lie."

He gave her hand a reassuring squeeze. "I've known Ned Stiles for most of my life, and you've known that lad for not much more than a few hours. If it comes to placing one word against another I know where I would put my faith. Don't allow yourself to be so easily deceived, my dear. If I'm wrong, I'll freely admit it and do whatever I have to do, and you must be prepared to do the same."

"Well, it's plain to me, uncle, that you're far more prepared to accept the word of this Stiles person than that of Matthew Pearson." She took his arm as they went down the stairs.

"What I believe matters little. If Ned denies it and young Matthew persists in his claim then it will be for the magistrate to decide," he said resignedly.

The doctor arrived an hour later and confirmed that Matthew had sustained nothing worse than severe bruising and a broken nose, but thought it best he remained in bed for the remainder of the day, which meant another night in the comfortable embrace of Millwood House. While Grace expressed her complete satisfaction at the arrangement her uncle paced the drawing room floor with his hands clasped firmly behind his back.

"A bad business all round." The remark was addressed as much to himself as his niece. "I should much rather be telling Sir Roderick Mortimer his son is a cowardly thug than pointing an accusing finger at Ned Stiles."

"If it's troubling you so much, uncle, send for the man now and get it over with." It pained Grace to see her uncle so troubled over something that appeared straightforward. "I still don't see why you find it so difficult to accept what Matthew has said."

"Because you don't know both men as I do," he replied bluntly. "If you did then you would know why." He slapped a hand angrily against his thigh. "I'll speak to Ned in the morning to give the lad a chance to change his story."

Grace sighed and shook her head. "Why should he if he's telling the truth?" She stood in front of him and looked deeply into his eyes. "I hate for us to disagree, uncle, and I understand why you should feel a loyalty towards this man Stiles, but surely Matthew has no reason to lie."

Haveringham placed a placating hand on Grace's shoulder. "Don't be in too much of a hurry to judge either man until you know them better, my dear. Now, I think there's nothing more to be said about the matter until I speak with Stiles in the morning."

Ned Stiles heard about the attack in the morning from the stable boy who had found Matthew lying on the path the night before. He enquired at the kitchen and found out that the lad was confined to bed in one of the guest rooms and was likely to be so for the next few hours at least. With nothing requiring his urgent attention on the estate he went back to the stables for his horse, casting a casual eye at the gig standing in the corner of the yard.

He rode at a steady canter, stopping only to exchange a quick word with one of the labourers working on Hibberd's Farm. When, a few minutes later, Rose Budden opened the kitchen door the shocked look on her face was palpable.

As Ned explained what he knew of the attack, Rose held her hands up to her face, and when he had finished she let out a little gasp of horror.

"I just thought he had too much to drink to get himself home," she said with a shake of her head. "I knew he was a bit too straight talking for those nobs, but he didn't deserve that. How bad is he?"

"Pretty bad by all accounts." Ned shrugged his shoulders. "Perhaps it's wrong of me to say as much, but it might do him a bit of good, knock some of that cockiness out of him." A devilish twinkle lit up his eyes. "Maybe he'll not be fit enough to come home today, and that being the case would you have any objection if I called on you again tonight?"

Rose scowled. She owed Matthew few favours, although she still felt some measure of responsibility towards him, if only for the sake of his mother's memory. She smiled wistfully. "I wish things could be different between the two of you, Ned, it would make all our lives so much easier. Perhaps you could ask to see him, make your peace."

"I'd be more than happy to make things right if I knew what was wrong in the first place," he replied openly. "He didn't take to me from the first time we met, and hasn't made it easy for me to feel any different about him. But if you think I should see him then I will, just for you, Rose. I'll call at the house when I've finished my day's work." He gave her a sly wink. "But you haven't given me your answer yet."

"My answer?"

"If I find out he's spending another night up at the house, can I call on you?"

She pursed her lips. "Ned Stiles, if I didn't know better, I would swear you planned all this."

"Perhaps I did." He laughed as he turned away. "Now, I've work to do."

About an hour after the doctor had left Millwood House Ned dismounted in the stable yard and left his horse in the care of a groom, telling him he would be no more than fifteen minutes and to keep the horse saddled.

In the drawing room Grace had tried to interest herself in a book while her uncle continued to pace, still clearly agitated by the present state of affairs.

"Please uncle, sit down and try to calm yourself," she said finally, slamming the book shut. "Matthew's not badly hurt and surely that's the most important thing."

"No Grace, that is not the most important thing," he snapped, glaring down at her until her startled expression softened his tone. "I'm sorry, my dear, I didn't mean to be so brusque with you." He sat down opposite her and pulled the chair closer. "I'm convinced the lad is lying, but why? Does he think that by blackening Ned's name he'll put himself in favour with me? If that's the game he's playing then it will be the worse for him."

"Well, I just hope you're not putting too much store in this man Stiles. Does he really deserve so much loyalty?"

Haveringham was prevented from replying when Jenkins silently slipped into the room. "I'm sorry, sir, but Mr Stiles is here, wanting to see young Mr Pearson. Am I to show him up?"

There was a moment of indecision before Haveringham could reply. Was it the action of a guilty man to ask to see his victim? He thought not, and it only reinforced his belief that his long serving estate manager was innocent. He puffed out his florid cheeks and raised his eyebrows as he considered the question.

"No, have him wait for me in the library," he said eventually.

Grace looked across at him questioningly. "Might I come with you, uncle? I should like to hear what he has to say."

Haveringham shook his head vigorously as he got to his feet. "I think it best you stay here. This is going to be difficult enough as it is." He placed a hand on her shoulder. "Don't worry, my dear, if he really is guilty, I shall find out. Whatever other failings he may have I believe Ned Stiles to be an honest man, he'll tell me the truth of it."

Grace watched him as he left the room, praying he would not be disappointed by the man in which he had so much faith.

When Stiles was asked to wait for his master in the library, he believed it was because Matthew's condition was far worse than expected. The thought even occurred to him, albeit briefly, that it may be so bad as to allow his relationship with Rose Budden to go forward unhindered. The notion quickly vanished and he admonished himself for the thought.

"Good evening, Ned," said Haveringham as he closed the library door behind him. "How was the day?"

Stiles gave a respectful nod. "Pretty fair, sir. Milk yield's up, as we suspected," he replied, surprised by the arbitrary question given the circumstances of his visit. He scratched the back of his head. "I heard about the Pearson lad and came by to see how he was. Not too bad, I hope."

Haveringham studied the man hard before waving a casual hand towards one of the wing- backed chairs. "Sit yourself down, Ned. Will you take a whisky?"

"Thank you, sir. I didn't mean to disturb you, I just thought to enquire after the boy and be on my way."

Haveringham had his back to him as he poured the drinks. "Truth be told, Ned, I'm already disturbed. This whole damned business has disturbed me, and that's a fact." He turned and handed over a generously filled glass. "The lad's not badly hurt, thank God, just a few bruises and a broken nose, that's all." His lips curled into a cynical smile. "And an injured pride, I shouldn't wonder."

"Any idea who did it?" asked Stiles, sipping at his drink.

Haveringham reflected on the question while rolling the glass between his hands. "Well, I thought I did. I thought it was all cut and dried. There was a spot of bother last evening between the lad and Sir Roderick Mortimer's boy, Giles, and a few of his friends. Seemed straightforward enough."

Stiles shifted uncomfortably in his chair, although he couldn't quite understand why. Perhaps there was something in the tone of his master's voice that caused the unease. "But it wasn't him, is that what you're saying, sir?" he enquired pensively.

There was a noncommittal expression on Haveringham's face as he fixed his employee with a withering stare. "I'm not sure, and that's where I was hoping you could help. I fully intended to speak with you in the morning, but we may as well get it sorted now."

"Sorry, sir, I don't see how I can help, unless you think some of the hands had something to do with it."

"I need to ask you something, Ned. Where were you last night?" The deep furrows in his brow were a clear indication the question weighed heavily on him. "I'm sorry to ask it, but I need to know."

Stiles sat forward in the chair, his features similarly creased. "I don't understand, sir, you surely don't think I had anything to do with this. What's the lad said?"

Haveringham held up a hand. "Don't take on, Ned, but the boy said it was you who gave him the beating, you and some of the hands. I don't believe him, of course, but I have to ask."

Stiles slammed the glass down on the table and leapt to his feet. "That's bloody ridiculous, I never went near him. Oh, I've come close to it right enough, and no one would blame me, but I never touched him, I swear."

"I told you, I don't believe him," he indicated that Ned should sit down again, "but if there was anyone who could vouch where you were then it would clear this matter up straight away."

"Oh, there's a few that would swear I was with them last night for the price of a pint, but I've done nothing and don't feel the need to defend myself," he said, still burning with anger. "The lad's lying and if you'll let me speak to him, I'll get it sorted."

"Not tonight, Ned. I'll speak to him again in the morning, but if he still insists then it's up to the magistrate to decide. I'm sorry, but if there's nothing more you can tell me then that's the way it lies."

Stiles looked down at the floor and shook his head. "I was home all night on my own. There's nothing more I can say." Slowly he raised his head. "You say you thought it was the Mortimer boy, sir, has anyone spoken to him about it?"

Haveringham sighed. "I sent a note over to Sir Roderick, but you know the man, Ned. Even if the boy is guilty, it'll go no further. I'm sorry, but if young Mr Pearson won't point the finger in that direction, then there's nothing more I can do." He got to his feet. "Now, you had best be off home and leave it in my hands."

As he returned to the drawing room Haveringham couldn't help thinking that Ned Stiles had not been entirely truthful. Not that he believed the man to be guilty of the attack, but he had known him long enough to have some misgivings.

Grace looked around expectantly as he entered. "Well, what did he have to say for himself?"

He shrugged his shoulders. "Exactly what I expected him to say."

"He denies it."

"Of course, he denies it, what else would he do? The man is innocent."

"And Matthew Pearson is a liar, is that what you say, uncle?"

"He's mistaken, I'll allow him that. Now we let the magistrate decide." He was still holding his glass and finished the whisky in a single swallow. "Sometimes I curse the day I invited Matthew Pearson into this house."

Grace threw down her book and stood up to confront her uncle. "How can you say that, Uncle Rufus? Matthew is guilty of nothing, he's the victim. I don't understand you. First you introduce me to him, and then you suggest he is some kind of monster."

He caught hold of her arm, more coarsely than he intended. "Of course, you don't understand. How could you? You may have learnt many things useful to a young girl at that posh school, but they taught you nothing about human nature. It takes years to understand that." His anger mellowed as he sat her back down. "I don't wish to be harsh or condescending, my dear, but your behaviour is a

139

little naïve. It's not a failing, it's quite natural. You've led a very sheltered life up to now, protected from the cruel and cunning ways that come naturally to others."

"Are you saying that Matthew is like that, cruel and cunning?" She turned her head away, unable to face him. "I think it's you who is being cruel, uncle."

"That's not what I'm saying, and it's your innocence that's twisting my words. I won't be judged, not by you, and certainly not until you've had the good grace to hear me out." He poured himself another drink before sitting down opposite her. "Matthew Pearson has a fire burning inside him. Much of the time it just smoulders, but sometimes it flares up and consumes not just him, but those around him. I'm not saying that it is a bad thing, it's rare to find such passion in one so young. Matthew's passion is the land, he was born to it, and no doubt he'll die for it, but he'll also destroy anyone who gets in his way. He infected me with his enthusiasm, and that's why I foolishly allowed myself to become involved with him, against my better judgement, and the advice of my lawyer." The remark brought a vague smile to both their lips. "I can see he has infected you in much the same way, and that is why I feel it right to caution you against becoming too involved in his ambitions. A man with such passion can be dangerous. Once he sets his sights set on a target he'll let nothing stand in his way."

Grace leant towards her uncle, an incredulous expression moulding her face. "Are you saying that Matthew has made a target of me?"

Haveringham chuckled. "Oh Grace, you are such a sweet, innocent child." He patted her arm. "I'm quite sure young Mr Pearson will have no difficulty in making a target out of you, as will every other young man in the county. You're both beautiful and eligible, and any man would be a fool not to desire you, but Matthew has his sights firmly set on far greater game." His eyes narrowed at the quizzical expression on her face. "My estate, girl, that's the prize he's after, my estate."

She cupped a hand to her mouth. "Surely you must be teasing me! You think he sees me as a means of getting his hands on your estate? Why, we met only last evening, he had no time to think of such a preposterous notion."

He continued to chuckle, tapping the side of his nose. "There you are again, you see, jumping to the wrong conclusion. He had designs on my property long before he knew of your existence, although, now you mention it, I shouldn't be at all surprised if the fellow sees you as a faster track into my shoes."

She scowled back at him, pouting her red lips to full effect. "Now you really are teasing me, uncle. Anyway, what has any of this to do with that man Stiles, surely there's nothing to be gained from falsely accusing him?"

All humour left Haveringham's face. "Nothing, directly, but in his head he sees Ned as holding him back from his rightful position. Ned's position. He thinks by getting rid of Ned he'll step straight into his shoes, and then into mine. The lad has a fertile mind, but at the moment it's growing all the wrong crops. I don't want to be heavy handed with you, but don't give him any cause to hope where you are concerned."

Grace smiled sweetly. "I might be naïve when it comes to men, and I can see that you have my interests at heart, but I can't help thinking you have him wrong."

"Well, I'll speak to both of them again tomorrow and see if I can't get to the bottom of it before it goes much further."

When Ned Stiles left Millwood House an early evening gloom had descended over the estate which did nothing to raise his spirits, and certainly left him in no mood for company. He kicked his heels into the flanks of his horse and set off at a steady trot towards his cottage on the edge of the estate.

He had lived alone in the cottage for more years than he cared to remember, ever since Rufus Haveringham had raised him to his present position, and he had never before given any thought to the possibility that his life would ever change. He had always commanded the respect of both his employer and the workers he commanded, and, while it had been mostly a solitary life, it suited him.

Haveringham had been generous in his support, there was no question of that, but it was not enough. Matthew Pearson had been a thorn in his side ever since he had first made his acquaintance, and had upset the equilibrium of his life, and now he was threatening his very future. He was still some distance from home but he pulled back on the reins, bringing the horse to a standstill. Was it really the time to brood alone?

In the kitchen at Hibberd's Farm Rose went about her chores while labouring under the added burden of anxiety. Since Ned's visit earlier that day she had been distracted from her routine, alternately by concern over her employers injuries and what they would do to his unstable mind, and the response Ned would be expecting to his proposal if he returned that evening. For the past hour she had spent much of her time glancing nervously out of the window, not knowing who to expect, or who she wanted to see.

When she heard the sound of hooves echoing on the stone flags of the yard, she felt an uncontrollable fluttering in her stomach as she waited to see who came through the door.

Without waiting to be invited in Ned threw open the door and stamped heavily into the kitchen, snatching the cap from his head and throwing it onto the table.

"I hadn't thought to see you," she said breathlessly, disturbed by his manner. "Have you seen young Matthew? How is he?"

"The lad's fine by all accounts. Better than he ought to be."

"Well, it's plain enough that something's upset you. Have the two of you had more words?" She helped him off with his coat and ushered him towards the parlour.

"I've seen nothing of him," he muttered angrily, staring down at the floor as he took his place next to her on the settle. He shook his head despairingly. "He's a bad one, Rose, there's no question of that."

"What is it, Ned, what's happened?" She placed a hand on his shoulder but refused to look her in the eyes.

With his head still bowed he massaged his furrowed brow. "He told the master it was me, that I was the one who did for him." Slowly he turned to face her, hatred etched into his features. "I'll tell you straight, Rose, I wish I had."

"That don't make sense, Ned," she said, wide eyed with disbelief. "Why would he do that?"

"Why indeed! The lad's not right in the head, that's why. He out to get rid of me and he can't wait for me to go natural. He wants rid of me now." He thumped his knee with his fist.

"But what about Haveringham, what does he have to say? Does he believe him?"

Ned shrugged his shoulders. "It doesn't make any difference what the master believes, it's my word against the lad's. The damage has been done."

Rose's curiosity was aroused. "But you were here last night, it couldn't have been you. Did you tell Haveringham that?"

"No, Rose." There was a finality to his tone. "I won't have you dragged into this. It's between me and the lad, and I'll get it sorted in the morning." His expression softened as he took her hands in his. "Now, let's not have any more talk of it this evening. We've got little enough time and I won't have it wasted on him."

142

"And what future will we have, Ned, with this hanging over us? Young Matthew is always going to come between us, making more trouble for you and …" She stopped herself. The thought of what Ned would do if he knew of the outrage she had already suffered at Matthew's hands was too terrible to contemplate.

"Then all the more reason for you to leave here, Rose." Without realising it he was shaking her by the arms. "I can look after you, but not while you're still living here with him. There's no knowing what he's capable of."

Rose was well aware of what Matthew was capable of, yet she clung tenaciously to the silent promise she had made to Emily Pearson. "I know that what you say makes good sense, but I can't just abandon him, it don't seem right, not after he took me out of that hovel I was in and put some flesh back on my bones."

"Damn you Rose for your stubbornness," he snapped at her, although his frustration was immediately regretted. "You try to see the good where there is none, and it will be the undoing of you if you're not careful."

She smiled at him. "You're right, Ned, we shouldn't be arguing over this, we should be enjoying the time we have together." She searched his face with her eyes, seeking out the tenderness she knew existed behind the anger. "Stay the night. Neither of us should be alone to brood on a day like this, not when we don't have to."

The suddenness of the invitation shocked Rose almost as much as it did Ned, and neither knew how to respond. It had been a spontaneous offer born from a need for friendship, and once made, she prayed that she would have no cause for regret. For several lingering moments the two were stunned into silence and through her hands she could feel the trembling in his.

"I'm so sorry," she blurted out before he could speak. "I should never have said such a thing. What on earth must you think of me?"

As the shock faded, Ned's face gradually creased into a broad grin. "Oh, my dear Rose, you should know what I think of you. There's nothing more that could make this day worthwhile than to spend the night with you." He stopped abruptly, his face flushed. "I'm sorry, am I taking too much for granted? Did you mean under the same roof, or in the same bed?"

Rose lowered her head, sharing in his embarrassment. "We're neither of us getting any younger, Ned. I think the time for modesty between us is long since past, don't you?"

In Rose's bedroom they stood either side of the bed, facing each other in the flickering candle light. It was a moment of mutual awkwardness as Ned fiddled nervously with the buttons of his waistcoat and Rose pulled the ribbons from her hair and shook it loose about her shoulders. While he was able to give temporary relief to his coyness by sitting on the edge of the bed with his back to her as he unlaced his boots, she made best use of the time to slip off her dress and climb into bed without him seeing.

He seemed almost relieved when he got up and gazed down at her, the counterpane pulled up to her chin. "I'll put the candle out, if you don't mind," he muttered as he fumbled with the buttons of his shirt. "I swear, Rose, I've not been this frightened since I don't know when."

From within the sudden blackness of the room there came a muffled laugh followed by the rustling of material as Rose removed her drawers and let them fall to the floor. "Like two young virgins," she said, still giggling. "And not at all like the Ned Stiles I remember."

He slid in beside her, avoiding any direct contact with her body, and unsure of what was expected of him. "That was years ago, Rose," he replied, his voice hoarse and anxious. "And if that's the Ned Stiles you're expecting then I fear you're going to be sadly disappointed."

She rolled over and found his face with the tips of her fingers, stroking his whiskered cheeks. "I expect nothing of you but your company," she whispered into his ear. "Any more than that will come naturally when we're both ready. A woman takes her pleasure from having her man close by her side, to feel his affection."

Slowly their erratic breathing subsided into a gentler rhythm and they were able to relax comfortably into each other's arms, kissing tenderly and stirring emotions that had for so long lay dormant.

"This is like a dream to me, Rose. I'm sure I shall awake and you'll not be there." He pulled her closer as if to assure himself that it was real. The involuntary hardness that pressed against her stomach surprised him as much as it excited her. "If you'll not expect too much I'll try not to disappoint. It's been a long time." There was a tremble in his voice, and his hands, as he raised the shift that separated their nakedness. Cautiously he manoeuvred his weight.

"Hush there, we've got nothing to prove at our time of life," she whispered, stroking the back of his neck as he eased himself into the willing dampness of her womanhood. "I've had the excitement, it's the affection I need now."

They moved slowly, without urgency, and when the final wave of passion swept over them, they both sobbed softly together in the dark. No other words passed between them and they fell into a deep, contented sleep that lasted until the first fingers of daylight edged their way onto the bed.

***

It was somewhat earlier in the morning when Matthew awoke in the now familiar surroundings of his comfortable bedroom. It had been a long, sound sleep, undisturbed by any pangs of conscience over the false accusations made against Ned Stiles. His dreams were filled with pleasant thoughts of Grace, that continued as he lay in bed staring into the pre-dawn gloom. Arrogantly, he had convinced himself that she had taken his side and would, therefore, persuade her uncle to do the same. It had been an inspired idea, evolved in a split second at a time when his brain was still recovering from the beating he had been given. He smiled to himself, then winced as the pain in his nose returned to remind him that he was still far from full fitness. Gingerly he tested his joints and muscles; both were stiff, although less painful than the day before. Slowly he sat up as his good eye became accustomed to the darkened room and he looked about him with a self-satisfied smile.

It was while he was sitting there that the first glow of dawn appeared visible through a gap in the curtains, the time when he would usually be preparing for the day's work. But there was nothing usual about his present circumstances and he was happy to take full advantage of any opportunity to be gained.

He must have fallen back to sleep because he suddenly became aware of another presence in the room. He blinked his eyes open to see Jenkins by the side of the bed holding a tray and looking down at him with an expression that showed no hint of sympathy or respect.

"I've brought you some breakfast," he said, placing the tray on the side table. "The master wishes to know if you feel well enough to leave your bed." He went over and opened the curtains before turning back to face Matthew. "That being the case he wants to be sure that you will see him before leaving the house."

Matthew looked at the tray of food and then at Jenkins with a barely concealed smirk. "How you must hate having to wait on me," he sneered. "Well, perhaps you should get used to it. You can tell your master I will be getting up when I've eaten and that I will see him before I leave." He smiled. "And you can give Miss Grace the same message if you see her."

Jenkins made no reply, although it was clear what was passing through his mind. He gave a curt nod of the head and left the room.

The shirt Matthew had worn on that fateful night had been laundered and his suit brushed clean and pressed, all now hanging from the door of the wardrobe. When he had eaten his fill of the food he belched loudly as his stomach fought to digest its extravagant contents. Slowly he climbed out of bed, carefully flexing his arms and legs that had been inactive for so long. Every part of him seemed to ache, and the temptation to return to bed was almost irresistible, but he persevered, taking short, tentative steps around the room.

Dressing was an effort, and when he had finished, he inspected himself in the long mirror on the inside of the wardrobe door. There was none of the elation he had felt two days earlier, and he recalled the guarded admiration of Rose Budden. What would she think of him now? Did she even know what had happened to him? Stiles would have told her, he was sure of that, but any pleasure they took from his predicament would be short lived.

He opened the bedroom door and peered out into the panelled landing. It was deserted so he ventured out, wondering at first which way to go, until he could see the top of the staircase. He walked stiff legged towards it, until a door he was passing, suddenly opened and he stopped. The one person he was hoping to see that morning came out of her room immediately in front of him and gave a little gasp of surprise.

She was dressed in a long, brown velvet skirt with a matching tight-fitting jacket. Her hair was tied back with a golden ribbon making her look older than Matthew remembered. She was dressed for riding yet the clothes did nothing to detract from her natural beauty.

"You startled me," she said with a questioning look. "Are you sure you should be out of bed? How are you feeling?"

Matthew forced a pained grin. "Probably better than I look, and much the better for seeing you."

She smiled back at him. "Then I'm pleased on both accounts." The smile faded as her face creased into a frown. "I believe Uncle Rufus wanted to see you before you left. He spoke to that man Stiles last night and he wants to speak to both of you this morning."

"He still doesn't believe me, does he?" Matthew said resignedly.

"He's very loyal to Stiles, it's difficult for him." As Matthew limped towards the top of the stairs, she took his arm in support. "But I'm sure when he sees you like this, he'll change his mind."

Matthew was less convinced. "What about you? What do you believe?"

"It doesn't matter what I think, but if you really want to know, I believe you." She cast her eyes up to him as they progressed slowly down the stairs. "You're quite sure it was Stiles?"

His head snapped around to face her. "If you need to ask then I don't think you do believe me. It was him and I'll say so to his face if you want me to."

"I'm sorry," she said defensively, looking away. "I just have to be sure, that's all. Perhaps when Stiles has a chance to think about it, he'll own up."

Matthew made a loud huffing noise. "I don't think so, not a man like that." They had reached the bottom of the stairs. "Perhaps you could come with me to see your uncle. He's bound to take more notice if you're with me."

She laughed dryly as she gave him a sideways look. "Oh, I think you overestimate the influence I have over my uncle." She gave a little pout. "I know he would do anything for me, but he still sees me as a little girl who has no understanding of such things. I'll come with you if you like, but I can only tell him what I think, and that won't carry much weight."

Haveringham had just finished his breakfast and was busily pruning the dead and dying leaves from his prized plants in the conservatory. If he heard the pair entering, he chose not to notice and carried on plucking with a solemn concentration. Not until Grace spoke did he deign to acknowledge them.

"Uncle Rufus, look who I found wandering around upstairs," she said with exaggerated enthusiasm.

"Feeling better, I see," he replied without emotion. His eyes narrowed when he noticed the hand that supported Matthew. "Perhaps if you're able to stand unaided I should like to speak to you, alone. You will excuse us, my dear, won't you?"

She slipped her hand from Matthew's arm and went over to her uncle. "I think Matthew would like me to stay," she said in a low voice. "I believe he feels a little intimidated by you."

Haveringham looked past her at Matthew. "Does he indeed," he retorted loudly, "that seems unlikely. If he's telling the truth then he's nothing to fear from me."

"But uncle, he feels that you favour Stiles over him and that he won't get a fair hearing," she persisted, trying to keep the conversation between the two of them. "I believe he's telling the truth and I should like to stay."

Still keen that Matthew should hear him Haveringham snorted loudly and raised his voice again. "I've already said, it matters not a jot what either of us believe. If he persists in his accusations then it's for the magistrate to decide." Addressing Grace, he lowered his voice. "Now, my dear, if you will excuse us, I really must insist on speaking to him alone. I've sent for Ned Stiles and I'll be speaking to him as well."

Knowing that any further pleading would only serve to aggravate her uncle she gave Matthew an apologetic shrug of her shoulders and swept out of the conservatory.

With his niece gone Haveringham continued with the nurturing of his plants, and whether by design or not he kept his back to Matthew.

"Do you remember the conversation we had in this room on the morning you came to me with your proposal?" he said, as though he were recalling the moment himself. "Do you remember what I said to you then?"

Matthew gave the question some thought and then replied slowly, "you said I would have to change if I was going to survive."

"And how much have you changed since then?"

Matthew made no reply. He had no immediate answer.

"Just as I thought," Haveringham went on. "You've made no effort to adjust to your new circumstances, and there's certainly no compromise in your attitude towards those who seek only to advance your position in society." He turned to fix Matthew with a steely glare. "My niece may be swayed by the bluntness she mistakes for honesty, and it's easy to see why she may favour you over a worthless fop like Giles Mortimer, but she's a naïve young girl and easily deceived." He bent his head closer. "We both know what happened that night, and why. You were your usual ungracious self and Giles took exception. But that doesn't excuse what we both know he did, and despite his father's standing I would have done right by you. But no, that wasn't good enough for you, you saw an opportunity to bring blame and dishonour on a man whose only crime was to carry out his duty to me." His eyes narrowed in anger. "And now you try to use my niece to further this cause."

For a while Matthew was unusually reticent, perhaps silenced by the truth. However, it did not last long and any regret or misgivings he felt soon passed.

"I might have known you'd side with Stiles," he snarled. "Why can't you believe me when you know how he's had it in for me ever since the first time we met in that barn. He knew I was coming here the other night and he was jealous. He was outside, waiting for me to leave."

Haveringham waved a dismissive hand. "That's enough. We'll go through to the library and you can hear what he has to say. After that I'll wash my hands of it and leave it for the law to decide." Angrily he strode away, leaving Matthew to trail in his wake.

Outside, in the stable yard Stiles was dismounting from his horse, his mood greatly lightened by the unexpected, but pleasurable, night he had spent at Hibberd's Farm. He was not at all surprised to be told that his master was waiting to see him, and with the past twelve hours having given him a clearer perspective on the situation he approached the meeting with equanimity.

When Jenkins showed him into the library, he was careful to avoid any eye contact with Matthew and instead simply gave his master a formal nod of acknowledgement.

From behind his desk Haveringham glared at both men in turn before letting out a heavy, resigned sigh. "Well, gentlemen, I don't suppose either of you have anything to add about this unpleasant business." His eyes bored fruitlessly into Matthew's conscience. "I take it you are still persisting with your story that Ned here is responsible for your injuries?"

Matthew was unrelenting in his obduracy. "Of course, I am. Why shouldn't I?" He jabbed an accusing finger towards Stiles. "He did it all right, him and his cronies."

Still refusing to look at Matthew, Stiles calmly addressed his response to his master. "Like I said last night, sir, I had nothing to do with this. The lad might have his reasons, but he's a liar."

"And who was it who threatened me not a few days since, and in my own home as well?" snapped Matthew, red faced with anger.

"It was nothing but words, sir," Stile replied in the same emotionless manner. "He was being abusive to a lady and I saw fit to say something."

Matthew laughed scornfully. "A lady! She's nothing more than a trollop who does for me. His fancy woman by all accounts. He came to the house uninvited and when I told him to leave, he threatened me."

For a brief moment Stiles felt a rush of rage sweep over him and he clenched his fists. For the first time he looked his adversary in the face. Then, accepting that he was being goaded into a violent response he relaxed and turned away.

"Like I say, sir, it was just words. There was nothing meant by it."

"And the lady, Ned, is there anything in that?" Haveringham enquired curiously.

"An old acquaintance, sir, nothing more."

"It looked a lot more when I caught them together," retorted Matthew. "I'd say the two of them were very well acquainted."

Stiles remained quiet, refusing to rise to the bait, but his patience was wearing thin. "Begging your pardon, sir, but could I speak with you alone? I'm admitting to nothing, but there's things that need to be said, in private."

Haveringham huffed loudly. "Well, if it will to get this damnable matter settled then I'm prepared to listen to anything." He cocked his head at Matthew. "You'll be wanting to get off home. You can't go about your duties dressed like that."

"No, if he's got anything to say I want to hear it," protested Matthew, angrily glaring at Stiles. "He could tell you anything and you'll believe him if I'm not here to defend myself."

"Damn you man." Haveringham thumped the desk violently with his fist. "It's Stiles here who is defending himself against your vile accusations, so you'll have the good grace to let him have his say in peace."

Such was the threat contained in Haveringham's words that Matthew felt compelled to obey. "Have a care what you say," were his parting words to Stiles as he turned towards the door. Looking back before he left the room, he was further disheartened to see neither men were taking any notice of him.

"Well, Ned, what have you to say?" asked Haveringham, settling back into his chair.

Stiles stared straight ahead, his eyes twitching nervously. Since early that morning, or possibly earlier, he had given deep thought to this moment, and what he would say, but now the time had come he found it hard to put his decision into words. He wrung his cap in his hands.

"Like I've already said, sir, I had no hand in this business with the lad, but in a way, it's done me a service."

Haveringham was watching him closely, noting his discomfort. He waved a hand towards a chair. "Sit yourself down, Ned, I can see there's something more troubling you."

Stiles nodded his gratitude as he sat, nursing his cap in his lap. "This is difficult, sir," he began falteringly. "The fact is I've made up my mind to leave, move on if you like."

Haveringham appeared stunned. "Leave, that's nonsense!" he said, shaking his head in disbelief. "No, I won't have it, Ned. This business with the lad is no small matter, but it will all come down on your side, you mark my words. I'll not have you throwing away a lifetime's work on the word of that young devil. It would be like an admission of guilt. He will have won."

Stiles allowed his head to drop forlornly. "It's got nothing to do with winning or losing. The fact is, sir, I've got only a few more good years left in me and I've been given the chance to do something with them." He looked up, almost apologetically. "Part of what the lad said was true. The lady in question has become more than just an acquaintance, and if I'm to make anything of it then it has to be away from here."

The grim expression on Haveringham's face gave way to a vague smile. "You old dog, you've kept this very quiet. I can't pretend I'm not disappointed, I thought you and I would see out our days on this estate, but I can see your mind is made up so I'll not put any arguments in your way. But where will you go, have you thought about that?"

"My sister, Mary, you know of her, sir. She's been a widow woman for some years now, and it was always understood that I would move in with her when my time here was done."

"And the lady, will she be going with you?"

"It's not been talked about yet, but I have great hopes." There was a lively twinkle in his eyes as he spoke.

Haveringham took a deep, expressive breath. "You'll be a great loss to me, Ned, I can't deny that, and until you go, I'll cling to a hope that you'll change your mind. But that's a false hope, I know, and I'm putting my own needs before yours." He came around from behind the desk, his hand extended as Stiles stood up. "You'll leave here with my best of wishes and a little money to set you up."

He clapped a hand on the older man's shoulder and when he spoke again his voice was heavy with emotion. "You'll be sorely missed, and not just by me."

Stiles gave a wry grin. "There'll be one who'll not miss me, that's for sure."

"Oh, he will. If he thinks your going will give him free rein then he'll be making a grave mistake. This has all been a bit sudden and I've not yet decided how to deal with young Master Pearson. I've made precious few errors in business and it grieves me to think I've made one with him."

"Well, if you want my opinion, sir, I think he's got the makings, but he's like an unbroken horse. It's going to take a firm hand to tame him."

"And that's what he'll get, you can be sure of that.

Chapter Ten

"Well?" Grace was waiting anxiously by the foot of the staircase, delaying her morning ride and impatient to see how Matthew had fared in his meeting with her uncle and Stiles. The raised voices she had heard coming from the library seemed to her a clear indication that there was to be no easy settling of the matter, and when Matthew appeared, the thunderous look on his bruised face only served to harden her assumption.

It was as though she were invisible to him, ignoring her, as well as his aches and pains, and striding purposefully past her on his way through to the kitchen and out of the house.

"Matthew, wait," she called after him, running to catch up. "Please, tell me what happened."

He stopped abruptly at the top of the stairs leading down to the kitchen area, his pale eyes wild with fury. He jabbed a finger in the direction from which he had come. "That man and your uncle are up to something. Why else would they want to talk in private?" He spat the words at her, making her recoil in alarm.

"No, you're wrong, I'm sure of it," she replied unconvincingly, placing a calming hand on his arm. "He probably wants to confess but was too embarrassed to do it in front of you, that's all." It was a side of Matthew she was seeing for the first time, but naively assumed it was due to his being wronged. "You're angry, I can understand that, but my uncle is not a vindictive man, he'll not side with Stiles if he really is guilty."

"Guilty! Of course, he's guilty," he snapped at her, snatching his arm away and limping down the steps. "It sounds like you don't believe me either. I might have known you lot would stick together."

Mrs Rafferty, the cook, looked up from her food preparation as Grace followed Matthew through her kitchen, but she quickly turned away when he gave her a threatening glare. The two maids exchanged questioning glances before pretending not to notice the pair.

"You're being very unfair, Matthew," protested Grace when they were out of the house and walking down to the stables. "Unfair on Uncle Rufus and unfair on me. I believed what you told me, but now I'm not sure you deserved it, not after what you've just said."

"Well, you can prove you believe me by speaking with your uncle and convincing him that Stiles is guilty." He spoke without looking at her, his words harsh and uncompromising. "And you can find out what the two of them have been talking about."

"I'll do nothing of the kind," she said defiantly, placing her hands firmly on her hips and letting him walk on ahead. "I'm trying hard to be your friend, but I'll not be used as a pawn in your fight with this man Stiles. And I'll not have you speaking badly of my uncle. Just remember, my first loyalty will always be to him." She ran after him and caught up as they reached the yard. Her horse, a handsome chestnut, was already saddled and waiting beside the mounting steps, and she took the reins from the groom. "I'll speak to you only when you're ready to apologise," she said from the saddle while Matthew waited for the groom to harness Sally to the gig.

Matthew was given no chance to respond as she flicked the reins and the horse set off at a steady canter. By the time the gig was harnessed she had disappeared from view and he feared he had missed his opportunity to make amends. Viciously berating the groom for his tardiness, he snatched the reins and laboriously climbed up onto the gig, groaning from the stabbing pains that shot through him. Wincing as he guided the gig from the yard, he was contrite enough to realise that he had done himself no favours, when favours were the one thing he needed most.

Rose Budden was hanging out washing and pulled down on the clothes line to peer over the top when she heard the sound of the gig approaching. It was the moment she had been dreading ever since Ned had tenderly kissed her goodbye earlier that morning, leaving her struggling with the dilemma of her situation. Of course, she wanted to be with Ned, under any other circumstance she would have jumped at the opportunity, and it was only a misplaced duty towards her old friend that had placed the weakest of obstacles in her way. Now, as the gig bounced into view and she could see the brooding expression on Matthew's bruised and florid face, that obstacle began to crumble.

Without a single word of greeting or a glance in her directly Matthew climbed stiffly down from the gig and went straight into the house. Rose finished hanging out the last of the washing before following, and, by the time she entered the kitchen, he had stripped to the waist and was washing at the sink. His discarded clothes that had cost him so much money lay in a heap on the floor, the same clothes that were expected to elevate him into higher society now relegated to a useless pile of rags. Automatically Rose picked them up and laid them over the back of a chair.

While she went silently about her business, he finished washing and went upstairs to change into his work clothes, and by the time he returned his mood appeared little changed. With the bandage removed she could see his blood red eye and the surrounding area purple and puffy. She avoided looking directly at him for fear of provoking an angry reaction, although the softness of her nature forced a small amount of pity. Hoping he would leave without speaking she was disappointed when he stopped at the door and looked over his shoulder.

"I suppose that fancy man of yours has been sniffing around while I've been away," he hissed, the corner of his mouth curling into a sneer. "Well, I don't expect he'll be troubling either of us for much longer."

Her determination not to respond was severely tested and she found it impossible to remain silent any longer. She pointed to his swollen face. "You think that by falsely accusing him of doing that you'll drive him away? You're a fool, Matthew Pearson, a troubled and dangerous fool. If your mother was still alive she would be ashamed of you."

"If my mother was alive you would still be living in that hovel I found you in, and starving to death, so you remember your place woman or you'll be begging for food in the poor house."

It was a threat that no longer carried weight. Ned's offer had freed her to speak as she wished without fear of being cast back into her previously impecunious existence.

"I'll not be begging from you or anyone else, not any more. It's you who will need to look to himself when I tell him up at the big house that Ned Stiles was here with me when he was supposed to have done that to you." She took some satisfaction as his face twisted with rage. "Oh yes, he was here all right, and last night too if you want to know. I don't expect Ned to say anything to defend himself, he's too much of a gentleman for that, but I'm not ashamed to say, in fact I'd be right proud to."

A fresh wave of burning pain swept through Matthew's broken nose as his nostrils flared, and in a fleeting movement he stepped forward and grabbed hold of her arm with one hand while he brought the other down hard across the side of her face.

"You lying bitch, you're just saying that to protect him," he screamed at her as he raised his hand again. "Anyway, who's going to believe a trollop like you?" He struck her again in exactly the same place bringing a scarlet weal to her cheek and a small trickle of blood from the corner of her mouth.

Through tear filled eyes she glared defiantly at him. "You can beat me all you like, but it won't make you less of a liar, or any more of a man." She turned her face, daring him to hit her again and as he raised his hand, she braced herself.

He wavered long enough for strong fingers to clamp themselves around his wrist, pulling him around. Before he even knew what was happening a balled fist smashed into his broken nose bringing a fresh flow of blood. A cry of agony broke from Matthew's lips until a heavy blow beneath the ribs forced the air from his body.

"That's for the lies you told about me," said Stiles through gritted teeth, and as Matthew bent forward the gnarled fist caught him in the side of the head. "And that's for laying a hand on this lady here."

Matthew dropped to his knees, his hands protecting his battered face. Stiles was about to swing his heavy work boot into Matthew's exposed body when Rose threw herself between the two of them.

"Don't, Ned, that's enough, you'll only get yourself into more trouble and he's not worth it."

"If I end up swinging for that bastard it'll be worth it," breathed Stiles, massaging his hand. "Begging your pardon, Rose, but I can't abide cowards or liars and he's more of both than any man I've met." He held open his arms and she launched herself into his embrace. "You can't stay here, not any more, you're to come away with me now, and I won't hold with any arguments."

His intervention had made any argument impossible, and, together with Matthew's behaviour, all her choices had been effectively removed. "I've only a few bits and pieces," she said, her words quavering with emotion. "We can be gone from here in a few minutes."

As she started towards the stairs, she glanced hesitantly at Matthew still on his knees and holding his face. Ned followed her eyes. "Don't worry about him, he'll not trouble you anymore."

True to her word, Rose was soon back down in the kitchen, her few possessions rolled into a bundle and tucked under her arm. She had made sure not to take anything that once belonged to her friend, and what was left made Ned give a sorrowful shake of his head.

"Not much to show for a lifetime's toil," he muttered.

Rose cast a contemptuous glance at Matthew, now sitting hunched over the kitchen table. "Perhaps not, but I still have my self-respect."

"You'll cause us no more trouble, lad," said Stiles to the back of Matthew's bowed head. "If you do, I'll come back and finish you."

Out in the yard the gig was still where Matthew had left it, Sally more than content to chew lazily on the tufts of grass that grew up between the flagstones. Stiles hitched his own horse to the back of the vehicle before helping Rose up onto the seat.

"He'll not mind us borrowing this. I'll leave it where it can be found." He climbed up beside her and smiled contentedly. "This is where I belong from now on Rose my love, by your side."

She returned the smile, adding no small amount of affection, but winced when the cut on her lip reopened, drawing a trickle of blood. Stiles took a handkerchief from his pocket and gently dabbed the wound. She took his hand in hers and held it to her face. Neither spoke, but what passed between them in that moment needed no words.

How long Matthew sat slumped at the kitchen table he had no idea, but the shadows had stretched the length of the room before he roused himself and went over to the sink to throw cold, reviving water onto his tender and swollen face. The burning sensation in his nose when he breathed made his eyes water and his damaged eye was all but closed. The day that had begun so promisingly in the bedroom at Millwood House had now turned into a nightmare of missed opportunity and painful humiliation. The one certainty that broke through the haze of his torment was that Stiles would pay for what he had done, and soon.

Although it was still only early evening he went upstairs, stripped off and lay on the bed where he closed his eyes. Immediately he was haunted by a vision of Stiles, whose bodiless head hovered before with, floating in a blackened sky. Matthew opened his eyes briefly, and when he closed them again, he forced himself to think of Grace, but became wracked by regret that he had not treated her with more humility. She was now the undeniable key to his future and he needed to nurture her friendship if he was ever to achieve his ambitions. Before falling into a deep and troubled sleep he vowed that, once he had dealt with

Stiles, she would become the shared focus of his affections, her and the vast Millwood Estate.

He was rudely awakened by the pre-dawn crowing of the cockerel down in the yard, and as he slowly lifted his aching head from the pillow he cursed the bird and pledged to wring its neck.

Less than an hour later he was outside, trying to remember if he had unharnessed the gig the day before. As the events of the previous day began to drop into place, he was forced to conclude that both the horse and carriage should still be there, where he had left them. He strode down to the shed, expecting that one of the farms hands had found them and obligingly stabled them for the night.

With no sign of either, Matthew scratched the back of his head before turning his attention to Roscoe who snorted derisively at his approach. The horse shook its head vigorously as the tack was placed on him, giving Matthew the impression that even the beast was taunting him.

He led the animal outside and climbed onto the saddle, his complete body rebelling against the effort. Allowing Roscoe to set his own pace he set off slowly towards the lower pasture where he knew at least one of the hands should be working on repairing a fence.

In fact, both men were there, one holding a fence post while the other drove it into the ground with a sledge hammer. The noise from the blows concealed the sound of the approaching horse and it wasn't until Matthew was almost upon them that one of them gave his mate a look of apprehension and they both stopped working. They disliked being away from the safe routine of the estate, and even more they disliked their new master. With Stiles they knew where they stood, but Matthew was harsh and unpredictable, showing none of the fairness they were used to.

"Have you seen my gig?" he snapped as the two men respectfully touched the peak of their caps.

They exchanged cautious glances. "We did see it yesterday, sir," ventured one nervously, pointing away into the distance. "It was Mr Stiles that was drivin' it, and there was a woman too. Couldn't quite see who, though."

Matthew gave them a vague nod of acknowledgement, accepting the news with little surprise and a good deal more anger.

"And beggin' yer pardon, sir, there was somethin' else too," said the other man apologetically.

Matthew was pulling the horse's head around and about to gallop away. "Well, what?"

"One of the grooms from over yonder." He jerked his head in the general direction of the estate. "Says master there wants to see you, urgent like."

"When was that?"

"Yesterday, late in the afternoon it was, about tea time." He looked to his mate for confirmation and the man nodded.

"Then why didn't he come and find me?"

The man shrugged. "Says 'e did. Called at the house 'e said. Couldn't get an answer."

"Damn the pair of you, and get back to your work." Matthew dug in his heels and galloped away. If it was at all possible for the previous day to get any worse it seemed it just did.

Haveringham's temper, sorely tested by the events of the past few days, was placed under further strain when Jenkins announced that Matthew was waiting to see him. He was sat in the drawing room engrossed in the daily newspapers, a time when he was loathed to be interrupted. He took an avid interest in the affairs of the day since he was no longer able to get down to London as often as he would have wished, and the papers were his one link with the society which was once a great part of his life. He sometimes regretted that the estate occupied so much of his time and energy, a situation made worse by Ned Stiles' sudden departure. Now the instrument of his foul mood was waiting to see him.

"Have him wait in the library, I'll be there when I'm ready," he snapped at the unfortunate Jenkins before returning his attention to the news.

For Matthew the wait seemed interminable as he paced the floor, taking a desultory in the rows of books while trying to decide if his cause would be best served by making a grovelling apology or levelling further accusations against his nemesis. He was erring towards an apology when the library door was flung open and Haveringham strode in, his expression anything but conciliatory.

"Well, what is it you want now, to add to the damage you've already done?" he demanded, even before the door had closed behind him.

Immediately Matthew knew an apology would be the sensible course. "I'm sorry, but I understood you wanted to see me."

"Needed, not wanted," was the emphatic response. "I needed to see you yesterday, and yesterday was when I expected you." He sat down at his desk and studied the injured face before him. "You appear to have suffered a relapse, perhaps that's the reason you were unable to come."

Matthew shuffled uncomfortably and stared down at the floor, unsure of how much the man already knew. "A misunderstanding, that's all," he mumbled.

"Yes, I know. I spoke to your misunderstanding yesterday. I know exactly what happened and I've no interest in listening to your version of events." Even as he looked down at the floor Matthew could feel the condemning eyes that were burning into him. "You've caused me great distress and worry, both personally and with regards to my business. Because of you I've lost a good and loyal man, and one I shall be hard put to replace."

Matthew's head shot up, his interest pricked. "You mean Stiles?" he enquired tentatively.

"There's only one man I value to that degree. Of course. Ned Stiles."

"Are you saying he's leaving?" He tried to conceal his delight. "He told you that?"

"He has, despite all my efforts to make him change his mind."

With some self-confidence returning Matthew smiled inwardly. "So, he decided to go rather than face the magistrate. Is that the arrangement he made with you?"

Haveringham's face took on a purple hue as his expression turned thunderous. He thumped the desk violently with both fists. "You insolent young …" Such was his fury that the words caught in his throat and he was forced to take a few deep breaths before he could continue. "I should have you horse whipped for the way you've behaved." His inflamed eyes narrowed under the heavy brows. "I regret having met you, and I particularly regret our agreement, but at the moment there are more important things to concern me than you and your arrogance. This estate is my life's work, as it was for my father before me, and I'll not see it suffer as a result of your despicable intrigues. At the moment I appear to be stuck with you until I can find a suitable replacement for Ned Stiles, so you will have to carry on the best you can. But have a mind, lad, I shall be watching you very closely."

Any smugness he now felt quickly evaporated and Matthew's mouth dropped open. "What do you mean replacement? We have an agreement, I'm to take over when Stiles goes."

"You were to take over when he retired, that was our agreement, and only if you were ready." His voice contained an air of sadness and bitter disappointment.

"You are very far from ready, and after your recent behaviour I have doubts you ever will be. You have a meanness about you Matthew Pearson, and a passion for self-destruction I find hard to comprehend. I don't think I shall ever be able to place any trust in you."

"But that's because I was never given the chance to prove myself. Stiles wouldn't give me any responsibility, and neither will you. So how am I to prove myself?" It was an impassioned plea rather than a protest, and stopped short of begging. "Give me another chance and I won't let you down. You have my word on that."

"And is your word worth anything, I wonder." Haveringham shook his head grimly. "I'm giving you a chance by allowing you to continue until a replacement is found, but let me down again and I'll have no hesitation in putting paid to any aspirations you may have." He got up from his desk and waved his hand in a perfunctory manner. "Now, get out and earn the money you get from me. And remember, I shall hear about everything you do from now on."

Matthew turned meekly to the door, his arrogance and argumentative attitude severely curtailed, and certainly no progress made towards self-advancement. All he had to rely on now was the conviction of his own ability, and with an obvious need to demonstrate that ability to Haveringham being an overriding priority before his position was usurped by a threatened newcomer. Admitting he had been a fool to think he could win against such a man was just a start, now he had to prove his worth.

"And one more thing," said Haveringham, stopping him at the door. "You'll pursue no further interest in my niece. I won't have her used in any more of your devious little games." His mouth showed traces of a wry smile. "Besides, you'll have little time now for anything other than hard work."

***

As the months passed and summer drifted into autumn Matthew came to realise just how little he knew about the management of a large estate. The work had proved relentless, making more and more demands on his time and energy, and all the while Haveringham was peering over his shoulder, goading and criticising at every opportunity. Many days he lacked the will to return to his own home and would fall asleep in one of the barns, only to rise at dawn to begin another unforgiving day.

If Haveringham was impressed or influenced by this dedication and stubborn determination he never let it show, instead constantly reminding Matthew that his position was purely temporary and that he had received news of a promising candidate, or that a man with splendid references had made his acquaintance. Whether or not it was true, made little difference to Matthew, he simply threw himself into his work with even greater vigour, driving himself to the point of exhaustion.

Although keeping her distance, either by choice or on the strict instructions of her uncle, Grace viewed Matthew's single mindedness with growing concern. Her uncle had kept from her most of what had happened between Matthew and Stiles so she had no reason to harbour the same depth of distrust, and her concern was developing into an affectionate sympathy.

For his part Haveringham had done what he could to divert her interest in other directions, arranging for her an endless round of social engagements on the speculative assumption that sooner or later she would be smitten by a more desirable suitor. But for Grace the likes of Giles Mortimer and his friends held no attraction. They were far too superficial and obsequious for such an independently minded girl like herself, especially when their interest appeared equally interested in her and her inheritance.

It was a morning in late autumn as she returned from her morning ride that she passed Matthew as he was leaving the stable yard. It was the first time in several weeks that she had been that close to him and was unpleasantly struck by his gaunt appearance, his pallid, sunken cheeks and dull, hollow eyes. Forsaking the attention she usually lavished on her horse when she returned from her ride, she threw the reins to a groom and ran into the house.

Haveringham was in the conservatory carrying out the daily pruning of his beloved plants when Grace burst in, throwing her hat carelessly onto a chair. "It's not right, Uncle Rufus," she blurted out breathlessly, unbuttoning her coat.

He looked around at her almost casually, peering over the rim of the glasses he had recently taken to wearing. "Not right, my dear? What's not right?"

"I've just seen Matthew, he looks dreadful, not at all well." Her tone implied a blame. "I think you've been driving him too hard, uncle, and you know you've no intention of replacing him, not while he's doing the work of two men."

Haveringham gave her a patronising smile. "He's doing only what he's employed to do, Grace, nothing more. He insisted taking on the duties even though I warned him he wasn't ready, and it seems he's proving me right."

"But you set out to punish him. You blamed him for Stiles leaving and you set out to punish him." She went over to her uncle and placed her hands on his shoulders. "I know you think he did wrong, and perhaps he did, but driving him into an early grave will benefit neither of you. Please, can't you say you've forgiven him for whatever it is you think he's done?"

He took hold of her hands and gave them a gentle squeeze. "How can I forgive a man for something he's yet to admit to. He needs to learn that humility is not a weakness, and that success comes only from hard work. I'm sure the day will soon come when he will have both."

Grace cocked her head and looked at him inquisitively before her face broke into a broad grin and she jumped up and down. "Oh, Uncle Rufus, you're such a wicked man. I was right, you never had any intention of replacing him, you just wanted to teach him a lesson." She broke free from his grasp. "I must go and tell him."

Haveringham scowled fiercely. "Yes, I did mean to teach him a lesson, a harsh one. He deserved nothing less. And as for telling him, you'll do no such thing. When I think he's earned any approbation then it will be from me, not you." He watched her excitement fade into a frown and a pout. "I'm sorry, my dear, but you shouldn't be concerning yourself with matters like this. Young ladies should be following more genteel pursuits."

Her pouting grew more pronounced. "But what is there for me to do here." She stepped away, her expression excessively sulky. "I feel so useless, uncle, with nothing to do. If you could just find me a job it would be a way of repaying all your kindness."

He cupped her chin in his hand. "I need no other repayment than your company, and your happiness."

"But you already have my company, and if you find me something useful to do then you will have my happiness too," she said earnestly. Her green eyes twinkled excitedly. "In a month it will be Christmas, let me make all the arrangements."

"I'm afraid since your dear aunt died Christmas had been a rather dull affair," He sighed apologetically. "There have been very few arrangements to make."

"Then this year it will be different." She bent forward and kissed him on the cheek before turning and skipping away.

For Matthew the work continued unabated, despite the shortening days and worsening weather. With no obvious sign of any concessions in Haveringham's attitude towards him he felt he still had much to prove, and saw no reason to indulge in the festive spirit.

The only encouragement he had received had come from Grace who now smiled and waved at him whenever their paths crossed while she was out riding, although no words passed between them. It was just three days before Christmas before the pair finally spoke, when Grace intercepted Matthew as he rode up a track leading to one of the many silage barns dotted about the estate to provide winter feed to the livestock.

It was early morning and still barely light. A fine drizzle that had started before dawn had suddenly intensified into a steady downpour and they were some distance from the house.

"You shouldn't be out in this," he said, the rain washing the sleep from his eyes. He pointed towards the barn. "We'll take shelter in there."

She nodded and followed him up the track, into the cover of the open sided barn.

"That was fortuitous," she said, indicating the barn as she shook the rain from her hat. As her horse nuzzled the side of Roscoe's neck she laughed. "Well, they seem to be friends."

Matthew cuffed the rain from his face. "And what about us, are we friends?"

She took the opportunity to study him, her face hardening into a frown. "I'm not sure. You've not made it easy for me to like you."

"And your uncle has told you to have nothing to do with me," he said bluntly, fixing her with eyes now red and heavy with tiredness.

"He was hardly likely to encourage us after what happened with that man Stiles." Her lips parted into a thin smile. "But at least you've had the chance to redeem yourself with your work. I think Uncle Rufus is impressed, although he would never admit it to you, and he might even be ready to forgive."

Matthew cocked his head to one side. "Why, what has he said?"

She grinned teasingly. "Nothing that will excite you I don't expect. He has asked that you join us for Christmas, as our house guest."

Matthew remained obdurate. "He asked, or you persuaded him?"

"What does it matter, you've been invited and we both hope you will accept." She seemed offended by his lack of enthusiasm. "Perhaps you've made other arrangements?"

"And would you be disappointed if I had?"

"I'm sure I don't care whether you come or not," she retorted impatiently. "My uncle just wanted to reward you for all your hard work. This has nothing to do with my feelings." She turned away. "Do as you please, Matthew, that seems to be the way with you. If you would rather not ..."

"I didn't say I'd rather not," he quickly interrupted. "You can tell your uncle I will be pleased to accept. And you can tell him I promise to be on my best behaviour."

"Perhaps you shouldn't make promises you find hard to keep. I don't think my uncle or I can forgive you all your failings.

While Matthew was still musing over her remark she pulled on the reins and turned her horse out of the barn. He watched as she galloped off down the track, the sudden change in his fortunes lightening his mood.

For the rest of the day, he was in thoughtful mood, trying to interpret some underlying meaning in the invitation. Was it Haveringham or Grace who wanted him there? Either way it presented a new opportunity to redeem himself after the episode with Stiles had gone so badly wrong.

That evening he rode into the yard of Hibberd's Farm completely fatigued, but feeling much more positive about his future. He led Roscoe into the shed, not bothering to light the lamp that provided the sole illumination in the old building, and went straight to the empty stall. Such was his tiredness that he failed to notice the figure that stepped into the open doorway until he heard the scraping of boots on the stone floor.

"Who's there?" Matthew swung round.

The figure stood where he was, the moonlight reflecting off a line of brightly polished buttons easily visible against the scarlet tunic.

"Surely it hasn't been so long that you don't recognise your own brother." John stepped into the shed. "Season's greetings, Matthew. How are you?" He patted Roscoe's head affectionately as he held out his other hand.

"What are you doing here?" asked Matthew bluntly, refusing the hand and walking to the door.

"Aren't you going to unsaddle him?" John called after him, taking hold of the reins.

"I'm too tired, you do it."

After settling Roscoe into his stall, and speaking gently to Sally, John followed his brother into the house where he found him slumped in their father's chair.

"Thank you for the warm welcome, brother," he said with undisguised sarcasm. "I didn't expect a brass band, but a handshake shouldn't be too much to ask."

"I didn't invite you and you didn't answer my question," grunted Matthew, staring morosely into the empty fireplace. "What are you doing here?"

John took his place on the settle and unbuttoned his tunic. "I'm on Christmas furlough. I thought you would be on your own and we could spend a few days together." If Matthew had taken the trouble to look at his brother, he would certainly have noticed he was no longer the fresh-faced youth that had left home almost nine months before. The boyish looks had been replaced by a firm jawed maturity, moulded by the discipline of army routine and enhanced by a thin, wispy moustache. "But now that I'm here I've a feeling I shouldn't have bothered, that it no longer feels like my home."

Matthew stretched and yawned loudly. "Have you forgotten, this isn't your home any more. You gave up that right when you sold out to Haveringham. It's a shame you didn't think about me then."

John shook his head forlornly. "Can't you ever forget the past, Matt? You've still got the farm, and a good deal more into the bargain. Why can't you let bygones be bygones?"

"What I've got is through my own efforts and no thanks to you and Paul, so don't expect any gratitude from me." He scoffed scornfully. "Besides, I'm not going to be on my own at Christmas. I've been invited up to Millwood House, so you've wasted your time coming back here."

"So it seems. I should have known better." He went to get up. "I don't suppose you've heard from Paul? Did he get to South Africa all right?"

Matthew shrugged. "He went, that's all I know. Why should he write to me?"

"Perhaps for the same reason I came here." He stood up. In his polished boots his head almost touched the ceiling beams. "I was hoping we could put the past behind us and be friends again, but I was wrong, and I'm sorry I trespassed into your grand new life. I suppose you'll not object if I spend the night under your roof? I've a friend in Northampton who's been more of a brother to me than you, and a mother who's handy in the kitchen by all accounts. I'll go there in the morning." He went through to the kitchen where his kitbag was lying on the table and took out a package. "I've bought you a present, although I don't suppose you'll appreciate it." He went over to the stairs. "I'll say goodnight to you, Matt, and a merry Christmas, just in case we miss each other in the morning."

Matthew made no effort to respond, instead he continued to stare into the cold, dead fireplace, a perfect reflection of his soul. Too tired to move, yet desperate for his bed, he waited until John had finished moving about before going up.

It was still dark outside when Matthew crept from his bed the following morning. He gave no thought to disturbing John, although it suited him to leave the house before his brother rose, if only to avoid continuing the conversation from the previous evening.

Downstairs he eyed the package on the table with muted interest, but instead of giving in to any curiosity and ripping open the wrapping he decided to rummage through the contents of the kitbag. It contained nothing but a change of clothes, a well-thumbed copy of Lady Bellair's 'THE TRANSVAAL WAR', his pay book and some letters written to Paul with the envelopes unaddressed. It seemed that John was relying on him having news of their brother. For no apparent reason Matthew took one of the letters and stuffed it into his jacket pocket before returning the rest of the belongings to the bag. After a hurried breakfast of bread and cheese he left the house for another long day's work.

It was a few hours later with bright sunlight filtering through the bedroom window when John awoke.

Washing at the kitchen sink brought back many memories of his previous life and he found it hard to believe he was now the soldier he had dreamed so long to be. How many times had he stood there with the hubbub of daily life playing out behind him? Now all was silent, the spirit of the house long since departed, and it was with a sense of relief that he would be spending so little time there.

He finished dressing and had another sad tour of the house. Matthew had done nothing to make it a home It was now merely a place to sleep and eat with all vestiges of a family abode removed. Out in the yard he breathed in the fresh, cold air and smells, feeling an invigorating familiarity, more than he had felt inside the house. He had intended to leave first thing for Northampton, but there was a need within him and he strode over to the stable shed. As he expected Roscoe was gone, but Sally tossed her head and snorted loudly in recognition of the boy she had taught to ride. True, John's ability had long since outgrown her sedate nature, but a close affection remained between them. He took her head in his arms and she nuzzled into him, pushing him back against the side of the stall. He needed no further encouragement.

After saddling her he led her outside where he swung nimbly onto her back, and with a deft flick of the reins he turned her out of the yard and onto the soft turf of the meadow beyond. In the cold air Sally's breath formed into small clouds which quickly dissipated with the steady movement of her head.

At a leisurely canter they headed up onto the wooded knoll that Matthew had considered his own, unaware that both his brothers treated the site with the same reverence, where John had often dreamed of military glory in some far-off land, and Paul had agonised over his decision to leave the farm at the appropriate time. Now, it seemed, all three of them had gone some way to achieving their individual goals, yet John was still at a loss to understand why Matthew continued to carry his resentment like an unshakable burden.

John walked Sally around the top of the knoll, taking in the changing panorama, a patchwork of pastures and ploughed fields stitched together with an intricate arrangement of hedgerows and fences. Herds of cattle and sheep peppered the landscape, taking advantage of the last of the winter grass, and with his hand shading his eyes against the bright sunshine John took in every detail as if it would be his last chance to do so.

Across the small river that separated the farm from Haveringham's estate he could clearly make out a lone rider, too far away to be identified, but with a riding style that did not mark them out as an estate worker.

"Come on Sally girl," he said, patting her neck before flicking the reins. "Let's go and see who rides like that."

Needing little encouragement, Sally set off at an unusually brisk pace down the hill as John set a course to head off the rider at a point where the river could be easily forded. For a time both riders were level, running parallel with the river between them, each trying to outpace the other, but Sally was no match for the fine looking chestnut and John waved to call off the chase and spare his mount.

As they slowed John pulled on the reins and Sally splashed through the shallow water of the river and easily climbed the low bank on the other side. While both horses shorted an acknowledgement and steamed freely in the cold air their riders viewed each other with a cautious curiosity.

"Don't you know you're trespassing?" said the girl in an overly stern tone.

"Oh, I don't think Mr Haveringham will mind too much," he replied with a confidence gained from his military training. "And what about you, I suppose you have his permission?"

The girl laughed, wrinkling her nose. "Oh, I can assure you I do." She pushed her hat from her head revealing auburn hair and a beautiful face with cheeks still flushed from the ride. "So, you know my uncle, do you?"

"Your uncle! Mr Haveringham is your uncle?"

"Why should that surprise you?" she asked, closely studying the surprised expression of his face.

"I'm sorry, I didn't mean … I was led to believe he had no relatives."

"You speak as though you know my uncle well." She cocked her head thoughtfully to one side and slowly her lips broke into a broad grin. "I know who you are, you're Matthew's brother, I should have known from the uniform. I'm sorry I don't recall your name. I'm Grace, by the way."

John snatched his cap respectfully from his head. "Good morning Grace. It's John, and I'm surprised my brother has even mentioned me."

She frowned guiltily. "He didn't. Uncle Rufus told me about you, and your other brother, …"

"Paul."

"Yes, Paul. Isn't he abroad somewhere?"

"South Africa. At least I think so. We've heard nothing from him." John felt comfortable talking to her, overcoming any previous shyness he had felt around the opposite sex. "How well do you know Matthew, is he a friend of yours?"

She smiled wryly, shaking her head. "He's not the easiest of people to be friends with," she said cautiously, afraid to offend.

John laughed. "You know him well enough then."

"I thought I did. He's to spend Christmas with us so perhaps I'll see how he really is. He's been so busy these past months so it will be a good time to find out about each other." She bent forward and stroked her horse's neck. "What about you, are you home for Christmas?"

"On leave, but not at home," he told her wistfully. "I thought to keep Matthew company on the farm, but he told me of his invitation so I'm off shortly to Northampton to spend the time with an army friend."

"But that's so silly, the two of you should be together," she retorted before placing a finger thoughtfully to her lips. "Why don't you come too, I'm sure my uncle won't mind."

John sighed. "I'm grateful to you for the offer, but I don't think it would be a very good idea." He gave an apologetic smile. "There's been a lot of bad feeling between us since our mother died, and Matthew has never forgiven us for wanting to sell the farm. I'm not sure he ever will. I was hoping for a reconciliation when I came home but he made it very clear last night that Paul and me will never be a part of his life again." He made a sweeping motion with his arm. "This is all Matthew is interested in, nothing more."

Grace looked at him through saddened eyes. "Perhaps if you spent Christmas together it would help mend things between you," she suggested hopefully. "I can't believe he has no forgiveness in him, especially at this time of year. Please, can't I persuade you?"

John shook his head. "I should hate to be responsible for spoiling your festivities, but thank you for the invitation. I hope we can meet again under more pleasant circumstances, but tell Matthew that I wish him well and that he gets everything he wants for himself."

She nodded, her face displaying a sympathetic understanding. "I wish you could tell him yourself, I think it so sad when families are divided. I have some experience of it myself." She twisted in the saddle to face John and held out her hand. "I suppose I should go. Uncle Rufus has left me to make all the arrangements and there is still so much to do. I'm so pleased to have met you, John, and I wish you well." Her face radiated a warmth as he took her hand. "I'll do whatever I can to make things right between you."

John watched as she galloped away, and wondered whose influence would be the greater. He couldn't help fearing for the girl.

Chapter Eleven

"Merry Christmas, Matthew," cried Grace with childlike excitement as he was shown into the drawing room by a sour faced Jenkins.

The room was festooned with great bundles of berry laden holly, gathered from the estate. A large Christmas tree, decorated with colourful baubles, stood obtrusively in one corner, beneath which were a few brightly wrapped presents.

"A merry Christmas to you." He returned the compliment with none of her enthusiasm as he viewed the decorations with a jaundiced eye.

Christmas at Hibberd's Farm had traditionally been a muted affair; their father was a mean, miserly man who viewed unnecessary expense as an extravagance, his only concession to the day being a glass of beer and the slaughter of two chickens. Matthew had inherited some of those traits. However, he did have in his hands two packages, each expertly wrapped by an obliging shopkeeper.

"I've bought you and your uncle a gift," he said with a note of embarrassment as he handed them to Grace. He watched as she went to place them under the tree. "Aren't you going to open yours now?"

"Oh no, not yet! Mother and I always opened our presents after dinner and Uncle Rufus has agreed that we should do the same."

"And where is your uncle?"

"He's in the ballroom with some of the estate workers. He's giving them a small gift and a glass of sherry to thank them for all their hard work during the year. Apparently, he used to do it every year until my aunt died, and then it stopped." She gave a self-satisfied smile. "I persuaded him to continue with it." She waved her hand towards an armchair. "Come and warm yourself by the fire. As soon as uncle is finished, we'll be off to church."

"Church?"

"Yes, of course. Do you not go to church, Matthew, not even on Christmas day?" She looked at him with indignant surprise.

"Not often, I don't have the time." He stared reflectively into the crackling log fire. "Mother used to go with my brothers, but our father wasn't a churchgoer. He said it was hard work and not prayers that brought rewards, and I suppose I must take after him."

Grace was beginning to understand some of what John had told her. "Well, you should make time," she scolded, wagging a finger at him. "I've nothing against hard work, but you need to look after your spiritual needs as well as your earthly ones." She studied him hard. "Perhaps you could offer a prayer for your two brothers, that they are both safe and well, wherever they are."

"I know where they are, and I'm sure they're doing well enough without any help from me, of God" He gave her an enquiring look. "Why should you mention my brothers? What do you know about them?"

"Only what my uncle has told me, because you never talk about them. I know that John is in the army and that Paul is in South Africa. I also know there is a lot of bad feeling between you."

"Did your uncle tell you that as well?"

"Only some of it." Her tone was still questioning. "This is your first Christmas since your mother died. Wouldn't you have liked to share it with your brothers?"

Matthew grinned sardonically. "My brothers have chosen their own lives with little regard for me, so why would they want to be with me now?"

"Even John?"

Matthew's pale eyes flashed inquisitively. "Why should you mention him?"

"Because I met him a few days ago, when I was out riding." She paused to allow him the opportunity to explain, but it was a pointless gesture. "He looked very handsome in his uniform. And he rides well too."

"Why were you talking to him?" he asked angrily.

"He came home to spend Christmas with you," she went on, ignoring his question. "I invited him here, but he thought it would upset you." She fixed him with her green eyes. "Why would he say that, Matthew?"

He looked away, continuing to gaze into the fire. "I don't know. I told him I had no right to invite him here. Perhaps he misunderstood me."

Before she could question him further the door swung open and Haveringham swept into the drawing room, his face flushed from a morning's excess of sherry. He beamed broadly when he saw the pair of them sitting either side of the fireplace.

"What a splendid seasonal picture you make," he boomed. "A very merry Christmas to you, lad."

Matthew got to his feet and gratefully held out his hand. It was the first civil words he had received from the man in a long while, and they came at a timely moment.

"And the same to you, sir."

"You look undressed, lad. Has my niece not offered you a drink?" He gave Grace a reproving look. "No one should be without a glass of sherry on Christmas morning."

"There's not time, uncle, we should be leaving for the church. I don't think the Reverend Martin will approve of us arriving late with the smell of drink on our breath."

Haveringham nodded solemnly. "Quite right as usual, my dear. Matthew, find Jenkins to have the carriage brought round."

The Reverend Oswald Martin was a short, fat, obsequious man with a bald head and a bulbous, heavily veined nose. It struck Matthew, when he first saw him, that he was no stranger to sherry himself. With his hands clasped together in front of his protruding stomach he nodded profusely as Rufus Haveringham and his small party approached the church door along the narrow path that wound its way through the haphazard arrangement of gravestones.

Inside the church they were ushered up a twisting staircase that led to the Haveringham family pews in a small gallery that looked down onto the main body of the ancient church, and the top of the heads of the congregation. It was no warmer inside than it was out, and a damp mustiness hung in the air, infused with the aroma from several burning candles.

Matthew looked out over the gathering with a feeling of superiority, which very soon melted into boredom at the long and predictably tedious sermon on the need to spread joy and goodwill to all mankind that he felt was directed entirely at him. And when it came to the carols it was as much as he could do to mumble his way through the words. It was with a heavy sigh of relief that he greeted the end of the service.

"Didn't you find that uplifting, Matthew?" asked Grace as they stood to one side while her uncle chatted animatedly with the reverend, and many of the congregation as they filed from the church.

In some things Matthew was bluntly truthful and he found it difficult to disguise his real feelings, even on Christmas day. "I told you, I don't often go to church, and now I know why." He jerked his head towards the reverend. "Look at him, spouting his empty words, a man who's never done a proper day's work in his life telling other folk how to live theirs."

"Why do you have to be so bitter and cynical, Matthew?" It was the question she had wanted to ask in the drawing room before they were interrupted. "Why can't you allow a little goodwill into your life, instead of shutting it out?"

Again, she was denied an answer when her uncle suddenly detached himself from the throng by the church door and hustled them down the path to the waiting carriage. "A fine service," he said with dubious conviction. "A fine service indeed."

When they returned to Millwood House, they settled back into the drawing room and more sherry, both of which Haveringham insisted perfectly matched the occasion.

"A warm room, a mellow drink and pleasant company, everything Christmas used to be," he said in a reflective, sonorous tone. He settled himself into his favourite armchair and beamed at the young couple sitting opposite. Quite suddenly his mood took on a more serious aspect as he directed his attention at Matthew. "I never thought the two of us would be sharing a glass like this, not after the way you conducted yourself." He rolled the glass around in his hands. "You caused me much pain, lad, and that is not something I can easily forgive or forget. Because of your despicable actions I lost a good man, one I thought I should never be able to replace." He noticed that Grace had opened her mouth to speak, but he held up his hand. "I know my niece has always spoken up in your defence, but I fear she speaks from a position of misplaced infatuation and is blind to certain aspects of your nature."

"But, uncle!" protested Grace before she was stopped again by another perfunctory gesture.

"Don't interrupt me, girl," he said, with any intended curtness muted by the sherry. "You can have your say when I've finished." He returned his attention to Matthew who now believed he was about to discover the real reason for his invitation. "Like I was saying, because of you I lost a good man under the most unpleasant of circumstances, and one I feared I could never replace. I was determined to make you pay for what you did and in doing so perhaps it was my intention to break you, your body and your spirit. I think I was very nearly successful, in one aspect at least." He emptied his glass and handed it to Matthew to be refilled, which he did unflinchingly. "I don't think I quite have the

174

ownership of your spirit just yet, but I think you have learned some valuable lessons these past months, and I'm prepared to place some of my faith in you as I always hoped I could."

Some of Matthew's growing pessimism started to abate as he handed back the filled glass, but he thought it best to say nothing as he resumed his seat.

"And that's not all is it, uncle?" said Grace, hardly able to contain herself. "Tell him, please, or I shall."

Matthew's gaze flicked between the two of them, first at Grace's excited and self-satisfied face, and then at her uncle's vexed look of defeat.

"You may as well. I could hardly let it be otherwise," said Haveringham with a resigned sip of his drink.

"You are to be the new estate manager, isn't that wonderful," she gushed uncontrollably. "Uncle Rufus thinks you've deserved it. What do you say to that?"

"What I say," said Haveringham, breaking into her celebratory mood, "is that I'm yet to be fully convinced. I'll admit that you've earned back some of my confidence, but you've yet to regain my respect."

"Oh, Uncle Rufus, don't be so mean. Matthew, tell him he can trust you, that he has nothing to worry about."

"I can tell him if you wish, but it would prove nothing. If I do need to prove myself further then I don't know what more I can do." He fixed Haveringham with what he hoped was a look of unreserved sincerity. "What I've done these past months is only what I told you I could do, and, now that you've given me the chance, what I shall continue to do. As for your respect, sir, I can only gain that by working your land and turning the profit from it you expect. I know of no other way."

Grace clapped her hands together in delight. "Bravo, Matthew. That was a good reply, wasn't it uncle?"

"Like I said, my dear, your judgement is clouded by infatuation," he replied thoughtfully. "But I believe Matthew, and we understand each other. Isn't that right, lad?"

Matthew nodded, although he said nothing. There would always be a dark cloud of doubt hanging over their relationship, but it suited him to let Grace believe he had been fully redeemed. For the time being that was enough.

"I'll do nothing to cause you to regret your decision."

"I hope not, lad." Haveringham put down his glass, rested his head back in the chair and closed his eyes. Within the minute he was snoring loudly.

Grace exchanged an amused glance with Matthew. "What would you like to do now?" she asked. "Do you play chess, or would you prefer to read?"

Matthew shrugged his shoulders. He had never found much time, or inclination, for either. "I suppose you could teach me chess," he replied casually, preferring the intimacy of the first over the more prosaic and solitary act of the second.

With infinite patience, and in hushed tones so as not to wake her uncle, Grace explained the art of chess, taking Matthew through the moves and importance of each piece and detailing the need to plot several moves ahead and to anticipate your opponent. Using the first game as an example she quickly outmanoeuvred his clumsy attempts to contain her moves, and giggled as he sulked whenever each of his pieces left the board. But by the second game he was learning, his quick and devious mind well suited to the cunning that formed a greater part of the play, and when it eventually ended in a stalemate he took it as a seminal victory. He beat her in the third game, which annoyed her less than his boastful claim that he could now beat anyone.

"It's not such a great feat, Matthew," she warned him. "I'm not a very good player. Besides, we were taught at school to be humble in victory and gracious in defeat."

"There's nothing humble about winning," he replied jubilantly. "Winning is something to be proud of, and losing is for those who deserve it."

She watched as he laid up the board for another game, the burning fire of ambition in his eyes plain to see.

"You frighten me sometimes, Matthew," she said apprehensively. "I liked you because you were different, more honest, than the other young men I've met, but I'm beginning to wonder if it really is honesty or just the lack of respect for the feelings of others."

He smiled back at her, but it lacked any real warmth. "Feelings are a sign of weakness. If you feel nothing then nothing can hurt you. It's a kind of defence."

"So, you feel nothing towards anyone, your brothers, my uncle … me?"

He looked at her, his cold eyes betraying no emotion other than contempt. "As far as my brothers are concerned, I have the same feelings for them as they have for me. They're just dreamers, chasing some romantic notion of a life that doesn't exist, and they resent me because I wouldn't share in their dreams. They knew what the farm meant to me, yet it didn't stop them from trying to sell it and to hell with me, so why should I have feelings for them." He glanced over at the slumbering figure in the chair. "Your uncle is a good enough man, I'm sure, but he is only really interested in profit, not people."

"That's not true, he does care about people, those that work for him, me, and even you if you let him." She lowered her eyes that were close to tears. "And me. Do you regard me with that same coldness? Was my uncle right, would you use me to get whatever it is you want?"

Before Matthew could contemplate his response there was a loud snort as Haveringham stirred from his sleep, rubbed his eyes and looked about him.

"Matthew grinned smugly. "Now you'll not know."

"Goodness me, I must have dozed off." Haveringham sat up and stretched. He blinked his eyes free of sleep and cast them over at Matthew. "Not know what, lad?"

"If he could beat me at chess, uncle," Grace replied quickly. "We were about to have another game, but it's almost time for dinner."

Haveringham checked his pocket watch against the clock on the mantel. "Indeed, it is. I hope you have a good appetite, lad, Mrs Rafferty will not take it kindly if we don't do justice to all her hard work."

"You will answer me," Grace said with quiet determination as the pair followed the old man from the drawing room.

The centrepiece of the dining table was a goose, complete in every respect apart from its lack of feathers and the roasted golden brown of its skin. It sat on a large silver salver, swimming in a sea of exotic fruits. As Matthew sipped at his soup, he felt the black eye of the bird on him, studying him judgementally, and he was pleased when the first course was over and Haveringham took a knife to the roasted inquisitor.

Whenever Matthew thought he could eat no more another course was produced which he felt obliged to accept graciously, anxious to keep his host in good humour. No such obligation burdened Grace who nibbled delicately at the small amounts that were placed in front of her, and sipped at the same glass of wine throughout the meal.

It was only Haveringham who managed to comfortably consume everything on his plate with practised ease before looking forward to the next course, and when he was finally confronted with a mountainous portion of Mrs Rafferty's Christmas pudding, he seemed almost disappointed. For Matthew it was a moment of rejoicing as he forced down the last spoonful of the dark, rich dessert and pushed his dish away with a heavy sigh that made Grace smile.

"I have to say," said Haveringham, belching loudly, "that I have not enjoyed Christmas dinner so much since my dear wife passed away, and I can only put that down to the present company." He cast his heavy eyes about him before they settled unsteadily on Matthew. "It was my niece's idea to invite you here today and I did have my reservations about the wisdom of it, but I'm delighted to say that she was right, your presence here gives the occasion a family atmosphere, and that is what Christmas ought to be." His words were laboured and slurred, but they had the ring of sincerity about them.

Grace relaxed and smiled at him. "If it were not for your generosity, Uncle Rufus, neither of us would be here today, so we both have much to thank you for. Isn't that right, Matthew?"

He nodded his response, but before he could put his thanks into words Haveringham held up his hand. "The pleasure has been all mine. What a lonely old man I should have been if it wasn't for the two of you." He picked up his glass with a flourish and waved it in the air. "A toast, I think. To youth and prosperity."

"To youth and prosperity," echoed the other two, Matthew less enthusiastically.

"It's been an eventful, and trying, year for all of us," he went on after draining his glass, "particularly for the two of you, losing someone very dear to you, while I had the misfortune to suffer the departure of a loyal and trusted friend." He had sunk into a sombre, reflective mood and failed to notice the sudden look of consternation on Matthew's face. "I did blame you for that, lad, but it's time to put the past behind us and look forward to the New Year."

He called for more wine and they toasted the prospects for the coming year, he with relish while the other two exchanged searching glances, both acknowledging that their immediate futures were bound inexorably to the benevolence of the man they shared a table with. Grace accepted the situation with equanimity and gratitude, while Matthew could only brood on the fact that his future was in the hands of someone other than himself.

"And what of you, lad, what are your wishes for the New Year?"

"To do the best I can for you, and our land," Matthew responded with hollow conviction while mulling over what his true answer should be. "I want nothing more than that."

"Nothing for yourself? Most commendable," remarked Haveringham with a hint of sarcasm. He turned to Grace. "And what of you my dear, are your aspirations a little more selfish than our young friend here?"

"Not selfish, uncle. I already have more than I need." She gave him a wan smile. "I wish only to be happy." She shot Matthew a harsh glance. "But not at the expense of others."

"Is that what you think of me?" questioned Matthew, content to rise to the challenge. "You think I use others to achieve my ambitions?"

"I think you are capable of that," went on Grace undeterred, "although it may not always be your intention to do so." She breathed deeply before continuing. "Not since I've known you have you shown any real feelings of affection, so it is only natural to assume you have none to give."

"A harsh assumption perhaps, but an honest one I'll warrant," interrupted Haveringham who had been trying to follow the exchange. "I accused my niece of being blinded by infatuation, but I think I was wrong, she appears to have the measure of you, lad. The question is, are you prepared to prove us both mistaken?" He took another large swallow of wine. "You've certainly impressed me these past months with your hard work and commitment, but what are you going to do about trying to impress us with your qualities as a human being?"

Matthew's lips curled into a thin smile as he nodded his head. "I'm beginning to wonder why you invited me here when that's what you think of me." He looked directly at Grace. "Did you invite me out of pity, or was it an attempt to save my soul from eternal damnation?"

"I think any pity would be wasted on you, Matthew Pearson," snapped Grace, stung by his question. "In fact, I think any attempt to gain your friendship would be a waste of time."

Haveringham held up his hand to silence them. "All this bickering is playing havoc with my digestive juices. I think we should pursue a more amicable conversation over brandy and cigars." He waved over Jenkins who had been in inconspicuous attendance throughout the meal. "You can go and have your Christmas dinner with the others, I won't be needing you any more today." When Jenkins had thanked him and left, Haveringham lifted himself a little unsteadily out of his chair. "We'll continue in the comfort of the drawing room, and this time I'll allow no serious talk."

As Grace slipped her hand under her uncle's arm and escorted him from the dining room Matthew trailed sullenly behind with the clear feeling that his

179

acceptance into their society was far from given. Grace was family, something he could never be, unless he could persuade them both he could change. He smiled to himself. It was not beyond his capabilities.

Haveringham poured two brandies and offered one to Matthew before settling back into his favourite chair. As he warmed the glass in his cupped hands he beamed up at Grace. "A splendid meal, my dear, and now I think it's time we opened our presents." He turned to Matthew, as if struck by a sudden thought. "Will you join me in a cigar, lad?"

Matthew looked doubtful. It seemed inappropriate to refuse, but even more so to make himself looked foolish. "It's not something I'm accustomed to, but I'm happy to give it a try," he said obligingly.

Grace was on her knees sorting through the brightly wrapped packages arranged around the base of the tree as her uncle put his glass down on the hearth and hauled himself out of the chair. He had taken no more than a few steps towards the box of cigars on a small side table when he suddenly stopped and clutched at his chest. The blood had drained from his face which was drenched in small droplets of perspiration and his breathing became laboured and erratic. He let out a sharp cry of pain and sunk heavily to his knees before falling forward wheezing loudly.

Grace screamed and leapt to her feet. "Uncle Rufus! Oh, my dear God, what's happened to him?" She dropped to her knees beside him, shaking him violently by the shoulder. "Uncle Rufus!" she sobbed.

Matthew dragged her to her feet. "Run to the kitchen and fetch Jenkins. I'll stay with him."

"Is he going to die? I can't leave him. We have to do something." She was gripping him by the arms, frantic with worry, willing him to make it right. "Please help him."

"He'll be all right, just go and fetch Jenkins. If it's happened before he might know what to do. There may be some medicine." He dragged her towards the door. "Just go, there's nothing you can do here."

When she had left, he went over to the old man and rolled him over onto his back. His breath was coming in short sharp gasps and his face had turned an ashen grey. His eyes were open, yet unseeing, and seemed to be focussed directly on Matthew hovering over him. How old and pathetic he looked, and no longer a threat, thought Matthew. In that split second a terrible thought struck him. What if the man should die? Would his position be better or worse? He had no way of knowing. He eyed the heavy, brocaded cushion on one of the chairs. There was a sure way to find out. But before he could reach any decision Grace burst breathlessly into the room followed closely by Jenkins.

"I've sent a lad for Doctor Colley, sir," said Jenkins, addressing his remark directly at his prostrate master, in case there was any misunderstanding with Matthew. "He's had a turn like this before, miss. I think we should get him up to his bed."

She was kneeling at her uncle's side and turned her tearful eyes up at Matthew. "Will you help Jenkins get him up the stairs?" she pleaded.

Matthew nodded. "If you think he should be moved," he replied obdurately. "Perhaps we should leave him where he is until the doctor's seen him."

"He needs to be made comfortable," insisted Jenkins, with a blatant disregard for Matthew's advice. "Begging your pardon, miss, but that's what Doctor Colley said last time."

"Then that is what we should do," she said decisively, scrambling to her feet while keeping her eyes firmly fixed on her uncle. "Matthew, take his head and Jenkins can take his feet. And be careful with him, please."

Even before the large meal he had just consumed Haveringham was not a small man, and now he was considerably heavier, but between them Matthew and Jenkins managed to get him up the stairs watched by a distraught Grace, Mrs Rafferty and a couple of the kitchen maids. Haveringham was a much respected master, and the expressions of concern on the faces of his staff were palpable.

Up in the bedroom Grace stood to one side with her back to the bed as the two men struggled to remove her uncle's clothing and get him into his nightshirt. When they had finished she dismissed Jenkins.

"Finish your dinner," she said with a grateful smile, "but show the doctor up as soon as he arrives."

"And what about me?" asked Matthew when Jenkins had left. "Would you like me to go too?"

Grace sat on the edge of the bed holding her uncle's cold, clammy hand. "I would like you to stay, at least until the doctor gets here. I'm so afraid, Matthew, I don't know what I should do if anything happened to him."

"You heard what Jenkins said, it's happened to him before. Too much to eat and drink I shouldn't wonder," said Matthew, trying to maintain an air of supportive concern. "I'm sure he'll be right as rain in the morning."

"But he looks so ill." Grace was stroking the limp hand, holding it up to her cheek. "Do you really think he'll be all right?"

Matthew stood by the other side of the bed, pondering on the possibilities this sudden turn of events had opened up for him. What he thought about the seriousness of Haveringham's condition was of less consequence to him than what would happen if he were to die. He nodded his head and gave Grace a reassuring smile.

It was nearly two hours later when Doctor Colley arrived. He was a short man of slim build and wearing a dark green velvet suit and gaily decorated waistcoat, an outfit clearly designed for the festive occasion and not a professional visit. He showed not the slightest degree of annoyance at having his holiday interrupted, having enjoyed the patronage of the Haveringham family since first setting up practise in the area, and from that patronage had gained many more affluent patients.

As he was shown into the bedroom Grace got up off the bed and went over to him. He took her hand and raised it to his lips. "Well, my dear, not the Christmas day either of us had in mind, I suspect," he said in a well cultured voice. He gently patted her on the arm. "Let's see if we can make it a little better."

He approached the bed and seemed to notice Matthew for the first time, peering at the lad over the top of his glasses. "If I'm not mistaken there stands the last reason I was called to this house."

Before Matthew could respond the doctor had dismissed the minor distraction and turned his full attention to his present patient. Ushering Grace and Matthew to the far side of the room he set about examining Haveringham in a calm and confident manner. He sounded his chest and looked into his eyes, all the while giving a whispered commentary that went unheard by his anxious audience.

When he had completed his investigation, he stood up, flexed his back and coughed. As Grace cautiously went over to stand by his side, he pursed his lips. "It's his heart, I'm afraid," he said quietly. "It's something I've warned him about in the past, but he's a stubborn man and has paid no heed to my advice."

"But he is going to get better?" demanded Grace. "He's not going to die, is he?"

"We are all going to die, Miss Haveringham, but most of us try to postpone it as long as possible. Your uncle seems intent on inviting the good Lord to take him sooner rather than later."

"Is there nothing you can do for him?"

"I have done what I can, but now that he has you to keep an eye on him perhaps it is you that can do more good than me. Persuade him to rest more and eat less, and between the two of us we may be able to delay the inevitable for a while longer. See that he stays in bed and I'll be back to see him tomorrow. In the meantime, someone should stay with him during the night and send for me should his condition worsen."

"Don't worry, Doctor Colley, I'll stay with him."

Once the doctor had departed, she resumed her place beside the bed, taking her uncle's hand in her own. Suddenly she felt quite alone and frightened, wondering what would become of her should the worst happen.

The death of her mother had created a vacuum in her life that her uncle had quickly filled with his generosity, providing her with the security she assumed would last forever, but now she was faced with the prospect of being alone once again.

Bathed in its funereal darkness the bedroom offered little comfort as Grace looked down on the lifeless form of her uncle, tears of sorrow slowly rolling over her cheeks as she prayed for his recovery. Then, as if in answer to her prayers, she felt a movement in her hand as he gave it a feeble squeeze, and on his pale, aged face was a weak smile.

"Oh, Uncle Rufus," she cried, leaning forward to kiss him lightly on the forehead. "You gave me such a fright."

His chest rose and fell as he struggled to speak. "You're not to concern yourself, my dear." The words were slow and laboured, but despite the imploring expression of Grace's face he persisted. "Don't believe what that old fool Colley tells you, he's just a quack. There's nothing much wrong with me."

"Please uncle, don't speak. The doctor says you're to rest, and I'm going to make sure you do." She placed a finger against his lips and straight away he closed his eyes. Within a few moments his breathing became more regular and she knew he was asleep.

She slipped her hand from his loose grip and stood up and went to the door. Outside on the landing she met Matthew, who was returning from showing out the doctor. He appeared suitably concerned.

"How is he?"

"He's sleeping now," she replied, her face lined and tense. "I'm going to stay with him tonight. I just came out to fetch a blanket."

"Is there anything I can do?" he asked, walking with her to her room. "Would you like me to stay with you, to keep you company. I know you think I don't care about anyone other than myself, but I've a lot to be grateful to your uncle for, and if I can repay him …"

She turned to stare deeply into his eyes, willing herself to have belief in him. "If that is what you truly want then I should be pleased of the company. I think it will be a long night."

Each hour in the darkened bedroom passed more slowly than the one before, and the battle to stay awake became increasingly difficult to overcome. Grace and Matthew exchanged brief whispered conversations during the course of the first few hours of the night, but they consisted mainly of vacuous and irrelevant platitudes. Eventually Grace submitted to her fatigue and fell into a fitful sleep. Matthew pulled the blanket up around her shoulders before settling down on the window seat from where he could watch them both. Every now and again he felt obliged to keep a check on Haveringham's breathing, while still contemplating the consequences should the ailing man's life slip away from him during the night.

Grace managed to sleep for several hours, but was woken before the first grey streaks of dawn broke through the small chinks in the heavy drapes that covered the window when Jenkins came into the room carrying a tray. She sat up with a start, the blanket falling to the floor. At first, she was disorientated and looked about her in alarm, trying to remember where she was.

"I fell asleep," she muttered, her voice laden with shame. As Matthew joined her at the bedside, she glared at him. "You should have woken me."

"It's all right," he assured her. "He slept all night. I've been keeping watch on him."

"I've brought you some tea, miss," whispered Jenkins, placing the tray quietly on the table. "If you would like to get some sleep, I'll arrange for someone to sit with the master."

Grace nodded her thanks. "I think I should like to stay with him myself, at least until he's awake."

When Jenkins had poured the tea and left, Grace gave Matthew a thin smile of gratitude. "Thank you. I don't know what I would have done if something had happened to Uncle Rufus during the night. I should never have forgiven myself." She reached out and took his hand. "I think I may have judged you too harshly. I'm sorry."

Her touch sent a shiver of anticipation coursing through him, although not the warm glow of affection Grace may have wished for. "Perhaps I'm not the ogre you had me for." The smile on his lips was mainly for his own benefit. "Who knows, you may even learn to trust me."

"You should get some sleep," she said to him before returning her gaze to her uncle. "With Uncle Rufus so ill, you will have to carry more of the burden. You need to look after your own health."

He gave a dry laugh. "There's nothing wrong with my health, but you're right, I ought to get some sleep. Would you mind if I stayed at the house until we see how he is?"

"Of course, I wouldn't want you to go." She watched him as he went to the door. "Matthew, I truly am sorry."

She remained in a pensive mood long after he had gone, and as her uncle slept on, her thoughts were split between the two men who now featured so prominently in her life. The prayers she had earlier made exclusively for the recovery of her uncle were now spread wider to include something for herself.

"Shouldn't you be in bed, it must still be so early?"

The voice was weak and hoarse, yet it broke through the gloom and into her distracted thoughts with a suddenness that sent her heart racing.

"Uncle Rufus!" she exclaimed, breathless with shock. "You almost scared me to death."

"What are you doing here?" he asked as she moved from the chair to the edge of the bed.

"It was Doctor Colley's instruction that someone should stay with you."

"I told you, Colley's a fool. It was nothing more than a touch of indigestion," he said irascibly. "Have you been there all night, girl?"

"Yes, and Matthew too, but I fell asleep during the night while he kept watch on you. I made him go to get some sleep himself." She gently stroked his hand. "And it wasn't indigestion. Doctor Colley told me it was your heart, and it's not the first time this has happened. He's coming back later to see you, but you're to stay in bed, and I'm going to make sure you do."

"I've never heard such nonsense, there's nothing wrong with my heart, it's as sound as a bell," he blustered, and as if to prove the point he tried to pull himself into a sitting position. But the exertion proved too much and he flopped back down onto the pillow, gasping for breath. "I'm not ill and I won't be treated like an invalid. Help me up, girl."

She placed a restraining hand on his shoulder. "Please uncle, if you won't do what the doctor ordered then do it for me. I couldn't bear it if anything should happen to you." Pleading tears filled her tired eyes as she lay her head down next to his.

"Oh, my dear girl, don't upset yourself so. There's plenty of good years left in me yet."

She sat up and wagged a finger in his face. "In that case you can spare a few days to rest in bed, and I won't brook any argument."

He raised his eyes in exasperation. "The simple logic of a woman. How can I argue against that?" He gave her a patronising smile before his pale face gave in to a concerned frown. "But what of the house, and the estate? They don't run themselves, you know."

Grace gave an annoyed shake of her head. "Stop worrying uncle, please. I'll speak to Jenkins and Mrs Rafferty. I'm sure between the three of us we can stop the house from falling down. I wanted something useful to do, and now I have it. As for the estate, don't you now have a new manager? I'm sure Matthew is more than capable, and this will be his opportunity to prove it. You have to trust him sometime, you know."

As she rearranged his pillows, he studied her drawn, tired face. "And what about you, my dear, do you trust him?" He took hold of her hand. "Have the two of you settled your differences, or merely postponed them on my account?"

"Perhaps we were too quick to judge him yesterday. I think he may have changed?" There was a note of guilt in her voice. "When I fell asleep last night, he stayed awake to watch over you, so he must care something for you."

"Unless he was just protecting his own interests," breathed Haveringham cynically.

"Uncle Rufus!"

"I'm sorry, my dear. If you think he has some compassion in him then the least I can do is to give him the benefit of the doubt. I shall want to speak to him later, but now I should like to sleep, and I think you should do the same." He noted the look of concern that flashed across her face. "Oh, don't worry, I'm not going to do anything foolish while you're gone."

She straightened his covers and kissed him again. "I'll tell Jenkins to keep an eye on you, just in case."

It was early in the afternoon when Grace woke up with a start. A thin shaft of wintery sunlight pierced the otherwise dim room and caught her face as she sat up. The sudden brightness hurt her eyes and she turned away, trying to gather her thoughts. Noting the time from the small travel clock on the table next to the bed she jumped up, angry with herself for sleeping so long.

She was still wearing the same clothes from the previous day so she stripped off, washed quickly at the wash stand in the room and dressed without giving any thought to what she should wear. Her only concern was for her uncle, and whether she had missed the doctor's visit.

She almost ran along the landing to her uncle's room, and was relieved to see he was still sleeping soundly. Silently closing the door, she went downstairs to find out what she could from Matthew or Jenkins.

With no sign of the former she went through to the kitchen where she found Jenkins talking to Mrs Rafferty.

"Has the doctor been yet? Have I missed him?"

They both turned to meet her anxious gaze and Jenkins shook his head. "We expect him any time, miss," he said confidently. "I have been keeping a close eye on the master and he seems comfortable enough."

Grace nodded her thanks. "And Matthew, Mr Pearson, have you seen him?"

"He's out on the estate, miss. Would you like me to send someone to find him?"

"No, thank you, I'll speak to him later."

She went through to the drawing room and looked with sadness at the presents still lying under the tree, a sorry reminder of the past twenty-four hours.

Unable to settle, it was a relief when Doctor Colley arrived and was able to reassure her that her uncle was in no immediate danger, provided he followed a strict regime of bed rest and diet, a prescription that did not sit well with the patient, but which Grace was determined to enforce.

The doctor had not long gone when Matthew returned to the house. "How's your uncle?" he asked as Grace met him in the entrance hall.

"Tetchy, from having to stay in bed, but looking a lot better."

"I know how he must feel. It would take a lot to keep me in bed."

Grace took him by the arm and led him to the bottom of the staircase. "He wants to see you, but you're not to stay too long." She shot him a warning look. "I don't want him tired or upset."

With due deference to her orders Matthew gave her an assurance before going up the stairs. Haveringham was propped up on several pillows, a half empty bowl of thin soup and some uneaten water biscuits sat on the side table.

Haveringham waved a hand at him. "A fine Christmas this has turned out to be. See what I'm forced to eat, a pauper's meal."

"There are some that would count that a good meal," commented Matthew.

"Perhaps so, but I didn't ask you up here to lecture me."

"I suppose not. Is there anything I can get for you?"

"Of course, there is, but unfortunately nothing I'm allowed, thanks to that fool of a doctor." He waved Matthew towards a chair. "What must I look like lying here, old and feeble, I shouldn't wonder," he added with bitter frustration.

Matthew nodded in sympathy. "I'm sure it's for your own good."

"It seems everyone knows what's best for me, including you," sighed Haveringham as he turned his face listlessly towards him. "But I'll tell you this, lad, and it's to go no further than this room. I felt the cold hand of death on me last night, and I'd be a fool or a liar to say I wasn't afraid."

Matthew looked suitably grave. "It must have been frightening, but you seem much better now, and you'll be up and about in a day or two, I'll bet."

"I might be old, lad, but I'm far from stupid. This was just a warning, the next time I may not be so lucky." He beckoned Matthew closer. "That's why I have to be certain my affairs are in order at all times."

Matthew felt puzzled as his nerve ends tingled with anticipation. "I'm not sure why you tell me this, sir. I'll manage the estate well enough, you only have to give me any instructions you think necessary and I'll carry them out. But your private affairs …"

Haveringham thumped the bed impatiently, appearing uncharacteristically scared. "Don't you see, that's just the thing, I may not be around to give the instructions." He put his hands up to his face, as though he were trying to imagine the world without him. "I've no fear of dying, not for myself, but I have Grace to think about now, I have to provide for her. She's so very young and vulnerable, and without me she'll be taken advantage of. Everything would be lost. I could have depended on Ned Stiles if he were here, he knew the way of things, but he's gone and I couldn't die easy."

Matthew was still puzzled. "Why do you tell me this, when I know you still have no trust in me?"

Haveringham fidgeted restlessly in his bed, no longer able to act from a position of dominance, and he felt exposed. "I find it hard to trust what I don't understand," he said, searching Matthew's face for answers that eluded him. "I wish I knew the truth of you, lad, then perhaps I could rest easier. If it was only you and me it would be a finely matched contest with a clear winner, but now I fear you have an unfair advantage which troubles me no end." His dull eyes were still firmly focussed despite his laboured speech. "I have little experience in the nature of women's emotions, but I fear that once their affections are set in motion, they become difficult to restrain. Do you understand what I'm getting at?"

Matthew got up from the chair and slowly walked around to the other side of the bed. He knew exactly what Haveringham was getting at, and it caused him some satisfaction. He smiled dryly as he nodded. "You think Grace has affections for me and that I'll use that advantage to get the better of you."

"I'll say that about you, lad, you have a fine grasp of things, and that's what worries me." He allowed his head to drop exhausted onto the pillow, and his expression was dark with anger. "I can't prevent the way she feels, and I've no idea of your feelings towards her. I doubt you would tell me the truth even if I asked, so I'll not bother."

Matthew gave a non-committal shrug of his shoulders. He was enjoying the situation, feeling he could now manipulate events from a position of strength. "If Ned Stiles were still here it's him you would be talking to now, not me, and not about Grace. The pair of you would be discussing the number of lambs expected in the spring, or the latest price of beef, so why not have that same conversation with me, because those are my concerns now. I'm flattered you worry that Grace has feelings for me, and whether or not I have the same regard for her has no bearing on my loyalties to you, or my responsibilities to your estate. You've judged me harshly these past months and I'm sure you had good reason, but I had hoped that could all be put behind us, and that now was the time to trust each other. You have my solemn word that I'll no more take advantage of your present disability than I would of Grace's affections, and if that's not enough then there's little more I can do." He allowed himself a moment of self-indulgent smugness before continuing. "Besides, I'm well aware of her loyalty to you and I know she would never pursue any interest in me without your permission or blessing, and neither would I."

Haveringham let out a bitter laugh that brought on a violent fit of coughing. "Permission! That girl has a will that is far stronger than mine, so I doubt anything I say will have any influence over her." He stopped to recover his breath. "But I've been struck by your recent commitment and I'm prepared to let bygones be bygones. Now you have my hand on it." He raised his hand weakly and Matthew took it, surprised by the firmness of the grip. "But take a care, lad, and don't give me cause for any further grief. And just so you know, I've sent for Miles Fennymore to bring my affairs up to date."

As the old man released his grip, Matthew gave him a sardonic smile. "So, there's still to be a limit to your trust. I suppose I should expect nothing less, and I only hope time will prove you wrong."

"No more than I do." He waved Matthew away. "Now, be about your business, I need to sleep. But remember what I have said."

As he closed the bedroom door behind him Matthew's face broke into a broad grin. It had been an extraordinary Christmas.

He found Grace waiting impatiently in the drawing room and as soon as he entered, she threw him an anxious look. "I hope you haven't tired him," she said sternly. "I know how it is with you men when you start talking business."

Matthew held up his hands. "We spoke little of business. Most of your uncle's concerns were for you, but I think I left him reassured."

"Reassured, … about me. Why?"

"He's afraid of what will become of you should anything happen to him, that you'll be taken advantage of."

She tipped her head to one side as she studied him carefully. "By whom, you?"

He responded with a convincing frown. "He still has his doubts about me, particularly where you are concerned."

"And are his doubts founded or unfounded?" she asked cautiously, walking over to him and fixing him with a hard stare.

Her closeness tormented him and he wanted to take her in his arms. "What I want may please you and displease your uncle, so whatever I do is bound to cause concern to one of you. The question is, who."

"Why not please me and prove my uncle wrong at the same time, then everyone will be happy."

She had made her feelings clear and Matthew responded by taking her by the shoulders and kissing her lightly on the cheek. She turned her face until their lips met.

Chapter Twelve

The New Year begun much as the old one had ended as far as Matthew's work was concerned. With seemingly tireless dedication he continued to impress Rufus Haveringham with the way he managed the estate, but which in turn placed a growing strain on the young man's burgeoning relationship with Grace. And with the coming spring, and all the extra work that entailed, there was to be even greater demands on Matthew's time and energy.

Since that first kiss at Christmas, Grace's attachment to Matthew had grown in tandem with her uncle's improving health, until she felt able to vent her frustration on the old man.

"It's so unfair, uncle," she told him one blustery March morning as they sat down to breakfast. "I get to see so little of him."

"And does he feel the same?" he asked blandly, peering at her over the top of his spectacles. "Is it his wish to spend more time with you?"

The question took her by surprise. It was one she had not yet asked Matthew, or herself. "I suppose he does, I don't know for certain." She looked questioningly at him. "Why do you ask, has he said something to you?"

Haveringham put down the newspaper he had been trying to read and smiled at his niece. "He speaks to me of nothing but the estate. What's in his heart is a mystery."

"And it will stay a mystery all the while he is so busy. All I want is for us to spend a little time together, but whenever I think we might, there is always something urgent that needs attending to." She stared imploringly across the breakfast table. "Is there nothing you can do to lessen the burden of work?"

Haveringham puffed his pale cheeks. Since his illness he had aged ten years and the obvious suffering of his niece weighed heavily on him. "It's a demanding task he has taken on, even more so for someone so young and with so little experience. You forget, my dear, that it was you who championed his claim to the manager's position, when I was still to be convinced he was ready. Now, it seems, you're suffering the consequences of the faith you placed in him."

Her head dropped to her chest as she accepted her share of the blame. "I know, but how much worse would it have been if you had passed him over for another manager? No, he deserved the chance, even though it comes at such a high price." She raised her eyes, allowing a few pleading tears to trickle down her face. "Are you sure there is nothing you can do?"

There was a long silence as Haveringham considered her appeal. Even though he had little regard for Matthew's plight, the grief it was causing his niece gave him sadness. "I'm sure there is something that can be done," he said finally. "Leave it to me, my dear."

Two days later Matthew entered Millwood House through the kitchen for one of his regular meetings with Haveringham. The old man would have much preferred to have those meetings out on the estate where he could see for himself the state of his business without relying completely on Matthew's glowing version. But Doctor Colley, supported by Grace, still forbade him any physical exertion or active involvement in anything that was likely to cause him stress.

As Matthew took his seat in the library, he couldn't help noticing that Haveringham appeared rather more pensive than of late. The reports he had given so far since the beginning of the year optimistically predicted an increased yield in all areas of the farm, and there was nothing to suggest that it would be other than a good year. But the face that looked at him across the desk hinted at a darker prediction.

"I'm impressed," said Haveringham when Matthew had finished making his usual report. "You seem to have everything well in hand."

Matthew nodded his thanks while waiting tentatively for a caveat to be added. "If the weather holds then I think we should have a very good spring," he added cautiously.

Haveringham toyed with some papers on his desk as he looked hard at Matthew. "Yes, my boy, you seem to have everything in hand in all areas, but one."

Matthew narrowed his eyes questioningly. "I think, sir, every part of the estate will turn a good profit this year. If there's anywhere you think I've misled you then I'll be happy to hear of it."

"There is, but I doubt you'll be happy to hear about it," he replied cryptically. He drummed the top of his desk. "All of your reports tell me everything I need to know of the lands that have been familiar to me since my birth, but nothing of my most recent acquisition, Hibberd's Farm."

Matthew sat up, his fingers tightening around the cap clutched in his hand. "Hibberd's Farm? What of Hibberd's Farm?"

Haveringham gave a wry smile. "Surely you don't think I rely purely on your reports to tell me what I need to know. Oh, I know what a splendid job you've done since the sad departure of Ned Stiles, and I've no doubt that the estate will flourish under your control, but at what cost?"

"If I've neglected my own farm, it's only because all my time is taken up with my work here," said Matthew defensively. "If you'll allow me more men then I know I can bring it into profit."

"There'll be no more men, and I'm afraid there'll be no more Hibberd's Farm," the old man said bluntly, tapping at the papers in front of him. "It comes down to a simple choice."

Matthew was about to leap to his feet in protest but changed his mind, remembering how he had fared in previous confrontations. "Choice, what choice?" he asked fearfully.

"That the farm is absorbed into the estate. It can no longer operate as an independent entity, even with the free labour you've enjoyed this past year. It is simply not profitable." He gave what he believed to be a deep, sorrowful sigh. "The other choice, alas, would be to sell it and cut our losses."

This time Matthew could no longer restrain himself. "Sell it! You can't. We have an agreement."

Again, Haveringham tapped the papers in front of him. "If you had bothered to read that agreement carefully you would know that I can." He pushed the papers forward. "Perhaps you would like to read them now?"

Matthew eyed them sullenly before shaking his head, realising how hasty he had been in accepting them. He was well aware of the clause, yet had chosen to ignore it, naively supposing it would never be enforced. "I can make it profitable, I know I can. I just need more time," he pleaded. "I could invest some money, pay for more labour."

"Don't be a fool lad," scoffed Haveringham. "No bank would advance you money against such dubious security, and neither will I. You'll simply be throwing good money after bad." He waved at Matthew to sit back down. "Just look at the advantages, lad. You'll have money in your pocket and more time to pursue other interests."

"But I won't have the farm. I'll not let it be sold and I'll find the money to make it work. I just need the extra time."

Haveringham shook his head resignedly. "You have until the end of the year, lad, and no more."

Any optimism Matthew had recently felt regarding his future had been severely dented, yet he was not beaten. The end of the year was still some way off and a lot could happen in that time to change his circumstances, or Haveringham's mind. He had found a way to rid himself of Ned Stiles and this was just another problem to be resolved.

***

As spring drifted unnoticed into summer nothing more was said about the sale of Hibberd's Farm and Matthew became more sanguine about his future. He felt that Haveringham's threat was just a hollow attempt to make him work ever harder, and have even less time to further any designs he had on Grace. But if that was the old man's design then it was sadly flawed.

With summer came the longer days when Matthew could begin his work earlier in the day, and with the lengthening evenings he suggested to Grace that she ride out to meet him at whatever part of the estate he found himself. They could then spend an hour or more wandering the quiet fields and woods, or along the river bank when she would allow him to hold her hand while she talked endlessly about trivial, womanly things that held little interest for him, although he did indulge her by feigning some degree of attention. Whenever possible he would try to turn the conversation towards the subject of her uncle, subtly enquiring if he had said anything concerning her inheritance, or what would become of the estate in the event of his demise. If she became suspicious of his motives Matthew would become suitably offended by her accusations and explain that he feared for her future. Afterwards he would avoid seeing her for several days and then blame his absence on her. She would apologise profusely and beg his forgiveness.

"I just wish I could make you happy," she said to him one evening after such an absence. They were walking by the river with the sun a deep orange ball delicately balanced on the edge of the horizon, casting long shadows across the water from the far bank. "I know I'm just a silly girl, but sometimes you seem so impatient with me."

"I have a lot on my mind," he replied, suitably apologetic as he took her hand in his. "You know your uncle intends to take my farm at the end of the year, and how much that means to me." He turned his head to face her. "But I don't mean to take it out on you, I'm sorry."

"As long as that's all it is," she warned, smiling. "I'll speak to him, I promise. I know he'll listen to me."

The smile vanished when Matthew snapped at her. "No, you can't do that. He already thinks I make use of you, to get what I want. I'm doing what I can to earn his trust and if you go to him now, it will ruin everything." His tone softened. "Besides, I'm sure it won't come to that, I'll find a way to save my farm, somehow."

He stroked her cheek affectionately before they walked on, and he even found himself making some complimentary remark about her complexion and the effect of the setting sun shining through her hair.

She smiled up at him and squeezed his hand. "This is the best time of year, and my favourite time of day," she sighed. "I wish it could stay like this forever."

"We can't stop the seasons from passing," he replied with a farmer's bluntness. He pulled her to a stop, slipping off his jacket and laying it on the grass close to the river bank. "Summer has its purpose though, as do all the seasons."

"Matthew Pearson, I think you're quite the most unromantic person I've ever met," she said with an exaggerated pouting of her lips as she sat down. "Is there anything to soften your heart that has nothing to do with farming?"

"It's all I've ever known, or wanted," he replied distantly as he sat down beside her. He picked up a dead twig and idly threw it into the river, watching as it drifted slowly away.

"That's not very flattering," she said, resting her head on his shoulder and gazing up into his eyes. "Is there no room for anything else in your life?"

He gave her the hurt expression that never failed to fill her with guilt. "Is it so wrong to have ambition? It's easy to be patient when you already have everything you want."

The poignancy of the remark was not lost on Grace. "Like me, you mean? Are you jealous of me, Matthew, is that why you are like you are?"

He stared intently at the river. "Well, you do have everything you could possibly wish for. A fine house to live in and all the clothes you need. And when your uncle dies all this will be yours. What more could you want?"

Grace sat upright and glared at him. "That's a wicked thing to say! If you think all I care about is money and clothes then you know nothing of me. I wouldn't want any of this if it brought only unhappiness." She placed a hand on his cheek and forced him to look at her. "What about you, Matthew, would you still care about me if I had nothing?"

He smirked at her serious expression. "Would you give it all up for me, if I asked you to?"

"Would you want me to?" she responded intently, sadly shaking her head. "I don't think it is me who needs to prove their feelings, do you?"

"And I wouldn't dream of asking you to," he said softly, his pale eyes burning deeply into her emotions, melting some of the doubts and worries that had plagued her.

He placed a hand on her bare shoulder and eased her back onto the grass. She made no protest when he slid his arm beneath her neck, cradling her head as he bent forward until their lips met in a lingering, passionate kiss that left her breathless and reassured. She wrapped her arms around his neck, fearful perhaps that it was all a dream that would evaporate if she allowed it to. They kissed again with even greater abandon. Through her closed eyes she saw the imperious, disapproving face of Miss Loxley and she was overcome with a feeling of delicious guilt.

At the finishing school she had talked about and giggled over such moments, and now she fully understood what it was the other girls pretended to know. Senses that had so far lay dormant were now coursing through her body, creating sensations that threatened to run out of control. Suddenly and with no warning she tensed and her back arched as Matthew's hand touched her breast with an almost imperceptible lightness. Her nipples hardened against the cotton shift she wore beneath her dress. She shuddered with excitement, knowing that she should stop him yet submitting to the exquisite pleasure that swept in waves through her body. Her breathing came in short, sharp gasps each time their lips briefly parted.

In that moment she was lost in a delirium that could only have been true love and she failed to notice that his hand had left her breast and was sliding slowly and gently over her stomach and then the soft roundness of her belly before descending down into the fertile valley of her womanhood, protected from his touch by only a few layers of thin summer cotton. In a few seconds love was lost to lust, but while her body found it hard to resist, her heart fought for control. She twisted her head away and reached down for his hand.

"No, Matthew, not this, we mustn't," she breathed, her voice and body trembling uncontrollably.

Matthew sat up, his face displaying a disappointed bewilderment. "What's wrong? I thought you wanted me to prove how I feel about you, and you to prove how you feel about me."

"I do, Matthew, really I do." Tears of shame and frustration filled her eyes and she looked away. "But not like this, it isn't right. If you feel the same as me then you will understand." She got to her knees and stroked his cheek with the back of her hand. "If we gave everything to each other now there would be nothing left to give, nothing to look forward to." Her face flushed an even deeper shade of red. "I wanted you then just as much as you wanted me, but what would you have thought of me afterwards if I had given myself to you so readily?"

He got to his feet, took hold of her hand and pulled her up. "It's all right," he said sullenly, "it's time we were getting back anyway. The sun's gone and the air's getting damp, I don't want you getting a chill."

She tugged at his arm as he went to walk away. "Matthew, please don't be angry with me." Her wet eyes pleaded for his forgiveness. "I do love you, and when the time is right, I'll willingly give myself to you. Be patient, just for now."

"Patient! You sound just like your uncle, he's always telling me I should be patient."

He strode away and she was forced to run after him, holding tightly onto his arm as he walked briskly back to where they had left the horses.

"Why are you so angry all the time," she pleaded as they walked. "Every small thing seems to upset you so, and it frightens me, it really does. We should be so happy together, yet you always seem so unhappy and dissatisfied. What is it you want?"

Matthew stopped abruptly and spun around to face her in the fading evening light. He no longer appeared so angry, instead he looked like a petulant schoolboy. "I'm sick of people telling me I have to wait. All my life I've had to be patient, waiting for the things I really want, when others seem to get them so easily. And every time I have them within my grasp they slip away again."

"What things, Matthew?" she asked earnestly. "If you mean me, I'm not going to slip away. Just because I'm not ready to give myself to you it doesn't mean you've lost me. You should know that."

He placed his hands on her shoulders and felt the shiver that ran through her. "I do know, and I'm sorry. I have to learn to be more patient, especially with you." He rubbed the top of her arms. "Come, it's getting chilly. I'd better get you home."

She smiled up at him as they walked, their arms around each other.

As summer passed inevitably into autumn the bond of affection between Grace and Matthew appeared to grow on a solid base of trust and understanding. He made no further attempts on her innocence that she now dreamed of losing on their wedding night, and for that he earned her further respect. They were halcyon days, that for Grace could only culminate in a lifetime of blissful marriage. Matthew had become everything she knew him to be.

For Matthew it was a side of his nature he was more than happy to present and have accepted, both by Grace and her sceptical uncle. But the side he was anxious to remain a secret was concealed from view within the dingy confines of the narrow backstreets of Daventry where he took the pleasures denied to him by the restraints imposed by his sweetheart.

When his work was finished, and he could make suitable excuses to Grace, he would ride over to the town where the price of a few tots of cheap gin or a hot meal would buy him the few minutes of gratification he craved. To the older, full bosomed women that Matthew favoured, the fair haired, handsome young man was a welcome change in their bed to their fat, sweaty regular clientele. After a few pints in the shabby ale houses he could have his pick of any of the women plying their trade in the stale smelling, smoke filled bar, and, having made his choice, he would accompany them back to a grimy room to use them as he wished.

Apart from the few shillings they demanded he owed them nothing. The pleasure was all his and he took it as fast and aggressively as the mood took him.

"Just as long as yer don't mark me face, lovely," was the only restriction they placed on him as he ripped away their worn and stained clothing while they lay submissively on the stinking mattress. "You give it to me good and proper if that's what yer want, but just watch me face." Then they would close their eyes and chew on their lip as he kneaded their sagging breasts and bit into their nipples before thrusting hard into them.

For a few extra coins he could stay the night and indulge himself as often and as brutally as he wished, his youthful body and willingness to pay for the privilege guaranteeing their compliance. He had no obligation to please, and in the morning he could leave with his conscience clear and his lust satisfied. He readily excused his behaviour as being for Grace's benefit, and he would return to his duties with a renewed vigour.

Sheltered from that part of Matthew's life, Rufus Haveringham and his niece saw only the man dedicated to proving his worth to one and devotion to the other. What more could they ask of him, and how much more had he to offer? For Grace the only worry that existed in her mind was that Matthew would never find the time to ask for her hand now that her uncle openly spoke to her as though no other conclusion was possible.

The only cloud that remained in an otherwise clear sky was the vexed question of Hibberd's Farm. Despite Matthew's optimistic opinion that the subject had been forgotten, it was a subject never far from Haveringham's mind, and as the year drew to a close he knew it was a problem soon to be addressed. When he first broached the subject with Matthew it was for romantic rather than economic reasons, to free the lad to pursue a more active interest in Grace. Unfortunately, it had the opposite effect, driving Matthew with even more determination to hold onto the land. But, even with the use of the additional pastureland it offered, the farm could not continue to be run in its present state and, one way or another, it would cease to exist. Never one to shirk his responsibilities when it came to business Haveringham's only hesitation came from Grace's pleadings.

"Is there nothing that can be done, uncle?" she begged again one morning as they sat at the breakfast table. She had known for some time that the problem had tormented her uncle and it severely tested the loyalties she owed the two men in her life.

"This is business, not spite, my dear," he replied, trying not to sound patronising. "If there was another way, do you not think I would take it? I've been as tolerant as any man could be, but the farm is a worthless drain on Matthew's time and my money, both of which should be of interest to you."

"I'm not worried about the money, uncle," she responded tartly, "but it's Matthew I worry about. I know what the farm means to him."

"And do you not think I don't? I said I would not speak of it until the end of the year, but the time for delay is over and it's best dealt with now, today." He pushed his plate away, his appetite gone. He reached across the table and patted her arm. "Would you like to ride out and tell him I should like to see him, as soon as it's convenient. I'll leave it up to you if you want to tell him why, but it might be better if you left it to me."

As she walked slowly down to the stables her thoughts were consumed with the impending meeting, which was almost certainly destined to upset the delicate equilibrium of the relationship she had with the two men. Knowing that her uncle's decision made good business sense was little consolation, and the extra time Matthew had to spend with her was, of course, welcome, but she feared it came at an unacceptably high price. Matthew's volatile nature, combined with his obsession with the farm was likely to blight the progress she had made in securing his affections. If only there was another way.

While her horse was being saddled, she enquired with the stable lad if he knew of Matthew's whereabouts, but he had not been seen that morning so she made up her mind to take a route that would intercept him should he be coming from home. Perhaps, she thought, they would meet by the river, a place that had become special to her since that summer evening when they had walked by its banks and where passion had almost overwhelmed her. She trembled each time she thought of that moment.

A chilly breeze accompanied the watery late October sun, blowing a shower of golden brown leaves from the trees. Soon it would be winter once again, with its cold days and long, dark nights, inevitably made worse by the prospect of Matthew driven to moroseness by the loss of his farm. Grace pulled the hood of her riding cloak over her head and wished it could be summer again.

At some distance from the river, she suddenly drew in the reins and came to a halt beneath the broad branches of a beech tree. She could see Matthew some way off and galloping towards her at a furious pace, the steam from his horse's flanks rising into the cold air. She wondered why he was in such a hurry; even with his heavy work load she saw no need to force Roscoe along at such a frantic pace. Volatile and angry, she thought, would he never change?

As he got nearer, she steered her horse out from the cover of the tree in case in his hurry he had not seen her, but even as she stood in his path he showed no sign of slowing. Raising her arm, she waved to him, beckoning him to stop, yet he came on at the same frenetic pace, hot breath streaming from the flared nostrils of his horse.

"Matthew," she cried out, throwing back the hood of her cloak. "Matthew, please, wait."

With barely a glance in her direction he continued on so she dug in her heels and took off after him. With his horse nearly blown she had no trouble catching up with him.

"Matthew, what on earth is the matter with you," she shouted as they drew level. "You saw me there. Why didn't you stop?"

"What is it?" he shouted back angrily, not even looking at her. "I'm late, I've got things to do." He finally brought his horse to a standstill.

She tried to manoeuvre her horse so she could face him, but he swung Roscoe around to avoid her. "There you go again, so bad tempered for no reason," she said breathlessly. "Can't you even bear to look at me, what's happened?"

"I told you, I'm in a hurry, that's all." Slowly he turned his head and Grace gasped as she saw the deep scratches covered with dried blood that ran across his cheek.

"Your face! What happened to you?"

He threw his hand up to hide the wound. "It's nothing. I took a shortcut through the coppice and scratched it on a branch," he muttered defensively. "Anyway, why did you stop me? What do you want?"

"I'm not sure I want anything, not with the mood you're in," she retorted indignantly. "But Uncle Rufus wants to see you when you have time, and I hope you're in a better frame of mind, he won't take kindly being spoken to the way you've just spoken to me."

Matthew glowered at her from beneath the peak of his cap. "What does he want to see me for?" he asked cautiously, aware that it could not be one of their regular meetings. "Is it about my farm?"

"Perhaps. I don't know," Grace replied guardedly. "Will I see you later?"

He nodded sulkily. "I'd better be going."

With no further explanation, or apology, he flicked the reins and galloped away leaving Grace to stare after him, wondering if she would ever understand the complex nature of the man she loved unreservedly, or if he would ever be truly happy.

Early that evening as the light was fading and a damp mist descended over some of the lower lying fields Matthew left his horse at the stables and made his way up to the back of the house. He went into the scullery and washed his face in one of the stone sinks before inspecting himself in a mirror hanging from the wall. He was anxious to present a less spectral visage to Rufus Haveringham than the one witnessed by Grace earlier.

As he turned away from the mirror one of the kitchen maids came into the room and raised her eyebrows at the sight of him. "Good Lord, Master Matthew, what on earth's happened to you?"

Apparently, his appearance had not been greatly improved. "Mind your own business. Where's the master?"

She shrugged her shoulders and went through to the kitchen where Jenkins was discussing the evening meal with Mrs Rafferty. On hearing the exchange, he excused himself from the cook and joined Matthew in the scullery.

"I was told to expect you," he said with his usual distain for the young man. "You're to wait in the library while I tell the master of your arrival."

Haveringham was in the conservatory with his niece and accepted the news from Jenkins with a curt nod and a heavy sigh. He had been made aware of the earlier meeting between Matthew and Grace and was far from impressed, although it had served to stiffen his resolve regarding Hibberd's Farm. Grace had made a case for Matthew's defence, once again blaming his mood on the pressure of work and the desire to succeed, but her uncle was having none of it.

"That's not good enough," he had replied furiously. "I don't care what he has to put up with, I won't have him being disrespectful to you."

His anger had lessened little during the day and before he left the conservatory Grace took hold of his arm. "Perhaps I should come with you," she said anxiously. "I don't want you getting too het up, remember what Doctor Colley said."

He gave her an assuring smile and patted her hand. "Don't you worry yourself, my dear, I promise I shall stay calm, no matter what happens."

"Well, if I hear any raised voices, I shall be straight in," she warned.

Matthew was pacing the library floor, his cap wrung tightly in his hands and every now and then he would give his thigh an angry slap. He had had many meetings with Haveringham since the question of selling the farm had been raised, but his instincts told him this time was different, that he had not been ordered there to discuss mundane estate business. It was almost with a sense of relief when the door finally opened and Haveringham strode purposefully into the room. The look on the old man's face told Matthew that his instincts were probably right.

"I have to say," Haveringham said with no pretence of a formal greeting as he took his place behind the desk and gestured towards a chair, "that I'm far from happy with your behaviour this morning. Your general lack of respect is well known, and to some degree tolerated, but when it affects my niece, I won't have it."

"And I'll apologise as soon as I see her later," put in Matthew defensively. He patted his cheek. "I had a small accident and was late for work. It's a poor excuse I know, but …"

Haveringham stopped him with a raised hand. "What goes on between us is business, pure and simple, and business has a way of sometimes causing discord, but we keep it between ourselves. Do you understand what I'm saying?"

Matthew wasn't sure, but he nodded anyway.

"I take it you know why I've asked for this meeting?" he went on, pressing the tips of his fingers together as if in silent prayer, while Matthew felt his heart begin to race in nervous anticipation. "We spoke some months ago of your farm and its drain on my finances, not to mention your time, and here we are again about to have the same conversation. It's now time for action."

"But you gave me until the end of the year to find the money to invest in it," protested Matthew vehemently. "I said I'll find the money and I will."

Haveringham let out a long, exasperated breath. "Well, the fact that you've done nothing about it up to now doesn't give me cause for optimism. I told you that no bank will advance you money on that property, and if you have tried you will know that I'm right." He relaxed his severe expression and sat back in the chair. "Look, lad, I know what that land means to you, but you have to give it up, it's the only way you'll ever have peace of mind." He patted the top of the desk pensively. "And I have to remind you that I own two thirds of the property and can force the sale if I need to."

"But not until the end of the year. You agreed to that." Matthew stopped short of begging.

"And I'll keep to that agreement, but I'll extend you no more time. At the end of the year that land of yours will either be sold or absorbed into the estate." He got up from his desk and went over to a small side table that contained some glasses and a decanter of brandy. He poured two glasses and handed one to Matthew. "Come, lad, let us not fight over this. Life is too short for me and too precious to you for us to spend so much of it arguing over such matters when there are far more important things we should be talking about."

204

Matthew gave him a questioning look, disarmed by the sudden change of manner. "More important! What can be more important to me than my farm? It's the most important thing in my life?"

"Is it indeed!" snapped Haveringham, the disappointment on his face palpable. "I was rather hoping it had been relegated at the very least to the second most important thing in your life."

Matthew felt himself flush with embarrassment. A trap had been laid for him and he had walked straight into it. "Of course, I wasn't thinking," he stuttered. "But it's because of Grace that I need to keep the farm. Don't you see that?"

"No, lad, I'm afraid I don't."

"It may not seem obvious to you," he began slowly and deliberately as Haveringham perched himself on the edge of the desk to face him, "but I'm very much in love with Grace. It wasn't my intention to say anything to you, not yet, but now I feel I'm forced to." He paused to give an affected sigh. "It's been my intention to ask your permission to marry Grace, but I wanted to wait until I had made a success of the farm, as well as my work for you. I wanted to come to you as a man of independent means and not as someone who was only interested in her inheritance. If I lose the farm then all I have is my employment with you, and although I'm grateful to you for that I shall always feel in your debt and that's not how I would wish to start married life. Can you understand that?"

Haveringham's expression remained implacable. "And have you mentioned any of this to Grace?"

"No, of course not! I wouldn't, not until I had spoken with you. Like I said, I was waiting until I had secured the farm."

Haveringham allowed himself a cautionary grin. "If she feels about you the way I believe her to then it will matter little to her whether you are a man of independent means or not. Despite what she may, or may not, inherit Grace is not impressed by material wealth. She is, though, swayed by the idea of love and affection, both for you and, I trust, for me. She is very aware of the economic difficulties attached to your farm, and I can assure you it would please her enormously if I were to relieve you of the worry of it." He held up his glass as if in a toast. "So, for her sake as much as mine, why not simply agree to give it up and settle for a life of contentment."

Matthew sipped thoughtfully at his brandy. "But surely, sir, if it were possible to have both, contentment and the farm, wouldn't that be for the best?"

Haveringham shook his head with weary frustration. "Have you not listened to anything I've said, lad. I'll put no more of my money or labour into that land, and you'll not find the money to invest."

"But if I could?" persisted Matthew to the obvious annoyance of the old man.

With a heavy sigh Haveringham put down his empty glass and jabbed a menacing finger at Matthew. "You have until the end of the year, and no more. And, remember one thing, whatever happens I'll not tolerate Grace being subjected to another vitriolic outburst as she was this morning. If you are going to have any future with her, and at the moment that is very much in doubt, you need to curb that temper of yours, otherwise I'll place every obstacle in your way and there will certainly be no wedding."

Matthew stood up and held out his hand, a smug smile on his face. "You have my word on it, sir," he said with uncharacteristic humility. "And I will get the money, you have my word on that too."

"Fine words, but it's deeds that count with me, especially where my niece is concerned." Reluctantly he accepted Matthew's hand. "Now, I think it's time you spoke to her of your intentions before she develops some of the doubts I still have." He indicated the scratches on Matthew's face. "And I hope she never has cause to resort to something like that."

Still smiling Matthew shook his head. "Just an accident."

Fanny Tomlinson rolled over on the rickety iron bed and lifted her head just enough to inspect, with some satisfaction, the small pile of coins on the wooden packing case at her side. Leaning forward she lifted the ragged hem of her worn, stained skirt to inspect the bruising on the tops of her heavily veined legs, deciding they looked worse than they felt, despite their tenderness to the touch. It was nothing more than she was used to given her line of work. Men liked to be rough, it was in their nature and made them feel superior, and once they were aroused the bastards couldn't help themselves. And what was it with men and breasts? Why did they have to bite them like a hungry infant? She rubbed them vigorously before swinging her fat legs around to sit on the edge of the bed. She looked again at the pile of coins. At least it was enough to keep her in gin for the next few days if she couldn't get a paying customer.

It was a few minutes before she dared to drag herself off the bed to inspect her face in the broken piece of mirror propped up over the mantelshelf. If it looked only half as bad as it felt it would be a few days before any man would pay the full price of her services. The bastard, why couldn't he have left her face alone? After all, she hadn't stopped him from brutalising her in every other way.

When she did eventually pluck up the courage to peer through her jaundiced eyes into the dirty glass she quickly turned away again. Her bottom lip was split open and swollen to twice its usual size and dried blood caked her nose which she was sure was broken. The bastard! She looked down at her grimy finger nails and forced a painful smile as she saw the evidence of her revenge.

The brashness Matthew had displayed in front of Rufus Haveringham was left behind in the library of Millwood House, and an immediate declaration of his intentions towards Grace was the last thing on his mind. In a few months his beloved farm would either be sold or become a lost part of the vast estate, and that was something he could not allow to happen. The silent promise he had made his dead father would be upheld, at any cost.

As he made his way back down to the stables his mind was consumed in feverish activity as he considered, and rejected, every possibility that would defeat Haveringham and his plans.

It was only when he was in his own home and sitting at the kitchen table lost in his forlorn thoughts that an embryonic idea began to develop in his deviously fertile brain. He leapt up from the chair, rushed upstairs and began a frantic search of the bedroom. After several minutes, and with a cry of jubilation, he found what he was looking for.

The letter, that for no apparent reason he had taken all that time ago from John's kitbag, was now an important part of his plan, not for its endearing contents, but for the address it contained.

Matthew sat back down at the table with pen and paper and set about composing one of the few letters he had ever written in his life, but possibly the most important.

Brother

You will probably be surprised at hearing from me and if you think it is because I now wish to ingratiate myself to you it is not. I have heard from our brother in South Africa who has some financial difficulties and is asking for our help. He makes no mention as to the extent of his problems only that it is important he receives urgent funds as soon as possible so I can only assume it is serious. As you know I am in no position to help him myself as all my money is tied up in the farm and should you feel that it is too hazardous to risk your own inheritance then I will write back and tell him so. It is only because of your special relationship with your brother that I felt it only proper to let you know of his circumstances. I will await your reply before writing back.

Regards
Matthew

He read through the text several times before giving a satisfied grin and addressing the envelope. The letter contained no degree of warmth that John would have regarded as suspicious, yet it hinted at desperation that would appeal to the loyalty he had for his older brother. Matthew nodded smugly as he folded the letter and placed it in the envelope.

It had been an inspirational plan and, while he did not expect to hear from his brother for several weeks, Matthew was confident of a positive response and was now able to face the immediate future with considerable optimism. Once the farm was running at the profit he expected from the investment, he could replace the money and, provided Paul remained in South Africa, no one would be any the wiser.

Haveringham viewed Matthew's lighter mood with mixed feelings, while Grace firmly believed it was leading to an imminent proposal of marriage. She constantly questioned her uncle to see if he had heard anything to confirm her belief, but he remained annoyingly obdurate, refusing to believe that anything of significance had occurred and that Matthew had merely come to terms with the inevitability of the fate of his farm.

When the letter did finally arrive Matthew could hardly bring himself to open it, fearing that the wrong response would close the door forever on his aspirations. He sat in his father's chair in front of the cold fireplace of the parlour turning the envelope over and over in his hands, convinced that John would refuse to part with his money. But the letter felt bulky, too bulky to be a simple refusal, and with that thought now firmly planted in his mind he ripped open the envelope. Inside were two further envelopes, one addressed to him, which he opened with trembling fingers, spreading the letter on his lap.

Dear Matthew

I was pleased to hear from you even though I wished the circumstances had been different. It would make me so happy if you and I could be friends and I still live in that hope. It was a relief to hear that Paul is at least alive and well although I was sorry to hear of his troubles. Naturally I will do anything I can to help but as we are about to leave barracks to take part in lengthy exercises on Salisbury Plain there is little I can do personally. I have enclosed a letter to the bank instructing them to release to you whatever amount you think necessary and trust that you will make all the arrangements to send it to him. I just hope our efforts are not in vain. Please let me know if you hear further from him and if you let me have his address I will write to him when I can. Meanwhile look after yourself brother.

Kind regards
John

Matthew read the letter two more times before cheering loudly and throwing it triumphantly into the air. It had contained everything he dared to hope for, and more, and there was now nothing to stand in the way of his independent future.

The following morning, as soon as he was able, he rode over to Daventry and nervously presented the letter John had obligingly written to the bank manager, fearing that something might still go wrong. After carefully comparing the signature on the letter with one John had already lodge with the bank. the manager gave instructions to his chief clerk to prepared a draft for two thousand guineas, the amount Matthew felt appropriate for his needs.

As he pocketed the draft and made his way back towards Millwood House Matthew marvelled at how simple it had been, his only regret that he had not thought of the scheme a lot sooner, so saving himself months of unnecessary distress. But that was all behind him now and he looked forward to his meeting with Rufus Haveringham with some relish.

In the library a few hours later Haveringham viewed the draft on his desk with some suspicion before fixing Matthew with a penetrating gaze. "And how did you come by this amount of money? Not by dishonest means, I hope."

It was a response that did not take Matthew too much by surprise, given the old man's lack of trust in him. "Isn't it enough that I've managed to raise the money," he replied arrogantly.

"No, it is not," rapped Haveringham, tapping the draft with his finger. "If I thought for a single second that this money was the result of anything underhand then any agreement we have would be cancelled."

Matthew took on a hurt expression. "You still don't trust me. Well, you've no need to worry. The money was a loan from my brother, John. He has no immediate need of it and I promised him a good return on his investment."

"A rash promise. I just hope he's not going to be disappointed." He frowned as he inspected the draft. "This money will buy you a year, or two at the most, and you still may lose the farm. You will need to use it wisely or you are doomed to failure."

"I won't fail," he insisted before breaking into a patronising grim, "if you advise me on how to invest it to best effect."

"And since when have you bowed to any advice," said Haveringham sternly. "No, lad, it's time to make your own decisions, and make your own mistakes. Like I said, this money will buy you time, and nothing else. Make the most of it."

"I will, but now I have urgent business elsewhere. Would you excuse me?"

Without waiting for a reply Matthew went in search of Grace. Having secured one part of his grand scheme it was now the time crown his success with the ultimate prize.

Grace was coming down the staircase as Matthew strode across the hall. She had just changed out of her riding clothes and was looking forward to a quiet read in the drawing room before lunch. Seeing Matthew, she gave him a puzzled look before breaking into a broad smile.

"What are you doing here this time of the day?" she asked as he waited for her at the bottom of the stairs. "Uncle Rufus said nothing about seeing you today."

"That's because he wasn't expecting to see me." He grinned back at her. "I had something important to say to him and it wouldn't wait."

Grace felt her stomach lurch with excitement and her breast began to heave behind the tight bodice of her dress. "And what was that?" she asked breathlessly.

He took her by the arm and led her to a discreet corner beneath the staircase. Grace could barely contain herself, willing the words from his mouth.

"I have the money," he said jubilantly. "I have the money and I'm going to keep the farm."

The trembling lips that were readying themselves for a reply twitched with abject disappointment, and the eyes that were wide with anticipation narrowed with disbelief.

"Oh, that's good news. I'm really pleased for you, Matthew."

"But that's not all." He took her hand in his and fixed her with his pale eyes. Immediately some of the disappointment left her and her heart lifted a little. "I've been waiting for the right time to ask you, and there's no better time than now."

Her lips quivered. "Ask me what?"

"I've already spoken to your uncle and he's given me his blessing." His mouth was dry and he swallowed hard. "Now I'm asking you, Grace. I want you to be my wife."

For a moment all she could do was to stare at him, her lips moving in muted acceptance, although there were no words. Without warning she burst into tears, sobbing convulsively while Matthew could only watch and wonder what it all meant. He was about to offer her some comfort when she threw herself at him, her arms around his neck in a tight embrace, and amid the sobs was a nervous laughter.

"And I want to be your wife more than anything in the whole world." The words were punctuated with loud, joyous sobs and the tears continued to roll over her flushed cheeks. She covered his face with wet, passionate kisses before they finally broke apart. "You don't know how happy you've made me. Let's go and tell Uncle Rufus, he'll be so pleased."

Although he couldn't share in her faith, he looked forward to seeing the expression on the old man's face. It had certainly been a good day.

Chapter Thirteen

The Witwatersrand, Transvaal, South Africa
May 1899

A range of low hills that runs for nearly two hundred miles through the Transvaal, that was Witwatersrand. Few people had paid it much attention, that is until 1886 when an Australian miner discovered what would soon become the greatest gold reef in the world. Already rich in diamonds, South Africa now attracted a further influx of speculators, adventurers, those looking to make their fortunes in a land that offered seemingly unlimited opportunities. From all parts of the English-speaking colonies, Australia, New Zealand, Canada and, of course, the British Isles, men who had mining in their blood, and those who thought the gold would be there just for the taking, flooded into the Afrikaner controlled territory to stake their claim to the riches of the land.

It was into this strange, alien world that Paul Pearson had arrived on a wave of feverish optimism, to become just another of the hundred thousand Uitlanders, outsiders, who had trekked north from the Cape.

Now he stood on the top of a small hillock scanning the dry, dun coloured veld for the tell- tale cloud of dust, his bush hat held above his head, shading his eyes from the bright early winter sun. When he could see nothing but miles of scrub and rocky outcrops he sighed heavily and started back down for the umpteenth time that day. It was getting late, probably too late to expect Frank until the following morning. With the uncertainty of events that were escalating between the Cape and the Transvaal government it was an anxious time, and Paul could not properly relax until he knew Frank was safe.

He had only just reached the bottom of the hill and resigned himself to not seeing his partner until the following day when he was stopped in his tracks by an excited shout.

"Boss Triffic comin', boss." Joseph, the Cape Coloured engine captain was perched on top of the mine shaft housing where he had been happily greasing the pulley wheels. He was now pointing out towards the east.

Paul turned and ran back up the hill and stared intently in the direction of Johannesburg. At first, he could see nothing, his eyes not so well adjusted to the monotone African landscape as the young native boy. Finally, and with relief, he could just make out what Joseph had seen, a small, insignificant cloud of brown dust that hovered motionless above the horizon, too far away to be distinguished, but too large to be a single horseman.

It was several more minutes before the discernible shape of the high sided wagon, drawn by four oxen, was unmistakable, and Joseph began waving and shouting wildly.

Paul laughed as he took off his hat and waved it in the air. "Tell the boys we'll be having fresh meat tonight," he shouted up to the boy who was scrambling down from the housing with the agility of a monkey.

"Yaas boss," grinned Joseph as he scampered away.

Paul waited by the collection of tin huts that provided the living accommodation for himself, Frank and the small army of native labour, huts that provided little heat during the cold winter nights but baked their inhabitants under the hot summer sun. It was not what he had imagined when he left the relative comfort of Hibberd's Farm, and neither had it been quite the success he had hoped for. But he had no regrets, except perhaps one, and he thought about her constantly.

As Frank pulled back on the thick leather reins the wagon drew to a halt, the oxen snorting and poring at the dusty ground with their hooves.

"It's getting late," said Paul, slapping the rump of the nearest animal as he looked up into the bearded face of the giant Cornishman. "I thought you might be staying in town for another night."

Frank wrapped the reins around the brake handle and jumped down, his boots kicking up clouds of dust. "I might have done before, but since that business back in January it's not a place I care to hang around in for too long.

"No letters, I suppose," Paul asked hopefully.

Frank took off his hat and slapped it against his thigh. "Sorry, m'dear," he replied in his thick Cornish accent.

Paul sighed. He had written to both Matthew and Jenny, but he had no way of knowing if his letters had been delivered, except by receiving a reply. It was no surprise to him that he had not heard from Matthew, he expected little else. But Jenny? Her parting words still echoed in his ears whenever he thought of her, and that was most days, and even though he had all but given up hope of hearing from her she still stirred a longing within him.

Frank recognised the disappointment and gave Paul a hearty slap on the back that almost sent him reeling into the dust. "Don't worry, m'dear, maybe next time."

Paul gave him a weak smile and nodded. He had developed a great affection for the big man, knowing that had it not been for him he would probably either be dead or on his way back to England.

**

Paul had hardly arrived on the bustling quay of Cape Town harbour when he was overwhelmed with the first feelings of being lost and alone. There was little excitement at having accomplished the first stage of his great adventure, only the urge to take the first vessel back to England and throw himself into the arms of Jenny. All the romantic notions that had driven him to the southern hemisphere were as distant as the village of Weedon Bec, and the faces that passed him in the busy streets were strange and friendless. Even the news that greeted him offered little cause for optimism; since the great discovery of 1886 most of the more profitable gold mines had been taken over by the big conglomerates. The opportunities for the small, independent mines had passed, he was too late.

Dejected by the news, yet still determined to see for himself, Paul had made the arduous three-day train journey north, to the burgeoning town of Johannesburg, established on the back of the gold, deep beneath the Witwatersrand.

When Paul arrived in the town, he found it as unappealing as his prospects of a prosperous future. It lacked any of the charm of Northampton, with most of the buildings linked in some way to the mines or the miners who worked them. There was a predominance of cheap hotels and bars to accommodate the growing labour force, and to relieve them of their wages, since there was little else to do with their leisure time.

Paul quickly realised that, with his lack of experience of mines or mining, he was at a disadvantage, and with only useless, worked out mines available to purchase it would be folly to invest his money recklessly. It seemed that his whole purpose of coming to South Africa was rapidly evaporating, giving him less and less reason to stay. But for Paul the alternative offered no more attraction. To return home was an admission of defeat, and after the rift it had caused between himself and Matthew, he could well imagine his brother's delight if he returned with nothing more than a sense of shame, and a large hole in his inheritance.

To preserve his capital, as well as to give him an insight into the mining industry Paul had found employment as a clerk in the assay office of one of the Company mines. The work was monotonous and uninspiring and the days passed slowly, but he was imbued with the conviction that the longer he stayed in Johannesburg the more likely an opportunity would present itself. That opportunity came in the gargantuan and unexpected shape of Frank Trevithick.

While the days passed slowly, the nights were an eternity of boredom as he sat alone in the bleak, rudimentary bungalow he rented.

What the town lacked in the more refined social amenities it more than made up for in sleazy bars where a man could drown his sorrows alone or in the company of those who shared a similar existence. On the days when Paul was at his lowest ebb, when the visit to the post office had proved fruitless, he would seek solace, if not company, in one of the bars frequented mainly by English Uitlanders.

It was a two-storey building of timber construction with a tin roof and made no pretence at comfort. The upper floor offered cheap accommodation for the multitude of itinerants who passed through the town, while the lower floor was a single large room with a counter that ran the length of the back wall. A number of crude wooden tables and chairs were scattered about the bar, many baring the scars of the numerous brawls that would break out with the smallest of provocation.

The day that was set to change the direction of Paul's life had begun as every other. He had arrived at work with the same resigned dissatisfaction that accompanied him every morning. The manager of the assay office, a small, mean faced Welshman who had never shown any inclination of friendship towards Paul, greeted him with even more contempt than usual.

"A word, Pearson, if you don't mind," he whined as soon as Paul stepped foot into the building. The manager, Hubert Price, jerked his head in the direction of his office. "In there."

Without a word, Paul raised his eyebrows and followed the man into the small area partitioned off from the main office where Paul and the other clerks carried on their work.

Once they were inside the manager kicked the door shut and turned on Paul. "I suppose you know what this is about?" he said, his beady eyes searching Paul's face for an answer.

Paul shrugged, used to the man's petty-minded demands. "I'm afraid I don't, Mr Price," he replied calmly. "Is there something wrong?"

Mr Price's pinched face contorted with an apoplectic expression. "Wrong! Of course, there's something wrong. Why else would you be here?" He went over to his desk and snatched up a sheaf of papers waving them in Paul's face. "This is what's wrong, Pearson, this."

With the papers still being waved in the air there was no way for Paul to identify the source of the complaint against him and he shrugged again, nodding at the papers. "Well, if you'll only show me then I'll know why I'm here."

"Damn you're insolence, Pearson." He thrust the papers in Paul's face. "This is your fault and I won't have any argument." He pushed the papers into Paul's hand. "Look at them, just look."

Refusing to be goaded into a row, Paul took the papers, an assay report, and he cast his eyes over them before handing them back without comment.

Price glared at him. "Well, what have you got to say?"

"What do you want me to say? It's got nothing to do with me."

The manager drew himself up to his full height, yet barely reached Paul's shoulder. "And who do you think is responsible?" he hissed, pointing to the bottom of the page. "The report is wrong and your name is on it."

Paul looked again and smiled. "It is, but I didn't write it. You can see whoever wrote the report has crossed out their name and written mine underneath. Any fool can see that." He looked through the glass partition at the three other clerks working away at their desks and pointed. "I suggest you ask him, it's his writing."

The clerk in question must have sensed the accusation being levelled at him and raised his head, a smirk creasing his thin lips. He was a pale, ferret faced youth who happened to have as an uncle none other than Hubert Price, and Paul suspected it was not the only time others had paid for his mistakes.

"Don't you dare try to put the blame on others," breathed Price, prodding Paul in the chest with a bony finger. "I've taken as much of your insolence as I can stand."

"And I've taken as much of your mean minded, miserable face as I can stand." Paul snatched the report from the manager's hand and tore it into shreds. "And that's what I think of that."

Price's face turned purple as he gathered up the strips of paper scattered about the floor, trying to assemble them into some sort of order. "This is sabotage, I'll have you prosecuted."

Paul gave a dry laugh, amused by the sight of the manager scrabbling around on the floor. "Do as you please, I'll be easy enough to find."

And that's how Paul found himself out of work and sitting at a table in a corner of the shabby bar, staring at a half empty bottle of cheap brandy. Around him there was an ebb and flow of conversations punctuated by an occasional argument that was settled by drunken amicability or a brawl. All of this Paul ignored, content to finish the brandy alone and lose himself in the fog of inebriation and self-pity. The first few glasses of the rough liquid burnt his throat, but as he persevered, a numbness set in that seemed to engulf his whole body.

He was only vaguely aware of the person who joined him uninvited at the table, and when he looked up from the bottle, he met the heavily made-up eyes of a woman. She smiled at him and slid a glass across the table.

"You were looking a bit lonely, love," she said in a very cockney accent, helping herself to a drink, "so I says to meself, Maudie girl, go and cheer the gent up."

Paul studied her for a moment before retrieving to the bottle. "I'm content with my own company, if it's all the same to you."

As she finished the drink in a single gulp, she gave him a sly wink. "Not been out here too long and feeling a bit homesick, I'm betting." She lowered her head and tipped it to one side until her eyes met his and nodded knowingly. "I thought as much. Seen it all too often with you young lads, away from home for the first time. And I'm betting there's a pretty girl back home waiting for you and the fortune you've come to make. Going to get married, I shouldn't wonder." She waited for Paul to nod his agreement before pouring herself another drink and raising the glass. "This helps, of course, but it ain't everything, and it don't make up for the company of a good woman, and that's a fact. There ain't no substitute for that."

Paul dragged the bottle back to his side of the table. "Look, miss, I don't want to be rude, but I'm not in the mood for any company at present, so if you wouldn't mind." He cast his eyes around the smoky room. "There's plenty here who would be far better company than me."

"That's as may be, but none as 'andsome as you, sweetheart. Besides, I know better, 'cause I've seen it all before. You might think you want to be left alone, but I knows better than that." She went to take another drink but Paul clamped his hand around the neck of the bottle. Her breasts, that hung loose beneath the low bodice of her dress, quivered as she chuckled loudly. "I know what men miss most when they're away from home, and it ain't their mother's cooking."

"I told you," said Paul, emphatically thumping the table with the bottle. "I just want to be left alone."

She threw her head back in an exaggerated display of indignation. "Look, love, I don't know who you think you're talking to, but I ain't no slut. I'm a respectable woman." She leant further across the table, giving Paul an understanding smile and a clear view of her ample cleavage. "I was only tryin' to be nice 'cause you looked like a gentleman who deserved it. I'm not generally so forward as this, but if it's a bit of privacy you want we could take this bottle here back to your place and have a nice little chat without any interruptions."

"Voetsak," shouted Paul angrily, again slamming down the bottle and attracting the attention of those around them. "If you don't understand plain English then maybe you'll understand that."

"Well, I ain't never been spoken to like that before."

"An' I 'eard it too." A rough-looking man with a large, round head and deformed nose barged his way through the crowded room and stood menacingly by the woman's side. "I don't take kindly to anyone what talks like that to my wife."

Paul stifled the urge to laugh as he looked up at the man. "Your wife!"

"That's right, dearie, his wife." The woman sniffed loudly, smarting from the affront to her sensitivities. "And he don't like men talking to me the way you just did. Ain't that right, Stan?"

Stan leant across the table, his stale breath as offensive as his manner. "I don't, so unless yer want me to give yer a beating in front of all these," he swept his hand around the bar at all the customers now taking a keen interest in the budding argument, "I suggest we go out the back and settle it man to man."

Already angered by the intrusion of the woman into his solitude, Paul could easily have risen to the challenge. The man was of moderately heavy build, but he was older and looked out of condition, not much of a challenge in a fair fight. Yet despite this, Paul was reluctant to give him the pleasure. "I didn't know she was even married," he said, mildly apologetic. "I thought she worked here and if I insulted her, I'm sorry, I just wanted to be left alone."

"Well, yer apology ain't worth a toss to me," shouted Stan, attracting a larger audience eager for some entertainment. "It looks t'me that you're a coward as well, so I'm goin' t'give yer a beating anyway."

There was a ripple of encouragement through the crowd which gathered in intensity when Paul leapt to his feet, his fists clenched. He spoke through gritted teeth. "All right, if it's a fight you want you can have it." He jerked his head towards a side door. "Let's go and get it over with."

Stan held up his hand to silence the clapping and cheering that had broken out. "This is between me an' the lad 'ere, so I don't want no interference from you lot." He winked and gave them a toothless grin. "I'll be back t'buy the drinks when I've seen t'him."

There was another outbreak of cheering as the two of them pushed their way through the throng of customers. If Paul had been thinking clearly, he would have considered the possibility that he was being drawn into a carefully contrived trap, but the effects of a half-bottle of brandy had dulled his senses, and between Hubert Price, his nephew, the woman and her husband, he was ready to release a torrent of pent up anger.

Stan led Paul through a side door that opened into a narrow alleyway that ran between the bar and the adjacent building. The front was open to the street but the back was blocked by a high fence, allowing only one way out. Stan walked to the back of the alley, merging into the shadows of the encroaching dusk. Still fired up Paul took off his jacket and threw it onto the ground, approaching his opponent with clenched fists raised ready to defend himself.

Stan noticed the menacing look of determination on Paul's face and grinned slyly as he cocked his large head to one side. "Yer don't need t'get yerself 'urt, yer know. There's another way t'settle this."

Paul was in no mood for small talk. "It's not me who's going to get hurt, so let's just get on with it."

219

Stan backed up against the fence, glancing nervously over Paul's shoulder. "Look, it's simple see. Yer jest 'and over yer money an' we'll say no more about it."

Paul gave a snort of derision and brought his fists up higher. "And why would I want to do that?"

"That's why, cock." Stan gave a jerk of his head in the direction of the street.

Assuming it to be a bluff Paul ignored the remark until he heard the scuff of muffled footsteps approaching down the alley. He gave a brief glance over his shoulder and in that instant, everything became clear, why Stan had showed such bravado. In the fading light he could see the two men who were now no more than ten yards away. He looked around for a means of escape, but there was no way out except past the newcomers.

He had the presence of mind to place his back against the side wall of the bar to prevent himself from being attacked from the front and back. It was still going to be a poorly matched contest, but at least he could face all three of them. When his two mates were close enough Stan found the courage to put himself within range of Paul's poised fists.

"Yer still wants t'hang on t'that money of your then?" he enquired, his lips parting in a toothless sneer. "Well, let's see 'ow long it takes yer t'change yer mind."

Paul made no reply as his eyes flicked defiantly between the three of them, waiting for them to make the first move.

"Yer've still got time t'save yerself from a good hidin' if yer jest 'and over yer money. Me mates 'ere won't mind missin' out on their bit o' fun, long as they get paid."

Paul remained alert and stubborn. He gritted his teeth. "If you want it, you're going to have to take it."

"Brave words m'dear from someone as outnumbered as 'e."

The remark was made by none of the three men confronting him, and any small hope Paul still clung to drained from him when he glanced over at the new arrival. He was a huge man, standing a good head and shoulders above the other three and his bulk almost filled the width of the alley, blocking what little light still filtered through from the street.

What was hidden from Paul was the look of anger that flashed across Stan's face. "Bugger off, this ain't none of yer business. This'n 'ere insulted me missus, 'an me 'an me mates is goin' to teach 'im some manners."

"Well, 'e won't mind I hanging around to watch the fun then, will 'e," said the big man with a chuckle in his voice. "E aren't got no objection to that, have 'e?" He addressed the question at Paul.

Even though there was something strangely reassuring in the big man's tone Paul was still tense, his nerves raw. "I'm not in much of a position to make you go, am I?" He jerked his head at the three men surrounding him. "But it depends on whose side you're on."

"Well, I aren't made up I mind on that," he replied in his curious accent.

"I told yer, bugger off," snapped Stan, shuffling agitatedly from one foot to the other. "This ain't none of yer business an' we don't want yer 'ere."

"And 'e'll be making I go then?" The big man had positioned himself behind Stan's two mates and his presence seemed to make them anxious.

"OK, but jest stay out of me way," said Stan with a nod to his mates. "Let's get on wiv it then."

Holding his fists up to cover his face Paul braced himself for the expected assault, twisting from left to right to see who would attack first, but before it came there was a sickening crack followed by a stifled groaning. The big man was holding Stan's two mates by their coat collars and, with frightening ease, had cracked their skulls together. When he let go of them, they sank to the ground like two sacks of potatoes.

With Stan's attention momentarily distracted, Paul took the initiative and rammed his fist as hard as he could into the man's face, splitting open the bridge of his misshaped nose. With a shriek of agony, Stan threw his hands up to his face, but that discomfort paled into insignificance as Paul swung his boot into Stan's groin. With an even louder cry of pain, he slumped to the ground where he rolled around sobbing and clutching at his crotch.

"Aren't e going to finish him off?" enquired the big man, giving his two unconscious victims a kick in the ribs. "They would have left e for dead."

"I think they've learned enough of a lesson," answered Paul, massaging the bruised knuckles of his right hand. "Thanks for your help, by the way." He bent over the two prostrate men. "They're not dead, are they?"

The big man shrugged his broad shoulders and chuckled. "Shouldn't think so, but it'll be a long time before they know it. But we'd better make ourselves scarce before the Zarps come nosing around, I can't afford to be stuck here in Jo'burg for days answering their stupid questions."

When they reached the end of the alleyway they peered cautiously up and down the street. There were still a number of people about but no one seemed interested in them so they walked briskly away, anxious to put some distance between them and the three chastened men in the alleyway. They walked without speaking until Paul's companion ducked into the narrow space between two shops and leaned against one of the buildings gasping for breath.

"Have 'e got some place we can go?" he asked, clutching at his chest. "I can't go running around the streets all night, I aren't as young as I used to be."

"I've got a place down at Florrie's Chambers, near the Salisbury mine." Paul led the way back out onto the street and through the thinning throng of people.

Described as bungalows, Florrie's Chambers was a row of tin roofed buildings that were little more than sheds. One of them had been Paul's home since soon after he arrived in the town. It offered only a basic degree of comfort, but more importantly to Paul, it gave him the privacy not found in the crowded hotels. After more than twenty years of sharing a bedroom with his two brothers the thought of doing the same with strangers held little appeal.

Inside was a single room with a small area curtained off for sleeping. The remainder of the space was for living, cooking, eating and washing. The sparse and battered furnishings came with the accommodation, although Paul had added a few refinements like a second-hand rug, and curtains at the windows.

"It's not much," apologised Paul as he lit an oil lamp hanging from a bracket on the wall. "But it's not much worse than I was used to back home."

As the lamp cast its glow around the room Paul took the first real opportunity to study his new friend. That he was big was already obvious, at least six feet six tall with a chest like a barrel and shoulders that filled the doorway. Beneath the slouch hat he wore was a mass of thick, black hair, and a similar beard covered the lower half of his face. His heavy brows shaded a pair of lively brown eyes that twinkled in the yellow glow of the room. Despite his intimidating bulk there was nothing threatening in his demeanour, in fact he gave off an aura of calm friendliness. His trousers were tucked into the riding boots that were common amongst the diggers, and inside his open jacket Paul could see the butt of the pistol tucked into his belt.

"Thank you again for helping me back there," said Paul, offering his hand. "My name's Paul Pearson, and I'm in your debt."

"The pleasure was all mine, m'dear. There's not much to keep a man entertained in this miserable town, and even less out on the Rand with just a lot of kaffirs for company." He took Paul's hand in a powerful grip and shook it vigorously. "Frank Trevithick's the name and I'm pleased to meet you." His eyes flicked around the bare room. "Wouldn't have a drop of drink in the place, would 'e?"

Paul grinned. He liked the man's openness. "Only some local brandy I keep for medicinal purposes. It does a good job of numbing the boredom but I wouldn't recommend drinking it for pleasure."

"Anything that's not work is a pleasure to I," retorted Frank, the thick hair around his mouth splitting with a broad smile as Paul gestured towards a chair.

For well into the night the two of them sat in animated conversation, talking in detail about their respective lives, both before and since leaving England. Paul spoke in endearing terms about his brothers and parents, of his life on the farm and his reasons for leaving. When he came to his brief reunion with Jenny, tears of emotion welled up in his eyes, which Frank diplomatically pretended not to notice. He ended with his frustrated plans to make his fortune in gold and return home a wealthy man.

Then, as he listened to Frank, he realised how mundane and sterile his life had been by comparison. Frank was the son of a Cornish tin miner. His father was killed in a mining accident when Frank was still a young boy, and when his mother died the same year from pneumonia, he was sent to live with an uncle, a Falmouth fisherman. From the age of ten he went to sea, first as a galley boy until he learned his craft, the brutally hard life turning him from a puny lad into a sea toughened young man.

But the life at sea did not suit him, the harsh weather and the smell of fish his constant companions. At the age of fifteen he was given the unfortunate opportunity to return to a life on land when his uncle was swept overboard during a violent storm. With his aunt unable to keep him he walked the fifteen miles back to Illogen, the village of his birth, where he found lodgings with a friend of his father, and started work in the West Tolgus mine.

For three years he toiled underground, hacking the tin ore from deep beneath the Cornish landscape, and by the time he was eighteen he had grown substantially in both stature and experience. He also had the looks to attract the admiring glances of the mine manager's daughter, but when the relationship became serious to the point of intimacy it brought down the wrath of the manager and an end to his employment. It was then he took the decision to join countless thousands of others in seeking a life elsewhere.

By the time Frank had reached the point in his story, when he arrived in Cape Town nearly ten years earlier, Paul was struggling to follow the thread, falling victim to the preceding hours of drinking. He had a vague recollection of Frank telling him something of a mine before the glass slipped from his hand and he fell asleep.

When he awoke it was daylight outside and he was lying fully clothed on his bed. It took him a minute or two to gather his thoughts and remember the stranger who had come to his aid, the same stranger who must have carried him to his bed. He sat and held his throbbing head in his hands until his brain could catch up with the events of the previous day. The thought occurred to him that he was probably late for work until he remembered he had no work to go to, a situation that had placed him in his present sad state.

Carefully he stood up and took a few unsteady steps, expecting to see Frank asleep in the chair where he had last seen him. But the room was empty, Frank had gone. Paul felt a sense of loss as he threw some cold water on his face and rinsed out his stale mouth. He had made no friends since arriving in the country, and Frank was the first to show him any real kindness. He peered through the grimy window in the hope of seeing the big man returning with breakfast, only to be disappointed.

He went outside, the bright sunshine stinging his eyes and sending a sharp pain shooting through his head. He needed something to settle his stomach and ease the pounding in his brain so he made for the familiar surroundings of Mary Kelly's coffee house just a few streets away. It was where he usually had his breakfast before work.

After ordering a strong coffee he sat at a table by the window massaging his temples while he waited for the recuperative beverage to arrive. When the girl set the cup down in front of him, he breathed in the fresh aroma and nodded his thanks. As soon as it was cool enough, he drunk it down and immediately ordered another.

"Looks like e needed that."

Paul turned on the chair as the words, and now familiar accent, startled him and looked up into Franks grinning face. "How did you know I was here? I thought you would be back out on the Rand by now."

"It was just luck I saw e. I was coming back to see e and there e were. Besides, I aren't had my breakfast yet and I never travel on an empty stomach." To emphasise the point, he gave his belly a hard slap. He shouted over to the waitress. "Bacon and eggs, m'dear, and lots of it, and whatever my friend here is having."

Paul held up his hands and shook his head at the girl. "Nothing for me, the thought of eating anything makes me feel sick."

"More coffee then." He laughed raucously and pulled up a chair, sitting down opposite Paul. "If I hadn't found e I would have hung around until I did." He leaned across the table as if he had some secret he wanted to share. "I've got a proposition I want 'e to hear."

Paul waited for the waitress to remove herself out of earshot. "A proposition?"

Frank nodded, his eyes set in a serious expression beneath the heavy brows. "That's right. I did a lot of thinking after 'e fell asleep last night." He looked about him furtively as though he expected others to be interested in what he had to say. "Do you remember I telling 'e about my mine?" he said in a low voice.

Paul gave the question some thought as his head began to clear through the effects of the coffee. "Vaguely. I know you said you had a mine, but that's all."

"I wouldn't tell this to another soul, but I think I can trust e, and I hope you can do the same with I." Again, he gave the room another sweep with his distrusting eyes as Paul waited with rising curiosity. "Can I trust e, Paul?"

"That's for you to decide, Frank, but if you want my word not to repeat anything you tell me, then you have it." Paul stared hard at his new friend, feeling he was on the verge of something new and exciting. "What about the proposition?"

A big hand reached across the table and gripped Paul's arm. "E didn't come to Africa to work in some damned office, you told me that, and I'm going to give 'e the chance to do what you came here to do, mine." His hand tightened of Paul's arm. "There's not many independents like me left out on the Rand, all the workable mines were bought up by the likes of Wernher, Beit and Rhodes, men with the money to invest, and the time to sit back and wait for their profits. Any they didn't buy weren't worth having."

"Except yours," interrupted Paul sceptically.

Frank's eyes lit up. "That's the thing, m'dear. It was finished when I bought it, that's why I got it so cheap. Old man McFarlane, the man I bought it off, thought it was finished, said I was mad to buy it, but he was quick enough to take my money."

"So why did you buy? You must have had a reason."

Frank gave a deep, frustrated sigh. "The future of the goldfields lies in the deep mines, like Geldenhuis. It's no good scratching under the surface. But the deeper e goes the greater the costs, that's why most of the smaller mines have closed down, or sold out to the big conglomerates." He lowered his voice even further. "I'm close to a big reef, I know it, but I need money to carry on. That's why I came to Jo'burg, to raise some capital, but the banks aren't interested. They won't take the risk, or have been warned not to."

Paul rubbed his forehead thoughtfully. "So, you want me to invest my money? I don't know much about mining, but it sounds to me you need a lot more than I could offer."

There was an enthusiasm building in Frank that was intended to cut through Paul's obvious scepticism. "I know it's a risk, but isn't that why e came to Africa in the first place. If I could give e a guarantee I would, but all I've got is a gut instinct and a good gang to boys who have worked the last two months without pay." He sat back on the chair as the girl put down a plate of food in front of him. "What do e say?"

There was no immediate response from Paul as he sat nursing the coffee cup in his hands. He had no reply. True he had come to Africa to risk his money in the goldfields, and how much more of a risk would it be to throw in with the man sitting opposite than to trust in his own instincts. Had Frank really saved his life, or was he part of the same elaborate plot to relieve him of his money? How could he be sure? Not only was this the land of opportunity, but also of opportunists, and Paul had no way of knowing if Frank was the genuine character he seemed to be.

"Well, what do e say, m'dear," prompted Frank, unable to contain his impatience, "your money for an equal share in my mine? I'll not make you any false promises, a year from now we'll either be flat broke or rich men. Only a small amount of luck will make the difference."

Paul took a further moment to consider the offer before his face broke into a broad grin and he held out his hand. "You're right, I didn't come to Africa looking for promises, just for an opportunity."

After shaking Frank's hand and parting with his money, Paul spent the next few months wondering if his investment, and faith in the big man, had been justified. There was no questioning Frank's unstinting optimism and the industrious and uncomplaining qualities of the native workforce, but there was still no gold to justify all their hard work. 'One more month, m'dear' was Frank's mantra, accompanied by his infectious smile and determination. But was that enough to persevere in where so many others had failed, that was Paul's constant fear.

Then, after more than a year of finding nothing but a handful of insignificant nuggets, it seemed that Frank's confidence was justified when Joseph returned from deep beneath the Rand and excitedly whispered something into his boss's ear. Frank's reaction was to throw his mighty arms around the boy's neck and bounce him up and down. All the signs pointed to the major seam that Frank always knew existed, and at last they could look forward to a return on all the money and toil they had invested. And, more important to Paul, he could begin thinking about a triumphant return to England and the new life he planned for himself and Jenny.

But following close behind the clear blue skies of success came the dark storm clouds of dissent over the Transvaal. The Uitlanders, the outsiders, who ran and worked many of the businesses in the Afrikaner territory were allowed to do so unmolested by the government of President Kruger in Pretoria, but many of their rights were severely restricted. The qualification to vote in the Transvaal was fourteen years residency, a bone of contention between Kruger and the British High Commissioner in Cape Town, Sir Alfred Milner.

There were those in London who viewed the Transvaal through envious eyes, seeing it as the next step in Britain's expansionist plans for Southern Africa, a view which Milner enthusiastically embraced. The Franchise Question, the law which set the qualifying period for the right to vote for some sixty thousand colonists was becoming an increasingly serious issue between the two governments, with the talk of war rumbling on the horizon. There had already been a number of violent clashes between the Uitlanders and the Boers, most notably the shooting of Tom Edgar, an English boilermaker, by the Zarps, the Johannesburg police.

Disappointed at having received no news from home Paul walked back to the bungalow he shared with Frank. "What's the news from town," he asked despondently. "More talk of war, I suppose."

"More talking, that's all. Apparently, Milner's meeting old Kruger in Bloemfontein, for all the bloody good it'll do." Frank put a comforting arm around his friend's shoulder.

"You never know," responded Paul as his spirits lifted a little, "Kruger knows he could never win a war against Britain, he's bound to back down."

"Maybe, maybe not, but if it does come to war, it'll be the likes of e and I who'll end up the losers. How long do you think it'll take to get an army up here, those bloody Boers would have us out of here long before then." He stopped at the door of the bungalow and took off his hat, using it to beat the dust from his clothes before going inside. "I'll tell e something though Paul, m'dear, I'm not going to fret over it tonight. There's a few bottles on the wagon, and that drive's given I a hell of a thirst." He laughed loudly and gave Paul another slap on the back. "There's no sense in worrying about what might never happen."

For the next few hours, the two men allowed their concerns and disappointments slip away on the flow of coarse brandy until Frank fell into a noisy, alcoholic sleep. Left on his own Paul's thoughts returned to conflict and home, and he knew that sleep would remain a stranger for some time yet.

He went outside to take a walk in the cold, clear winter air, something he often did when he felt troubled, or simply wanted to be alone. Slowly he climbed one of the small rocky outcrops that surrounded the mine and sat down on a large boulder, smiling to himself at the sound of childlike laughter that drifted across from the Kaffir's accommodation on the far side of the compound. How he envied their apparent simplistic attitude towards life.

As usual he sat facing the north, towards England, imagining he was back home in the soft warmth of Jenny's embrace, a thought which brought a few tears of emotion to his eyes. Even the majestic array of bright stars in the clear black sky did little to lift the heavy feeling of remorse that always filled him on such occasions.

"You want some company, boss Paul?"

So lost was he in a far off world that Paul failed to hear the native boy who had climbed up behind him. He spun around at the sudden intrusion. "You startled me Joseph, I was miles away."

"Miles away, boss? But you was here." Joseph looked at him with a puzzled expression on his coffee coloured face. He pointed down towards the compound. "I seen you from down there."

Paul laughed briefly. "It's just a figure of speech, Joseph. I am here, but my thoughts were somewhere else." He gave the boy a wistful smile. "I was thinking about my home."

"I understand, boss." He sat down next to Paul. "I sometime go away too, miles away when I lay down to sleep."

Paul was beginning to warm to the interruption. "And where do you go, Joseph? Is there somewhere you call home?"

Joseph stared longingly out across the veld. "This is my home now, boss, with you and boss Triffic." He spoke with such sincerity that Paul knew it was heartfelt and true. "But I sometime think of me brothers an' sisters I one time had. I wonders boss what 'as become of them, if them still alive or no."

As the boy spoke Paul felt a surge of guilt at his own self-pity. He had never given a thought that behind Joseph's ever cheerful smile and willingness to please lay a past full of sorrow. "What happened to them Joseph, do you know?"

Joseph lowered his head and shook it sadly. "Them took from me when I was jest a little'un, boss. But I still remembers me sister cryin' when theys went. I cried too, boss, but I was jest a baby then."

"I'm sorry, Joseph." Paul swallowed hard at the lump that had formed in his throat. "Maybe someday you'll find them again, or they will find you."

"Maybe, boss." In the bright moonlight his teeth flashed a brilliant white as he smiled before his expression turned more serious. "Kaffir boys sayin' there goin' to be war boss. Is they right?"

Paul turned away from Joseph's enquiring gaze. "I hope not, but it is possible, I'm afraid. The English boss from Cape Town is going to meet Mr Kruger I think, so we'll just have to wait and see. Anyway, you tell the boys not to worry about such things, it won't affect us at all." As a sudden gust of chilled air swept across the top of the hill Paul shuddered and turned up the collar of his coat. "It's getting cold, time we were getting back inside, Joseph."

"You right, boss. You an' boss Triffic always right." He gave Paul a wide grin as they started back down. "G'night, boss."

Chapter Fourteen

It surprised few people, Uitlanders and Boers alike, that the talks in Bloemfontein between Milner and President Kruger achieved little success. Despite Kruger's concession in reducing the qualifying period from fourteen to seven years, Milner's intransigent stance always meant that the outcome of the meeting had been established beforehand. It was Kruger's firm conviction that his opponent was less concerned with the rights and interests of his country's subjects than his ambition to annex the gold rich Transvaal to the British controlled territories.

When the meeting broke up after five days of talking it was Milner's belief that only a show of force would be sufficient to make Kruger back down further. In anticipation of such a reaction the president had, for some time, been strengthening his own war machine, buying a quantity of field pieces from the French and, more particularly, the Germans who had shown a good deal of sympathy with his cause. From the moment Kruger arrived back in Pretoria the prospect for war seemed, for many. to be very real.

In Johannesburg the first signs of panic were becoming evident as shops and businesses began putting up shutters, while the more affluent began moving their valuable portables south, beyond the reach of the Boers.

By August the trickle of refugees through Johannesburg's railway station had turned into a flood as thousands fought to catch trains to Cape Town. Carrying just what they could reasonably manage they packed into carriages and cattle trucks, leaving behind the remainder of their possessions in the vague hope that they would return in a few months when the troubles had passed.

Paul had viewed the exodus with growing dismay and frustration. The mine into which he had sunk so much time and money was about to repay them with interest. The rich strike in which Frank had displayed so much faith was at last within their grasp. and it was heart breaking to think that everything was about to be lost due to the greed of one government and the determination of the other.

"What do you think we should do?" he asked Frank following a brief trip into the town to assess the latest developments. "Most of the mines are shutting down and the talk is that the Boers will expel all the English once the fighting starts."

"Let's not be too hasty, Paul m'dear," Frank replied with his usual equanimity. "It's still just talk and might not come to that. We just wait and see what happens, and if they try to kick us out then we'll give them an argument."

Reluctantly Paul was forced to nod his agreement. "I don't see why we should be forced to give up everything we've worked for, not without putting up something of a fight." He looked about him at what they had achieved and his determination became ever more resolute. "Not without a fight."

Frank gave a loud belly laugh, as he did in the face of any serious situation. "After seeing e the first time in that alleyway I should've guessed e wouldn't be frightened off by a few Dutchmen. I would have been disappointed if e'd have said any different."

So, for the following few weeks they carried on as normal as the deteriorating situation allowed. Out on the Rand things still felt very much as they always did, with little evidence of the gathering storm clouds, but in the town the impending hostilities were being acutely felt. As more shops and businesses closed, basic supplies became more difficult to obtain, and queues for the trains heading south grew longer. The clamour for available spaces for the three-day journey increased with each day, with the Uitlander Council paying the fares of those who had no money.

In early October the Volksraad, the Pretoria parliament, issued a four-point ultimatum to Britain, and unless all four conditions were agreed to within forty-eight hours there would be a declaration of war.

It was during this short period of grace that Joseph's sharp eyes picked out something on the veld and pointed anxiously at an approaching cloud of dust.

"Riders come, boss," he shouted as Paul and Frank emerged from the lift cage into the bright sunlight. "Many riders, boss. Maybe soldiers."

"Boers more like," muttered Frank with a resigned air as his eyes became accustomed to the brightness. "I've been expecting them."

"What do you think they want?" asked Paul, hoping to be persuaded from the obvious answer.

"What do e think they want?" replied Frank with unnatural curtness. He held up his big hand to shield his eyes from the sun. "Judging by the size of the cloud it's not a social visit."

"It might not be as bad as we think," commented Paul optimistically as he scanned the horizon. "We're no threat to them. They might just leave us alone."

Frank's dust laden beard parted with a broad grin. "Believe in fairies too, do e lad?"

They stood in silence, watching as the riders grew closer, and when they were about two hundred yards out Joseph counted about a dozen burghers, all armed with a German Mauser rifle and a bandolier of ammunition slung across their shoulder. It was clear, even at that distance, that Paul's optimism had been premature.

As the horsemen rode into the compound, they spread out into a wide arc in front of the two Englishmen, their bearded faces set in firm determination beneath their slouch hats. For a few moments the two sides faced each other in an apprehensive silence until one of the burghers in the centre of the arc walked his horse forward a few paces and took a folded paper from his coat pocket.

He glanced at the paper before returning his cold stare to the two men. "Which one of you is called Trevithick?" he demanded in his guttural Afrikaner accent and struggling with the pronunciation of Frank's name.

The big man took a step forward and raised his hat in mock respect. "That'll be I, m'dear."

"You be the owner of this mine." It was a statement of fact and not a question.

"Half owner, m'dear," said Frank with a sarcastic grin. "If e were to read the deeds properly e would see I have a partner, young Mr Pearson here."

The burgher looked back at the paper and shrugged his shoulders. "It make no difference to us, you both English." He stood up in his stirrups and looked around the mine workings and the various buildings. "Who else work here?"

Frank pointed to where Joseph was standing a few yards away, anxiously watching the proceedings. "Just the boy there and about twenty Kaffirs."

The burgher sat back in his saddle and gave the two Englishmen a cold look of contempt. "You have to leave," he grunted with a casualness that gave the command an even greater menace. "You and the boy. The Kaffirs we will find work for."

232

Frank took another step forward and glared up at the burgher. "I'm not going anywhere," he hissed defiantly before turning to Paul. "What about e, m'dear, are e going anywhere?"

Paul shook his head, albeit with uncertainty. He couldn't see how they would be allowed a choice by the heavily armed men. He scanned the semi-circle of riders and was struck by how similar they all appeared. The bearded faces beneath their hats all bore the same humourless fixed expression, and to a man they wore the same drab coloured clothing that blended perfectly with the dun-coloured veld. As well as the rifles they carried, most had a pistol tucked into their belts.

With no interest in entering into a discussion the head burgher stabbed his finger at the two Englishmen. "You not read the newspapers, English, there going to be war. All English must leave the Zuid Afrika Republik, that is the order of the Volksraad."

There was a ripple of movement through the line of horsemen as they sensed a resistance to the orders they had been sent to enforce. Paul glanced nervously at them, but his greatest fear was reserved for his partner who was clearly in no mood to back down. He knew it would take little provocation for the burghers to react with force, recalling the incident back in January at the amphitheatre outside Johannesburg when a Boer mob brutally broke up a peace meeting of Uitlanders while the police looked on and did nothing. Now, with a state of war only a day away it would take only a spark of resistance for the burghers to use their firearms.

"If we leave what will happen to our mine?" he asked in an effort to defuse the situation, and to pre-empt a violent response from his partner. "Will we be able to return when the war is over?"

The head burgher shrugged again. "That for the Volksraad to decide when we won the war. If we allow you to come back it be on our terms and your Mr Milner have nothing more to say." He urged his horse a few steps closer to the Englishmen in an effort to intimidate. "You have one day to collect the things you take. We come back tomorrow, escort you back to Johannesburg." With that he wheeled his horse around and galloped off, followed by the others.

As they stood watching them disappear into the distance Paul puffed out his cheeks and gave a deep, resigned sigh. "That's it then, I suppose. At least we now know where we stand." He shook his head sadly. "We'd better start packing."

For a second Frank stared back at him, the sparkle gone from his eyes. "That's it then, is it m'dear, just like that?"

"We've got no choice, Frank, you heard what he said, and you saw their guns. They're not going to take no for an answer." He gripped Frank's arm to stop his friend from storming away. "You saw them, Frank, if we try to put up a fight, we'll either end up hurt or dead, it won't matter much to them. At least if we leave here alive, we can always come back when the war's over. It can't last very long, they're only a bunch of farmers and they'll be facing the best army in the world. Just a few months and we'll be back, and we won't have a lot of Afrikaners telling us what to do."

Frank shook his arm free, his anger slowly subsiding. He spoke slow and thoughtfully. "I don't know, e may be right. But don't e underestimate them Boers when it comes to fighting." He gazed into the far distance. "You may be too young to remember what happened back in eighty one. They caught us good and proper with our trousers down, and they can do it again." He placed a powerful arm around Paul's shoulder. "I know e's no coward, and you make good sense, I suppose, so e have my word that I won't go making any trouble tomorrow, just as long as they do the same." He led Paul back towards the mine head. "There's a lot to do to get this place shut down so we'd best be getting to it."

***

By noon the following day the two men, with Joseph's help, had gathered together everything of value that they were able to load onto the ox wagon. Frank had warned Joseph to keep the Kaffirs in their huts until it had been decided what was to happen with them. He didn't want them thrown into a panic by the sight of the armed Boers, knowing of the history between the two factions.

It had been raining lightly all morning so there would be no dust cloud to warn them of the advancing burghers. When there was nothing left to do but wait, Paul climbed to the top of his favourite outcrop to keep watch. He wiped the boulder dry with his bush hat and sat down, instantly recalling the conversation he had with Joseph and wondering if the lad would ever find his family. It also made him realise how fortunate his own life had been by comparison, and it remained only a matter of choice for him to be reunited with those who were precious to him. It put into sharp perspective the troubles that had hung over the compound since the previous day.

It was not long before his sombre thoughts were dispelled by some movement far out on the veld. At first it looked like a solid mass advancing from the east, and it was still some time before Paul could identify individual horsemen, and he idly made a futile attempt to count their number. The only thought that struck him as he hurried back down to warn Frank was that there appeared to be more riders than the day before and that it would be a mistake to offer any resistance.

"They're not taking any chances then," commented Frank bitterly when Paul had told him what he had seen.

When the riders eventually converged on the compound Paul could see that there were, perhaps, a few more armed burghers, but added to these were three officers of the Johannesburg police, a sergeant and two corporals. There were also three other horsemen, similarly dressed to the burghers but conspicuous only because they were unarmed.

Again, the burghers fanned out into a wide arc with the three policemen taking up a position at one end, and the unarmed men a safe distance behind them.

When they were all in place, the leading Burgher again nudged his horse forward with a satisfied nod in the direction of the loaded wagon. "I'm pleased to see you not make any trouble, English. That would have been very foolish."

Frank strode forward and grinned up at him. "We thought it was time we took a short holiday. I've heard that Cape Town is where everyone is going this time of year."

The Burgher's stern face broke into an uncharacteristic smile. "Very funny, English, but I think for you it will be a very long holiday." He pointed to the wagon. "I see you are ready to leave, that is good, but I hope you have done nothing to compromise the working of the mine."

"What do e mean by that?" demanded Frank, his mood hardening.

The Burgher waved forward the three unarmed men. "It is necessary for us to keep mine working. We need gold for our war against you people. These men are mine engineers, they will see if it worth keep going or destroying. They will be in charge."

"I don't think so," shouted Frank, taking a firm grip on the horse's bridle. "We have agreed to leave, not to have any Tom, Dick or Harry playing around with my machinery. If this mine stays open, I will be the one running it, not them."

"That will not be possible," replied the Burgher calmly. "You are English and not to be trusted to work the mine for the benefit of the Zuid Afrika Republik. No, if your mine worth anything it will be well looked after."

"And you think I'll let my mine be used to finance your bloody war effort against my country? Do e think I'm a traitor?" With one hand still gripping the bridle he reached up with the other and grabbed at the Burgher's jacket, ready to drag him from his horse.

Paul raced forward to intervene as the other horsemen raised their Mausers. In a few short moments the situation had deteriorated from tense into dangerous, and it would take only the smallest act of aggression for them to open fire. He threw his arms around Frank's huge torso and tried to drag him away from the horse and rider.

"Don't, Frank, come away. There's nothing more we can do."

"Isn't there?" breathed the big man, brushing Paul away like an irritating insect. "If we can't work the mine, neither will they."

By the time Paul picked himself up from the damp ground Frank was striding purposefully towards the mine head. The leading Burgher shouted out an instruction and the three policemen broke away from the end of the line and galloped in pursuit of the big man who broke into a run. As Frank reached the entrance to the engine house one of the corporals leapt agilely from his horse and brought him down with a flying tackle, but before he could receive any help from his two companions Frank had rolled over and knocked him unconscious with a single blow to the jaw.

From behind the loaded wagon Joseph took in the scene, wide eyed with fear. Frank had been more like a father to him than a boss, and the affection the boy felt for the big man was urging him to take some sort of action.

By now the other two policemen had dismounted and while the sergeant covered Frank with his pistol the corporal set about him with the butt of his rifle. The first blow caught him across the shoulders, which had little effect as Frank tried to scramble to his feet, but when the corporal tucked the butt against his shoulder and took aim he was forced back onto the ground.

The sergeant cocked his pistol and in a moment of blind panic Joseph ran from the cover of the wagon. "Look out, boss, look out, I'm comin'," he screamed, running forward.

236

Equally panicked by the shouting and sudden movement from behind him the sergeant became confused and indecisive as he turned his gaze from the struggle taking place at his feet to the wild-eyed coloured boy bearing down on him.

Paralysed into inaction, and conscious of the Mausers that were directed at him by the Burghers, Paul could only let out a hoarse cry of warning, but it went either unheard or unheeded and Joseph kept going with even greater determination until he was only about twenty yards from the group.

As Frank and the corporal continued to roll about on the muddy ground for control of the rifle the sergeant brought up his pistol and took aim at Joseph running frantically at him.

"No!" screamed Paul as the gun went off with a sharp crack.

The first shot caught the boy in the right shoulder, and while he slowed momentarily it failed to stop him and he ran on, his arm hanging limply by his side. With the boy almost upon him the sergeant rushed his second shot and the bullet took Joseph squarely in the chest. A looked of pained shock flashed across his young face and he took a few more steps before his legs buckled and he dropped to his knees.

"I'm comin', boss," he gasped before collapsing onto his side where he lay still.

As the struggle with the corporal continued Frank heard the shots and saw Joseph fall. With a bellow of rage, and an even greater surge of strength, he threw the officer from him and sprang to his feet. Consumed by a burning desire to kill, he gripped the barrel of the pistol with one hand while clamping the other tightly around the sergeant's throat, forcing him back against the tin wall of the engine room. The policeman had no answer to the fury that was squeezing the life from him as he breathed with a rasping wheeze and kicked out in a last desperate act to free himself.

Behind Frank the corporal was swinging his rifle like a club and brought the stock down on the back of Frank's head with a force that would have smashed the skull of a lesser man. It took two further blows before the big man's strength began to desert him and he sank to the ground, taking the sergeant with him.

After the second shot had been fired Paul had finally shaken off his stupor, and a fear of being shot himself, and raced over to where Joseph had fallen, cradling the boy's head in the crook of his arm. The light had gone from his eyes although his bloodied chest rose and fell spasmodically.

"Boss Triffic OK?" he gasped weakly, his wide eyes staring blindly up at Paul.

"Yes, Joseph, he's fine," lied Paul, aware of the drama being played out only yards away. Anguished tears rolled over his cheeks as the life pumped from the boy's chest and there were only moments left for him. "Everything's all right now."

The boy forced a pained smile. "All OK now, boss. Maybe I see my brothers an' sisters." With those final words there was one last spasm and his body went limp.

Sobbing with uncontrollable grief Paul laid the body gently on the wet ground. There was nothing more he could do for the boy, and now Frank became the focus of his immediate concern. Still in shock from the death, he felt sick when he saw his friend lying prone on the ground, a pool of blood from his head mingling with the dark mud. Terrified that Frank too had been killed he threw himself down on the ground beside him and was relieved to hear a shallow, laboured breathing.

"He needs a doctor," yelled Paul, staring up into the glazed eyes of the sergeant.

"He need hanging," responded the officer coldly, still having problems with his own breathing.

The leading Burgher, who had watched the entire drama from the saddle of his horse with no outward display of emotion, walked the animal over to where Frank lay. "He was a fool, English," he said impassively. "He is lucky to be alive. A weaker man would be dead by now."

The Burgher ordered one of his men to fetch the wagon, and with the help of a corporal, Paul lifted Frank onto a small space at the back where he found an old sheet, which he ripped into rough bandages. After dressing the wound as best he could he was ordered at gunpoint up onto the seat next to the corporal who took the reins.

"Come, English, we go now," said the Burgher.

Paul threw him a shocked look, pointing at Joseph's body still lying where he had died. What about him?" he said, his voice trembling with emotion. "I can't just leave him there."

The Burgher jerked his head towards the back of the wagon. "The need of your friend is greater," he replied with cool practicality before indicating the three engineers, who had dismounted now that there was no threat to their safety. "They will see to the boy."

It was a heart-rending decision, and Paul agonised over what to do before he was forced to curse the Burgher for being right. If Frank was to have any chance of survival there could be no delay in getting him some medical attention, and reluctantly Paul climbed up beside the policeman.

The journey back to Johannesburg was slow and tortuous. After Paul's pleading, the Burgher agreed that they could take a longer, more even route, so avoiding the rougher terrain. Every mile or so he would scramble over their belongings to check on his friend's condition and replace the soiled bandages. Frank's breathing was irregular and Paul prayed that they would reach the town in time. The thought of losing both of the people who meant most to him in this foreign land filled him with an overwhelming dread and a realisation that in such a short space of time his life had been transformed from one of hope to that filled with grief and wretchedness.

The sense of relief he felt at finally reaching Johannesburg, with Frank still clinging on to life, was tempered by the uncertainty that hung over them while they were there. Paul was grateful that the leading Burgher ordered the corporal to take the wagon straight to the hospital where Frank was placed onto a stretcher and carried into a ward. The doctor, a Welshman called Davis, was a tall, wiry man with wild hair. Despite his youthful face he presented a steady, confident manner. The Boers had apparently allowed him to stay because of their own lack of qualified doctors in the face of an impending war, and he seemed to command some degree of respect.

"Is he going to be all right?" asked Paul anxiously when the doctor had completed his initial examination.

The doctor gave a non-committal shake of his head. "Difficult to say. His skull's fractured and he's lucky to still be alive in my opinion. But he's lasted this long, and if there's no infection … who knows."

"It make no difference," sneered the Zarp corporal, who had been ordered to stay with them. "He going to hang anyway."

"Well, there's no need for either of you to stay," said Davis, ushering them both from the ward. "He won't be going anywhere for some time, and even then, it might be in a box."

"You better come with me then," ordered the corporal, taking a firm hold of Paul's arm. "We not finished with you yet."

Paul was taken to the police station where he was reacquainted with the Burgher who had been in charge out at the mine. His name was Christiaan De Kock, a Field-Cornet with the Lichtenburg Commando. Without his bush hat, rifle and ammunition bandolier he appeared less intimidating, yet he still glowered at Paul through stern eyes.

"You have caused us much trouble, English." He spoke in his usual matter of fact tone of a man who took trouble in his stride. "But now it is time for you to leave our country like the rest of your people."

Paul threw him an incredulous look. "My friend is in the hospital. I'm not going to leave him there," he replied with quiet determination.

De Kock gave him a cynical smile. "If your friend survives, he will stand trial for the attack on the policeman. If you stay it will be the worse for you. There is no point." There was a clear warning attached to the last remark.

"I'm not going. If there's going to be a trial then they're the ones who should be facing the hangman." He gave a curt nod at the corporal. "They murdered the boy and tried to kill my friend. No, Mr De Kock, I'm staying for the trial. At least there will be one witness in Frank's defence."

"Like I said, English, you are a fool. Haven't you heard the news, the time for the ultimatum has passed, my country and yours are now officially at war." De Kock took him by the arm and led him into an adjoining room, away from the watching officers. "I'm sorry for what happened to the boy and your friend, but I do not think it will do you or them any good by staying. I am leaving here myself tomorrow to join the rest of my commando at the Natal border, and when I am gone, I can no longer guarantee your safety." He glanced across at the open door and the room beyond where the policemen were talking in low tones. "Do you understand what I am saying?"

Paul followed his gaze to the doorway and nodded his understanding. The killing of Tom Edgar was brought vividly to mind, and if he remained in Johannesburg there was a good chance that something unfortunate would happen to him, and the outside world would never get to hear about what happen to Frank Trevithick and Joseph out on the Rand. The best chance of helping his friend now lay in reporting the incident to the British Authorities down at the Cape.

"I'm grateful for the advice, Mr De Kock. But what about by friend, Mr Trevithick, do you really think they'll make him stand trial?" He kept his voice low, knowing the policemen in the next room would be less sympathetic than the Burgher.

De Kock bit his fat lip pensively. "If he lives, he will, you can be sure of that," he said slowly, keeping an eye on the doorway. "There is much bad feeling here with the English. Your Mr Milner has caused us a lot of trouble. But you should not worry about the trial, your friend is very sick and will be in hospital for a long time." Paul thought he caught a glimpse of a wry smile behind the Burgher's thick beard. "Besides, the doctor is a countryman of yours, he will see your friend receives the best attention." He patted Paul's arm. "There is a train leaving tonight for Cape Town, make sure you are on it."

When they returned to the other room De Kock spoke firmly to the policemen in Afrikaans, assuring them that Paul would be leaving Johannesburg that night and would be no further trouble to them. After much discussion with the senior officer, it was reluctantly agreed to let him go, while making it very clear that Frank would remain under guard.

De Kock insisted on accompanying Paul back to the hospital. "Take what you need from your wagon, English," he said ruefully, "and I will find a safe place for the rest of your things. The wagon we will take for our needs. I hope you understand."

Paul stared dubiously at the man as they walked along the darkened street. "Our countries are now at war, Mr De Kock, we're supposed to be enemies, so why should you be concerned about what happens to me, or my belongings?"

The Burgher shook his head sadly. "I am a farmer, English, not a soldier. I was ordered to leave my wife and young children on my farm to come and fight a war many of us do not want. You and I are both victims of our government's argument, so I know how you must feel."

When they reached the hospital De Kock insisted on going with Paul to see if there had been any change in Frank's condition. The doctor shook his head gravely as he led them through to the ward where they stood around the bed and stared down at the unconscious man, his head heavily swathed in fresh bandages.

"There's not much more I can do for him but wait." He looked pointedly at Paul. "If you're a religious man you could try praying."

"Will he be able to hear anything I say to him?" asked Paul, leaning over the bed.

"He's in a coma, we don't know what he's aware of. You can talk to him if it makes you feel better, but don't expect anything in return."

Paul sat on the edge of the bed and took Frank's great hand in his. "I don't know if you can hear me, my friend," he said with a voice trembling with emotion as tears filled his eyes, "but if you can I want you to know that you are the first true friend I have ever known. I have to leave Jo'burg, not because I want to, but because it's the best for both of us if I go. You're in good hands here, and as soon as it's possible I'll be back and we'll both make our fortunes. I promise you that." The tears streamed down his cheeks and dropped onto Frank's face. He squeezed his hand, willing a response yet expecting none. "I'll be thinking of you all the time I'm away, and I'll pray for your recovery."

De Kock placed a comforting hand on Paul's shoulder and spoke quietly to him. "Come, English, we have to go now and get you a place on the train. If you are still here tomorrow the police will certainly arrest you. Say goodbye to your friend."

Slowly Paul stood up and let Frank's hand slip from his grasp before wiping away the tears. "Goodbye, Frank. I'll be back."

After collecting all he could carry from the wagon Paul went with De Kock to the railway station. The platform was packed with people fighting for places on what was expected to be the last train out of Johannesburg before hostilities broke out. Most were clutching their pathetic belongings, the only goods with which to keep them going in the uncertain future that faced them. The confused and frightened looks on their faces told the story of their bitter resentment at having to leave, while at the same time relief at being given the chance to escape to a place of safety.

"Do you have money?" shouted De Kock above the clamorous noise as they pushed their way through the throng at the entrance to the station.

Paul nodded in reply. Before the troubles had reached their obvious conclusion, he had withdrawn what money he had left from the bank. It had proved to be a wise decision.

"Good," replied the Burgher with a satisfied grin. "The station master is a distant relative of mine, and even in these difficult times money speaks louder than a gun. He will get you a seat, for a price."

It was another hour before the train from Klerksdorp came lumbering laboriously into the packed station and rumbled to a halt amidst a great hiss of steam. Paul had spent the time with De Kock in the relative comfort of the station master's office. The Burgher had told his relative that Paul was a political undesirable, and anything that could be done to expedite his removal from the Transvaal would be viewed favourably by the Volksraad. Combined with the excessive price paid for a ticket, that was enough to guarantee him a seat on the packed train.

"Good luck, English," De Kock shouted up from the platform, a sad smile on his face.

As the engine built up a head of steam and jerked its way out of the station Paul forced his way through the carriage to get to an open window. He reached out and took the man's extended hand.

"Thank you for all your help, and good luck to you."

He stayed at the window waving until the train cleared the platform and began to pick up speed as it steamed south across the open veld towards Vereeniging and the Vaal River. With a feeling of desolation and hopelessness he settled into the cramped seat that was to be his home for the next three days.

In the dim light of the packed carriage, he looked around at his motley collection of travelling companions and wondered if they were all leaving under similar circumstances to himself. The self-pity and sadness that engulfed him as the miles separated him from his friend was probably shared by most that had been forced to leave, especially the children who had probably known no other home. But added to his own emotions was the guilt of leaving behind a dear friend who, baring a miracle, he would never see again.

Apart from the relentless rumbling of the wheels on the track, the carriage was awash with noise; babies who cried incessantly for food or attention, women complaining about the cramped conditions and lack of privacy, and men who cursed everyone but themselves for their misfortunes. Someone from the rear of the carriage made the loud and unhelpful remark that the Boers had threatened to blow up the tracks as soon as the train had passed into the Cape Colony, provoking the women into further wailing that they would all soon be dead.

Never before in his life had Paul felt so miserable, feeling sure he would never be able to endure the next three days in such debilitating conditions, and, while having some degree of sympathy for the young families forced to give up their established life in Johannesburg, he still sunk ever further into a quagmire of remorse.

When the ordeal was finally over, and the train rolled safely into the shade of Cape Town station on a warm spring afternoon, Paul welcomed it with the same numb relief as the rest of his travelling companions, who now seemed as familiar to him as his own family. But instead of joining them in their manic rush to leave the train he stayed in his seat until the carriage was empty. He wanted to experience a few minutes of peaceful solitude, to reactivate his thoughts that for three days had been engaged in the sole occupation of self-recrimination.

He got up from his seat and stretched his aching limbs and joints free of the stiffness that had plagued him since that first night on the train. Outside the station he embraced the bright sunshine until he was swept along on a tide of humanity that seemed to be driven by the single purpose of having somewhere to go, leaving him as the sole flotsam of indecision.

Cape Town was a hive of frantic activity as it struggled to contain those arriving from the troubled hinterland, as well as the passengers and goods being disgorged by the ships that packed the crowded harbour beneath the shadow of the majestic Table Mountain. The busy streets were lined with beautiful wooden fronted colonial styled houses with broad verandas to the upper floors and gardens filled with exotic plants.

From the station all roads seemed to lead down to the harbour and Paul soon found himself amongst the congested mass of warehouses, dingy drinking establishments, that catered for the needs of dock workers and seamen, and dubious looking hotels that provided a bed and little else.

Despite of his urgent need to report on the circumstances of his leaving Johannesburg to the British Authorities, the necessity to find a room was greater. He had few clothes other than those he was wearing and they, like the rest of him, had suffered severely from the stresses of the journey south. To present himself in front of a well pressed official in his present state hardly seemed ideal, and was unlikely to impress upon them the seriousness of his business.

The first two hotels he tried, although in no position to comment on his appearance, cast him aside like an unwanted vagrant with the excuse that they were full to overflowing. At the third he dropped his belongings onto the bare wooden floor in front of the small reception desk and sank into a small wickerwork chair. As there was no one in attendance Paul reached across and struck the bell with his hand. There was no immediate response so after a short wait he struck it again before resting his head back and closing his eyes. With only a few hours of uninterrupted sleep during the whole train journey he was losing the battle with fatigue and felt himself slipping into a deep slumber.

"We are full, you have to go away." The voice was distant and indistinct, but enough for Paul to force his eyes open and turn his head to the reception desk.

"I need a room, and I'm not moving until I get one," he found himself saying.

From where he sat, he could just about make out the head and shoulders of a small Indian man, his black hair slicked back like a shiny skullcap. "I told you, we are full, we have no rooms. You will have to try elsewhere," he said in impeccable English.

"I've tried and there is nowhere else." Paul sat up to get a better view of the little man. "You were my last hope."

"Then your situation is hopeless." He made an exaggerated show of fiddling with something behind the desk. "Now please go, I am very busy."

Paul got to his feet and stood in front of the desk, forcing the little Indian to take a step backwards. "I don't mind sharing, just as long as I have a bed. I've got important business here in Cape Town and I need a room. Do you understand?" He stopped short of thumping his fist down onto the desk.

The Indian raised his eyebrows and snorted indignantly. "I understand perfectly and I am sorry, but there is still nothing I can do." He gave a dismissive wave of his hand. "Now, will you please go away."

"I have money. I can pay, if that's what you're worried about. I can even pay double if it will get me a room." Paul reached into his pocket and jingled the coins.

The resolute expression on the Indian's face softened noticeably. "Double?"

Paul nodded and held out a handful of gold coins. The man stared hungrily at them before apparently being struck by an inspired thought.

"Perhaps there is a room," he said with a simpering smile and pressing his hands together. "I had quite forgotten the guest who is leaving today." He gestured towards the chair. "You will wait here and a room will be ready for you shortly.

Paul heaved a grateful sigh and, as the Indian came around from behind the desk and scurried up the narrow wooden staircase, he settled back into the chair and closed his eyes again. For the first time since before leaving the Transvaal he felt able to relax.

But the pleasure was to be short lived as a sudden outbreak of excited and angry voices from somewhere above his head brought him back to the reality of his situation. Paul sat up and looked towards the stairs, and a few minutes later amidst much shouted protests appeared an elderly Jewish man struggling to put his jacket on with one hand while dragging a battered suitcase in the other. He was being hurried along from behind by the Indian holding a bundle of clothes.

As the two of them reached the hotel lobby the Indian gave Paul and ingratiating smile. "Your room will soon be ready, sir."

Paul could only stare in disbelief as the Jewish man was forcibly ushered towards the door and out onto the street, still loud and verbal in his protestation. When the door was slammed shut behind him the Indian returned to the desk, straightening his waistcoat and running his fingers through his dishevelled hair.

"If you would like to sign the register, sir," he said still smiling as he indicated the dog- eared book. "And shall we say three days in advance."

Paul looked guiltily at the doorway. "I didn't expect you to throw someone out to make room for me."

"It is not a problem, sir, the gentleman had merely forgotten he was supposed to leave today. Now, if you'll just sign the register, I will show you to your room."

Although ashamed of himself for benefitting from another's misfortune Paul was too weary to reject the opportunity of a comfortable bed, and trailed behind the Indian as he led him up the stairs to his room.

"I am sure you will be satisfied with the accommodation," said the Indian as he threw open the door. "It is a very pleasant room, and from the window you can see the harbour. Now, if there is anything else you require, please let me know."

"I'd like a bath," replied Paul, throwing his belongings onto the bed. "A hot bath."

"And for a very reasonable sum it can be arranged. The bathroom is at the end of the passage and I will let you know when it is ready."

When the man had left, Paul took in his 'pleasant' surroundings. Apart from the bed, which looked far from comfortable, there was just a wardrobe with no door, a small table by the window and a chair, but to Paul it was indeed luxury. He took off his jackets and boots, his feet revelling in the freedom, and listened contentedly to the rhythmic groaning of the bed as he manoeuvred his body into the lumpy mattress. Within a few minutes he was sound asleep and free from the stresses of the past days.

Chapter Fifteen

During each of the next three days he spent in Cape Town Paul made the journey up to Government House, where he was passed from one minor official to another, all of whom listened to his story with feigned sympathy before telling him there was nothing they could do, that the Transvaal was beyond the influence of British power until the war against the Boers was won. Any notion that Paul had that he would be granted an audience with Sir Alfred Milner was quickly dispelled, the great man had far more important issues to attend to than the fate of one British citizen in Johannesburg. Paul was bluntly reminded that war brought many casualties, and that his friend could only be regarded as one of them.

The main preoccupation of the High Commissioner at that time was the threatened invasion across his eastern border by the Boers from the Orange Free State, or that the Cape Afrikaners themselves would give in to their loyalties and rise up against their British masters. Then, to add to Milner's woes, came the news that the towns of Kimberley and Mafeking were under siege, and, in addition to which, the great imperialist and mining magnate Cecil Rhodes was trapped inside Kimberley and threatening to hand the town over to the Boers if an early relief was not forthcoming.

A few days later General Penn Symonds is mortally wounded at Talana Hill in Natal and General White is forced to retreat back to Ladysmith. The war that Milner had fought so hard to orchestrate was barely two weeks old yet the start could hardly have been more ignominious. The only bright speck on an otherwise bleak horizon was the news that the new Commander-in-Chief, General Sir Redvers Buller, was about to arrive in Cape Town aboard the SS Dunottar Castle.

It was a time of frenetic activity and speculation in the city, and the earlier boast that the war would be over by Christmas was no longer mentioned. The big question on most lips was how a force of undisciplined farmers could inflict such defeats on what was recognised as the finest army in the world. Buller would answer that question quickly and decisively, that is what everyone expected. But for Milner, the protection of his borders with the Boer states was the first priority.

Paul's thoughts were led back and forth by the sway of public opinion, but the one constant that remained firmly on his mind was the fate of his friend all those miles away to the north. For him it was a time of fretting and indecision; he had no idea how best to serve Frank, and after giving up on expecting any help from Government House, he spent his time walking the streets of Cape Town in a confused state, trying to make some sense of the events over which neither he nor the military might of Britain appeared to have any control.

Almost daily, ships were arriving in the crowded anchorage of Table Bay, bringing in fresh troops from England and India. For most of the soldiers it was only a brief stay before continuing their journey around the coast to Durban where they were needed to halt the Boer invasion into Natal.

For a while Buller's arrival helped to calm the uncertain atmosphere and speculation that existed in Cape Town, but his presence alone was not enough to prevent many of the refugees from losing hope of ever returning to the lives they had made for themselves in the Transvaal. Those who could afford it were booking passage on the troop ships for the return journey to England, to consider their futures in calmer, safer surroundings, and perhaps return when the war was won. For Paul the choice was more agonising and emotive; he had the money for his passage, and good reason, with the desire to see his brothers and Jenny almost overwhelming. But his desire was tempered by his loyalty to Frank, and how best to serve his needs.

Added to these choices was a further option that merely compounded the indecision that had plagued Paul since his arrival in the town. Many of the refugees flooding into the Cape Colony, especially the single men, were being enlisted into the volunteer units, to be given the tempting opportunity to help win back what they had lost. It was an almost perfect option that should have required no second thought. The chance to strike back at the Boers should have filled Paul with patriotic enthusiasm, to repay them for what they did to his friend, yet still he hesitated.

For days he wrestled with his conscience, trying to understand why it was not simply a clear choice, and the inescapable conclusion he came to was that war was morally wrong. He had followed all the imperialistic tub thumping from men like Milner, but the voice that was now influencing him most was that of

Christiaan De Kock. What if it was an unwanted, and unwarranted, war, forced upon them by the power mongers in both governments? What if many of the Boers took the same view as De Kock? How would he feel about having to kill them?

These were the questions that haunted Paul for every hour he remained in Cape Town, but he knew he stood no chance of finding peace until he made a decision. He made a silent and painfully sincere apology to his friend and booked passage on a ship sailing on 16th November.

Early in that month all talk in Cape Town revolved around Buller, and what he would do to reverse the gains made by the Boers in northern Natal, and to lift the sieges of Kimberley, Mafeking, and now Ladysmith. It seemed to Paul during those days that everyone was preoccupied by the war while he was busy making preparations for the journey home.

He spent most of that time down at the port, watching the troops and their equipment arrive. There were sun tanned veterans direct from India, men who had served with Lord Roberts in Afghanistan, come to teach the Boers the same lessons they had taught the tribesman in Kabul and Kandahar. Then, in stark contrast, were the fresh-faced lads straight from England, away from their homeland for the first time and wide eyed with excitement, ready to plunge themselves into this great adventure for which they had trained so long.

Paul watched with great interest as they assembled their equipment on the quayside before being marched away to their barracks accompanied by much cheering and flag waving from the crowds that had gathered along the streets. For Paul, being there had a particular poignancy, anyone of those young men proudly marching in their new khaki coloured uniform could so easily have been his brother. Although his own feelings were mixed. Paul knew that his brother would want to be there. It had always been John's ambition to serve Queen and Country, and for him there would have been no room for moralising, it would simply be a matter of duty. No longer would John be the boy Paul remembered as he watched those passing by; many were the same age as his brother, but in their uniforms, they were all men.

Two days before he was due to depart for England Paul was down at the docks as usual, although the news he had heard that morning gave a far greater significance to his being there. During the night the SS Nubia and Harlech Castle had arrived, carrying with them officers and men of the 58th Regiment, men from his home county of Northamptonshire, under the command of Colonel Denny.

As soon as he heard the news a surge of nervous anticipation had shot through him, making him shake visibly with excitement. Was it possible that John would be with them? To see his brother at a time when his spirits were at their lowest ebb would be the ideal tonic, yet at the same time he hoped John was still safely back in England, safe from the horrors of war.

By the time Paul walked anxiously along the quayside the soldiers were assembling into their companies, a sea of excited, expectant faces partly hidden beneath the rim of their pith helmets, responding to the barked commands of the non-commissioned officers. There were a few occasions when Paul was sure he recognised a face only to be disappointed as he was met by the surprised look of a stranger.

As his disappointment grew, his searching became more urgent. Once the troops were marched off the quay and up to their barracks the chance of finding his brother would be lost. He resorted to calling out his name in the hope that someone who knew John would respond, but whenever he got too close to the formed-up ranks, he was politely, but firmly, ushered away at the point of a swagger stick. Then quite unexpectedly, standing in the shadow of a warehouse stood a soldier who could possibly have been his brother. The man had taken off his helmet to wipe the sweat from his forehead, someone who looked very familiar, yet with the unfamiliar bearing of a soldier.

With his heart pounding inside his chest, Paul pushed his way through the military throng, ignoring the shouted protests that followed him. "John! John Pearson, is that you?"

The soldier turned, a stunned expression on his face, hardly able to believe what he was hearing, and not immediately recognising the man bearing down on him. The heavily bearded face beneath the bush hat bore a vague familiarity, and the voice was strangely similar to that of his brother, yet the coincidence was too much to contemplate. But the man was calling his name.

"John, is it really you?" With unrestrained joy Paul threw out his arms, tears rolling down his cheeks to be lost in the thick growth of hair.

"Paul!" John stared back opened mouthed in disbelief. "My God, it is you!"

"Of course, it is, didn't you recognise me?" He threw his arms around his brother's neck, clasping him tightly to his chest as he sobbed with uncontrollable emotion.

As the audience of bemused soldiers looked on, Paul and his brother continued to embrace until John remembered where and who he was and forced them apart, conscious of the restraints imposed upon him by his military training.

"What are you doing here, in Cape Town?" he asked as they held on to each other at arm's length. "I thought you would be up north in the gold fields."

Paul was still so overcome with the joy of seeing his brother he found it difficult to reply. "The Boers had other ideas," he said breathlessly, keeping a firm grip on John's arms. "That's what you and your mates are doing here." Instantly all traces of happiness faded from his face as he was reminded that this was destined to be a short and strained reunion. "I'm on my way back to England. I was hoping to see you there."

John freed an arm and waved it at the soldiers massed along the quay. "And miss all the fun! No Paul, this is where I have to be."

It was all still a dream to Paul until he was shaken back to the reality of their surroundings by the abrupt voice that barked out behind him.

"What's goin' on 'ere, Corporal? Who's this civilian?"

As Paul turned, John stiffened in response to the question. "This is my brother, Sergeant Miller. I didn't know he would be here. We haven't seen each other for two years."

The sergeant narrowed his eyes, his moustache twitching. "And you're a soldier, lad. Soldiers get used to being parted from their kinfolk. Now, get fell in with yer mates."

"Couldn't we have just a few more minutes please, sergeant?" pleaded Paul, giving him an impassioned look.

Clearly a man with some compassion for the men under his command, Sergeant Miller gave a rueful smile. "I'm sorry, sir, but the army don't give a toss for the wants of you an' me. All I knows is if we're not ready to move when the officer tells us we'll be for it."

As John obediently gathered his kit together and prepared to take his place in the ranks, the sergeant took Paul by the arm and led him away from the line of soldiers. It was a moment of abject misery as the joy of seeing his brother was snatched away from him.

Recognising the familiar pain of farewells, the sergeant gave Paul a fatherly smile. "Look, sir, I can't make any promises, but when we get to barracks, I'll have a word with the duty officer, see if we can't get your brother a pass out for an hour or two." He gave a cautionary wink. "Like I say, no promises, but be at the gate about six o'clock."

Effusive in his words of gratitude Paul watched with tear filled eyes as the entire regiment marched smartly by on their way to the barracks on the edge of the town. For a while he kept pace with his brother's company until he was forced to let them go.

With irritating predictability, the time passed at a snail's pace that afternoon as all Paul's hopes hinged on the good will and persuasiveness of Sergeant Miller. As six o'clock sharp he presented himself at the gates of the barracks to be challenged by the sentry who barred his way at the point of a rifle. After explaining his business Paul was ordered to stay where he was while the sentry disappeared into the guardroom beside the gate. A moment later he returned, accompanied by the guard sergeant.

"You can wait inside, sir, if you like," said the sergeant, a round-faced stocky man with a similar military moustache as Sergeant Miller. As he was led into the guardroom Paul wondered if the moustache was handed out with the three stripes. "Hoping to see your brother then, sir?"

Paul nodded, grateful for the brief distraction during his anxious wait. "That's right. We just met by chance, down at the port."

"Well, I hope you won't be disappointed, it ain't easy getting a special pass." He offered Paul the use of a chair. "Been in the country long, have you?"

"About two years. I'm off back to England in a few days." He peered out of the window for any sign of his brother.

"You're the lucky one then, sir. I've only been here a few weeks myself, but they say it's a devil of a country for fighting in." He sat himself down at the table opposite Paul and leant forward with an enquiring look. "They say them Boers are slippery customers, not like real soldiers. They say you never see them when they're shooting at you. Is that right, sir?"

"I couldn't say, sergeant, I've not been shot at by one," replied Paul reservedly, vividly recalling his recent encounter with the Johannesburg police.

The sergeant was clearly amused by the remark and roared with laughter, although Paul was unable to share in the hilarity as he nervously awaited news from the sentry.

After what seemed like an interminable period of time there was the crunching of army boots on the gravel outside and Paul leapt to his feet, secretly praying that the sentry was not alone. He almost wept with joy when John appeared jubilantly clutching a slip of paper which he presented to the sergeant.

"Good old Sergeant Miller," he said, a broad grin spread across his face. "It's only an hour, but it's better than I expected."

The two brothers embraced again before walking out through the gates excitedly firing questions at each other, making the most of their precious hour. Such was the ferocity of the questioning that one was asked before the previous one was answered, and it was quickly decided that John would speak first while Paul listened.

He recounted his early days of army life, the endless drilling and harsh discipline that drove out all remnants of civilian youth and turned him into the professional soldier that Paul hardly recognised as his brother. The barrack room taunting of the older men and lack of privacy had hardened his sensitive nature and he felt ready to fulfil the role for which he had trained so hard. With undisguised pride he pointed to the two stripes on his tunic, explaining that because of his enthusiasm and obvious leadership qualities he had become the youngest corporal in the regiment, a promotion that had brought a degree of resentment amongst some of his colleagues.

Also, the army had quickly recognised his ability as a horseman and he was now part of the newly formed Mounted Infantry, a unique unit in the army that was part foot soldier and part cavalry, set up to combat the hit and run tactics of the Boers. Yes, the army had been everything John had hoped, and now that he was about to prove himself in battle, he could want for nothing more.

He spoke with noticeably less passion when he told Paul about the previous Christmas when he had returned to their home to spend the holiday with Matthew, only to be rejected. It was only then that the two were struck by a sense of guilt; it was the first time Matthew's name had been mentioned.

"Why did the two of you not write?" asked Paul, without any intended recrimination. "I sent several letters to Matt and never got a single reply."

John shook his head sadly. "He still bears us a lot of ill will. He never replied to my letters either. The only time I heard from him was when you wrote asking for money. You must have heard from him then." He stopped walking and looked hard at Paul. "You did get the money, I suppose?"

Paul returned his brother's gaze, his eyes narrowed. "What money? What are you talking about? I've never asked for any money."

John's eyes widened in disbelief. "But you wrote to Matt saying you were in difficulties and asking for him to send you money. I sent him a letter for the bank, to use the money from my share of the farm."

Paul shook his head woefully and turned his head skywards. "Dear God, Matt, what have you done?" He gripped his brother's shoulder. "He's deceived you, John. He's cheated and deceived you out of your inheritance. I can never forgive him for that, and I'm just thankful that I'm on my way back to England. With any luck I can save your money for you."

"I'm not worried about the money, Paul, he can have it if he needs it that badly. It just makes me so sad and angry that he feels the need to deceive us." He gave Paul an imploring look. "The money really isn't important, so please don't do anything you might regret later, not on my account. I've made a will, just in case something happens to me, so the money would have been yours and Matt's anyway. Just don't make any trouble for yourself."

Paul patted him reassuringly. "You've got a soft heart, John. I don't know how you ever became a soldier. Don't worry, I promise not to harm him, even though it won't be easy." He took out his pocket watch and a pall of sadness enveloped him. "It's nearly time for you to be getting back, I don't want to be responsible for you getting into trouble."

As they walked slowly back to the barracks it was Paul's turn to tell John some of what had happened to him since arriving in South Africa, putting particular emphasis on the tragic death of Joseph and the sorrow and guilt he felt at leaving Frank in Johannesburg.

"It doesn't sound as though you had much choice," sympathised John as they reached the barrack gates. "But if I ever get up that way, I'll find out what I can, I promise."

"I only want you to promise me one thing, that you'll keep your head down when the bullets start flying, that's all," smiled Paul, knowing it was a pointless request. "Be safe, not a hero."

"I'll try to be both." The two brothers threw their arms around each other in a final embrace of farewell. When they pulled apart there were tears in their eyes. "It was hard enough parting from you that first time in England, but this is so much worse. I love you dearly, Paul."

With those parting words he turned and strode briskly through the gates and away to the barrack blocks. Not once did he trust himself to turn and wave while Paul stood watching him as he disappeared from view. For several more minutes

Paul lingered outside the gates, feeling alone and desolate, just as he had when he was forced to leave Johannesburg. How many more partings would he have to endure?

In a few days he would be leaving South Africa, perhaps for good, but that thought was inconsequential when compared with the prospect of never seeing his young brother again.

John was given little time to indulge in remorse. Within days of arriving in Cape Town his regiment received orders to entrain for the Orange River. They were to be part of Lord Methuen's 1st Division who had been tasked with relieving Kimberley.

As the eight thousand men assembled at the river with all the impedimenta that accompanied such a field force, the sight filled John with a sense of awe as well as pride. He had taken part in exercises on Salisbury Plain, but this was something much greater, that carried with it a heavy burden of responsibility, with the outcome being scrutinised by more than just their colonel.

It was now the 20th November. The following day they would cross the river and begin the seventy-mile march on Kimberley. Among the younger and less experienced soldiers there was still the excited anticipation of their first battle. It was to be a game filled with thoughtless acts of heroism, and the knowledge of certain victory. For the older men who had seen it all before, the reality was somewhat different. It was noise, smoke, blood and death, and win or lose there would be no lasting glory, just the memory of friends they had lost.

It was largely a force of foot soldiers that, Methuen had under his command with less than a thousand mounted troops. During the first few days of the march the Mounted Infantry were used for reconnaissance patrols, riding out over the flat, dusty brown veld and up onto the rocky kopjes that broke up the otherwise bland landscape. The patrols, though essential to the security of the column, were usually uneventful, although for John they provided a welcome distraction to the routine monotony of the march.

In the evening, when the column halted for the night, was a time for reflective thought, sitting around the camp fires discussing the events of the day and speculating on what they could expect once the sun rose again. The younger men, on their first campaign, would question the older veterans on their experiences, only to be surprised by the lack of bragging and shows of false bravado. Men who had faced death rarely found anything to brag about.

On the evening of that first day when they had crossed the river and set up camp on the north bank, John sat down to write a letter to Paul. In it he set out all the feelings and emotions he was unable to put into words before they parted. It was not so much an outpouring of sentimentality but a maturely written account of his thoughts. He made it plain that, while he could never condone what Matthew had done, he did not hate him, and hoped that Paul would understand. He told Paul that he accepted the risks he faced as a soldier, although he could face death a little easier knowing his two brothers were not enemies. When he had finished, he wrote with similar sentiments to Matthew.

In the morning they broke camp before dawn, leaving behind their tents, and piling the fires high with brushwood and acacia branches to disguise their departure from the prying eyes of any Boer commandos.

After marching for twelve miles the column halted for breakfast at a place called Finchams Farm. The farm had been long deserted, but it was a convenient place to stop, just long enough for the men to rest, enjoy a mug of tea and eat a hastily prepared meal. But for John the rest was to be even more short lived. Before he had finished his tea he was interrupted by the thud of horse's hooves and a spray of gritty dust.

"Get five of your men into the saddle, Corporal Pearson, we've got a reconnaissance."

John threw the dregs of his tea onto the ground and sprung to attention, looking up into the firmly set face of Lieutenant Rogerson. While some of the men grumbled at the orders John threw at them, he was personally pleased to be spared the constraints of the march, even if only for a few hours. Besides, he liked the lieutenant, he found him approachable and a good officer. Although no more than a few years older than himself he came from a solid military background and commanded the men under him in a confident, reassuring manner.

Amongst the others on the patrol were Private Barker, a rough, thickset Brummie, a barrack room bully who resented John's rapid promotion; Private Caulkin, a dull-witted lad for whom the army provided the family and home he had never known in civilian life; and Private Dobson who had joined the army soon after John and had become his firm friend. John had spent the previous Christmas with Dobson's family.

Once they were mounted and clear of the camp the lieutenant explained to John the purpose of their patrol. From the limited intelligence available to Lord

Methuen, it was thought that the first Boer resistance would be met at Belmont, about a dozen or so miles further up the railway line. It was Methuen's plan to make a night approach, followed by an assault at dawn to capitalise on his most precious weapon, surprise.

Maps of the area were notoriously unreliable, therefore the more information they had of the terrain ahead the fewer the problems and delays they were likely to encounter on the march. The orders for the patrol were to follow the railway line for a few miles and then to strike off in a north-westerly direction until they could see the kopjes, the low rock strew hills, which protected Belmont, and where it was expected the Boers would be waiting. They would then turn east, re-cross the railway before heading back south to meet up with the column. A straightforward, but important patrol, it was assumed.

For nearly two miles they rode parallel to the track before the lieutenant gave the order to strike out across the veld. The early morning sun was already hot and there was only the slightest hint of a breeze, and as they rode at a steady canter it was left to the horses' hooves to stir up the dusty ground.

"A pleasant day for a jaunt, corporal," commented the lieutenant as the pair rode side by side. "But we mustn't lose sight of the fact that we're here to observe and take note of the lie of the land."

John nodded his understanding. "Do you think we'll see any of the enemy, sir?"

The officer raised his eyebrows as he stared intently into the distance. "Truth be told, corporal, I'm not sure I know who the enemy really are. It's not the army we're usually pitched against, but don't be fooled into thinking they're just a lot of farmers. We thought that nearly twenty years ago and learnt a bitter lesson."

"So, what happens if we come across any of them?" asked John, confused about exactly who they would be fighting."

The lieutenant gave a dry laugh. "We assume the worst, but hope for the best."

As the morning wore on, they found little to arouse any fears in that isolated part of the Cape Colony. They passed one or two Afrikaner homesteads scattered about the area of their patrol, the occupants of which giving little indication if their sympathies lay with their neighbours living no more than ten miles to the east across the border in the Orange Free State. Lieutenant Rogerson erred on the side of caution, preferring not to risk any provocation by giving the farms a wide berth. Instead, he scanned them from a distance through his binoculars before recording their existence on the map he carried.

About an hour or so after leaving the railway line they approached a low, shallow sided kopje and Rogerson order the five troopers to wait at the bottom while he and John rode ahead to the top of the rise to reconnoitre the land beyond.

"Can't be too careful," muttered the officer as the two men reined in their mounts.

As the lieutenant pulled the binoculars from the leather case slung at his side John stood up in his stirrups and scanned the surrounding landscape, and the first thing he noticed was a scattering of buildings no more than a hundred yards away off to their left. He pointed them out to Rogerson.

"Looks like another farm, sir."

The lieutenant nodded and focussed his glasses on the small collection of buildings, a brick- built house with small windows and tin roof, and a few more outbuildings which were either barns or stables. There was no sign of any activity around the buildings and Rogerson was about to suggest that they skirt the farm and continue on with their patrol when the loud crack of a rifle shot rang out. He let out a shocked gasp and clutched at the right side of his chest before slumping forward across the neck of his horse.

Shouting at the others to keep under cover of the kopje John grabbed the reins of the lieutenant's horse and galloped back down, praying that the officer stayed in the saddle. With the help of his friend Dobson, he pulled Rogerson off the horse and made him as comfortable as possible on the ground.

As the rest of the patrol dismounted John ordered two of them around the side of the hill to keep an eye of the farm from the safety of whatever cover they could find while he checked the officer's wound. The lieutenant had been hit high in the chest, just below the shoulder, and was bleeding freely. With no field dressings between them John pulled out a handkerchief, formed it into a pad and stuffed it inside the officer's tunic.

John looked about him, suddenly and acutely aware that he was now in command.

"We can't stay here, the lieutenant needs medical attention, but I don't think he'll make it back to the column without getting his wound dressed first."

"Bugger 'im," snorted Barker, his voice weighted with its usual belligerence, "what about us?"

"You'll do what needs to be done," snapped John. It was not the first time Barker had questioned his authority, but this was the first time he had done so while in action, and he was in no mood to tolerate any resistance to his orders. "We'll have to clear the house and get the lieutenant out of this sun."

"But we don't know how many of the bastards are in there," sneered Barker. "If we rush the house, we'll be cut down before getting ten yards." He looked to the others for support, but only Caulkin nodded his agreement.

"There can't be that many, probably only one," reasoned John, edging forward to where the other two were watching the farm. He looked pointedly at Barker. "We'll move in from two sides, you and me from the left and three of you from the right. One stay with the horses and the lieutenant and I'll send someone back to help bring him in when it's over. With a bit of luck there'll be no windows at the side of the house and we can get in close without being seen."

"A bit of luck! Is that the best you can do, corporal," retorted Barker as the two set off.

Moving in short, crouching runs they circled wide, making use of what little cover the barren ground provided until they drew level with the side of the house. John was right, there were no windows, and as they went further forward, they could see the end of a narrow veranda that ran along the entire front. Keeping low to the ground they moved in closer, expecting with each yard to hear the sharp crack of a Mauser and feel the burning thump of a cartridge.

When they reached the side of the house John pressed himself close to the building, listening for any sound to indicate they had been seen. Taking a deep breath to steady his uncertain nerves he swung his leg over the veranda rail and, ducking below the window, he beckoned Barker to join him.

Keeping tight to the wall the two men edged along the veranda towards the open doorway. With the cuff of his tunic John wiped away the beads of sweat that threatened to blur his vision as he tried to recall if there was anything in his training that covered such an action, but was forced to conclude that caution and common sense were the only essential tactics. From the other side of the house, he could hear the approach of the other three men.

With a trembling hand John cocked his rifle and gave Barker a slight nod, then he was through the doorway, swinging the barrel of his rifle left and right as his eyes became accustomed to the gloomy interior. Barker was right behind him and he could clearly hear the man's heavy breath.

Just as it became apparent that the room was empty there came the sound of shattering glass and a loud, jubilant shout from Dobson.

"In the bedroom, John, we've got them covered."

Cautiously the two men crossed the room that seemed to serve as both kitchen and parlour. They entered into a narrow passage with an open door at each end. John indicated to Barker that he should check the room to the right while he edged slowly towards the door on the left. At first, he could see only the faces of the three soldiers at the window and the barrel of Dobson's rifle which he jabbed towards a corner of the room, hidden from John's view by the open door.

Stepping smartly into the room John swung his rifle around at three people who were huddled into the corner, a woman with her arms tightly wrapped around the shoulders of two children, a boy and a girl. The woman was tall, but with a slight frame hidden beneath a shapeless black dress, and probably younger than her prematurely grey hair suggested. Her thin face showed a mixture of contempt and fear as she started jabbering excitedly in her guttural Afrikaans. The girl, who John judged to be about eighteen years of age, was doing her best to calm the woman and turned her cornflower blue eyes on John in a pleading look. The boy was three or four years younger than the girl and had kept up a defiant gaze on the soldier standing before him.

"Check the outbuildings, but watch out for yourselves," ordered John to the men at the window. "If it's all clear bring the lieutenant and the horses down."

Barker had now joined him in the bedroom and his mean, menacing expression set the woman off in a fresh bout of verbal anxiety. John indicated that they should move away from the corner and sit on the bed from where the boy continued with his defiant stance until the girl spoke in heavily accented English.

"Are you going to shoot us?" she asked, clutching hold of the woman's bony hand.

"We're going to shoot the bastard what done for our officer," hissed Barker, his thick lips curled into an evil grin as he thrust the barrel of his rifle in the girl's face.

Although the woman was unable to understand the words, Barker's tone and actions were enough to set her off wailing.

"We're not going to shoot anyone," John assured her, with a stern look of rebuke at Barker. "We just want to be sure that no one shoots at us."

Still obviously agitated the woman spoke urgently to the girl, indicating that her words be translated for the benefit of the soldiers.

"My mother says …" began the girl hesitantly with quick glances at the woman who nodded her head. "My mother says she does not care what you do to her, but she begs you not to harm my brother and me."

Despite the tension that existed between them John managed a smile. "Tell your mother we mean none of you any harm, we just want the man who shot our officer. If you know where he is it would be better for all of you to give him up."

As the girl translated John's words the woman began to sob uncontrollably and pulled her son closer while he continued to glare his defiance at the soldiers.

"You do know where he is?" John asked the girl quietly. "If it's your father tell us where he is. The other soldiers are searching outside and if he tries to resist he could get shot."

The girl shook her head while keeping a nervous eye on her mother. "My father is not here, he is away."

"Yeah, fighting against us somewhere, I expect," sneered Barker. "If there ain't anyone else here then it has to be one of you, and I know who my money's on." He glared directly at the boy.

For the woman his remark needed no translation and she spoke urgently to her daughter who stared back at her in alarm.

"Come on then, who was it?" demanded Barker.

The girl breathed deeply as her mother urged her to speak. "My mother says it was her who shot your officer. She is sorry, but she only did it because she was afraid you were going to hurt or kill us."

"The British don't make war on women and children," snapped John, offended by the suggestion. "Now, where's the rifle?"

The girl spoke to her mother before replying. "It is under the bed." She looked imploringly at John, her blue eyes pleading for leniency. "What will happen to us?"

"I don't know, that's not for me to decide. It will probably depend on whether the lieutenant lives or not. I could tell my superiors that it was an accident, that your mother only intended to frighten us away."

"It was not an accident, I wanted to kill you all," shouted the boy before his mother let out an anguished cry and slapped him hard across the face.

To John the confession came as no surprise. The boy's hatred of the British had been apparent for the whole time they had been in the house. It was likely that his father had joined up with the local commando in the Orange Free State and he resented the fact that he had been ordered to stay behind to tend the farm. As the other soldiers returned from searching the outbuildings John got his three prisoners up off the bed and ushered them through to the parlour.

His friend Dobson reported that they had found no one and that Caulkin and the other men had gone up to the kopje to bring back Lieutenant Rogerson and the horses.

As Barker toyed with the Mauser he had retrieved from under the bed, John kept watch on the woman and her two children until Caulkin and one of the other privates carried the wounded officer across the veranda and into the room.

"Take him through and put him on the bed," John told them, making a quick assessment of the officer's condition. "He's still bleeding."

While the soldiers were briefly distracted the boy broke free from his mother's grasp and made a grab for the Mauser, trying to snatch it from Barker's hand. But he was no match for the brutish soldier who snatched it back and smashed the butt into the side of the boy's head, sending him reeling backwards.

Barker dropped the Mauser on the table and brought his own weapon up into the firing position. "Young tyke! Want me to put a bullet in him, corp?"

As the woman screamed in terror John placed himself between Barker and the boy. The girl ran across the room and dropped to her knees in front of John. "Please don't shoot him, he's only a boy."

"No one's going to shoot anyone," said John, staring pointedly at Barker. He turned to Dobson. "Keep an eye on them, I'm going to see to Mr Rogerson."

In the bedroom John sat on the edge of the bed and carefully unbuttoned the officer's tunic. His handkerchief was soaked in blood and doing little good. He stared down at the wound with a feeling of helplessness. Even if he was able to stem the flow of blood the arduous journey back to the column would be too much for the lieutenant to endure, even supposing they could keep him in the saddle.

As John pondered what best to do the lieutenant's eyes flickered open and he reached up, his fingers weakly plucking at John's tunic. "You should leave me here, corporal, and make your way back to the column."

"I can't do that, sir. The people here hate us, I don't trust them. I'm going to send back to the column for an ambulance. I think that's for the best."

Before the officer could demand that John carry out his order his head dropped back and he lapsed again into unconsciousness.

"Is there anything I can do for him?" John swung around to see the girl standing in the doorway with Private Caulkin immediately behind her. "My uncle was a doctor in Cape Town. I used to spend a lot of time there. That's where I learned to speak English. I also learned how to dress a wound."

She went away and returned a few moments later with a bowl of water and some clean cloths which she tore into strips. John looked on in silent admiration as she ripped open the lieutenant's shirt and set about cleaning the wound with the tender professionalism of a trained nurse. When she had finished, she asked for John's help to sit her patient up so that she could apply the bandages.

Afterwards they lay him carefully back down onto the bed and John gave her a nod of gratitude. "Thank you. It's good that you don't share your brother's dislike of us English."

Sadly, she looked down at the bare wooden floor. "My brother did what he thought was right. He is angry that our father left him behind when he went off to join the commando. Afrikaner boys are taught to shoot and ride when they are very young and Johanne is as good as any of the men, but our mother would not let him go. She thinks fighting is bad, and so do I."

John took the opportunity to study her closely, and, despite her plain cotton dress and unkempt hair, she had a pretty face not yet ravaged by her hard life and harsh sun out on the veld. Her skin was tanned and freckled, but her high cheek bones and small nose perfectly complimented her blue eyes, giving her a youthful attractiveness. In a few years she would begin the premature aging that came with her heritage, but at that moment she held John's admiration.

"That's very good, very professional," he told her as he buttoned the lieutenant's tunic. "Perhaps you should become a nurse."

"I would like that very much," she replied guardedly, "but I will be a farmer's wife instead." She glanced anxiously at the bedroom door. "I must go back to my mother. She is very frightened."

When they returned to the parlour John took the decision to send two of the troopers back to the column for a field ambulance and for instructions of what to do about the Boer family. It was clear to John that the boy had acted in defence of his mother and sister and had it not been for the lieutenant's condition he would gladly have left them in peace. But the army took a different view of acts of aggression and the decision would not be his.

John would have preferred to rid himself of Barker's company, but he couldn't trust the man to report accurately what had happened so he allowed the belligerent Brummie to wander about amongst the outbuildings where he could do little harm while he sent his friend Dobson back to the top of the kopje to keep watch. This left Caulkin to watch the family while he went out onto the veranda.

After several minutes the girl came out of the house. "I'm going to the barn to milk the goats," she said to him with the vaguest hints of a smile on her pale lips. "I thought you and your men would enjoy a drink."

John smiled back and nodded his gratitude. "That's very kind of you."

Caulkin edged out onto the veranda, his eyes flicking between the girl and the two other members of her family. "Shouldn't I go with her, corp, just to make sure she don't get up to nothin'?"

John wondered what it was that Caulkin thought she might get up to, but agreed when he considered that the woman and her son would be better guarded by himself.

He moved to the doorway from where he could watch the two of them as well as being able to see what was going on outside. Barker was still wandering about between the various buildings in a desultory fashion looking bored and unpredictable, while his dim-witted mate followed the girl into one of the barns.

John turned his attention on the boy who was still displaying a look of arrogant defiance, sensing he was watching a boiling pot, knowing that it was bound to boil over, but without knowing when.

"We are not afraid of you British," said the boy with a haughty tone to his accented voice. "Our commandos will soon drive you back to Cape Town and into the sea."

John shrugged his shoulders and smiled benignly back at him. "Perhaps," he replied, unwilling to enter into a pointless argument.

As the three of them settled into an uneasy silence John began to wish he was back at the column, suddenly preferring the boring routine of the march to the strained atmosphere of his first command. Keeping watch on a group of civilians was proving to be more stressful than what he imagined real soldiering would be, and he prayed that the two troopers would find the column without any delay and return before dark.

He was deeply immersed in making mental preparation for spending a night at the farm when he was brutally interrupted by a series of short, sharp screams coming from the direction of the barn.

"Stay here," he ordered, snatching up his rifle as the woman and her son leapt to their feet. "Stay here, or I'll shoot you."

As he jumped the veranda steps and raced across the twenty yards to the barn, he cursed himself for letting Barker and the girl out of his sight. At the barn door he was met by Caulkin who made an attempt to bar his way.

"It's all right, corp, it ain't nothin', just a bit of a lark, that's all," he said with a stupid grin that showed a row of black, decaying teeth.

"Get out of my way, Caulkin," shouted John breathlessly, pushing the halfwit private to one side.

As John tried to get past, Caulkin lunged at him, pulling him back. "Albert don't want t'be disturbed. You'll 'ave t'wait yer turn."

Without any further warning, John swung the butt of his rifle hard into the private's gut as muffled screams continued from the back of the barn. As Caulkin sunk to his knees, John strode through the barn, his eyes slowly adjusting to the dull light inside the building while he searched out Barker and the girl.

There were a number of partitioned stalls, most housing tethered goats that munched contentedly on bundles of straw. Then his attention was drawn to a stall at the very end of the barn from which bare legs kicked out. The girl was lying on her back, squirming and struggling to free herself from Barker who was kneeling astride her, pinning her arms above her head. The bodice of her dress had been ripped open, exposing her small breasts which Barker was feverishly kissing. She gave a pathetic whimper as he tried to force her legs apart, but had the determination to bite into his lip when he tried to kiss her on the mouth. He cried out in pain, releasing one of her arms to bring his fist up.

John dropped his rifle onto the straw and grabbed Barker's wrist, pulling the private backwards off the girl.

The evil intent on Barker's face was clear as he turned on John, blood trickling from the corner of his mouth. "Bugger off, Pearson, rank don't count here. You'll have to wait yer turn."

"Clear out of here, Barker. Get outside and take Caulkin with you."

As the girl pulled the tattered remnants of her dress together Barker got to his feet and glared at John, licking the blood from his lip. "I ain't goin's nowhere yet. I ain't finished with her."

Clutching the bodice of her dress to her chest the girl stood up and edged around until she was standing behind John. She would have run for the entrance but Caulkin was still there, one hand massaging his stomach.

Barker had his fists raised, and even in the gloomy barn there was no mistaking the vile determination on his face. "You'd better step aside if you know what's good for you, Pearson, 'cause me and Caulkin are goin' to have her, even if you don't want to." He jerked his head towards the end of the barn. "You'll make yerself scarce if yer don't want no part of this."

"Don't be stupid, Barker. Get out of here now and I won't say anything more about it." Behind him he could hear the girl's heavy, fearful breathing. Her fate lay in his hands and he wasn't sure he was up to the task. "Get out now, that's an order."

Barker's response was a harsh, cynical laugh. "An order! This ain't no army business. Now get out of me bleedin' way."

He threw his weight at John, catching him off balance and pushing him to the floor of the barn. Using the advantage of his size he kept John pinned to the ground with one hand and slammed the other fist into the side of his jaw. John was stunned for an instant, but before another blow could knock him senseless John brought his knee up into the other man's groin, making him give out an agonised cry. Taking advantage John punched upwards into Barker's face, hearing the sickening crack of bone as he caught his nose. John took hold of the private's tunic and mustering all his strength threw him sideways into the straw. In that second John jumped to his feet and went to retrieve his rifle, but Caulkin had beaten him to it and had his foot firmly planted on the weapon and his own rifle trained on the corporal.

"Don't be stupid, Caulkin," hissed John, his chest heaving wildly. He took a few steps forward, his hand held out in front of him. "Don't make it any worse for yourself, you don't have to do what Barker tells you."

"No, but you do," sneered the voice from behind him.

The words were immediately followed by a short warning scream from the girl, and John spun around in time to see Barker almost upon him, his bayonet in his hand and raised ready to strike. It was too late to move out of the way as the lethal eighteen inches of steel arced downwards through the air. John was frozen with fear as he waited for the fatal blow, but there was the sudden crack of a rifle which seemed distant and unreal. When John dared to look again, he saw Barker reeling backwards from the force of the cartridge, his hand clutched to a bloodstained wound to his chest and a shocked look on his face.

As Barker sank slowly to the floor John looked around and was surprised to see his friend Dobson framed in the doorway of the barn, his rifle still raised in the firing position and a thin wisp of smoke drifting from the barrel.

He gave John a brief nod of his head, and when he spoke it was with an unnatural calmness. "I couldn't let him do for you, John, could I?"

Overcome by a wave of incomprehension, John could only look from Dobson to the body of Barker lying on the bloodied straw. He had not even noticed that the girl had run from the barn, and when he was finally able to shake himself from the stupor that shrouded him, he knelt by the prostrate soldier and felt for a pulse.

"Is he dead?" asked Dobson, a touch of anxiety entering into his voice.

John looked around at his friend and nodded, realising that it could so easily have been himself lying there. "Thanks, George."

When John rose to his feet he found Caulkin with his foot still on the rifle, but now he was trembling visibly and there were tears in his eyes. John took him by the arms and shook him roughly, dragging him out of the barn where the girl was being comforted by her brother and sobbing mother.

"Take them back into the house, George," John said quietly to his friend, "and see how the lieutenant is."

As Dobson ushered the three of them away John turned on Caulkin, swinging the private around to face him. "You know I'll have to make a report about this when we get back to the column," he said sternly, his eyes fixed on the man's traumatised face. "So, you'd better make up your mind whose side you want to be on. Remember, Barker's dead, so it'll be your word against mine and Dobson's if you try to protect him."

Caulkin was still trembling and scared. "He said it would just be a lark, a bit of fun with the girl, that's all. He said he would see to me if I tried to stop him, but I didn't mean it to be like it was. I see he was trying to kill you. Dobson didn't have no choice, I'll tell 'em that."

"See that you do, or I'll have to tell them about your part in all this," growled John angrily. He shoved Caulkin away. "Now, get up on that ridge and keep watch."

When John returned to the house, he found George in the parlour keeping a watch on the woman and her son. "Where's the girl?"

Dobson jerked his head towards the bedroom. "She's seeing to the lieutenant, he's still unconscious." When John was close enough for him to speak being overheard, he said quietly, "what do you think is going to happen to me, John?"

John patted his friend on the shoulder. "Don't worry, George, you only acted in my defence, and Caulkin will vouch for that too." He gave a thin smile as he crossed to the bedroom, turning as he reached the door. "And thanks again."

The girl was sitting on the edge of the bed checking the lieutenant's dressings and looked up as John entered.

"How is he?" he asked, overcoming the shame he felt over Barker's actions.

She gave a non-committal shrug of her shoulders. "He is very weak, I think from the blood he has lost, but I think he will live, God willing."

John sat down on the opposite side of the bed. "I'm so sorry for what happened to you in the barn." He bit his lip as he recalled the scene that had met him. "Barker was a bad lot and I should have kept him away from you."

"You must not blame yourself, we have bad people as well. What you did for me was very brave so you have nothing to apologise for." The smile that she gave him faded into a concerned frown. "My mother is very frightened about what will happen to Johanne when the soldiers come here for this officer. She thinks they are going to take him away, and if they do, I am so afraid it will kill her."

John reached across the bed for the girl's hand and was pleased that she allowed him to take it. "I'm only a corporal so it will not be for me to say, but I will speak up for him and I think they will see that you have been punished enough.

When the pair joined the others in the parlour the girl relayed to her mother what John had said to her and it brought a nod of grateful acknowledgement. There followed a long period of tentative silence, broken only by a few brief conversations between the girl and her mother. The boy was no closer to accepting the presence of the soldiers and still glowered at them throughout the long afternoon.

The dying embers of the sun were settling on the horizon when Caulkin came scurrying down from the kopje to report that he had seen riders coming from the expected direction of the column. John went back with him until he was certain that it was a troop of lancers and not a body of Boers that were heading towards them.

Ten minutes after he returned to the house the lancers galloped into the farm and trailing behind them John was relieved the see the horse drawn field ambulance.

While the medical orderlies rushed into the house to attend to the lieutenant, the captain in charge of the lancers dismounted and took John to one side to listen to his report. Having no knowledge of the incident involving Barker his primary concern was for his fellow officer and he went inside to see for himself.

It was only after he had done so that John discreetly spoke to him and, together with Dobson, took him into the barn where he explained the circumstances of Barker's death.

"And the girl and Private Caulkin will confirm all this?" he asked gravely when John had finished. John nodded. "Well, there will have to be an enquiry when we get back to the column, but if you want my opinion the shooting was unavoidable."

John smiled thankfully. "What about the family, sir, what will happen to them," asked John as they left the barn in time to see the lieutenant being carried on a stretcher to the ambulance.

"What do you think should happen to them corporal, that they should be shot?" The captain gave him a caustic look. "We need the goodwill of these Cape Afrikaners. My orders are to confiscate any weapons and nothing more. Then we'll leave them to get on with their miserable lives."

John heaved a sigh of overwhelming relief, and while the captain supervised the removal of Barker's body John went to tell the girl the good news. She wrung her hands with joy before translating for her mother. The woman wept with gratitude and threw her arms around her children and even the boy discarded some of his contempt in favour of a thankful smile.

"I wished we could have met under different circumstances," John said to the girl as the medical orderlies carried Barker's body to the ambulance. "Perhaps you could tell me your name so that at least I can take some pleasant memories away with me."

She smiled, a beautiful, radiant smile that seemed completely at odds with the present events and surroundings. "It's Katerine, Katerine Reinecke. I too would have liked to have known you in a time of peace. Perhaps, when the fighting is over, and our people are no longer enemies, we will meet again." She went over to him and kissed him lightly on the cheek which brought a round of coarse cheering from the mounted lancers. "I know my brother and father would not approve, but I do not care."

When John was mounted and ready to leave, he gave her a wave. In just a few hours the girl had made a deep impression on him and he was already considering the possibility of returning once the war was over, if he survived.

As they were about to ride away the girl ran to him. "I don't know your name," she cried.

"John Pearson," he shouted back as they galloped away.

Chapter Sixteen

It was late in the evening when John and his party arrived back at the column. Both he and Private Dobson had been warned by the captain to say nothing of what had really happened back at the farm and that the official report would probably confirm that Barker was killed in the same minor skirmish with the Boers in which Lieutenant Rogerson had been wounded. It would have done nothing to placate the war sceptics back home to know that a soldier had been killed by one of his comrades during the attempted rape of a young Boer girl, or that an officer was seriously wounded by a teenaged boy.

When they re-joined their company, both John and George remained stubbornly tight-lipped against the barrage of questions that were thrown at them regarding what had happened during their protracted patrol. Once the questioning abated John settled down to write a further letter to Paul, wanting to commit to paper some of the more pleasant memories of the day, as though preserving them should they be lost. Most of all he wanted Paul to know about Katerine, because that was the memory he most wanted to cherish in an otherwise unpleasant day, and by writing her name it made her real and permanent. Of course, he could say nothing of what really happened, but it was enough just to mention her. Also, with the attack on Belmont now being planned by Lord Methuen and his first action imminent there was a real possibility that her memory would die with him and he could not allow that to happen.

For the attack on Belmont, John was to re-join his regiment, leaving the mounted men of the Lancers and Rimington's Guides to cut off any Boer retreat after the infantry had cleared the kopjes surrounding the town.

There was little time for rest that night as they prepared to move out of their camp in readiness for a dawn attack, but poor preparation and intelligence meant that it was already light before the attack could begin.

For Corporal Pearson and many of his comrades it was to be their first real taste of battle, and as they waited for the order to advance there was an eerie silence within the ranks as each man dealt anonymously with his private thoughts and fears. Those who did speak cracked bad jokes and laughed loudly to disguise their nervousness, and some mouthed silent prayers to a God they had dismissed for most of their lives. As they finally received the order to move off, the only emotion common to all was a bond of comradeship.

With the Northumberland Fusiliers to their left they moved forward over the dead ground at the base of the kopjes where, under covering fire from the Guards Brigade, they were to swing around and attack the hills from the north.

But they were attacking an invisible enemy. Two thousand Free State Boers under the command of Jacobus Prinsloo were well hidden amongst the rocks on the kopjes and poured down a deadly rain of fire on the advancing troops while giving the British nothing to shoot back at. The Boer marksmanship was deadly; these were men practically born with a rifle in their hands and they used the Mausers with terrifying effect. Even the veterans amongst the British troops found the accuracy of the fire unnerving. They were more used to standing face to face with their enemy, to see the men they were shooting at and where the iron discipline of the army counted. Now, as they scrambled over and around the rocks men were dropping, screaming with pain as bullets ripped through their bodies or jagged shards of rock tore open their flesh.

As the Northamptons, urged on by their company commanders, increased their pace they almost trampled over the prone bodies of the Scots Guards taking cover at the base of the hill.

"Were the hell are they?" shouted a sergeant of the Northamptons to a guardsman who was searching frantically for something to aim at.

The man raised his eyes and shrugged in dismay as he continued to search. The Boers were masters of concealment, and the new smokeless powder they used in their cartridges gave no clue as to their positions.

For John, clambering over the boulder side of the kopje, this was the reality of soldiering, what he had been born to do, and the only thing that mattered now was winning their objective. With the familiar faces of his mates around him he led a small group up the steep slope where every few seconds brought fresh casualties, when a soldier would scream with pain, thrown backwards by the force of a bullet, or throw his hands up to his face when the bullet struck a rock and a needle-sharp splinter would gouge out his eye or rip open his cheek. This was soldering at its bloodiest, and not the text book manoeuvres of the field manual. Close friends became unrecognisable strangers beneath a bloody mask of gore, and there was nothing to be done for them except to win the day so that their agonies were not entirely in vain.

"Come on men, remember Majuba," was the encouraging cry from an officer whenever the advance looked like faltering, or collapsing completely, and from the ragged line would come back the shouted reply, "Majuba," and they would struggle on, and die. This was real, bloody war, and the high cost of victory was the dead and the dying.

But there was to be no victory at Belmont that day. There was to be no glorious finale to a heroic bayonet charge at a fleeing, terrified enemy who would rather throw up their arms in surrender than face British steel. By the time the troops reached the top of the kopjes the Boers had gone, abandoning their positions in favour of another battleground on another day of their choosing. This was to be the pattern of this war, chasing an invisible foe across limitless miles of barren veld, and the only trophy a growing roll-call of dead and wounded.

For John and his comrades as they made their way wearily down off the hills after such a fruitless, wasted climb was the consolation that they, at least, were still alive.

In the camp that evening there was no excited recounting of individual acts of bravery, only muted mutterings about friends they remembered seeing fall, and a delayed feeling of guilt that it had not been them. Some of the men resolutely tried to start up a singsong, but there was little enthusiasm for it and it soon petered out into a sullen, angry silence.

John sat on his own, trying to finish the letter he had begun the night before, grateful that he was able to do so. Against the background of the battle and the grotesque loss of life that day the meeting with Katerine and the events at her farm seemed distant and irrelevant, yet, in a way, it gave a balance to his letter, showing that even in the dark depths of war there was also some light and hope.

Two days later, ten miles north of Belmont at a place called Graspan the Boers dug in again. But it was to be a frustrating and pointless repeat of the previous battle, with the Boers taking to their ponies before the infantry had a chance to close with them, and when the cavalry set off in pursuit they were embarrassingly driven off by a rear guard action. There was nothing in the text books that prepared field commanders for the hit and run guerrilla tactics they were facing and it led to a bitter frustration felt by all ranks.

If there was any advantage gained from these two battles it was that the column was moving ever closer to its real goal, the besieged town of Kimberley.

But how many more fruitless actions they would be involved in, and how much more loss of life they would have to endure before the objective was reached were questions no one was prepared to speculate on.

There was a sour mood amongst the men that Lord Methuen led on towards the Modder River, beyond which lay the Magersfontein and Spytfontein Ridges. If the Boers were going to make a final stand before Kimberley that was where it would be, and it raised hopes that finally there would be the opportunity for a real battle.

Scouting parties of lancers and Rimington's Guides were sent out to assess the Boer strength, but the reports that came back varied wildly from a few hundred to several thousand as it was impossible to pin down the irregular units who seemed to lack any clear cohesion, except when it came to fight. Preferring to err on the side of caution Methuen accepted the higher figure.

The Boers had blown up the railway bridge and were digging in on the southern bank of the river, an encouraging sign that they were finally planning to stand and fight. Any plans that Lord Methuen had for a flanking movement was abandoned in favour of a straight drive for the river, giving his men hope that, at last, they may be given the chance to set eyes on their opponents.

However, for John and his comrades the excitement and anticipation of finally getting to grips with their enemy was to be short lived as they learned that the Northamptons were to be held back to guard the camp and railway line. When the news was given, no amount of praise for their bravery in the two previous actions could make up for the disappointment they felt.

"Just our damned luck," commented John bitterly, angrily kicking at the dust on the ground. "It looks like being the first real action and where will we be, playing nursemaid."

"Don't be too keen to get yer 'ead blown orf, corporal," said a grizzled old sergeant who had seen service with Kitchener in the Sudan. "There'll be plenty of chances for that, don't you worry."

That was of little consolation to the men of John's regiment as the other troops marched out of camp to take up their positions for the advance. Who would be the ones covered in glory when the Boers were driven back from the river to the very edge of Kimberley.

Glory! There was no more glory to be had at the Modder River than there was at Belmont or Graspan. As usual the Boers were well concealed, this time in the natural cover of the steep river bank, and when the Guards Brigade advanced over open ground, oblivious to the men lining up the sights of their deadly Mausers, they were scythed down like corn in a fierce hailstorm of bullets, and with little cover their only option was to throw themselves to the ground where they lay for hours baking in the searing sun. There they came under attack from another army, ants, while the kilt clad Scots Guards had the skin burnt from the backs of their legs.

To the west of the railway track the 9th Brigade under Major-General Pole-Carew suffered a similar fate, being fired on from both the front and from some farm buildings on their flank. In all, eight battalions were tied down by the lethal firing from an enemy they could not even see.

Unable to advance or retreat, and without food or water, the Guards were held there all day, and if not shot they ran the risk of sunstroke or dying of thirst. And to add even more gloom to an already disastrous day, news came during the afternoon that Lord Methuen had been wounded and that General Colvile was now in command.

The only success of the day, if indeed it could be described as such, was credited to Pole-Carew who had driven the Boers from the farm buildings and went on to lead some four hundred men of the Loyals and Argylls across the river and into the village of Rosemead, only to rewarded with the ignominy of being fired upon by his own artillery.

With the Guards still pinned down to the east there was no other way forward, and as night fell any further plans to advance were abandoned. Staying true to their favoured tactics the Boers crept away under cover of darkness, leaving five hundred British dead in their wake.

Back at the camp the men of the Northamptons received the news that filtered through to them with growing disbelief and dismay, and a certain amount of relief. And when the weary, hungry and wounded soldiers began drifting in with their own first-hand accounts of the debacle the disbelief expanded into outrage and anger.

"I don't mind being shot at," grunted a Guards sergeant ruefully as he helped in a wounded colleague, "if I've got something I can bleedin' shoot back at. Laying out in the bleedin' sun all day and being shot at by a load of bleedin' farmers ain't my idea of a bleedin' war."

That sentiment just about summed up the feelings of most of those who had taken part in the action that day, and it began to appear to many that they may well die in that damned country without once setting eyes on the enemy that killed them.

Although the way was now clear to continue the advance on Kimberley it was decided, for various reasons, to stay at the Modder River for a further twelve days. During this time the Engineers repaired the bridge, Methuen recovered from his wound and reinforcements arrived. But John was to witness little of this.

Twenty-five Boer prisoners had been taken during the fighting, and they were to be taken under escort to the Orange River Station from where they would be sent by train down to Cape Town. John's section of Mounted Infantry under the command of Lieutenant Forster had been given the escort duty and, while it could not match the excitement of battle, it gave the men the chance to exercise their horses.

After a midday meal the prisoners were loaded onto two ox drawn supply wagons for the fifty-mile journey south. They took with them sufficient supplies for three days, although the lieutenant confidently expected to be back in two. Like John, the lieutenant had come to Africa to fight the Boers and did not intend missing out on any of the action by playing guard to a 'crowd of scruffy dirt farmers'.

"Keep the wagons moving at a good pace, sergeant," he ordered when they had barely cleared the camp. "I want to be over the Orange River by this time tomorrow."

"Yes, sir," snapped Sergeant Wilkinson, spurring his horse forward until he was level with the lead wagon. "You 'eard the officer, private, don't spare the whip on them bullocks."

The soldier cracked his whip above the heads of the lead oxen, but it would take more than that for them to increase their lumbering pace. He shrugged his shoulders and settled back onto the hard wooden seat to enjoy the journey as best he could. If the officer wanted more speed let him give the order to the beasts.

By dusk they were just north of Graspen, and only when the dark made their progress too hazardous did the lieutenant give the order to halt and make camp. He was unhappy with the progress they had made that day and would have travelled on through the night if it had been at all possible.

The prisoners were let down off the wagons and secured with manacles around their ankles. As he fastened the ends of the chains to the wagon wheels John couldn't help but have some feelings of pity for them. There was nothing to identify them as prisoners of war, no uniform, only the drab garb they would have worn when working their farms, and these were dirty and threadbare from weeks spent in the field. Beneath their thick, full beards their faces displayed no emotions, nothing to show what was in their thoughts. During that first day they had sat stone faced in the wagons with hardly a word passing between them, just staring at some unidentifiable point in the distance. They had been taken during Pole-Carew's assault on the farm buildings forward of the Modder River and now they were destined to sit out the remainder of the war miles away from their farms and families. If they harboured any regrets, anger or hatred it was impossible to tell.

Lieutenant Forster allowed no fires that night, fearful of attracting the unwelcome attention of any Boer patrols that may have been in the area. Instead, they had a meal of cold bully-beef and biscuits, with the promise of a hot meal in the morning.

John had been given charge of the first watch and set his guard to patrol a perimeter about fifty yards from the wagons while he took up a position from where he could keep watch on the horses and the prisoners.

After the stifling heat of the day, the evening air felt cool and refreshing at first until night forced the temperature down to a shivering chill and John wrapped himself in a blanket. The Boers, he noticed, seemed impervious to the cold. They were hardy men, well used to the extremes of their homeland weather. Most appeared to sleep soundly on the hard baked ground, accompanied by a rhythmic snoring and the occasional clinking of chains as they turned in their sleep. The only other sound that cut through the still night air was a constant harsh, hacking cough from one of the prisoners. John had noticed it during the day, but in the quiet of the night it sounded louder and more persistent. He wondered how the other prisoners managed to sleep through it.

With a concern for the ailing prisoner, and that his comrades would awake and cause trouble John wandered over to where they lay.

"Are you OK?" he asked the man, although doubting he could understand.

The reply came in a blank stare and a further fit of coughing.

"Would you like some water?" he persevered, stooping down by the man's feet.

"He can't understand you, English," came a gruff voice from further down the line of prisoners. "He says it is just a cold, but I think it is more serious. He should have stayed on his farm where he belongs. Where we all belong."

John slipped the blanket from his shoulders and offered it to the man who gave him a curt nod and said a few words in his native Afrikaans.

"He thanks you, English, and so do I," said the translator. "Perhaps we can all get some sleep now." It was a bland statement of fact, devoid of humour and gratitude.

The camp was roused the following morning just as the first orange tinge of dawn crept above the eastern horizon. They arranged to move out straight away, the lieutenant wanting to cover a few miles before they stopped for breakfast. He thought it would be safer, and also avoid the need to feed the prisoners again before he handed them over at the Orange River railway station.

As the wagons and their escort progressed over the dusty grassland John made a point of positioning himself close to the sick prisoner who was still convulsed with fits of coughing to the obvious annoyance of his fellow travellers. The man should be in hospital, thought John, not on his way to a prison camp, and he wondered if it would do any good to point out that fact to the lieutenant. He concluded that in all probability it would not. The man was simply another casualty of war.

Perhaps, because of his encounter with Katerine and her family, John felt compelled to take a greater interest in the prisoners than the other members of the escort. Where they probably saw them simply as the elusive enemy they had failed to come to grips with at Belmont and Graspan, he saw the men in their dark clothes and long greying beards and thought they looked more like prematurely aged preachers, more capable of delivering a fiery sermon than a deadly aimed bullet. They certainly did not resemble any soldiers of his imagination, yet he knew they were going to be difficult to defeat.

As John rode alongside the wagon the man who had acted as translator during the night beckoned him closer. "You should not concern yourself too much with him, English," he said with a nod at his sick comrade. "He would shoot you if he had the chance."

John gave a short laugh. "And I would probably shoot him too if we met on the battlefield. War makes killer of us all, but we shouldn't forget how to behave like civilised men when the fighting stops."

John pulled his horse away from the wagon, common sense dictating that seeing these men as anything other than the enemy could impair his judgement when he did have to face them again across the battlefield.

They were travelling parallel with the railway line and by mid-morning had passed Belmont where Lieutenant Forster called a halt. He allowed a fire to be lit and, despite the warmth of the morning, the soldiers welcome the chance for a mug of hot tea.

The Boers too seemed thankful for the opportunity to stretch their legs and enjoy a hot meal. Even the man with the cough appeared to have benefitted from the warmth of the sun and showed some gratitude for the hot drink, although he hardly touched his food.

They had not been manacled, and when they had finished breakfast were allowed the freedom to wander about in a confined area under close guard while preparations were made to move out.

Instead of flexing his limbs with the other prisoners the sick man seemed content to stand motionless, staring fixedly out over the veld at some point towards the south-west. Such was the intensity of his gaze that John wondered if perhaps his home lay in that direction and that he was thinking longingly of the family he had left behind. When the prisoners were herded back onto the wagons, he was reluctant to be moved and hung back until the very last moment.

The first wagon was already loaded and moving off when Sergeant Wilkinson bellowed an order at the mounted private closest to the sick man.

"Get that man up onto the wagon, private, before I 'ave yer guts for garters."

As the soldier guided his mount alongside the prisoner the man suddenly started a violent fit of coughing, bending double and apparently unable to catch his breath. Assuming he would need help clambering up onto the back of the wagon the private dismounted and took him by the arm. He had no sooner done so when the Boer straightened up while swinging his fist into the side of the private's jaw, and in a single movement he had grabbed the horse's reins and swung up onto the saddle. His agility had defied his age and condition, and before a single shot was fired after him he was lost in a cloud of dust kicked up by the horse's hooves.

John had been sent back by Sergeant Wilkinson to get the second wagon moving when the prisoner took off no more than twenty yards from him. He pulled up his horse sharply as Lieutenant Forster barked out an order.

"Corporal Pearson, take a man and get after him. You can catch up with us further down the track."

George Dobson was closest to him, and wanting someone with him he could trust John shouted at his friend to follow as he spurred his horse forward.

The Boer had a good start and a better knowledge of the landscape, but the country adjacent to the railway track was relatively even and they could keep him in sight. John was equally confident he could match the man in horsemanship. Not wishing to blow their horses in a protracted pursuit John was content just to keep the Boer in sight as they headed in a south- westerly direction, and their quarry was apparently making no attempt to throw them of his trail; it seemed his only concern was to stay ahead.

As they reached the top of a rise John reined in his horse, allowing Dobson to catch up while keeping the Boer in sight.

"Where do you think he's heading?" asked George breathlessly.

John gave his friend a knowing look. "My guess would be home, and if it was up to me, I'd let him go. He's not much of a threat to us in his condition."

George gave a hollow laugh. "He was fit enough to lay out Jenkins back there. Come on, before we lose him."

As Dobson galloped off down the far side of the rise John followed on reluctantly. What difference would one sick Boer make on the outcome of the war? But John was a soldier first and foremost and orders were to be carried out unquestioningly. He soon overtook his friend, taunting him to keep up.

Conscious that at any time they could come across armed locals sympathetic to the Boer cause John kept to the high ground whenever possible, and when the escaped man made his way around the side of a low kopje John led his companion up the shallow side to the top from where he could clearly see the ground ahead. It was then that a sudden and shocking realisation struck him, sending a wave of nausea surging through his stomach and he slumped forward, supporting himself on the horse's neck.

As Dobson joined him, he frowned at the sight of his friend's blood drained face. "Are you all right, John, you look like you've seen a ghost?"

Without speaking John raised a hand and pointed down the far side of the kopje at the collection of farm buildings.

George stared hard for a moment before letting out a loud gasp. "Bugger me!" he exclaimed, taking off his helmet and cuffing the sweat from his forehead. "Is that where the bastard's gone? Bugger me!"

John was breathing heavily, and not just from the exertion of the chase. He stared wide eyed at his friend with a look of utter disbelief. "Of all the people it could have been! Why?"

George returned a blank look. "What are you going to do, John? He's still a Boer, and an escaped prisoner."

John shook his head in dismay. There was nothing in his rigorous training that could have prepared him to weigh this duty against conscience. No one told him that he would have to consider moral duty over military expedience, and make decisions like this. In that moment he knew it would be far easier to test a soldier's courage than his conscience.

"You wait here, George, I'll go down alone," he said finally after making an agonising decision. It was then that he wished his friend had been the corporal.

"Don't be bloody daft, John. You might know these people, but they're still Boers and they're still the enemy. It will be much safer if there's two of us."

John shook his head, his expression adamant. "No, wait here and cover the house. I don't think he's got any intention of running, but if he gets away from me you know what you have to do."

Before George could argue further John dug in his heels and started at a steady walk down off the kopje towards the farm.

"Watch out for yourself," George shouted after him, slipping his rifle from across his shoulders.

As before, John approached the house in a wide arc in case the boy had got his hands on another rifle. His heart was thumping hard against the wall of his chest, and not just from the fear of being shot at. Foremost in his thoughts was the prospect of seeing Katerine again, and what her reaction would be to his unexpected reappearance.

He rounded the side of the house and cautiously dismounted in front of the veranda to one side of the opened doorway. From inside he could hear raised, animated voices, some loud sobbing and the man's hacking cough.

Tethering his horse to the veranda rail he slowly approached the door, standing to the side of the opening with his Lee-Metford rifle held at the ready.

"Katerine," he called out, while not presenting a target to those inside. "Katerine, it's me, John Pearson."

At the sound of his voice the house fell to silence, even the coughing stopped. Then there was the soft tread of footsteps slowly crossing the parlour floor, and a moment later Katerine appeared in the doorway, her face showing the same look of shocked disbelief that John's had displayed minutes earlier. Her eyes were red from crying, and when she saw it really was the man who had saved her from certain rape a fresh flow of tears rolled over her flushed cheeks.

"I prayed it would be you, but I did not dare to believe it could be," she cried pitifully, clutching her hands to her breast.

At the sight of the girl, John fought desperately to maintain some military discipline, although when he spoke his voice was shaky with emotion. "I couldn't believe it either, that we would see each other again so soon."

She stepped out onto the veranda and glanced nervously about her. "How many of you are there?"

He smiled reassuringly. "Just one. My friend, George." He looked past her into the house. "That man, he's your father?"

She nodded her reply. "You've come to take him?"

"I've got my orders." He took a step inside the parlour and paused. "Are there any more guns in the house? I don't want anyone to get hurt."

"We only had the one your men took away. We have nothing else. You have my word on it." She followed him inside and took hold of his arm. "Why must you take him, he is very sick? I do not think he will last long in your prison."

"Take me to him," he ordered in a calming voice before urging her to lead the way through to the bedroom.

The man was lying on the bed with his wife sitting by his side while the boy stood framed by the window, the same defiant look on his face. At the bedroom door Katerine indicated that John should wait.

"Let me talk to them, but as you can see, he is very sick."

John did as he was asked while keeping a firm eye on the boy. Katerine sat on the end of the bed and spoke softly to her parents. During the conversation the woman turned her red, tear filled eyes on John who could hardly bring himself to return her pitiful gaze.

After several minutes of discussion in which Katerine had done most of the talking, she got up off the bed and went over to John. "I have made my father promise that he will take no further part in the war if you will leave him here with us." She pointed at the pathetic figure on the bed. "Look at him, he is no danger to you."

Looking at the man John was forced to agree, but within the grief laden scene two things dominated; he was a soldier and he was bound by duty to his queen and country.

"I'm sorry, I have no choice."

Then the boy spoke in his native Afrikaans, his voice loud and forceful despite his youth. Whatever he said brought a fresh outpouring of woe from his mother.

John looked to Katerine for a translation, but she appeared reluctant to repeat his words and her face was tight with anguish. John urged her to speak.

"Johanne said if you leave our father here, he will go in his place."

John looked directly at the boy and spoke firmly. "The officer you shot is going to recover. We have no interest in you and your place is here with your family."

As Katerine translated her mother managed a thin smile of gratitude at John which was short lived when he spoke again for the girl to pass on his words.

"Your father is an escaped prisoner of war and it is my duty to take him back."

The man raised his head a little off the bed and turned towards the doorway as his wife slipped a supporting arm beneath his neck. He appeared to have aged, even in the short time John had known him, and when he spoke the words were interspersed with the dry cough. Whatever he said brought plaintive cries from the woman and her daughter, while the boy continued to glare at the soldier. The man had barley finished speaking when Katerine shouted at him with a pleading anger.

Lowering her husband's head back onto the bed the woman got up and beckoned to her son as she went to the door.

"We are all to go into the parlour," Katerine said to John while still staring hard at her father.

The woman dropped into a chair, her head held forlornly in her hands. The boy remained impassive, although John suspected he was putting on a show of bravado, and Katerine paced the floor, tense and full of bitterness.

John took her by the arms in an attempted to steady her. "What did your father say to make you react like this? Tell me."

Her mouth opened to speak, but the words failed to materialise and it was left to her brother to explain the family grief.

"My father says he knows you can take him by force if you want to, but he says he wants you to shoot him here so he can stay with his family."

John could feel the trembling in Katerine's body as he looked from her to her brother and then at their mother. "And is that what you and your mother want, that he should die here in front of you rather than on the battlefield or in a prison camp?"

"We would prefer him not to die at all," said Katerine in a barely audible voice. "But what happens to him is in the hands of you, and God, not ours."

For several moments John was incapable of rational thought. He was a soldier and expected to kill the enemy, but not in cold blood in front of his family. His obvious choice was to drag the man off the bed, throw him onto a horse and see him on his way to prison. That would be his duty.

"Wait here, all of you. Is that clear?" he said firmly, striding determinedly back to the bedroom.

To make sure he was not interrupted John closed the bedroom door and stood with his back to it as he faced up to the most difficult task of his army career so far. From the bed the man stared up at him through hollow eyes that gave away nothing of his feelings, no fear of death and certainly no pleading for his life, just the impassive acceptance of whatever hand he was dealt.

In the parlour the woman held her two children close to her as Katerine spoke quietly, but with an urgency, as she tried to offer some assurance to a mother almost broken by grief. Even Johanne had thrown off some of his bravado and sunk his face into his mother's shoulder. When the sharp crack of the rifle echoed through the house, the woman's fingers clutched at Katerine's dress with such intensity that the fabric was close to ripping. A heartrending, high pitched cry broke from her lips, and the boy's head turned sharply towards the bedroom. He had tears in his eyes.

When John came back into the room the first he saw was a look of bitter hatred on Katerine's face and he swallowed back on the bile that rose in his throat. The woman jumped up off the chair and stared hard at him for a second before pushing past to get to the bedroom, followed closely by her son. Before Katerine could join them John caught her by the arms and held her back.

"Let me go," she sobbed, "I have to be with my father."

"In a minute," replied John firmly, "but I must speak to you first." She fought to free herself from his grip, but he shook her until he had her attention. "You must dig a grave for your father and plant a cross. Do you understand me?"

Her expression was a mix of confusion and open hostility. "I understand that you have killed my father in cold blood. Of course, we will bury him, we are not animals."

Her hatred was almost impossible to bear although he knew he was able to endure it as he held onto her arms.

Partly submerged in a cloud of dust George Dobson came galloping down from the kopje just as the woman appeared back in the parlour. The look on her face added even more confusion to Katerine's state of mind; a smile of unrestrained gratitude was the last thing she had expected to see.

The woman said nothing as she walked unsteadily across the room and kissed John on the cheek while she gripped his hand. Katerine looked from one to the other as a slow realisation seeped into her brain and she ran towards the bedroom. When she returned, she ran to John, throwing her arms around his neck and kissing him several times just as George reined in his horse outside the house.

"Don't forget, do as I said." John spoke to her in a soft, firm voice.

She nodded her understanding while her mother added a few words. "How can we ever repay you? Mother gives you her thanks and will pray that God protects you."

From the back of his horse George looked down on the touching scene. "I heard the shot. Is everything all right?"

John looked hard at the girl before turning to his friend. "The prisoner was shot trying to escape. We'll leave the family to their grief."

George's eyes narrowed in doubt, but he said nothing as John ushered the two females back into the house.

"I have to go now, but, if it is at all possible, I will come back," he said, addressing Katerine earnestly. "I don't know what will happen to me or how long the war will last, but when it's over I want to come back to you, if you want that."

She nodded furiously, and the tears that rolled over her cheeks were no longing of sorrow. "Of course, I do. I will wait for as long as it takes."

As they rode away George looked questioningly at his friend. "What really happened back there, John?"

John gave him a shocked expression. "Exactly what I told you, George, the prisoner was shot while trying to escape."

Without any further exchange on the subject the pair galloped off towards the east with the hot afternoon sun on their backs, and soon they were within sight of the railway track. They turned south and caught up with the lumbering ox wagons and escort just as dusk was approaching.

Lieutenant Forster listened to John's report, accepting it without reservation or any corroboration from Private Dobson. To him it was more important that the man would no longer be a participant in the war than that the British would be forced to keep him fed for the foreseeable future.

"You had better find one of the prisoners who understands English and tell him what happened to his comrade," he said to John. "We don't want them thinking he got away."

As John rode up to the wagon containing the Boer who had previously acted as translator the man gave him a curt nod of acknowledgement. "You did not succeed in bringing him back, English," he said blandly.

"No, but I think he will be happier where he is now."

"And his family, will they be happy too?"

"They will be in mourning, but only while it is necessary." John gave the man a wry smile before wheeling his horse away and joining George at the rear of the wagons.

They continued for another hour and as night closed in around them they reached the Orange River. Soon they would be relieved of their prisoners and free to return to the column in time to take part in the greatly anticipated relief of Kimberley. For everyone else in the escort it had been a relatively uneventful episode of their army life, but for John it had been an opportunity to examine his own character. His duty had been tested and found wanting, but even if he could no longer claim to be a good soldier, he at least consoled himself with the assurance that he was, perhaps, a good man.

When they handed over the prisoners to the guard commander at the Orange River Station John watched them go with a feeling of pity. It was a stark fact that they had shot at, and probably killed, British soldiers, but he could no longer look upon them as a hated, faceless enemy. Like himself, they were men doing what they had been ordered to do. They were just like himself.

Early the following morning they set off back to the Modder River and the prospect of glory in the coming battle, and John prayed that when it came to killing another Boer, the man would forgive, as the last one had done.

Chapter Seventeen

When Lieutenant Forster's guard detail arrived back at the Modder River camp nothing much had changed. They had expected, and hoped, to find it a frenzied hive of activity, preparing for the final push on Kimberley, but instead it was very much as they had left it a few days before. In fact, it was to be another ten days before any advance was made as Lord Methuen recovered from his wound, giving the Boers more time to happily dig in along the base of the Magersfontein Ridge.

For the soldiers in the camp, the waiting and tedious daily routine was no better than the fighting, and with Kimberley only twenty miles away they were anxious to get to grips with the enemy that had so far eluded them, while inflicting grievous losses.

Only the occasional mounted patrol provided John with some relief as he brooded endlessly on the events of the past few days, events that had little to do with the accepted norms of soldiering. He had been in South Africa for only a short time, yet in those weeks he had discovered more about life and his own character than he had in all the years spent on the farm. That he had a brother who was a liar and a cheat had been a harsh lesson, and the sight of men dying of horrific wounds, although an acceptable aspect of his trade, had gone some way to hardening the softer side to his nature, but his association with Katerine and her family had brought into question his commitment to a military career. For the time being, though, he was still a soldier, and with more battles to be fought he had to push such doubts to the back of his mind.

And the chance for the next battle came on Sunday 10th December. That afternoon the artillery opened fire on the slopes of the Magersfontein hills, the pounding of the Howitzers, and the deafening blast of the 4.7inch naval gun was like a well-orchestrated overture to the action in which the men of John's division would soon be embroiled.

Again, Methuen insisted on a night advance, followed by a dawn attack, and at midnight the Highland Brigade marched out of camp under cover of a violent thunder storm that raged overhead. It was not the auspicious start the troops had hoped for. As they marched out by companies the men were roped together to avoid the risk of getting lost in the pitch-black night.

By dawn they were within a half mile of the base of the ridge, but before they could extend into their line of advance the Boers opened up from the row of narrow trenches they had dug at the base of the hills. Far from being decimated or routed by the artillery fire as was expected they had suffered few casualties and were now pouring their deadly fire into the packed ranks of the Highlanders.

Once again, the British troops had been caught in the open and could do nothing more than to throw themselves onto the ground, and pray. As before the Boers were so well concealed that there was nothing for the Highlanders to shoot at, and if the Scotsmen did raise their bodies to aim they became an instant target. From early that morning until late into the afternoon they were forced to lie there, and those that were brave enough to attempt an advance, or foolish enough to retreat, rarely made it more than a few yards.

In order to try and relieve the pressure on the exposed infantry Methuen sent out what little cavalry he had in a flanking movement around the sides of the hills. With the Mounted Infantry were the 12th Lancers who were more accustomed to charging down on a standing line, or running through the fleeing stragglers of a routed enemy than picking their way over the boulder strewn ground of the Magersfontein slopes. But, if Methuen thought the sight of the Lancers would be sufficient to drive the Boers from their hiding places, he was to be sorely disappointed.

While the Lancers proved to be ineffectual the Mounted Infantry were bound by no such restrictions. They were first and foremost foot soldiers and as soon as they came under fire from the slopes they dismounted and deployed amongst the boulders, looking for a way to drive forward.

"Stay close, George," John shouted to his friend as they scrambled forward, seeking a position from where they could return the Boer fire.

All around them men were running, crouching down as they sought what cover they could find amongst the rocks. All the while Mauser bullets kicked up little spurts of dust or threw splinters of rock flying in all directions, but most found their target and there was a scream of shocked pain and a soldier would throw his arms in the air before dropping to the ground, his khaki uniform stained with dark red.

"This ain't nothing like Salisbury Plain," called out George from his position behind a jagged edged boulder a few yards ahead of John. "No one told us it would be like this."

To his left was the now familiar figure of Sergeant Wilkinson who had been with them on the guard detail down to the Orange River station. He was gallantly urging the men forward, all the time exposing himself to the savage enemy fire. Several bullets ricocheted off the rocks around him, and for a time it seemed that he was blessed with an invisible shield which encouraged those closest to him to stand up and charge forward. It was sheer folly. No sooner had they broke cover when they were cut down. It was as though the Boers had allowed the sergeant to live in order to provide them with a ready supply of willing targets.

The hand of fate had placed itself on John's shoulder and he decided to wait as he looked for another way through the withering fire.

But it was George who saw it first. "Over there!" he shouted above the noise of battle, pointing to a spot about twenty yards ahead and slightly to their right.

John rolled over onto his side so that he could see the top of a shallow rise lined with a number of small boulders that could be manoeuvred into a makeshift wall with embrasures through which they could fire from the prone position.

John nodded that he understood his friend's intention, but before he could move out of his cover George was already going forward in a low crouch. He had already covered about half the distance to the top of the rise by the time John had scrambled to his knees in preparation of following during a brief lull in the enemy fire.

Apart from George, the only other soldiers John could see were those already dead or wounded and he was suddenly deaf to the sound of battle raging along the slopes of the hills. Breaking from cover he zigzagged after his friend in an adrenalin fuelled scene of what he had always imagined war to be. But when reality returned George was lying on his back at the top of the rise, the front of his tunic already stained with his blood.

John let out a mournful cry and instinctively threw himself onto the ground. "No, George, not you." For what seemed like an agonising eternity he lay on the ground, immobile with indecision, not knowing what to do or whether his friend was alive or dead. "Stay where you are, George," he shouted with ill-considered stupidity. "I'll come for you."

He lay still on the stony ground incapable of clear thought. Someone from the Boer lines must have seen him drop to the ground because bullets were kicking up the dust around him. Perhaps it was the same Boer who had shot George, thought John, and it was only a matter of time before the marksman found his target. Using his legs and elbows he snaked forward, the rough ground tearing at the front of his tunic as he inched closer to his friend several yards to the front. When he had covered half the distance he raised his head, just enough to look ahead. With immeasurable relief he could see the spasmodic rising and falling of his friend's bloodied chest, the sight spurring him to greater effort as he continued edging forward.

"Hang on, George," he breathed as he reached his friend's side, "I'm going to get you back."

George's head rolled listlessly to one side and his dull eyes looked into John's face. "You're a bloody fool, you should have stayed where you were," he breathed, his words barely audible.

John managed a brave smile and patted George on the shoulder. "We're both bloody fools for being here."

Staying flat to the ground John looked about him for help, but found none. Anyone capable of giving assistance had either moved forward or fallen back to safety. Holding his rifle in one hand he took a grip on George's webbing with the other and began the muscle sapping task of dragging his friend to cover. Minute by minute and inch by inch they moved at a snail's pace towards the boulders that a short time before had given him shelter. Several times they had to stop while John recovered his strength and all the while bullets buzzed through the air or struck the ground around them.

By the time they were within sight of their goal John's strength was spent, he had nothing left for the final effort. His only chance now was to get to his feet and carry George the last few yards. He threw his rifle behind the boulders and got up onto his knees in readiness to stand up. He hooked his hands under George's limp arms, took some deep breaths and got to his feet, lifting George with him. Oblivious to the sudden increase in the intensity of the bullets buzzing around them John hauled his friend to where his rifle lay, and it was only when he thought they were both safe that the searing pain tore through his leg.

At first John thought it had been caused by the exertion his muscles had endured, until he felt the warm flow of blood that was running down his leg beneath his trousers before seeping out through the material.

With one final effort he dragged George behind the nearest boulder and dropped to the ground exhausted, George's head falling into his lap.

The bullet had buried itself deep into John's thigh and the blood pumping from the wound made him feel weak and light headed. Soon he would be too weak to look after his friend. He undid his belt and fastened it tight around the top of his leg, the way he had been taught in training. He then unbuttoned George's tunic, and it was clear from the position of the wound that unless he received urgent medical attention he was bound to die. An overwhelming feeling of helplessness swept over John as he fought to maintain his own consciousness and knowing that with the battle still raging around them it would be some time before help could reach them.

"Just lay quietly, George," said John through his own pain, not knowing if his friend could hear him.

As George's breathing became noticeably weaker his eyes flickered open, searching wildly for John's face. He was clinging to a life that was rapidly slipping away from him, yet he appeared calm and resigned. "Do something for me, John," he gasped, reaching up and clutching the sleeve of his friend's tunic. "Tell my mum I died like a man, tell her ..."

Those were his last words, and as his final breath escaped through pale lips John cradled George's head close to his chest and allowed his tears to flow freely.

"I'll tell her, George."

This was not John's romantic vision of battle, not the heroic sacrifice of life in the name of Queen and Country. This was a young man paying the ultimate price so that rich and powerful men could become richer and more powerful. With one last hug he laid his friend on the ground he had given his life for.

Forcing back his grief and anger John took out his bayonet and ripped open the leg of his trousers. The limb felt numb and he was wracked with a sudden fear that he would soon lose consciousness only to awake and find that the limb had been hacked off by an army surgeon. He had to stay awake long enough to tell them, no matter what the consequences, they were not to take his leg. He would rather die that let that happen.

As the noise of the battle continued to rage about him John lay with his back resting against a rock while he kept himself occupied releasing and tightening the tourniquet as he had been taught, each release bringing a fresh flow of blood from the wound. How long he sat there he had no idea before a peaceful stillness settled over him.

The battle for the Magersfontein Hills was just one of three disasters to beset the British forces in what was to become known as 'Black Week'. Although many of the troops maintained their positions throughout the night no further advances were made, and the following morning the Boers were still firmly entrenched in their positions. An armistice was called to allow both sides to collect their dead and wounded, after which Methuen withdrew his troops back to the Modder River. There had been nearly a thousand casualties amongst the British, with more than two hundred killed and many more to die later from their wounds.

The operating tables in the field hospital were awash with blood as a constant stream of wounded men were carried in by the orderlies to be treated as best they could by the over-worked surgeons. There was no time to spare for the luxury of delicate surgical procedures or lengthy discourses on the best form of treatment, for many of the wounded the exigencies of war meant only one thing, amputation, with the need to save lives resulting in a growing pile of discarded limbs.

When it was John's turn to be carried into the tent, he was still unconscious and seemed likely to remain so, having lost a considerable amount of blood. An orderly cut off his trouser leg and cleaned the wound of its congealed mass of blood and dirt before stepping aside for the surgeon to have a better look.

"Unlucky devil," muttered Surgeon-Major Bryce with a resigned sigh as he felt around the area of the wound. "Would have had him back in the field in a few weeks if the bullet had gone clean through, but the bone's been smashed.

"Comin' off is it then, sir?" responded the orderly with similar resignation.

The surgeon gave a weary shrug of his shoulders. "Most likely, but not yet. He's lost too much blood and I doubt he'll survive the operation." He inspected the wound more closely. "I'll get the bullet out and cauterise the wound, then you can put the leg in splints. If it gets gangrenous then we won't have a choice, but it would make a nice change to save one."

John's leg had been reprieved by his own debility, but for how long only time would tell, and it was a considerable time later when he was to discover its fate.

His first awareness was the smell, a nauseating blend of stale urine and antiseptic. But with the smell came the realisation that he was still alive, death would have had a healthier aroma. Following closely behind the smell came the pain, an excruciating throbbing from somewhere in the lower part of his body.

He suddenly remembered his leg. The bastards, they've taken my leg! How could he have fallen asleep? How could he have been so stupid? He wanted to open his eyes but was afraid of what he might see. If they had taken his leg there was no point to his life. But how was he to know?

Slowly, cautiously and terrified he open his eyes and the first thing he saw was the green canvas canopy hanging over the bed. He turned his head to one side and saw the man in the next bed, although what he really saw was the bandaged stump where there was once an elbow. Sickened by the sight he quickly turned the other way.

"Watcha mate," said his neighbour on the other side in a cheerful cockney accent. The man's head was heavily swathed in bandages. "Yer awake at last then."

John studied the man hard. Apart from the bandages, he looked whole enough. No part of him appeared to be missing. "Hello," he replied, still not fully awake to his surroundings. "Where are we?"

The soldier gave him a curious look and grinned. "Field 'ospital, chum. Where else would yer be?"

John looked at the canopy, closed his eyes and tried to think. Gradually, and painfully, he began to remember. The attack on the ridges. The incessant firing and shouting, and men dying. Men dying! George was dead! George Dobson, his friend, had died in his arms out there somewhere on the slopes of the hills. He opened his eyes again; that part of his life was too dreadful to relive. He had to concentrate on the present.

He looked again at the cockney patient. It was time to learn the truth. "How bad am I?" he asked, afraid to look for himself. "Did I lose my leg?"

The man laughed and pointed at the canopy. "What d'yer think's under that mate, a stuffed elephant?" He sniffed and cuffed his nose. "Mind you, I think it's still a bit touch an' go. They're still debatin' it."

Nervously lifting his head from the pillow John reached down and raised the edge of the canvas canopy. With a heavy sigh of relief, he saw that his leg was still there, hanging in a sling a few inches above the bed with splints either side and the whole thing encased in heavy strapping. As tears of joy sprang from him, he bent forward, gently touching it to make sure. It hurt like hell, but what did that matter, the pain would go and he would still have his leg. He patted it thankfully, with a silent promise that he would never again take it for granted.

"Don't yer get too attached to it, mate," said his new cockney friend, nodding his head at the man on the other side of John. "'e 'ad 'is arm before it started turnin' black."

John threw an anxious glance at the bandaged stump. "Why, what have they said?"

"They 'aven't said nothin', mate, not in front of me, but I've seen 'em sniffin' at it."

John's face creased into a curious frown. "Sniffing at it?"

The soldier gave a knowledgeable nod of his head. "That's right, mate, sniffin' at it they was. There ain't no better way of tellin' gangrene than the smell. First sign of it an' off it comes."

John's brief spell of relief rapidly turned to alarm. "Did they smell it? Did they say they can smell it?"

"I told yer, mate, they don't say nothin' to me. We're always the last to know what's wrong with us." He took a pipe from the small chest beside his bed and stuck it in his mouth. "No point worryin' about it, not 'til it 'appens." He tapped the bowl of his pipe. "Ain't got a light, 'ave yer?"

Ignoring the question, John lay back on the bed. He was determined they were not going to take his leg, gangrene or not. Even if it killed him, he wanted to be buried whole. He made a vow that he would not sleep until he was sure his leg was safe.

He spent the next few minutes taking in his surroundings. The hospital tent contained about two dozen beds, or low metal framed cots, arranged in two rows, one down either side. Every one of them was occupied. Most of the patients appeared to have a missing limb and John found it easier to count those who were still whole, and he wondered how it was he had been spared the surgeon's knife.

"You'll know soon enough," said his new friend, as if he was reading his mind. The man pointed to the open end of the tent. "It's time for 'is nibs to do 'is rounds."

John turned his attention to the end of the tent where the surgeon-major was conferring with the orderly in charge. He continued to watch closely as the pair moved from bed to bed down the opposite side of the tent, and took in the range of reactions from the patients as the doctor made his judgment of their condition. For some of the soldiers there were open displays of relief and joy, while others sunk their heads into their pillows to hide their distress.

Eventually it was the turn of John's cockney neighbour and the orderly unwound the bandages from his head for the surgeon to inspect the wound. Having done so, he gave a satisfied nod of his head and offered the man a few congratulatory words. It translated into bad news for the soldier. He was going back to his regiment.

"But me 'ead still 'urts, sir."

The protest went unheeded.

John felt a slight anger that the man should complain that he had been pronounced fit. Didn't he know how fortunate he was compared to others in the tent?

When the surgeon stood at the end of his own bed John tried to appear indifferent to the muted conversation being conducted over his condition. Inside, his stomach was churning with fear as the fate of his leg hung in the balance.

At last, the surgeon gave John a piercing look, as the orderly peeled back the canopy. "Good to see you with us, corporal. How do you feel? Is the leg giving you much pain?"

"No, sir, not much," he lied.

The surgeon smiled at his orderly. He had been a doctor too long to be deceived. "Don't try and hide the pain, lad," he said, prodding the leg and watching as John winced. "Pain can be a good friend to someone like you. It was a pretty bad wound and I would be surprised if it wasn't giving you hell." His smile broadened. "But it's my guess you would rather have the pain than be parted from the leg."

John nodded enthusiastically. "You won't have to take it off, sir, will you? Not now."

As he was speaking the orderly was unravelling the bandage under the watchful eye of the surgeon. "I might not have any choice, and if I have to I will." Unaware of the fear that spread across his patient's face he inspected the leg and added, "but only if I have to."

With no further comment the surgeon moved on to the next bed and the missing forearm while the orderly summoned a subordinate to replace the strapping on John's leg. The new orderly was a fresh-faced youth who looked barely old enough to be away from home, yet he worked in a confident manner and appeared to take great pride in his work.

"How long will I have to stay here?" John asked him as he worked.

The youth gave him a look that implied he knew but that it would be a professional offence to tell. "Not for me to say, mate, but it don't look like you'll be going back to your regiment. Not in my opinion, anyway."

It was comforting enough for John that the orderly did not appear to react to any offensive smell that may have been coming from the leg.

Having just been discharged by the surgeon the cockney soldier had been removed from his bed and helped into his uniform before being ushered from the tent.

He gave John a brief wave. "Good luck, chum."

Within minutes a new incumbent was being stretchered in to occupy the vacant bed. He was a sergeant of the Black Watch, another amputee who had lost his right leg below the knee. John was surprised to see he was fully conscious and assumed he had been treated elsewhere and had been brought there to recover.

As the orderlies placed him on the bed the sergeant looked across at John and winked. "How are ye doing, laddie?" he enquired with a cheerfulness that made John ashamed at his own self-pity. "Damn mess up on yon hills d'ye no think?"

John nodded his agreement. The tent was full of men suffering as a result of the mess up on those hills, men who would be crippled for life for so little gain.

The Scot appeared to harbour no bitterness at the loss of his leg. "I'll no be dancing the reel until I grow a new one, y'ken." He laughed heartily as he pointed to his bandaged stump.

John was warming to the man. It was reassuring to have such an ambivalent character for company.

"What do you think will happen to us now?" he asked. "The orderly thinks I won't be going back to my regiment, and I don't suppose they'll keep us here."

The sergeant peered at John with a fatherly concern. "Why d'ye fret so, laddie. Ye're out of the war now so that's not for greeting over."

"Will they send us home, back to England?"

The sergeant grinned. "England may be home to you, laddie, but it's nae mine. The army will send ye where it suits them to send ye, so just enjoy the wee rest and wait and see."

John waited, and a few days later he had his answer. For those with wounds deemed too severe to render them incapable of an early return to active service there was to be a transfer to a military hospital further south. Rail transport had been organised and stretcher bearers ferried the patients in procession down to the Modder River station to be placed aboard the specially prepared carriages.

For John, and his travelling companion the Black Watch sergeant, the destination was to be East London on the coast in the Eastern Cape Colony.

They arrived at night in the middle of a violent thunderstorm, and their transfer from the station to the hospital was delayed until some covered wagons could be found. It had been an uncomfortable journey, the rolling of the train and the lifting on and off stretchers had done little to ease the pain in John's leg, and there were times when he thought he would pass out. He was still in fear of losing his leg and fought to stay conscious throughout the journey, although common sense should have dictated that nothing would have happened to him on the train.

When he was finally settled onto the hospital bed, he allowed himself the luxury of closing his eyes as he waited for the throbbing pain to subside. When he first heard the woman's voice he ignored it, thinking he was asleep and dreaming, but when she repeated her question, he knew he had been awake all the time.

"Is there anything you need?"

He opened his eyes and was looking into the face of a nurse who was standing over him.

"Is there anything you need, corporal?" she repeated impatiently, annoyed at having to ask for the third time. "The doctor will see you in the morning, but if there's anything I can get you now please say so."

John managed a thin smile. The sight of the nurse was something of a surprise, although he could think of no reason why. Perhaps he had been too long in the company of men to consider that women had any place in the theatre of war.

"It's just my leg," he replied, feeling the need to indicate the heavily strapped limb. "If you could give me something for the pain?"

"I'm sorry I can't," she said with a professional detachment. "You can ask the doctor in the morning. Now, if there's nothing else, I suggest you try and get some sleep."

Sleep! Is that the best she could manage? thought John. He raised his head to take in his new surroundings. All the walls were whitewashed giving the ward an appropriate sterile appearance, and while the wall behind him had a few windows the wall facing him had none, and all he had to look at was the three lines of beds. Above each bed hung a tubular shaped mosquito net that was draped over the iron bed head when not in use. Between each bed was a small table.

All around him men were moaning and calling to the nurses for assistance. For most, their needs were genuinely medical, but for others the soft tone of a female voice held their own healing properties. Like the canvas ward on the Modder River, his present accommodation contained a good percentage of limbless patients and again he had reason to consider himself fortunate, as long as no one sniffed at his leg.

Confident that the limb was safe until the doctor came around in the morning, John closed his eyes in an effort to get some desperately needed sleep, but each time he managed to doze he was dragged back to sensibility by another plaintive cry for attention.

By the morning he had managed to snatch just a few hours of interrupted sleep, and as he was about to succumb again, he was prevented from doing so by the nurse bringing his breakfast.

"How did you sleep?" she asked, with no apparent interest in the answer.

"What time is it?"

"Six o'clock." She placed the bowl of porridge on the table. "When you've eaten your breakfast, I'll bring you some water and you can wash. The doctor will be around at nine o'clock, so please don't try to get out of bed until he says you can." She delivered the words like a well-rehearsed speech that had been given many times before.

As she helped him to sit up, he took the opportunity to study her. She had a round face, not beautiful but certainly not plain, plump red cheeks and brown eyes. John thought she was about his own age and with a maturity that probably came with the uniform. As the army made men out of boys so her profession made women from girls.

"What's your name?" asked John as she fussed over him.

"It's none of your business," she retorted indignantly. "You just call me nurse, and I'll call you Corporal Pearson." She bustled away leaving her patient flushed with embarrassment.

"Don't worry about her," called the soldier softly from the next bed, "she's like that with all of us. Not that she's stuck up or anything, but I think she's a bit frightened of us." He gave John a knowing wink. "Got no experience with men, if you know what I mean."

"Thanks," responded John, grateful for the support. "I was only trying to be friendly. I'm John Pearson by the way."

The soldier held up a hand in acknowledgement. "Jimmy Morrison, 1st Manchesters. Got one in the stomach up at Elandsslaagte. What about you?"

"I was with Lord Methuen's division up on the Modder River. Got shot in the leg trying to take the Magersfontein Ridge."

"Bit of a disaster from what I hear," he said cynically. "It's some of the bleeding officers what want shooting if you ask me."

John returned a humourless laugh and got on with eating his breakfast. Afterwards he propped himself up on his pillow so that he could watch the morning activity in the ward. Whenever he felt sleepy, he closed his eyes, only for his head to be filled with a kaleidoscope of emotions that combined with the noises around him, forcing him to abandon any attempt at sleep.

Foremost amongst the visions that haunted him was the face of Katerine. She appeared with a persistence and vividness that made him believe she was with him in the ward. Entwined with hers were the faces of his two brothers, and that of George Dobson uttering his last words that he repeated over and over again. But despite his tiredness, John remained awake, helped by the cold water brought by the nurse which he threw into his face in a vain attempt to wash away all the bad memories.

Drawing some strength from the resilience and resoluteness of his fellow patients, who were clearly far more debilitated than himself, he resolved to shake of the self-pity that had clung to him like a damp shirt, and take a more positive view of his condition.

By the time the doctor appeared on the ward to make his rounds John's spirits had improved and even the pain in his leg had responded to his lighter mood.

When he arrived at the foot of John's bed the doctor ordered the round-faced nurse to remove the strapping, and to a running commentary of low mutterings he studied and prodded the wound. Although tender to the touch John gritted his teeth and grinned.

"It's healing all right, isn't it, doctor?" he said positively.

"They made a good job of cleaning the wound. It's healing well enough," he replied in the non-committal way of his profession. "It's what's going on with the bone that's of more concern to me, corporal."

"But it will mend? I will be able to walk and ride again?"

"We can only keep it splinted and hope for the best. Time will do the rest, so you'll just have to be patient."

Patience, that was a quality reserved for older men, men for whom the passing of time could proceed at a leisurely pace. How much time would pass before he could be sure of his future? And where was he to spend that time, in South Africa or back in England? Both prospects threw up their own penalties and rewards. To forsake Katerine in favour of his brothers, or be confined in a foreign country with his family so far away, that was the choice.

When the doctor had gone, he called for the nurse. "Could you get me a pen and some paper, I want to write a letter."

"A letter? I hope you've thought carefully about what you want to say," she warned mildly, possibly reading the torment in his face. "The folks back home don't want to be upset unnecessarily, so don't be going on too much about how you're suffering. Just tell them that you've got a bit of a wound and you'll be right as rain before long."

"Is that your professional advice?" asked John, bitterly resenting her opinion. "Tell them anything as long as it's not the truth."

"Now you listen to me, corporal," she said, wagging her finger at him, "you may think you're the most hard done by soldier in here, but I assure you, you're not." She cast her hand around the ward with an anger that was not necessarily directed at John, but more at the merciless results of war. "Will it do those back home any good knowing about all this, about how much their sons and husbands are suffering? They'll know soon enough." She looked away, shame faced. "I'll get you the paper."

If she had deliberately set out to humble him then she had succeeded, and by the time she returned he wanted to apologise, but changed his mind.

"Thank you," was all he could offer, and she responded with a smile and a wink.

Each day the pain in John's leg eased and he was able to think more positively about his future, although he accepted the fact that it would not be a future in the military. But there was more to his life now, and he thought constantly of his two brothers, and Katerine, especially Katerine.

As Christmas came the nurses did their best to raise the spirits of their charges, and for those who could attend there was a service in the hospital chapel. John contented himself by remaining in the ward with his own thoughts which now included his friend George Dobson, and the mother who would be grieving the loss of her son at this poignant time of the year.

By the new year he was hobbling around the ward with the aid of crutches, and with his new found mobility came the news that he was to be sent back to England to complete his recuperation. He received the news with mixed emotions; the joy at seeing his brothers again being tempered by the miles that would separate him from Katerine. While the other men accepted their news with unreserved delight John suffered long periods of sullen contemplation.

"What's wrong with you now, corporal?" demanded the nurse as she made up the bed next to him. "You're going home and you've still got a face like a wet week. Is there nothing that makes you happy?"

"I was just thinking, nurse, that's all," he replied absently.

"Well, you shouldn't, it doesn't do you any good," she snapped, vigorously shaking the pillow she was holding.

He turned his head a little and watched her as she went about her duties. "Can I ask you something?"

She eyed him suspiciously, throwing the pillow on the bed. "That depends on what it is."

"Why won't you tell any of us your name?"

"What good would it do you to know? Would it make your wounds heal any quicker or take away the pain?

"It would be a lot more friendly than calling you nurse. What harm can it do?"

She came around to the side of his bed and stood staring down at him, her hands on her broad hips. "That's what you think, is it?" She leaned over and put an arm around him, making him more comfortable. "If we were back in England now, in a park for instance, and I put my arm around you like this, what would you be thinking?"

John felt a hot flush of coyness at the question. "I don't know. I should think it was because you liked me, or was in love with me even."

She removed her arm and stood up. "And do you think I'm in love with you, Corporal Pearson?"

His cheeks glowed a deeper shade of scarlet. "No, of course not. Why should I?"

"Because I put my arm around you. Don't you think that I love you?"

"You were only doing your job, that's all. You do it to all the men, you're a nurse."

She stepped back from the bed, folded her arms across her chest and nodded cockily. "Exactly! If I let you call me Molly or Mary and I called you Bob or Jack you would stop seeing me as a nurse. I would be your friend." She unfolded her arms and pointed an accusing finger at him. "You're one of the lucky ones, corporal, you're going home soon, but a lot of the soldiers who come in here will never be going home again. I've already seen a lot of young men die, and I expect I'll see a lot more before the war's over. I've got all the friends and love ones I need back home and it would grieve me to see any of them die, so I don't need any more here. I couldn't care properly for all these men if they were my friends, and I certainly couldn't watch them suffering. Do you understand now?"

John lowered his head and nodded ashamedly. She had made him feel foolish, not only because he had failed to see her reasoning, but because he had allowed himself to believe in an impossible relationship with Katerine.

"Have you never felt anything for any of your patients, even though you knew it to be wrong?"

The question must have sparked something inside her. She raised her brown eyes and clasped her hands together. "I'll tell you this, only because I think you have your own reason for asking." She fussed around him, straightening the bed, trying to appear occupied with her duties. "It was soon after I had finished my training," she said quietly, scanning the ward for prying eyes. "There was this young man in the ward, no more than about twenty he was, and a right handsome devil too, all the nurses thought so. He wasn't a local lad, been visiting the town on some business or other and got taken ill, I forget what with. Anyway, the long and the short of it is I felt sorry for him because no one came to visit. Sometimes I used to sit and chat with him when I was off duty. We got on like house afire. Well, this went on for a few weeks and we got to know each other pretty close, and when he was well enough, I used to walk with him in the grounds. It was summer, and one day we were out walking and he slipped his arm around my waist, like I did you. But he said he loved me, and being a silly young girl I told him I loved him too. I probably thought I did.

"Then it suddenly came over all dark and there was this almighty thunderstorm and we ran for cover in this old summer house. There was no one else there, just me and him, and we started kissing and cuddling and …" Her cheeks flushed with shame and she looked away. "Anyway, a few days later he was well enough to go home, and I thought he would give me his address and say that we could visit each other. But then this girl turns up to collect him and I says to her 'are you his sister?' and as cool as anything she says 'of course not, love, I'm his wife'. All he said to me before he went was 'thanks for looking after me so wonderfully, nurse'. Since then, I vowed I would never tell a patient my name, and you're the first person I've ever told this to." She leaned over, pretending to adjust his pillow. "I hope I haven't told you just to satisfy your curiosity, corporal, that it's been some use to you."

John felt a deep sympathy for the girl and wanted to reach out for her hand. He could only imagine the hurt that had been dealt her, but was grateful to her for confiding in him. How wrong had he been to make his promise to Katerine, and what would she suffer from the promise she had made to him? Neither had it in their power to make good on those promises they had made, and in a few weeks he would be back in England and Katerine would be condemned to scan the bleak veld around her home in the vain hope of seeing him galloping towards her at the start of their life together. How long would her hope last?

He made a pledge there and then that during the voyage home he would write to her, releasing her from the promise she had made and begging her forgiveness. He had no expectation that she would receive the letter, but the writing of it would be proof of his intent, and ease his conscience.

When he left the hospital, the round-faced nurse was there to see him off. He wondered if it would be appropriate to kiss her on the cheek, but while he was considering it, she came forward and kissed him.

"Take good care of yourself, Corporal Pearson," she whispered with a warm smile.

"Take care of yourself, nurse."

Chapter Eighteen

Northamptonshire
December 1899

Matthew rode towards Millwood House at a leisurely pace. There had been many false alarms over the latter part of the year concerning Rufus Haveringham's health, and there was no reason for Matthew to suppose that this latest one would be any different. Grace's message sent via a groom had been full of alarm and urgency, but Matthew easily convinced himself that this was just her natural concern for her uncle. She had clung tenaciously to the hope that he would survive to a ripe old age, while Matthew harboured prayers for an entirely different outcome.

Since the old man had suffered his severe attack nearly two years earlier, there had been many occasions for alarm, when Matthew was poised to accept the mantle of total responsibility, only to be disappointed by the master's recovery. But each attack had taken its toll, leaving Haveringham a little more debilitated. Matthew had noted this decline in health and so had Grace, although she tried to dismiss it in public. Her uncle no longer had the energy to pursue the affairs of the estate as rigorously as before, leaving many of the more stressful duties to Matthew, who stepped into the role with relish.

While he now had much of the power he craved, Matthew still held a deep-seated resentment. Having authority over the estate workers was one thing, but the house and land still remained firmly in the hands of Rufus Haveringham, and only when he was married to Grace could Matthew confidently expect the entire property to slip conveniently into his grasp. The old man's stubborn refusal to allow the couple to set a date until he was fully satisfied of Matthew's irrevocable commitment to his niece, and that the lad could turn Hibberd's Farm into profit, festered like a cancer within the younger man. Although the farm now showed promise, Haveringham still had sleepless nights and an erratic heart rhythm out of concern for his niece.

Each time Haveringham's health had given rise to concern, Matthew had been summoned to the house, and each time he had been imbued with optimism, only to have it dashed. Grace was well aware of Matthew's growing frustration. Her betrothed lacked any subtlety where emotions were concerned. There had been numerous acrimonious exchanges between the couple, and on each occasion Grace had done her best to pacify him with reminders that her uncle would soon allow the marriage to go ahead. Matthew accepted her assurances only because he knew she was right. Haveringham's health was undeniably in decline and he would want to see his niece married before he shook off his mortal coil. Matthew had no option but to wait.

His walk from the stables was taken at the same leisurely pace that had seen him travel from the furthest reaches of the estate, and as he reached the hallway through the back of the house Grace was coming down the staircase, her face full of anxiety and streaked with fresh tears.

"I was expecting you sooner. He's much worse this time," she sobbed, taking Matthew by the hand. "I've sent for Doctor Colley, I was so worried about him." She turned and led him back up the stairs. "He's asked to see both of us and he's never done that before."

"You shouldn't worry so much, you should know your uncle by now." He tried not to sound harsh or patronising, but found it hard to disguise what he really felt. "He probably just wants to give us our orders for the next few days until he's better."

She turned on him at the top of the stairs, her red rimmed eyes tearing into him. "Matthew, that's a horrid thing to say. He really is ill this time, and I know what you think, but I want to get married just as much as you and I think that's why he wants to see us together."

Matthew's spirits rose at the suggestion and he kissed her lightly on the cheek. "All right, I'm sorry. Come on, we had better not keep him waiting."

She gave him a weak smile as they hurried on to the bedroom.

As they entered, Matthew felt the darkened room had the aura of death about it, reminding him of the day his mother had died. He approached the bed expectantly, only to be greeted with the rasping breath of a man refusing to give up on life.

Haveringham appeared to be asleep, but as Grace sat on the edge of the bed he opened his eyes, although they were dead and unfocussed, trying to assimilate his surroundings. He looked blankly at Grace as she leant over him, responding little when she took hold of his hand. Only when she put it to her lips and kissed it did he show any sign of acknowledgement. He brushed her cheek with the back of his hand and gave a sigh of pleasure.

"How are you feeling, uncle?" she asked, holding back her anguish.

He turned his head a little towards her, his mouth opening and closing as he sucked in air as if the effort had strained his breathing. Grace bent closer to catch any words that came out.

"Matthew is here with me, uncle," she said softly, encouraging him to speak. "But if you're too tired we can come back later when you've rested."

He seemed agitated by the suggestion and gripped her hand as he gulped in air. "It's all right my dear … we have to talk." He paused, further strained by the effort. "This is … getting the better … of me. There's not much … time."

The tears of sadness were even harder to restrain. "Nonsense, uncle, you've got lots more years yet. I've sent for Doctor Colley, he'll tell you as much."

"It's my body and … I know best," he went on impatiently, gripping her hand tighter. "Now, girl, listen … to me, this … is important." He waved his other hand in the air to beckon Matthew closer to the bed. "I want to see the … two of you … married. I promised myself … I would, but we … can't leave it much longer. Matthew?"

"Yes, sir."

"I want you to … swear you'll be a good … and faithful husband … to Grace."

"You have my word, sir," replied Matthew with a well-rehearsed sincerity. His thoughts were already racing ahead, beyond the wedding and towards to fulfilment of his ambitions. "It's all I've ever wanted."

Haveringham struggled with his laboured breathing caused by both his health and the words that weighed heavily on him. "Then the two of you … had better start making … your arrangements. I think the early … spring would be a good time … for all of us."

The pronouncement should have brought unreserved joy to Grace's face but she simply turned it towards Matthew. "The spring would be perfect for us, Uncle Rufus," she said quietly while waiting for Matthew to nod his approval. "That will give you time to get properly well again. I won't hear of anyone but you walking me down the aisle."

Having given his approval to proceed with the wedding plans. Haveringham settled back onto his pillow. "Now, my dear … I should like to … speak to you alone."

Grace threw a cautious glance at Matthew who simply shrugged his shoulders. "Wait for me downstairs," she said to him, "we have much to talk about." As soon as he had left, she looked hard into her uncle's drained features. "You still don't properly trust him, do you?"

The old man patted her hand. "We can't choose those … we fall in love …with." He said slowly and deliberately. "But you are the one … who has to be sure, … and if you are … I shall trust in your judgement." He beckoned her closer. "What I have to say now … concerns only you. My lawyer, Mr Fennymore, is in … possession of a box. When I'm gone … you must ask him for it."

"A box, uncle?"

"Yes, girl, a box. Things you … should know about only after … my death."

"But what things?"

He shook his head wearily and closed his eyes. "You must go now, my dear, … I am tired and you have … a lot to do." As he finished speaking his hand slipped from hers and he was asleep.

By the time Grace re-joined Matthew he was seated in the library, a glass of whisky in his hand. It would have been difficult shielding his euphoria behind a solemn mask of concern while in her company, but alone he could fully savour the moment.

He jumped up as she came sweeping into the room. "That was all a bit of a shock," he said, holding up the glass. "I needed this."

She stood close to him, looking up into his pale eyes. "He mustn't die, Matthew, not yet." She rested her head against his shoulder. "What I want most in the world, other than to marry you, is for him to be well again."

"Then we must make sure he gets all the rest he needs," he said with a secret smile, gently stroking her hair. "I shall take full responsibility for the estate and leave you to make all the arrangements for the wedding. By the spring he'll be fit enough to walk you down the aisle, you mark my words."

She did, and they encouraged her, not because she necessarily believed in them but because they came from Matthew, and more than anything else she needed to have faith in his support, as vacuous as it may have been. Despite her uncle's lingering misgivings, she was still in need of the emotional crutch.

The tears that again welled up in her eyes were now less sorrowful. "It will be a wonderful wedding, Matthew. I just wish we both had more family to share it with. If only your two brothers could be here, that would make it perfect. Perhaps you should try and write to them."

He took her by the shoulders and held her at arm's length. "I've got all the family I need right here," he snapped. "They deserted me when I needed them most, and I don't need them anymore. It's just going to be you and me, and the fine sons we'll raise." He gazed out over her shoulder into the inviting vision of the crumbling House of Haveringham, rising again under the hand of its new master. "What was it your uncle wanted to speak to you about in private?"

"What? Oh, nothing of importance," she replied vacantly. Her thoughts were still with her uncle and the forthcoming wedding. She hated deceiving her future husband, but it was better than the questions he was bound to ask. "Domestic matters, that's all."

He set aside any curiosity. "We must set a date. March, I think. What about you? Is it too soon, or not soon enough? I think the sooner the better. And a small affair, we don't want anything too extravagant, we have to think of your uncle."

Grace found Matthew's sudden and unexpected enthusiasm for the wedding quite overwhelming, and while it would have been easy to allow herself to be swept along by his apparent exuberance, she felt the need for caution. "Let's not decide on a date until we hear what Doctor Colley has to say," she said apologetically. "I'm as excited as you, but I can't think about anything else while Uncle Rufus is so ill. You do understand, don't you Matthew?"

He smiled back contentedly. Now that the final barrier to their marriage had been lifted, he could afford to be a little magnanimous, but not for too long. A premature funeral would only serve to delay and complicate matters. "I'll leave it entirely up to you."

She threw her arms around his neck and kissed him full on the mouth. "Oh Matthew, I love you so much. We'll set a date soon, as early as possible, I promise."

Doctor Colley's professional opinion, when he came, was that the health of his patient would be best served with a stay in hospital where full time care could be administered to him. Even in his weakened state the cries of protest from Rufus Haveringham echoed through the house. If he was going to die it would be in his own bed and not in some sterile room surrounded by a lot of strangers.

At the risk of damaging his patient further the doctor thought it best not to press the point.

"His heart is weak," he told Grace on the landing outside the bedroom. "I have serious doubts that he will survive another severe attack. He needs complete rest, free from any worries." He took Grace by the arm and led her to the top of the stairs. "I know how imperious your uncle can be, but you simply must be forceful with him if he is to make any progress." Noticing the strain on the girl's face he gave her a kindly smile. "With a bit of luck and a lot of care he could have a few good years. A lot depends on you."

"Don't worry, doctor, we'll all make sure he does as he is told," she said firmly.

From the bottom of the stairs Matthew waited with interest. In his mind Rufus Haveringham was already deceased, and as soon as the wedding was out of the way there would be no need for the old man to cling onto his life, his purpose would be served. But until then Matthew would do all that was expected of him, tell Grace everything she wanted to hear and be the attentive son Haveringham had always longed for. How enjoyable the next few months would be.

It was ten days before Christmas when Paul stepped off the train at Northampton station, almost at the end of his exhausting journey.

The month-long sea voyage had helped to acclimatise his body from the heat of a South African summer to the damp chill of the English winter, but as he stood on the windswept platform he shivered in the cold air. Perhaps it wasn't just the cold, he thought to himself as he turned up the collar of his coat, perhaps it had something to do with the prospect of seeing the two people he had had no contact with for more than two years.

He picked up his bags and walked briskly to the station exit. What he needed was a drink, both to warm his bones and to settle his strained nerves. The long sea voyage had given him time to think and to focus his mind on matters he still had some control over. Leaving behind Frank and John had torn at his emotions, but as the days at sea passed with the miles he was able to come to terms with the parting and to concentrate on his reunion with Matthew, and in particular Jenny. Why she had not replied to his letters he had no idea and that was the disappointment that had plagued him most during his absence. Now, he was soon to discover the reason, the resolution of a two-year old puzzle.

It was early evening when he left the station and he stood in the midst of the people who bustled past him, his mind a confused state of indecision. The need to see Jenny was paramount, but the journey and a recent lack of sleep did not leave him presented in the best light. If her feelings for him had faded then his current appearance was hardly likely to invigorate them. He turned his attention to the hotel next to the station, the warm yellow glow from the windows spreading their welcome into the street. It made good sense to spend the night there and hire a gig in the morning so that he arrived in Weedon Bec clean and refreshed.

He pushed open the door to the bar with his shoulder and struggled inside with his bags. A gentle hum of conversation greeted him and he breathed in the heavy aroma of pipe smoke and stale beer. There was nothing in the world that smelt and sounded like an English tavern, he thought.

"Evening, sir," said the portly landlord, his drooping moustache curling upwards into a warm smile. "It's a cold one out there right enough, and if you don't mind my saying you look like you're feeling it. What can I get you?"

Paul unbuttoned his coat and nodded an acknowledgement. "I'd like a room for tonight if you have one, and if not, I'll take a brandy anyway."

The moustache twitched smugly. "I can do you both, sir. Is it just for yourself?"

Paul nodded. "Yes, the room and the drink. Unless you'll take one with me."

"That's very generous of you, sir." He waved a chubby hand towards the fireplace. "If you'd like to warm yourself by the fire while you have your drink I'll have my boy take your bags up to the room."

Paul took off his coat and made his way over to the large, open fireplace where he settled himself into a high-backed chair, and cupping the glass in his hands. The flickering, crackling flames had a warm, hypnotic effect and with a few large sips of brandy inside him Paul was finally able to feel his body relax into the homely atmosphere of the bar. It was as though all the worries that had been part of him those past weeks were being sucked up the chimney along with the smoke.

"Will you be wanting supper, sir?" The landlord had appeared like a phantom at Paul's shoulder, breaking through his stupor. "Only we have some excellent rabbit pie."

Paul threw him a startled glance. "What? Oh yes. Thank you."

"Then it'll be ready for you in an hour in the dining room." He indicated a door on the other side of the bar. "If you want to go up to your room in the meantime, I'll have my boy show you the way."

By eight o'clock Paul had finished his meal. The landlord was right, the rabbit pie had indeed been excellent. In fact, the whole meal was the best he had eaten since the one he had shared with Jenny and her family.

Afterwards he went back into the bar to enjoy another drink before retiring. He wanted an early start the next morning, expecting it to be a long and eventful day.

"Is there somewhere close by I can hire a gig?" he enquired of the landlord as the man poured him a pint of ale.

He stroked his moustache thoughtfully before slapping his hand down on the counter. "Why bless me, yes. Old Bert Foley's stables not two streets away, he's got an old gig he hires out sometimes. Seen better days, but I expect it'll suit your purposes. I'll send my boy around first thing in the morning so he can get it ready for you. Save you a bit of time."

Paul thanked him and took the drink over to his place by the fire, hoping for a few more reflective moments before he retired for the night.

Many of the customers who had occupied the bar earlier had now left and there was no more than a half dozen scattered about the room, engaged in a low murmurs of conversation. Apart, that is, from two women standing at the counter, their loud, coarse voices cutting through the gentle ambience. The landlord had already spoken to them when their ribald comments seemed likely to cause offence to his clientele and the reputation of his hotel. He warned them to manage their language or leave.

For a time, they appeared to respect his wishes and stood quietly, casting a contemptuous eye around the bar, assessing the sorry potential for business. One of them was urging her friend to leave, to seek out more lucrative pastures, when the other, her eyes alighting on Paul, made a whispered remark. The other woman looked across and gave a non-committal shrug. The first one spoke again and made a move in Paul's direction until her friend grabbed her arm and warned her away.

Undeterred the woman shook her arm free, pushed her friend away and sauntered unsteadily across to where Paul sat. She squinted down at him through small, deeply lined eyes framed in sagging, blotchy skin.

"Don't I know you, dearie?" she demanded, her hands planted firmly on her pronounced hips. She threw her scarf back to give Paul a better look at her florid face. "If you're from over Daventry way I believe we may have done business in the past."

Reminded of the previous time his private thoughts had been rudely interrupted, and the ensuing consequences, Paul looked up angrily. "I'm sorry, I've never seen you before."

Her eyes narrowed further. "Are you sure, I don't generally forget a face." She glanced over to her friend. "Here Flo, I'm sure this is the gent, ain't you?"

Preferring not to be involved, the other woman shook her head. "I dunno, Fanny, it were more than a year since. Just leave the gent to 'is drink."

"I could swear on me old man's grave it's 'im," she persisted, continuing to scrutinise him closely. "Got good cause to remember, ain't I."

"Look, I don't know you, I've never set eyes on you before." Paul turned away from the leering face. "Besides, I've been out of the country for more than two years, so go away and pester someone else."

"Maybe I was mistaken. Maybe 'e 'ad fair 'air," she finally conceded, huffing loudly. "'andsome devil 'e was though, a bit like yerself mister, if yer don't mind me sayin'."

Before Paul could respond the landlord intervened, worried he would lose a paying guest.

"Right, I warned you. I don't want your sort in my hotel." He took her roughly by the arm and propelled her forcibly towards the door where her friend was already waiting. "I'm sorry you've been bothered, sir."

Paul assured him that no harm had been done, but quickly finished his drink and went up to his room. Compared to his expectations of the following day this was an inconsequential matter, although it did set him wondering on the improbable notion that the woman had mistaken him for Matthew. A notion he quickly dismissed as absurd.

Despite all the imponderables that cluttered his brain Paul managed the best night's sleep since leaving Cape Town, and was downstairs at breakfast by the time the sky turned a drab shade of grey.

True to his word the landlord had arranged for a gig to be waiting for him at the stables, although the nag that had been harnessed to it seemed less up to the task than the vehicle itself.

It was a dull morning and a clinging dampness hung in the cold air as Paul steered the gig out of the stable yard and onto the cobbled streets of Northampton. He shrunk into the warmth of his coat, but realised it was not merely the weather that chilled him as he shook the reins to urge a little more speed from the old horse.

Ever since his parting from Jenny Conners he had imagined a thousand times how their reunion would be and had longed for that time to come. He was not returning under the successful circumstances of his dreams, and it was inevitable that he would return to South Africa at some time in the future, but to be given the chance to reassert his feelings for her would surely keep their relationship secure, until he could give her everything he had secretly promised her. In a few hours he would know the truth of her feelings towards him, while he listened to the plausible reasons why she had not replied to his letters. He tried to keep his thoughts positive as he guided the gig along familiar roads towards Weedon Bec.

Even in winter with the trees stripped bare of leaves the countryside through which he passed contrasted favourably to the dun-coloured veld of South Africa, and the closer he got to his destination the more comfortable he felt amongst his surroundings, and no longer a stranger in his own land.

As he neared the village, he began to look for faces that he recognised on the farm carts he passed on the road, or on those who stepped aside as he guided the gig down the narrow lanes. The beard he had grown while away had now been removed, but still he attracted no welcoming waves, or shouts of greeting, and he began to feel that after all he was a stranger.

Then he was in the village and in sight of the Farrier's Inn, the sign hanging motionless in the still air. As he halted the gig outside, he sensed an aura of sadness hanging over the building, perhaps because no one had rushed out amid a mix of laughter and tears of joy that had been the essence of his imagined return, But no one knew he was coming, so this is the reality.

He stayed seated on the gig as he pictured the scene inside. Jack Conners would be busy preparing the bar for another routine day, while Jenny helped her mother in the kitchen. Unaware of the shock awaiting them they would be carrying on with their mundane daily routines. But there was another possibility. Unable to bear the waiting and succumbing to the cautionary remarks from her mother that Paul was unlikely to return, Jenny had gone away again and started a new life elsewhere.

With that thought prompting him into activity Paul jumped down off the gig and secured the reins to an iron ring set in the wall. Better to know the truth than to agonise over the possibilities.

Even though the inn was not yet open to customers the door to the bar was unlocked and as he stepped inside his boots echoed on the bare boards of the floor and he stopped dead, for fear of causing anyone a scare. Slowly he walked across to the counter, looking and listening for any sign of life, while his heart thumped inside his chest and his stomach churned with uncertainty. Had Jenny kept her word and waited for him, or had she been lured away by the more immediate and certain offerings of a new suitor?

At the back of the bar was the door to the cellar. It was open, and as he waited Paul could hear the heavy tread on the steps coming up from below. He backed away into the shadows of the dimly lit room for no other reason than to delay the inevitable. Seconds later Jack Conners appeared in the doorway carrying a mop and full bucket. Watching, without being seen, Paul noticed how the man had aged a good ten years in the past two, his hair was completely grey and his face drawn and heavily lined. Eyes that were once lively were now dead within the hollow sockets. Without a glance in Paul's direction Jack shuffled out into the yard and there was a slopping of water as the bucket was emptied, followed by a clattering as it was dropped to the ground. Moments later Jack returned to the bar and as he was about to go upstairs his attention was suddenly drawn to the still figure in the corner.

"Sorry, sir, we're not open yet. Come back in an hour," he mumbled apologetically.

"It's not a drink I'm wanting, Mr Conners," replied Paul, emerging from the shadows.

Jack blinked as the stranger approached, trying to recognise the face he thought he should know. "I'm sorry, I … My eyes aren't what they were."

Paul smiled nervously. "It's me, Mr Conners, Paul. Paul Pearson."

Jack continued to stare as though he were looking at a face that should not have been there, and one he wished was not. "It is you, lad, isn't it? We weren't expecting … We thought …"

Paul was expecting surprise, shock even, but there was something in this welcome that was neither. "You thought you would never see me again, I expect," he said, trying to help the landlord through whatever indecision was inflicting him. "Well, here I am, and I'm pleased to be back."

Paul held out his hand, and the reluctance with which the old man took it further demonstrated the awkwardness of the occasion. Any temptation to ask after Jenny stuck in Paul's throat, somehow it didn't quite feel appropriate, and it was left to Jack to relieve him of the burden.

"We got all your letters, lad. They're in a drawer upstairs. We should have written back, I know, but Mary thought it best we didn't. She was so sure you wouldn't be back."

Paul looked at him with an uncomprehending expression. "But if she got my letters, why didn't she write back?" He looked for the answer in her father's face, but only sorrow looked back at him. "She is here, isn't she? She's quite well?"

Jack Conners took a grip on Paul's arm, as much to steady himself as to offer any reassurance. "You'd best come upstairs, lad, we can talk proper up there."

Enshrouded in a sense of foreboding Paul followed the old man up the narrow staircase, both gripping the handrail for support. Something was very wrong, even a fool could see that, something far worse than that Jenny had met a new lover, or even got married. If that was the case, he resolved to accept the fact with magnanimity and bid the Conners a gracious farewell.

"The wife will be in the kitchen," said Jack in a hushed voice, glancing anxiously towards the far end of the landing. "We'll talk in the parlour, there's no sense in disturbing her."

Paul wondered why the old man was so keen to exclude his wife from their meeting as he was led into the parlour and the door quietly closed behind him.

Jack Conners waved him towards a chair before crossing to a cabinet and pouring two glasses of whisky. "I don't usually, not this early, but this ..." He handed Paul a glass and sat down opposite. "We really never expected to see you again, Mary and me. Perhaps that's what we were hoping."

"But I said I would be back, I promised Jenny. Didn't she tell you?" With increasing concern, he stared hard at the landlord. "Where is she, Mr Conners?"

As Jack toyed agitatedly with his glass, he kept his eyes fixed firmly on the worn rug under his feet, unable to meet Paul's withering gaze. "It was a good few months after you left, lad," he begun in a slow, pained voice. "She was taken bad, a bit of influenza we thought. That's what the doctor thought too until it got much worse and she had to go into the hospital." His hands were shaking and he took a long swallow of the whisky. "Of course, by then we knew it was pneumonia, and by that time there was nothing much anyone could do." Tears filled his eyes at the recollection and he emptied his glass. "She passed away late in the February."

Paul felt stunned and sickened by the news. Nothing had prepared him for this, and he had no words to offer in return. There was nothing to do but drink his whisky.

Jack took a few deep breaths before going on. "We got your letters but she wouldn't let us write to you while she was ill. She said we weren't to burden you, there was nothing you could do. Then, after she died, it was Mary who said we shouldn't write, even though I knew it would have been the right thing to do. I'm sorry, lad."

Paul gave a vague nod that he hoped expressed a forgiveness and understanding that he still had no words for.

"I know it's not right, but in her way, I think Mary blames you for what happened to our Jenny."

Paul was still trying to come to terms with Jenny's death when he was hit with this other devastating blow. "Me! She blames me when I was thousands of miles away? You said yourself there was nothing I could have done."

Jack Conners rolled the empty glass around in his fingers and his eyes never left the floor. "I know the wife won't forgive me for telling you, but it's not right to keep it from you, now that you're here." What he was about to say must have affected him deeply because he struggled with his breathing. "You see, it wasn't just the pneumonia that took her. The doctor said she was strong enough to get through that. It was the baby."

Paul almost dropped the glass he was holding. "The baby!"

"When she was taken ill, she was expecting a baby. Your baby, lad." For the first time his tired eyes met Paul's as the last few words escaped on a rush of expelled air, the pressure on the old man released.

Paul wanted to leap from his seat, to raise his voice in anger at the secrets that were kept from him, but Jack had suffered enough, that was plain to see, and now there were further questions to be asked.

"And what of the baby, did it die too?"

"There were some complications before it was born. They had to operate on our Jenny. It was the operation and the pneumonia that killer her, she wasn't strong enough for both."

"But the baby," persisted Paul, trying to maintain some sympathy for the old man, "did it live?"

Jack was giving some thought to the answer when the parlour door slowly opened and a little girl with frothy brown hair and wearing a pink pinafore dress came tottering into the room. She stood unsteadily holding onto the door handle and giggled happily when she saw her grandfather. Then her wide eyes fell on the stranger and a look of fear crossed her pretty face. She squealed and ran from the room.

Paul threw a questioning look at Jack and was about to go after the girl when the old man held up his hand.

"Please, lad, don't," he begged. "The wife don't know you're here, and it wouldn't do to go rushing down there. It would only upset the two of them."

"But she's my daughter, my flesh and blood," protested Paul, staring hard at the open door. "I've a right to know her."

"I know and I'm …" His words tailed off at the sound of heavy footsteps on the landing.

Mary Conners stood in the doorway, glaring at Paul, the little girl wrapped in her arms. Like her husband she had aged, almost beyond recognition, but it was pure anger that Paul saw above anything else.

"I knew he'd be back some day, didn't I say so." She spat the harsh words at her husband, despite the contradiction to what she truly believed. It was now Paul's turn for her venomous tongue. "Why did you have to come back, you've no right here."

"That's not fair, mother," responded Jack meekly in Paul's defence. "The lad had a right to know. I told you, we should have written to him."

"Just you hold your tongue, Jack Conners, you're as much to blame as him, letting him stay here under our roof so he could entice our girl into his bed. You men are all the same."

"No!" shouted Paul, unable to hold himself in check any longer. "No, that's not right, and it's not fair. I truly cared for Jenny and it breaks my heart that she's dead. It wasn't like you said, she came to me willingly, and if I had been told about the baby and her illness I would have come back and married her. I swear to God I would."

Paul got up and took a step towards them, but stopped abruptly when the girl started to cry, burying her head in Mary Conners' chest. The woman backed away, clutching the child to her.

"You'll not take her from us. You've taken one daughter and I'll die before I let you take another."

Paul made no further move towards them and the girl ceased her crying, turning her tiny head coyly to him. He smiled at her and gradually the fear faded from her face and she returned a beautiful smile of her own. Her eyes were big and as deep blue as his own, but in all other respects she was a striking image of her mother. He wanted to reach out and take her in his arms, to tell her he was her father, but to do so would be wrong and confusing for the child. Jack and Mary Conners were the only parents she had known and he could do nothing to change that.

"I've no wish to take her from you, Mrs Conners," he told her, a wave of emotion getting the better of him. "I know what she must mean to you after the loss you have both suffered, but can I ask you what you have called her."

Mary Conners looked back at him suspiciously, as though parting with the name was tantamount to giving away some small part of the child. She glanced across at her husband who nodded his agreement.

"I suppose there's no harm in telling you that," she said grudgingly. "We've called her Rosemary, that was Jenny's other name and it's what she wanted. We know our Jenny's gone, but it makes us feel like part of her is still here."

"Rosemary, that's a lovely name," said Paul reflectively. He reached out to stroke the child's hair, but thought better of it. "She's a lovely child too and must remind you of Jenny every time you look at her. Mrs Conners, I wish with all my heart that things had worked out better for all of us. I would have made Jenny a good husband, and Rosemary a good father." He could no longer prevent the tears of regret that burst from him at the thought of what could have been and the realisation he had come home to nothing. "I'll leave it to you to tell her whatever you think is best, but I'll never forget Jenny or that I have a daughter. Never."

Jack Conners pulled his tired body from the chair and placed a comforting arm around Paul's shoulders.

"We've done our crying, lad, and there's no shame in it for you. We know she's your daughter, yours and our Jenny's, but she's all we've got left now while you've still time to make another life for yourself. We won't stop you seeing her, if that's what you want, but all we ask is that you let her be our daughter for the years we've got left."

Paul wiped away the tears with the back of his hand as he nodded his acceptance. "Things are best left as they are, I know that," he said between sobs. "I'll do nothing to upset you or the child. She's got a good home here with folk who love her. That's more than I could give her at the moment." He reached out and stroked the girl lightly on the cheek, and Mary Conners made no move to prevent him. Rosemary gave him a sweet smile, blissfully unaware of the pain surrounding her arrival in the world. "I'll go now," he said quietly, "but I should like to visit Jenny's grave if you've no objection."

Jack patted Paul on the shoulder as he followed him from the room. "We can't deny you that, lad, you've done your duty by us. She's close by in the churchyard, you'll have no trouble finding her."

Before he descended the stairs Paul turned and took a last lingering look at his daughter before allowing her to pass from his life.

Jack Conners said nothing until they were out on the road, when he held out his hand in a more conciliatory manner. "All this time the wife and me have fretted over your coming back. Every time the door opened, I expected it to be you. It was a time we both dreaded, but now it's happened I can't tell you what a relief it's been." He squeezed Paul's hand with genuine sincerity. "You're a good lad Paul Pearson and I grieve for you as much as I do our Jenny. I wish you well. God bless you."

Paul drove the gig at no more than a slow walking pace to the tiny churchyard, giving himself time to reassemble his shattered thoughts. In the past hour he had been dragged from anxious anticipation into a mire of unimagined sorrow. In such a short time he had lost a sweetheart and gained a daughter who would be inaccessible to him.

As he walked morosely amongst the sorry looking headstones, he read the pitiful inscriptions that converted death from an intangible state into something that was final and irrevocable. Not until he saw Jenny's name carved into the stone slab would he truly believe that she had gone.

When he found her, she was lying in a quiet corner of the graveyard beneath the shadow of a willow tree that in summer would give her shade, but for now had covered her in a blanket of brown and shrivelled leaves.

Fresh flowers had been propped up against the headstone and Paul wished he had some token of the love he was so desperate to give. Instead, he stood with his head bowed in silent prayer, begging her to forgive him for not being there to keep her safe and for the grief he felt he had caused her parents. He asked also that he had her blessing for leaving their daughter in the care of her parents, that it was the proper thing to do. He consoled himself that Jenny was in complete agreement.

For several minutes he stood there conducting his one-sided conversation, answering his own questions with replies he knew Jenny would have given, until he reached the inevitable conclusion that she had gone and he was left to deal with life alone. Now those he cherished most were either thousands of miles away or beyond the reach of his affections.

The tears he shed beside her grave were not all for Jenny, many were for his own self-pity.

Chapter Nineteen

The day that had begun with such great expectations now offered little more to Paul than the dismal prospect of an acrimonious meeting with his brother. When he left the churchyard his first thoughts were towards a return to Northampton where he could allow his grief to drown in the bar of the hotel while he contemplated an early return to South Africa. At least there he could make some positive contribution towards recovering his mine and the affections of the friend he left behind.

But a greater power than grief worked on his intentions and he found himself directing the old gig back to his former home. So, by late afternoon, he pulled the carriage to a halt in the yard at the back of the house as a gloom descended over the surrounding landscape, setting a suitable backdrop to his return.

What he expected, or hoped for, he had no idea, except some vague notion that he needed to see Matthew, either to clear the animosity that existed between them or sever their relationship once and for all. After speaking to his brother, he would allow fate to deal with the situation as it wished, he no longer cared.

He pushed open the kitchen door and stepped inside, taking in the eerie familiarity. Nothing much had changed in the years he had been away. The room was still devoid of the life and warmth that had died with their parents. It seemed that Matthew had done nothing to turn the house into a welcoming home, apparently content to devote all his energies to the land he was so obsessed with.

Paul wandered through to the parlour, trailing his hand over the back of his father's chair as he stared into the cold, lifeless fireplace, trying to conjure some of the pleasant memories of his youth. In that instant he had the urge to stay, to spend the night there, whether Matthew would welcome him or not.

He found some wood stacked in the yard and lit a fire in the hearth. At least he could rekindle some warmth, if not a welcome. He also found some meagre food in the larder and helped himself, and, when he had finished eating, he settled down in his father's chair to await Matthew's return.

The heat from the fire and the gentle creaking of the chair had a mellowing effect on his raw emotions and, while much of the sorrow remained, some of the bitterness slowly begun to subside. Before he fell into a light slumber, he felt sure he could now face Matthew free from some of his anger.

It was a fitful sleep, broken my every noise he heard or imagined, but by late that evening Matthew had not yet returned home. The fire was almost dead and Paul's body was stiff and aching. Upstairs was his old bed where he could sleep properly and face the new day more resolutely than he would see out the old.

He climbed the stairs and thought of all the times he had done so in the past, trying to calculate how many times that had been. By the time he reached the top he realised it was an impossible task. He hesitated outside his old bedroom, not for any reason of nostalgia but because if Matthew came home and caught him asleep, he would have him at a disadvantage. Their first meeting would be difficult enough without that.

His mother's room seemed a little different than he remembered, although there was nothing he could identify as having changed. Unaware that the bed had since been occupied by the unfortunate Rose Budden, he undressed and climbed in beneath the sheets. The bed felt cold and damp, much as it must have done when his mother had died. He quickly dismissed that thought, preferring instead to occupy his mind with the memory of Jenny. Soon, he succumbed once again to his fatigue.

Paul woke the next morning, as he had done countless times, to the choking cry of the old cockerel. He sat up, prepared to face another day of toil on the farm, until his senses returned and he remembered where he was. The room was still in darkness and there was no sound of movement elsewhere in the house. Paul thought it strange that Matthew was not yet about, he had always been the first out of bed and ready for work. Cautiously he threw back the covers and got dressed, expecting at any moment that his brother would come bursting into the room, demanding to know what he was doing there. Even if he came home late Matthew must have seen the strange horse in the shed, the gig parked in the yard and Paul's bags where he left them in the kitchen.

The door to their old bedroom was open, as it had been the night before, and there was no indication that Matthew's bed had been slept in. Paul lingered a moment before going down and washing at the sink, a further reminder of his previous life.

Outside, the day was dawning grey and dreary with a chilling breeze sweeping into the yard from across the open pastureland. Paul found the fresh air invigorating and breathed deeply, filling his lungs with its Englishness. But apart from the freshness there was nothing in the smells of the farm that filled him with any regret for the choices he had made. The misfortunes that had befallen him since he left, had not been of his making, and now that he was back he could think only of leaving again.

He walked over to the shed that served as a stable. There was still no sign of Sally or Roscoe and the hired nag had made herself at home, lazily chewing on some fresh hay. It would have been easy to harness the horse to the gig and leave without setting eyes on Matthew, and he doubted his brother would be bothered by the fact, but, if nothing else, there was the question of John's money to be addressed. and Paul would consider it a failing if he left the country with the matter unresolved.

He led the horse outside and was in the process of tightening the harness when he was interrupted by a harsh voice from over his shoulder.

"Oi, what are you doin' 'ere?"

Paul looked around to see a lad of about eighteen, dressed typically as a farm hand, his weather worn clothes looking as though they had been handed down from an older sibling.

Paul returned the lad's questioning gaze. "I was looking for my brother, but it doesn't look like he's here."

"Who are you then?" enquired the lad with a sideways look at the stranger.

"Matthew Pearson's brother. Do you know where I can find him?"

The lad's face broke into a cheeky grin as he reached under his cap to scratch his head. "You been away or somethin'? Don't you know 'e spends most 'is time up at the big 'ouse nowadays?"

"You mean Millwood House, Mr Haveringham's house?"

"Of course. Don't you know your brother's been walking out with the 'averingham girl." He tapped the side of his nose and gave Paul a sly wink. "There's talk of a weddin', but I don't know as that's right. Anyway, we 'ardly ever see 'im about 'ere these days."

Paul stared blankly at the lad. Events seemed to be overtaking him at a rate he found difficult to keep up with. "Are you sure it's my brother, and who is this girl?"

The lad nodded confidently. "It's Mr Matthew right enough. Been actin' like the cat what's got the cream from what I 'ear." A look of concern crossed his spotty face. "Don't tell 'im I said that, he'll skin me. Anyway, that's all I knows."

Paul thanked the lad, and assured him he would say nothing. Already stunned by the devastating news of the previous day this latest turn of events left him with the feeling that there was little justice left in life. While he had been separated from all he held dear, Matthew, it seemed, had been gifted more than he was worthy of.

The lad obligingly helped Paul as he finished harnessing the gig. "Are you really his brother?" he asked cautiously. "Only I never heard talk about you." He snorted loudly. "But 'e don't say much about anything, only to give us our orders an' shout a lot."

Paul made no comment. It was clear that Matthew's good fortune had done little to improve his temperament.

With a further assurance to the lad that any opinion he had of his master would remain safe, Paul set off for Millwood House. He had no doubt that the lad was telling the truth, as he knew it, but large estates like Haveringham's were rife with rumours that tended to expand with each retelling. The fact of Matthew getting married was hard enough to digest, but who was this girl? As far as he knew Haveringham had no living relatives, the man had made a point of telling as much during their dinner together, so surely that part of the rumour had no basis to it.

He was still pondering on all these things as he steered the gig up the sweeping drive to the house. The groom who took the reins suspiciously, wondering if he ought to direct the visitor around the back. He changed his mind when Paul strode purposefully past him and up the steps to the door.

But the air of authority he must have displayed merely camouflaged the nervousness that churned his stomach as he tugged at the lion's head bell pull.

Jenkins viewed him with a mixture of condescension and curiosity. The face had a vague familiarity, although the clothes marked the visitor more as a tradesman than an invited guest.

"I'm looking for my brother, Matthew Pearson," said Paul before the man servant could question his right to be there. "I was told he might be here."

Jenkins' expression was unmoved. "I'm not sure where he is at present, but if you care to wait inside I'll enquire."

He moved aside to allow Paul into the hallway, and after closing the door he walked slowly away to somewhere at the rear of the house. Paul took in his surroundings, vividly remembering the last occasion he had been there and the events that had brought him back.

He was quickly dragged back to the present by Jenkins' return. "You can wait in here," he said coldly, pushing open the library door. "Someone will be with you directly."

As the door closed behind him and he idly perused the rows of books Paul couldn't help but wonder who that someone could be. He pulled out a leather bound copy of Homer's Iliad and flicked in a desultory fashion through the pages, remembering the stories he had heard as a boy, the siege of Troy and the heroic deception of the wooden horse. Now it was he and John who were being deceived, but not by a devious enemy, by their own brother. He now knew how the Trojans must have felt.

How many minutes he waited he had no idea, and the suddenness with which the girl swept into the room took him by surprise, and he guiltily slid the book back into its place on the shelf. For several tense moments the two stared at each other in silence, both questioning the identity of the other.

"I'm sorry," said Grace, recovering first. "I didn't mean to stare, but when Jenkins said it was Matthew's brother, I naturally assumed it was the younger one, John."

"You know John?" It was an involuntary question. His brother had made no mention of her when they had met in Cape Town.

"Yes, briefly, when he was home on leave. It must have been two years ago now." She took a few steps across the room before stopping and clapping a hand to her mouth. "Oh, do forgive me, how rude." She held the hand out to him. "I haven't even introduced myself. I'm Grace, Rufus Haveringham is my uncle."

"I'm Paul, Matthew's older brother, but I expect you already know that." He took the hand and looked hard into the face, so attractive and so familiar.

She smiled at him, a thin apologetic smile. "Matthew speaks so little about his family, I'm afraid." She offered him a chair and they sat facing each other. "I know there was some trouble between the three of you over the sale of your farm and that Matthew was very bitter, but I hope that is all now passed, that you can all be friends." Her bright eyes betrayed a lively enquiring mind. "Have you been abroad, South Africa, or somewhere? Your brother John told me that."

Paul nodded reflectively. "I was, until the Boers drove us out. John's there now, trying to win my mine back for me. We met in Cape Town, just before I sailed for England."

"How exciting," she said enthusiastically, clapping her hands together and begging him to tell her everything of his adventures.

All he really wanted to do was to hear about Matthew, but she made him feel so at ease that he gave into her wishes and related, in broad terms, what had happened to him since his arrival in South Africa and the events that had forced him to return home. As he spoke, she listened intently, enthralled at his every word. All the while Paul tried to recall where he had met her before, because he knew that he had.

"What an adventure," she commented excitedly when he had finished. "It all makes my life here seem so dull." Her eyes widened with concern. "But please, don't think I would change it. You must know that Matthew and I are to be married in the spring, just as soon as my uncle is well enough."

"I did hear about the wedding, but I wasn't sure if it was true. And your uncle, I'm sorry to hear he's not well. Nothing serious, I hope?"

Sadness clouded her eyes. "It's his heart. The doctor says he must have complete rest, but it's not easy for a man like him."

Paul smiled knowingly, remembering what a vigorous man Rufus Haveringham had been. "It must be very difficult, with the house and estate to take care of. I know Matthew works for him now so I hope he's of some help."

"Works for him!" she exclaimed with a chuckle. "Matthew manages the estate now, as do I the house. We are quite a team, your brother and I, so it shouldn't be a surprise to anyone that we are to be married."

"But marriage should be more than just a business arrangement," declared Paul with mock concern. "I think love should play its part as well. I suppose you are in love?"

As she carefully considered her reply her face took on a far-away look. "Very much," she said tenderly, "and he with me. It would be so perfect if it wasn't for my uncle's illness."

It was hard for Paul to accept that she held Matthew in such high esteem. Had he hidden his true character so well that she too had been deceived, or had he really changed? It was doubtful that she was aware of his cruel deceit over John's money, or that it would make any difference to her feelings. She appeared completely besotted with the man she was soon to marry.

"And what are your plans now?" she asked as he was still thoughtfully toying with an angelic image of his brother.

The question had taken him unawares. "I have no plans. I came back to England because I had to, and to settle a few things here, but beyond that …"

He would have liked to tell her about Jenny and Rosemary, but it was too soon and too personal. He did not know Grace well enough for her to share in his sorrow.

"I had thought to go back to South Africa, to offer my services to the war effort. It seems the right thing to do considering I still own half a mine out there."

"But you can at least stay for Christmas. Have you got accommodation?"

Paul shrugged his shoulders. "There's our old house. It belongs to Matthew now, and your uncle, and if they have no objections, I could stay there until I can make other arrangements."

She wrung her hands together. "Nonsense! You'll stay here with us. Matthew already has a room here, it's so much more convenient for him, especially since my uncle's recent attack." She noted the look on Paul's face and gave an embarrassed giggle. "Oh, there's nothing improper in it, I assure you, it's simply an arrangement of convenience."

"I never for a second thought otherwise," replied Paul, grinning. He sighed. "But as for your offer, I'm not so sure. It could cause trouble for you with Matthew."

"This has nothing to do with him, you're to be my guest, and I insist. Besides, I'm sure he'll welcome you. Two years is a long time to hold a grudge. Do you have any luggage?"

"Everything I was able to salvage from South Africa is back at our old house," he replied cautiously, hardly daring to believe that Matthew had changed so much.

"Then you must go and fetch it," she ordered with the authority forced upon her by her uncle's illness. "I shall be expecting you here for dinner and I'll be deeply offended if you don't come. It's going to be such a wonderful surprise for Matthew as well. You two must have so much to talk about."

So much indeed, thought Paul as he said his goodbyes to Grace, while Jenkins looked on through more amenable eyes. Perhaps Grace's influence had indeed spread throughout the house to include the staff as well as his brother.

As he drove the gig back down the drive Paul couldn't help admitting to a twinge of jealous irritation. Was his brother truly deserving of such good fortune? Grace was a beautiful young woman, and with the added attraction of her probable inheritance, she could surely command the attention of the most eligible bachelors in the county, yet she had accepted Matthew's hand. The logic and justice of it escaped Paul as he drove back to Hibberd's Farm, but the fact remained that there was to be a wedding in the spring and Matthew was set to achieve more than his ambitions could have ever conceived.

It was only when he was clear of Millwood House, and driving through the quiet lanes, with only the cathartic clip-clopping of the horse's hooves and the occasional bird cries to break the silence, did his thoughts drift from his brother and back towards Jenny and his daughter. How could the fate that had been so kind to his brother have been so cruel to him? Paul looked up at the grey, unyielding sky, tears streaming down his cheeks.

"Oh, dear God, why?" he screamed in an outpouring of pent up grief.

Instead of going straight back to the house he took the track that crossed Hibberd's Farm and led down towards the river, to a spot beneath the trees where he and Jenny had experienced the guilt and thrill of their first kiss. It was there that an infantile friendship had blossomed into a juvenile love. He found the same patch of grass where they had sat on the warm summer afternoon, and which was now covered in a layer of moss and dead leaves. He kicked the leaves away and stood in quiet contemplation of that time so many years and lifetimes away. How much more would that kiss have led to if they had not been discovered by his brothers who, hidden behind the trees, whistled and shouted at them? Would they have gone on to explore the forbidden secrets that had more recently contributed to Jenny's death? Again, he kicked angrily at the leaves. Why should Matthew have what had been denied him?

He stayed at that place for some time because he could think of nothing he would rather do. He could have gone back to that cold brick edifice that used to be his home, and wait there until it was time to return to Millwood House, but he no longer had a stomach for the place. An option would be to go back to Northampton and enjoy the friendly company offered by the hotel while he decided on his future. But the choice that appealed most was the one most likely to offend his brother.

He took one last look around that magical place before climbing back up onto the gig, flicking the reins and setting off at a steady pace from his past. Jenny was gone from his life now and nothing could bring her back, even though her memory would live on through his daughter, and he was sure neither would want him to mourn forever.

At the house there was still no sign of Matthew, or any evidence he had been back there. Paul stayed long enough to gather up his belongings before taking a last lingering look around the place, unsure if he would ever return. He contented himself with all the pleasant memories as he closed the door on them and left.

On the way back to Millwood House he occupied the time trying to recall where and when he had previously met Grace, a thought that had haunted the deeper recesses of his mind since earlier that day. That she was to be related to him in marriage was a fact that he would have to accept, yet it still grated that it was Matthew who had prospered most from the sale of the family farm.

When he arrived at Millwood House, Jenkins overcame any reservations he had and showed Paul to one of the guest rooms that had been prepared for him. It was furnished modestly in comparison to the other parts of the house that Paul had witnessed, yet it still offered a level of comfort he was unused to. It was easy to see what had motivated Matthew to set his sights so high.

He washed at the washstand in his room and changed out of the clothes he had been wearing for far too long. Those simple acts made him feel not only refreshed but more resolute to face whatever welcome his brother chose to give him. Despite Grace's assurances on Matthew's behalf Paul knew that first meeting would be a trial for all three of them.

He went downstairs and was met in the hallway by Jenkins who showed him through to the conservatory where Grace was dutifully tending her uncle's treasured plants. A watery late afternoon sun had broken through the clouds to spread its rays onto the glass roof, adding a touch of gold to Grace's auburn hair and further highlighting her natural beauty. Her eyes sparkled with unreserved delight when she saw Paul.

"Back so soon," she remarked with a teasing smile.

He grinned back at her, immediately infected by her warmth. "I can always go away again if it's not convenient. I'm sure my brother would prefer it if I did."

She stopped what she was doing and wagged a finger at him. "Now you listen to me, Paul Pearson, I won't have talk like that, not in this house. Whatever differences you and Matthew may have had are long forgotten, I'm sure. He's got far too many other things to worry about nowadays."

Paul doubted that was true but kept those feelings to himself. "Is he back yet?"

"I never know what time to expect him, he works such long hours." There was a hint of dissatisfaction in her voice that suggested she thought Matthew might prefer his work to her company. She tossed her hair back and gave Paul one of her disarming smiles. "But I'm sure we have more than enough to talk about until he comes home."

She led him through to the drawing room and ordered tea, and, until it arrived, they sat in an embarrassing silence which suggested that, whilst there was indeed much to talk about, neither wanted to be the first to ask what they both wanted to know. The subject common to them both was, of course, Matthew, but Paul knew that any conversation concerning him was bound to end in controversy. He was anxious that nothing was said to sour the mood between him and his future sister-in-law.

Grace was the first to break the awkward silence. She leaned forward in her chair and fixed Paul with an engaging look. "Tell me about South Africa," she asked with genuine interest. "I only know what I've read in uncle's newspapers, but I want to know what it's really like."

Paul remained pensive. It was a safe enough subject, yet difficult to know where to begin. "A land of extreme contrasts," he began wistfully. "It's a land of great opportunity and unimaginable suffering. Men have made immense fortunes, but there's more poverty than you could ever imagine in London or Birmingham. It's a white man's country, Grace, with precious little room for the natives. We've taken everything from them and given little back in return. Only what we don't want." His eyes glazed a little as he pictured himself back there. "It's also a land of barrenness and beauty, heat and cold, black and white, and each fighting with the other for the right to survive." His head dropped to his chest and he sighed heavily. "I could talk about it for hours and you still wouldn't know what it's really like. You need to be there, to experience it for yourself."

Grace was sitting on the edge of the chair, her chin cupped in her hands. "You make it sound very romantic," she said softly. "I wonder if I shall ever go there."

Paul appeared puzzled. "Why should you want to? You've got everything here you could ever want or need. People go there to find what they can't have here, not out of idle curiosity."

"And what were you looking for, Paul?" she asked bluntly.

He drew a deep breath. "I was looking for something more than I had here, something more rewarding. I always knew the farm would never be my whole life. Perhaps I was looking for adventure and a fortune."

"And did you find either of those things? I know the war forced you home, but before that, were you happier than you would have been if you had stayed here in England?"

It was a question that had no answer. "If I was to measure happiness by satisfaction and achievement then the answer is possibly, yes. But it wasn't just the war that brought me back, it only determined when. I could never have turned my back on England forever."

"England, or your brothers?" she asked directly. "Surely you would never turn your back on them?"

"No, of course not! I know Matthew and I are not as close as brothers should be, but I couldn't imagine never seeing him again. And John, well I love him dearly." At the mention of his youngest brother Paul's eyes misted over and he made a silent prayer for his safe return.

"And no young lady pining for your return, or did you leave behind a broken heart in South Africa?"

Paul raised his eyebrows and shook his head. It would have been an ideal opportunity to unburden his grief on her, to share the sorrow that was still so raw. But his relationship with Grace was new and tentative, and she already carried enough responsibilities on her young shoulders.

"No young ladies, either here or in South Africa, so why don't you tell me about you and Matthew. I know nothing about how you met, or what has been happening here while I've been away."

"I shall leave Matthew to tell you about what he's been doing. I know little enough about it myself, except that it takes up too much of his time. As for how we met, well that was at a reception here in this house that my uncle gave in my honour when I first came to live here." For a moment she seemed lost in a reverie of that time before she was interrupted abruptly by the sound of voices from the hallway. She sat up and listened, her eyes widening. "There's Matthew now. Wait here, I'll bring him in, it will be such a wonderful surprise for him."

A surprise certainly, mused Paul as she left the room. But wonderful? Had Matthew really changed so much that he would welcome his brother back with open arms? Paul got to his feet, prepared to meet him with all previous grievances forgotten, for the time being. How long they remained hidden was up to Matthew.

As the two brothers faced each other Grace waited expectantly in the doorway, barely able to contain her excitement. But what she witnessed only left her bitterly disappointed.

"So, you're back again then," commented Matthew coldly.

"It's good to see you, Matt." Paul held out his hand and managed a thin smile.

When Matthew made no effort to accept the hand Grace rebuked him sharply. "Matthew, shake hands with your brother and don't be so rude."

Reluctantly Matthew held out his hand. "There, my dear, does that make you happy?" he sneered sarcastically.

Paul felt an anger rising within him as he saw the embarrassment that flushed her face. "It's all right, it's no more than I expected. I knew I should never have come so perhaps it's better I left now before either one of us says something we'll regret."

"You will not," Grace snapped emphatically. "I invited you to stay, Paul, and I'll not have you leave because Matthew insists on behaving like a spoilt child." She took Matthew's arm and glared up into his face. "You've got no reason for this, and I won't allow it. Just forget the past and treat him like the brother he is."

Seeing the discomfort she was suffering Paul stepped forward. "I came here to see you, Matt, not to fight with you. Just for Grace's sake can't you at least pretend to be pleased to see me?"

"Is that the only reason you came back?" Matthew asked bitterly. "I find it hard to believe you came all this way just to see me. I suppose you've lost all your money and came back to see what you could get from me."

The muscles in Paul's face twitched and his fingers curled into fists. He wanted nothing from his brother, except an explanation, and it was only Grace's presences that prevented him from demanding that. Any hope Grace had given him that Matthew had mellowed had been dispelled in a few minutes, and all he wanted now was to retrieve John's money and leave Matthew to get on with his life. He felt sorry for Grace, but he would have to allow her to make her own mistakes.

Grace was close to tears, unable to make sense of Matthew's intolerance. "For pity's sake, why do you have to be like this?" She placed a hand gently on his arm. "Paul is the one who has lost everything, not you. I don't understand why you're still so angry when you've got so much."

Matthew's lips curled into a thin, sardonic smile. "Is that what you really want, for me and my brother to be friends?"

"Of course, I do," she replied with an imploring look. "But more than that, I want you to want it too. Please Matthew, shake hands with Paul, and this time mean it."

As the two brothers faced each other she fidgeted anxiously. It was a moment beyond her comprehension, her cloistered life had given her no understanding of what really went on within families. It was to her great relief that Matthew finally relented and held out his hand which Paul took, although she chose to ignore the emptiness in the gesture.

"You see, brother," said Matthew, his tone supercilious, "with a good woman behind you anything is possible." He placed an arm around Grace's waist and pulled her to him. "And what do you think of my bride to be?"

"I think you're a very lucky man, Matthew." There was no denying the honesty in that reply. "You must be well satisfied with the hand fate has dealt you."

Matthew laughed scornfully, pulling Grace even closer. "Luck and fate have nothing to do with it. I've got only what I deserve, what I've worked hard for. Isn't that right, my dear?"

Grace smiled up at him, but there was uncertainty in her face. She had often witnessed his change of moods, when a single word was sufficient to turn good humour into rage.

"I've told Paul how hard you work, especially so since Uncle Rufus' illness." She gave Paul an assuring smile. "I'm very proud of him, you know. I should hate to think what a mess the estate would be in if it wasn't for Matthew's hard work."

Matthew grinned arrogantly at her. "I could stand here and listen to you flatter me all evening, but I have to go and change before dinner." He made a great display of kissing Grace full on the lips. "Keep my brother company for me, won't you my dear."

When he had gone, she let out a loud, exasperated sigh. "I'm sure it's just tiredness that makes him like he is," she said, making an unconvincing defence. "He can be very caring and gentle when he wants to be."

"You've no need to make excuses for him," Paul assured her. "He's my brother, remember. I've known him a lot longer than you, and it would have surprised me if his welcome had been any different."

At dinner later that evening the conversation was muted, polite and uncontroversial. All Paul's contributions were guarded so as not to be open to misinterpretation by his brother, and Grace continued to place emphasis on Matthew's finer qualities. It soon became clear to Paul how easily his brother had shaken off his resentment of wealth and had slipped, just as easily, into the assumed role of master. But, while Jenkins appeared to readily accept instructions from the young mistress, he still baulked at Matthew's authority.

After diner Grace excused herself. She wanted to devote some time to her uncle's needs before retiring for the night, leaving the two brothers to enjoy a glass or two of brandy alone, in the hope they would use the time to build a new friendship. Before she left, though, she asked if Paul would accompany her on her morning ride. His response was to look dubiously at Matthew.

"Of course, you should." Matthew gave a magnanimous wave of his hand. "I want the two of you to be friends." It was a wine fuelled gesture that Paul feared would have repercussions for the girl the next day.

In the drawing room Matthew looked completely at home, nursing his brandy much to Paul's concealed amusement at how completely his brother had embraced his new life. Matthew had drunk freely of the wine over dinner and was now attacking the brandy with the same relish. He sat in the chair with one leg slung rakishly over the arm.

"Well, what do you think of my new home?" he asked with an arrogant flourish. "Not what you expected, eh?"

"It's not your home yet, brother," replied Paul with a note of caution. "But I have to admit you've done well for yourself. I just hope you appreciate it."

"Appreciate it! You talk as though I've been given something I don't deserve." He took a large swallow from his glass. "I might have known you would be jealous."

"I'm not jealous, Matt. A little shocked, but not jealous. I'll not deny you've done better than I expected. I'm sure Mr Haveringham is not a man to hand out rewards lightly, so I've no doubt you've worked hard for your position here."

"But it's Grace, isn't it?" Matthew cut in sharply, wagging a finger at Paul. "You think I'm not good enough for her."

Paul narrowed his eyes warily; Matthew was spoiling for a fight but he was equally determined not to give him the pleasure, not while his brother was full of drink.

"I think she's a lovely girl who deserves a husband who will love her and treat her well." He peered hard at his brother. "You do love her, Matt, don't you?"

Matthew finished his drink and flashed a sardonic smile. "Who couldn't love a girl like that," he said tauntingly. "You could love her, couldn't you?"

With the question designed solely to provoke a reaction Paul refused to reply and simply sipped reflectively at his drink. With the lull in the conversation Matthew's eyes slowly closed and the glass slipped from his hand. Leaving his brother where he was Paul went up to bed.

The next day dawned with a grey mistiness enveloping the estate, but by the time Paul came down to breakfast a hazy sunshine was forcing its way through the thin clouds.

"A perfect day for riding," Grace said cheerfully as she joined him. "Uncle Rufus is looking so much better too. I shall soon have trouble keeping him in bed." She laughed. "He was so much more manageable when he was weaker, but I'm not complaining. I just wish he was his old self again."

"He's a fine man. Perhaps I could look in on him sometime, if he's up to it." Paul helped himself from the silver salvers laid out on the dresser. "He does know I'm staying here, doesn't he?"

"Yes, I told him yesterday when you went to collect your things. It would really cheer him up to have someone new to talk to, I know how fed up he is with the same old faces. day after day, and nothing to talk about but the affairs of the house and the estate. Some fresh conversation is just the tonic he needs." She sat down opposite Paul at the breakfast table. "When we come back from riding, I'll take you up to see him and you can tell him first-hand what is happening in South Africa. He makes me read the daily dispatches from the newspapers so I know how interested he would be to hear from someone who was actually there."

As they walked together down to the stables. she questioned him on what he and Matthew had spoken about the previous evening. She was anxious that they had not argued, and stressed to Paul how important it was to her that the brothers should be friends. Paul smiled and assured her that not a single cross word had passed between them.

Once they were mounted Grace led the way across the estate and down towards the river that formed the boundary between her uncle's land and Paul's former farm. She continued along its bank until she reached the spot where she had met John two years before.

They slowed to a walk as they followed the river bank and Grace made a point of showing Paul the exact place where she and John had spoken.

"I still don't quite understand why Matthew refused to invite him to stay with us for Christmas," she said, looking at Paul inquisitively for the answer. "I knew that Matthew was still very angry over the sale of your farm, but surely that's not the only reason for all the bitterness between you?"

"If you knew our father then you would better understand Matthew. For both of them the farm was the most important thing in their lives."

"More important even than family?" she asked incredulously as she turned her horse away from the river.

"It wouldn't be right for me to speak ill of our father, he was a good man in many respects. But Matthew, well, that's something you'll have to discover for yourself, if you haven't already." He turned in the saddle to study her reaction, fearing he had said too much. "I'm sorry, that probably sounded harsher than I intended. My father was a good man really, but he was a farmer first and a husband and father after that. I just fear Matthew has inherited those same qualities and it will take someone stronger than our mother to change him."

"And you don't think I'm that person?"

Paul laughed, if only to disguise his doubts. "I didn't say that. You seem to be a very strong minded young lady, but you will need to remind Matthew constantly where his first duty lies."

Grace gave a heavy sigh. "I already have some experience of that. I sometimes think he forgets I even exist. Do you think he will ever change?"

"That depends a lot on you, but I think you've got quite a battle on your hands."

They left the river and lower pastures behind them and rode at a steady canter up onto higher ground from where they could see out over much of the estate. It was an inspiring sight compared to the meagre acreage of Hibberd's Farm, yet, thought Paul, against the vastness of the veld it seemed quite insignificant. He could easily see, though, how Matthew could have risen to the challenge of managing such a thriving business, an opportunity that for most men of

Matthew's ambition could remain only a dream. The thought that one day his brother would be master of all this was almost unthinkable to Paul.

He glanced across at Grace as she stared out into the distance, deep in her own thoughts. She was a rare example of beauty and innocence that any man would covet, and he prayed that she would be neither hurt nor tainted by his brother's influence. He felt a sudden surge of pity for her that could so easily have compelled him to tell her everything she should know about Matthew, but that would only leave him open to accusations of spite, envy or lying.

Paul flushed with guilt when he caught her studying him, as though she could read his thoughts. "You seemed so far away." she said smiling. "Were you thinking of South Africa?"

He returned the smile and shook his head. "No, something much closer to home, and before you ask, it's nothing I care to talk about."

She pouted with feigned disappointment. "Matthew never talks to me, and I hardly ever know what's in his mind. I was hoping you would be different. I need someone other than my uncle I can talk to."

"I'm sorry, I didn't mean to sound evasive, but there are some things better left unsaid. Of course, we can talk. I've had little enough female company in the past few years. It's just that I would prefer to talk about something other than Matthew."

"It's agreed, and if it's female company you've missed then I'll make it my duty to try and remedy that. I don't have too many girlfriends yet, but I'm sure I can find someone to suit you." She had a mischievous grin on her face until she recognised that Paul had remained sombre. "I'm sorry, have I said something I shouldn't?"

"No! No, not at all." His response was unconvincing. "It's all right, really. It's just that … well, never mind." He wheeled his horse around. "We ought to be getting back."

She came up beside him. "Paul, wait a moment." Her tender eyes searched his face for an explanation. "Look, if I've said anything unkind or insensitive, I'm sorry, truly I am. I can see I've upset you, and if it's something you don't want to talk about, I understand." She reached out and gently touched his arm. "But if you ever need a sympathetic ear then I want you to know you can speak to me in complete confidence."

In a spontaneous reaction Paul took her hand and for a brief second their eyes met and it was then that he remembered. "The train," he shouted jubilantly, making her start. "It was on the train from London, that's where I first saw you."

She stared at him with a puzzled expression as she searched her memory.

"You sat opposite me in the carriage," he went on. "You were with an older woman, a bit of a harridan, I think. She didn't approve of me. Not a relative, I hope?"

Grace laughed out loud as she too remembered. "Yes, it is you. I knew when I first met Matthew there was something familiar about his looks. Isn't it incredible that you should turn out to be his brother."

"It's been troubling me ever since ever since I first saw you at the house." He was still unwittingly holding on to her hand and she had made no attempt to pull away. "You know, I thought about you often after that, but I never thought we would meet again."

"I thought the same too," said Grace before it struck her that the admittance could be misconstrued, and she drew her hand away. "I'm sorry, you're right, we should be getting back. Uncle Rufus …"

They rode back to the stables in an awkward silence that was only broken when they walked back up to the house. And only then did they speak about that most English of things, the prospects for the weather and its effect on everything imaginable.

"I have to check on Uncle Rufus," she said as soon as they were inside. It was as though she needed an excuse to be free of Paul's company. "I'll see if he would like you to go up."

Paul waited in the library, randomly flicking through the pages of a number of books, none of which held any interest for him. His mind was elsewhere, on Jenny and his daughter, and on Grace. Had something happened while they were up on the high ground? Whether it had or not, he felt some sense of guilt. He had a sudden compulsion to leave, to allow Grace and Matthew to get on with their lives, to make their own mistakes undisturbed by any influence he might feel obliged to inflict upon them.

He was still undecided when Grace returned. There was nothing in her expression to suggest she shared in his in his guilt, in fact she appeared completely at ease.

"Uncle Rufus is resting comfortably. He seems to be getting a little better each day," she said with strong note of optimism. "I told him you would go up after lunch and I know he has much he wants to ask you, but please don't let him tire himself."

"Of course," he replied absently, replacing the book he was holding. "Grace, I hope you don't think …"

Perceptively she held up a hand to stop him. "I think you and I can be good friends, Paul. It would really please me if we could. And John too when he comes home."

Paul nodded knowingly. Perhaps that was possible.

Chapter Twenty

Paul's reunion with Rufus Haveringham proved to be an animated experience for both of them. For Paul it was an opportunity to divulge a side of his time in South Africa that would have been too unpalatable for Grace, and of no interest to Matthew. Despite his weakened physical condition Haveringham's mind had lost none of its sharpness and he made a lively contribution to the discussion. His knowledge of world affairs greatly impressed Paul, who was interrogated vigorously on the on all aspects of the current situation. It turned out they both held similar views on the war and that it would ultimately lead to the undoing of Lord Salisbury's government.

So intense was the debate that the afternoon slipped away until Grace came to remind them of her warning, insisting that it was time for her uncle to rest.

"Nonsense girl," he barked at the suggestion. "This has done me more good than your fussing could ever do. You don't know how refreshing it's been talking about something other than the damned estate. It's a pity your young man isn't a bit more flexible in his thinking, it might make him a bit more human."

"That's unfair of you, uncle," she retorted, appearing deeply hurt by the slight on her betrothed. "I know Matthew can be a bit difficult at times, but he does have many other virtues, as you well know."

Haveringham held up his hand submissively. "I'm not arguing with you, my dear, but at his age there should be more to a young man's life than just work. Ned Stiles always found time for other things, and so should he, especially since the two of you are soon to be married." He leaned forward and whispered into her ear as she adjusted his pillows. "Have the two of you set the date yet?"

"We'll set the date when I'm sure you are going to be well enough to walk me down the aisle." She smiled tenderly and kissed him on the cheek. "And that will be never unless to start doing as you are told and get some rest."

He shook his head resignedly as he lay back. "Well, don't leave it too long." He pointed upwards with an unsteady finger. "I'm in no great hurry to see you wed, but there's someone up there who seems pretty eager for my company." He laughed at her disapproving look then inclined his head at Paul. "Just see he comes back to see me tomorrow, we've still a lot more to talk about."

Grace made the promise before ushering Paul from the bedroom. She was pleased that the two of them had got on so well, it had given her uncle a renewed interest in life, despite the unfavourable comparison between the two brothers. She was suddenly struck by the fear that her uncle would come to favour Paul over Matthew, a situation with which she could foresee some difficulty.

The arrangements for Christmas proceeded under the cloud of Haveringham's continuing disability, although he insisted that none of the festivities be spared on his account. With the big day only a week away the house was awash with frantic activity, with Grace ably supervising every detail.

The tree was being delivered the following day and she asked Paul if he would help her with the decorations, knowing full well Matthew's natural aversion to anything frivolous. Paul was pleased to agree, since he had set aside any awkwardness he felt following that morning ride, and he was again able to feel at ease in her company. When Matthew had arrived home that same evening, she had made an open display of affection towards him, throwing her arms around his neck, like she was trying to dispel her own doubts as well as Paul's.

The following morning, she went riding before Paul was dressed. He watched her from his bedroom window as she hurried down to the stables as if anxious to avoid his company.

On the morning that the tree was delivered Paul helped Jenkins and one of the gardeners install it in its usual place in the drawing room. Afterwards he went to sit alone in the library where he mused further on the unlikely relationship between Grace and his brother, reaching the irrefutable conclusion that the marriage would be set on shaky foundations. If Grace's expectations for a happy life lay in the hope that Matthew would miraculously change once they were wed then, in Paul's view, she was clutching at a very small straw. However, he was equally determined not to interfere, and if Grace did harbour any doubts they would have to be dealt with by her alone. When he heard her returning from her ride, he quickly buried his fears in the spirit of the season.

"Come on," said Grace excitedly as she threw open the library door. "Come and help me decorated the tree."

As they worked, she chatted endlessly about everything, yet about nothing in particular, as a sister would to a brother, or a girl to her friend. Paul joined in as best he could, but he found it a little too artificial, as though she was using it as a barrier against her vulnerability. It became all too obvious to him that, whenever the conversation took a personal tack, she would go off at a tangent onto a different, safer topic. It was a relief to Paul when they had finally finished and she stood back to admire their handiwork.

"It looks beautiful," she declared after fussing with one or two changes. "I just hope Uncle Rufus will be able to come down and see it."

For the remainder of the day Paul avoided spending any time alone with her as far as was possible without arousing her suspicion. The strain of discussing irrelevant subjects was taxing him and he was grateful for the few hours spent during the afternoon with Rufus Haveringham. Afterwards he went for a walk until it was dark.

At dinner that evening Paul announced that the following day he would be going to Northampton to return the gig and that he expected to be gone for most of the day.

"Why don't you take Grace with you," suggested Matthew with a generous sweep of his hand. "I'm sure she would welcome the chance to get away from the house and do some shopping."

Paul and Grace exchanged conflicting glances.

"I'm not sure that's such a good idea," replied Paul sharply. "It's a long drive and the gig's not at all comfortable. Besides, I was going to borrow a horse from the stables for the ride back, and I couldn't ask Grace to do that."

Matthew emptied his wine glass with a flourish. "Then I'll have one of the grooms meet you with the landau and you can both ride back in comfort." He put down the glass heavily to emphasise his insistence.

"I really would like to do some shopping, and it would make a pleasant change from being stuck in the house all day." She looked across at Paul. "If you wouldn't mind, that is?"

She had placed him in an impossible situation. And did she really want to go shopping or was she simply bowing to Matthew's wishes? Paul smiled and nodded.

They set off the following morning under a sky that promised a dry day with the sun making fleeting appearances through a thin blanket of pale grey cloud. It had been arranged that the landau would meet them at three o'clock outside Northampton station, which would give them a few hours in the town, sufficient for Grace's purpose, and testing for Paul.

But despite his concerns he found it pleasant having some company on the long drive, when even the most guarded of conversations broke the tedium of the journey. As they drove along the road Paul impressed Grace with his knowledge of the countryside, identifying many of the birds that swept overhead or picked at the fields and hedgerows for a sparse winter meal. She was also touched by his passion as he described the hardships of rural life that persuaded him to leave the land in favour of adventure overseas. The only time Matthew's name was mentioned was by Grace when she complained that he never spoke to her of such things. Then the subject was changed and the conversation resumed.

In return for Paul's contribution, she spoke in detail about her schooling in Switzerland, of the schoolgirl antics of the friends she feared she would rarely see again. Paul wondered if that last remark had some reference to Matthew, and the reason their mother was never encouraged to have any close acquaintances. It only added to his conviction that the couple were seriously mismatched, and the more he listened to her the greater his conviction grew. So consumed did be become with his thoughts that when she addressed him directly, he had to ask her to repeat herself.

"I'm sorry," she said, taking the blame. "You must find my silly chatter so tedious after all your adventures. I should learn not to talk so much."

Paul assured her that she was in no degree tedious and apologised for not giving her the attention she deserved. He promised it would not happen again, while she insisted on not holding him to his promise. It was on that lighter note that they arrived in Northampton.

Once he had returned the gig to the stables, he asked her if there was anything in particular she wanted to do.

"Just to look in the shop windows will make a nice change from the past few weeks," she said, her eyes alight with childish anticipation. "Not that I've minded in the least looking after Uncle Rufus." They stood looking up and down the cobbled street that was busy with shoppers. "I need to buy Matthew something for Christmas. What do you think he would like?"

Paul grinned and shook his head. "I've no idea. I remember when we were young our father sometimes made us something out of odd pieces of wood. It was the only thing he really did for us. One year he made Matt a toy plough which he treasured for years. He may still have it for all I know."

She pursed her lips. "Well, he's not getting a plough from me, or anything else to do with farming," she declared so seriously that it made Paul grin. "Let's just look. I'm bound to see something to suit him."

As they walked, she casually slipped her arm in his, and it was so natural that he neither objected nor felt threatened. At nearly every shop they stopped and peered through the window at the array of goods on display. Paul made her giggle at the comments he made, and his naivety on the subject of women's fashion was a constant source of amusement, and she gently chided him on his ignorance.

When they came to a gentleman's tailors she dragged Paul inside on a sudden whim, and asked the assistant to show her some kid leather gloves. From the selection he laid out for her perusal she selected a tan pair that buttoned over at the wrist and ordered two pairs.

"Two pairs?" questioned Paul.

"Yes, two pairs indeed," she retorted.

Further along the same street she tugged at his arm as they were passing a dress shop. "I need to buy some under garments," she said in a hushed voice that contained only a hint of embarrassment. "Will you come in with me or do all men have an aversion to such things?"

Paul felt himself flush, although he suspected she was teasing him and would have been shocked if he agreed to accompany her.

"I can't answer for all men, but I think I would prefer to wait out here, if you don't mind. I'm still old fashioned enough to believe there are some things that should remain private, especially between unmarried couples."

While she was inside the shop Paul paced the pavement, trying to obliterate from his mind the vision of Grace and the delicate secret of her underwear. But this was only replaced by a hideous jealousy that the secret would soon be shared with his undeserving brother. To distract himself from those thoughts he began to look in the windows of the adjacent shops before his attention was drawn to a particularly brightly lit window across the street. It was a toy shop and the window was crammed with a huge variety of toys for both boys and girls. He crossed for a closer look and was immediately drawn to the centrepiece of the display, a large doll with long blond hair tied with two pink ribbons. She wore a matching pink dress trimmed with white lace and a scarlet sash. The wide blue eyes seemed to be staring directly at him, even when he moved to one side. He went to turn away, but a sudden impulse took over and he found himself inside the shop and asking the shopkeeper to take the doll from the window.

"For you daughter, is it, sir?" the shopkeeper asked, as he laid the doll carefully in the box and placed a sheet of tissue over it before replacing the lid. "She'll be thrilled with that when she opens it on Christmas Day. It'll be a treat to see her little face light up when she sees it. Well, merry Christmas to you, sir, and to your family."

Paul nodded curtly and left the shop. He cursed the man for his insensitivity, even though he was blameless. He crossed the street and waited agitatedly for Grace to finish her shopping.

When she came out, the first thing she noticed was the impatient expression on his face and naturally assumed she was the cause.

"I'm so sorry I took so much time. It was very selfish of me." She glanced down at the box half hidden behind Paul's coat. "You've been doing some shopping of your own, what have you bought?" She craned her neck to see. "Is that a doll? Paul, you've bought a doll! Who is it for?"

He viewed the box with a look of surprise, as though it had miraculously appeared. He had given no thought to explaining its presence, and now he felt like a child caught misbehaving.

"Yes, ... It's a doll," he mumbled with no idea of what he should say. "It's a present for ... I'm sorry, Grace, I can't say."

Her face creased in puzzlement. "It's a secret, I'm sorry, I didn't mean to pry." She smiled to let him know she understood. "There's no shame in buying a doll for someone, and you don't need to tell me if you don't want to."

Paul looked about him despairingly. It would be so easy to lie to her, to invent a child of a friend, yet for some reason that escaped him he wanted her to know the truth. That she was deserving of his honesty.

"There's a tea room a little way back down the street," he said urgently. "Would you mind if we went there."

Without any further questioning she took his arm, although her eyes took in his pained expression. Inside the tea room he led her to a table in a quiet corner, away from the other customers and Grace waited patiently until the young waitress had taken their order and returned with the tray. The nervous silence continued while Grace poured the tea and Paul pretended to take an interest in everything except the beautiful girl sitting at his table. Grace could only watch, and wait.

"The doll," he began in a hoarse whisper, glancing down at the box beside the chair. "It is a present, but not …" The strain in his face was clear and Grace felt ashamed at wanting to know. "It's for a little girl I barely know, who until a few days ago did not even exist to me." He massaged his eyes with the tips of his fingers, and when he took them away there were tears. "It's for my daughter." He looked across at Grace as though asking her forgiveness at his weakness. After that he was unable to stop himself and told her everything, like it was important for her to know. He wanted to unburden himself of every heart-rending secret and by doing so, allowing her to share some of the pain.

Grace listened without interruption, her face set in a mask of sympathy, moistened by her own tears. By the time he had finished they were clutching hands across the table, their fingers locked by a common feeling of grief.

"I'm so sorry for you, Paul." Her voice was weak and shaking, and the comment was a pointless platitude, but the silence had been unbearable and she could think of nothing else to say.

He simply nodded his appreciation. "I never intended that anyone should know." He breathed deeply to regain his composure, conscious that there were other witnesses to his weakness. "But when I saw the doll, I knew I had to buy it for her. I wanted her to have something from me."

"Yes, it's right that she should. She only knows her grandparents, and I understand how they must feel, but you are her father, they can't deny you that." She flashed him a brave smile. "When will you take it to her?"

"I thought perhaps tomorrow, or the day after." In truth he had given it no thought and it was only then that he realised it was something he would have to do.

"Why not today, on our way home?" Her eagerness to help had suddenly overtaken the need to respect the rawness of his feelings. Her fingers tightened on his. "I'm sorry, I wasn't thinking, you'll want to go on your own."

Paul forced a weak smile. "No, I'd like it if you came with me. I think it would be more bearable if you were there." He stared down at the table top. "Yes, we'll go this afternoon. I think it's best done straight away."

They stayed in the tea room until it was time to meet the landau, any notion of more shopping having been lost in a thick mist of emotion. A strong bond of friendship had been built over that past hour, and when Paul insisted that she told no one of his daughter it was as though that single secret had rendered the bond unbreakable. When their hands finally parted, their thoughts remained joined by that secret.

Dusk had dropped its cloak over the landscape long before the landau pulled up outside the Farrier's Inn, where the only lights that showed came from the upstairs windows.

"It doesn't look like it's open yet," remarked Paul, less confident about the visit now that they had arrived. "I'll have to knock."

Grace caught hold of his arm as he was about to climb down from the carriage. "Shall I wait for you here?"

He got down and held out his hand. "No, come with me. Now that you know about her, I want you to see her for yourself, and then you won't always be wondering what she looks like."

He helped her down and knocked on the inn door. As they waited, Paul tried to curb the tremor that had engulfed him, fearing that he had made a dreadful mistake. He wanted to leave, but felt a compulsion to knock again. It brought mixed feelings when a dull yellow light brightened the bar window and seconds later came the sounds of bolts being drawn.

Cautiously Jack Conners' face peered out into the gloom as Paul stepped forward. "Oh, it's you, lad," he said with a mixture of surprise and wariness. "I thought it was an impatient customer, that's why I didn't hurry myself."

"I'm sorry to disturb you, Mr Conners, but I've got a Christmas present for Rosemary. Would it be all right with you and your wife if I gave it to her?" He held out the box for the landlord to see.

Jack Conners looked anxiously over his shoulder, knowing full well what his wife would say. "I suppose it will be all right," he said hesitantly, opening the door wider. He stepped aside to allow Paul in. "Can't see what harm it can do."

Paul took Grace by the arm and eased her into the doorway. "I've someone with me, Mr Conners," he said as Grace stepped into the dim light of the bar. "This is Miss Haveringham, she and my brother are to be wed."

Jack gave her a respectful nod. "Pleased to meet you miss. Come through, both of you."

He led them through the bar to the bottom of the stairs when he stopped to face them. "They're both in the parlour," he said in a low voice, "so I reckon we'll hide this present away before the little 'un sees it." He took the box from Paul and tucked it under the stairs before going up.

Mary Conners was sitting in a chair, a sewing basket on her lap as she stitched the hem of a dress. The little girl was on the floor, playing with a rag doll that had once belonged to her mother. They both looked up expectantly as Jack entered.

"We've got some visitors for our little Rosemary," he announced with some reservation. "They've brought her a present, a doll by the looks of it."

Mary Conners looked up at them over the rim of her glasses and gave Paul and Grace a curt nod as they crowded in behind her husband. When Rosemary saw them, her eyes widened and she scurried on her hands and knees behind her grandmother's chair from where she peeped out at them.

"Bless her," laughed Jack, "she's a shy one and no mistake." He was repaid with a cutting look from his wife. He waved his guests towards some chairs. "Well, sit yourselves down and I'll get us a glass of sherry. What about you, mother, will you join us in a glass?"

"I'll not, if it's all the same," she replied coldly. "We need to keep one sober head in this house now we've got responsibilities."

Paul and Grace exchanged awkward glances and Jack raised his eyes to the ceiling, all three perhaps wishing they were elsewhere.

While Jack was arranging the drinks Rosemary remained behind the chair, every now and then peering out suspiciously at the visitors. When she caught them looking at her, she quickly pulled back, only to repeat the process moments later until in the end it became a game and she began to giggle as her confidence grew. Encouraged by Grace's infectious smile the child eventually ventured out into the room and edged her way closer to where the pair were sitting. She sat on the floor, looking up from one to the other before being drawn towards Grace, reaching out to touch the velvet softness of her skirt.

"She seems taken with you, miss, I'm blowed if she ain't. Do you see that, mother?" Jack Conners was doing his utmost to break down the hostility that his wife used as a barrier to her fear of losing the child.

"It didn't take you long to find someone to replace our Jenny," Mary said bitterly without looking up from her sewing. "You come here with your fancy woman and your presents thinking you can take our baby away after all the promises you made."

"And I meant it, Mrs Conners. You don't …"

"No, this is my fault, lad," interrupted Jack Conners, angrily facing his wife. "You've got this all wrong, mother. This young lady is Miss Haveringham, she's to wed Paul's brother." He turned apologetically to Grace. "I'm sorry, miss, I should have introduced you right away."

"It's all right, really," insisted Grace, gently stroking Rosemary's hair as the child sat contentedly at her feet. "I do understand how you feel, Mrs Conners. Paul has told me all about your daughter and you have my sympathies, but you mustn't blame him for her death, or accuse him of trying to take the child from you. I wanted to come here with him, to bring the present, but I can see it was a mistake, and now I think it best we leave."

She gave Rosemary a last pat on the head before getting to her feet. Jack Conners shook his head sadly as he followed his visitors to the parlour door and took the hand Paul had offered him. Overcoming all her previous shyness the child had tottered after them and stood clinging on to the bottom of Grace's coat, looking up with wide, imploring eyes that only the hardest of hearts could ignore. Not wishing to cause further offence, Grace looked to Jack, expecting him to take the child to her grandmother.

"You can pick her up if you want." The words came not from Jack, but from his wife. "I don't suppose it can do any harm."

So unexpected was the gesture that Paul could only stare at the old woman in disbelief, but Grace needed no second bidding and she bent down to scoop Rosemary up in her arms, kissing her on the cheek. The girl responded with a childish smile as she played with Grace's hair.

"I know what you must think of me," went on Mary Conners with no hint of self-pity, "but that child there is all we have left of our Jenny, and there's nothing on God's earth that will make us give her up."

"And I've already made it plain that I'll make no claim to her," protested Paul as he stroked his daughter's cheek with the back of his hand. "But I would like the right to visit her, and to bring her presents. I don't think that's too much to ask."

Jack reached out and patted Paul's shoulder. "Me and mother know that, lad, and we wouldn't want to stop you from seeing her." He looked sadly at his wife. "It's not so bad for me, I've got this place to occupy my time, but Mary's only got the child now and it would break her heart if she was taken from us."

"You don't have to make excuses for me, Jack Conners, I can speak for myself if I have to," retorted his wife with proud indignation. "The lad knows the right and the wrong of it. I can see that now, so we've no need to talk of it anymore." Her taut features softened a little as she looked at the child content in

Grace's arms. "Pass her to him, girl, he's earned the right to hold her, if he wants."

Paul glanced at Grace with uncertainty. It was a moment he had thought about often since first seeing his daughter, and now she was being held out for him to take. As Rosemary showed no signs of shying away, he gingerly reached out and took her, grinning nervously as he did so.

"Hello, Rosemary," he said softly, feeling a rush of emotion surging through him. He wanted to tell her that he was her father and that he would always be in her life, but he had no right to that, yet. Instead, he contented himself with holding the child close to his chest and absorbing the warmth from her little body.

The child was not his to keep and he quickly realised that the longer he held her the harder it would be to give her up. He passed her back to her grandfather.

"She's certainly taken to the two of you," laughed Jack, taking the child and swinging her to and fro in his arms. "She don't generally take to strangers."

Strangers! To Paul it was an odd choice of word to describe her father, yet Jack was right, he was a stranger, and perhaps it would be more appropriate for him to remain so.

"We really should go," he said quickly. "A merry Christmas to you, and to you Mrs Conners, and thank you."

"And a very merry Christmas to you, lad, and the young lady. God bless the two of you."

Paul gave Rosemary a lingering kiss on the cheek. "And a merry Christmas to you, my love," he whispered.

On the drive back to Millwood House Paul sank into an abyss of reflective silence. Respecting his mood Grace made no attempt to engage him in conversation, although she desperately wanted to talk about his daughter, to tell him what a beautiful girl she was and how fortunate he was to have her. But instead, she contented herself with a feeling of sadness and pity that the child would not be a part of his life through her formative years. She tried to imagine how it would be to have a daughter like that, and wondered if she and Matthew would be similarly blessed.

It was almost time for dinner when the landau drew to a halt at the end of the drive and Grace became acutely aware that they were much later arriving home that they should have been. As Jenkins let them in, she asked if Matthew was yet home.

"In the drawing room, I believe, miss," he replied with no pretence that his opinion of Matthew had mellowed over the previous few years.

As they passed through the hallway Grace caught a glimpse of herself in the huge gilt framed mirror that almost covered one wall. "I look a frightful mess," she declared with a look of horror, although Paul would have disagreed. "I must go and change before dinner, and look in on Uncle Rufus." She took him by the hand. "Would you be a dear and keep Matthew company until I come down?"

Suppressing the opinion that Matthew was fortunate to have her, whatever her appearance, he reluctantly agreed. He doubted his brother would welcome his company any more that he relished it himself.

He found Matthew slumped in a chair, in his now familiar pose of draping one leg over the arm. In his hand was a glass and on the small table at his side was a decanter of whisky. By his flushed and heavy-eyed features, Paul judged that he had already drunk more than was good for him. That opinion was reinforced as he crossed the room with Matthew's mean and unfocussed eyes following him.

"Home at last," he hissed sarcastically, raising his glass in a mock toast. "What have you and my woman been up to all day?"

Paul ignored the question. He was in no mood for unnecessary confrontation. He took the chair opposite and gave his brother a look of contempt.

"Well, aren't you going to answer me?" persisted Matthew, pouring himself another drink. His mouth curled into a drunken leer. "Or is it something you can't tell me about, a secret?"

"She's in her room dressing for dinner, and you know full well where we've been, since it was you who insisted she come with me." Even the satisfaction of knowing that he and Grace shared a secret was not sufficient to stop him resenting the implication of the question. "You shouldn't drink so much, Matt, you know that stuff always gets the better of you."

Matthew gave a loud, disdainful snort. "Nothing gets the better of me, brother, nothing and no one." He waved his hand unsteadily at the ceiling. "Even old Haveringham tried, and look what happened to him. And do you know why, because I'm better than all of you."

"You're drunk, Matt, so I'll excuse what you just said, but you'd better stop before you go too far." Paul got out of the chair and went to take the decanter from the table, but before he could do so Matthew snatched it up and clutched it

351

to his chest in childish defiance. "Give it to me, Matt, before you end up making a fool of yourself."

To Paul's surprise Matthew handed him the decanter, a stupid grin on his face. "Here, have a drink yourself, and tell me all about your day with my beautiful bride to be."

Paul took the decanter and placed it out of reach on the mantle shelf. His determination to avoid a fight was waning, but the things he wanted to say to his brother were best left unsaid until he was less angry and Matthew less drunk.

"Well, I'm waiting, dear brother," went on Matthew, his words slurring. "I'm waiting to hear what kept you both out so late. Did you seduce her, is that why you're late, and is that why she can't face me?"

"You know, Matt, sometimes you disgust me," said Paul with a quiet calm that belied the rage that was welling up inside him. "You might not think much of me, but at least have some respect for the girl who loves you and who's going to be your wife. I had hoped the years might have changed you, and given you a sense of decency, but I was stupid to think such a thing, you're still the arrogant, uncouth person you've always been."

Matthew finished his drink in a single swallow and swung his leg over the arm of the chair to sit up. "Still the same? Oh no, brother, I have changed, believe me." He spat the words vehemently as he stared up at his brother through red, hazy eyes. "There was a time when you could push me around and tell me what to do, but no more. I'm master here now, with more power than you'll ever know, and you don't like that. You're jealous, that's why you're trying to take Grace from me."

"You're drunk, and what's worse, you're stupid and you're drunk. You've no idea what you're talking about, but I'll tell you this, Matt, if I could find a way to stop Grace from marrying you I would. She deserves better than you, someone who would marry her for love and not for all this." He swept his hand around the room. "You don't love Grace, and I doubt you even know the meaning of the word, and the only reason you're marrying her is to get your greedy hands of her uncle's land and money."

Matthew let out an evil, hollow laugh. "And is that what you're going to tell her? Do you really think she'll believe you?" he mocked, holding out his empty glass. "Pour me another drink, there's a good chap, and then you can run along and tell Grace what a bad person I am."

"Oh, I've no need to tell her, she'll find out soon enough, especially when you're as drunk as you are now. I just hope it's not too late."

"Get me another drink, damn you." Matthew lunged forward out of the chair.

Paul caught him by the shoulders and pushed him back down. "You've had enough. For pity's sake, just look at yourself."

Matthew was beyond any reasoning. He threw down his glass and hurled himself at Paul, clamping his hand around his brother's throat.

"I know why you came back," he breathed, his face full of hatred. "You want to stop me from getting what's rightfully mine."

Paul gripped his brother's wrist, trying to break the tightening hold. "You don't know what you're saying It's the drink that's doing this to you." Matthew's response was to squeeze harder until Paul began to cough as the air was choked from him. "Matt, for God's sake stop."

In desperation Paul reached out, pressing the heel of his hand under his brother chin and pushing back with all his strength as the room around him became distant and blurred. In Matthew's crazed state Paul knew that only luck or brute strength would prevent his passing out and it was the former that came to his aid. With his legs unsteady through drink Matthew tripped against the small table and began toppling backwards, taking Paul with him, and as they fell to the floor Matthew's head struck the edge of the marble hearth with a sickening crack. He let out a loud gasp before releasing his grip and lying limp and still.

For several seconds Paul lay on top of his brother, recovering the breath that had been forced from him. Slowly he raised himself onto his knees and stared horrified at the prone body beneath him. In that dreadful moment he feared Matthew was dead, and the overriding thought in his head was the fear that Grace should think he had killed his brother.

In a frantic effort to free himself of the guilt he shook Matthew violently by the shoulder. "I'm sorry, Matt, this wasn't my fault."

He almost wept with relief when he heard the laboured breathing and saw the gently rising and falling of Matthew's chest. Carefully he raised his brother's head and held it to his chest, feeling the warm dampness of blood on his fingers. "I'm sorry, Matt, truly I am."

The door to the drawing room opened and Paul readied himself for Grace's dramatic reaction.

"I heard a noise and wondered if something was wrong." Jenkins stood in the doorway just as Paul was getting to his feet. He looked at the still figure on the floor and raised his eyebrows. "Is he …?"

Paul shook his head numbly. "He fell and hit his head. He's unconscious."

Jenkins walked slowly across the room, picked up the glass and sniffed at it indignantly. "We should take him up to his room," he said with a detached air of indifference. "I'll get someone to help me with him."

"No, I'll help," snapped Paul, "and I think we should send for the doctor. He's bleeding."

"I'll see to it when we've got him to bed." There was little urgency in his voice, further demonstrating the poor regard with which he held Matthew. "I'll take his legs, shall I?"

Between them they carried Matthew up the stairs and reached the landing just as Grace was coming out of her room. She let out a horrified shriek when she saw the two men carrying Matthew's limp and sagging body towards her.

"What happened?" she cried, breaking into a run. "What's the matter with him?"

Paul was too upset and too afraid to speak.

"He fell, miss, apparently," said Jenkins without emotion. "He hit his head." They carried on to Matthew's room and laid him on the bed. "I'll send a lad for Doctor Colley."

Once Jenkins had left, Grace bent over Matthew, fussing with the collar of his shirt, her face drawn and anxious. "What happened, have the two of you been fighting?" she asked without giving Paul so much as a glance.

He watched helpless as Grace took a towel from the washstand and carefully placed it under Mathew's head.

"He had been drinking. He was already drunk when we got back," Paul felt obliged to say, as though it were his fault. He helped take off Matthew's boots. "We did argue, Grace, and I'm sorry for that. But this was an accident, I swear."

Between them they made Matthew as comfortable as they could and Paul was aware that the closeness that had developed between him and Grace during the day had been badly dented by this unfortunate event.

"I'll stay with him until the doctor comes," she said tearfully. "I don't want him to be alone when he wakes up."

"I'll stay with you, unless you would prefer it if I went."

354

She was brushing the hair away from Matthew's face, the tips of her fingers gently tracing lines across his cheeks. "No, of course I want you to stay." She gave him an uneasy smile. "You have as much right to be here as me. What was it you were arguing about, nothing to do with me, I hope?" Her tone suggested there was still some blame to be apportioned.

Paul made no reply. He was standing on the other side of the bed and turned to gaze out of the window. Even though it was dark outside and he could see nothing except his own sad reflection he stared past that and into the black void beyond. It was as if he were looking at his own future, an impenetrable blackness through which there was no visible light. At that moment he was struck by the undeniable fact that he had nothing left in his life, while his brother, now lying unconscious on the bed, had been blessed with more good fortune than most good men deserved.

How easy it would be to tell Grace what Matthew was really like, what words had passed between them that led to the current situation, and the things he had done both before and since she had begun her infatuation with him. But that would be unfair, even someone like Matthew had the right to defend themselves. And how would Grace receive the information, would she even believe it? He doubted it, although he owed Grace some explanation.

"He was drunk and argumentative. You should know how he can be sometimes." He was speaking to the face in the window, addressing himself as much as Grace. "I should never have come here. I knew there would be trouble between us. It goes back since long before the farm was sold, before our mother died, and it's not something that's easily forgotten, or forgiven. It's not something that will go away, Grace." He slowly turned to face her and found her staring back at him.

"I can't believe that, Paul, nothing can be so bad that it can't be mended." In the dull light from a single lamp, he could still see the sad disbelief on her face. "You must mend it, Paul, you must."

He cast his mind back to that time when it was only the pleadings of his mother that prevented him from beating Matthew to death. In the intervening years he had been grateful for that, but now he was not so sure.

"Is that what you were fighting over when this happened?" she asked timidly, as if scared of the answer. "Can it never be resolved?"

Slowly he crossed to the bed. "The answer to both questions is no. This is something that can never be resolved, not while I'm still alive to remember it. The best I can promise is never to speak of it."

"And now it's going to haunt me and my marriage to Matthew. Do you think that's fair?" She stood up to look Paul full in the face. "I know that life has been cruel to you these past few years and Matthew has gained so much, but don't let resentment spoil what I have found, I beg you."

When he looked into her pleading, tear filled eyes it was almost impossible to refuse her anything, yet she was asking too much, and with genuine sorrow he shook his head.

"I said I would never mention it again and I never will, unless Matthew forces me to. What I want most is for you to be happy and I'll do nothing to jeopardise that. This will remain between me and Matthew."

"But it will still be there," she protested bitterly, "and it always will be. Perhaps the three of us can talk about it, lay it to rest. You can make it your wedding gift to me and I will make sure Matthew becomes the brother you want him to be."

He turned his face away from her in an act of self-chastisement. "No, I'm sorry, Grace. You're asking too much of me and the impossible of yourself. If it was in my power to make this go away then believe me I would in an instant, but it's not just mine to forgive and all I can do is to ask you to understand."

"No, Paul, it's you who is asking too much." She gripped his arm and spun him round, her face flushed with anger. "I so much wanted us to be friends, and when you told me about your daughter, I thought we were, that you could trust me with such a secret. Now you ask me to understand something you can tell me nothing about, something that can never be spoken of. I'm sorry too, but I think I was expecting too much from our friendship, and your staying here will be a threat to my marriage."

"You want me to leave then?" he asked quietly.

"No," she replied quickly, shaking her head. "But I'm afraid of what will happen if you stay here." She sat on the edge of the bed and lifted Matthew's limp hand to her cheek. "I pray to God that he will be all right, and I believe that you meant him no harm, but the next time it might be worse, either for you or him, and I couldn't bear that."

"Nor should you have to." He wanted to make it right for all of them, but there were no words that could do that. Instead, he had to be content to salvage what he could from the damage caused by his return. He sat next to her on the bed. "I will go. I think it will be for the best, but I need to ask a favour of you first. There is something I need to speak to Matthew about that has nothing to do with this other business, but important nonetheless. It will have to wait until he is well enough, so I'm asking your permission to come back, perhaps in a few days."

"No," she said firmly, "that's quite out of the question." In the dim light she searched his face to make some sense of everything that had happen that day. "I don't want anything to spoil Christmas, not for us or for Uncle Rufus. You will stay with us until after the holiday and say nothing to Matthew that will cause any unpleasantness. Can you promise me that?"

Paul sighed heavily and looked down at his brother who seemed to be breathing more evenly. "I'll stay and I'll say nothing, you have my word on that."

It was her turn to sigh, a long and wistful sigh. "This is not how I imagined it would be when you first came here. I've never known what it is like to have a brother or sister, but I always thought that if I had we would be the best of friends, someone I could turn to when there was no one else. But seeing you and Matthew together has destroyed that illusion."

"I'm sorry for that, and you shouldn't let it. I'm sure most brothers and sisters are the best of friends, and what you see with me and Matthew shouldn't be regarded as normal. Look at me and John, I can't imagine anything destroying our friendship, so don't judge everyone in the same way."

Her face creased in confusion. "Would it have been the same with Matthew if it were John here now, instead of you? That Christmas, when he was home on leave and Matthew wouldn't invite him to stay, was that for the same reason?"

Paul shook his head. "Thankfully John has no knowledge of that, and, God willing, he never will. I can't answer for what Matt does or thinks, it could only have been to do with the sale of the farm and his bitterness over that. To speak for John would be too presumptuous of me."

"Even to save me from a bad marriage?" She stared down at the floor as she spoke as though shamed by the question.

"What is it you're asking me, Grace?" He reached out, took her chin in his hand and turned her head to him. "What is it you want me to say, that Matthew isn't the man for you, that you shouldn't marry him?"

She refused him a reply, keeping her eyes lowered.

"Grace, if you've any doubts about Matthew you should talk to him about them, or postpone the wedding. You shouldn't be discussing them with me."

"I didn't have any doubts," she said tearfully, "at least not until you came here, and I don't know why I should have them now. I've never doubted my feelings for him, only his for me, and even those had faded. I thought that when you arrived the two of you would confide in each other the way brothers should, and that you would assure me of his love. I know it was childish and underhand of me, but I so wanted to be sure."

"And now you think that anything I tell you about him will only be designed to put you off marrying him. What is it you want most, Grace, to be talked into marriage, or talked out of it?"

Her tears turned to a pitiful sobbing and Paul felt compelled to put an arm around her shoulders. "I don't know, I really don't know."

In an involuntary movement they both looked down at Matthew, as though expecting him to provide the solution, but he remained oblivious to the drama he had created.

"You have to make up your own mind, Grace. I know Matthew and I are not the best of friends, but he is my brother and despite everything I have enough regard for both of you to not see you ruining your lives."

"You must think I'm a stupid young girl." She wiped away the tears with the back of her hand and forced a smile. "I wanted so much to be grown up and ladylike, and since my uncle's illness I thought I was, but now …"

Paul placed a finger lightly against her lips. "You are very much a lady, Grace, a beautiful and intelligent one. And you'll make the right decision, you wait and see."

She sniffed back the tears and threw back her head as she got up from the bed. "I wish the doctor would hurry up. Where on earth could he have got to?"

Chapter Twenty-One

It was early the following morning before Doctor Colley finally arrived at Millwood House. He had been some miles away attending a 'particularly interesting birth'. Grace had stayed by Matthew's bedside until after midnight, and when she fell asleep in the chair Paul had carried her through to her own room, covered her with a blanket and returned to keep a vigil until the doctor arrived.

Matthew had slept soundly through the night, and by the time Doctor Colley saw him he appeared completely recovered, apart from a pounding headache and a small cut on his scalp. He remembered little of the previous evening and Paul saw no good reason to remind him, leaving the bedroom as soon as the doctor had finished his examination.

Out on the landing he almost collided with Grace who had just woken and was hurrying to be at Matthew's side.

"Why did you let me sleep?" she rated him angrily.

Paul thought her unnecessarily harsh. "The doctor's just seen him, he's all right. A sore head, nothing more."

"Well, you should have woken me when the doctor came." She brushed past him and disappeared into the bedroom.

Paul stood alone on the landing, massaging some life into his tired face. It seemed that everything he and Grace had spoken about the night before had been pushed to the back of her mind by an overriding concern for Matthew, a concern Paul thought never more undeserving. But he was too tired to take issue with her, persuading himself that he could best serve everyone by keeping out of the way. He went to his room and slept.

Apart from Matthew's remarkable recovery, there was more good news for Grace. Doctor Colley had taken the opportunity to look in on his other patient, announcing that he had made sufficient progress to be allowed downstairs for a few hours each day. As soon as she heard, Grace instructed Jenkins to make the arrangements and by the time she had returned to give Matthew the news he had already dressed and left the house.

While Paul slept fitfully through the morning, and Matthew went about his usual business, Grace had her uncle installed in the conservatory where she hoped the weak sunshine, magnified by the domed glass roof, would put some colour back in the old man's cheeks. Haveringham watched her closely as she tended his precious plants, refusing to admit that she had kept them in remarkably good order during his confinement.

Matthew returned to the house at midday to take some more of the tablets the doctor had left for him. Grace was still keeping her uncle company, although the old man was more interested in his newspaper than engaging with her in idle conversation. Nevertheless, she insisted on remaining at his side, should he require anything.

As soon as she saw him Grace ran over to Matthew. "What on earth are you doing, you should be in bed." She raised herself up on her toes and kissed his forehead. "How is your head?"

"It hurts like hell, but it doesn't stop me from working." He walked with her over to where Haveringham was sitting, a blanket across his lap. Any surprise at seeing the old man out of bed remained hidden. "I think we should lay off some of the herders," he said without ceremony, "now that we've reduced the size of the dairy herd."

"For pity's sake, Matthew," snapped Grace impatiently. "Uncle Rufus doesn't need to be troubled with things like that, not now."

Haveringham put down the newspaper and held up his hand. "It's quite all right, my dear, a little stimulation will do me no harm at all." Over the top of his glasses, he fixed Matthew with a piercing stare. "Now, you listen to me, young man, they'll be no lay-offs, not while I still have control of this estate, and especially not at this time of year. Most of those men have been with me since they were boys, I know them by name. Come the spring the herd will be up again and we'll need all the men we have, possibly more. If they haven't got enough to do find them other duties, after all that's what you're paid to do."

"Well, if that's what you want, it's your money you're wasting," he said sullenly before turning away and muttering under his breath, "for now." Grace followed as he strode away. "I'll see you this evening," he told her testily.

"It's a pity that bang on the head didn't knock some humanity into him," commented Haveringham when Grace returned. "And some manners."

"I'm sure he's only got your best interests at heart, uncle," defended Grace unconvincingly. "He has a lot on his mind at the moment, and I'm not sure his brother being here is helping him."

"Well, I should be a lot happier about your wedding if you were marrying a man who was a bit more like his brother."

Any opinions she had on the subject Grace kept to herself.

Between brief periods of sleep Paul's thoughts were fully occupied. Whether or not he harboured any inappropriate feelings for Grace, the one thing he was sure about was that the marriage to his brother was wrong. And to make matters worse he suspected that she knew it too. He had done his best to warn her and, apart from telling her everything, there was nothing further he could do. Besides, he had others who were more deserving of his concern; a young daughter who one day would be entirely dependent on him; a brother fighting a war in a far-off land who may now even be dead, and a friend who could have suffered the same fate. All three would need him one day, and that is where the greater part of his responsibilities lay.

He stayed in his room until after noon when he went for a walk. It was while he was roaming the estate that he took the decision to go again to Northampton the following day. Having made up his mind to leave Millwood House immediately after Christmas he saw no advantage in spending those last few days in resentful isolation. It was bad enough that Grace and her uncle were forced to suffer Matthew's dark moods, without him adding to the general air of despondency. In an effort to make amends for any offence he may have caused, he decided he would buy presents for Grace and her uncle, and even for his brother. Any disharmony in the house during the festive season would not be of his making.

He left early the following morning, before breakfast, borrowing a horse from the stables, and was in the town by mid-morning, browsing the now familiar shop windows.

He had discovered during his conversations with Rufus Haveringham that the old man had a predilection for a particular brand of Havana cigars which, apart from London, were only available from one shop in the town. Although he felt sure neither Grace nor Doctor Colley would appreciate the gesture, the old man was deserving of some reward for all his suffering.

With one present taken care of he gave some careful consideration to what he should buy Grace. He needed to find a delicate balance between something that would prove useful but not so personal as to be misinterpreted by Matthew. For Paul it was a difficult decision and he was finally led to his choice when he passed a shop he had been in a few days before. Also, he was in a town raised around the leather trade so what more suitable than a pair of pig skin riding gloves. As the assistant placed them in a box Paul allowed himself to hope that each day Grace wore them, they would remind her of his existence.

Matthew was to prove the most difficult. Even as a child he cherished only toys that had a practical application. He had not been an easy boy to please, and now, as a man, he was even less so. While Matthew had given him no reason to do so, Paul wanted to leave his brother with some offer of conciliation.

It was only as he was casually peering into the dusty window of an ironmonger's shop that the solution stared back at him. When they were young their father owned a knife; he had used it to carve the toy plough given to Matthew as a Christmas gift. The boy had constantly pestered his father to let him have the knife, but he never had the opportunity. It was lost somewhere on the farm before their father died and was never found. The knife in the shop window was almost identical down to its carved bone handle and six-inch blade. The choice was never more obvious.

He left the shop and looked down at his packages with smug satisfaction. In little more than an hour he had completed his shopping and was ready to face the journey home. As he walked slowly back to Mr Foley's stable where he had left the horse, he was feeling not just pleased but more confident that, when he returned to Millwood House, the atmosphere would be less strained.

He turned into a narrow lane that led down to the stables and had to step aside as a customer lurched out of a public house into his path. But it was not the customer that put the thought into his mind, it was the heady smell of the tavern that wafted out into the street. There was nothing like the aroma of ale and tobacco smoke, or the sound of convivial conversation to attract a man with a thirst. And Paul had a thirst for English beer that he had missed during his time in South Africa.

There was nothing inside to match the welcoming comfort of the Railway Hotel. The bare wooden floor was sticky with spilt beer and the air was heavy with smoke that stung the eyes. A few dozen customers were crowded into the small bar area, a mix of leather workers and local tradesmen making the most of the time and money available to them.

No one gave him a second glance as he pushed his way through to the counter and ordered a pint of mild ale from the landlord, whose only acknowledgement was a grunt and a nod. To avoid being jostled Paul took his drink to a corner of the bar and rested his elbow on a shelf as he sipped with relish the dark liquid. After the trials of the past few days, he now felt sufficiently relaxed to think about Matthew and Grace with less resentment and sadness. It occurred to him that he had entered into their lives uninvited and had no right to intervene in the decisions both were old enough to make for themselves. Whatever the future held for them it was not his to change, especially since his own future stood on such shaky foundations.

"So, it's you again, dearie." The scratchy voice had made another unwelcome intrusion into his thoughts. "Remember me, do you?"

Slowly Paul put down his drink and turned to face the woman. "Please leave me alone, I've already told you I don't know who you are." He tried to dismiss her with a wave of his hand. "Just go away, will you."

"I knows you, though, and where you're from. Hibberd's Farm, over Weedon Bec way. Right, ain't I?" She chuckled smugly as she caught sight of Paul's curious expression. "I suppose you're wondering 'ow I knows that. Well, I slipped a ha'penny and a quick feel to the lad at old Foley's stable, he told me." She cackled some more as Paul's curiosity turned to annoyance.

"What is it you want from me?" he asked angrily, scanning the sea of customers to see if anyone was taking notice. They weren't, but he was no less furious and he thrust his face close to hers. "Whatever you think I've done you're wrong. I've been out of the country for two years and I've never set eyes on you until a few days ago. Now go away and leave me alone."

He tried to turn his back on her, but she took his arm and pulled him round. "I've been asking round. Your name's Pearson, and you've got a brother. He's the one I'm after." Her bloodshot eyes narrowed as she squinted at Paul. "It was 'im what gave me a right good seein' to a while back. Off work for days after that and lost me plenty of business 'e did."

Paul shook his arm free and glared back at her. "I'm sorry for what happened to you, but it's still got nothing to do with me." He hurriedly forced down the remainder of his drink and prepared to leave. Could he never have a drink in peace without being pestered by a woman. "Don't ever bother me again."

She followed him to the door and shouted after him even when he was out on the street. "If I ever set eyes on 'im again, I'll do for 'im. You tell 'im that."

Paul walked briskly to the stables, intent of having a few harsh words with Bert Foley and his lad. But, more than that, he had once again been reminded that his brother was capable of harm that would inevitably come back to destroy the love that Grace undoubtedly had for him. Paul cursed himself for going into the public house, and he cursed the woman and he cursed his brother.

Instead of riding directly back to Millwood House he needed time to calm his anger and took a detour through Weedon Bec. It was not his intention to call on the Conners, although Rosemary was seldom far from his thoughts, but he had another reason to visit the village.

He dismounted outside the small post office and tied the horse to the tether post outside. Mrs Juniper, the post mistress, had held the position for as long as Paul could remember, and as she peered at him through her round spectacles, he could swear that her appearance had not changed.

She gave him a smile of vague recognition. "Master Paul, isn't it?"

"Hello, Mrs Juniper," he replied, concealing his despondency behind a cheerful grin. "How are you keeping?"

"Oh, fair to middling. And what of you, and those brothers of yours?"

"They're fine, at least I think they are. John's away fighting in South Africa," he said with an element of pride. "That's the reason I'm here."

"I rather thought it was." She turned away to search the wall of pigeon holes behind her. "I wondered who it was you knew in foreign parts. She pulled out two letters and handed them to Paul. "Young John, well, well, I can't hardly believe he's old enough for the army."

He gave her a hollow laugh, took the letters and bid her good-day. With the letters tucked away in his coat pocket to be enjoyed later in the privacy of his room, he climbed back on the horse and rode at a leisurely pace through the village. As he passed the Farrier's Inn. he gazed longingly up at the parlour window and conjured up the image of Rosemary playing happily on the floor, blissfully unaware of the love he had for her. In a day or so she would be playing with the doll he had bought for her and he wondered if his love would ever be returned. Sadly, he carried on along the street. He had one further stop to make before going on to Millwood House.

He stood at the foot of Jenny's grave in silent vigil before telling her that their daughter was well cared for and growing into a beautiful little girl. He wished both of them a merry Christmas and shed a tear for his loss.

In the short time that remained before Christmas everyone in the household, with the obvious exception of Matthew, made some pretence at rejoicing in the festive spirit. Grace had apologised to Paul for her brusque treatment of him on the morning after Matthew's accident, and in return he assured her that it had been forgotten. Rufus Haveringham was making the best he could of his enforced sobriety, although Paul caught him more than once trying to entice Jenkins to leave the sherry decanter within his reach. There had been very little direct conversation between Paul and Matthew, with Grace acting as a reluctant intermediary, a role she accepted only to have them talking amiably by the big day.

When that day finally dawned, Grace announced that the three of them were to attend the morning church service, a tradition that had been firmly re-established since her arrival. Jenkins was instructed to keep a close eye on her uncle. But, at the last minute, Paul told her that he had decided not to go, a decision, he insisted, had nothing to do with any unresolved issues with his brother.

"Jenkins has enough to do," he told her while Matthew was elsewhere. "I'll sit with your uncle until you get back. And I think it will be good for you and Matthew to spend some time together, even if it is just in church."

Grace bit back on any disappointment she felt and thanked him for his consideration.

Rufus Haveringham had been installed in the drawing room, between the fireplace and the Christmas tree. "I love this room," he said wistfully to Paul, indicating that he should take the chair opposite, "especially at this time of year. When my dear wife was alive, we would entertain all our friends in here before dinner." His old eyes glazed over when he thought back to those halcyon days. He leaned forward in his chair. "Have they gone to church?"

Paul smiled back and nodded. "Is there anything I can get you?"

The old man peered around him furtively. "A small dry sherry would be most welcome," he said with a wicked grin.

Paul looked questioningly at him. "I'm not sure you're allowed that."

"Of course, I'm not allowed it, why else would I be asking for it," he said with mock impatience. "Good God man, one glass isn't going to kill me, and even if it does it will be well worth it." He waved his hand weakly towards the cabinet. "What's the point of living a life that doesn't allow a man one glass of sherry on Christmas Day."

"Just one then," said Paul, sympathetic to the old man's condition. "But don't tell Grace I gave it to you or we shall both be in trouble."

Haveringham insisted that Paul join him and together they sat by the fire enjoying the sublime pleasure of a forbidden indulgence.

"Tell me, lad," said Haveringham after savouring the first few sips of his drink, "how are you managing to pass your time here? Not too tedious, I hope? I doubt that brother of yours is much company for you, he's far too engaged in his own purpose to worry about others."

"I've been well enough looked after, sir," Paul assured him, "your niece is the perfect hostess." His expression hardened. "But you're right about Matthew. I've not known anyone as pre-occupied with work as he is. I just hope he's prepared to change a little once he's married."

Haveringham's tired face further creased into a frown. "Yes, it's not natural in a lad of his age, told him so often enough too, but he takes no notice." He fixed Paul with drooping eyes. "What do you make of this marriage to my niece, is he going to make her a good husband, or is he just getting wed to my property?"

Haveringham's directness was something Paul had admired in the old man, but now it had placed him in an impossible situation. It was a question he preferred not to answer.

"If you're asking me, does he love her then, in truth, I really don't know. He's my brother so the answer should be simple, but Matthew's changed so much these past years I fear I don't know him anymore." He stared into the fire, seeking inspiration from the flickering flames. "I do have a high regard, though, for a woman's intuition, so I'm sure Grace will make the right decision when the time comes."

"I wish I could be assured of that." He sipped reflectively at his drink. "How does it go, 'there's none so blind as those who will not see'. You should have seen her when she first came here, an innocent girl straight out of boarding school. Almost overnight I watched her blossom into the beautiful young lady you see now, and it grieves me that I may not be around to enjoy her for many more years." He paused to take some deep breaths, and Paul realised just how much pain and anxiety must be locked up in his failing heart. He went to interrupt but the old man held up a hand. "I want to be certain that when I go, her happiness is assured and her future set on the right course. I've done all I can to make sure she'll be well provided for, but money isn't everything. Do you understand what I'm saying?"

Paul understood perfectly, he had the same concerns himself. But what did Haveringham expect of him, an admittance that his brother was a cheating and violent blackguard who was not to be trusted? Even if he knew it to be true, he could not bring himself to say as much, whatever he thought of Matthew's true motives. Also, Haveringham still relied heavily on Matthew's ability to manage the estate during his incapacity, and for that reason alone he was due some merit. Only one person could decide on Matthew's suitability as a husband.

"I'm sure Grace is sensible enough to decide for herself. She's been closer to Matthew than I have these past few years," was all he was prepared to offer.

Haveringham gave a dubious grunt before badgering Paul for another sherry on the pretext that the first had made him feel so much better. Reluctantly Paul agreed, reasoning that one more drink was probably less damaging than a protracted disagreement.

"And what about you, lad, what are your plans for the future?" he enquired as Paul handed him the glass. "You'll be going back to South Africa, I suppose, as soon as this damned war is over?"

Paul sighed heavily. "I don't see that I have any choice. Everything I have is tied up in that mine. I just hope there's something left of it when our lads have given those Boers a lesson."

"When!" retorted Haveringham, clearly disgruntled with the news. "Buller's made a right pig's ear of it so far. And Methuen hasn't even managed to get that man Rhodes out of Kimberley." He gave a short humourless laugh. "They said it would be all over by Christmas, but it's a pity they didn't say which Christmas."

"I've had some letters from young John. He said the men were looking forward to the fight, but the way it's going he may feel a bit differently now." The letters from his young brother and the talk of the war had brought home to him how much he missed John, but it had also provided a welcome distraction from other, more recent, events. Haveringham's words faded into the distance as he offered up a silent prayer for his brother's safety, adding a hope that he would be home soon.

For Paul the time he spent in the drawing room with Rufus Haveringham was a most enjoyable part of the day. It also gave him hope that the time Grace had spent with Matthew that morning would put his brother in better spirits. But as soon as the pair returned from church it was clear that the word of God had not spread to everyone in the Haveringham family pews.

"It was a good sermon, uncle," announced Grace with at pretence at cheerfulness as she swept into the room. "It was all about seeking out the good in our enemies and finding love in those who wish us ill." She switched her attention from Paul to Matthew who was standing sullenly in the doorway behind her. "I think we can all learn a lesson from that."

Matthew's response was to help himself to a large glass of sherry and he continued drinking until dinner was announced.

In the dining room Matthew ensured that the mood remained strained, although Grace did her utmost to maintain a spirited conversation, ignoring his muted contribution.

Since her uncle's illness it had been her fervent hope that he would be able to join them for Christmas dinner and had stressed to Mrs Rafferty that the usual meal would need to be moderated to accommodate his strict diet. The old man complained bitterly at the meagre portions and the lack of taste, but gave Paul a sly wink when he was allowed only one glass of wine. In deference to the restrictions placed upon him Grace and Paul moderated their own drinking, while Matthew felt bound by no such constraint, and drank freely throughout the meal. Grace gave up on the disapproving looks even before the main course was served. It was not a day to provoke more discord, and she relied on the effects of the drink to improve Matthew's disposition.

When the meal was finally over the relief on Grace's face was palpable, her expression not wasted on Paul as she ushered them all back into the drawing room for the ceremonial opening of the presents.

With the excitement of a young child, she sat on the floor next to the tree passing out the gifts and squealing with delight when she found one with her name. Haveringham made a particular point of thanking Paul for the cigars, even though it attracted a look of mild rebuke from his niece. There was a lighter moment when Paul realised that one of the pair of gloves Grace had bought was for him, and that he had bought her the same.

"We must both be of similar minds," she giggled, a remark that bypassed Matthew.

He did, however, take more than a passing interest in the knife, and even managed a brief nod of thanks at his brother.

That, then, was Christmas at Millwood House, neither auspicious nor disastrous. For Matthew, an annoying interruption to his working life, for Grace, a lost opportunity to bring harmony to the house, for Paul, a reinforcement of all his previous doubts, and for Rufus Haveringham a solemn conviction that it was to be his last.

"Will you come riding with me this morning?" Grace asked as she sat with Paul at breakfast the following day.

He gave her a cautionary look. "Do you think that's a good idea? I'm not sure Matthew would approve."

Matthew had already left the house earlier that morning with a vague explanation to Grace that there was urgent estate business that required his attention. She thought it was unlikely, but offered no objection and was rewarded with an unexpected kiss.

Paul agreed to her request, albeit against his better judgement, and found himself rushed through the meal and down to the stables with a speed he found unsettling.

Despite the strain that the previous day had placed upon her, Grace was in surprisingly good humour, and as soon as they were in the saddle, she offered to race Paul down to the river, with the loser having to pay a forfeit. Although always open to a challenge Paul had misgivings about the forfeit, fearing she had contrived some plot involving himself and Matthew. Nevertheless, he accepted and they set off at a gallop.

Once they were out on the open pastureland Grace's five-year old chestnut forged ahead of its much older stable companion. Paul pulled his cap down further over his forehead and spurred the horse to greater effort.

Grace looked back over her shoulder and grinned. "I'll wait for you at the river," she shouted.

The fields through which they passed were separated by low hedgerows or ditches and Grace's horse cleared them with practised ease, her riding skills honed by the many hours spent in the saddle since arriving at Millwood House. Gritting his teeth Paul encouraged his own horse at each obstacle, less confident in his own ability.

Grace was two or three lengths ahead as they fast approached a hawthorn hedge that was a good three feet high, a greater challenge than all the others they had taken, and while she took it effortlessly, Paul's mount began to falter and lose its stride. By the time it reached the take off point its courage failed completely and it slewed to the right, throwing Paul onto the top of the hedge. His thick winter clothing saved him from any real harm, but the shock made him shout out in alarm, and by the time he had rolled off the hedge and checked his body for injury Grace had pulled her horse around and was laughing at him from the other side of the hedge.

"I'm sorry," she said with mock concern, "but I didn't know you couldn't ride. If I had I would have suggested an easier route." She watched with continued amusement while he went to retrieve his horse. "I think we had better abandon the race, but you will still have to pay the forfeit."

They went on to the river at a more sedate pace. "Don't you want to know what the forfeit is?" she asked.

Having overcome his embarrassment Paul smiled nervously. "I expect you're going to tell me. I've already made a fool of myself once and I think I'm about to do it again."

"Don't worry, it's no worse than falling off your horse."

"Maybe not, but I think it's your way of asking for something I might otherwise refuse."

"That's very perceptive of you."

"That must mean I'm right."

Without replying she turned her horse and led the way along the bank to where the river was shallow enough to ford, and they waded across onto Hibberd's Farm. Paul wondered if this was all part of some pre-planned strategy.

"I've decided to set a date for the wedding," she blurted out as soon as they reached the far bank. She spoke as though the news had been a burden to her and she was glad to be rid of it.

The raised eyebrows beneath the peak of Paul's cap needed no further explanation as he reined in his horse.

Her face creased. "Was it really that much of a surprise? Perhaps you had already made up your mind that I wouldn't marry him?"

He puffed out his cheeks. "Have you told Matthew?"

She shook her head guiltily. "Not yet, I wanted to speak to you first."

"But why? If you've already made up your mind you don't need my blessing."

"It's not your blessing I want Paul, it's your understanding, and your help."

"My help!" He urged his horse forward until he was level with her. "The other evening you wanted my help in finding out how Matthew felt about you, and I told you it was something you would have to discover for yourself. You must have decided, otherwise you wouldn't be marrying him, so what more help can I be?"

She hung her head. "I know this terrible thing that exists between the two of you can't be resolved, you told me that, and you can't tell me what it is." Slowly she raised her head until their eyes met. "I want to know if this thing is so terrible that, if I knew of it, I couldn't marry him."

Of all the questions she could have asked this was the one he feared most, possibly the only one he was unable to answer. "Is that my forfeit?"

"It's part of it," she admitted, "but I do have another favour to ask."

"Well, I hope that part is within my power because I can't give you an honest reply to the first."

"I believe you already have."

He would have liked to tell her that everything would be all right between her and Matthew, and more than that he wanted to believe it too.

"What's done is done and nothing can change that, so if you love him, you must do what your heart tells you is right." He prayed she could not read what was in his thoughts. "What of this other favour?"

"You're angry with me, I can see that, but it's my life, mine and Matthew's, and I know he can change. I want you to have faith in him too, that's my other favour."

"To have faith?"

"I want you to be the first to congratulate him when I announce the wedding date at dinner tonight. I want you to offer him your hand and to give us your blessing."

He gave a cynical smile. "Of course, I will offer him my hand, and I'll give you both my blessing, just don't expect him to accept either, not from me. The last time I offered him my hand he had to be persuaded to take it, do you think it will be any different this time."

"Yes, it will," she replied emphatically, "because I think much of what ails Matthew is insecurity and he hides it with his aggressiveness. Once we set the wedding date that will change, I'm sure of it. Perhaps for the first time since your parents died, he will feel part of something."

"If you truly believe that then who am I to argue," said Paul, his bitter resentment hidden behind a thin mask of resignation. "You have my word, I will be the first to congratulate him, and I'll certainly wish you both the best of luck."

With that he clicked his tongue, flicked the reins and dug in his heels. The horse took off at a gallop, leaving Grace staring after them with the certain conviction that she had demanded too much from him.

Paul kept up the fast pace until he reached the stables, throwing the reins to a waiting groom and striding off into the house. He went straight to his room with the intention of packing his bags. He was still considering what to do when there was a light tapping at the door. When he ignored it, Grace let herself in and stood in the doorway.

"I don't know if I should feel angry or insulted, leaving me the way you did," she said, close to tears as he remained with his back to her, staring out the window. "I wanted so much for us all to be friends, but it's clear that's not going to be possible. What is it, Paul? Are you jealous of Matthew for what he's achieved, or is it more than that? Whatever it is I think you owe me an explanation."

He spun around to face her, but found he was unable to look her in the eyes. "Jealous! Yes, I am jealous. That first time I saw you, on the train, I thought you were the most beautiful girl I had ever seen, and I did think about you after that." He sat down on the edge of the bed and cradled his head in his hands as though hiding his shame. "I never expected to see you again, and when I went off to South Africa, I thought only of spending the rest of my life with Jenny. I don't know if I loved her, we had so little time together before I went, but I cared deeply for her and would have married her, and been a good father to Rosemary." He turned to face Grace as she sat next to him on the bed. "Now I feel so ashamed because I have these feelings for you. Ashamed because you're betrothed to my brother, and ashamed for being unfaithful to Jenny's memory."

He felt her hand resting gently on his shoulder. "It must have taken a lot of courage to tell me that," she said softly, "and if you think I've done anything to encourage you then I'm truly sorry."

Paul shook his head. "No, you've done nothing, this is all my doing, and if I had no doubts about you and Matthew then I would have said nothing at all." He resisted a strong temptation to take her in his arms. "I've made up my mind to go back to Africa. There may not be much of my life to go back to, but it will be more than I have here."

Grace gripped at his arm, her eyes pleading through the tears. "Will you at least stay for the wedding, it would mean so much to me, and I'm sure Matthew …"

"I can't." he interrupted abruptly. "You must know that. I'm sorry, Grace, I just can't."

The words cut through her like a knife. "When will you leave?"

"I don't know, in a day or so, I suppose. I'll go to London and stay there until I can arrange a passage." His sad expression begged her forgiveness. "I think the sooner I go the better it will be for everyone. At least it will be one less thing to upset Matthew."

"It seems so unfair, that I should have all this to look forward to and you have so little." There was a real sadness in her voice. "I can well understand how you must feel, but please don't think ill of me."

"Think ill of you! How could I ever do that? It's you who should think ill of me for all the trouble I've caused between you and Matthew." Their closeness was making him feel uncomfortable and he got up from the bed. "I want you both to be happy and I think that will be easier if I'm not here."

"And will you come back?"

"I don't think I could go if I thought I should never come back, after all, I've got a daughter who might need me some day." He returned to the window to gaze out over the bleak winter landscape. "Perhaps we could write and you could tell me if you've seen her, and let me know how she is. I'll leave it up to you what you tell Matthew."

When they all sat down to dinner that evening only Paul and Grace were privy to the news she was about to announce. She had said nothing to Matthew except that it was important he was home on time and properly dressed, instead of sitting down in his work clothes, as he often did. Since her uncle's confinement there had been a relaxing of the usual formalities, something she was keen to rectify, especially now the old man would be joining them. Some of the excitement and anticipation she had felt earlier had been muted by her conversation with Paul, although she would not allow that to spoil the occasion.

"Perhaps a little more on my plate this evening," Haveringham pleaded as Grace tucked in his napkin." I've been wasting away these past weeks, and if nothing's done, I'll have no clothes that fit me."

"A little more, perhaps," she replied softly, wagging a finger at him. "I need you to be completely well by the spring."

His dull eyes twinkled as he gave her a knowing wink.

Grace had warned Jenkins to allow them a few minutes after the soup before serving the main course, praying that Matthew would not start berating the man servant for his tardiness. He had been away from the house for most of the day, yet Grace had resisted asking what had occupied him for so long, instead sympathising at his tired and vexed appearance.

He had barely exchanged a word with his brother or Haveringham, offering only a curt reply when spoken to. Behind an outward display of composure Paul was seething, more so because he knew how smugly Matthew would react when Grace made the announcement. He wondered if she appreciated how hard it would be for him to offer Matthew his hand.

No one noticed the slight inclination of the head that Jenkins gave to Grace as he cleared the soup dishes. When he had left the room, she got to her feet and, while Matthew made no response, she waved at Paul and her uncle to remain seated.

"I know this is unusual," she said, smiling directly at her uncle, "that it's not customary for a woman to speak at the dinner table, but on this occasion, I'm going to break with tradition and I hope you'll excuse me." As they all watched her with varying degrees of curiosity her eyes moved discreetly from Paul to Matthew. "Now that Uncle Rufus is well on the road to recovery, I think it's time Matthew and I made firm plans for our wedding." She looked affectionately at her betrothed, hoping for something in return, but got no more than a self-satisfied curling in the corner of his mouth. "I should like to propose the twenty third day of March. I have always dreamed of a spring wedding and with God's grace I will have it."

"That's lambing time," said Matthew blandly as Grace continued to look expectantly down at him, "but I suppose we'll manage well enough."

"Damn you, lad, and damn the lambing." It was Haveringham who had got to his feet, thumping the table with his fist. His face was florid as he supported himself. "For once in your miserable life can't you put someone else before your selfishness." He gasped for breath and was forced to sit down again. "I'm sorry my dear, I know I gave my blessing to this marriage, but that young man of yours is sorely testing my resolve to let it continue. I was prepared to give him the benefit of the doubt, but if this is how he repays my trust …"

"I'm sure Matthew didn't mean …"

"I can speak for myself," said Matthew, slowly getting to his feet, his gaze fixed on the old man. "I'm well aware of your low opinion of me, that you think me a poor husband for your niece. But let me ask you this, what would you prefer, some feckless aristocrat who would gamble and squander away her inheritance, or someone prepared to work hard to ensure its future growth." He turned his attention to Grace. "I don't find it as easy as some to express my feelings, but that doesn't mean I have none, and if you think I have more interest

374

in farming than you it's only because I want to protect what would one day be yours."

"And yours too, no doubt," put in Haveringham dryly.

"And that's what really troubles you," went on Matthew. "You think my only interest in Grace lays in this house and the land that goes with it." He glared hard at the old man, his cold, pale eyes narrowed. "If you disinherited her tomorrow, I would still marry her."

Grace let out a squeal of delight while Paul got up from his chair and walked around the table, his hand extended.

"Then let me be the first to congratulate you, Matt. You and Grace."

Surprisingly Matthew took the hand and shook it vigorously, savouring his moment of triumph, as even Haveringham was forced to reconsider his opinion. Grace threw her arms around Matthew's neck, planting a lingering kiss on his cheek.

"You see, uncle," she gushed, as tears of joy rolled over her flushed cheeks. "There's no need for you to worry, your estate and my life are both in safe hands." She turned to Paul who was still at her side. "If only you could stay for the wedding, then everything would be perfect."

"You're not thinking of leaving us, are you, brother?" said Matthew with exaggerated disappointment. "Who else would I have for a groomsman?"

"I'm sure your day will be everything you both want it to be whether I'm here or not," remarked Paul with an impassioned glance at Grace. "All I ask is that you treat her with all the consideration she deserves."

"He will, or he'll have me to answer to," barked Haveringham, still having trouble with his breathing. He waved at Jenkins who had just returned to the dining room. "Some champagne when we've finished eating."

"I don't know when I've ever been so happy," declared Grace, an arm around the waist of both brothers. "How fortunate I am to have such three wonderful men in my life."

Not as fortunate as Matthew, thought Paul.

Paul had lay awake for most of that night, restlessly tossing and turning in his bed as he tried to rid his mind of thoughts of the forthcoming marriage. He knew the match was wrong, and now his brother had skilfully deceived Grace, and perhaps her uncle, into believing that he was working purely towards her future security.

He got out of bed long before it was light. The time for sleep had long passed. There was too much laying heavy on his conscience. In the past few years alone, he had abandoned much that had become dear to him, and now he was about to do the same again. He had made up his mind to leave that day, but before that he had one more thing to do.

The clock on the landing showed it was a little after six o'clock and the house was quiet apart from a rhythmic snoring coming from Haveringham's room. Paul smiled to himself, he had come to admire the old man and believed that only poor health had prevented him from protesting more strongly against the wedding.

Downstairs the only sounds that broke the silence were the low voices filtering through from the kitchen. He went down the steps and along the narrow passageway to where Mrs Rafferty and one of the maids were preparing breakfast.

"Have you seen my brother this morning?" he enquired.

The cook and the girl exchanged cautionary glances before Mrs Rafferty replied. "Master Matthew? No, sir, not this morning. But if you'd like some breakfast, I can have it on the table for you in a few minutes." She waved the girl away to lay a place on the kitchen table. "It'll be no trouble, sir. Master Matthew often eats down here when he's about early. Probably be down himself shortly I shouldn't wonder."

"Thank you, if it's not inconvenient," he said gratefully. He wanted to catch Matthew before he left the house and this was as good a place as any.

"Poached eggs on toasted bread, that's his favourite," went on Mrs Rafferty as Paul sat at the large table. "I'll do the same for you, if you like?"

Paul nodded. He had little appetite that early in the morning, but while he waited for Matthew it seemed a less obvious way to do so.

He was still eating when he heard the heavy tread of work boots coming along the passage and there was an involuntary knotting in his stomach as he pushed the plate away.

"Well, well!" exclaimed Matthew, standing in the doorway with his hands on his hips. "I didn't think to see you down here at this time of the morning." His face showed none of the surprise the remark suggested. "Hoping to catch the early worm, were you?"

Paul raised his eyebrows. "I think I just have."

Matthew gave a dry laugh. "Still bitter about my engagement to Grace, are you?" He sat down at the table opposite his brother and gave the cook an impatient look. "Anyway, why are you up so early, not thinking of leaving without saying goodbye, were you?"

"Not at all, Matt, just the opposite in fact."

Matthew glared across the table at him. "And what's that supposed to mean?"

"It means I got up early so as not to miss you." It amused Paul to note the sudden change in his brother's mood. "Oh, don't worry. I will be leaving soon enough, though, today, in fact, but not before you and I have a serious talk."

"We've got nothing more to talk about. We said all we had to say to each other before you went halfway around the world." He kept his cold eyes on Paul as Mrs Rafferty put his breakfast down in front of him. "Well, what is it you want to say?"

"It's something best left until you've finished your breakfast and we're on our own. I'm quite sure you won't want our business to be common knowledge."

"You can speak freely, I've nothing to hide," he replied loudly, smirking in the direction of the two women, and Jenkins who had just entered the kitchen. "Come on, brother, say what you've got to say."

Paul shook his head. "No, not here. Outside when you've finished eating. I'll be down by the stables." He got up, thanked Mrs Rafferty for his breakfast and left.

While he waited Paul arranged with one of the grooms for him to be driven to Northampton later that day. Afterwards he paced the stable yard, going over in his mind how he would broach the delicate subject with Matthew before he decided on a direct approach. As soon as he saw his brother Paul strode across to meet him, away from prying ears.

"You'd better be quick," retorted Matthew as Paul took him by the arm and led to around to the side of the house. "I've got work to do."

"I won't take up any more of your time than I need to." They stopped on the narrow path close to where Matthew had his unfortunate encounter on the night of Grace's reception. "Did you know I met young John in Cape Town before I sailed back to England," he began, taking pleasure from the paling of his brother's complexion. "It seems he had more luck in corresponding with you than I did while I was away. At least you exchanged one letter with him."

"So that's it, you're going to accuse me of stealing his money?"

"Well, didn't you? And as if that's not bad enough you used my name to do it."

"I needed that money to save my farm," Matthew sneered arrogantly, free of any guilt. "It was of no use to him. The army provides everything he needs."

Paul felt his insides churn with anger. "And that makes it all right, does it? If you had asked him for the money, he would have lent it to you without question, because that's what John is like. You can't just take everything you want, Matt to satisfy your personal greed." Unable to look his brother in the face he turned away in disgust. "Is that what Grace is to you, another part of your grand plan, a means to your own selfish ends."

Matthew snorted contemptuously. "That's what this is really all about, isn't it? It's not John's money that bothers you, that was just an excuse. Ever since you set eyes on Grace, you've wanted her for yourself, and you'll do anything to stop me from marrying her."

Paul's eyes flared with uncontrollable rage as he rounded on his brother, grabbing the lapels of his jacket. "You might have fooled Grace with your little speech last night, her uncle too, but you didn't fool me. You've got no love in you, except for yourself and the land, and yes, I do have some feelings for Grace, and one of them is pity because she's let herself be deceived by a miserable wretch like you." He pushed Matthew away, afraid he would allow his temper to bubble over into violence. "You know, nothing would have given me greater pleasure than to give you both my sincere blessings, and it would have been my wish to see you happily settled. But not content with your own miserable existence, you're going to condemn that lovely young woman to the same life." His finger nails dug deep into the palms of his hands as his fists clenched tight and he fought the urge to strike his brother. "Do you think Grace would still want to marry you if she knew the truth about you?"

"The truth or the lies? She wouldn't believe either."

The veins in Paul's neck throbbed as Matthew's lack of remorse pushed him to the limit. "Perhaps not, but it might be enough to plant the seeds of doubt. Does she really love you that much?" He began to walk away before turning back. "I am going today, and I'll say nothing to her before I go, but if I hear she is in any way unhappy in her marriage then she'll know the truth, about everything."

As he strode away Matthew ran after him, spinning him round. "You bastard, you think you can blackmail me." He spat the words into Paul's face, his fist raised threateningly. Then he lowered his hand and reached into his jacket pocket and when he pulled it out it was holding the knife Paul had bought him. He opened the blade and held the point to Paul's throat. "If you ever try to speak to her, I'll kill you, I swear it."

Paul managed a cynical smile. "I wondered how long it would be for you to stoop to threats like this. Is this what your life has become, Matt, full of deceit, anger and violence?" Not once did he avoid Matthew's hateful stare until he lowered his eyes to the blade of the knife. "It may come to this one day, that one of us has to kill the other, if you keep to this path you're on." He took hold of his brother's wrist and pushed the knife away from his throat. "Now, I'm going to pack, so I'll say goodbye and leave you to decide how it will be between us."

It was with a sense of relief that there was no sign of Grace by the time Paul had finished his packing, perhaps the champagne of the previous evening had taken its toll on her. He was in no mood to invent a reasonable excuse for his sudden departure, but before leaving he went to the library where he found pen and paper and wrote the following letter.

Dear Grace

You must know how very much I wanted things to be different between Matthew and me, and it would have given me so much pleasure to see the two of you happily wed. But I cannot pretend to be happy when I'm not, and I leave fearing for your future.

It seems a cowardly thing, leaving without saying a proper goodbye, but sometimes I think I am a coward, always running away from my responsibilities and I only hope you can forgive me.

I still have this hope that Matthew will turn out to be the husband you deserve, but I beg you to keep a tight rein on your own emotions, until you are sure.

I promised I would write, and I will as soon as I find somewhere to stay while I await passage to South Africa, for that is where I feel my future lies.

I must go now so take good care of yourself, and give my kindest regards to your uncle and my wishes for his speedy recovery.

God bless you

Paul

He read the letter through, and when he was satisfied, he folded it and tucked it into an envelope.

Out in the hallway he met Jenkins coming up from the kitchen. The man servant viewed the bags in Paul's hand. "You're leaving us, sir?" he said courteously.

"Yes, and thank you for everything. Could I please ask you to do one last thing for me, would you please see to it that Miss Grace gets this letter after breakfast."

Jenkins gave him a low nod of acknowledgement as he took the letter.

Paul left through the back of the house and went quickly to the stables, pausing only for a brief glance over his shoulder. He had arrived expecting so much and was now leaving with so very little.

Chapter Twenty-Two

London celebrated the start of the new century under the heavy cloud of depressing reports coming out of South Africa. Mafeking, Kimberley and Ladysmith were all still under siege, with no optimistic probability of an early relief, a situation most of the population and politicians found difficult to understand or explain.

Yet the celebrations went on, and as the bells rang out at midnight Paul joined with the throng outside the public house in the Walworth Road where he had spent the evening in the company of his new friend and benefactor. Amidst the peeling of bells and a cacophony of ships' horns from the nearby Thames the two men had joined in with a tumultuous rendition of Auld Lang Syne between fits of uncontrollable revelry as each tried to stop the other from sprawling into the road.

It had been a long night of heavy drinking which had provided Paul with a welcome relief from the taut emotions experienced over the previous days. For a few hours, at least, he was able to put those unhappy memories to one side and to forget about the weeks to come, a few hours to be free of worry. And for that he had his friend to thank.

For Paul, the train from Northampton offered no cheerful prospect of a pleasant journey, with most of the compartments being full of people excitedly talking of a merry Christmas spent with friends and family. With the holiday yielding little in the way of a warm glow he walked the length of the train in the hope of finding an empty compartment. The best he could find was one containing just a single passenger.

The man was a little older than himself, he judged, with a round, open face that glowed with a ruddy, fresh complexion. He was twirling the ends of his thin moustache, but stopped to beam broadly as Paul entered the compartment. His whole demeanour suggested a friendly disposition, although Paul responded with a curt nod of the head as he lifted his bags up onto the rack. If only he had stopped to buy a newspaper at the station, he thought as he sat down opposite the man.

He stared out of the window, at the fringes of the town before passing fields and hedgerows, a bleak landscape that reminded him too much of the pointlessness of his life. In a further attempt to discourage any conversation he closed his eyes, even though he knew it would be impossible to sleep, the events of the morning ensured that.

"Home or away?" His efforts had been in vain, the stranger had spoken.

Too polite to ignore the intrusion Paul opened his eyes. "I'm sorry, did you say something?"

"Nothing important, old chap, I merely said, home or away." There was nothing offensive or demanding in his tone, his voice was kindly and cultured.

"I'm sorry, I don't understand."

The man laughed heartily. "Of course, you don't. No reason to, but it's quite simple really. Anyone travelling on a train is either going home or away from it." He leaned forward in his seat, peeled off a glove and held out his hand. "Gilbert Bullivant, and in my case it's home."

Reluctantly Paul took the hand, noting the firm grip. "Paul Pearson, and if you really want to know, it's neither."

Releasing Paul's hand, the man's face creased into a quizzical expression. "Don't wish to be nosey, old chap, but how is that?"

This was exactly what he was trying to avoid, and Paul sighed deeply within himself. "I'm neither going home nor going away from it."

"In that case," persisted the man, "a natural curiosity forces me to ask where exactly you do reside, or are you simply a transient with no fixed abode?"

Paul returned to the view from the window. "I don't wish to be rude, but if it's all the same I would rather not discuss my present circumstances with someone I've known only for a few minutes."

Not to be put off the man slid along the seat until he was directly in front of Paul. "You must excuse me, old chap, but I'm a keen student of humankind, and if you don't mind my saying, I think you would be doing yourself a service if you were to discuss your 'present circumstances. Unburdening yourself would be a great favour to both of us." He was staring hard at Paul's reflection in the window. "Tell me I'm wrong and I'll shut up, leave the compartment even."

It was a tempting offer, yet deep down Paul knew the man had the measure of him. Despite being a stranger there was something in him to inspire a certain comfort. "No, you're quite right," he returned, with some reticence. "It's not been the best of times for me."

There was a brief glimpse of jubilation in Bullivant's polished face before his expression darkened into concern. "I'm sorry to hear that, old chap. Anything you care to talk about? You know what they say, a trouble shared, and all that."

"I don't think so. There's nothing much I can do about it, so there's no point …"

"Quite understand, old chap. Not something you want to talk about to a stranger." He sat back in his seat, apparently no longer interested. "But if you feel you want to, then I'm your man. We've plenty of time before we reach London."

By the time the train had puffed and ground its way to a halt in St Pancras Station, Paul had involuntarily poured out his heart to his new friend and felt the better for it. Gilbert Bullivant had proved to be a most attentive and sympathetic listener, giving support instead of advice, and as they stood on the busy forecourt of the station preparing to go their separate ways it was a sad parting.

"Perhaps we could keep in touch," said Gilbert, pumping Paul's arm. "Where are you staying while you're in London?"

"Well, that's another thing," replied Paul almost ashamed. "I've yet to find somewhere."

Gilbert beamed with delight. "Then consider it a problem no more, old chap." He slapped Paul soundly on the shoulder. "I live with an old aunt in Walworth, she's more rooms than she knows what to do with. Always talking about taking in a lodger or two, and I know for a friend of mine her rates would be very reasonable."

"If you're sure, I wouldn't want to impose on her."

"Nonsense, you would be doing us both a great favour."

Gilbert was going to brook no further argument on the subject, and before he realised what was happening Paul was being dragged along to the cab stand. Less than an hour later he was standing on the pavement in front of a once imposing three storey terraced house whose façade would be enhanced with a coat of paint. Gilbert had moved there when his uncle died, to allow his aunt to keep the property, which alone she could never have afforded to do.

The aunt greeted Paul like a distant member of the family returning into the fold.

New Year's Day and for Paul the suffering only began when Gilbert came into his room with a cup of coffee. The New Year had progressed into early afternoon with no active participation from Paul, and he was more than content to allow it to continue in the same vein.

"Come along, old chap, this is no way to begin a new century," boomed Gilbert with inordinate cheerfulness. "Up you get and we'll go out and face the world together."

Paul peered at him through the puffy red slits that were once his eyes. "Shouldn't you be at work?" he asked in a hoarse whisper.

"Not today, old chap. Today I'm devoting myself entirely to your salvation and restitution." He laughed out loud and Paul shrank back beneath the bed covers where the sound of his friend's voice was less offensive to his ears. "Come on, drink your coffee and we'll go for a brisk walk to clear away the cobwebs, and you can tell me what plans you have for the New Year."

An hour later, and despite all his objections and protestations, Paul had been coaxed and cajoled out of bed and was dressed and ready to leave the house, but still very much against his will and delicate constitution.

"I thought we might leg it down to Peckham Rye," announced Gilbert as the first few breaths of cold, fresh air assailed Paul's lungs. "It's no great distance, but it will give us the chance for a decent chat."

As they set off down the Walworth Road towards Camberwell Green, Gilbert took a devilish delight in ribbing Paul over his incapacity for alcohol while assuring him that he would feel so much better by the time they returned.

"So, my dear fellow, what are you going to do with yourself now?" he asked, once he had dispensed with his views on Paul's health. "Are you still as intent on returning to that wretched country the Dutchmen are so keen to keep for themselves?"

As his head slowly cleared in the icy winter air Paul was able to give the question the consideration it deserved. "I don't see that I have any choice. Apart from what's left of what little I was able to bring back with me everything I possess is still there, not to mention a partner I had to leave half dead in a Johannesburg hospital. I don't even know if he's still alive, but I owe it to him to go back to find out, even if it takes my last farthing to get there."

"Brave words well spoken, my friend, but aren't you forgetting one little thing."

"Sorry?"

Gilbert looked askance. "The war is still going on, you know. It might not be as easy as you think to get back there."

"I haven't forgotten the war at all," said Paul with a hint of annoyance. "I've got a brother out there in the army, remember." As they rounded Camberwell Green he stared wistfully into the distance. "Soldiers are dying out there for the rights of men like Frank and me, and if I don't go back then it will all be for nothing."

"I'm not doubting your commitment, Paul, only your common sense. It could be some time before you get passage. They're bound to give priority to the military. Have you thought of that?"

In truth Paul had given very little thought to the finer details of his plans, since they had progressed no further than beyond the need to go. It had taken Gilbert's detached logic to bring home the difficulties that faced him, and by the time they entered the open expanse of the Rye, where the cold wind stung his face, a dark gloom had descended over Paul which even his friend's ebullient nature failed to lift.

There was no better news the next day when Paul presented himself at the offices of the Union Castle Line in the City. From behind his counter the booking clerk shook his head gravely. "I'm sorry, sir, but there won't be any berths available for at least two months."

"Two months! Surely there must be some way of getting there, what about other shipping lines?"

"I can't answer for other lines, sir, but I think you'll find them all the same. There is a war going on, you know."

He needed no further reminding of that and with his despondency still intact he returned to Walworth.

"Two months is no great time," Gilbert offered when he arrived home from work that evening. "And there are far worse places to spend it than here with me."

Paul gave him a grateful smile. There was some truth in what his friend said, he was probably as happy as he could be, under the circumstances. And it would at least give him time to correspond with Grace before he left.

When Grace received the letter, Paul had left for her with Jenkins her first reaction was one of general annoyance, that he had left without the courtesy of a final goodbye. But, having read it through a few times, she reached the conclusion that his motive had been to spare them both some unnecessary grief, and she instantly forgave him. It was only later that evening, when he returned from work, that Grace spoke to Matthew of his brother's leaving, and he reluctantly admitted that he had seen him that morning, making a vague reference to their argument.

"Why didn't you say so?" she demanded of him. "Was it because of you he left so suddenly?"

"That had nothing to do with me, he had already made up his mind to go when I saw him."

"And what was it you argued about?"

"It was nothing," he replied, dismissively waving his hand in her face. "You know how he is with me, he's jealous of what I've got and that's all there is to it."

For the sake of peace Grace let the matter rest, although for the next few days she regarded Matthew's increasingly attentive attitude with mild suspicion until she eventually concluded that the change in him was due to the setting of the wedding date. Also, she thought, perhaps Paul had been right, that his continued presence at Millwood House only inflamed the situation and that his leaving was more for her benefit than his own.

Even so, she missed Paul and the company he provided for both her and her uncle, and she would not give up on the fervent wish for him to be there on her wedding day. Just as important to her was that he kept to his promise to write, and she made regular visits to the post office in Weedon Bec. She longed to write back with the news that he had been entirely wrong about Matthew who, she was now sure, would prove to be the ideal husband for her.

It was now the arrangements for the wedding that occupied much of her time. The church, the invitations, the wedding breakfast, there was so much to do, and with just a few months to have everything ready. Her uncle's casual observation that he hoped their guests would not place an improper interpretation on the hastily arranged marriage fell on stony ground. She would not be distracted from her mission. And his suggestion that she might consider a short delay fared little better, as far as she was concerned the date was now set in stone.

Haveringham had made no significant progress in his recovery since Christmas and Grace feared that another relapse would cause the wedding to be delayed indefinitely, should something happen before the big day. As much as she cherished her uncle and his continued wellbeing, she was acutely aware of the strain on her relationship with Matthew that any delay would inevitably bring.

Therefore, she allowed the old man no involvement in the stress laden tasks that occupied her each day, with the exception of his advice when it came to preparing the guest list. Inviting the 'right people' was so important.

"There are two types of guests," he informed her solemnly, "those by virtue of my long acquaintance with them, my friends, and those whose good offices could prove to be of benefit to you in the future."

"You mean those in a position to grant us favours, uncle?" she responded indignantly.

He smiled benignly. "I suppose I always expected your marriage would bring together two of the most powerful families in the county, whichever the other one might be, and that it would not depend so heavily on the financial strength of just one side. Your young man brings nothing to this union but himself, and while I appreciate that love is a powerful motive, I doubt that it is enough to sustain you should all else fail." He patted her on the arm. "I fear for your future, my dear, especially if I'm no longer around to …"

She tutted loudly and placed a finger to his lips as she rearranged the cushion behind his head. "Nothing is going to go wrong, and besides, you will always be around to look out for me. Now, rest quietly before dinner."

Outside the drawing room the confidence she had displayed in front of her uncle was exchanged for the concern she truly felt. She had done everything possible to protect the old man from the stresses of daily routine, particularly in the affairs of the estate. She had repeatedly reminded Matthew of the need to take greater responsibility, and when he arrived home that evening, she mentioned it again.

"Then I'm damned if I do and I'm damned if I don't," he said bitterly. "He gets angry if I don't consult with him over everything, and if I do go to him, I have you to answer to. What am I expected to do?"

"I know how difficult it is, but you can see how weak he is still, and I want him strong enough to be at the church, otherwise I shall have to postpone the wedding."

It was of no consequence to Matthew if Haveringham was at the wedding or not, his early demise would be a welcome event, but not before he was married to Grace. So, he gave her his solemn promise he would do nothing to impede the old man's recovery.

Grace's spirits rose markedly when she received the first letter from Paul. She took it straight upstairs to read in the privacy of her room. Despite the feeling of guilt, she had already determined that, should she hear from him, she would keep it secret from Matthew. It was for the best, she told herself.

It was just a short letter, telling her how well suited he was with his accommodation in London and of the unavoidable delay in his plans to return to South Africa. He made no reference to anything that had occurred between himself and Matthew before his departure, in fact there was nothing in the letter that could be regarded in any way controversial. There were, however, two aspects of the letter that delighted her enormously; the first was that she had an address to which to reply, and the second was the possibility he may still be in England at the time of her wedding. It only remained for her to persuade him to attend.

When she had finished reading, she immediately sat down to pen a reply. In it she told him how the plans for the wedding were progressing, a report on her uncle's health and of the mundane events that occupied her days. Her only submission to sentiment was an expression of regret that he found it necessary to leave Millwood House without a personal farewell. Of Matthew she mentioned only that he was in good health. It had been a somewhat trite exchange, but it was a beginning.

There was nothing that went on in the environs of Weedon Bec that the village post mistress, Mrs Juniper, knew nothing about. If not the instigator of local gossip she certainly did nothing to impede its progress through her district. She knew long before the official announcement in The Times of the forthcoming, yet unlikely, marriage between the niece of Rufus Haveringham and the Pearson boy. She knew also, although who was she to judge, that he was already living up at the big house but, to her knowledge, in separated rooms, and that the other Pearson boy, the older one, was staying there for Christmas and had now returned to London. She knew all this.

But, if Mrs Juniper's gossiping was vexing to some, it also proved providential to others, for when letters arrived at her post office addressed to Paul Pearson she knew exactly what to do with them. If anyone had a forwarding address it would be Miss Haveringham, or her intended.

The letters were duly passed on to Millwood House where Grace agonised over whether she should tell Matthew. To do so would be a virtual admittance that she was already in contact with Paul so, for the sake of harmony, she decided to send them on to London with a covering letter of her own.

The strain on Paul's finances caused by his enforced sojourn in London had been lightened by the further help of his new friend, Gilbert Bullivant, who had found him employment as a clerk with a grain merchant in the City. The job offered no more stimulation than that of the assay office in Johannesburg, but it helped to pass the long winter days and preserve what was left of his savings. On one day a week he would spend his lunch break trawling the shipping line offices in the hope of finding an earlier passage, but the news remained depressingly bleak.

After a month he was beginning to come to the conclusion that his time spent in London was a time lost from his life, unproductive and wasted, and his only consolation was the fact that there was little else he could do. When he admitted as much to Gilbert, his friend appeared suitably hurt and Paul was forced to offer profuse apologies.

"You must think me so ungrateful," he told him. "After all, without your help I would have had nowhere to live and no money to live on."

"Think nothing of it, old chap," he replied with genuine sincerity. "I've no idea what it must be like to be in a position such as yours. I've never felt safe venturing any further away than Birmingham." He took a small packet from the dresser in the parlour and handed it to Paul. "Maybe there's something here to bring a little cheer to your life. It arrived today and I recognised the handwriting. It always seems to bring a smile to your face."

Gilbert was right, a letter from Grace was always a welcome experience, but this was more than a letter and he accepted the packet with rising anticipation.

"I'll open it later, after diner," he said, much to Gilbert's disappointment.

Later that evening he sat alone in his room turning the packet over in his hands, trying to guess what it contained. Finally, he broke the seal and took off the wrapping to find a small bundle of letters. He first read the one that was obviously from Grace which merely repeated much of what had been said before, as well as admitting to a growing feeling of loneliness during Matthew's long absences from the house. It would have been easy for Paul to translate her admission of as a yearning for his company.

From the postmarks and the writing on the envelopes it was clear that the other letters were from John, and as he opened the first one Paul's hands shook.

That his young brother was still alive there was no question yet he was nonetheless nervous at what he was about to read. Why was he being so stupid? He put it down to the strength of love he had for his brother.

As he read the first letter, he smiled at some of the humour, yet other paragraphs brought him close to tears at the vivid pictures of war painted with his words. But it was the contents of the last two letters that had the most profound effect on Paul, the ones in which John told of the loss of his close friend and of his own wound. The fact that he glossed over the seriousness of the injury led Paul to the clear conclusion that it was far more severe than was mentioned.

With the last letter came the news that John was coming home. He was being transferred to the military hospital at Woolwich, just a few miles from where Paul was staying. The letter had been written just prior to John's embarkation for England and he was expected to arrive at Woolwich early in February. He may already have arrived.

The Royal Herbert Military Hospital was a grand, impressive looking building occupying a prominent position at the crossroads of Shooters Hill and Academy Road, just above Woolwich Common. On the Saturday morning after receiving John's letter Paul stepped off the omnibus in Beresford Square in Woolwich, opposite the main gates to the Royal Arsenal, deciding to make the last leg of his journey on foot. It was a cold crisp morning, ideal for walking, and the added incentive of seeing his brother put an extra spring in his step.

His route took him up the hill past the historic headquarters of the Royal Artillery and as the ground levelled out across the common Paul's initial excitement began to turn to worry. John had said only that he had been wounded and Paul's mind began to conjure up images of horrific injuries, even of amputations. If that was the case, how would he react? He tried to dismiss the thought from his mind, within the hour he would know.

He had kept the news of John's return from Grace, there was no point in causing her unnecessary alarm. Also, there was the strong possibility she would feel compelled to pass the news on to Matthew, provoking further friction between them. All these things went through Paul's mind as he covered the last mile.

It was possibly the largest building he had seen outside London, and as he stood outside, looking up at the countless windows, he wondered which, if any, was shedding sunlight onto his brother. He had no way of knowing if John had actually arrived, some unforeseen circumstance may have delayed his return, or worse, the wound may have proved fatal. It was with a sense of trepidation that he was directed to the main reception.

The initial news was encouraging. John had arrived and was in a ward on the second floor. As he climbed the stone staircase Paul was struck by the sights and smells that assailed his senses. Everywhere he looked there were men hobbling unsteadily on crutches, trying to manage with one leg, and others learning to light a cigarette or pipe with the use of just one hand. Then there was the sickly smell of carbolic and antiseptic masking the stench of gangrene and other infections.

On each floor the scene was the same, dispelling the illusion that the higher he went the lesser the infliction.

At the door to the ward Paul hesitated. He was almost within touching distance of his brother, yet he was afraid to go further, afraid of what he would find. Through the glazed door he could see the rows of beds, some with men sitting on them chatting happily to their mates. Other beds were empty, their occupants shuffling around the ward with varying degrees of disability. Paul looked for his brother, but there was no sign of him amongst the scene of ailing humanity. His heart beat faster as he pressed his face closer to the glass.

"Can I help you? Are you looking for someone?"

Startled by the sudden interruption Paul spun round. "I'm sorry," he mumbled to the nurse who had appeared behind him. "I'm not sure I'm allowed to be here, but I had a letter from my brother saying he was being transferred here. I was hoping to see him."

"Your brother?" Her expression was stern, although not intimidating.

"Yes, Corporal Pearson, John Pearson. Is he here?"

She pushed open the door to the ward and Paul followed her in. "We do have strict rules about visitors, you know. We can't have people turning up here at any time, upsetting our routine." She went over to a large blackboard fixed to the end wall and studied the list of current patients. "Come far, have you?"

"Yes, quite a distance," Paul lied. He tried to look past her at the list. "Is he here?"

She traced her finger down the list before giving him a nod. "He came in two days ago, last bed on the right." She stared at Paul through narrowed, questioning eyes. "Quite a distance, you said?"

He nodded sheepishly. "Just a few minutes, that's all I need."

"And a few minutes is all you'll get, or we'll both be in trouble." She gave him a sly wink.

He thanked her warmly and walked slowly between the two rows of beds. Some of the patients eyed him with curiosity while others raised a hand in a brief acknowledgement. Paul was struck by the dignity with which they all seemed to accept their injuries, however serious, and as he looked for John, he could only hope his brother had been imbued with the same resolve.

Arriving at the end of John's bed, Paul could barely bring himself to look. He had seen the tell-tale depressions in the beds where limbs no longer supported the covers. In his letter John had said only that it was a leg wound, and as Paul now shifted his gaze up the length of the bed, he found himself expressing his relief in a broad grin and watery eyes.

John was dozing, and Paul quickly wiped away the tears as he approached the side of the bed. He was reminded of the numerous times in the past when he had to wake his brother in the morning, but now, instead of looking down on that boy, he saw only a man. In those few months since they last parted company John had aged immeasurably, and even though the moustache had now gone there was a defined maturity to his features. If the horrors of war had done that to his looks, Paul wondered, what had it done to his mind?

He pulled up a chair close to the bed and sat down. He was torn between waking his brother and wasting the short time they had just to watch him sleep. He reasoned that John had plenty of time to sleep so he shook him gently by the shoulder until his brother grunted and turned his head, although his eyes were still closed.

"What time is it?" he muttered distantly.

"It's time you were getting up, little brother." They were the familiar words Paul had spoken countless times before.

With a start the eyes flickered open, staring up into the face that was smiling back at him.

"Paul!" With a look of disbelief, he lifted his head from the pillow. "Paul, it's really you!"

"In the flesh."

John dragged himself into a sitting position and the two of them embraced, slapping each other repeatedly on the back. "You got my letters then? I wasn't sure where to reach you."

"It was only by luck. I got them just this week. I'm staying here, in London." He glanced cautiously up the ward. "But don't say anything to the nurse, I told her I had quite a journey getting here otherwise I don't think she would have allowed me to stay."

"Why aren't you staying at the farm, is there still trouble with Matt? You have seen him, haven't you?"

Paul nodded, his expression solemn. "Yes, I have seen him, but I don't want to talk about him now. We've only got a short time and I want to know about you." He looked down at John's legs beneath the covers. "How badly are you hurt?"

John gave him a weak smile. "Not as bad as some of the poor devils in here." He patted his leg. "At least I've managed to keep this."

"And you'll be fully fit soon?" Paul asked optimistically. "Do you want to tell me how it happened?"

"There isn't that much to tell." He gave his brother a brief description of the action with most emphasis being placed on the sorrow at losing his friend, George Dobson, rather than on his own misfortune. He told of his transfer to the hospital in East London and of the nameless nurse, smiling reflectively as he recalled his conversations with her. "Then they sent me back here." He gripped hold of Paul's arm. "But tell me what's been happening since you got back. What of Matt?"

Conscious of the anxious looks he was getting from the nurse Paul quickly gave an account of his stay at Millwood House, but for John's benefit leaving out some of the more contentious issues. Most of the talk was of Matthew's forthcoming marriage.

"Marriage!" exclaimed John, louder than he intended, drawing more attention from the nurse as well as some of the other patients.

"Yes, I think you met her. Grace Haveringham, Rufus Haveringham's niece."

John cast his mind back. "The girl on the horse! But she's beautiful."

"Yes, she is," Paul replied gravely. "And soon to be rich too." He gave a dismissive shake of his head before fixing his eyes on John. "But what of this girl of yours? You wrote so affectionately of her in your letters. What was her name … Katherine?"

"Katerine," he corrected wistfully. "Such a beautiful, sweet, innocent girl."

"You talk about her as though she is dead."

"She might as well be for all the good I can be to her now." As he thought of her, his eyes misted over. "I had this dream that we would finish the war in a few months and the two of us could be together. I promised to return to her when the war was over, and she promised to wait."

"Perhaps they'll send you back when you're fit enough," said Paul, trying not to sound patronising while preferring that his brother remained safe at home.

John gave a cynical laugh, throwing back the covers to expose his heavily strapped leg. "Fit enough! Does it look like I'll ever be fit enough? I'll be lucky if I can walk again without the aid of a crutch."

Paul stared miserably at the leg. "Oh, John, I'm so sorry. You never said how bad it was, I had no idea."

"And I never intended that you should. I thought the doctors over there were all wrong, that I'd be walking by the time I got back here. The bone's too badly damaged, it will never heal properly. The best I can hope for is to be a cripple all my life. Do you think I would want Katerine to see me like that?" He burst into tears. "Do you think she would want me like that?"

Paul placed a comforting arm around his brother. "If she cares half as much about you as you seem to care for her then she will want you however you are."

The nurse appeared at the end of the bed. "I'm sorry Mr Pearson, but you really must go. The doctor is due for his rounds soon, and if he …"

Paul turned and nodded his understanding. "I have to go now, John, but I'll be back next week and we'll have a serious talk about your future. I won't have you giving up before the fight has even started."

After a final embrace Paul left, stopping at the end of the ward to look back and wave.

"Saturday afternoon, three o'clock," said the nurse. "That's the official visiting time."

"Thank you, I'll remember that." He shot a parting glance at his brother. "Take good care of him, nurse."

On the way back to Walworth, Paul was struck by the sudden realisation that providence, and not the war, had delayed his return to South Africa. The opportunity he had been given to see John far outweighed all other considerations, even Frank Trevithick. It was a controversial conclusion, but Frank's fate had probably already been decided and his being there would make little difference. Of course, he would return, but for the time being John was his priority.

When he arrived back at the house he wrote immediately to Grace, thanking her for the letters and giving her details of his meeting with John, leaving it up to her whether or not she passed the news on to Matthew.

There was now more purpose to Paul's life. In the weeks that followed it was John's recuperation that occupied his thoughts and not the self-pity of previous few months. Even the hours spent at the grain merchants passed more quickly.

Gilbert noticed, with satisfaction, the marked change in his friend's spirits, so when the letter arrived from Grace and the troubled countenance returned he felt obliged to ask why.

"Is everything all right, old chap. Not bad news, I hope?"

Paul paced the floor agitatedly, waving the letter in the air. "It's this, from Grace, I don't know what to do about it."

"Anything I can help with?"

Paul sighed and slumped heavily into the chair. "She's asking me … no, she's begging me to go to the wedding. And she wants me to take John too, if he's up to it."

Gilbert eyed him curiously. "Is there something you've been keeping from me? I know you and your brother don't get on, and from what you've told me I can quite understand that, but he is still your brother, and I think you owe it to the memory of your parents to be there, because who else does he have. And what about your younger brother, does he not have the right to decide?"

Gilbert had a way of making everything appear simple. "I suppose so," admitted Paul reluctantly. "But there's so much hostility between us, and with John too. I wouldn't want that to spoil the day for Grace, or her uncle."

"And is that the only reason, old chap?"

"What do you mean?"

Gilbert gave him one of his smug grins. "I don't suppose jealousy has anything to do with it?" He flicked his eyes at the letter in Paul's hand. "I've seen the effect those have on you my dear fellow."

Paul lowered his head and turned away. "She's a sweet girl, Gilbert, and I'm afraid Matt is just using her for his own ends. She deserves better and I find it hard watching her throw her life away like that."

"All the more reason for you to go I should think. If you don't, she'll think you care nothing for her, that you can't be bothered, and I know you Paul Pearson, you'll only regret it afterwards."

Gilbert made good sense. He always did. "I'm being selfish, aren't I? The only person I've been thinking about is me. You're right, I should go. And if John is able to come with me it may be the last time we are all together."

***

It was three weeks after his first trip to the hospital that Paul arrived for his weekly visit, with more on his mind than his young brother's progress. There had been some improvement in John's mobility, but not as much as Paul would have hoped for, as he was only able to take a few steps with the aid of two crutches, and apart from the obvious pain there were increasing signs of bitterness and resignation.

Paul took the stairs two at a time and arrived on the landing outside the ward breathless and anxious. The nurse who had granted him the favour on his first visit was sitting at her desk just inside the door. He could see John lying on his bed so he tapped on the window to catch the nurse's attention. She turned and smiled as Paul beckoned her outside.

"It's past three o'clock, Mr Pearson, why don't you just go in?" she asked with a puzzled expression on her freckled face. "Your brother needs something to cheer him up."

"Why, what's the matter with him?" he asked, concerned.

She shook her head. "Nothing more than with most of the others in here. Some men cope well with their injuries, many don't."

"Do you think a change of scenery will help him?" he asked hopefully. "Do you think he would be allowed out of here for a few days?"

Again, she shook her head, more purposefully this time. "That's not for me to say, you would have to speak to his doctor, Major Kemp." She pointed down the corridor. "He's here now, if you want to see him, third door on the right."

Paul thanked her and she returned to the ward as he was struck by a moment of indecision. If there was a chance that John would be allowed out then it was right that he be given the choice of attending the wedding or not, but if the doctor was firm in his refusal, then there would be no point in mentioning the invitation.

His tentative rap on the door was immediately answered.

"Come," snapped the authoritative voice from inside the office.

The major was a heavily bearded man who Paul thought looked a lot older than his actual years. He was sat at a desk busily writing as Paul entered.

"What is it?" he asked without looking up.

"I'm sorry to interrupt you, doctor," Paul said nervously.

The doctor looked up, his deep set eyes expressing surprise at the sight of a civilian. "What can I do for you Mr …?"

"Pearson, major, Paul Pearson. My brother is Corporal Pearson, he's in the ward just down the hall."

"Quite." he said abruptly. "But I don't have time to discuss my patients with members of their family. I'm sure the duty nurse can tell you all you need to know."

"I understand, but I've already spoken to the nurse and she referred me to you. If you could just give me a minute?"

The doctor huffed and reached for a sheaf of papers hanging from the wall behind him. "Pearson you say?" The thumbed through the papers. "What is it you want to know?"

"He seems to think that he's going to be crippled for the rest of his life. Is that right, or is there a chance he'll make a full recovery?" He looked hard at the doctor.

The major referred to his notes, sucked his teeth and slowly shook his head. "There was too much damage done to the bone. We repaired it as best we could, but it's always going to be deformed, shorter than the other leg. The best your brother can hope for, I'm afraid, is a pronounced limp. Does that answer your question?"

"Yes, but I do have another. How long will it be before he can be discharged?"

The doctor tapped his medical notes with his fingers. "That depends as much on his state of mind as his physical condition. A permanent disability is a difficult thing to come to terms with, especially for someone as young as your brother. He needs to be able to cope with both before he leaves."

Paul took a deep breath. "The only reason I asked, doctor, is because our other brother is getting married in a few weeks, up in Northampton. Is there any possibility he would be able to leave for a few days to come with me?"

The major considered the question for some time before replying. "Physically I see no reason why he shouldn't, it would do his leg no damage, in fact the enforced exercise is exactly what he needs. But don't expect him to be enthusiastic about it, there's a certain stigma attached to infirmity, he probably feels some sense of shame." Behind the beard the doctor smiled. "If you can persuade him to go it can only do him good."

As he shook the doctor's hand Paul thanked him profusely. It only remained to convince his brother, and as he approached the bed his feeling of elation was tempered by a lingering doubt.

John was awake, sitting up on the bed, his questioning eyes following Paul's progress through the ward.

"Where have you been? I saw you talking to the nurse." There was resentment in his voice.

Paul tapped the side of his nose. "I've been talking with your doctor, Major Kemp."

"Why? Been checking up on me, have you? Think I've been swinging the lead?" he asked bitterly.

"Not checking up on you, John, I know how serious your injury is." He sat on the edge of the bed. "I wanted to ask him when he thought you would be ready to leave here. He says that physically you're ready to leave at any time."

"And where would I go? I'll tell you, straight in front of the medical board to be told the army has no further use for me."

"I can't answer for the medical board, John, we didn't discuss that. I only know what the doctor told me. He thinks it would be good for you, and your leg, to get out of here for a few days." He waited for a positive response but got none. "How do you feel about that?"

"Get out of here! And what would be the point of that?" he said, dejectedly staring down at the bed. "I've nowhere to go and I can get all the exercise I need walking up and down the ward. At least in here no one stares at me."

"And you think everyone outside is going to stare at you, like you're the only one who's disabled," snapped Paul angrily before relenting. "Look, John, I know how much the army meant to you, and I can guess at how angry you must feel, but it's no good hiding away feeling sorry for yourself. Sooner or later, you'll have to leave here and get on with your life."

"So, what do you expect me to do, act like nothing's changed?"

"No, but you can start thinking about your future."

John thumped the mattress with his fist. "Future! What future?" He stared bleakly up at the ceiling. "I've got nothing left, Paul. Matthew's taken most of my money, I'll be pensioned out of the army and I've lost the only girl I'll ever love." He looked his brother in the face. "Tell me, where's the future in all that?"

Paul wanted to tell him he was wrong, that his life would be so much better once he left the hospital, but he was in no position of offer any such guarantee.

"Perhaps I shouldn't have come. I'm supposed to cheer you up, but all I've managed to do is to make you feel worse." He got up from the bed. "It might be better if I leave."

John reached out and caught his arm. "No, Paul, please wait. I'm sorry, don't go yet." He forced a smile and patted the bed. "Please, sit down. The only thing I have to look forward to is your visits, and they're short enough as it is."

Relieved, Paul sat back down. "Then perhaps you need something more to look forward to." He paused to compose himself. "I had a particular reason for seeing the doctor when I came today, before I saw you."

John gave him a quizzical look. "Not just checking up on me then?"

"We've received an invitation," he began hesitantly "well, a demand really, from Grace Haveringham. She wants us at the wedding."

"And you think we should go, after what Matt's done?"

Paul thought carefully, there were many things John was still unaware of. "I think it's our duty to go. Matthew has no family other than us. If our mother was alive, we would have no choice but to go, but I didn't want to make any decision until I had spoken to you."

John thoughtfully massaged his damaged leg. "It's a chance to make things right, I suppose, for the three of us to be together again. But I'm not sure I'll be allowed. I'll need to get permission and I don't know …"

"Why do you think I went to see your major," interrupted Paul with a mischievous grin. "He thinks it will be good for you, an important step on your road to recovery, and your rehabilitation to the outside world."

John almost choked on the emotional laugh that caught in his throat. "That sounds like an order, I shall have to go."

Chapter Twenty-Three

Gilbert Bullivant was turning out to be an even better friend than Paul could ever have imagined. The favours he commanded extended far beyond the boundaries of cheap accommodation and sources of employment to the far-flung realms of comfortable carriages suitable for the transportation of invalids from the hospital at Woolwich to St Pancras Station.

"The very least I could do, old chap," he said, fending off the gratitude heaped upon him.

"But you've done so much for me already, Gilbert, and I don't know how I'll ever be able to repay you. Everything I own is in that mine, and if I can't get back to it I'll have nothing."

"Nothing!" retorted Gilbert angrily, his moustache twitching. "Only a man without friends or family can truly say he has nothing, and you have a small, but significant, amount of both." He took Paul by the arm and led him to the door. "Now, go to your wedding, or be damned."

Thanks to Gilbert's good connections and generosity the journey to the station was as comfortable as it could possibly have been for John. Officially still a soldier and entitled to wear the uniform he did so with immense pride. With the train only half full and the sympathetic response of the other passengers he was able to sit in the compartment with his leg supported along the length of the seat, getting up from time to time to relieve the stiffness the doctor had warned him to avoid.

At Northampton they checked into the Railway Hotel, the landlord immediately recognising Paul. "A message arrived for you this morning, sir," he said, handing him an envelope.

John eyed it suspiciously as they sat in the bar waiting for their room to be prepared. "Who knows we are here?"

"Only Grace, and possibly her uncle," replied Paul as he broke the seal. He read the letter while the landlord brought them each a glass of brandy. "It looks like there's been a change of plan. I had thought to go straight to the church tomorrow, but Grace wants us to collect Matthew from the farm. She's arranged a carriage for us."

"Taking a bit of a chance, isn't she," retorted John with a wry smile. "I thought she might be afraid that we would do something nasty to him before he gets to the church."

Paul smiled back. It was good to see that some of his brother's humour had returned. "I think she's still hoping it will be a chance for reconciliation, not fighting. I suppose we ought to be on our best behaviour, if only for her sake."

John winced as he adjusted the position of his leg. "That's fine with me, but I've been through too much to be scared of him anymore. And I certainly won't let him have the better of me."

Paul looked across the table at his young brother and saw the face of a resolute man staring back at him.

The small church was bedecked with garlands of spring flowers, daffodils, bluebells and tulips. Haveringham had wanted more exotic blooms sent up from London, but Grace had insisted that the ceremony was not overwhelmed by ostentation and that her uncle could have his way with the evening arrangements when he would be free to impress his guests. The service was hers and Matthew's and should reflect their own simpler upbringing.

During the morning her mood swung wildly between ecstatic excitement and blind panic. She worried about everything. Was her hair perfect? How did her dress look? Were all the carriages properly organised? Was someone attending to her uncle? Had all the arrangements been made for the evening? Her worries were endless. But the one worry that occupied her most she mentioned to no one. How would it be between Matthew and his two brothers, all together again for the first time in three years?

At the expedience of tradition, reinforced by Haveringham's insistence, Matthew had been forced to spend the night alone at Hibberd's Farm. He had grown too accustomed to the cosseted luxury of Millwood House and now viewed his former home with unrestrained contempt. In a few hours his life was to change forever, and that thought had kept him awake for much of the night. Only one more obstacle remained to hamper his climb up the ladder of blind ambition, and nature would take care of that soon enough.

Unaware that the carriage Grace had arranged to take him to the church would also be occupied by his two brothers, he got himself ready, with the smug satisfaction that all his plans were proceeding exactly as he imagined. All that was expected of him was to be a doting husband to a beautiful young woman who clearly loved him. He could manage that.

It was a bright spring morning with a clear blue sky and only a stiff northeast breeze prevented it being perfect for the wedding. As the carriage drew away from the Station Hotel Paul warned the driver to avoid as far as possible any ruts and bumps, and to go no faster than was necessary to complete the journey on time. John stoically assured him that he could endure a little discomfort to see his brother wed, and it would be worth it to see him trussed up for the occasion.

When they arrived at the farm the driver climbed down to call for Matthew, and Paul asked him not to mention his other two passengers. He wanted to surprise his brother.

"Aren't you more afraid that he wouldn't come out if he knew we were waiting for him?" asked John, massaging his leg. "Will you be with him at the altar?"

Paul shrugged his shoulders. "I think Grace hoped I would be, but it's up to Matthew. I could stand it if he can."

As the driver waited by the door to the house both Paul and John strained for a first glimpse of their brother, anxious to savour not only his sartorial splendour but also his initial reaction to their presence.

When Matthew finally emerged from the house, scrubbed clean and wearing a new black suit made for the occasion, John's first impulse was to laugh. "He's put on a bit of weight since I last saw him," he commented with a broad grin. "Something about his new life must suit him."

Paul silenced him with a stern look. "Best not upset him any more than he's going to be."

Matthew appeared strained and uncomfortable, constantly tugging at the stiff collar of his shirt as he walked towards the carriage. Beneath his well combed blond hair his face was ruddy and vexed, not the pleasantly nervous countenance expected of a groom on his wedding day. If there was any surge of fresh emotion when he first set eyes on his brothers nothing showed in his face, although there was just a small hesitation in his step.

While the carriage door was held open for him Matthew stepped up inside without a word of greeting and only a cursory glance at John's stiff leg laying along the seat. He sat down opposite, next to Paul.

"Not surprised to see us then, Matt?" It was John who felt the need to speak.

As the carriage drew away Matthew's gaze was not at his brothers but towards some unknown point in the distance.

"You're not here for me. I know you've been writing to Grace, and I might have known she'd persuade you to come."

"Is it so strange to you that we should want to be at our brother's wedding," said Paul. "You're right, Grace did ask that we come, but for your sake, not hers."

"And I suppose for my sake you'll do your best to ruin my day." He turned his bitterness on John. "I bet you can't wait to tell everyone that I stole your money."

John felt his anger rise, made worse when the carriage wheel hit a rut, sending a sharp pain shooting through his leg. "Isn't that what you did, or were you just investing it for me?" He rubbed his leg. "If you had just been honest enough to ask me, Matt, I would have given it to you. You didn't need to cheat."

"You'll get it back, all of it, and with more interest than you'd get from the bank." His first vague sign of contrition showed in his face as he inclined his head towards John's leg. "Looks like you got yourself wounded."

"He's going to be crippled, Matt," cut in Paul with a well-intentioned intervention that sounded unduly callous. "He's going to need all his money now that his soldiering days are over."

"I told you, he'll get it back," snapped Matthew.

"And I can speak for myself," retorted John with a sharp look at the other two. "I think we should stop all this squabbling and remember the occasion. This is Matthew's day and we should respect it." He lifted a crutch and jabbed it at Matthew. "But that doesn't mean I've forgotten what you've done, and I'll expect you to keep your word."

Paul raised his eyebrows. "Well spoken, little brother, looks like the army has taught you diplomacy as well as fighting."

"And isn't there something that you need to say to Matt as well?" asked John, raising his left hand and extending the third finger.

Paul nodded and glanced tentatively at Matthew. "I take it you've no groomsman, no one you could trust to hold the ring?"

The remark brought a chuckle from John, and even Matthew found it hard to ignore the veiled sarcasm.

"I had to manage well enough on my own when the two of you left, and have done ever since."

"That may be so, but I can imagine how lonely it will be waiting at the altar on your own. I won't force you, but if you want some company, I would be pleased to provide it."

"Pleased, but not honoured. I suppose that's too much to expect," grunted Matthew, gazing down at the floor of the carriage.

"We've still got a long way to go, Matt, but it would be a start."

With no pretence at gratitude Matthew nodded. He reached into his jacket pocket and pulled out a small box which he handed to Paul.

"I'll get her a better one when I'm a man of substance. Shouldn't be too long now, old Haveringham isn't getting any better."

Both Paul and John could feel their hackles rising at Matthew's cold sentiment, although they said nothing. It seemed that any hoped for improvement in his nature was not to be, but they were too close to the church to provoke further argument. The narrow path leading up to the church from the lych gate was lined with estate workers, their wives and children. Much to Matthew's chagrin Haveringham had ordered that they be given time off to see the bride arrive and leave the church, although few would raise a cheer at the groom's arrival.

Inside the church the pews on the bride's side were already full with close friends, and with Matthew conspicuously lacking in these, the seats of his side were occupied by some school friends of Grace.

The Reverend Martin stood outside the church door, nodding and smiling in his overtly obsequious manner at all the guests as they arrived, reserving his most ingratiating posturing for those whose influence could offer him a more propitious living in the future. Rufus Haveringham was a man of enormous influence, but he was also very sick, which had placed the reverend in something of a dilemma. He had never taken to Matthew and seriously doubted that he could rely on his patronage when the time came.

He held out a limp hand as Matthew walked self-consciously up the path followed by his two brothers.

"Mr Pearson, what a wonderful day for a wedding," he gushed, his head bent lower than was necessary. He peered around Matthew at the two men standing behind him. "And these will be your brothers. Will one of them be standing with you today?"

Matthew shuffled awkwardly. He would have preferred to say no, but tradition and Grace's unspoken wishes had persuaded him otherwise, and he jerked his head at Paul.

"He will."

Heads turned, following the three brothers as they walked slowly down the aisle, John's crutches echoing harshly above the muted conversations.

"They're all talking about me," muttered Matthew, fidgeting nervously as the three took their place in the front row of pews. "I know what they're all thinking, but just wait until I'm master, they'll have plenty to talk about then."

"Does it matter what they think, or say. The only thing that matters is that you and Grace are marrying for the right reasons." Paul looked hard at his brother. "You are, aren't you Matt?"

"What do you think, of course I am. Anyway, they can say what they like, they'll be coming cap in hand to me sooner or later."

Paul and John exchanged cautious glances, it wasn't quite the reassurance they were looking for, but it was too late now. A ripple of excited noise ran through the congregation and all heads turned to the back of the church. To an accompaniment of sighs, gasps and clapping, Grace appeared in the doorway, encased in a sphere of coloured light as the sun pierced the circular stained glass window above the alter. She looked even more beautiful and virginal than she had done before, swathed in white silk and lace, her face covered by a fine veil weighted down with a row of diamond beads. At her side, beaming as proudly as was possible, stood Rufus Haveringham, the strain of the occasion bravely hidden behind a façade of pure joy.

As the small organ ground out its first stentorian notes the pair began the slow walk down the aisle followed by two more school friends who acted as her attendants. Matthew leapt to his feet, unable to resist the temptation to watch her progress, and for anyone with their eyes not fixed on the bride they may have noticed a thin smile of success on his lips.

It seemed to take an eternity for Grace and her uncle to finally stand before the altar, and all the while Matthew kept her in his gaze, giving Paul hope that, perhaps, there was still room for love in his brother's heart.

While Grace appeared outwardly calm and serene, Haveringham was puffing and sweating profusely. In deference to his condition Grace had asked that Reverend Martin kept the service as brief as possible. As an added precaution Jenkins and Doctor Colley had slipped unnoticed into the back of the church.

The service proceeded with equal amounts of speed and dignity as Grace kept one eye anxiously on her uncle who sat on a chair just a short distance behind her. While she spoke her words with concise confidence, Matthew had to be prompted on a number of occasions as he stumbled over his vows. He was visibly relieved when it was finally over. As he kissed his new wife tenderly on the cheek Grace mouthed a silent 'thank you' at Paul.

As the couple turned to begin the slow procession back through the church a man and woman moved away from the dim corner where they had been standing and quickly slipped out of a side door. For one of them it had been an emotionally charged experience, and the other a chance to wish the bride all the luck in the world.

Outside the church the newly-weds stepped into the bright sunshine to a round of excited clapping and cheering, given more impetus, perhaps, by the incentive of a few shillings. While most knew little of Grace, except that she was a Haveringham, their affection for the groom was sadly lacking.

The pair walked slowly down the narrow path, Grace acknowledging with a wave and warm smile the best wishes shouted from the crowd, while Matthew stared straight ahead, wanting no part of the approbation he saw as a debt they would expect to be repaid. He wanted nothing from them other than the hard work they were paid to do, and they should expect nothing of him.

The carriage to take them back to Millwood House had been decorated with white satin bows and the horses had white rosettes attached to their bridles. As Grace gave a final wave to the crowd before climbing aboard a woman pushed her way through the throng and stood in her way. Her attention seemed to be focussed more on Matthew as she peered at him through narrow, yellowed eyes.

"What do you want?" gasped Grace, taken aback by the woman's sudden and aggressive appearance. She took a tighter grip on Matthew's arm. "Who are you?"

"Ask yer new 'usband, dearie," she sneered, her cracked lips curling at the corners. "And I'm come t'give yer both a little present. For you, dearie, I wish yer luck, and for 'im …" She hawked and spat forcibly into Matthew's face before being dragged away by a few of the estate workers.

Hoping the incident had gone unnoticed by those following on behind Matthew hurried Grace into the carriage as he wiped his face on the sleeve of his jacket. But Paul, walking some yards behind with John and Rufus Haveringham, had seen the woman and recognised her from the two previous times she had crossed his path. John too had seen, but was prevented from commenting by a severe look from his older brother.

"Who was that?" demanded Grace as she rearranged her dress in the carriage to prevent Matthew sitting on its flowing train.

"A mad woman, who do you think," he snapped, urging the driver to be on his way.

"But she seemed to know you," persisted Grace. "Are you sure you don't know her?"

"I've already told you I don't. She's probably the wife of a worker I had to dismiss. How do I know."

He made it clear that the subject was closed and they completed the journey back to the house in moody silence. For Grace the happy memories of a perfect beginning to the day had been wiped away in that incident, and as she brooded on it, she wondered how much more of Matthew's past remained lurking in the shadows. She resented the secrets kept from her by someone supposed to be her friend and was now her family.

When they arrived back at the house, she tried to drive those concerns to the back of her mind as she awaited the return of her uncle and the other guests. As Paul helped the old man from the carriage, she fussed around him until he sent her away with a firm rebuke.

"This is your wedding day, girl, and you've more important things to attend to than nagging me into an early grave. You've a husband to nag now, and guests to take care of, so go and do one or the other."

The ballroom had been laid out for the wedding breakfast and Grace took her place at the top table with a sullen looking Matthew at her side. With her uncle on her other side, they were joined by Paul, John and the two friends who had acted as her attendants.

By necessity Haveringham's address was reduced to a sincere vote of thanks to those who had attended, a summary of his niece's many and obvious attributes and his hope for a long, prosperous and happy marriage.

Breaking with tradition Grace insisted on replying, thanking her uncle for his selfless generosity and expressing the hope for his early return to full health. She also made a strong point of thanking Matthew's two brothers for their welcome attendance. When the whole room stood and applauded her efforts Matthew felt obliged to do the same. His speech too was brief, delivered with the expected reluctance and commenting on the difference in the social standing between himself and his bride, with the mooted observation that it was a sign of the times, a social advance in a new century. It brought a desultory ripple of appreciation from those of the guests who firmly believed that social boundaries were sacrosanct. It was now up to Paul and his impromptu speech to bring back a smile to the faces that had been left smarting from the predictions of the groom. While Paul had to admit to knowing little of the bride, he was able to give a long and detailed account of his brother's journey through life since his arrival in the world. Of course, he only mentioned that which was likely to cause maximum embarrassment to his brother, much to the delight of the guests who enjoyed watching the young man squirm. But most of all it delighted Grace who feigned sympathy for her new husband throughout his ordeal.

When the meal was over the room was cleared in preparation for an evening of music and dancing, and an opportunity for the guests to jostle with each other for the distinction of being the first of offer the couple a place at their dinner table.

While her uncle went to rest Grace was saddled with the dual duties of bride and host, which kept her fully occupied for long after the meal had finished as she conferred constantly with the imperturbable Jenkins over the arrangements for the evening. In the meantime, Matthew was happy to wallow in his new found status, readily discussing modern dairy practices and the relative merits of mechanised farming with those now more ready to listen.

When the group of musicians struck up for the first dance Paul and John were more than appreciative of the further embarrassment to their brother as he took to the floor for a Viennese Waltz, specially selected by Grace. Clearly, he had been given a few fundamental instructions, but his stiff, jerky movements did little to compliment the graceful turns and swirling of his wife.

"Isn't that a treat to watch," laughed John, grateful that he had the perfect excuse for not making a similar spectacle of himself.

The two school friends of Grace had looked expectantly at Paul for a partner, but he shook his head guiltily. "I'm sorry, but I'm no better than my brother, and as I'm not obliged to dance it would be a favour to you that I didn't try."

It was no great disappointment for them as they were soon whisked away by other young rakes anxious to make themselves better acquainted.

It was only after an hour and several dances that Grace found herself free to join the two brothers. "I'm so pleased you were both able to come," she said breathlessly, taking them by the hand. "I've been longing to talk to you all day."

She gave John a long compassionate look. "I was so sorry to hear about your wound, it must have been dreadful."

John gave a resigned shrug. "There's plenty worse off than me."

"And what about you, Grace," cut in Paul, still holding on to her hand, "are you truly happy now that you are finally married?"

She gazed fondly around the room until her eyes settled on Matthew talking earnestly with a group of local landowners who previously would not have given him the time of day.

"Look at him," she said wistfully. "This is what he was born to, and this is what makes him happy."

"But it's not his happiness that concerns me, it's yours," Paul said, a little tetchy at her response. "He's got everything he wants now, but what of you? How much of him will be yours?"

"Don't judge him too harshly, Paul." Her green eyes pleaded for his understanding. "He's going to need some time to get used to all this, just as I did when I came here, and I know, despite everything you think, he loves me."

"Perhaps we should ask him" said John, inclining his head to one side. "It looks like he's finally got time for us."

Matthew sauntered across the ballroom floor, nodding a curt acknowledgement to those offering their belated congratulations.

"Suddenly remembered you have a wife now?" mocked John. "You can't be married to two women you know."

"What do you mean by that?" snapped Matthew tartly.

"I think what he means is that there's more to your life now than just farming," explained Paul. "Spare some time for Grace, and some love as well, if you can manage it."

"Paul, please!" exclaimed Grace, red faced. "Matthew knows full well where his duties lie, don't you, dear?"

Whether it was for his brothers' benefit or not, Matthew put an arm around his wife's slim waist and drew her close, kissing her passionately on the lips.

"I'm enough of a man to give Grace all the love she needs, and still have time to carry out all my other duties." He smirked before kissing her again.

"Matthew, you don't need to prove anything to me," she said, blushing coyly and turning away.

"Well, he still needs to prove it to me," responded Paul obdurately.

"You just can't get over your jealousy, can you? I've got everything I want and you two have nothing, and it galls."

"Matthew, enough, that's unkind. I'm sure Paul was only jesting with you." She was growing increasingly irritated by the way the conversation was going. "Now, please, for my sake, shake hands with your brothers."

There was a tense moment before Matthew offered his hand. "I suppose I can afford to be generous to my poor relatives," he said smugly.

Paul and John took his hand, although there was no warmth or sincerity in the gesture.

"I think we should be getting back to Northampton," said Paul with a quick glance at John. "We have an early train to catch in the morning, and I don't want to tire John."

"Do you really have to go so soon? I was hoping that you would stay the night at least. There is so much we have to talk about."

"If they have to go then we shouldn't delay them," said Matthew bluntly. "Now that they've seen how happy we are."

Grace could see that Paul's mind was made up. "Please come and visit us as soon as you are able," she said to them imploringly. "And please, write."

As he shook hands with the two brothers, Haveringham looked tired and drawn, the day had taken its toll. "So pleased you were able to come," he said affectionately. "I know it meant a lot to Grace. And Matthew too no doubt. If there is anything I can do for either of you please don't hesitate to ask."

Paul thanked him for his generous offer and wished him a speedy recovery.

"I hope he still has enough wit to keep a close eye on Matthew," he said as he helped John up into the carriage that had been provided for them.

"You don't think Matthew can ever change, do you?" asked John wryly as he made himself comfortable. "And just how early is this train in the morning?"

"I don't think he's capable of change. And, as for the train, it's early enough."

Chapter Twenty-Four

"Not quite the wedding I had in mind for you, my dear," gasped Rufus Haveringham breathlessly. Grace and Doctor Colley had helped him up the stairs, and now that the doctor had left, Grace was fussing with his pillows. "You deserved so much better."

Soon after Paul and John had left, she had insisted that her uncle should retire, an opinion strongly reinforced by the doctor. She was worried by how tired he seemed to be, the strains of the day etched deep into his sallow face.

He gave his chest a feeble thump with his fist. "This damned heart of mine has ruined what should have been the most memorable day of your life," he whispered angrily.

"The day was perfect, uncle," she assured him with a gentle kiss on the forehead. "All that could have made it better would have been a dance with you. Now, get some sleep while I go and see to our guests."

By the time she returned to the ballroom some of the guests were making their excuses to leave, feeling no obligation to remain after the departure of their host. There was no sign of Matthew to join with her in offering their thanks, so Grace sent Jenkins to look for him.

"He has so little experience of such occasions, as do I," she told the guests coyly as they made little effort to hide their impatience behind understanding smiles. "But we will learn in time, and hope to be the perfect hosts in the future."

When Matthew finally appeared, he did little to convince her that her hopes would be speedily realised. He made only the smallest pretence at having enjoyed their company, and it was only Grace's urgings that forced him to thank them for their gifts.

"Thank God that's over," he said when he had seen the last of the guests out of the door, and listened with raised eyes and a heavy sigh as the rattle of carriage wheels grew fainter on the gravel drive.

"You could have made an effort to be a bit more agreeable," retorted Grace with tired resignation. "Those are my uncle's dearest friends, and our neighbours. They'll be a part of our lives even more now."

"Pompous oafs, the lot of them," he scoffed with a dismissive wave of his hand. "They can be your friends if you like, but they'll never be mine." He walked back into the ballroom and slumped down at one of the tables, ordering a passing footman to bring him some champagne. "And they know nothing of farming," he shouted as Grace hovered uncertainly in the doorway. He held up his glass to her. "Aren't you going to join me, after all this is supposed to be our wedding day?"

She shook her head. "It's been a long day and I think I should like to retire." A burning redness rose up in her cheeks, and inside the lace gloves her hand felt clammy. "Will you be coming up?"

He tapped his glass against the neck of the bottle, giving her a wry grin. "And let this go to waste! You go and see to yourself, I'll be up soon enough."

Grace closed the bedroom door behind her and stood there leaning against it, staring bleakly around the room. It had been her room since first arriving at Millwood House and she had enjoyed its opulent comfort that contrasted so dramatically with the monastic starkness of the boarding school. Over the preceding months her contentment had been heightened by the prospect of sharing its comforts with a husband, and as she had lain alone in her bed, she had often imagined him sleeping peacefully by her side, wrapped in his warm embrace. She had thought also of the passion that for so long had been held in check, only to be unleashed on her wedding night.

Now that night had arrived and she felt none of the sensations she anticipated, only a numb foreboding. There would be no nervous giggling as her trembling fingers fumbled with the buttons of her dress, and no tender words of reassurance from a new husband anxious to calm her fears. She had no way of knowing how a wedding night was supposed to be, but she knew enough to be certain that the bride should be neither alone nor frightened.

She felt angry and cheated as she ran across the room and threw herself onto the bed, fighting back the tears that no bride should ever have to shed. "Damn you, Matthew, damn you," she cursed through trembling lips as she pounded at the pillows.

She was still lying there some time later, overtaken by fatigue and sadness, when the bedroom door quietly opened and Matthew stood silhouetted in the doorway. The room was in darkness, but from the light on the landing he could see her still lying face down on the bed, enveloped in the voluminous folds of her wedding dress.

Unsteadily he approached the bed and knelt down beside her, and as his eyes became accustomed to the dark, he was able to take in her sleeping form and wondered why he had been so reluctant to take what was now his inalienable right. He reached out and ran his fingers through her long hair, feeling the bare skin on the back of her neck. She let out a little murmur and her head twitched at his touch, and when he ran his hand across her bare shoulder, she rolled over to face him.

A slender shaft of moonlight broke through a gap in the drapes that allowed her to make out his face, and as he looked down into hers, she was convinced of the tenderness and remorse in his eyes.

"Matthew," she whispered, smiling up at him. Was she about to experience the moment she had dreamed about for so long?

He slid his hand beneath her head and she raised it up to meet him, their lips locking together in a long, passionate kiss. She became aware that her whole body was trembling and her insides churned as his other hand urgently explored those parts of her body so far denied him.

With his appetite whetted by her kisses and his inhibitions stunted through drink he groped clumsily and frantically at the fastenings of her dress, tearing at the delicate material when it refused its access to her body. As his efforts became coarse and urgent she gently pushed him away.

"No, Matthew, not like this," she said hoarsely, her throat dry. "Let me get undressed."

Before he could protest, she had rolled out from beneath him and off the bed, disappearing from his view behind a lacquered screen that had been placed in the room that morning for just this very purpose. Although in her romantic imaginings Matthew had slowly and seductively undressed her, she knew that in reality when the time came, modesty and shyness would prevail and the screen would be her protection from both.

The provocative rustling of material as she undressed served only to inspire Matthew to tear off his own clothes, and when he was completely naked, he slid beneath the cold, silk sheets.

When Grace emerged from behind the screen, she was wearing a long, flowing white satin nightdress that dipped at the front to reveal the deep cleft between her high, firm breasts. The filmy fabric clung tenaciously to every curved of her slim body, and as she stepped into the shaft of moonlight, she looked every bit the statue of a Greek goddess.

She stood still next to the bed, her chest heaving, her breathing erratic. She could never have imagined this moment would have invoked such a reaction; she was supposed to feel excitement, nervousness even, but not fear. Matthew threw back the covers on her side of the bed and in doing so exposed his body. In the dim light she could see the smile on his face. Quickly sliding in next to him she pulled the covers over them and lay on her back, taut and trembling. Immediately his hands were upon her, exploring her body through the thin, sheer fabric of her nightdress. Soon he would be upon her, expecting her to be ready. But she wasn't, neither in mind nor body. She needed to be coaxed slowly and tenderly towards that final submission, as she had been so many times before, in her dreams.

He pressed against her and she could feel is hot breath on her face and the hardness of his manhood in her side.

"Please, Matthew, not yet," she pleaded, tugging away the hand that was forcing its way into the valley between her tightly clamped thighs. "I'm not ready yet, please be patient."

He responded by sliding the nightdress from her shoulders, covering the bare skin with urgent kisses behind the retreating material. She allowed him to uncover her breasts and tensed as he cupped them roughly in his hands, sucking hard on the erect nipples. Then, to her horror he shifted his weight on top of her, his leg between hers, trying to force them apart.

Even though there had been no lessening of her panic her will was beginning to break and she allowed him access to that secret place. She parted her legs just a little and he manoeuvred himself into position, pulling up the bottom of her nightdress. He lowered himself down onto her and she let out a little cry that begged him to be gentle as he probed, seeking entry. No one had told her what she should expect, only that it was her duty as a wife, and now that the time had come to fulfil that duty she faced it with unrestrained trepidation, not expectation.

With none of the tenderness or affection of her dreams he thrust against her womanhood, but instead of being warm and receptive it was dry and resistant. The harder he tried the more tense she grew, and with it came the pain.

"Please, Matthew, stop, it hurts." She tried closing her legs and pushed against his shoulders to force him off, but he was too heavy and too insistent as the tip of his manhood probed ever harder to plunder her virginity. "For pity's sake, stop," she sobbed, her fists now hammering at his body while she writhed beneath him to get free of the pain. "I don't want this anymore, please stop."

"You're my wife, damn you," he breathed, unrelenting in his efforts. "If you really loved me, you would want this."

"I do love you, Matthew, you know I do," she cried, "but it hurts so much and I'm so frightened. Please stop now."

With his face contorted with anger and frustration he threw himself off her and lay on his back breathing heavily. Grace covered her naked body, shamed by her own failure, yet distressed by her husband's lack of understanding and affection. She had no idea that giving herself to him would have been such a painful experience, there had been no one to warn her and now she felt cheated, robbed of her dream. She reached out to Matthew, wanting him to take her in his arms and tell her everything would be all right, and assure her that, when they were both ready, it would be the most perfect, sensual experience imaginable. Instead, he pushed her arm away and got up off the bed.

"Matthew, where are you going?" she asked in a hushed, strained voice as she watched him searching for his clothes and pulling on his trousers. "I do love you, please come back to bed."

He returned to the bed and bent his face close to hers. "You don't know how to love," he sneered at her. "If you did, you wouldn't force me away like that. I'll come back when you can love me like a proper wife."

In the dark she heard him storm out of the room, and as the door closed, she turned her head into the pillow, the downy softness muffling the uncontrolled sobbing and soaking up the tears. She could not imagine feeling any more wretched than she did in that moment and wondered how much of the blame was hers. Perhaps it was only a dream and that the reality was pain and not pleasure, that it was a woman's duty to suffer for her marriage. No, she couldn't let herself believe it was so. That day by the river, when she could so easily have given herself to Matthew, that would have been the dream, the perfect experience.

She continued crying long after Matthew had left, the turmoil in her head banishing any thought of sleep until, after a few hours, she gave in to exhaustion.

In his own room Matthew lay on the bed knowing exactly who to blame for the present predicament. Even the whores of Daventry took pleasure from him above and beyond their financial gain. And Molly, the kitchen maid, who devoured him with the appetite of a voracious sow, did so with no expectation of any other reward. So why had his own wife found it so impossible to grant him the favour of her body when others were so willing?

He lay there, tense with a frustration that refused to subside, that sleep could not relieve. Still wearing only his trousers he slipped quietly from the room.

The house was still, just the familiar rumbling of snoring coming from Haveringham's room. Softly he crept along the landing, as he had done many times in the past, and mounted the narrow service stairs that led to the attic bedrooms. At the top he stopped to listen, but all he could hear was his own noisy breathing.

Molly Turner, the jolly, plump kitchen maid, slept soundly in her bed with only her head visible above the covers. Little tufts of ginger hair poked out from beneath her nightcap and her pleasant, round face looked deceptively serene and innocent as she slept soundly after a particularly busy day. As Matthew stepped out of his trousers and gently pulled back the blanket, he was the last one she would be expecting this night. Usually she held herself in readiness, knowing how impatient he would be to take her, and she would welcome him into her bed. But this night would be different and he was very conscious that she could easily cry out at the shock of finding his naked body next to her. As she stirred to his touch, he clamped a hand over her mouth while the other groped at her beneath the coarse cotton nightdress. Suddenly she realised it was not a fanciful dream and her big eyes widened with the surprise as he removed his hand from her mouth and silenced her with a rough kiss.

She shook her head in disbelief. "Master Matthew, what are you doing here?" The shock turned rapidly to alarm. "This is your wedding night, why aren't you and Miss …?"

He put a finger to her lips. "My bride hasn't learned how to be a wife yet," he whispered into her ear. "Perhaps she should come to you for some lessons."

Molly looked frantically at the bedroom door. "But what if she comes looking for you and catches us. I'll be out on me bleeding ear."

Matthew grinned as he tugged urgently at the nightdress. "Don't worry, there'll be no one looking for me tonight, so you don't need to be sparing with your favours just because I'm a married man."

Molly giggled nervously as he pushed her down onto the bed, and she accepted him into her with a little whimper of forbidden delight. She would spare him nothing, and the pleasure would be all the more intense now that he firmly belonged to another.

Paul quietly opened the door to John's room at the Railway Hotel. He smiled to himself when he saw his brother was still sleeping soundly. The train to London was not due until after lunch and it was still very early, too early to wake him.

The horse Paul had ordered the day before was saddled and waiting for him in the yard at the back of the hotel. It was a clear spring morning, the chill air invigorating, causing his nostrils to tingle as he breathed deeply to clear his lungs and bring life to his body. A perfect morning for a ride, he thought.

He had spent a night disturbed by thoughts of Grace and Matthew, and all the other worries that seemed to be constantly on his troubled mind. He knew that soon he would be able to return to South Africa and to do so without one last visit to his daughter was unthinkable. He wanted one more vivid memory to carry with him on his long journey.

For Grace the night had been no less fitful, and the dawn brought with it little more in the way of comfort. The dream of waking that first morning entwined in her husband's tender embrace, delirious in the knowledge that she was now a woman, had been denied her, and all she was left with was the abiding nightmare of her wedding night.

As a narrow shaft of daylight penetrated the room, she lifted up the covers and looked down at her body. It still looked the same. Was she still a virgin? Had all that pain been for nothing? Not knowing was almost as agonising as the suffering she had endured, but even worse was the fear of going through it all again. What she had been through had nothing to do with love, or passion, it was a brutal assault by the man who only a few hours before had sworn to care for and protect her. She was further desolated at the thought of it becoming common knowledge below stairs. Could she ever live with the disgrace?

She got out of bed. Her legs felt weak and the bruising on her thighs was tender to the touch. When she ordered her bath to be run, she was forced to berate the maid for her suggestive giggling and sent her away before undressing. She was in no mood for frivolity.

Downstairs Jenkins made a point of telling her that Matthew had left the house at his usual hour, his tone suggesting that he was a somewhat surprised by

417

the adherence to routine on such a day. In Grace's mind it was further evidence of her failure as a wife.

"Is my uncle awake yet?" she asked Jenkins as he served breakfast. "I didn't want to disturb him."

"He was still sleeping a short time ago, miss, when I looked in on him."

"Miss? Aren't you forgetting, Jenkins, that yesterday was my wedding day? I am no longer a miss." Never before had she spoken to the staff so harshly and the rebuke brought a shocked response.

"I'm very sorry, miss … ma'am, it won't happen again. I'll make sure all the other staff are aware."

She gave an embarrassed smile. "No, I'm the one who should be sorry, Jenkins. I should never have spoken to you like that. It's just that … well, never mind. If you could make up a tray, I'll take it up to my uncle when I've finished breakfast."

As she drew back the heavy curtains and allowed the bright morning sunlight to flood his bed, Haveringham blinked open his eyes. Grace was struck once again how old and frail he looked, the sallow skin of his face hanging loose from his once plump, ruddy cheeks.

She helped him as he sat up. "Good morning, uncle," she said with forced cheerfulness. "How are you feeling?"

He coughed several times to free his lungs. "No worse than I ought to be," he wheezed, holding onto her arm. "But what of you, my dear, how does it feel to be a married woman?"

"I'm not sure I should feel so very different, uncle," she replied indignantly. It was just the sort of enquiry she was hoping to avoid, although aware of its inevitability. "Do I appear any different to you?"

He gave a sly chuckle. "Oh, it's not a difference you can see, it's more how you feel inside. I can still remember how I felt after my dear wife and I were wed. Very fortunate and very happy. I hope it's just the same with you."

"I've been married for only a few hours, uncle, so surely you don't expect me to feel so very different so soon."

"And what of that husband of yours, how does he feel?"

"You will need to ask him that yourself," she said tartly. "It certainly hasn't kept him from his work, if that's what you mean."

"It's not, and you know it, my girl." He gave her a sharp, enquiring look. "Is everything as satisfactory as it ought to be, you have no regrets?"

She avoided his gaze, preferring to stare at the floor while his yellowed eyes continued to probe for an answer. "I've no regrets, Uncle Rufus," she said quietly, hiding any uncertainty behind a weak smile. "And I'm quite sure Matthew has none either." She was sitting on the edge of the bed and gave him a sideways look. "How should I feel, uncle? I thought I should feel different, but apart from the blessing of the church and the well wishes from all the guests I feel nothing has changed. I'm just the same as I was before."

The old man took hold of her arm in a feeble grip, his expression stern, yet fretful. "If that is the case then the fault can only be your husband's. I don't wish to be intrusive or insensitive, my dear, but the wedding night can be a testing time for any young couple and it's up to the man to appreciate the delicate needs of his bride." He needed to be blind to miss the flushing in her cheeks. "I'm sorry, I've gone too far, these are things a girl should discuss with her mother, or older sister, but you have neither to turn to. Nevertheless, I hope you understand my meaning." She nodded coyly before he continued with a glint in his watery eyes. "We were about the same age as you and Matthew when we got married, and just as innocent, but nothing could persuade us that we were too young, or too inexperienced, to get wed. We loved each other and that was all that mattered to us. It was a grand affair, as you can imagine, and that day was the most important of our lives. We danced well into the night, not wanting it to end. We were determined that our whole life would be just as happy and nothing would ever change. Yet, the following morning we were hardly able to look each other in the face." He lifted her hand to his face and held it tight to his cheek. "You see, Grace, even though weddings are made in church, in the eyes of God, marriages are made in time. It's a whole learning process that ends only when one of you are dead. Don't use anything that happens on that first night as the yardstick for your whole married future, just use it as your first lesson, and learn by your mistakes." Tears rolled over her cheeks as he kissed her hand, and he nodded his head perceptively. "I'm sure nothing has happened that can't be put right with time," he told her gravely.

She laid her head on his chest. "Thank you, Uncle Rufus."

As their train steamed clear of Northampton Station John looked enquiringly across the carriage at his brother.

"You still haven't told me where you went this morning," he said, his eyes narrowing suspiciously. "Anything as secretive as that can only involve a lady. Am I right?"

It was difficult not to notice how quiet Paul had been since returning from his early morning jaunt, and all enquiries John had made of the landlord had achieved nothing, and Paul had been no more forthcoming.

"It is a lady, isn't it?" he declared jubilantly when Paul stubbornly refused to be drawn. "Well, what a dark horse you are. Come on, tell me all about her, or is she such a dragon you're too ashamed."

Paul sat forward on his seat, his chin resting in his cupped hands. "I can't tell you what there isn't to tell. But if it amuses you to presume, then who am I to spoil your little pleasure."

"I see," said John with feigned solemnity. "Perhaps it's a little too delicate to talk about in such a public place as a railway carriage, after all you don't know who might be listening, a husband maybe."

"For pity's sake, John, will you not keep going on about it like some childish schoolboy," snapped Paul, wringing his hands. "If you must talk, please change the subject."

John knew his brother well enough to recognise that something was troubling him, and that it would be foolish to continue with the teasing, although it also concerned him that there should be secrets between them. For the next hour they exchanged only desultory comments until the subject of the war was mentioned and Paul's spirits seemed to rise.

"Have you seen the latest reports?" he said with muted enthusiasm. "Now that they've relieved Ladysmith and Kimberley, and with Bloemfontein taken, it can only be a matter of time before the Boers surrender." But it only took a cursory glance in John's direction to see that the news had been received with rather less emotion. "Oh John, I'm sorry, I wasn't thinking, except of my own selfishness."

John flashed him a reassuring smile. "Don't worry yourself about it. I've indulged in all the self-pity I intend to, and from now on I'm going to look to the future."

"And have you decided what it is you're going to do?"

John shrugged and shook his head. "Not exactly, but I'll not be too badly off with the small pension the army will pay me and what little money Matthew hasn't taken."

"But where will you live, have you thought of that?"

He grinned cheekily. "Oh, I know a very nice house in need of a sympathetic tenant, and close enough to our brother to be a constant reminder of the money he owes me."

"Our old house!" Paul sat back in his seat and gave his brother a sideways look. "Do you really think Matt will agree to your living there? He's got a very strong sense of what belongs to him."

John gave a dry laugh. "I think he'll be agreeable enough when he finds out I still have the letter he sent me asking for the money. I don't think it's something he'll want his new wife or father-in-law finding out about."

Paul smirked. "And I thought Matt was the only devious one in the family.

Later that evening, as they prepared to part company outside Woolwich Arsenal Station, Paul took his young brother in his arms as if they were saying their final farewells.

"I've enjoyed the time we've spent together these past few days." There was a tremor in his voice.

"There'll be plenty more when you come back from South Africa," John assured him, holding back his own sadness. "You'll be a rich man and we'll have such a celebration."

With a sudden burst of inspirational laughter Paul shook his brother by the shoulders. "I have it," he shouted, as passers-by turned to stare. "Why don't you come to South Africa? As soon as the war is over, and I'm settled I'll send for you."

Steadying himself on his crutches John smiled his gratitude, but shook his head. "What good would I be out there, it's not a country for cripples. I'd just be a burden to you. No, Paul, if you're going to make anything of your life you won't need the extra responsibility of someone like me. Besides, that country has too many unhappy memories for me."

They embraced again before Paul helped his brother into a cab and watched despondently as it progressed slowly up the hill towards the common and the hospital.

His own journey to Walworth was a lonely, unhappy one, and he was pleased to be back in Gilbert's ebullient company. His friend insisted on being given every last detail of the wedding before Paul was at last allowed to his bed.

The booking office of the Union Castle Line was as busy as ever when Paul made his next lunchtime visit there. The booking clerk recognised his now familiar face in the queue and gave him an encouraging nod.

"Haven't seen you for a while, sir," he said as Paul stood expectantly before him. "I thought you may have taken your business elsewhere."

Paul shook his head. "No, I've had other business to take care of. What news of the sailings?"

"Well, things have improved a bit. Perhaps it's because the war's taken a turn for the better." He thumbed through his sailing schedules. "It looks like I could get you a berth about the middle of May."

"The middle of May? Nothing before then?"

The clerk bit his lip and looked doubtful as he checked again. "If you're in that much of a hurry to get out there I could offer you something in steerage," he said apologetically. "There's the Warwick Castle leaving Southampton on 27th April, that's the best I can do."

"I'll take it," replied Paul without hesitation.

"But steerage, sir. Are you sure?"

Paul answered him with a determined stare that left the man in no doubt, and the booking was made.

Now, at last, he could begin to make some firm plans for his future, and that evening as soon as he arrived home, he sat down to write a letter to Grace. Afterwards he surprised Gilbert with the suggestion that they should go to the public house to celebrate. His friend accepted the news with a mixture of resignation and sadness.

"I shall miss you, my friend," he said, raising a glass to Paul, "but I fear you need to lay this ghost once and for all if you are to have any chance of getting on with your life."

Paul slapped him heartily on the shoulder. "And I shall miss you too. I could never have got through these past months without your support, and words of wisdom."

Paul's last visit to Woolwich before leaving for Southampton coincided with John's final discharge from the hospital. Although his leg was stiff, and occasionally painful, he had discarded the crutches and was now able to walk quite steadily with just the aid of a stick. He was waiting for Paul in the hospital grounds, taking full advantage of the warm spring sunshine. He was also keen to show off his new found mobility, outwardly appearing in good spirits.

"Well, look at you," declared Paul, beaming proudly and throwing out his arms. "So, what happens with you now?"

John's face took on a more serious expression as they shook hands. "I go before the medical board on Monday morning and they'll tell me what I already know, that I'm no longer fit for active service. Then I'll be sent back to Northampton for my discharge."

"Is there no chance you'll be allowed to stay in?"

John pursed his lips and gave a non-committal shrug of his shoulders. "They may offer me a position of clerk in the paymaster's office, or in the stores where my disability won't be a hindrance, but that's not for me. I joined the army to be a proper soldier, and if I can't be that then I want no part of it."

"Well, my offer to come to South Africa is still open, so please promise me you will at least think about it."

He shook his head solemnly. "You have my word I'll consider it, but I'm making no promise beyond that."

Paul's letter reached Grace at a time when she was in need of his companionship and council, not news of his impending departure from the country. He was about to sail out of her life when his presence could have made such a difference. But then she chided herself for her selfishness. She had determined her own future against his better judgement and now he had the right to pursue his own destiny. Perhaps it was for the best, for how could she hope to shape her own future unless she was allowed to do so by herself, and in her own way.

She wrote back saying how much she would miss his company, and then lied about how well married life favoured her. Pouring out her unhappy heart would have been so much more honest, and may even have caused Paul to rush to her side, but that would have been callous and it would also have been an admission that he had been right all along. The last thing she needed was his condescending sympathy.

Since the wedding Matthew had thrown himself even deeper into his work, to the exclusion of almost everything else. His control over the running of the estate was almost total, and with Haveringham little improved, there was no one to countermand his orders and decisions. There was also no one on the estate left in any doubt about who was now the master. Grace saw little of him during daylight hours, and in the evening, he was either too tired or had not the inclination to talk to her.

After the experience of that first night, Matthew had made no further attempt to share her bed, preferring to sleep in his own room or slipping quietly up the back stairs to enjoy the uncomplicated pleasures afforded by the servant's quarters. For Grace it was a lonely existence, made worse by the pretence she was forced to display in front of her uncle and the closer members of her staff. Her only comfort were the words of advice the old man had offered, that time would resolve any marital problems.

For a week or more she allowed the situation to continue, occasionally making tentative approaches to her husband with a few tender words and a touch of the hand, but each time he shunned her advances, leaving her feeling hurt and humiliated.

Finally, she decided she could bear it no longer, that the blame did not entirely belong to her, and whether Matthew agreed or not, they would have to talk about it in a calm and adult manner.

"This can't go on," she ventured quietly as they sat one evening in the drawing room after dinner.

Matthew looked up from the newspaper he was pretending to read and stared at her dispassionately. "What can't go on?" he asked blandly.

"You know very well, this … us," she replied, determined not to sound angry. "We're supposed to be married, yet here we are more strangers now than we have ever been."

"And I suppose I'm the one to blame for that. Was I the one to push you away on our wedding night, the one night when a man and wife are meant to share a bed? No, Grace, you're the one who insisted on making strangers of us, not me."

She fought hard to maintain her composure against his provocation. "You don't need to keep reminding me of that night, Matthew, it's not one I'm proud of, or likely to forget. I'm sorry I disappointed you, but surely I'm deserving of a little understanding, and another chance."

"Another chance! To do what, push me away again?" He threw the newspaper on the floor and glared across at her. "What makes you think it will be any better next time?"

"I don't know, but if we don't try, we'll never know. Perhaps if you weren't so rough, if you were a bit more patient with me." This was so much more painful than she could have imagined, with Matthew showing no sign of contrition.

"So, it's my fault then, for wanting to make love to my wife. Do you know nothing of a man's needs, that he can't simply turn his feelings on and off to suit the wishes of a wife who can't make up her mind."

"That's so unfair." She finally snapped. "You know how things are with me, that I don't have the experience of the other women you might have known, but I'm your wife and deserving of some respect."

He gave a sardonic laugh. "I thought that's what I was doing, respecting your wishes by staying out of your bed. I don't know what it is you want from me."

"I want the husband I thought I was marrying," she said, composing herself by breathing deeply. "We made our vows in church to love, honour and obey. Did they mean so little to you?"

"I don't think you ever believed that I loved you, but you married me anyway," he sneered arrogantly. "As for the other two, well I think it's a case of the pot calling the kettle black. Where was the honour and obedience when you forced me from the marriage bed?"

"One night, Matthew, it was just one night." He had driven her beyond the point of self-control, and the tears broke free from her eyes. "What about every other night since? Do I mean so little to you that you can't bear to be with me?"

He got up from his chair and kicked away the newspaper, scattering the pages about the floor. He stood over of her as she hid her face in her hands.

"That's right, shed some tears," he said coldly. "Isn't that what all women do when they know they're in the wrong?" He sat down again and bent forward. "I'll tell you why I haven't returned to your bed, it's pride. Being rejected once, on my wedding night, was bad enough. I couldn't bear the thought of it happening again."

"I don't believe you." She took her hands away and stared defiantly at him. "I did love you, I still do, and if you just showed me the consideration I deserve, then I'm sure I could prove it to you." She wiped away the last of her tears. "I don't know what else to say, and I don't know what more you want from me."

"I want what any man should expect from his wife, what my father expected from my mother. She never denied him anything."

"How would you know that? Were you there when they were first married, to know that she didn't go through what I'm going through now?" She was determined not to be driven back on the defensive. "I was willing to give myself to you, but it's not my duty to endure the pain of your rough treatment. I'm sure it's not supposed to be like that." She picked up the sampler she had been working on, diverting her attention to the delicate stitches. "Anyway," she continued casually, "marriages are not just made in bed, it's companionship and loyalty, and if we don't have those then I see no point in continuing."

Matthew's pale eyes narrowed. "What do you mean by that?"

"I've decided that a marriage without affection or friendship is no marriage at all, so I'm going to speak to Uncle Rufus about asking Mr Fennymore to arrange an annulment." While appearing to concentrate on her embroidery she raised her eyes a little to gauge his reaction. "I shall speak to him in the morning, and under the circumstances I think it best you move back to your farm."

Matthew remained silent. Apart from forcing her to accept the blame and to beg for his forgiveness, his position was now the one under threat. But she was bluffing, surely.

"You won't do that. You said only a minute ago that you love me, and to throw that away after so little time, and for so little reason, will only look badly on you. I've done my best to be a good husband so it's you who failed as a wife."

She shook her head in disbelief. "Still as arrogant as ever. You've only ever given your best to your work, I don't think you really wanted a wife." She put down the sampler and got up from the chair. "Whether you believe me or not is of no concern, I shall speak to my uncle in the morning and can only imagine what he will say. Now, I'll leave you to brood on all my failings, and to think about your future."

She swept from the room, biting her lip to prevent a further flood of tears until she was well away from Matthew's domineering gaze. In the privacy of her room, she sat on the bed and allowed the tears to flow as she bit into her knuckles. Anger and frustration had combined to force the confrontation with her husband, but now she wondered if she had gone too far. Had her impetuosity pushed them so far apart for there to be no way back, or had she saved herself from a lifetime of misery? By the morning she would know.

Slowly she undressed, her mind in a confused state of self-doubt and conviction. She climbed into bed still clinging to a vague notion that the marriage could be saved, but how, she had no idea.

It was impossible to sleep and she lay in bed trying to find some small glimmer of light at the end of a very long and dark tunnel. For what seemed like hours she lay there, listening to the sounds of the house before eventually drifting into a light sleep. How long she slept she couldn't tell, it may only have been minutes, but she suddenly became aware of a presence in the room. Her eyes probed the dark until she could make out the shadowy figure standing at the foot of the bed.

"What do you want?" The words escaped her dry mouth in a hoarse whisper.

"I've been thinking about what you said. Is that what you really want, to end the marriage?" Matthew came around to the side of the bed.

She sat up in alarm, pulling the covers over her bare shoulders. "What I want is the chance of happiness with a husband who loves me in the way I love him. If I can't have that then I would rather be on my own."

"And you think I can't give you that." It was not a question, but a statement. He sat on the edge of the bed, stopping short of reaching out to her. "I make no excuses for my low birth and lack of breeding. I don't have the social graces of your uncle's family, and I may never be the kind of gentleman he would have wanted you to marry. But that doesn't mean I can't love, and I do love you, Grace."

He couldn't see the sceptical expression on her face. "Do you, Matthew, or are you just frightened you might lose everything?" She cast an arm around the darkened room. "All this?"

He lowered his head. "I don't blame you for thinking that, and I don't deny I've got ambition, but it would all mean nothing to me if I lost you."

They were the words she had longed to hear, but was there any truth in them. "How can I believe in you when you've done nothing to prove how you feel?" She backed away as he leant towards her. "Do you think it will take only one night of passion to undo all the hurt you've caused me? If that's all you want from me then I dare say there are plenty of girls to suit you better."

He pulled away. "Aye, but none that I would wish to wake up with in the morning. You were right in what you said, how will we ever know what we mean to each other unless we try." He slid off the bed and dropped to his knees, his hands clasped together. "That first night I was cruel and insensitive. I wanted you so much and didn't know how to wait. Next time it will be different, I swear it. I just want the chance."

All the time he had been at her bedside she dared not look directly at him, knowing how susceptible she had always been to the forlorn expression that had softened her heart so many times in the past.

"Just words, Matthew. How am I to know they mean anything?"

"You don't, unless you allow me to show you." He reached out and found her hand beneath the covers. "Let me spend this night with you, and if in the morning you still feel the same, I'll come with you to see your uncle and we can finish this together." He squeezed her hand. "But I'll not give you up without a fight."

Slowly she turned to face him and met the pale eyes that seemed to burn his sincerity deep into her soul. "And you'll not try to force me to do anything I don't want?"

"I'll not try or force you to do anything at all. I just want us to spend the night together."

As Matthew released her hand Grace allowed the bed covers slip from her shoulders. "One night, Matthew," was all she said before turning away as he undressed.

As he climbed into bed next to her, she could feel the heat from his body and shivered nervously. She feared she had been too hasty in accepting his assurances, although it was too late to change her mind now. In her heart she knew he was merely responding to the threats she had made, and now she was faced with the consequences. But they were acceptable consequences if they brought him back to her.

He made no attempt to touch her, but she could sense his nakedness and longed to reach out for him as her heart beat with a pounding rhythm. Perspiration made the satin nightdress cling to every curve of her body, and it moved with her as she turned to face him.

"Can we pretend this is our wedding night," he said softly as their hands met in the narrow space between them. Their fingers entwined and he edged his body closer, daring to reach out with his free hand to stroke her shoulder. "I'll do only what you want."

Her whole body trembled to his touch, and her breathing came in short, sharp gasps as his hand snaked behind her neck and he drew her face to his. When their lips met it was without resistance or regret and she remembered how easily his kisses could reduce her to submission. She put her arm around him and felt it tingle to the touch of his bare flesh. With none of the urgency of that first night his hardness pressed into her belly and instead of fear she was aware of a new and sensuous sensation deep in the pit of her stomach. The nipples of her breasts were hard and sensitive against the smooth fabric and her mouth was dry against his. She drew away slightly to make her breathing easier.

She allowed him to run his hand down her arm and over the gentle rise of her hip until it rested on her thigh. She knew what she wanted him to do, yet she was afraid to offer any encouragement. The involuntary swelling and moistness between her legs urged her to remove the final barrier and invite him to make a

428

woman of her, and when he slid the thin material over her skin it served only to heighten her desire.

Matthew kissed the side of her neck, not hard or forcibly, but with the soft tenderness of a lover, and she responded by rolling over onto her back, her leg wrapped around his. This then was the dream, and more. It was as though her body no longer belonged to her and she was happy to give it to him, which she did with a low moan as he entered her without resistance in a wave of intense pleasure that swept through her whole body.

She moved with him as though it was the most natural thing to do, with each thrust bringing an entirely new sensation. Tears of pure joy and release rolled over her cheeks which Matthew wiped away with a light touch of his fingertips. When the eruption came it was something shared by both, and for Grace it went way beyond the expectations of all her fantasies as she felt her heart would burst. When it eventually subsided, it did so with a warm glow of absolute contentment.

For several minutes they clung to each other in a breathless silence, neither wanting nor daring to move, as though doing so would break the spell of such a magical moment.

When he finally moved his weight from her it left behind an emptiness that needed to be replaced with a firm embrace that lasted throughout the night. Not a word was spoken before they fell into a deep, satisfying sleep, and Grace did so in the knowledge that she had lived the dream and that from now on everything would be perfect.

The following morning, instead of waking up alone, Matthew was by her side. When she opened her eyes, his face was close to hers and he had a smile on his lips.

"Thank you," she said softly, and without another word she lived the dream again, because it was what she wanted, what she would always want.

After that his attentiveness towards her, although not always spontaneous, was sufficient to feed her belief that she now had a solid base for their future together.

Chapter Twenty-Five

Transvaal, South Africa
May 1900

Since the capture of Bloemfontein, the Free State capital, on 13th March, Lord Robert's forces had been pushing steadily northwards until, on 26th May, his western flank under the command of Ian Hamilton crossed the Vaal River and attacked the Boer positions at the town of Doornkop. It was the last battle in the drive on Johannesburg.

The Boer leader in Johannesburg, Commandant Krause, was now ready to surrender the town and, provided Roberts gave him an assurance that he would be allowed twenty-four hours to withdraw his army, he would ensure the mines remained intact. Roberts agreed, and on 31st May the British troops marched down Commissioner Street towards the law courts to a generally cordial welcome from the gathered crowds.

Amongst those who watched the procession was a tall bearded man who neither applauded nor jeered the passing soldiers, but viewed them with an apparent indifference. He looked on no less dispassionately as the Vierkleur was hauled down to be replaced with the Union Flag. As Lord Roberts took the salute with Commandant Krause at his side, the man left the celebrations to all the others as he turned down a side street and disappeared amongst the buildings.

Six months earlier.

The police sergeant paced the hospital corridor, his patience pushed to the limit by the prevarication of the Uitlander doctor. It was the same sergeant who had been in attendance when the Boers had taken possession of Paul's mine, and he was as anxious now to get his hands on his prisoner as he had been that night when the man was first admitted. He was going to be executed anyway, so what did the state of his health matter. But, frustratingly, he had his orders, only the doctor could decree when the man was fit enough to leave the hospital to face trial.

As far as the sergeant was concerned the man was fit enough, and languishing in his bed under the protection of a fellow countryman. Why could his superiors not see that? The pair of them deserved shooting, if only to spare him any further waste of his time. But his opinions counted for little in the eyes of his superiors; if the war went badly for them there were many who still remembered the Tom Edgar affair, and any further injustices would have to be accounted for.

But the sergeant was not to be put off, and for the past month he had presented himself at the hospital two or three times a week, if only to satisfy himself that his prisoner had not been allowed to escape. Now he was forced to wait as the lanky, wild haired Welshman completed an operation.

After waiting for more than fifteen minutes his patience finally gave out and he went striding down the corridor in the direction of the ward. Frank looked up and grinned as the officer burst in through the double doors at the far end of the room, it was a performance he had witnessed many times before. As the sergeant strode through the ward Frank returned his attention to the book he had been reading, blatantly ignoring the man's presence, even as he stood at the end of the bed.

"Get up," he ordered in Afrikaans, which Frank pretended not to understand. "Get up immediately."

The harsh voice had attracted the attention of a passing nurse who came marching up to him. "Stop your shouting, sergeant, or you'll have to leave," she demanded, wagging a finger in his face. "There are sick people in here and I won't have them disturbed."

"Sick people!" His beard parted in a cynical grin as he jabbed a finger at Frank. "This man isn't sick. Get his clothes, I'm taking him with me."

The nurse stood her ground. "This man can't leave until the doctor says so, you know that. So, leave him alone and get out of the ward."

"Not without my prisoner." The Zarp sergeant snatched his pistol from its holster and pointed it at Frank's still bandaged head. "Now, get this man's clothes, nurse, or I'll take him as he is."

"You'll do no such thing, sergeant." The doctor stood in the doorway, his deep Welsh voice resonating through the ward. As he strode between the beds he nodded at the nurse. "Go back to your duties, I'll see to this." He fixed the sergeant with determined eyes, glaring at him across the bed. "What the hell do you think you're doing, threatening my staff and patients like this? Put that gun away and get out of my hospital."

431

The officer's mouth twisted in rage. "We both know this man is well enough to leave, so why do you continue to shield him? I could have you arrested for harbouring a fugitive."

"He's hardly a fugitive since he's not been found guilty of anything, yet," said the doctor scornfully. "So, the choice is yours, take both of us, or leave, because I'm not ready to discharge him. Is that clear?"

The sergeant's face flushed through his thick beard. Having lost the initiative, he felt humiliated in front of witnesses. He thrust his face towards the doctor. "Just remember, you're a Uitlander just the same as he is." He waved the pistol threateningly. "The streets of Johannesburg can be very dangerous, especially for foreigners, so I would take great care, if I were you." He turned the weapon back on Frank. "I'm sure he'll be ready to leave by the end of the week, don't you?"

With a final flourish of the pistol, he turned and marched out of the ward.

"Ignorant oaf," the doctor muttered after him.

"But a dangerous oaf all the same," commented Frank as he watched the retreating officer. "I shouldn't take his threat too lightly if I were 'e." He reached out for the doctor's arm. "Looks, 'e can't go on protecting I much longer without 'e getting into trouble. They're going to take I sooner or later, and the longer I stay here. the more trouble it'll be for 'e."

Davis frowned thoughtfully, his face creased in concern. "You know what's going to happen to you if you go with them. They'll fabricate so much evidence against you that the only outcome will be an appointment with the hangman. And if you try to get away, they'll shoot you for trying to escape. Your best hope is for me to keep you here until the British take the Transvaal."

"But that could be months away, the way things are going," said Frank, grinning mischievously. "Anyway, who said anything about going with them. E heard what he said, I've got 'til the end of the week before he comes back. I could be miles away by then."

Gravely, Davis stroked his long chin. "They've got their spies watching this place day and night, you'll never get out of here without being seen. And then they'll shoot you for certain."

Frank's grin widened. "They'll have to see I first. I know I'm a big enough target, but I haven't lost my wits and I can easily slip past they bastards."

"And if you do get out of here, where will you go?" The doctor had grown to like the big Cornishmen and his concern was genuine. "There's few people left in the Transvaal prepared to hide someone wanted by the Zarps."

Frank shrugged his broad shoulders. That was something to worry about only when he was clear of the hospital. "I've got a few more days to think about that," he laughed.

The following afternoon, as the doctor was doing his rounds of the ward, Frank beckoned him over. "I'm going out tonight," he whispered. "Could 'e leave my clothes in the washroom before 'e goes this evening. I don't want the other patients seeing I getting dressed, I don't know who I can trust."

"Have you thought about where you'll go?"

Frank gave the doctor a knowing wink. "That's not for 'e to worry about; the less 'e knows, the better."

"Well, I think you're a bloody fool, but I'll not try and talk you out of it, I know how stubborn you Cornishmen can be." He gave his patient a nervous smile and a pat on the shoulder. "Good luck to you."

During the remainder of the afternoon and that evening Frank tried to behave as normal as possible, reading his book between periods of dozing, and all the time his mind was turning over all the hazards attached to his escape. He had reasoned that if he was seen and shot his position would be no worse than it was now. Besides, it would be months at least before the British took the Transvaal, given all the reverses they had suffered since the war began, and the doctor's protection receding with each day. There was no other way, in a few days the sergeant would be back, probably with a doctor prepared to give the diagnosis he was looking for.

Just after midnight, when he was quite sure all the other patients in the ward were sleeping and there was no sign of any nursing staff, he slipped out of bed and made his way quietly to the washroom that was situated off the corridor between the men's and women's wards.

A single dim lamp illuminated the corridor, but once inside the washroom the only light came from a narrow shaft of moonlight through two high windows. Frank allowed himself a moment as his eyes became accustomed to the darkness, but even so, he was forced to grope blindly beneath the row of stone sinks for the clothes that should have been left for him. He suffered a moment of panic when there was no sign of them stuffed between the pipes, and when he searched the linen cupboard with no more success, he started to curse the doctor for betraying him. The only other possible place to search was a large wicker basket on wheels that was used for the dirty laundry, but as he lifted the lid he froze when he heard footsteps in the corridor outside. Quickly he shuffled over to the furthest corner from the door and crouched down in the shadows, trying to conceal the whiteness of his nightshirt behind the sinks. As the door opened and a nurse entered Frank knew that if she lit the lamp on the washroom wall he would be discovered, and even if she didn't, he was sure she would hear the heavy pounding of his heart. He clenched his fist. If she did see him, he would have to knock her out, as regrettable as that might be, but needs must. As he pressed himself further into the corner, he could hear her lift the cover from the lamp and he readied himself to rush her before she could raise the alarm. Just when he was silently apologising to her for the attack there was a distressed cry from the women's ward. With a bad-tempered muttering the nurse replaced the cover on the lamp and left the room.

Sweating profusely and shaking violently Frank struggled to his feet and tottered over to the basket where he threw the contents onto the floor. Amongst the towels and bedding he found his clothes, and breathing deeply with relief he stripped off his nightshirt and the bandages around his head and quickly got dressed, conscious that the nurse could return at any moment. Within a few minutes he was ready to leave and pulled open the door an inch or two, peering up and down the corridor. It was empty, but to get to the main entrance he had to pass the women's ward and as he slipped out of the washroom the nurse came out of the ward directly in front of him. For a moment the two stared at each other before Frank gave her his most endearing smile. Her eyes narrowed suspiciously until he blew her a kiss. She threw back her head indignantly before going about her duties, muttering something about men.

At the main entrance Frank paused, listening for any sign that his absence had been discovered. All was quiet and he pulled open the heavy door, realising for the first time how weeks of inactivity had left him feeling weak. He breathed in the fresh night air that swept through the gap, a welcome change to the stale, sterile atmosphere of the ward. He opened the door a little further, staring out into the night for any evidence of prying eyes, knowing full well that anyone watching the hospital would be well hidden. He had no option but to take a chance.

The steps from the entrance led down to a driveway which skirted a lawn, beyond which was a high wall that separated the hospital grounds from the road.

If anyone was watching they would need to be inside the wall to see him leave the building and if they were, it was already too late to turn back.

He slipped out of the door and down the steps, but as he reached the driveway he stumbled, his legs unused to supporting him, and he fell heavily onto his knees. He cursed loudly as he picked himself up and hurried unsteadily into the shadow of the wall. Two large stone pillars stood sentinel either side of the driveway and he pressed himself into the shadow of one of them as he looked out into the road. It was too quiet, any movement instantly visible to a watching Zarp spy.

As he stood there the warnings of Doctor Davis became painfully acute. He had given no real thought to his escape or made any plans beyond getting out of the hospital, and now his mind was a whirl of indecision. One thing, though, was certain, he couldn't stay where he was, anyone leaving or entering the hospital was bound to report his suspicious behaviour. He had to take his chance or go back to the ward.

It was while he debated his situation that fate threw out a helping hand. Out of the silence came the sound of loud voices and raucous laughter from further down the road. To see who they were would have meant exposing his position, but he could tell the voices were getting closer, coming in his direction. An embryonic plan began to develop and he prayed they would continue towards him and not turn off into a side road. From the noise they were making he judged there were at least four or five of them which gave a little more substance to his plan. The waiting seemed interminable, but at last they drew level with the entrance.

They were a rough looking lot, part of a road mending gang that had spent the evening drinking their way through a week's wages, the sort of men who would just as soon split your head with a bottle as drink with you into oblivion.

Frank smiled to himself. The coarseness of their shouting was unmistakeable in any language. The progress they made along the street was understandably slow as they weaved from side to side, supporting one another as they went. As they passed the entrance to the hospital Frank prepared to make his move, slipping out of the shadows to push his way in between them, throwing his arms around the shoulders of the men either side of him. One of them turned to stare at him, but any suspicion was lost in his blurry, unfocussed vision. Frank responded with a few well-chosen expletives in Afrikaans and the man roared with laughter, slapping him violently on the back.

As they all carried on in erratic movement along the street Frank looked cautiously over his shoulder. He thought he caught a glimpse of a figure moving out of an alleyway opposite the hospital to check on the source of the commotion, but being satisfied it was of no concern to him he moved back again.

Once they were well clear of the hospital Frank began to worry that the continuing noisy behaviour of his new friends would sooner or later attract the unwelcome attention of a police patrol. It was now time to make his own way. At the first opportunity he detached himself from their company and slipped into the darkness of a narrow side street. He walked quickly, and at the end he stopped in the shadow of a hotel balcony to catch his breath and take stock of his situation.

So far, he had been lucky, but if he was to remain free, he would need more than luck, he needed a plan and he had none. He knew of no one in Johannesburg who would risk taking him in for the duration of a war that could go on for months, even years. Besides, he had been a virtual prisoner for the past month and the prospect of a further incarceration did not sit well with him. His best hope was to get out of the town and make his way to the nearest British lines.

Leaving the Transvaal, and the mine that had almost cost him his life, was a heart breaking decision, without even considering the enormity of the task ahead. The nearest British garrison was a hundred and fifty miles away at Mafeking, and they had been under siege by the Boers for more than a month. To the south-east the situation was no better as the British were being forced back from the Natal border, and Ladysmith was completely cut off.

It all seemed so helpless, and as he stood beneath the balcony Frank was in half a mind to return to the hospital and take his chances with the court. Nullified by indecision he sank back against the wall of the hotel to consider his options when more voices broke through the silence of the night. These were not loud, drunken voices, but official voices raised in alarm, and were coming from the direction of the road that passed by the hospital. Was it possible his escape had been discovered, or was he just being paranoid and It was nothing to do with him? He had no way of knowing, but he was not prepared to take any chances with the freedom he had only recently gained. Steeling himself for a long trek, he resolved to put as much distance as possible between himself and the town by dawn, cautiously setting off towards the west.

Keeping clear of the main streets he was soon free of the residential and business area and was passing through the sparsely occupied outskirts with its scattering of ramshackle bungalows. Once or twice a dog barked, but no one came to investigate, and shortly afterwards he was out on the open veld. It was still dark, and in the distance, there was an occasional rumble of thunder, but Frank felt happier now that he was on the move, and as his legs regained their strength he was able to pick up the pace to a steady stride, accompanying himself with an unmelodious, yet comforting, rendition of the Helston Flora Dance. By the time dawn began to lighten the horizon he had put a few miles behind him and was satisfied it would soon be safe enough to stop and rest.

The sun rose higher, covering the dusty brown veld with a shimmering haze of early morning warmth that enveloped Frank in its embrace, giving him a sense of security. He knew it was still too dangerous to travel far during the day so he searched the landscape ahead for somewhere that would give him protection from the hot sun and inquisitive eyes.

There was little natural shelter in the rocky scrubland, just a few barren trees and acacia bushes, but the area was strewn with man-made monuments, evidence of efforts to scratch a living from the unforgiving soil. Old farm buildings had been replaced by mine workings, both long since abandoned, proof that where one livelihood had failed another did not succeed by right.

The sun was well clear of the horizon by the time Frank found somewhere suitable, a worked out digging called Good Hope Mine, a relic of the early days of prospecting when its name reflected the optimistic aspirations of all those who came to the Transvaal to make their fortunes. Now it was just a hole in the dry earth, surrounded by the rusting remains of the mine buildings, a few tin huts in varying stages of decay.

The smaller buildings, the ones originally used for storing equipment and explosives were completely empty, anything of value long since removed, leaving behind a flimsy shell that creaked and swayed in the slightest breeze. The largest building, the one used for living and sleeping still had the skeletal frames of the rough wooden bunks and there were even a few rotting mattresses. It was the best Frank could hope for, and with his wasted muscles far from back to their full strength he could not have covered much more distance in the full heat of the day. He chose a bunk nearest the door where the breeze that blew lightly across the veld would provide him with a little welcome relief. Selecting the least rotted mattress he threw it across the framework of the bunk and rolled up his jacket to make a pillow before settling down to recover from the fatigue that had drained the strength from body.

Despite the discomfort and the pungent stale aroma of the mattress he slept soundly for a number of hours, only waking when a gust of wind caught under a loose sheet of tin and sent it crashing into the side of the hut. Frank sat up with a start, imagining the sound to be a gunshot, that he had been discovered. It took him a moment to relate to his strange surroundings before rolling off the bunk and peering cautiously out the doorway. There was no sign of life, but in the distance, he could hear the indistinct thumping of a mine battery, and as he shaded his eyes from the sunlight, he could just make out a thin plume of smoke in the clear sky. It was not only a poignant reminder of his own lost mine but also that life was going on as normal despite the war that was raging further south.

He was rested, but now other needs had replaced his tiredness. His mouth was parched and stale, and the first pangs of hunger were beginning to niggle at his belly. If he was to survive his trek, he would soon need to find both food and water, a further flaw in his hastily contrived plan of escape.

The sun began to dip low in the sky as the afternoon drifted towards evening, and in another hour it would be dusk. While there was still sufficient light Frank made an urgent search of the other buildings in the hope of finding something useful, but there was nothing and he was in danger of slipping into another bout of irresolution. As he sat on the bunk, the shadows crept further into the hut until he was sitting in complete darkness. In desperation he began forming a vague notion that he should walk to the nearest mine where he could steal enough provisions to keep him going for a day or two. Beyond that he had no firm plans.

It was while sitting there that a distant sound caught his attention. He listened more intently, and as his heart began to race, he went to the doorway where he could just make out the unmistakeable grinding screech of a dry wheel hub on an ox wagon. His first instinct was to rush out and greet whoever was approaching with an impassioned plea for food and water. Instead, he stayed inside the hut and watched the progress of the wagon through a window opening.

As the wagon came into view Frank could just make out the driver in the encroaching gloom. He was a thickset, heavily bearded Boer, the brim of his slouch hat pulled down low over his face. Next to him sat a sullen faced young native boy. Behind them, piled high on the wagon, was an assorted load of supplies, probably for one of the mines commandeered by the Boers at the start of the war. For my mine, perhaps, thought Frank bitterly.

It was the moment for decision, and as the wagon skirted the far side of the mine workings Frank took it, slipping out of the hut and striding towards them, hailing the driver in Afrikaans. Startled by the sudden appearance of anyone in that deserted place the driver threw the reins to the boy and picked up the Mauser at his feet.

"Who's there?" he shouted nervously, cocking the rifle and pointing it at Frank's shadowy figure. "What are you doing out here?"

Frank held up his arms and walked slowed towards them, grinning at the driver. "I'm not armed, I just need your help." Keeping his arms in the air he continued walking.

"That's as far as you need to come," ordered the Boer when Frank reached the lead oxen. "What's your business out here?"

"Out here!" Frank let out a loud laugh, sweeping his arm over the black, barren landscape. "You don't think I'm out here by choice, do you?"

"So, what are you doing here then? This mine was abandoned years ago, it's worthless."

"I'm not interested in the mine, I just want something to eat and drink, and perhaps a ride back to civilisation."

"You're a Uitlander, I can tell by your accent," said the Boer suspiciously. "And you still haven't told me what you're doing out here."

"My horse threw me, it was frightened by something. I banged my head and was knocked unconscious. When I came around my horse was gone and I was left out here."

"No Boer would let himself be thrown from his horse," said the man with a strong contemptuous note to his voice. He levelled the rifle at Frank's head. "Are you English?"

Frank shook his head and smiled. "American. I was working the mines over at Elandsfontein, but got bored with it and thought I'd look for some new adventure. I was on my way to join up with Cronje's Transvaalers over in the west. That's where I was going when this happened."

"You're not going to be much use to him with no horse or rifle," sneered the Boer, still suspicious of him. He jabbed the rifle in the direction of the hut. "Is there anyone else with you?"

Frank shook his head again, wincing as a pain shot through it. "Just me. Look, if you could just spare me a little food and some water, and a ride to wherever you're going it would help me, and the cause."

For a while the man appeared unconvinced by Frank's story and looked as though he was about to abandon him there. "American," he said finally, sniffing loudly. He pointed the muzzle of the rifle towards the back of the wagon. "I suppose you can ride with us as far as we go and maybe you can get a meal when we get there."

Frank smiled in appreciation as he walked to the back of the wagon and climbed onto the tail board. "And what about a drink for now?"

As he took over the reins the Boer ordered the boy to pass back the water flask.

"And how far are you going?" questioned Frank as he settled himself between some sacks of flour and cases of tinned beef.

"Not as far as Mafeking, because that's how far you'll need to go if you want to catch up with Cronje." The Boer gave a humourless chuckle. "And you'll know where we're going when we get there."

Even though night had completed closed in around them Frank sensed an unnerving familiarity with the landscape, and he was beginning to think he had made a mistake in accepting the ride. But it was too late to change his mind now; if he was right, they were almost at their destination and he would once again become a prisoner. He could try and slip away in the dark, but a gnawing hunger and fear of a Mauser bullet in the back persuaded him that even the slimmest chance of carrying off a bluff was worth taking.

"Nearly there," called out the driver unnecessarily as Frank stared about him, picking out all the familiar features.

As the wagon rolled into the perimeter of the mine, Frank tried to remain optimistic that the engineers left there by the Burgers may not recognise him, although, given his size and the dramatic circumstances of his departure, he thought it unlikely. And even if the engineers failed to recognise him then, come the morning, the Kaffirs were bound to give him away. His best chance still lay in bluffing it out for the night, and while they were asleep steal some food and a horse and strike out for the border.

At the sound of the wagon's approach two men came out of the bungalow to meet them. "It's about time, Koos," said one of them intemperately. "We expected you hours ago."

"What's the matter with you Jacob, can't you sleep without a bottle of brandy inside you?" returned the driver, jerking his thumb over his shoulder. "I stopped to pick up a passenger."

With only the dull yellow glow of an oil lamp spreading its light from inside the bungalow it was impossible for Frank to make out the faces of the two men, and he took some comfort from the fact that they would be suffering a similar difficulty. He climbed down off the wagon, keeping as far as possible to the shadows.

"He's not a replacement then for De Groote?" asked the other man, peering hard at Frank.

"He's an American," replied the one called Koos. "Said he was on his way to join up with Cronje at Mafeking when his horse threw him."

The two men laughed mockingly. "I don't think the general will want anyone who can't stay on his horse," said Jacob, taking his turn for a closer look at the stranger. "I thought you Americans were supposed to be good horsemen."

They were close enough to see each other and Frank waited tensely for an exclamation of recognition. When none came, he breathed a sigh of relief and held out his hand.

"I'm sorry I'm not the replacement," he said, grinning broadly. "Like your friend said, I'm just passing through."

Jacob was staring hard at him. "Haven't I seen you somewhere before?"

As Frank stiffened the driver jumped down off the wagon. "He's been mining over at Elandsfontein, that's what he said."

"Well, I'm certain I've seen him somewhere before," persisted Jacob.

"The amount of brandy you drink, Jacob, it's a wonder you don't see two of everything," said the other engineer, slapping his companion on the back. As Frank forced a laugh the man gave him a sideways look. "So, you're a miner as well as a soldier. What's your name?"

Frank was conscious that Jacob still had a wary eye on him. "Probably a better miner than a soldier," he replied flippantly. "It's Thompson, George Thompson."

"Well George Thompson, I expect you're hungry. Come and eat with us." He turned to the wagon driver. "Koos, get some of the Kaffirs to unload the wagon then come and join us."

Still anxious that he was sure to be found out, Frank followed the two men into the bungalow, certain that in the full glare of the lamp Jacob's memory would return. Yet foremost in his mind was the risk that he would lose out on a meal. Inside it was much as he remembered, although far less tidy than Paul insisted on keeping the place.

"Please sit down, Mr Thompson," said the man, who introduced himself as Andries. He smiled charmingly as he waved Frank towards a chair. "We shall eat supper in a short while."

Jacob made a point of sitting opposite their visitor, all the while studying the stranger's face. When Koos returned he was holding a couple of bottles of brandy and tossed one to him. Dispensing with the formality of a glass, Jacob started on it straight from the bottle and Frank gave him an encouraging grin, while hoping the others would do nothing to dissuade the man from sliding into an early oblivion.

"Tell me, Mr Thompson," said Andries when they were all seated, "what part of America are you from?"

"Pennsylvania," responded Frank unhesitatingly. He had already planned that far ahead.

"Ah, then I guess you must be more familiar with mining coal than gold or diamonds," grinned Andries.

Frank smiled back and nodded. He knew he was being interrogated through a heavily camouflaged veil of sociability and was relieve to note that Jacob's interest was now wholly on the bottle and not on him.

"Have you been in South Africa long, Mr Thompson?" asked Koos, opening the other bottle and handing around the glasses.

"About thirteen years, soon after the strike of eighty-six." He held out his glass for Koos to fill.

"And you've been working in the gold fields since then?" put in Andries who Frank guessed was in charge of the operations at his mine.

Again, Frank replied with a nod as he took a large swallow of the fiery liquid.

Shortly afterwards one of the Kaffirs served their supper and showed no sign of recognising Frank. The food was an unappetising looking beef stew that contained a number of other unidentifiable ingredients, but while Andries and Koos took turns to shout abuse at the boy, Frank attacked the food with relish. He even drew Andries' curious admiration when he accepted a second helping that was left over when Jacob staggered away to his bunk, still clutching the bottle.

Once they had all finished drinking Frank felt more relaxed as the three of them settled down to an evening of pleasant conversation, and more drink. Having satisfied his hunger, and with the warming glow of the brandy working its magic on his insides, all his fears evaporated and it was as though he were back working his mine, and all the past weeks just an unpleasant dream. Whatever his fate in the morning, that was something to worry about when the time came.

"So, Mr Thompson, what are your plans now that you have no horse?" asked Andries as the bottle was passed round. "Back to Elandsfontein, perhaps?"

Frank gave a casual shrug of his broad shoulders. "I haven't had much time to think about it," he said with indifference. "It's a long walk to Mafeking, and like Koos here says, I won't be much use to the war without a horse, or a rifle."

The remark brought a thin ripple of chuckling from the other two until Andries' face took on a serious expression and he leant forward on his chair. "Why not stay here then? We could use a man with your experience, and you would still be helping the Boer cause."

Even in his mellow state Frank's startled reaction must have been apparent to the others and he took another large swallow to compose himself.

"It's not such an impossible idea," went on Andries, noting the look of surprise on Frank's face. He took a pipe from his pocket and began sucking on it reflectively. "When the Volksraad ordered this mine to be confiscated for its own purpose it sent out three engineers to take over the running from the Uitlander owners." He took the pipe from his mouth and prodded the stem towards the curtained off sleeping quarters. "Jacob is the only one of the original three to remain."

"What happened to the other two?" interrupted Frank. Suddenly the proposal seemed less improbable.

"Soon after the mine owners were taken away the Kaffirs began to rebel against the new regime. They refused to work and some tried to run away. One of the engineers, Willie van Horne, tried to stop them and was attacked with a spade. Jacob shot a few of them and the others were taken away. We were given a new lot."

"And the other one?" enquired Frank.

Andries shook his head sadly. "Poor old de Groote. It seems this place is cursed with misfortune. Soon after I arrived to replace Willie there was a cave in underground and de Groote was crushed to death, along with two of the boys." He stared ruefully at the sleeping quarters. "Now I'm left with Jacob who only manages a few days useful work each month, when the drink runs out."

"But what about Koos here?" Frank inclined his head towards the dozing figure in the chair next to him.

Andries smiled benevolently. "Koos is no miner, he just delivers our supplies. In the morning he'll be on his way back to Johannesburg and we won't see him again for another month."

Frank tried to clear the fuzziness from his brain to concentrate on such a preposterous idea. He had arrived at the mine through an unaccountable twist of fate, and with only the smallest hope of eluding capture, yet here he was being presented with an opportunity he could never have imagined. And what an opportunity; no one would think to look for him at his own mine.

"Then why not send Jacob back with him?" he said slowly, hiding any note of enthusiasm. "If he's of no use to you here then he's just another mouth to feed."

Andries sighed heavily. "Company, Mr Thompson, that's why. Even though he's drunk most of the time I can still talk to him and pretend he's listening. Does that make any sense to you?"

It made perfect sense to Frank who well remembered how lonely it could be out on the Rand, even with Joseph, and latterly Paul, for company. "And if I agreed to stay, what then?" he asked cautiously. "Would you still need his company?"

Andries eyed him questioningly, as though seeking out some ulterior motive in the enquiry. "Would that be a problem for you, Mr Thompson, a condition of your staying?"

Again, Frank gave an indifferent shrug to disguise his real intent. "He's not my responsibility, and I wouldn't presume to tell you how to run your mine, but I don't think the Volksraad would appreciate wasting their precious funds on someone as unproductive as him."

Andries tapped out his pipe on the leg of the chair. "You're probably right, but I can't force him to go. He has family up near Pretoria and that's why he drinks. He misses them badly. I'm sure he would rather be with them than slowly killing himself out here. He can go back with Koos in the morning if he agrees, and you and me can get on with the business of running this mine."

He held out his hand to Frank who took it unreservedly. If Jacob could be persuaded to go there would be no one at the mine who knew of his true identity, and it would be a month before Koos returned again. Frank had no reason to believe the wagon driver would even mention the American he had picked up on the Veld so, for the time being at least, he should be relatively safe. Not only that, he was back at his mine and best placed to reclaim it from the Boers once the war was over.

He was given a bed for the night, although he found it difficult to sleep, what with Jacob's loud snoring and his mind filled with a jumble of disparate thoughts.

In the morning Jacob was still sleeping soundly and Andries took the decision to send the man back with the wagon. While Frank and Koos carried the slumbering figure out to the wagon Andries packed his few belongings. When they laid him on the rough wooden boards at the back of the wagon Jacob stirred, staring through confused, bloodshot eyes at his colleague.

"You're going home, Jacob," Andries said softly, patting him on the shoulder.

Jacob gave a nod of vague understanding and fell back into a deep sleep.

After a quick breakfast Frank accompanied Andries on a tour of the mine, trying to appear suitably ignorant of its workings. He was told that production was down due to poor supervision of the native labour, although previously it had increased to above what Frank and Paul had achieved before the takeover. Frank guessed they had struck the rich vein he knew existed at a lower level, and this was confirmed when they went underground. Less encouraging was the information that the gold was collected every two weeks by a wagon with a police escort; the next collection being due in about ten days.

"Now that you're here we can work two full shifts," announced Andries enthusiastically when they came back up to the surface. "I couldn't allow Jacob underground. It was dangerous enough for him up here when he was drunk. Do you want to take the early shift?"

Frank was still preoccupied with the vexing question of the gold collection. "I'm sorry, what?"

"Which shift do you want to take, the first or second?"

Frank shrugged his shoulders. "You're in charge, you decide."

It was agreed that Andries would go underground first, giving Frank the opportunity for a good look around. He had noticed the night before, although deliberately avoiding giving it any undue attention, a newly installed strongbox. It was there, he assumed, the refined ore was kept while awaiting collection. He wondered if Andries would ever trust him enough to give him the key. He doubted it.

He was pleased when it was time for his shift. Andries found him some suitable clothing, although the seams strained against his large frame. But, after all the weeks of inactivity and the threat to his future, it was good to be doing something useful, even if he was contributing to the war coffers of an enemy who wanted him dead.

"It's all going very well, my friend." Andries made the unexpected remark one morning as the two of them sat down to breakfast about two months after Frank's arrival. "Production is increasing. You and I are a good team, the Volksraad should be pleased. What could be better?"

"What indeed," commented Frank, raising his bushy eyebrows.

He had to admit that, despite the man's Boer ancestry, he liked Andries, and they did indeed make a good partnership. Under different circumstances the operation of the mine would have been an unqualified success, although he did suffer pangs of guilt and betrayal when he remembered his true partner. It was during such periods of regret that he fell into a withdrawn silence, contrasting starkly with his usual ebullient nature. But if Andries noticed he generally made no comment, until that particular morning when Frank was perhaps more morose than usual.

"I thought we might increase the length of the shift by a few hours," said Andries casually, although Frank felt the suggestion contained an underlying importance. "How do you feel about that?"

Frank kept his reply equally non-committal. "You're in charge, Andries, you make the decision. I've no objection, but I don't think the boys will be too keen."

"The Kaffirs will do as they're ordered," retorted Andries with unexpected harshness, "but I would have expected more of an argument from you."

Instinct told Frank there was more on Andries' mind than a simple discussion on the time they spent underground.

"If you want an argument from me I won't oblige you. A few more hours underground would mean a few less hours of boredom up here. What's the difference?"

"A great deal of difference, my friend, it means we can increase production even further. I thought the idea of that might bother you."

Frank's eyes narrowed. "Why should it?"

Andries' expression remained stern for several seconds until his lips parted in a huge grin. "Why? Because it means more gold for the war effort. More guns and more ammunition to help drive the British out of the whole of South Africa. That's what I thought might bother you, George, … Or should I call you Frank."

Frank dropped the fork he was holding onto his plate and flashed his companion an uncomprehending glance. But before he could protest Andries held up a hand.

"It's all right, my friend, I've known for a few weeks now."

"But how?" Frank got up from the table and paced the bungalow, unsure of how he should react.

"Oh, I've always had my suspicions about you, your eagerness to get rid of Jacob, because he was the only one able to recognise you, and your exaggerated ignorance of the mine workings when one mine is much the same as another. And your familiarity with the machinery that I still find so temperamental. It was all enough to make me do some checking." He was closely watching Frank as he spoke and noticed a flicker of concern. "Some discreet checking, I might add. I've told no one about you."

Frank stared at his dubiously. "Why not? If you've been checking you must know I'm wanted by the Zarps. And weren't you worried I might kill you and make off with the gold, my gold?"

Andries waved a hand for him to sit down. "Like most Afrikaners, George, … I'm sorry, Frank, I'm a realist with a strong sense of self-preservation. I'm no traitor to my country, but I know that when the war is over it will be men like me who will be the losers, not the politicians. The longer the war goes on the more our people will suffer." He reached across the table and gripped Frank's arm. "Even when I first discovered who you were I never felt threatened by you, otherwise I would have had you arrested. I have grown to be fond of you, my friend, and I'm vain enough to believe you feel some friendship towards me. It is time now to put all our trust in each other and, how do you English say, place all your cards on the table."

"I don't see that I have much choice." Frank scratched his head through his thick, greying hair. "You're right, though, we are friends. I would never have thought of using force to stop you from giving me away, so I don't suppose we have much choice than to trust each other."

"But it's more than just friendship, Frank. Why do you think I arranged your shifts so that you were always underground when the gold was collected? It wasn't just to protect your identity." He looked cautiously around the empty bungalow, an unnecessary precaution. "It was to stop you from finding out that not all the gold we mined was going back to Pretoria. I've been protecting my future. Our future."

Any misunderstanding on Frank's part was now slowly being dispelled as the truth dawned on him and he let out a low chuckle. "You old devil, Andries. I would never have guessed."

There was no such humour in Andries' expression. "You understand, my friend, now that I've told you my life is also in your hands. If my countrymen found out what I've done my life would be worth no more than yours. So, you see, more than ever now we must have trust in each other."

Frank clasped the man's hand in a firm grip of reassurance. "I owe you my freedom, Andries, you don't think I would jeopardise that for a few ounces of gold, do you?"

Andries shook his head solemnly. "But it's much more than a few ounces, so much more. By the time the war is over we could both be very rich men, but it can't succeed unless I have your help." He fixed Frank with a steely stare. "Whichever side wins this war I will never be allowed to leave the Rand with a great fortune in gold, and at the moment I'm counting on the fact that the Boer cannot win. That being the case we will be ordered to either destroy the mines or hand them back to their original owners, like you. It will then be for you to decide what happens to the gold we have managed to acquire. There would be nothing stopping you from keeping it all for yourself. All I can do is to hope you will not forget our friendship."

Frank held on to the hand, shaking it resolutely. "If there's been any misjudgement between us then it has all been mine. I always took you for a patriotic Boer, not a capitalist like me. If we both survive this war then we will owe that equally to the other, and that is how we'll divide the spoils."

For the next three months production at the mine continued to increase, although the amount transferred to the Boer war coffers remained constant, an arrangement that appeared to satisfy all parties, and the longer the war went on the more satisfactory it became. By the middle of May, Frank Trevithick was under no illusion as to who the final victors would be. It seemed certain that, within the coming few weeks, most of the Transvaal would be under the control of the British forces. There was still much speculation, however, that the Boers may be panicked into dynamiting the mines, and in some of the larger ones, charges had already been laid in anticipation of the advance on Johannesburg.

Andries had become increasingly more agitated during those final weeks as he dealt with his greatly troubled conscience and personal loyalties. In the meantime, Frank remained quietly sympathetic to his friend's anxieties.

The last collection of gold was made during the third week of May by an escort of Burgers who told Andries that they would soon be evacuating north to Pretoria, and advised him to do the same.

"What do you think will happen when the British do arrive?" he asked Frank as they sat down to supper that evening.

"Much the same as happened in Bloemfontein, I shouldn't wonder," replied Frank, trying to make light of what clearly weighed heavy on his friend's mind. "Some flag waving and drum beating, then everything will be back as it was."

"But what about me? What do you think will happen to me?"

Gravely Frank scratched at his beard. He wanted to give his friend an assurance that as a non-combatant nothing would happen to him, but he had heard talk of the concentration camps that had been set up further south and there was no guarantee Andries would not end up in one of them.

"You could always apply to become a British citizen, in fourteen years," he joked.

Andries shook his head sadly. "I may have been dishonest, but I'm still a loyal Afrikaner at heart, and no amount of gold will change that."

"Maybe not, but if it's just your conscience that's troubling you then it will be just as easy to live with in luxury as poverty." He gave his friend a comforting pat on the shoulder. "You knew this is how it would be, what we've been working towards these past months. The amount of gold we kept for ourselves would have made no difference to the outcome of the war, and it didn't even belong to the Volksraad in the first place. Treat it as a gift from me to you, and then your conscience will be clear."

"That's typical of you English, you make everything sound so simple."

A few days later the rumble of artillery fire could be heard from the south, the battle for Doornkop had begun, the last show of Boer resistance before Johannesburg. Amongst those trying to hold back the might of Hamilton's column were Christiaan de Kock's Lichtenburg Commando, pouring down a rain of Mauser fire on the advancing Gordon Highlanders. But as the kilted soldiers began to take the ridge the awesome sight of the fixed bayonets destroyed the final resolve of the Boers and they broke rank and scattered. Those that were able to do so retreated back on Johannesburg.

Standing together at the mine head, Frank and Andries listened in silence to the sound of the battle as they watched the smoke drifting up from the burning grass across the veld.

Leaving Andries to his own private thoughts Frank climbed the low kopje, past the grave where the brave, foolish Joseph was buried. The firing was dying away, and from the top he could just make out riders coming in their direction. The first of the Boers were making good their escape. Most of them turned towards the east, but some kept coming, probably heading straight for Pretoria.

The first of the riders to pass stopped just long enough advise the pair to pack up their belongings and get out, and then they were gone, galloping off northwards. But a party of five or six Burgers stopped at the mine head just as Frank was coming down off the kopje. They were talking in earnest to Andries, asking him if he had any food to spare. As he disappeared into the stores hut to find some tins of meat and biscuits Frank saw no reason to stay out of their way, after all, had he not been working to finance their cause. He waved and shouted out a greeting as he approached.

"We heard the firing," he said, "how did the battle go?"

"There were too many of the bastards," one replied angrily. "They'll be in Johannesburg in two days."

The one who had asked for the food wheeled his horse around to face Frank and the two men stared at each other, one in shocked disbelief and the other in vague recognition.

The Burger broke away from the group and trotted his horse over to where Frank stood waiting. "It is you, English. What the hell are you doing here?"

It was only then that Frank remembered where he had seen the man before, it was almost on that very spot. Just then Andries returned with the sack of food and de Kock turned on him angrily while jabbing the muzzle of his rifle in Frank's direction.

"Do you know who this man is?" he shouted.

Before Andries could reply Frank ran between them. "No he doesn't, he thinks I'm an American, that's what I told him"

"He's been helping me run this mine," said Andries defensively, with a nervous glance at Frank. "If it wasn't for him, I couldn't have carried on here. We would have got nothing from this mine."

"This man is English, this was his mine before the war. Are you telling me he's been helping you dig the gold for us Boers?"

"It was either that or spend the war in one of your prisons," grinned Frank in an attempt to defuse the taut situation. He jerked a thumb at Andries. "This man's not to blame, I can be very persuasive when I want to be."

The other Burgers crowded around and one of them pointed his rifle threateningly at Frank's chest. "Do you want me to shoot the Englishman, Christiaan?" he asked coldly.

De Kock appeared tempted, but shook his head. "We're not savages, we don't shoot unarmed men." He glared menacingly at Andries. "But if I find out this man knows more than he's saying then I will personally take charge of the firing squad. What's your name, friend?"

"Schoeman, Andries Schoeman," he replied, too frightened to lie.

"Well, I hope you have a clear conscience, Andries Schoeman." With that de Kock spurred his horse forward and led his men away from the mine, brushing Frank aside as he went.

When they had gone Frank noticed his friend's face drained of colour. "Don't worry about them, they'll have forgotten all about you long before they reach Pretoria."

"You don't know us Afrikaners, Frank, we have very long memories, and very unforgiving hearts."

That evening Frank worried about his companion, the words of Christiaan de Kock had a disturbing effect on Andries and he remained withdrawn and sullen. With the British troops just a few miles away Frank urged him to discuss the arrangements for dividing up the gold and to give serious thought to what he should do and where to go.

"In the morning, we will talk about it in the morning," was the only reply he would give.

Eventually, and at Andries' insistence, Frank gave up his prompting and went to bed, although he found it impossible to sleep straight away. Something that remained outside his full comprehension lay heavy on his mind. Finally, he must have fallen asleep because he was aware of being woken by a loud noise he was unable to identify. Behind the curtain that closed off the sleeping quarters a lamp still burned, and from the thin glow Frank could see that Andries' bunk was empty.

Pulling on his trousers Frank went outside, anxiety gnawing at his stomach as he shivered in the chill night air. He knew something was terribly wrong, and when he called out his friend's name the only response was a babble of excited voices from the direction of the Kaffir's quarters.

With no moon, the night was quite dark and Frank went back into the bungalow to fetch the lamp. As the yellow glow spread over the ground Frank's attention was drawn towards the stores hut, and the dark shape lying on the stoep. The lamp swung wildly as he ran over to the hut and he felt sickened by what he knew he would find. The crumpled body of Andries lay there, the smouldering pistol still gripped in his hand.

Frank dropped the lamp and fell to his knees, cradling the blood-soaked head in his arms.

"You stupid damned Boer," he sobbed. "You were no traitor you stupid bloody Boer.

In the morning he buried Andries next to Joseph at the bottom of the kopje and stood at the foot of the graves reciting the Lord's Prayer. Before him now lay the bodies of two friends, both the victims of a war few wanted, and because of his cursed mine. What a price to pay for a fortune in gold.

When the British troops marched proudly down Commissioner Street a few days later Frank could find nothing to cheer about, he had no heart for celebrating what was for him a hollow victory.

Chapter Twenty-Six

Little did Paul realise that obtaining passage to Cape Town was to be the least of the obstacles to stand in his way before he was finally to reach the Transvaal. When he disembarked from the Warwick Castle, he found the streets of the town teeming with army personnel and vehicles, most of which were waiting to be sent up country.

Adding more confusion to the frenetic activity in the town was the news that Mafeking had been relieved a few days earlier. It appeared to Paul that there was nothing of less importance to the population of Cape Town than the travel arrangements of a lone English civilian.

Every single wagon and railway carriage leaving for the north was packed with troops and their equipment, leaving no spare place for those lacking any connection with the war. And even if room was available, it was doubtful that permission would be granted by the military authorities who insisted that the country beyond De Aar Junction was far too dangerous for private travel. As far as they were concerned there would be no question of anyone reaching Johannesburg until the war was truly over and all the Boer commandos had surrendered.

So, while he resigned himself to be stranded in Cape Town, Paul took a room at the hotel that had so obligingly accommodated him during his previous stay in the town.

The little Indian manager welcomed him back. "Will you be staying long, sir?" he asked with a simpering smile.

"Just as long as it takes to arrange transport to Johannesburg," he replied with weary resignation. "I could be here forever."

"Then we will be pleased to have you here forever, sir."

With failing optimism Paul pursued his enquiries daily, but no one seemed impressed or interested in the urgency of his business in the north. The war effort took priority over everything, and by the end of the first week Paul's resolve was beginning to weaken and he believed he had made a mistake returning to South Africa. Each evening he would return to the hotel looking more tired and dejected than the day before only, to be greeted with the same demoralising enquiry from the manger.

"Did you have any luck today, sir? If not, we will be happy to accommodate you for as long as you wish."

Or as long as my money lasts, thought Paul.

Then, at the end of May, came two pieces of news, convincing Paul that all barriers to his journey north would be removed. The first was that the Orange Free State, now renamed the Orange River Colony, had been annexed and was now under British martial law. The second, three days later, was that the Union Flag was now flying over Johannesburg and that Lord Roberts was pushing on to Pretoria, which was expected to be taken without much opposition.

Once more, and with greater determination, Paul went back to the railway station to speak to Colonel Palmer, the officer in charge of all train movements from the town. The closest he had managed to get to the officer in the past was the impenetrable and brusque sergeant of the Army Service Corp whose prime duty was to protect his colonel from the irrelevant and insignificant enquiries of civilian types.

"I'm sorry, sir, but the colonel is much too busy with military matters at the moment to be interrupted," he told Paul without even looking up from the sheaf of despatch orders he was thumbing through. "Perhaps if you could come back in a week or two."

"In a week or two, sergeant, I may not have anything to come back for. I had a gold mine in the Transvaal which may have been blown up by the Boers, and I also had a partner who I had to leave behind in a Johannesburg hospital and who may not even still be alive. If I don't get back there soon there will probably be nothing left to go back to and this bloody war will have all been for nothing."

"Now see 'ere, sir," said the sergeant, forced to drag himself away from the papers by the offence to his profession, "this bleedin' war ain't bein' fought for the benefit of you capitalists, so's you can go on makin' yer bleedin' fortunes. A lot of good men have got themselves killed or wounded for the likes of you."

"I know, my brother was one of them," replied Paul, his tone softened by the memory.

"Well, I'm sorry to hear that, and I'm sorry about your problems, but like I said, there's bugger all I can do about it." He returned to his papers. "You can't see the colonel, and that's that, so you'll have to excuse me, I've got more important things to attend to."

"Well, you go ahead and attend to them, sergeant, because I'm not leaving here until I've seen him, with or without your permission."

"Then you've got a long wait ahead of you, sir, because you won't get in to see him, not while I'm here."

"Is that so?"

Skirting the desk Paul had reached the door to the colonel's office before the sergeant could move out of his chair.

Colonel Palmer was a large, florid faced man in his late fifties and at the end of a largely inglorious career. He viewed his present posting as a slight on his perceived talents.

"What's the damn meaning of this," he demanded, glaring up at the intruder through small, beady eyes. "Sergeant!"

"I'm sorry, sir." The sergeant burst into the office behind Paul, grabbing him by the arm. "I did try and stop him."

Paul snatched his arm away from the soldier's grasp. "I have to speak to you colonel. I know it was wrong to come in here like this, but I was desperate. If you could just give me five minutes, please."

"Make an appointment with the sergeant, that's the best I can do," he huffed dismissively, cuffing his walrus moustache.

"But I'm here now, colonel. Just five minutes, I promise you."

The officer sniffed loudly. "Very well then." He waved the sergeant away and leaned back in his chair. "What's this all about, and make it quick."

"My name's Pearson, colonel," he began, and then went on to relate as quickly and concisely as possible all the events that had led him to be there, and why it was so important for him to travel up country.

For a while the colonel seemed patently unimpressed by the familiarity of Paul's problems, he had heard similar stories many times before, and only showed some glimmer of interest when Paul happened to mention his brother and the Northamptons. A look of nostalgia slipped across the officer's face.

"My old regiment," he said ruefully, and almost as an aside, staring vacantly into the distance. "Now I'm stuck here because the War Department have decided I'm no longer fit enough for active duty Northampton people, are you?"

Paul nodded, looking suitably sympathetic.

"Haven't been back there for some time myself. Miss the place." He got up from his desk to stare wistfully out the window at the railway tracks beyond. He turned back to Paul, a vague smile causing his moustache to twitch. "Don't suppose you know anything of an old devil named Haveringham?"

"As a matter of fact, I do," remarked Paul, greatly encouraged by the revelation. "We were neighbours. If fact my brother is married to his niece, so I suppose we are related."

"We were at Rugby together, you know. How is the old chap?"

Paul shook his head sadly. "Not too good when I last saw him. His heart, you know."

"Too bad, too bad. I must get up to see him some time." He turned away from the window and began pacing the floor, his hands clasped behind his back. "But you didn't come here to talk about that. What is it you want from me?"

"To get up to Johannesburg, colonel," Paul reminded him.

The officer shook his head vigorously. "Quite out of the question, I'm afraid." He went over to a large map of South Africa pinned to the wall. "There's an epidemic of enteric fever up around Bloemfontein." He prodded the area with his stubby finger. "And even if there wasn't, it would still be too dangerous. The damned Boers still have a lot of men active in the River Colony, blowing up tracks and attacking trains. Not cricket, I'm damned if it is. No, the best I can do for you is to give you a pass as far as Kimberley." He jabbed at the map again. "You'd be on your own after that, at your own risk. Can't do any better."

"Then I'm indebted to you, colonel."

Once the colonel had signed the pass Paul shook him warmly by the hand. As he went through the outer office, he waved the pass provocatively at the sergeant before going off to buy his ticket.

Two days later he was on a packed train as it left Cape Town station at the start of a six- hundred mile journey to the diamond town of Kimberley. It would still leave him a further five hundred miles of wild country to cross before he would finally reach his destination, but even so he was still glad to be on the move, and as Table Mountain disappeared from view he began to think once again of Frank and whether or not he was still alive.

He shared the compartment with a mixture of army personnel, government officials and a number of giggling young women on their way to serve in the military hospitals. Most of the conversations were tied to the recent British successes, but Paul took little part, preoccupied as he was by the uncertainties and anxieties he felt.

After passing De Aar Junction, where the line to Johannesburg branched off towards Naauwpoort, the train continued on its uneventful journey, rattling across the Orange River Bridge a few hours later. It was here, as they approached Belmont, that the track ran parallel with the border of the newly annexed colony a few miles away. There was a noticeable increase in tension amongst the soldiers, who were well aware of the attacks carried out on the railway, although it was unlikely there were any Boer commandos still active this far west.

Some of the soldiers in Paul's compartment began discussing the various actions that Methuen's force had fought in the area six months before, the same actions John had so vividly described in his letters. Paul had brought the letters with him and had read them over and over again during the sea voyage, and knew by heart the names of the places where each battle was fought. He knew too that not many miles away was the farm where John had met the girl who had clearly made such an impression on him. Katerine Reinecke. It had long since festered in the deeper recesses of Paul's mind that, should the opportunity arise, he would do what he could to find the girl, if only to explain to her why his young brother had not kept his promise to return.

Now the train, and fate, had brought Paul to within a few miles of where she lived, and when the train jerked and hissed to a halt at Belmont Station, he found himself in the grip of a dreadful dilemma. There may never be a better time to make good on the secret promise he had made to his crippled brother, yet, set against this, was a stronger commitment and his primary reason for returning to South Africa.

He had only a few minutes to make up his mind, and as the engine built up steam and the carriages jolted against each other and jerked forward he snatched his luggage from the rack and pushed his way through the passengers crowded around the door. Within seconds of making his decision he was standing on the platform watching the train rumbling down the track, leaving him stranded in that isolated town.

Belmont was nothing more than a scattering of tin roofed bungalows and a general store that also served as a bar, and as the train disappeared from view Paul had the sickening feeling that he had made a grave mistake. With no idea where the loyalties of the local population lay, he felt sure they would not take kindly to the prying enquiries of a stranger, and an Englishman.

He made his way to the store. If anyone could answer his questions it would be the owner. Whether he would be prepared to was debateable. Judging by the group of bearded, dour faced men who lined the stoep outside the store and glowered at him suspiciously Paul was pessimistic. Inside there was nothing to raise his expectations, the dim, musty smelling place offering no degree of a welcome. Many of the shelves were half empty, testament to the hardships brought on by the war and evidence that it was not just the combatants who were suffering.

As Paul looked about him the storekeeper emerged from the shadows behind the counter and studied him with the same distrusting eyes as those outside. He was tall and willowy with a heavily veined face behind thick grey whiskers that reached his chin. His age was indeterminable, anywhere between fifty and seventy.

"What can I do for you, friend," he asked in Afrikaans.

"Do you speak English?" asked Paul, insecure in his own knowledge of the language.

"Aye, I do," replied the storekeeper, his brown eyes betraying a concealed smile. "Well enough for a Scotsman at any rate." He studied Paul carefully, clearly surprised by the stranger's presence. "But what would bring a Sassenach to a place like this if he's not in uniform."

Paul continued to look around the store, in no hurry to state his true business. "I'm in need of a few things, I thought I could get them here."

"That still don't answer the question. What would you be doing in a place like this with the war still going on up yonder?" He rested his bony elbows on the counter and stroked his chin. He looked down at the luggage on the floor. "Why would you get off the train when there ain't much of anything here? Not to do some shopping?"

Paul glanced over his shoulder and noticed that some of the men from the stoep had gathered around the doorway. He moved further along the counter, indicating that the Scotsman should follow. "I'm looking for a family that have a farm close to here," he said in a low voice. "The name is Reinecke, do you know them?"

The Scotsman stiffened and Paul sensed an unwelcome movement from the doorway.

"And why would you be wanting to know?"

"I have personal business with them," replied Paul.

The Scotsman's eyes flicked towards the men in the doorway. "It's dangerous to ask questions like that, laddie, so you'd better have a good reason."

"I have, and you have my word that I mean them no harm. They would want you to tell me."

The Scotsman shook his grey head and let out a deep breath. "These are trying times. Old friends are now enemies, so you may not be as welcome as you think."

"But you do know them?" asked Paul hopefully.

"I did'nae say that, laddie, but you state your business and I'll see if I can stop them from taking too much of an interest in you." He jerked his head at the men who had now edged into the store.

Paul thought for a moment, although it seemed he had little choice. There were still many Afrikaners living in the Cape Colony and it was impossible to gauge where their loyalties lay. The Scotsman relied on them for his living and he couldn't afford to lose their trust. Paul leant closer to him and as briefly as possible gave his reasons for the enquiry. By the time he had finished the Scotsman was nodding his head gravely.

"Aye, we heard about what happened out there right enough. So, that young soldier boy was your wee brother, was he? I don't suppose he'll get any medals for what he did, but he'll no get a bad welcome if he ever came back here." He gave the men by the door a wave of reassurance. "I think they'll nae blame me for telling you what you want to know."

With the storekeeper's assistance Paul was provided with a horse and a young black boy to show him the way. But before setting off he returned to the store.

"I'd like to take them something, a gift," he said after receiving a curt nod of acceptance from the men on the stoep. "You know them, what do you think they would like?"

The Scotsman gave a dry laugh. "I've nae much here that would put things to rights out there. But if you're looking to take something a little food would nae go amiss." He waved his hand around the desolate shelves. "As you can see, we're a little short of a few things, but I reckon we can find something."

After filling a sack with some of the basic provisions that were still available Paul set off with his young guide for the Reinecke's farm. It was, he was told, about a two hour ride across the bleak, windswept veld that was heading into winter. It was mid-afternoon when they left and Paul was anxious to get there

459

before dark. The storekeeper had advised him that, should they come across any riders, he ought not to admit to being English, just as a precaution.

In fact, they saw no one, and as the light began to fade Paul and his guide breasted the kopje from where John had first seen the farmhouse about six or seven months before. Paul was heartened to see the dull glow showing through a small window from where the lieutenant had been shot. He felt the sickening spasm of anticipation as they started down at a slow pace.

As he approached the house the Scotsman's words began to gnaw at him. A lot could have happened to change the Reinecke's circumstances during those months, just as it had with John, and he may not be as welcome as he first assumed. He left his horse with the boy and indicated that he should wait.

The steps up to the veranda creaked loudly as Paul mounted them and he hesitated, not wanting to cause any undue alarm, or provoke a violent reception. When there was no apparent response, he carried on up the steps and stood to one side of the door, tapping on it lightly.

Soon he could hear nervous chattering coming from within, and footsteps crossing the floor.

"Who is there?" called out a woman's voice in Afrikaans.

Paul put his head to the door. "My name is Pearson, I'm looking for Katerine Reinecke."

The door remained closed, but Paul could hear the woman's voice which was quickly joined by another, a younger female speaking in a high pitched, excited tone. Suddenly the door flew open and the girl stood there, wide eyed and bursting with expectation.

"John, John Pearson." The words came out in a breathless rush, a mixture of thankfulness and disbelief. "I never thought to see …"

The words died on her lips as Paul stepped out of the shadows. "I'm sorry, I'm not John. I'm his brother, Paul. Are you Katerine?"

Gradually she overcame her disappointment and nodded her head. "I'm sorry, I just thought …" Her expression changed suddenly to one of concern. "Why have you come, is he …?"

Paul gave her a reassuring smile. "John's in England. He was wounded, they sent him back home."

From inside the house the woman spoke sharply and Katerine stepped aside, dropping her head apologetically. "I'm sorry for my bad manners, please come inside."

"Thank you, but first I have something for you." He went back to the horse to collect the sack of food before following the girl into the house. He placed the sack on the table. "It's just some food, but the storekeeper in Belmont said you might be pleased for such things."

Katerine looked inside the sack and spoke to her mother who rushed over to see for herself. She spoke to her daughter and there were unmistakeable tears of gratitude in both pairs of eyes.

"You are a kind man," said Katerine, "just like John. I never thought to see him again, although I hoped every day. I can't believe you have come. Please, sit down and tell me how he is." Her voice was breathless with excitement.

Paul looked sadly at the girl. She was very much as John had described her, although the deprivations she must have suffered during those past months had taken their toll. Her cheeks were pale and her face was thin and sallow from lack of proper nourishment. Her hair hung lank and dull, and through her dress he could see the bones of her shoulders. Paul felt a deep sorrow for her, just as he had done for his brother. They both deserved so much more than circumstances dictated.

"John was badly wounded," began Paul as the girl stared back at him in dread anticipation of bad news. "He was in hospital for a long time."

"But he is all right now?" she interrupted impatiently. "He will be coming back to South Africa?"

Paul lowered his eyes, unable to meet hers. He saw no point in hiding the truth, to raise false hopes, and he shook his head. "He is as well as he will ever be. The bone in his leg was too badly damaged to mend properly and he was forced to leave the army."

"But he is alive, and that is the most important thing." The relief on her face was palpable. "He promised he would come back for me when the fighting is over, but you are here so I know he will not come."

In an involuntary movement Paul reached across the table and took her cold hands in his. "Not because he didn't want to, Katerine, that's why I came here, to explain. His injury means that he will be crippled for the rest of his life." He watched her face as she digested the news. "He thought you wouldn't want him as he is, and that's why he won't be coming back for you."

Up to that point she had managed to keep her emotions under control, but now her face became more drawn, twisted with anguish. "But he promised! He promised he would come back for me, just as I promised I would wait."

"And he had every intention of doing so, believe me. He wrote to me, telling me all about you, and how he felt. But when he found out how badly he was hurt he felt he couldn't hold you to your promise."

Katerine turned to her mother, providing her with a few words of explanation before fixing Paul with her tired, watering eyes. "It wouldn't have made any difference to me," she said tearfully. "I love John, he was so kind to me, and to my family. It does not matter to me how badly he is hurt. I will always want to be with him."

Her reaction was nothing less than Paul should have expected. The way John had described her in his letters, and on his return home, should have awakened Paul to the depth of feelings she had for his young brother, and now he wondered if he had done her any favours by his visit, that she would be better off for knowing the truth.

He looked about him, at the bare walls of the room, the crude, sparse furnishings. "Where are the rest of your family?" he asked, hoping to draw the conversation away from his brother. "Your father and brother, where are they?"

Katerine spoke again to her mother, clearly seeking permission to speak of things that were liable to cause them distress. The woman said a few words and covered her face with her withered hands. Katerine addressed Paul in barely more than a whisper.

"My father died a few weeks after he escaped from the British soldiers. It was because of John's kindness that he was able to spend his last days with his family and not in a prison camp. We were able to bury him on his own land." She wiped away some tears with the back of her hand. "Soon after that my brother ran away to join the commando, we have heard nothing from him since. We don't know if he is dead or alive. My mother became so ill with worry, he is just a boy."

Paul's heart reached out to her. "I'm so sorry for you. It can't have been easy for just the two of you. Is there anything I can do?"

She shook her head, failing to find a smile of thanks. "Was it stupid of me for believing he would come back for me when our people are fighting against each other?" It was her turn to take Paul's hand. "When you see him again tell him he will always be in my heart, and that I will never give up hope of seeing him again.

Her simple faith and loyalty almost broke Paul's heart. "I'll tell him, you have my word on that. I will also tell him how foolish he is for giving up on someone as lovely as you." He got up to leave. "I'm on my way up to Johannesburg, but I should like to come back to see you again, if I get the chance."

Before Katerine could give him a reply her mother struggled to her feet and spoke harshly to her daughter. The rebuke brought a little colour of embarrassment to the girl's cheeks and she looked sheepishly at Paul.

"I'm sorry, but my mother has reminded me again about my bad manners." She toyed with the sack on the table. "You were kind enough to bring us this food, so the least we can do is to ask you to stay and share it with us. Besides, she has also reminded me that it is not safe for you to travel in the dark and you should stay for the night. You can have my brother's room and the boy can sleep in the barn."

Paul hesitated as he considered the logic of her argument, then, realising how hungry he was, he gratefully accepted. Also, the thought of travelling back across the veld in the dark held little appeal for him. Katerine was pleased too, it gave her ample opportunity to ask Paul endless questions about John, his life growing up on a farm, the things he liked and disliked, and particularly if he had known many girls in England. She also wanted to know in minute detail what he had said about her, if he still thought about her when he returned to his homeland. Paul gave her all the answers and assurances he could, knowing them to be the truth. He also knew that if ever a couple were meant to be together it was this innocent young girl and his equally innocent brother. It was in that instant that he made a secret pledge to do everything within his power to reunite them.

The following morning Paul rose early, ready to leave. Katerine and her mother joined him on the veranda. The girl neither made nor asked him for any promises, she simply kissed him twice on the cheek, one for him and one for his brother.

Back in Belmont Paul was once again forced to address his own problems. There were no trains through to Kimberly expected for at least three days, and the prospect of spending so much time in that bleak place held no appeal, especially when the urgency of his mission had resurfaced. Even at Kimberley he would have only accomplished half his journey.

When he asked the advice of the Scotsman, Grierson, the old man looked at him as though he were mad. The idea of a 'wet behind the ears Sassenach' making his own way across hundreds of miles of wild terrain struck him as being insane. He thought it more likely to find a sober man in Glasgow on Burn's night.

Then, with a twinkle in his eye he added, "but it's nae impossible, laddie, if you've a real mind to do it."

He raked around amongst his littered shelves until he found a tattered map which he laid open on the counter top. Indicating the spot that marked Belmont he traced the railway line northwards, through Kimberley to a place another forty miles further on called Fourteen Streams.

"See here," he said, a dirty fingernail covering the place. "If you can get yourself that far without getting shot by the Boers or the British, you can cut across country following the Vaal River. It'll take you within a few miles of Klerksdorp and the railway into Johannesburg. A man travelling on his own didn't ought to attract too much attention, and I reckon with a bit of luck you should be able to make it in five or six days."

Paul made a close study of the map. It certainly looked possible enough to him, but, as Grierson pointed out, he would make an easy target for a Boer bullet, or fall victim to the travel restrictions of the British authorities. His best chance lay in avoiding any unnecessary contact with anyone liable to ask him too many awkward questions, and to keep clear of towns.

"You'll need a good horse and a pack animal," went on Grierson, "and supplies for a week, just in case. I'm in no position to be charitable, laddie, but if you've the money I can get you everything you need."

"Then get it together for me, Mr Grierson," grinned Paul, hiding his apprehension. "I'll be leaving first thing in the morning."

Filled with the pioneering spirit that had first brought him to that country, and wrapped up against the cold drizzle that shrouded the veld in a thick mist, Paul set off early the following morning with Grierson's battering of warnings and good wishes still ringing in his ears. That he could find his way across this vast country was not highest on his list of concerns, his greatest fear was being mistaken for an enemy and shot out of hand by whichever side happened to cross his path. And of equal concern, was losing his vital supplies through any number of accidents that could befall him.

For the first day he followed the railway line past Graspan and over the Modder River Bridge which was occupied by a company of Engineers under the command of a captain. Paul showed the officer the pass signed by Colonel Palmer and he seemed impressed enough to allow Paul to pass unhindered. Once across the river he left the railway and struck off towards the northeast, crossing the border into the Orange River Colony, hoping to save himself at least half a day, as well as avoiding any unnecessary questioning at Kimberly.

It was a largely featureless landscape, criss-crossed by numerous small streams and broken up by a few low kopjes. There was little vegetation in the early southern winter which added to the barrenness that surrounded him.

Grierson had provided him with a canvas sheet from which to make a rough bivouac to protect him from the cold rain and cruel winds during his nights in the open. He rationed himself to two meals a day, one taken midmorning, and the other at night, both eaten cold as he feared a fire would attract unwelcome attention from anyone within a few miles.

He saw little sign of human life, giving a wide berth to any of the isolated farms he came across. It was a lonely and monotonous journey and at times he craved company. But with that company would come the risk. It was impossible to know who was friend or foe, until it was too late.

For the first two days he made what he considered to be good progress, then, late on the third day, he reached the Vaal River approximately thirty miles west of Bothaville. He followed the course of the river for a while until the encroaching dusk made it too dangerous to continue, and he was forced to camp for the night. The next day he would search for a suitable place to ford the river and cross, at last, into the Transvaal.

Greatly encouraged by his progress he celebrated with a good meal and then slept soundly until he was woken just before dawn by what he thought was thunder. He lay under the canvas sheet and listened for several seconds before he could finally interpret the noise, not as the continuing roll of thunder, but as the approaching rumble of hooves.

Leaving his shelter, he climbed to the top of a low ridge about fifty yards away. He could see nothing. The vast expanse of veld was still heavily cloaked in the last vestiges of night, although he was certain that riders were coming towards him, probably heading for the river. He ran back down to his camp and hastily loaded the pack horse before saddling his own mount, praying that, in the dark, he had left behind no tell-tale clues to his presence. He expected the riders were most likely Boers, travelling at night to avoid any British patrols, and that being the case the best he could hope for was to be left in the middle of nowhere with just his life intact.

He swung up onto his horse and set off at a gallop, following the river bank in a north-eastern direction, hoping to find some cover. The sky was beginning to lighten and soon he would be visible to anyone up to a mile or so away, and with the river still too deep to ford he would be trapped with no way to retreat. He began to panic, and for the first time since leaving Belmont he wished he had stayed on the train to Kimberley. He had been a fool to believe he was capable of making such a journey.

The impossibility of his situation struck hard, and with the pack horse holding him back he had no chance of outdistancing them. He couldn't give up his supplies, and if he continued to run it would only persuade his pursuers of his guilt. His best hope, he reasoned, was to stop and face them, and pray they would see him as no threat, and allow him to continue unmolested.

Paul turned his horse away from the river and up the gently rising ground to a point where he could see them, and be seen. At the top of the slope, he reined in his horse and scanned the rolling landscape. In the growing light he could just make them out, they were less than a mile away and coming on fast. He strained his eyes, but his vision was impaired by the cold wind blowing directly into his face. The riders had covered about half the distance before Paul allowed himself a sigh of relief. They were in a column of twos, not Boers but a British troop, Lancers, by the look of them.

Jubilantly Paul waved his arm in the air, anxious they should not mistake him for the enemy. At first it seemed they had not noticed him, so he shouted to them before starting down the far side of the rise to intercept them. A cry went up from the column and the officer in charge brought them to a halt a few hundred yards away.

"English, I'm English," Paul shouted as he continued towards them.

A sergeant and two troopers were ordered out to escort him in and he rode with them until he was in front of the officer who looked him over suspiciously while the escort remained close.

"Who are you, and what the devil are you doing out here?" demanded the officer, a captain who was well past his prime and sat his horse heavily and round-shouldered. "Don't you know there's a war on?"

"Of course, I do," replied Paul indignantly. "My name's Paul Pearson, and I'm on my way to Johannesburg."

"And what's your business there?" asked the captain, unconvinced of the stranger's identity.

"My partner and I owned a mine there before the war. I had to leave him behind in Johannesburg and now I'm on my way back there to find him and reclaim the mine, if the Boers haven't destroyed it."

"And what proof do you have that you're who you claim to be?"

Once again, the pass issued by Colonel Palmer was to prove invaluable, and as the captain had met the colonel, Paul's description of him was the final proof.

"I ought to take you back with us to Kimberley," went on the captain. "I can't leave you to roam about out here on your own, not when the damned Boers are still everywhere."

"I'm not roaming about, captain," insisted Paul, "I was looking for a place to cross the river, but I know exactly where I am."

"But the country's not safe, man," blustered the officer irritably. "We were on our way to reinforce the guard at Roodewal, but the Boers beat us to it." He shook his head with a tired resignation. "They captured an entire infantry regiment and fired what supplies they couldn't carry away with them. There was nothing we could do. If I were you, I'd forget about Johannesburg and come with us back to Kimberley."

"Well, if it's all the same to you, captain, I think I'll just carry on. I've got no interest in this war beyond finding my partner and getting my property back. I've got this far so I'm prepared to take my chances with the Boers."

The captain clearly had greater concerns than the safety of a single stubborn civilian. "Suit yourself, I haven't the time to stand here arguing with you." He gave a casual salute. "I wish you luck, I think you'll need it."

Wheeling his horse about he gave the order to move off, leaving Paul to watch as the column galloped off across the veld in the direction of Kimberley. When he could no longer hear the drumming of horses' hooves an eerie silence descended over him and he was once again left with his feeling of loneliness. A temptation to give up his journey and race after them almost overwhelmed him, but he shrugged it off and cursed himself for his weakness.

"No, damn it, no!" he shouted at the vast expanse of empty veld and turned his horse back towards the river, and the Transvaal.

For most of the day, he followed the course of the winding river, testing it whenever he spotted a likely crossing, but the early winter rain had already raised the level, and each place he tried defeated him. It was late into the afternoon when the most promising opportunity presented itself, and for the first time that day he had real cause for optimism. The river bank suddenly flattened out to form a shallow sandy beach that sloped gently into the water, and appeared to do the same on the far bank. He had to try. It may be his last chance to cross before the level of the Vaal was bolstered by the emptying of the Valsch River less than twenty miles upstream.

Taking a tighter grip on the rope attached to the packhorse he tentatively urged his mount into the water at an angle to the far bank so that the horses were not hit by the full flow of the river. By the time he reached the middle, the water was up to the animals' flanks and lapping over his thighs, but he was half way across and soon the chilling water began to subside and, with a loud whooping of success he threw his arms around the horse's neck. Minutes later he had reached the far bank, back once again in the Transvaal.

As he struck out for Klerksdorp, less than a full day's ride away, he uttered a prayer of thanks, and that evening he allowed himself the luxury of a fire to dry his clothes and have his first hot meal since setting out from Belmont. He ate well, ready for an early start the following morning.

Klerksdorp was typical of most small townships in South Africa, an assortment of tin roofed buildings. It was also the railhead for trains into the western Transvaal, and when Paul rode into the town late that day, tired but elated, he went straight to the station. The next train to Johannesburg was leaving at six o'clock the following morning.

With Lord Roberts once more in pursuit of the elusive Boer commandos as they fled northwards, Johannesburg adjusted quickly to its new masters and simply got on with its life.

When Paul walked out of the railway station, he was surprised to see that so little had changed since he had been forced to leave nearly eight months before. The greatest difference was the sight of British troops on the streets, and Paul was immediately struck with the thought that, had not John been wounded, they might even now be enjoying another emotional reunion. Apart from the presence of the soldiers there was nothing to remind Paul that the war was still continuing in the surrounding country. It was almost disappointing, as though he had been forced out under false pretences.

From the station he made his way through the familiar, and once again busy, streets intending to go straight to the hospital as being the best source of news of Frank. Since boarding the train at Klerksdorp, he had thought of little else but the fate of his friend, and now that he was about to find out, he wondered if he really wanted to know. Guilt and self-recrimination had plagued him ever since he had deserted Frank in the hospital, and if his friend had survived, would he now be in the mood to forgive. Of course, more than anything he wanted him to be alive, but as he mounted the steps up to the hospital entrance fear gripped him.

In the corridor Paul made enquiries with the first nurse he saw, but she had only worked there for three months and had no knowledge of Frank, although she knew the Welsh doctor, and yes, he still worked there and was currently making his ward rounds. She directed Paul to his office and invited him to wait. Unable to settle he paced the floor, keeping an anxious eye on the door as he waited for the doctor to return.

When Davis finally entered, he looked older than Paul remembered, thinner and excessively gaunt. His hair was still wild and turning noticeably grey. He peered at Paul over the top of his glasses, his face displaying a vague recognition.

"The nurse said I had a visitor," he said hesitantly. "Don't I know you?"

"Paul Pearson, doctor," he said, holding out his hand. "I was here when my friend was brought in, Frank Trevithick."

"Yes, of course," he said, pumping Paul's arm. "Well, I never expected to see you back here so soon."

"I had to come back, I had to find out about Frank," said Paul, almost too afraid to ask. "He did live, didn't he, doctor?"

Doctor Davis sat down behind his desk and invited Paul to take the other chair. Taking off his glasses he massaged his eyes before looking up at the ceiling and giving a little chortle of amusement. "Quite remarkable," he muttered as though to himself, "quite remarkable indeed."

"He survived then, he's alive?" Impatience was getting the better of Paul.

Davis gave a wry smile as he lowered his eyes until he was looking directly at his visitor. "Oh yes, he's very much alive." The words had a ring of incredulity about them. "Your friend seems to lead a charmed life, Mr Pearson. I doubt that anything other than old age will ever kill him."

"So, you've seen him since he left here?" asked Paul, his excitement rising. "How was he?"

"A lot better than he ought to be. I saw him just a few days ago, here in town, as large as life."

Paul clenched his fists and pushed them into his cheeks as he leant forward on the chair.

"Thank God, and thank you, doctor. Do you know where I can find him?"

"I should try out at his mine, that's where he's been spending most of his time by all accounts."

Paul leapt to his feet and shook the doctor's hand with renewed vigour. "Thank you so much, doctor."

He almost ran from the hospital. Gone was the feeling of fatigue and worry that had wracked his body for days, and all that mattered now was to find Frank and return to the life they had shared before the war had thrown their existence into turmoil.

Paul searched the town to find a stable that had a horse to rent. Most had been stripped bare, any worthwhile mounts having been commandeered by the fleeing Boers on their way through to Pretoria. Eventually he found a stable prepared to part with a round-bellied, aged nag that looked as though it was barely capable of leaving its stall. But in his euphoric state Paul was happy to part with the last of his money just for the chance of finding his friend.

This was the final lap, the culmination of an arduous journey that had begun in London weeks before, and one that he sometimes felt would never be completed. The news he had received at the hospital was better than he had dared to hope for, and could only be eclipsed now by their meeting.

Frustratingly the horse failed to recognise the urgency of the task she was being asked to perform and set her own pace. Dusk was descending by the time Paul was in sight of the mine, recognising the shape of the buildings and engine house silhouetted against the fading western light. He felt his heart racing, and a cold sweat broke out beneath his bush hat as he tried to rehearse what he would say.

Everything in the mine compound was silent, the only noise was the rattling of loose sheets of tin disturbed by the wind. There was no excited conversation coming from the Kaffirs' huts and no one had come forward to challenge him. Suddenly Paul was struck by the realisation that the doctor had been wrong, Frank had not been to the mine.

In the dim light it was impossible to see if the Boers had carried out their threats to destroy the mines, although, to Paul, everything looked as it should be, with the exception of life. He dismounted and strode over to the bungalow that used to be his home. There was no light inside, but a cursory glance told him that it had been lived in recently. By whom, was a question he couldn't answer. He was beginning to think it had been a wasted journey and he quickly sunk into a mire of despondency.

It was too late to even contemplate riding back to Johannesburg that night so he would stay and return in the morning. For the sake of nostalgia, he wandered about amongst the buildings, recalling the memories they held for him, mostly good, but some that brought a lump to his throat, especially when he thought of Joseph. The boy had died needlessly, his only crime a blind loyalty to his master. Paul wondered where he had been buried, feeling a need to pay his respects, and offering the apology he deserved. An impulse led him towards the low kopje from where he used to sit and dream of Jenny. If he was to choose a final resting place for the boy that is where it would be.

He quickly found the grave, in fact he found two, both marked with a carefully carved wooden cross, but he had no time to consider who the second may belong to when a slight movement at the top of the kopje made him start. Night had completely closed in by now and the figured appeared like a great ghostly apparition. Paul knew it could only be one person.

There was no more than ten yards between them yet neither made any attempt to rush forward in a welcoming embrace, that small distance was an immense gulf of disbelief. This was not how Paul imagined it would be, there were no wild shouts of joy, no hugging or back slapping, only a silent, heart tearing acknowledgement of the other's presence.

Paul moved first, cautiously stepping forward as though Frank was merely an illusion that would disappear when threatened, but when there was nothing but the two graves between them, he stopped.

"Hello, Frank," he said hoarsely. The words seemed totally inadequate, but they were the only ones to struggle past his trembling lips. "How are you?"

Frank remained silent and motionless, like a great carved monument, aloof yet protective. In that moment Paul felt like a trespasser in a world to which he had given up all rights by his leaving. Then, quite suddenly, Frank was upon him, rushing forward between the graves, throwing his tree like arms around Paul and swinging him off his feet.

"Paul Pearson, you daft bastard," he cried, crushing Paul to his barrel chest, "for pity sake!"

Tears of unparalleled joy flooded down Paul's cheeks. He could find no words to describe how he truly felt. "For God's sake, Frank, I'm so pleased you're alive."

Frank released him just enough to grip him firmly by the shoulders, their wet eyes meeting in a mutual expression of exhilaration. "Did 'e ever doubt I was alive?" he whispered, shaking his friend violently.

"I prayed, but it never seemed enough. I should never have left you, Frank, I'm truly sorry."

Frank clamped a big hand over his friend's mouth. "'E had no choice, I know that. Did 'e really think I would blame 'e for going?" He placed an arm around Paul's shoulders and led him back towards their bungalow. "We've got a lot to say to each other, Paul lad, but we've no need to waste words on apologies." He pulled Paul close just to reassure himself. "I need a drink to convince myself 'e ain't my imagination, and then we can drink 'til morning. It is 'e, Paul, isn't it?"

For hour after hour they talked, one listening intently to the other and then interrupting with endless questions of their own. One bottle of brandy followed another, but the intensity of the conversation nullified most of the effects of the drink, and when dawn broke over the mine, they were both exhausted, yet completely sober.

"So, what happens to the mine now?" asked Paul when all other conversation had dried. "Can we hire more workers and get on with production?"

"Is that what 'e wants to do?" questioned Frank, staring hard at his friend. "Is that why 'e came back?"

"I came back to find you, to make sure you were safe, but yes, I did hope we could restart the mine if the Boers hadn't destroyed it." As the first rays of daylight spread into the bungalow Paul felt there was something Frank was hiding from him. "Isn't that what you want too?"

Frank took a deep breath and slowly let out the air. "I never thought it would be necessary for anyone to ask I a question like that. Before this damn war started, I would have given my life for this mine, I very nearly did." His eyes narrowed. "But now I'm not so sure what I want. Two people I cared about are buried out there because of this mine, and now, suddenly, it doesn't seem so important to hang on to it."

Paul shook the tiredness from his mind. "But we can't just give it up, not with all the time and money we've put into it."

"Not give it up, Paul lad, sell it." Frank got up from the chair, stretched and went over to gaze at the dawn through the dirty window. "This will all be British territory soon, just like the Orange. That means more investment in the mines by the likes of Werner-Beit, and the others. We can't hope to compete with them,

Paul, we haven't got their resources." He turned to face his friend, his eyes fired by enthusiasm. "But what we have got is a damn good mine with rich seams for anyone with the money to dig it out. With the money from the sale, and the gold me and Andries hid away, we would both be rich men, Paul, rich enough to do whatever we wanted. What do 'e think, do 'e still want to be a miner for the rest of your life?"

Paul stared bleary-eyed at his friend, unable to absorb all he had said. This had come as something of a shock from a man who had mining in his blood.

"'E could go back home and provide for that daughter of yours," went on Frank while Paul was still turning over the possibilities. "This is no country for 'e, and these past months have left a bitter taste in my mouth. I think it's time for a change."

Paul massaged his forehead, he was too exhausted to put up an argument, even if he had one. "If I were honest with myself, Frank, it was you I really came back for, not the mine. I would have willingly given up my share for your safety, so to give it up now for a profit would be no hardship at all for me." He held out his hand and Frank readily accepted it. "Here's to our fortune, and our future, whatever it may bring."

"To the future, Paul my friend, to the future."

The words trailed into obscurity as Paul slipped into a deep, comfortable sleep. For him it was time to exchange reality for pleasant dreams.

Chapter Twenty-Seven

Northamptonshire
Autumn, 1900

Grace opened her eyes as the clock on the landing chimed four times. She reached across to the empty space beside her, clutching at the cold sheet where her husband should have been lying asleep. It was the third time in the past week that he had left her alone in the marital bed to spend the night in his own room, or elsewhere. She had tried to make sense of the vague excuses he had offered, that his work demanded he rose early and he wanted to spare her the disturbance, but the more she thought about them the more she realised that was all they were, excuses.

It was true that for several nights during the previous months she had sat up late with her uncle as his health continued to deteriorate, returning to her own room in the early hours of the morning, but never once had she disturbed her sleeping husband.

Insisting, on so many occasions, that his early rising was of no inconvenience to her, he merely fobbed her off with the same excuse and accused her of acting like a spoilt child. But there was nothing childish about the barren relationship that now existed between them; the passion of that night when she had given herself to him so completely was now a distant memory, and the times since when he had taken her, those first expressions of tenderness and affection had gone. Since then, he had used her to satisfy his own lust with no consideration given to her needs.

And then there were the whispers and sniggering amongst the kitchen girls below stairs, that stopped so abruptly whenever she appeared. That was not a figment of her imagination, it was proof that they knew, or guessed at, something. She should have asked, demanded an explanation as was her right, but fear of the answer prevented her.

But there were other, more important, issues that occupied her, after Doctor Colley was forced to tell her that her uncle was unlikely to survive beyond Christmas. All her time and energies were now lavished on his welfare and she pushed her personal problems into a convenient recess at the back of her mind. Making his final weeks as comfortable as possible was her prime consideration and there would be time enough to deal with Matthew when there was nothing else to command her attention. It was a miserable time for her, a time when she so desperately needed the support of a loving husband and got none. Whenever anything was said Matthew retaliated by saying that, with her uncle's end so near, his responsibilities to the estate increased. It was a lame excuse and only served to reinforce her resolve to sort the shortcomings in her marriage when the time was right.

But now it was four o'clock in the morning and Grace knew there would be no more sleep for her that night and, as on so many other mornings, she lay there analysing her miserable situation. A maelstrom of confusion and suspicions swirled around in her brain, and it was in those bleak hours before dawn that she did all her crying, away from her dying uncle and insensitive husband. In the morning she would once again become the mistress of Millwood House.

Any suspicions she had about where Matthew spent his nights could have been so easily dispelled with a visit to his room, but the truth would be an inconvenient distraction to the duty she owed her uncle. Uncertainty was a dreadful burden to carry, but less so than the weight of her uncle's unstoppable slide towards death.

Matthew lifted the fleshy arm that weighed heavily across his chest and slipped quietly from the bed. Molly Turner gave a nasal snort at the disturbance before turning over and continuing with her slumbering as Matthew climbed into his trousers and left the room.

Back in his own bed he thought of Molly and how much she pleased him, giving everything of herself and receiving in return her share of the pleasure, and the few shillings he gave her. There was nothing delicate or refined about her, just a wholesome earthiness that had attracted Matthew to the whores of the district. Grace was beautiful, there was no denying that, yet he found no warmth in her body, no enticing comfort he found in the more voluptuous women. No, Grace would provide him with the sons he needed and not the carnal satisfaction he craved.

It was a morning, about mid-November, that Grace slept later than usual, having spent much longer with her ailing uncle the night before. She heard the heavy tread of hurried footsteps on the landing outside her room followed by an urgent tapping on the door. She called out and Jenkins entered, his face strained.

"It's the master, ma'am. I've sent for Doctor Colley but I fear it might be too late."

With a gasp of dismay Grace threw on her dressing gown and ran to her uncle's room, where she found him lying on his back staring up at the ceiling through glazed, unseeing eyes. His breathing was barely audible, coming in weak, irregular gasps.

"I found him like this when I brought in his medicine," said Jenkins in an apologetic tone. "He seemed so much worse that I felt it necessary to send for the doctor."

"You were right to do so," Grace assured him, bending close to her uncle and stroking his brow. "He seems not to be breathing. Is there nothing we can do?"

"Perhaps if we sat him up, ma'am, it may help."

Between them they lifted Haveringham into a sitting position and propped him up on pillows. After a short while his breathing appeared to ease, and as Grace looked on, anxious and helpless, his lips twitched as though trying to form words. Nothing came other than a few hoarse coughs as he sunk back deep into the pillows.

Grace took hold of his cold, clammy hand. "It's all right, Uncle Rufus, I'm here," she said gently, holding back the tears that were so desperate to flood her cheeks.

He gave no outward indication that he was aware of her presence until his fingers flexed weakly against her skin and he half turned his head to her.

"It's me, uncle, Grace," she whispered, pressing her lips to his brow. "Can you hear me?"

He continued to stare vacant eyed before his pale lips parted in a thin smile and she knew that he could.

"Please don't try to speak. We've sent for Doctor Colley, he should be here soon."

As the smile faded from his jaundiced face, he tightened his grip on her hand, watery eyes pleading for her attention.

"Not much time," he gasped, those few words exhausting the breath in his failing lungs. He gulped in more air and with his free hand he beckoned her closer. "Tell me the truth, are you happy now?"

Grace swallowed hard, almost choking on the deceit that was to follow. "Yes uncle, I am, truly I am." She hated lying to him but it was no time for an admittance of the painful truth.

Haveringham nodded his satisfaction, and then he began tugging urgently at her hand. "Know your father," he croaked faintly, "heed his advice."

Grace stiffened as she struggled to comprehend. The words were indistinct, but she was sure of what she heard. "My father! Did you say my father, uncle? Who is he? I have to know."

A look of calm resignation replaced the strained expression on the old man's face as though he had said all that was necessary and was now content to let his life slip peacefully away. His eyes flickered before closing and his breathing, though shallow, set an easy rhythm.

"Please, Uncle Rufus, no," she begged tearfully, laying her head on his chest and hearing the final gentle beats of his heart. A long sigh escaped from his lips as he passed comfortably from her world into the next. "No, uncle, please don't go, don't leave me."

Jenkins placed a tender hand on her shoulder and when she turned to face him, he nodded slowly, his own eyes red and moist.

In the dismal hours that followed Grace felt more alone than she had done her whole life. Even the death of her mother had not affected her so deeply; then she had a circle of school friends to help cushion her grief. Now she felt she had no one, not even Matthew who could manage only a few insincere words of condolence before returning to the more important task of reasserting his claim to power. The king is dead, long live the king, he thought with a wry smile to himself.

Matthew's sole concession to that sorrowful time was to spare a few hours from his busy life to attend the funeral, which, at Haveringham's express wish, was a simple affair. At the graveside it was left to Jenkins to take Grace's arm and support her when she looked like fainting.

"I feel so ashamed of you," remarked Grace bitterly when the last of the mourners had left the wake. "Do you feel nothing at my uncle's death?"

Matthew's response was contemptuous. "Like you say, he was your uncle, not mine. You mourn him for as long as you wish, I have more important things to occupy my mind. I'm the master here now, remember."

Defiantly, she would not allow the anger he had provoked in her to overcome the grief she was feeling, a grief she knew would be with her for the remainder of her life. For the rest of that day, and for most of the next, she locked herself in her room, refusing to come out even to take her meals, and allowing no one but Jenkins to see her. During that time, she expunged from her all the emotions that had previously bound her to Matthew, and when she finally emerged it was to face a life totally devoid of any warm feelings towards him.

Two days later the lawyer, Miles Fennymore, arrived at Millwood House for the formal reading of the will. Although Grace did not wish it, the lawyer thought it best that Matthew be there to avoid any unnecessary further explanation, or misunderstanding, afterwards. It immediately occurred to her that her uncle had had the foresight to protect her inheritance and she gave the lawyer a concealed smile of gratitude. The only other person present was Jenkins, and when the four of them were seated in the library Fennymore took the documents from his case and cleared his throat.

"Despite the size of my late client's estate the will is, in essence, quite uncomplicated," he began, directing his address at Grace who, he assumed, would be his new client. "There is just one principal beneficiary." He inclined his head at Grace which brought an agitated reaction from her husband. Fennymore returned his attention to the documents before him. "There are a number of small bequeaths to some of the estate workers, the value of which I don't propose going into, but are dependant of length of service. Suffice to say I shall take care of them, if required to do so." Once again he looked at Grace and she nodded her assent. The next he read directly from the will. "To my friend, and loyal servant, Edgar Jenkins, I leave the sum of two hundred and fifty guineas and a pension of one hundred guineas a year following his retirement, and providing he continues to serve my niece as he did me."

As Jenkin appeared shocked Grace reached over and patted his arm, while Matthew glowered at the pair of them.

"A most generous gift," commented the lawyer, "but one, I'm sure, is well deserved."

Jenkins fidgeted on his chair with acute embarrassment. He had devoted all his working life to the Haveringham family and considered the treatment he had received from them was payment enough. He was completely overwhelmed by the bequest.

"I don't know what to say, ma'am," he said, emotion affecting his usually calm tone.

"I agree with Mr Fennymore," she told him. "My uncle thought a good deal of you, Jenkins. He valued your service, as do I."

Matthew continued in his sullen silence, waiting impatiently to discover how the will would assure his future, and power.

Fennymore cleared his throat again, studying the will in detail. "Now we come to the main portion of the will which deals with the balance of the estate. I shall read this verbatim so there can be no possibility of misinterpretation." He coughed loudly to emphasise the gravity of the occasion. "To my niece, Grace Pearson, nee Haveringham, I leave the residue of my estate, including the property known as Millwood House, all the lands attaching thereto and including all buildings, livestock, goods and chattels pertaining to the estate. Title to all such property shall remain exclusively with her until her death, at which time it will pass solely and equally to any children from the marriage. Should she die without issue the estate will pass in accordance with her wishes. It is my express instruction that there shall be no transfer by right to the husband of the marriage."

Unable to contain himself Matthew leapt to his feet. "What does that mean?" he demanded of the lawyer.

With a look of unguarded distain Fennymore maintained his composure at the interruption. "It means, sir, that your wife alone is the beneficiary of her uncle's estate, and that you have no claim by right of marriage, should anything happen to her."

So, the old devil has done it, thought Matthew, throwing Grace a sardonic smile. "Even from the grave he still doesn't trust me. Well, it makes no difference you can't run this estate without me."

Grace avoided his cold eyes and made no reply. Matthew was right, her uncle had never completely trusted him, and he had done nothing in return to prove the old man wrong. Even after death her uncle was looking out for her.

"Well," said the lawyer, rubbing his bony hands together, "I think that concludes the business of the will." He addressed the following directly to Grace. "Naturally I hope I can continue to be of service to you as I was to your uncle. Should you require counselling regarding the will, or any other matter, please feel free to call on me at any time."

As she took his hand and thanked him, she was struck by a sudden thought. "As a matter of fact there is one thing I should like to speak to you about, in private." She looked hard at Matthew and Jenkins. "If you will please excuse us." She waited for them to leave, which Matthew did with some reluctance as Jenkins held the door open for him. "Tell me, Mr Fennymore, is there anything belonging to my uncle in your keeping?"

Fennymore's thin face creased in a confused expression as he considered the question. "Why do you ask?"

"It's just that my uncle mentioned some time ago, when he was first taken ill, that there was a box left in your keeping, only to be opened after his death."

The lawyer continued to appear puzzled until a flash of recollection crossed his features. "Yes, of course, the box! It was so long ago I had quite forgotten about it." He tapped his temple with a finger. "As I recall the key to it is kept in his room, in a silver snuff box."

"I know the snuff box!" declared Grace excitedly.

"Would you like me bring it over here?"

Grace gave the question a brief though. "No," she said firmly. "I'll come to your offices tomorrow. Shall we say eleven o'clock?"

Instead of returning to work immediately after leaving the library Matthew hung about in the hallway, waiting for the lawyer to leave. Despite his display of arrogant indifference to the terms of the will he was far from happy at being excluded from what he believed to be a husband's natural rights. He was also aggrieved at the generosity Haveringham had shown towards his man servant, which he interpreted as a further snub to himself. For months he had looked forward to the old man's passing, and what it would mean to him, but now he felt slighted and cheated.

"So, what was this private business you couldn't talk about in front of me?" he demanded of Grace, while Jenkins showed the lawyer to the door.

"I should have thought it obvious that if I wanted you to know then I would have asked you to stay. As you so aptly pointed out, it was private business." She tried to pass him, but he stood firmly by the library door and caught hold of her arm. She glared angrily up at him. "Stop this foolishness, Matthew, and get out of my way."

The corner of his mouth curled into a cynical sneer. "I won't be cheated out of what's mine. I've worked hard to keep this estate going, and I've as much right to a share of it as you, or anyone else. What do you think it would be worth now if it wasn't for all my hard work?"

"Oh, don't worry yourself, husband dear, I've no wish to prevent you from improving my inheritance." She gave him a patronising smile. "You can go on living here, and I'll even suffer your little indiscretions, all the while it suits me." She shook her arm free and pushed him to one side. "Now, go about your business, and leave me to attend to mine."

Waiting until Matthew had stormed out of the house she went up to her uncle's room. It was the first time she had been in there since his death, and even though nothing had been touched, the room had an eerie coldness about it, and it made her shudder. For a moment she stood still in a silent vigil to his memory, recalling all the times she had been in there, and all the hours spent by his bedside. She knew that sooner or later she would have to sort through his personal belongings, but it was far too soon for such a painful task and for the time being she concerned herself with only the silver snuff box that had always sat on the walnut inlaid table by the window.

The lid of the box was delicately engraved with birds of prey, although Grace had never taken too much notice of it, or its workmanship. Now she picked it up and cupped it lovingly in her hands, holding it close to her chest as though it was the very embodiment of her uncle. She lifted it to her lips before finally taking off the lid to look upon the small, insignificant key. She took it out, twirling it in her fingers while trying to imagine what secrets it could unlock.

That night, unsurprisingly, Matthew crept into the marital bed. He was not so stupid, or arrogant, to ignore the delicacy of his situation, and that it was only his flimsy marriage that kept alive any hope he had of achieving his ambitions.

Grace had gone to bed early, leaving Matthew in the drawing room being comforted in his despondency by a bottle of the uncle's fine brandy. She had lain awake, not through any disturbing reason of her marriage, but because her mind was preoccupied by the possible contents of her uncle's mysterious box. It was only the sound of Matthew entering the room that drove such thoughts from her head, and it came as an unwelcome intrusion. She turned over so that her back would be to him.

She tensed when she felt him close to her, and, when his arm curled around her waist, she pushed it away.

"I thought this was what you wanted," he breathed, pressing closer, "a husband to share your bed."

"Being a husband is much more than sharing a bed otherwise you would be married to half the whores of the county," she replied bitterly, keeping her face buried in the pillow. "I was the one who married for love and you for convenience. Now I feel the same as you and I've no wish to change that, so you are free to spend your nights with whatever trollop you choose."

Matthew laughed as he continued to force himself on her. "Surely you're not going to deny me the right to father a child. At least you'll have someone to inherit all this, a son to carry on the traditions of such a noble house."

She turned over to face him, pushing him away as she did so. "Let you father a son to bring up in your own selfish image!" she hissed vehemently. "No, Matthew, I would rather give all this away than to be tied to you by children. I've no wish to bring up any children in this loveless marriage, and if you're so eager to father a son do it with someone else, I'm sure there's no shortage of willing candidates. If you want to use this bed for sleep that's your right, but beyond that we have no further obligation towards one another."

She rolled away from him, fully expecting that he would forcibly seek some selfish and vengeful gratification, but a few minutes later he left the bed and she heard the bedroom door close behind him. There was a clear finality to his leaving, that it removed once and for all any possibility of a reconciliation. She took some comfort in that.

In the morning she was surprised to discover that she had no regrets and was able to return her attention firmly on the intriguing contents of her uncle's box. She also began to think more about what he had said to her just before he died, 'know your father'. What had he meant? Was it possible there was a connection between her father's identity and what was locked away in the box? It was such a disturbing supposition that she was unable to eat breakfast.

So impatient and unsettled was she that by ten thirty that morning she was sitting in the outer office of Fennymore's chambers playing nervously with the fingers of the gloves Paul had bought her the previous Christmas. Every few minutes she would glance up at the wall clock only to discover that the hands had barely moved, and the lawyer was still engaged with his previous client.

Eventually the door to the lawyer's office opened and a ruddy faced rotund gentleman appeared looking less than content with the outcome of his appointment. But Grace paid him no heed as she looked anxiously at the aged clerk who beckoned her forward.

Fennymore leapt to his feet and greeted her effusively. "My dear Mrs Pearson, I'm so sorry to have kept you waiting." He waved her towards a chair. "Please, do take a seat." He rang a small bell on his desk and the clerk returned. "Some tea please, Squires," he ordered as he beamed at Grace. "I take it tea is acceptable?"

"Yes, thank you," she replied distractedly. "Mr Fennymore, I have the key, do you think we might have the box straight away."

"Of course," he said with a patronising smile. "This must all be most disquieting for you." He rang the bell again. "Squires, the tea can wait a moment, would you be good enough to fetch Mr Haveringham's box from the vault."

While they waited the lawyer took a snuffbox from a desk drawer and held it up. "Would you mind?" As Grace shook her head, he pinched a small quantity of the brown powder onto the back of his hand and took a large snort before repeating the process with the other nostril. "Ah, that's much better. The first sign of cold weather plays the devil with my sinuses."

Grace threw him a sympathetic smile as she wrung her hands impatiently beneath the desk, trying to contain the anticipation and apprehension that was building within her. And when Squires returned her gaze never left the innocuous looking box bound in burgundy leather which the clerk carefully placed on the desk in front of the lawyer. So engrossed was she in dwelling on its contents that she quite forgot the key until reminded of it by Fennymore. She searched her bag, and when she handed it over found her hand was shaking.

"Now we shall see," remarked the lawyer in his detached way, taking the key and trying it in the lock. "Ah, yes, there we have it."

He lifted the lid and Grace peered over the expanse of the desk to see inside. It contained, as far as was immediately visible, two documents of neatly folded parchment, each tied with green ribbon and sealed with red wax. Fennymore lifted them out and held them up for Grace to inspect.

"Your uncle's seal and, as you can see, they are quite intact. Do you wish me to open them?"

"No, I'll do it." She took the first one from him and, with trembling fingers, she broke the seal.

As she unfolded it, she could see straight away that the writing was not in her uncle's hand. She spread the document open on the desk and tried to take in the text in one go before steadying herself to read it line by line.

'I, Ned Stiles, being the natural father of a daughter born on 16th day of June 1879 to Miss Margaret Haveringham of Millwood House in the county of Northampton do hereby and forever relinquish all rights and claims to the said child and do swear an oath never to contact or make myself known to said child. In consideration of my accepting and abiding by the terms and conditions of this agreement I shall continue to remain in the employ of the Haveringham family until such employment be mutually terminated'.

Signed this day 30 June 1879   Witnessed my hand

Ned Stiles   Joseph Fennymore

Having read it once, she did so again and again, and with each reading came a growing feeling of disbelief and anger. Those few lines of text had robbed her of the right to a father who, at times, had been no more than a few yards from her. What right had anyone to deny her that, and why did her father agree to give up all rights to his daughter?

She threw the document across the desk at Fennymore. "Did you know anything of this?" she demanded angrily in an outpouring of deep resentment.

The lawyer slowly read the document and shook his head. "This was witnessed by my father. He dealt with all your uncle's affairs until he died some fifteen years ago. I knew nothing of this."

"Buy why? Why keep this from me for all these years? Hadn't I the right to know my father?"

Fennymore sighed, a long professional sigh. "It's not for me to judge the right or wrong of it, my dear, but you have to try and understand that for an old and revered family such as the Haveringhams there would be a great deal of stigma attached to a child born out of wedlock." He tapped the document with his finger. "This type of agreement is all too common, I'm afraid."

"But why would Mr Stiles sign such an agreement in the first place? If he and my mother were in love, why didn't they simply get married?"

Fennymore leaned across his desk, his hands placed in front of him. "You would need to know your grandparents before making any judgement on your mother and this man Stiles. He was an employee, not one of the establishment. I know your uncle had a high regard for him, but he was still just an estate worker. We now live in more liberated times where such marriages are more acceptable." He gave a loud snort which Grace took as a reference to her own marriage. "Your grandparents were very much of the old school, quite severe in that regard and would never have allowed the union, and by the time they died the damage would have already been done. If you are looking for someone to blame then direct your anger towards them, not your mother or father."

Unconvinced Grace shook her head. "But why keep it from me all these years? Why wait until there are no Haveringhams left?"

Fennymore shrugged his shoulders. "I suspect they were your grandparent's wishes." He took a handkerchief from his pocket and offered it to Grace. "Look, I'm aware of how painful all this must be for you, but what's done is done and nothing can change it. It's your future you have to consider now. It's none of my business of course, but what do you wish to do now?"

Grace wiped away a tear from her cheek and drew a deep breath. "My uncle's last words to me were 'know your father'. It seems clear to me that it was his way to make amends, that he wanted me to contact this man Stiles, but I've no idea where to look. Since he left my uncle's employ he could have gone anywhere."

"Don't worry yourself on that score, my dear, I'm sure we can be of assistance in that regard." His face took on a pinched expression as he handed her the other document. "Shouldn't we see what this one contains?"

She had not yet come to terms with the shock of discovering her father's identity and was unsure if she was ready for more distressing news. As she slowly unfolded the paper and recognised her uncle's handwriting she could only hope for some understanding. It was dated nearly two years after the first document and she took her time in reading.

'My dearest niece

It grieves me more than mere words can express how sorry I am that I must write to you thus. My own parents have now passed and, while I am bound by the oath I made to them, I would like it known that the decisions taken regarding your future were never mine.

You will know by now that your father is Ned Stiles, a good man who would have made you a good father. He did not abandon you by choice but by threat and I can only hope you will someday allow him the opportunity to explain the circumstances of your birth.

I can only imagine the hurt you must be feeling now, but I beg you to direct your anger at the dead, and not the living. Ned Stiles longed to be your father and, God willing, may be for the time he has left.

Speak to him if you will and I pray you may both find peace.

Take care my child

Your loving uncle'.

Tears rolled off her cheeks and fell in droplets onto the paper, if only she had been told before. So much of her life had been forfeited because of social prejudices and now she felt so badly cheated.

"Find him for me, Mr Fennymore," she sobbed purposefully. "Find him as soon as you can."

When she left the lawyer's chambers there was no greater purpose in her life than to discover the truth surrounding her birth, and the relationship between Ned Stiles and her mother. Had she been the product of a single night of lust or a child born to a couple bound in love but torn apart by shame and ignorance? She had to know the truth.

Too many thoughts occupied her mind to return immediately to Millwood House, she was in dire need of a distraction. As the carriage left Northampton, Grace directed the driver to take the road to Nobottle.

John Pearson gathered up the firewood he had been chopping and hobbled back to the cottage. It had taken him many hours of practice to wield the axe accurately without losing his balance, and now he was justly proud of his achievement.

"That should keep us going for a bit," grinned Peggy Dobson as he dropped the logs into a wicker basket beside the hearth. "Can't beat a roaring fire this time of year."

"I'll need to get in a good store of logs before the weather turns, I can feel the cold in my leg already. I don't know what it's going to be like once the snow's thick on the ground." Cautiously he lowered himself into the chair by the fireside and massaged his aching thigh. "I'd be a lot more use around here if it wasn't for this."

Peggy Dobson abruptly stopped what she was doing and came over to him, wagging her finger. "Now you listen to me, John Pearson, I wasn't expecting no unpaid servant when you came here. I'll always be in your debt for giving comfort to my Georgie in his last minutes and you being here is the nearest I can get to having him home. You've been a great comfort to me, and giving you a roof over your head is the least I can do to repay you. I appreciate the help you give, but you've no obligation where that's concerned so don't go feeling guilty."

When John had left the hospital to return to Northampton for his final discharge from the army Matthew had reluctantly agreed to his moving into their old home on Hibberd's Farm. Grace had protested that a room should be made

486

available to him at Millwood House, but John had declined the offer after noting his brother's reaction to the suggestion. Also, it seemed to him like an act of charity, which he was determined to shun as firmly, just as he did with sympathy. He preferred to look after himself on the farm.

Grace had visited him a number of times, even accompanying him when he first visited Peggy Dobson. John was grateful for Grace's support as he explained to the grieving mother as painlessly as he could the circumstances of her son's death. It was at that same meeting, when Grace told the woman how John was struggling to look after himself, that the idea was first mooted that he should move in with her. At first, pride had forbidden him to consider the idea, but both women put forward such a compelling argument in its favour that he was eventually forced to submit. He had not regretted the decision, and now he did what he could around the house by way of recompense.

It had proved to be a good arrangement for them both, for while the stalwart Mrs Dobson hid the pain of her grief behind a façade of joviality John understood the comfort she took from his company, as he enjoyed hers. Grace visited when she could, usually bringing with her little gifts of food and other luxuries that were beyond the means of their limited income.

This time, though, she brought no gifts, just two pieces of news, the impact from which she was still recovering. It was unlikely that John would have heard about her uncle's death, and now she had even more startling information to share with him. In John she found a good companion, replacing Paul as someone in whom she could confide. Like his brother John was a sympathetic listener, unlike her husband, and it felt right that he should be the first to hear about her father.

Mrs Dobson pulled back the worn curtain and peered through the window at the sound of carriage wheels in the lane. "It's that young lady friend of yours, Miss Grace." She wiped her hands on her apron and fussed with her greying hair.

"She's my brother's wife, Mrs Dobson," said John grinning, flushing with mild embarrassment. "You make her sound like my fancy woman."

"A fine looking woman nonetheless," she said with a knowing nod as she went to open the door. Mrs Dobson flapped her hands excitedly as Grace walked from the carriage. "Such a pleasure to see you again, miss. Come in and take a seat by the fire, you must be frozen."

John got to his feet and went over to embrace his sister-in-law and she gave him a light kiss on the cheek. "Hello, John, how is that leg of yours, still giving you trouble?"

"Getting better by the day. I can swing an axe now without falling over. Isn't that right, Mrs Dobson?"

"I'm saying nothing so I won't be accused of telling no lies," she replied, narrowing her eyes at him. "Sit yourself down, my dear, and I'll put the kettle on for a warming cup of tea."

"Take no notice of her," laughed John, "she fusses over me too much as well. Anyway, Grace, how are you?"

"I'm fine, John, thank you."

"And that brother of mine, is he behaving himself, being a good husband? And what of your uncle, is he feeling any better?"

"Goodness gracious me, young John, let the girl get her breath," shouted Mrs Dobson from the kitchen.

Grace stared into the fireplace, the flames highlighting the sadness etched into her face. "Uncle Rufus passed away more than a week ago. I'm sorry I didn't let you know sooner."

"Oh, Grace, I'm so sorry."

"Thank you." She turned her heavy eyes to face him. "That's one of the reasons I came here today, to tell you that."

Mrs Dobson came scurrying in from the kitchen. "You poor child," she said, placing a comforting hand on the girl's shoulder. "We both know how much he meant to you."

"I miss him terribly. He was so good to me, like a father." That last remark brought about a fresh flow of emotions and her spirits lifted a little. "But I have some other news, and you two will be the first to hear of it."

Barely able to contain herself she quickly related to John and Mrs Dobson details of her meeting with the lawyer and the extraordinary news she had just received. It all meant little to Peggy Dobson, but when Grace had finished John shook his head in disbelief.

"Ned Stiles!" he exclaimed, scratching his head. "I remember him. He chased me once when I was scrumping apples from your uncle's orchard. So, it's Ned Stiles who's your real father?"

"I find it all so incredible too, but it's the truth. All the time he lived on the estate and I never knew, and no one would tell me."

"And what do you intend doing about it?" asked John when Mrs Dobson went to deal with her boiling kettle. "Do you know where he is now?"

"Mr Fennymore, the lawyer, is going to find him for me. I have to go and see him, it was my uncle's last wish. I need to hear from his own lips why I have been without a father all these years. What happens after that I don't know, I suppose it depends on how we both feel when we meet, how we feel about each other after all this time. He must have known who I was when I came back to Millwood House so what must have gone through his mind."

As Grace took her tea John exchanged a cautious glance with Mrs Dobson. "And what about Matthew, will you tell him?" he enquired.

Grace appeared confused by the question. "I don't know, I haven't given it any thought." She gazed back into the fire and for a time seemed mesmerised by the crackling flames. It was several seconds later when she turned away. "I feel ashamed to admit it, but the only thing remaining of our marriage is my name." She spoke the words as though burdened by blame. "I've never spoken to you of the difficulties we've had, but I think you know your brother well enough to believe me when I say they are not entirely of my making."

"I think I know my brother well enough to be convinced that none of it is of your making," retorted John tartly. "Has he been mistreating you?"

"No, oh no!" she exclaimed. "At least, not in the way you suggest. But any love he had for me existed only in my imagination and I feel so used, deceived. I don't think I want to tell him about my father, deceiving him will be like my revenge. Besides, Matthew and Ned Stiles had no love for each other so it would serve no useful purpose telling him."

"I think it's such a wicked shame," announced Peggy, sadly shaking her head. "A lovely young girl like you deserves better." She glared at John. "If I ever set eyes on that brother of yours, I'll give him a piece of my mind, you see if I don't."

John and Grace looked at each other and burst into a spontaneous bout of laughter. "Thank you, Mrs Dobson." Grace reached out and squeezed the woman's hand, "but I'm well able to fight my own battles. I am grateful for your support and friendship, though, it's been a real tonic for me coming here."

She left the cottage an hour later with her spirits raised, knowing that she had, at least, two true friends on whom she could depend.

The house stood on its own at the bottom of a narrow lane, which was bordered on one side by a low hedge of hawthorn and on the other by a shallow ditch, beyond which were barren fields. The house was surrounded by a white painted fence and neatly kept gardens. On the gate was a sign, SWALLOW COTTAGE.

Grace climbed down from the cab and stared, first at the sign and then at the house. The excitement that had fluttered within her that morning when she left Millwood House had slowly transmuted itself into a chronic nervousness that gnawed at her stomach and made her feel sick. Unsure if there was anyone at home, or of the welcome she would receive, she instructed the cab driver to wait for fifteen minutes and if she had not returned by then he was to come back for her in two hours.

It had been almost three weeks since her visit to the lawyer, and the day before her current mission he had arrived at Millwood House with an address at which, he was reliably informed, Ned Stiles could be found. She had declined Fennymore's offer to accompany her, stating it was something she would prefer to face alone.

Telling only Jenkins where she was going, and instructing him to say nothing to her husband only that she was away for the day, she had left the house early for Northampton where she caught the train to the spa town of Leamington.

Now, clutching the piece of paper with the address, she stood in front of the house full of trepidation and conscious that the driver was watching her with more than idle curiosity.

At last, she gathered her courage together and lifted the latch on the gate. Pushing it open she walked slowly up the flagstone path which curved towards the cottage door and divided the neatly tended lawn. With her heart beating fast within her chest she took hold of the black cast iron knocker and gave the door a delicate tap. It was with a sense of relief that there was no immediate response, and she had to fight an urge to scurry away. It took another few minutes to pluck up more courage to lift the knocker again and give the door a more resolute rap.

A moment later Grace heard a woman's muffled voice inside. "Bless my soul, I'm coming," it said in an irritated tone. Footsteps hurriedly approached the door which was thrown open. The woman was short and plump, her round face was red from exertion and bore an annoyed expression which faded on seeing Grace. "Oh, my dear, do beg my pardon, I wasn't expecting visitors, except the baker's boy, and he knows how long it takes me to get down those stairs."

"It's quite all right," replied Grace as the woman looked her up and down with some suspicion. "I'm sorry to have disturbed you."

The woman continued to stare at her, as if trying to recall if she should know her before deciding she would need to ask. "What is it I can do for you, miss? Are you lost?"

"No, at least I hope not," replied Grace falteringly, giving the woman a nervous smile. "I was informed Mr Ned Stiles is supposed to live here. Is that right?"

The woman's face creased into a scowl. "And who would be wanting to know?"

"My name is Grace Pearson, Mr Stiles used to work for my uncle, Rufus Haveringham. I have some personal business with him."

The woman gave an indignant snort. "Personal business, is it? For more than thirty years my brother served that man faithfully and look how he was treated. If he's sent you here with an apology then he's a mite late."

"I know what happened with Mr Stiles, but my coming here has nothing to do with that. My uncle died recently and I've other business to discuss with your brother."

"I'm sorry to hear about your uncle, Ned always spoke highly of him." She stepped away from the door and gave a curt nod of her head. "You'd best come in and wait, they'll be back shortly."

She showed Grace through to a comfortable parlour, the room smelling strongly of lavender and as neat and tidy as the garden. The woman poked some life into the fire burning in the grate and offered to take Grace's coat before inviting her to sit.

Left on her own Grace fidgeted with her fingers as she waited, and stared about the room. The thought struck her that, had Stiles been at home, the worst would be over by now and she would know of his reaction, but he wasn't, and she had time to dwell further on what she would say when he did arrive. When she finally heard voices from the back of the house the sickly feeling returned.

From another room came the unmistakeable voice of Ned Stiles followed by the hushed tone of his sister as she warned him of their visitor. There was an audible exclamation from a third person, a woman. Grace wrung her hands as she anxiously watched the door.

With her stomach turning like a butter churn Grace got to her feet as the door opened and Ned Stiles stepped into the room, looking no different than Grace remembered, except perhaps a little greyer in his whiskers. Behind him stood a woman, a stranger, and both their faces reflecting Grace's own anticipation.

"Well, miss, this is all a bit of a shock, I must say." Ned shuffled forward uncomfortably, holding out his hand. "My sister has just told me about Mr Haveringham. I'm truly sorry, really I am."

Grace thought how strange it was that a father should greet his daughter in such a way before dismissing the notion. He would not be that until she allowed him to be.

"Thank you," she said weakly as she took his hand, "but you must know my visit here is not just to bring you that information. A letter would have sufficed."

Only Grace saw the instant alteration in his expression, a mixture of guilt and relief.

He turned to the woman. "Rose, would you be a love and see about some tea for our visitor." When Rose had left, he turned his attention back to Grace and beckoned her to sit. "I'm not sure I understand your meaning, miss," he begun hesitantly, taking the seat opposite. "My sister said you had personal business, but if it's nothing to do with your uncle's death I'm not sure how I can be of help."

Grace was in torment. Had the years of denial driven all thoughts of her from him, forcing him to forget her very existence?

"You know who I am?" She focussed her attention on the fire, unable to look at him. "My mother was Uncle Rufus' sister, who, I believe, you knew." She was giving him the opportunity to make a free admission. She wanted him to tell her he was her father. She turned her tortured face to him. "You did know my mother?"

Slowly and solemnly, he nodded. "Yes, miss, I knew your mother well. A very beautiful woman she was." To the guilt was now added sadness and regret. "What is it you're wanting with me?"

To admit that you are my father, to hear you say the word, that is what I want, thought Grace. "I believe you know what I want, why I am here." Her eyes were pleading with him. Was he going to force her to say? "I've been to the lawyer and seen the agreement you signed all those years ago."

The suppressed pain of twenty years of remorse pushed itself to the fore bringing tears to Ned's tired eyes as his head dropped into his hands. For several seconds he sat like that until the clattering of crockery on a tray brought him back from whatever emotion had engulfed him. He took a handkerchief from his pocket and blew his nose as he leapt to his feet. As Rose entered, he strode over and took the tray from her.

"Ned?" said Rose as he carried the tray to a table under the window. She had clearly noted the strained look on his face. "Ned, are you ill?"

He turned to face her, although it pained him to do so. "Rose, you know this young lady, Mr Haveringham's niece," he said, his voice hushed and trembling.

"Yes, of course," she retorted, "we were at her wedding."

Grace shot them both a startled look. "You were at my wedding?"

"Yes, miss … sorry, ma'am, we were both there, at the back of the church." Rose gave Ned a sideways look before turning back to Grace. "Ned said he had known you as a child and wanted to be there. We weren't invited, of course, but your uncle made sure we got in to hear you speak your vows. Very beautiful you looked too."

"My uncle knew as well!" It was all becoming unbearable for Grace and she covered her face with her hands.

"Rose, I haven't been entirely truthful with you," said Stiles, holding onto the mantle shelf for support. "When I told you I had known Miss Hav … Mrs Pearson as a child I wasn't being honest."

He can't even say my name, thought Grace, as she watched him struggle to explain. Why can't he just say he is my father? "He didn't know me as a child, not even as a baby."

"Ned, what is she's saying?"

"Sit down, please, Rose my love, it's time for me to speak plainly." There was a pitiful look of regret on his face as he straightened his back and clasped his hands behind him. He waited for Rose to sit, as though he feared the news would cause her to faint. "You should never have found out, not like this, but all these years I've both dreaded and longed for a moment like this, when the truth would come out." He went over and placed a steadying hand on Rose's shoulder. "Rose, this young lady is my daughter."

Rose's eyes widened until Grace was sure they would burst from their sockets. The woman clasped a hand to her mouth, and for what seemed like an eternity an ominous silence fell over the room.

Finally, Rose spoke. "But she's a Haveringham, Ned, how can that be?"

Ned Stiles lowered his head as a shame overwhelmed him. "That's something we must talk about together, Rose," he said in a dry whisper, "but for now you need to know it's the truth." He raised his eyes to Grace and she nodded her acceptance.

"We heard all sorts of rumours below stairs, but I never …"

"That's enough, Rose," said Ned sharply. "I'm sorry, love, but we don't need to speak of rumours, only truths." He took Rose's arm and helped her off the chair. "Would you mind if Grace and me spoke alone for a while, there's things that need to be said and it's best done between the two of us for now."

Still numb from the news Rose agreed, giving Grace a brief curtsey before quietly leaving the room. At the door she looked questioningly back at the two of them before closing the door behind her.

"I'm sorry if Rose said ... it's all come as a bit of a shock to her." He took his place again opposite Grace. "It's all a bit of a shock to me too, you coming here like this, but I can't imagine how you must have felt when you found out." He found the courage to study her face. "I can only think it must have been a disappointment to find you have a father that's no more than a common man, not high born." He shook his head desolately. "You should never have found out about me."

"Is that what you wanted? And don't you think I had a right to know my father, whoever he was?" Her voice was full of resentment. "All these years you've been denied to me because of some ridiculous agreement you made with my mother's family." She stopped when he began to choke on the tears he was holding back. "I'm sorry, but I didn't come here to blame you, just to discover the truth."

"You have every right to feel some bitterness towards me. What I did must seem unforgiveable to you now." His regret was overwhelming him. "Will you walk in the garden with me? I've spent all my life outdoors and I can speak more easily in the open air."

He went into the hall and fetched her coat, draping it around her shoulders. Outside they crossed the lawn and he led her to the back of the house where the garden was divided by narrow pathways into neat squares of flower beds and vegetable patches. They were accompanied by an awkward silence until Ned spoke.

"My sister is responsible for this," he said softly, extending his hand proudly around the garden, "but Rose and me spend a lot of time out here since we've not much else to occupy our time." It was clear to Grace that the garden was the last thing he wanted to talk about, but she allowed him the distraction and was pleased when he stopped and faced her. "It doesn't seem right for me to go on addressing you as miss, not now you know. Would it be appropriate if I called you Grace?"

It was all the encouragement she needed, and was waiting for. "I think, under the circumstances, it would be entirely appropriate." She smiled tantalisingly, feeling it would have been right even to slip her hand in his arm, although she resisted the temptation. He was still a virtual stranger to her. "I want to know about you and my mother. Did you … Did you love her?"

The face that had been full of remorse suddenly showed a flicker of light. "Yes, I did, very much, and I believed she loved me, she told me so. That was the tragedy of it all, that we loved each other so much. She was such a beautiful young woman and you are so much like her. Whenever I saw you out riding it almost broke my heart, I thought it was her. That's when I used to see her, when she was riding. I was never allowed to speak to her up at the house. Long before we were … well, I used to dream about her, not daring to believe we could ever be together." He paused when he felt Grace's wide, expectant eyes on him. "I was nothing more than a farm hand in those days, someone who should have known his place and not have any fancy notions above his station. Then, one day, she stopped and spoke to me. I could scarcely believe it, me a labourer and her the master's daughter." He shook his head as though the very idea of it still mystified him. He smiled wryly. "It turned out that she had her eye on me too, although we both knew there could never be anything between us, her parents would never have allowed it. But we used to meet, in private. One whole summer we had together, she would ride out to where I was working and we would sneak off into the trees where no one could see us." His cheeks flushed as he recalled those days. "We both felt guilty, of course, but it only added to the pleasure of being together."

Grace felt giddy as she absorbed every detail of their forbidden romance, and how close it could have resembled her own. She bit into her trembling lip as she fought to prevent the tears of happiness that began to roll down her cheeks. She now knew that she was not the product of a sordid lust, but a child born out of genuine love.

"Then, just before Christmas, she suddenly refused to see me again," he went on with a palpable bitterness to his voice. "I didn't even know she was expecting our baby. I found out that she had confided in her maid that she was frightened of what would happen to me when her father found out who was responsible for her condition. I was young and headstrong and all I cared about was her. Like a fool I went to your grandfather and offered to marry her." He winced visibly as he recalled that occasion. "I won't burden you with the details of what happened, but I still bear the scars of it to this day. They would have sent me away, but they were too afraid that your mother would follow, so, instead, when the baby was born the two of them were sent away to London."

"But I don't understand," interrupted Grace, "why didn't you go with her?"

He gave a hollow laugh. "Why do you think they made me sign that damned agreement?"

"You could have refused."

He gave her a cynical smile. "When the baby … when you were born, your grandparents insisted that you should go for adoption." He gulped back the emotion that almost choked him. "Your mother was so upset she threatened to kill herself, and it was only on condition of my signing that agreement that she was allowed to keep you."

Grace threw her hands up to her face and sobbed convulsively. "Oh, dear God, how could they have been so cruel?"

"All I ever wanted was to marry your mother and be a father to you, Grace. It almost broke my heart when you came back to Millwood House, and that's why I left without trying to clear my name. I couldn't bear the thought of being so close to you without being allowed to tell you who I was."

"So, you had nothing to do with that attack on Matthew?"

He shook his head. "Your uncle knew the truth of it, but he understood."

"But when my mother died there was nothing to stop you from contacting me."

"Your uncle loved you and he regretted what happened, but he also knew you would blame him for keeping the truth from you and that's why it was agreed that nothing would be said until after his death. He couldn't bear the thought of you hating him while he was alive."

They had reached the bottom of the garden where there was a seat. They sat together, each longing for the other to seal their new relationship with a tender touch, but there was still a gulf between them that the years had created and only time could heal.

"Would you forgive me if I can't yet find it in me to call you father?" It seemed strange that she should be so reticent when it was her who should feel guilt at her family's cruel actions all those years ago. "I need time to come to terms with my past as well as thinking of what to do with my future. Could I possibly call on you again when you've had the chance to explain everything to Rose and your sister?"

"There's nothing to forgive, Grace," he assured her. "And if I were never to see you again then it would be me I would blame, not you."

"I hope Rose is understanding when you tell her." She got up to leave. "Tell me, do you love her as you did my mother?"

He nodded guiltily. "And I think she feels the same about me."

"Then I'm truly happy for the two of you."

Chapter Twenty-Eight

Since returning from the visit to see Ned Stiles, Grace had become obsessed by the novelty of finally having a father in her life, and could give little attention to anything else. Even the difficulties within her marriage, and the constant arguments with Matthew had receded into relative insignificance as she thought endlessly on how best to progress her new found relationship. Whether she liked the idea or not, she now had a new family to consider and it was up to her how she wished to take advantage of that fact.

In the few days following her visit to Leamington she had spent much of her time alone, shut away in her room or in the library, deep in contemplation. How much different, she wondered, would her life have been if her mother had been allowed to marry the man she loved. Would she now be the mistress of Millwood House with the fortune that came with it? One thing she did know for certain was that wealth was no guarantee of happiness, the happiness that came from being brought up in the bosom of a loving family.

The final outcome of all her meditation and soul searching was the resolve to arrange another visit to Mr Fennymore, who appeared surprised by her unexpected appearance.

He pushed his surprise to one side and smiled graciously as she was shown into his office by the apologetic Squires.

"An unexpected pleasure indeed, Mrs Pearson," he said, taking her hand and raising it delicately to his lips. "I can only assume this has something to do with your meeting with Mr Stiles. I hope it wasn't too distressing for you?"

She reassured him with a smile as she sat down. "On the contrary, Mr Fennymore, it was most beneficial for both of us, I believe. I'm pleased I went, and now I have a very clear understanding of what happened. And that's the reason for my visit here today."

The lawyer gave her a questioning gaze as he took his place behind the desk and locked his fingers across his chest. "I'm not sure of what further service I can be in that regard, dear lady. Surely it's now a matter to be resolved between yourself and Mr … your father."

Grace leaned forward in her chair and planted her hands firmly on the desk. "He was wronged, Mr Fennymore, and not just by my uncle and grandparents but by my husband as well. I want to make some restitution."

Fennymore gave her his best professional frown. "What is it you intend?"

"I want my father properly compensated for all the wrongs he has suffered. I know I can do nothing to replace all the lost years he and my mother should have had together, but I can ensure that he spends the remainder of his years in comfort." She paused to choose her words carefully. "But more than anything I want him as my father, I want him to be part of my life, and me his. I know that is something only time will achieve and it will be up to me to devote that time, but more immediately I want to settle some money on him, to compensate him for the injustice he had to endure at the hands of my husband. I feel that is the least I can do."

The lawyer leaned back and stared at her, drumming his waistcoat with his fingers. "Well, there's little I can do to allow your father back into your life so I assume it is the financial arrangements to wish me to attend to. Had you any particular sum in mind?"

Grace met his gaze. "One quarter of my inheritance, I thought that fair."

Fennymore shot forward, his patronising expression having disappeared. "My dear young lady, do you have any idea how much that would be?"

"I was rather hoping you could tell me," she replied calm but firmly.

He massaged his temples to recover his composure. "Let me try to explain. The value of your inheritance is tied up inexorably in land, livestock and properties with much less in the way of liquid assets. Do you understand what it is I'm saying?"

"I may be just a young woman, Mr Fennymore, but I'm not a fool."

"I'm sorry, it was not my intention to suggest as much, I was just trying to point out that to raise a sum in cash of the amount you have in mind would entail selling part of your estates." He peered hard at her. "I assume it was a cash settlement you had in mind?"

Grace confirmed his assumption with a nod. "I quite understand the difficulties, and that is why I'm here, to seek your advice."

The lawyer shook his head in despair. "My advice would be to find another way to compensate Mr Stiles. To sell off part of the estate would create a number of problems, one part is very much dependant on another. Even a man such as myself, ignorant of farming, can see that." He took a deep, thoughtful breath. "There is only one piece of land that could be sold without causing too much harm."

"Hibberd's Farm?"

His beady eyes narrowed. "It seems to me you've already given this some thought."

"My uncle never really wanted that land, and neither do I."

"And what does your husband have to say about this?" he asked cautiously. "I take it you have discussed this with him, particularly as he still has a one third holding in the land."

"No, I haven't discussed it with him, but as far as I'm aware I don't need his permission to sell. Am I right?"

Fennymore sighed. "Yes, you are right, that was written into the agreement. Your uncle was most insistent on that. But even if you do sell there will still be quite a shortfall in your intended bequest. I have to council you to reconsider."

"Hibberd's Farm will be sold, there can be no argument on that, but the rest I will consider. Perhaps there are other ways I can make amends." She got up to leave. "After all, money isn't everything."

She left the lawyer's chambers with a feeling of smug satisfaction. She was under no illusion regarding Matthew's reaction to the proposed sale of his beloved farm, although she had never considered herself capable of such vindictiveness. Was she justified in her actions? She certainly thought so. She had no intention to telling him of her plans, assuming he was arrogant enough to believe it was merely a device to win back his affections. Nothing was further from her mind.

Despite the parlous state of his marriage Matthew was content to continue in the role of master, treating the workers under his control with the same harshness that had already earned him their contempt and mistrust. He accepted their dislike of him as the badge of his ultimate authority, the price of his success. To him everything was as it had always been, as it should be, with both his work and his marriage. It was this very attitude that convinced Grace to forge ahead with her plans.

Purely for the sake of appearance, Grace and Matthew continued to eat together in the dining room most evenings, but little passed between them of a personal nature. For her own benefit alone, Grace would enquire of him how well the estate was faring, expressing her doubts when his reply fell short of her expectations. It was not in her interest to allow him to think she lacked any understanding of his management of her inheritance. On the rare occasions when Matthew endeavoured to manoeuvre the conversation towards a more personal nature, she would simply scowl at him from across the table and continue with her meal.

It was a far from happy or ideal existence, nevertheless it suited Grace far more than it could have Matthew since she now felt in complete control of her life, and the secrets she kept from him only added to her fulfilment.

About two weeks before Christmas she made another journey to see her father, and this time the reception she received from his sister could not have been more cordial as she kissed Grace warmly on the cheek and ushered her in from the cold.

"You could have knocked me down with a feather when Ned told me about you," she said with flustered excitement as she ushered Grace into the parlour. "Imagine him not saying anything all these years. Brought tears to my eyes when he told me, I can tell you."

No sooner was Grace in the room when her father came in followed by Rose, tightly clasping him by the hand. Grace looked at the two of them nervously, trying to assess the effect the revelation had made on the pair's relationship.

"This must all be quite a shock to you," she said apologetically to Rose. "I hope my coming back here hasn't caused you any upset."

Rose smiled and turned lovingly to Ned, taking a tighter hold of his hand. "Bless you, no, my dear. There should be no secrets between a man and his wife, and him telling me like that, well, it's brought us closer together, if such a thing were possible."

Grace nodded her gratitude. "You've no idea the pleasure it gives me, being able to visit you like this. I hope I don't sound too presumptuous after so little time, but I think of you as my family, my only family now that my mother and uncle are both dead."

"Presumptuous!" exclaimed Ned's sister, Dolly, throwing up her hands. "Good gracious me, an honour I'd call it. To find out I've got a niece, and one as lovely as you, is an honour indeed."

Ned gently freed himself from his wife's grip and went over to take Grace in his arms. "I've never forgotten I have a daughter, but I did think I would take the secret of it to the grave. You've no idea how proud I feel to finally be able to call you daughter, and if you can find it in you to call me father then I too would be honoured."

Over her father's shoulder Grace caught Rose's eye and gave her a questioning look.

"It's all right, my dear," said Rose with a broad grin. "I'll not insist on you calling me mother."

The whole room erupted into a bout of joyous laughter, marking them, from that moment, as a family. All that afternoon they talked together and Grace fired endless questions at Ned about her mother and life at Millwood House before she was forced to leave. More than once, Grace found herself glancing across at Rose and was relieved to see no hint of hurt or jealousy on the woman's face, even when her husband spoke openly of his love for Margaret Haveringham. If anything, the jealousy belonged to Grace at the depth of love Ned and Rose now had for each other, a love she felt was beyond her reach.

"But what of Matthew, your husband?" enquired Rose when Grace had exhausted all her questions. It had been blatantly conspicuous that Grace had not once mentioned her husband, and knowing the man as she did, the question was tinged with concern. "How does he feel about this new family of yours."

Grace felt her face flush from a sense of guilt and shame. "I'm sad to say that I've not yet told him about any of this." She glanced awkwardly at her father. "You know as well as me how he will feel about it, how he feels about you. I shall have to choose the time carefully before I tell him."

"Then perhaps it's better he never finds out," said Ned, his face creased fretfully. "I'm satisfied enough just to keep this to ourselves if it saves you from any trouble. I beg you not to take any risks on my account."

Grace gave him her assurance and when she got up to leave there was no embarrassment as the pair embraced with the naturalness of a father and daughter, while Rose and Dolly waited for their turn to kiss her on the cheek.

"I've dreamed about this so often," said Ned tearfully as he saw her out, "but I never dared hope it could ever happen."

"I've dreamed about my father too," wept Grace, "and I could not have asked for a better one."

It was late into the evening when Grace arrived back at Millwood House and she was met at the door by a worried looking Jenkins.

"I'm so relieved you've returned, madam," he said as he took her coat. "There's someone waiting to see you. I told him you were out and not expected back until late, but he was very insistent, so I took the liberty of putting them in the library where they wouldn't be disturbed. I hope you don't mind."

"I'm sure you did the right thing, Jenkins," she said thoughtfully before adding. "Do you know where my husband is?"

"I believe he may have retired, madam, although I couldn't be entirely sure."

Retired perhaps, thought Grace, but to which bed? The thought remained with her for only a second before she returned to the burning curiosity of her unexpected guests. As Jenkins went about his duties, she wished she had questioned him further before walking in on an unwelcome surprise.

Slowly, she opened the door, and as soon as she stepped into the room a man leapt to his feet and gave her a respectful nod of his head. His face was familiar to her, although she was unable to straightaway recall the name.

"I'm sorry to have kept you Mr ... What is it I can do for you?"

"Conners, miss, Jack Conners, the Farriers. You came to see us last Christmas with young Paul, ... Mr Pearson." He spoke with a dry, tired voice and he had the drawn face of a man carrying the weight of the world on his shoulders.

"Yes, of course, Mr Conners. But what can be so important to make you wait so long?" A stab of fear suddenly struck her. "It's not the child?"

"In a manner of speaking yes, miss. There was no one else, no one I could turn to for help, and with you being a friend of Mr Pearson I thought of you." Although there was no hint of self-pity in his voice, he was clearly distressed. "I would never have troubled you, not for myself, but it was the little mite. I didn't know what else to do."

Grace stared at him in alarm, recalling the promise she made to Paul to look out for his daughter, a promise that had been pushed from her mind by her own personal troubles.

"Has something happened to her?"

Jack Conners turned his eyes towards a high-backed chair, tipping his head as he did so. Grace followed his gaze, peering over the back of the chair where the child was curled up between the arms, fast asleep and wrapped tightly in a pink woollen shawl. She stared down at the child with a mixture of incomprehension and compassion before turning to the old man for an explanation.

"Why have you brought her here? And where is your wife?"

He gripped the back of the chair with one hand while gently stroking the girl's hair with the other, tears falling into the hollow of his cheeks. "I'm sorry, miss, I know it's not fitting for a grown man to shed tears in front of a lady, it's just that …"

"It's quite all right, Mr Conners, really." She placed a hand on his arm. "Please tell me, what has happened?"

His lips trembled as they struggled to form the words. "Mary, my wife, she passed away sudden like, taken from us these three months since." Seeing how distraught he appeared Grace made him sit while she poured him a brandy. "She had her faults right enough, but she was a good wife to me, and a better mother to little Rosie here. We both miss her something terrible."

"I'm so sorry, for the two of you." She took the chair opposite and reached over for his hand. "I know what it is to lose someone close, but I don't understand why you have brought her here. What can I do? Is it money you need?"

His head was bowed, but he looked up sharply. "No miss, not money. They're going to take Rosie from me, they say I can't look after her proper. I love that child, miss, so help me I do, and I can't bear to see her put in an orphanage, for that's what they want to do. That's why I brought her here. If she can't stay with me then she belongs with her father. I just thought you might know how to get hold of him, you being his friend."

For his sake she held back her own tears of sorrow, although inside she fully shared his heartache. The thought of Paul's daughter taken from a loving home and thrust into the harsh regime of an orphanage filled her with horror. How anyone could believe she would be better off in such a place was beyond her comprehension.

"I've received only one letter from Paul since he returned to South Africa, and I've no way of knowing if my reply ever reached him. I'll write to him immediately, of course, but in the meantime, and if you are agreeable, Rosie will stay here with me. No one will dare try and take her while she's in this house, and you can visit as often as you wish. Would that be acceptable?"

A wave of relief swept across Jack Conners' drawn features, it was almost possible to see the burden being lifted from him. "Bless you, miss, you're an angel. I couldn't ask for more than that, and I know Rosie will be safe with you."

"I'll have Jenkins make up a bed for her in my room so she won't be alone and frightened when she wakes."

Without even touching his brandy the old man got up from the chair and went over to the sleeping child, running his fingers lightly through her hair before bending to kiss her on the cheek.

"I've only brought her with the clothes she's wearing," he mumbled apologetically, "if it's all right with you I'll bring some more of her things over tomorrow."

"Come over by all means," said Grace, smiling warmly, "but don't worry about bringing anything for her, except some favourite toys. It will be a great pleasure for me to buy her everything she needs, and I won't listen to any arguments. I know she will never be my daughter, Mr Conners, but I hope you'll not think ill of me if I pretend, even for a short while."

"I couldn't deny you anything, miss, not after what you're doing for me, and little Rosie here. God bless you."

Invigorated by her new responsibilities, Grace helped Jenkins make up the bed that he arranged to have carried into her room, and when he asked if he should carry the child up she insisted on reserving that duty for herself. It seemed to her, as she held the child close, that fate was playing a decisive hand in compensating her for the loveless marriage she endured. First by providing her with a father and then arranging for the child she had denied her husband. Was the tide of justice finally turning in her favour?

As the child slept soundly beside her Grace lay awake, struggling to keep a perspective on all the recent, and dramatic, developments in her life, while at the same time keeping a watchful vigil over her ward. Worried that Rosemary would awake in her strange surroundings, Grace spent a restless night listening to the gentle breathing in the bed next to hers and imagining that the girl was really her own daughter. When she extended those thoughts to the girl's father her heart began to race.

The clock in the hall struck midnight and there was a sound other than the child's breathing for Grace to focus on. A door opened and closed, followed by the creaking of the service stairs. It could have been Jenkins, or one of the other staff, but it sufficiently aroused her attention to climb out of bed and go to the door. Satisfied that Rosemary had not stirred she put on her dressing gown and went out onto the landing. There she listened as she struck up an argument with herself. Why was she bothering when she already knew that Matthew was not living a life of celibacy? But it was now a question of pride. He was flaunting his infidelity right under her nose, in her house.

She went to the bottom of the stairs, feeling like a sneak thief in her own home. She thought she heard the sound of whispered conversation and giggling, and as she crept up the stairs it became painfully clear that it was her husband's voice she could hear, and from which room it was coming.

By the time Matthew slid naked into her bed, Molly Turner had pulled her nightdress over her head and thrown it unceremoniously onto the floor, at the same time pushing back the bed covers to expose her heavy breasts. It had been several nights since his last visit and she was impatient for him, grasping him roughly by the back of the neck and forcing his lips onto hers.

"Damn you woman," he said breathlessly, pushing her away. "I'm the master here now and you'll do what I want."

He took one of her breasts in his hand and bit hard into the pulpy flesh. She let out a little whimper of pain and then giggled. "Aye, you're the master right enough."

She allowed him to take her with the coarseness she both expected and enjoyed as Grace stood outside the door listening to their loveless passion. Defiantly refusing to give in to a feeling outrage or jealousy she allowed their lust to stiffened her resolve to forge ahead with her planned retribution. Biting hard on her lip she ran back down the stairs, not caring who heard her.

Molly lifted her head from the pillow. "Oh, my good lord, what was that?"

"Lie still you bitch," responded Matthew angrily, thrusting her back down onto the bed. "I've not finished with you yet."

It was a few hours later when Grace finally fell into a deep sleep only to be woken early in the morning by an unfamiliar cry.

"Grandpa, where's my grandpa?"

Grace sat up with a start until she remembered the little girl who now shared her room. In the gloom she could see the child's bed was empty, and for a second she panicked. Rosemary was over by the door trying to turn the door handle.

"I want my grandpa," she sobbed.

Fully awake now, Grace jumped out of bed and went over to her, but the girl cowered back against the door.

"It's all right, my love" said Grace softly. She smiled and held out her hand, "I'm your friend. I'm not going to harm you." She held back, allowing the scared child to accept her presence. "Your grandfather has asked me to look after you. You're going to stay here with me for a little while."

Grace continued to hold out her hands in the hope that Rosemary would come to her in her own time, but the child stayed pressed against the door, her pretty face tight with fear, her red cheeks streaked with tears.

"My name is Grace. I came to see you once. Can I please be your friend?" She knelt down so as not to appear too intimidating. "Are you hungry, would you like some breakfast?"

If there was anything certain to win over a child's trust, thought Grace, it would be food. Slowly Rosemary lowered her head and gave a little nod. Watched anxiously by the girl, Grace got to her feet and went over to the pull cord hanging down beside her bed and gave it a sharp tug. Rosemary watched with infantile curiosity and little by little she edged away from the door and went over for a closer inspection of the cord, attracted by the purple silk tassel on the end. All the time she kept a wary eye on the woman who now appeared to be in charge of her life.

For several minutes she played with the tassel, intrigued by the fine threads that she ran through her fingers and held to her cheek. It was only when Jenkins tapped on the door did her fear return and she ran to her bed and pulled the covers over her. In an attempt to defuse a difficult situation Grace turned the interruption into a game by jumping into her own bed and pulling up the covers before bidding Jenkins to enter.

"We should like to take breakfast in our room this morning, Jenkins," said Grace with a mischievous grin and a sly wink at Rosemary. "Some porridge, I think, lots of sugar."

Jenkins smiled at the girl who peered suspiciously at him from over the covers. He nodded graciously. "Of course, madam."

"Oh, Jenkins," Grace called after him as he turned to leave. "The kitchen girl, Molly, I want her dismissed, immediately."

He looked around sharply. "Dismissed, madam?"

"Yes, immediately. She can have one week's wages, but no reference. I think that's fair, don't you?"

Jenkins gave her a knowing deferential nod. "More than fair, I should say, madam."

When he returned with their breakfast Grace asked him to arrange for the landau to be ready that morning to take her to Northampton, telling him that she would be taking the child to do some Christmas shopping.

"And have you taken care of that other business?" she asked him.

"It's all been dealt with, madam," he assured her.

It took some persuasion to get Rosemary to eat her porridge, but after the first few tentative mouthfuls, it would have been impossible to stop her until the bowl had been scraped clean. Grace watched her eat with immense satisfaction, feeling she was making real progress in winning over her confidence. A hot bath followed, which further cemented their friendship, especially when Grace playfully splashed her with water and Rosemary responded with excited enthusiasm. By the time they were ready to leave the house, the girl was secure in Grace's company, happy to hold her by the hand, although she constantly asked after her grandfather.

On the journey to Northampton, Grace chatted to her about all the sights they passed, replying to the girl's questions while keeping clear of any subject likely to provoke any unhappy memories. But any lingering anxieties Rosemary still harboured of her previous life were well and truly laid to rest once they arrived at the shops, with the brightly lit window displays of festive goods bringing squeals of delight. Her joy was heightened when they went inside the shops, but she was surprisingly undemanding and begged for nothing, accepting all the things bought for her with effusive gratitude.

On the journey home she fell asleep across the seat, her head resting in Grace's lap. Whenever the carriage wheels hit a bump or dip and she looked as though she would stir Grace stroked her long hair and cheek and whispered tenderly to her. As she watched her sleep, it was impossible for Grace to wonder if she could not become too attached to the girl, to think of her as her own daughter. That could never happen, she told herself, the idea was beyond consideration. Rosemary's father was in South Africa, and if he chose to stay there his daughter would eventually be sent out to join him, that was the sad fact that Grace had to come to terms with. Having suffered herself from not knowing her father Grace could not countenance the same fate for Rosemary.

By the time they arrived back at Millwood House Rosemary was fully awake and too excited even to consider the need to take her to bed. Instead, Grace took her to the library and read to her from a book they had bought that day. They were still there when Matthew arrived back from work.

He enquired of Jenkins if his wife was home before going to the drawing room, as he usually did, to pour himself a drink. But rather than sit alone brooding he preferred that evening to inflict his mood on Grace.

From beyond the library door he could hear Grace talking, and as curiosity took over, he pushed open the door. All he could see was the top of his wife's head as she sat in the chair with her back to him, and when she heard him enter, she stopped reading.

"Talking to yourself!" he exclaimed, his mouth twisted in a sarcastic grin. "Perhaps you're spending too much time on your own."

"Talking, but not to myself," she replied coolly. "And as for being on my own, surely that's not something that need concern you, since it never did in the past. Anyway, I think you are the one who will be more in need of company from now on."

"And what's that supposed to mean?" He crossed the room to face her but stopped abruptly when he saw the child curled up on Grace's lap. A look of fright shot across the little girl's face when she saw him. "Who's that girl?"

Grace gave him a smug smile and pulled Rosemary close to her chest. "Did you think you were the only one allowed secrets? It must be so infuriating to you that mine are better kept."

As he scowled down at them Rosemary threw her arms around Grace's neck and buried her face in her aunt's shoulder. "Don't be frightened, darling this is your uncle Matthew."

"Uncle, what do you mean, uncle? Who does this child belong to?" he demanded loudly.

"Do you have to be so aggressive, Matthew, can't you see you're scaring her." She rocked Rosemary in her arms. "This is Rosemary, Paul's daughter. It may come as a shock to you, to suddenly find out you're an uncle, but please try to behave like one."

"I don't believe you," he sneered derisively. "Paul doesn't have a daughter. I would have known. Who's the mother supposed to be?"

"That's of no concern, but you have my word, this is your niece." She placed a hand under the girl's chin and tilted her face for him to see. "She'll be staying here with me until I hear from Paul, so, whatever your feelings, you had better get used to the idea."

Matthew laughed forcibly, but without humour. "How ironic all this is. You couldn't have my brother, yet here you are saddled with his bastard offspring."

"Keep your voice down in front of the child. You can taunt me as much as you wish, if it makes you feel better, but I won't be goaded into an argument in front of her just to suit you." A self-satisfied thought occurred to her. "But since you have brought up the subject of desires, I think you will find yours a little curtailed from now on."

He gave her a cautious, puzzled look. "More riddles? Perhaps you'd better explain it, or is that another of your secrets?"

"Oh, it's no secret," she grinned, cuddling Rosemary to her. "You'll find there will be no more special favours from the kitchen in the future, I've had to dismiss one of the staff. Molly, I think her name was."

Matthew gave a sharp cough as the whisky caught in his throat. "I still don't know what you're talking about." He crossed to the table and poured himself another drink. "You might think you're being clever, but you're not," he added before storming from the room.

When Grace had given Rosemary her dinner, she took the child straight up to bed. The poor girl was so exhausted from the exertions and excitement of that first day in her new home that she could barely stay awake through the meal and fell asleep almost immediately. Grace sat with her for a while before changing and going down to join her husband in the dining room.

That evening he was even more sullen and reticent than usual, not even prepared to give any account of his day's activities, which was now the only common ground for any conversation between them. The silence suited Grace who now felt she firmly held the upper hand in their relationship and was content to keep her other great secret for a time of her choosing.

When she did speak it was to Jenkins as he cleared their plates. "Would you be good enough to tell Mrs Rafferty we will be nine for Christmas dinner this year," she said casually, although clear enough for Matthew to hear.

"Nine, madam?" queried Jenkins. "Yes, of course. I'm sure cook is quite up to the challenge."

When Jenkins had left Matthew glared across the table, his cold, pale eyes narrow and piercing. "And who are these nine people?" he demanded. "You've said nothing to me about inviting anyone."

"I thought you would be pleased to have some company, particularly as you seem so bored with mine," she replied mockingly. "If it was left to you, we would have no one here. And as to who they are, well you'll just have to wait and see."

Matthew huffed loudly. "It seems to me that there's nothing I have any control over any more. Perhaps I should move into one of the empty cottages on the estate as I'm no better than any of the others in your employ."

She smiled, taking a perverse pleasure in his self-pity. "I can't be held responsible for the low opinion you have of yourself, Matthew, but if you're not happy with my choice of guests then you're free to spend Christmas however, and wherever, you wish.

With that Matthew threw his napkin across the table, violently pushed back on his chair and strode from the dining room. Grace was left wondering if, perhaps, she had been a little too harsh with him, but when she recalled all the lies and deceit, both before and since their marriage, she considered her conscience clear.

By Christmas morning Matthew was still no closer to discovering who Grace had invited to join them for the day, stubborn pride had prevented him from asking further. Instead, he chose to brood alone in the drawing room while Grace took Rosemary to the church service.

At the church the child sat contentedly between her new guardian and her grandfather, tightly holding hands with both for fear they would abandon her in this strange and wondrous place where everyone seemed so full of unnatural joy. She was now old enough to know the day was special, but being with the two people who cared for her added an extra warmth to the occasion.

They were joined at the church by John, accompanied by Peggy Dobson. Grace had arranged a carriage for them earlier that morning, should John use his damaged leg as an excuse and change his mind about joining them. When the invitation had first been extended to him, John had dismissed it out of hand, as much for Grace's benefit as his own concerns, knowing that the antipathy it would cause in Matthew would rebound onto his wife. But Grace's persistence proved to be more powerful than John's objections and, with weight added by Mrs Dobson, he finally gave in and agreed.

"Would you really condemn me to spend Christmas alone with Matthew?" said Grace to conclude her argument.

When the five of them returned from church, Matthew was still seated in the drawing room, a glass in his hand and a bottle by his side. He hardly took any notice when Grace ushered in her guests, and grudgingly stood only when his wife pointed out that there were ladies present.

"I see that marriage has done nothing to improve your manners," remarked John, fearing he should never have been persuaded to come. "Living in a grand house doesn't make you a gentleman, you know."

"And what has the army made of you?" responded his brother vindictively. "A cripple?"

"Matthew, that's despicable," cried Grace. "If you've nothing civil to say then I would rather you keep quiet. I won't have our Christmas spoilt by your contemptible behaviour."

"Quite so, my dear." Mockingly he raised his glass to her before glaring around at his guests who looked away in embarrassment. "I thought you said we were nine for dinner. I may be an ill-mannered oaf, but I can still count." Pointing his finger, he made an exaggerated count. "We appear to be three short, or were you thinking of inviting some of the servants?"

"Well, that can be another surprise for you." Grace smiled smugly. "Just be patient, they'll be here in plenty of time for the meal."

For the next hour the group settle down to pleasant, yet muted, conversation in which Matthew took no part, preferring instead to devote his undivided attention to the bottle of whisky.

After some initial hesitancy Rosemary made friends with John who, despite his stiff leg, sat with her on the floor reading from a book of tales by Hans Christian Andersen. It was an immense relief to Grace how well the girl had adapted to her new life at Millwood House, and no one was more pleased to see Rosemary settled than Jack Conners. His old eyes never left the child as she sat enthralled by the stories, and it was difficult to know who enjoyed them most.

Neither Matthew nor the guests seemed to notice when Jenkins slipped inconspicuously into the room and whispered to Grace. She got up and asked to be excused for a few minutes, following the man servant out into the hallway. While John exchanged a wary glance with Peggy Dobson, Matthew took no interest in his wife's departure, the effects of the drink beginning to weigh heavily on his senses. John wondered if her leaving had anything to do with the surprise she had promised.

Several minutes of uncomfortable silence passed before the door opened again and Grace came in, giving a little nervous cough. Once she had their attention, she stood to one side to allow three more people into the room.

"I should like you all to meet my father," she said in a faltering voice, and taking Ned Stiles by the arm. She held out a hand to the two women. "This is his wife, Rose, my step-mother, and my Aunt Dorothy."

As John scrambled ungainly to his feet and Jack Conners pushed himself from the chair, Grace ushered the three newcomers further into the room. Only Matthew remained seated. But even the alcoholic haze that surrounded him failed to lessen the impact of his wife's dramatic announcement.

After Grace had made all the introductions she turned to her husband. "I know that you and my father are already well acquainted, but never as members of the same family."

Graciously Ned Stiles held out his hand, but Matthew knocked it away as he leapt to his feet, throwing the glass violently into the hearth.

"Is this another of your little games?" he screamed at his wife, while Rosemary began crying and ran to the comforting arms of her grandfather. "Do you get pleasure out of humiliating me?" He gripped Ned by the lapel of his jacket. "You were forced to leave here once and now I'm going to make sure you do again, for good this time."

While he tried to push her father towards the door Grace forced her way between them. John limped forward to pull his brother away.

"For pity's sake, Matt, leave him alone," he pleaded. "Haven't you shamed our family enough."

Far from calming him the accusation only served to incense Matthew further, and he threw John to one side. Grace cried out in alarm as John crashed to the floor, sending Mrs Dobson rushing to his aid, while Rosemary continued to cling in fear to her grandfather.

"I warned you that there would be trouble, that we should never have come," Ned said quietly to Grace. "Perhaps it would be for the best if we went."

"No," breathed Grace firmly, glaring at her husband with undisguised hatred. "You're my father and you've every right to be here." She jabbed an accusing finger at Matthew. "If he can't accept that then he's the one who should leave."

"And that's what you want, isn't it?" sneered Matthew through bared teeth. "I don't know what lies he's told you to make you believe he's your father, or to get his job back, but I won't go just to suit the two of you."

"If that's what you think then you've less sense than I gave you credit for," scoffed Grace. "Do you imagine I would allow my own father to work for me? He's entitled to so much more than that." She gave her father an assuring smile before turning back on Matthew. "I was not going to mention this yet, especially not today, but your behaviour now has left me with little choice. If you intend to stay then you had better be prepared to have a smaller estate to run in the future. I'm selling some of the land, including your precious farm, to give my father some of the compensation he deserves, for the years he has been denied a daughter, and for the hurt you did to him."

A stunned silence descended over the room as they all separately digested the ramifications of her decision. Even despite the deceitful behaviour of his own brother, John found it hard to believe that Grace was capable of such harshness, purely out of revenge. He stared at her with such incredulity that she found it necessary to explain herself.

"The farm isn't profitable, John, you more than anyone should know that. It was an economical decision and not an emotional one."

That may have gone some way towards satisfying John, but not Matthew. He gripped Grace by the wrist, bending her arm backwards. "That land belongs to me." He spat the words into her face. "It's been in our family for years, you can't just sell it. I'll die before I let you."

With those last words he pushed her roughly away and strode from the room, slamming the door behind him. As Grace massaged her wrist Ned put his hands on her shoulders and gave her an impassioned look.

"I don't want your money, or your land. All I ever wanted was my daughter, and now that I have her, I'm well satisfied. I'm grateful that you feel the need to make amends for what's happened in the past, but you hold on to your inheritance and do what you can to save your marriage."

Grace gave a deep, resigned sigh. "I think my marriage is beyond saving, and as for that damned farm, it has been the cause of so much unhappiness that I shall be pleased to be rid of it." She threw her arms around her father's neck and hugged him to her. "This is our first Christmas together and I don't want to remember it just for all the arguing and bad feelings." She looked to her other guests who seemed to share her sentiment. "I'm sorry for my husband's behaviour, for causing you all so much embarrassment, especially on a day like today. Please, let us try to forget what has been said and enjoy the rest of the day together."

"But what about your husband, my dear, should you at least go and try to make your peace with him?" It was Dolly who pleaded with her.

Grace shook her head sadly. "I wouldn't know what to say to him, and even if I could find the words, I doubt he would listen. I think it will be a better Christmas if we leave him to his own devices. But if he chooses to join us, I'll make him more than welcome."

"If I know my brother, we won't be seeing him any more today," added John. "The only company Matt wants right now is his own."

John was right. Grace learned later that Matthew had taken a bottle of whisky from the library and retired to his room where Jenkins had found him later that evening, unconscious on his bed.

For the rest of them, they managed to salvage some peace and goodwill from what was left of the day, even though Ned was persistent in his efforts to persuade his daughter that he neither needed nor wanted her money and that she should concentrate on trying to repair her marriage.

"My mind is made up," she told him at dinner. "There was a time when I would have been content just to know who my father was, but that was before I inherited all this." She swept her hand around the room. "I know my uncle had a high regard for you, and regretted the way you were treated, so I know he would approve."

"I know it's none of my business, and you're only doing what you think is right," said John reservedly, "but is there no other way than by selling Hibberd's Farm. I know Matthew was drunk and angry, but you shouldn't take his threat lightly."

"Surely you don't think he would kill himself over that farm!" exclaimed Rose, who was as aware as anyone of Matthew's unpredictable temperament.

"I think Matthew is capable of anything if he feels threatened." John directed his remark at Grace. "And it may not just be him that gets hurt."

"The lad's right," put in Ned, his expression full of concern, "please reconsider what you're doing."

"I will agree only to think about it," said Grace with an assuring smile. "Now, can we please talk about something more in keeping with the occasion, after all it is Christmas and we should all be celebrating." She raised her glass and they all followed, even little Rosemary, thrilled with her glass of cordial.

Chapter Twenty-Nine

The quayside at Southampton was thronged with people, those arriving and those waiting to leave, and those saying their farewells or waiting to greet loved ones. The passengers surging down the gangways searched out familiar faces in the waiting crowds, anticipation on the faces of them all.

With Frank leading the way carrying the portmanteaux, Paul kept a protective arm around the girl's shoulders and tucked himself in behind the large frame of friend. After such a solitary life, Paul feared the girl would be overwhelmed by the seething mass of humanity in a land so far from her own, and he assured her constantly that it would be less fraught once they were on the train to London.

After clearing their baggage through the customs shed the two men met up again to say their farewells. Frank had spoken vaguely about returning to his native Cornwall in an attempt to reacquaint himself with the girl he had given up all those years ago, although neither man thought it much of a promising prospect. Despite that, and the sadness of the occasion, Frank remained his usual ebullient self, and any sorrow he felt at the parting was well hidden behind his think beard and broad smile.

"Well Paul, my boy, this is it," he roared, slapping Paul heartily on the back. "I don't remember too much about the last time I parted with 'e so this is a new experience for I. I hope I don't make a damn fool of myself by blubbing in front of the young lady."

"I don't think you've ever cried in your life, you big oaf," laughed Paul, shielding his own sentiments with a forced grin.

"Won't change your mind then and spend a few days with I in Southampton?" asked the big Cornishman, knowing full well what the answer would be.

Paul shook his head. "Now that I'm back in England, I want to get home as soon as possible." He gave the girl a sympathetic glance. "Katerine has waited long enough to see my brother again so we'll be catching the first train to London."

"Well, I won't come with 'e to the station, I find them depressing places at the best of times." He enveloped Paul's hand in his. "I know we'll see each other again, but it doesn't make this any the easier, not after what we've been through together. Take care of yourself and I hope 'e finds some happiness." He flung his massive arms around Paul, squeezing the breath from him. When they broke apart, he took the girl to him. "Good luck to 'e my lovely, and don't take no for an answer."

After one more final embrace, and promises to write to each other, the two men parted to begin new and separate chapters of their already eventful lives.

After enduring the arduous journey back to Cape Town through a country still very much ravaged by the effects of the war, followed by the three weeks at sea, Paul and Katerine settled easily into the peaceful and relative luxury of a first-class compartment on the train to London.

For Katerine the excitement of travelling to a strange new country had been tempered by the pain of leaving her homeland and the apprehension of being reunited with a man whose feelings towards her may have cooled. Despite Paul's constant assurances of his brother's love for her, she would not be absolutely convinced. However, the long and draining journey, and the gentle rolling of the railway carriage soon replaced her fears as she slipped into a deep, comfortable sleep, her head resting on Paul's shoulder. Now she drifted through the events that had brought her out of her own land and deposited her in a new and wondrous environment.

When Paul had left her and her mother on the farm, she never expected to see him, or John, again. With her father dead and her brother away somewhere fighting with the commando, or even dead himself, it was becoming increasingly more difficult for the two women to survive alone out on the veld.

Weakened by the perpetual worry for her son and the lack of a nourishing diet, Katerine's mother had died a sad and broken woman about two months after Paul's visit. Katerine had dug the grave and buried her mother with her own hands.

In the hope that her brother would return Katerine had stayed on at the farm for a few more weeks before hunger and loneliness had forced her to close the door and abandon the only home she had ever known. Harnessing their last remaining bullock to the cart, she had driven herself and her few possessions into Belmont. There she found lodgings with a woman who had lost her own son and husband to the war and welcomed Katerine as someone with whom she could share her grief. Katerine passed her days and earned a little money by helping out at Grierson's general store.

The time she spent there was amongst the unhappiest of her wretched life, and most nights she would cry herself to sleep, thinking of all the loved ones she had lost, both living and dead.

So, one morning when she arrived for work at the store, she dared not believe it was true when Grierson told her that the Englishman who had visited her farm had arrived back in Belmont earlier that day and was asking after her. Knowing how the Scotsman loved to tease her, she refused to accept the truth of it until Paul returned a little later accompanied by Frank Trevithick.

Even when they told her how they had sold their mine before travelling overland to Mafeking and catching the train to Belmont just to find her, she had trouble believing it was not a dream. But that was only the beginning of the fairy tale, the two men now wanted her to go with them to Cape Town and from there take passage to England where she would be reunited with John. It had been too much for her to take in, it was her destiny to live and die a poor Boer girl. She had collapsed onto some sacks of flour and wept.

But dreams do come true, and when she opened her eyes and saw through the carriage windows not the stark, arid expanse of the veld but the rolling green hills of Surrey she had to look to Paul to be assured of its reality. As if reading her thoughts, he nodded his head and smiled back at her.

"We'll be in London soon," he told her. "A day or two there and then on to Northampton."

She returned his smile before settling back into her seat to watch the English countryside slip by.

Paul had intended to spend at least one full day in London, he wanted to see his good friend Gilbert Bullivant, desperate to tell him how he had fared since leaving the city all those months before.

If Katerine had been fascinated by all she had seen since leaving Cape Town then she was surely awestruck by the sights that greeted her when they walked out of Waterloo Station. If she thought the pace of life in the Cape capital was frenetic then she was quite unprepared for the noise and smells that assailed her senses, and the pedestrian and road traffic that threatened her person. To her it was a world in chaos, and when an old gypsy woman approached her with a tired looking posy of lavender she shied away and gripped Paul's arm.

"We'll have to buy it," Paul told her seriously, giving the woman a penny, "otherwise she'll curse us with bad luck."

Katerine stared up at him in alarm before they both broke into a fit of laughter.

Thirty minutes later the cab turned into the Walworth Road and soon after that Paul was helping the girl down outside the house of Gilbert's aunt as the cabbie unloaded their luggage.

Paul could barely suppress a broad grin as Gilbert threw open the door. Paul's friend stood open mouthed, unable to speak, which for him was a rare achievement, and when the initial shock transferred to an expression of sheer joy his manicured moustache twitched uncontrollably and he threw his arms out in welcome.

"Paul, my dear chap, this is wonderful," he cried excitedly until he caught sight of the girl waiting on the pavement at the bottom of the steps. "And with a young lady!" He took Paul by the shoulders and shook him. "You old dog."

Paul introduced him to Katerine and was quick to explain that his friend had completely misinterpreted the situation.

"Ah, that young lady," said Gilbert with an apology to Katerine.

He ushered his guests into the living room and within an hour he was fully familiar with everything that had happened since Paul had left him the year before.

"I'm delighted that everything has worked out so well for you," he said, clasping his hands excitedly when Paul finished speaking. "And now you've come home a rich man."

"Modestly rich," Paul was quick to correct him, embarrassed by such things.

With a sudden movement that made both Paul and Katerine start, Gilbert leapt to his feet, slapping a hand against his forehead. "I'd almost forgotten," he shouted, "I've been keeping a letter for you, from your sister-in-law. It must have arrived about two months ago." He left the room and returned a few minutes later clutching the letter. "I know it's from her because she wrote to me also. Her instructions were to forward it on if I had your address, or to keep it here should you return. I take it you've heard nothing from her?"

Paul shook his head, conscious that he had been remiss in staying in touch. He now turned the letter over in his hands before breaking the seal. As the others sat in silence, watching him, he read the letter to himself.

My dear Paul

As I have not heard from you for so long, I fear we may have lost contact completely. I hope sincerely that this is not so.

Because so much has happened here I feel I must make some effort to reach you and have therefore sent this letter to your friend, Mr Bullivant, in London should he have better information of you than I do.

You will no doubt be saddened by the news that my uncle died just before Christmas. I know you thought well of him as he did of you, which is more than can be said of your brother, my husband. It shames me to tell you that Matthew has proved to be a great disappointment and I fear our marriage is now doomed to fail. I feel it improper to go into personal details, but suffice it to say that I feel terribly deceived and let down.

But there is some good news. After all these years I have discovered the identity of my father. You will be shocked to learn it was none other than my uncle's former farm manager Mr Ned Stiles. You can only imagine my shock too, but it is so wonderful and comforting to finally know him. I am planning to sell off some of the land to make a financial settlement on him by way of compensation for wrongs that were done him. Unfortunately, the land I am planning to sell includes your former home, Hibberd's Farm. This was purely an economic decision, but as you can imagine it has done nothing to improve my standing with your brother.

John is managing well and is presently staying with the mother of an army friend killed in South Africa. He has been a good and comforting friend to me.

I have kept until last the news that most affects you. Your daughter Rosemary is presently staying with me at Millwood House under my guardianship. Unhappily her grandmother, Mrs Conners, died suddenly and, threatened with having the child taken from him, Mr Conners has entrusted me with her care. She is an adorable little girl and a good companion to me during these tiresome times. I am trying very hard not to allow myself to become too attached to her because I know she is not mine, but at the moment we are, to all the world, as mother and daughter. Naturally I am most anxious that you are made aware of this situation and I am desperate to hear from you.

It is my dearest wish that you should return to England, but if this is not possible, I have to know your instructions concerning Rosemary.

My love

Grace

Paul read the letter a second time, particularly the passage concerning his daughter. He then sat for several seconds in deep thought.

"Nothing wrong, I hope?" enquired Gilbert after a lengthy silence.

Paul looked up and stared blankly at him. "What? I'm sorry, Gilbert, but I'm not entirely sure." He tapped the letter lying across his lap. "I shall have to go on to Northampton first thing tomorrow."

Early the following morning Paul said an emotional farewell to Gilbert and by late that afternoon he and Katerine had arrived at Northampton Station. Paul would have preferred to travel directly on to Millwood House that same day, but Katerine had suffered badly from the rigours of the long journey from her former home, her condition exacerbated by the restricted diet she had endured. Already fretful of how John would react to her sudden arrival she begged Paul to be allowed one more night's rest before they finally met.

Remembering him well from his previous visits the landlord greeted Paul like an old friend.

"Would the young lady be your wife, sir?" he enquired, somewhat indelicately.

Paul gave him a sideways glance. "She would not, I'm afraid to say. We shall be needing two rooms, the best you have."

"My apologies miss," said the landlord as Katerine flushed and turned coyly away.

Once they had rested Paul escorted Katerine down to the dining room for supper. With the meal, he ordered a bottle of Burgundy and was amused as she winced at the taste of the unfamiliar drink. How innocent she was, he thought, and how lucky his brother was to find a girl with so much innocence who cared for him. He also saw in her the apprehensiveness she felt at the forthcoming reunion and he took every opportunity to reassure her.

"How can you be so sure he will still feel the same?" she said with growing anxiety. "It's been so long, he may have found another girl and even married her, and then what will I do?"

Paul reached across the table and patted her arm. "The way John used to talk about you, no other girl will ever be good enough for him. I can't wait to see his face when he sets eyes on you."

"I just wish I could be as sure," she sighed.

They had finished their meal and enjoying the last of the wine when Paul noticed a discarded newspaper on an adjacent table. "Would you mind?" he asked Katerine as he reached over for it. "I would just like to see what's been going on since I've been away."

He flicked through the pages, idly glossing over the headlines for any local news or gossip, stopping at the page listing local sales and auctions. One item in particular caught his attention and it instantly reminded him of something he had read in Grace's letter. With the newspaper spread open in front of him he sat for a while in deep contemplation until he suddenly remembered he was in company and threw Katerine an apologetic smile.

The following morning, he left Katerine at the hotel, telling her he had some business to attend to and that he would arrange for a carriage to take them to Millwood House. He returned an hour later and as soon as their luggage was loaded, they set off on the final stage of what had been a long and exhaustive journey. Both had much on their minds, but disguised the fact by chatting frivolously about everything except what was really important to each of them.

As they drove at a steady pace, Katerine never stopped marvelling at the lush greenness of the countryside through which they passed, and at the cheerfulness of the people they saw. It was all so very different from the life and homeland she had left behind.

When they finally drew into the long sweeping drive of Millwood House a loud gasp of amazement escaped Katerine's lips. "Surely this is a palace!" she breathed incredulously. "I cannot believe this is a house for just one family."

This was not simply a new country for her, it was a new and different life, so far removed from anything she could have imagined, so wondrous yet so frightening.

When Jenkins opened the door to them, she hid behind Paul, still unable to accept they had any right to be there. To her relief the butler greeted Paul with a smile of recognition and welcomed them inside where she could only gaze in awe at the opulence of her surroundings.

"The mistress is in the conservatory," said Jenkins with a quick glance over his shoulder. "Would you like to wait in the library while I tell her you are here?"

Paul thought for a second, his eyes glinting mischievously. "She's not expecting us so I think I'd like to go straight through and surprise her, if that's all right."

Jenkins raised his eyebrows and gave a knowing inclination of the head.

Since her uncle had first been confined to his bed Grace had taken on the responsibility of caring for his beloved plants and tended them with the same enthusiasm that he had lavished on them. To her they were the living embodiment of her uncle's strength and spirit and through them she felt he was still alive in the house.

She took no notice when Jenkins entered, and carried on watering the plants as though he were not there. Paul put a finger to his lips and waved the butler towards the door. Jenkins winked and nodded before quietly leaving, while the two visitors stood motionless, waiting tensely for Grace to discover their arrival.

"I'm sorry, Jenkins, what is it?" she enquired when she at last acknowledged a presence in the room.

When she turned to face them, she let out a loud shriek, dropping the watering can and throwing her hands up to her face. Water splashed down the front of her dress but she was oblivious to everything except the man who stood before her. Taking a few deep breaths, she could find no words to express her feelings, just a mixture of stunted laughter and tears of joy as she ran to Paul.

She threw her arms around his neck and kissed him repeatedly on the cheek while he held her tightly to him. Ignoring Katerine's presence, they whirled round and round in an impromptu pirouette that more than once almost sent them tumbling to the floor.

"Paul, I can't believe you are really here!" she exclaimed breathlessly when at last she was able to speak. "Why didn't you write and tell me you were coming home?"

"I thought you would enjoy the surprise," he laughed teasingly. "And here's another." He turned and took Katerine's hand. "This is Katerine, a friend of John's all the way from South Africa."

"Oh, I'm so pleased to meet you," declared Grace with genuine warmth, taking the girl's hand in hers. "Welcome to Millwood House. John has spoken so much about you I feel we are already friends."

Overwhelmed by the depth of her welcome Katerine smiled through a flood of tears. "Thank you. Everyone has been so kind that I can hardly believe it is all happening to me. How is John, is he well?"

"You can answer that for yourself when you see him," Grace said, leading her to the door. "Now, come through to the drawing room, you two have so much to tell me."

As Grace ushered them out of the conservatory Paul took her arm and drew her to one side. "I read your letter while I was in London," he said to her earnestly. "My daughter, Rosemary, is she really here?"

"Yes, safe and well, you'll hardly recognise her. She's sleeping at the moment. You can see her as soon as she's awake." She pushed him forward. "But now I'm impatient to hear everything that's happened with you."

As soon as they were comfortably seated in the drawing room with the tea Grace had ordered for them, she began pestering Paul for every little detail of his life since he left for South Africa. In return she recounted the events that had brought her marriage close to an end, leaving out only what pride or embarrassment prevented her from telling.

Katerine sat in silence, listening to all that was said, and from what she heard she had every sympathy for Grace, realising that even great wealth could not guarantee happiness. Paul could only shake his head at his brother's shameful and deceitful behaviour towards both Grace and her uncle.

"But what will you do?" he asked. "Surely you can't continue like this, you must be so miserable."

Grace cocked her head to one side and smiled. "I have a father now, a good home and some very dear friends. Isn't that enough for anyone?"

"But you married for love, Grace, don't you feel cheated?"

She shrugged her shoulders. "Perhaps I do, but then perhaps I was only deceiving myself. I was a silly young girl who thought she was in love with a man who loved her; perhaps we were both mistaken. Anyway, I've been more than compensated in other ways." She gave Katerine a sideways glance. "Now I think it's time we did something to reunite John with his sweetheart here. I know you've done enough travelling to last you a lifetime so I'll send someone to bring him here." She got up and placed a hand on the girl's thin shoulder. "If you'll both excuse me I'll go and make the arrangements."

When she had gone Paul watched with some amusement as Katerine squirmed in her chair, wringing her hand, her eyes flicking nervously around the room.

"Do stop worrying," said Paul with mock sternness. "If John is less than overjoyed to see you then he'll have me to answer to."

She forced a weak smile and said quietly, "it wasn't just John I was thinking about. This other brother you have, Matthew, he seems so different from you and John, I can hardly believe it is possible."

"Don't let the thought of Matthew frighten you. Even as a child he was never like John or me, he was more like our father."

"Your father was a bad man?"

"No not a bad man, just not a good father. I think he cared more about his farm than he did his family, and Matthew has inherited that same lack of feeling towards other human beings. I had hoped that being married would change him, but …" His words tailed off as he recalled all that Grace had told him.

Just then Grace returned and standing by her side, clinging to her dress, was Rosemary, rubbing the sleep from her eyes with the back of her hand. Even in her drowsy state she looked so pretty, her blond hair no longer a frothy mass, but flowing over her shoulders in ringlets. Disarmed by the sight of the unexpected company she quickly hid her face in the folds of Grace's dress as the pair progressed slowly into the room.

"What a beautiful little girl," declared Katerine to Paul, "is she really yours?"

"Yes, she is," replied Paul with proud sentiment bursting from him as he gazed at the child, "although I don't think she knows it yet." He held out his arms, but Rosemary would not be parted from Grace's side as he spoke softly to her. "I'm your father, Rosemary, don't you remember me?"

With no sign of recognition on her face Rosemary stared at him nervously until Grace bent to pick her up. "You'll have to give her time. Like me, she's never known her father. It takes some getting used to."

"Well, we've got plenty of time now," said Paul, reaching out to stroke the back of the child's hand. "I'm not going to leave you again, ever."

For the remainder of that afternoon the three of them sat chatting about all manner of subjects as Rosemary played happily on the floor until Paul was eventually able to coax her up onto his lap. Every now and then Katerine would glance anxiously at the clock, and more than once asking Grace how long it would be before John arrived. She stiffened visibly every time she heard footsteps in the hall, only relaxing when they faded away again.

Although she did well to hide the fact, Grace too was harbouring some anxieties of her own, fearing Matthew would cause trouble when he arrived back from work to find both his brothers waiting for him. An uneasy truce had existed between him and Grace since Christmas, principally because they spent so little time in each other's company, and restricting any conversation purely to affairs of the estate. The subject of Hibberd's Farm had been avoided by both, Matthew wrongly assuming her threat to sell to be a bluff just to keep him in line.

When the carriage arrived to collect him, John questioned the driver why he had been sent for. The driver could only repeat what he had been told to say, that it was a matter of the utmost importance and urgency. Having spent the morning tending the garden John hobbled upstairs to change, telling Mrs Dobson that it was likely there had been more trouble with Matthew and that Grace needed his support.

Peggy Dobson shook her grey head forlornly. "That brother of yours needs a boot up his backside," she muttered sharply.

When he came back down John was carrying a small bag. "Just in case I'm not back until morning," he told her.

"You just watch out for yourself, young John, he's a spiteful one," she warned.

John assured her it was probably nothing to be concerned about, but throughout the whole journey to Millwood House he pondered gravely on Matthew's continual capacity to cause trouble. When he arrived at the house, he limped up the steps as fast as his leg would allow.

Following Grace's instructions Jenkins showed him directly to the library where he was told to wait. It seemed strange to him that Grace wasn't there to meet him, given the urgency of her invitation, and instead of sitting he paced the floor to ease his agitation and the stiffness in his leg.

In the drawing room Katerine was suffering too, and when Jenkins came in and whispered into Grace's ear the poor girl looked as if she were about to faint.

"Is he here?" she asked, and when Grace nodded Katerine turned to Paul. "Will you come with me to meet him? I don't think I can do it alone."

"Of course, you can," encouraged Grace. "You've come all these thousands of miles to be with him so don't let your courage fail you now." She took her by the arm and led her to the door. "Go with Jenkins, he'll show you the way."

Katerine looked frantically over her shoulder at Paul, but he simply waved her forward. "Go on, it will be all right, I promise."

With leaden legs she followed on behind the butler, glancing back all the while to see if Paul had changed his mind, but before she knew it the library door was being opened for her and suddenly, she was alone and vulnerable. Despite everything Paul had said she was still unable to accept that John would be tied by the promise they had made to each other all that time ago, and now that the moment she had dreamed about was at hand she could not have felt less prepared. Her legs barely supported her and her stomach churned until she thought she would be sick, and the hands that would soon hold his shook uncontrollably.

Once he had opened the door Jenkins stood to one side and beckoned her to go in, but she could only remain where she was, trembling and pale. If she had been capable of any action her first instinct would be to run away and hide, but Jenkins encouraged her with a smile and eventually she found the strength to shuffle forward until she was standing in the doorway.

To distract himself from the speculation that was playing havoc with his mind John had been idly browsing the rows of books, just as he had done on the evening of that first visit. With his back to the door, he thumbed through the pages of a volume on husbandry, but his mind was firmly fixed on matters far removed from the demerits of intensive farming.

Preoccupied with Matthew's latest foray into disruptive behaviour he failed to hear the door open and was completely oblivious to the terrified girl who watched him, too scared to approach yet unable to turn away. It was John who moved first, vaguely aware that he was no longer alone. Casually he turned, and when he saw Katerine framed in the doorway he had to clutch the back of a chair for support.

Neither of them would ever be able to say how much time passed as they gazed at each other, unable to move, as though traumatised by the sight of a ghost. The colour had drained from John's face as he blinked in disbelief, and when he tried to speak, his mouth was dry and the words dissolved into a series of gasps.

It was left to Katerine to break the deafening silence. "Hello John, how are you?" She moved slowly and unsteadily into the library, her pale, dry lips parting to form a thin smile. By the time Jenkins closed the door on them they were no more than a few feet apart. "You do remember me, don't you?"

Tears ran freely down John's face and he held out a hand to her. "Katerine!" The name almost choked him. "Katerine?"

She nodded, sobbing convulsively as she accepted his hand in hers. "Yes, it really is me."

"It is ... I can see it is, but I can't believe ... how?" His words made no sense, he knew that, but where was the sense in any of this.

"I'm sorry, I have shocked you." She tightened the grip on his hand. "See, I am real. Your brother, Paul, he has brought me from South Africa."

She was real, he could feel the warmth of her breath on his face, her fingers wrapped around his, and the evidence of his own eyes, yet he was still afraid to believe.

"Katerine!" he whispered through trembling lips, enfolding her thin body in his shaking arms.

She clutched at his jacket, terrified that he would slip again from her grasp, and as she pressed her face to his, their tears mingled in a fusion of ecstatic joy. The time for fear was finally over.

Again and again, he whispered her name and they held the embrace until each accepted the presence of the other.

"I still can't believe you are really here." He stumbled over the words as he pulled away to look her in the face. "And Paul, where is he now?"

"He is here, in the house. They made me see you alone, and now I'm pleased they did." She ran her fingers lightly over his cheek, brushing away the tears. "Oh John, I was so afraid you wouldn't want me. I know about your leg and it doesn't matter to me. I love you so much."

"I've never stopped wanting you, Katerine. There wasn't a day that passed I didn't think of you, but I didn't dare believe I would ever see you again." He stepped back to admire her properly. She was thinner than he remembered, but just as beautiful, and the shabby dress she wore when they first met had been replaced by something more fashionable that concealed her thin frame and enhanced her beauty. How could he not want her? "You're here and I still can't believe it's true. We must go and find Paul, I've so much to thank him for."

With their eyes red from crying, and tears still streaking their cheeks they walked hand in hand to the drawing room where Paul and Grace had been waiting for them, exchanging speculative remarks on how the reunion went. All the assurances Paul had given Katerine during their journey from Belmont were made in good faith, but there was always an element of doubt that niggled at him. As soon as the couple entered the room that doubt immediately disappeared when the expression on their faces could be interpreted as nothing other than unreserved love.

Paul embraced John, sharing in his obvious elation. "It's good to see you again, little brother."

"It's good to see you too, Paul, and what a present you've brought me back." He cast his eyes lovingly at Katerine. "This is a miracle, nothing less than a miracle."

It probably began with the grooms, and confirmed by the kitchen and household maids, but by early evening the comings and goings at Millwood House during that day was common knowledge throughout most of the estate, reaching Matthews ears before he had finished his work. By the time he arrived back at the house he already knew to expect visitors and that one of them was his younger brother, but the groom at the stables could give him no information as to the identity of the others. He shrugged dismissively and strode on into the house.

It had been a particularly long and tiring day, so instead of taking his usual drink he went straight upstairs to bathe and change before dinner, which was not a refinement he regularly chose to adopt. He could not even be bothered to enquire of Jenkins if his wife was entertaining, since taking an interest in Grace's friends was one quality he was yet to embrace.

For the whole of the afternoon and into the early evening the animated chatter in the drawing room had continued unabated, regularly punctuated by bouts of girlish giggling and loud laughter as the four adults became better acquainted. Rosemary was now a firm fixture on Paul's lap, and even though she understood little of the significance of the occasion she joined in with the laughter. Although she was nearly three years old her relationship with her father was new and strange and Paul had no clear idea of how to move it forward, except by spending time with her. When Grace wanted to take her for her early dinner Paul asked if she could be allowed to stay up and eat with them. She relented, and when they all went through to the dining room Jenkins had arranged some cushions on a chair, seating the child between Grace and Paul.

When Matthew came down, he stood for a moment outside the dining room door listening to the voices coming from inside. He disliked guests, but more than that he disliked unexpected guests. He could recognise the voice of his young brother but the others he could not, and when he threw open the door his mood was already dark and brooding.

With his elbow he shoved the door shut and scowled at those sitting around the table as they turned to face him. Immediately Paul got up and went over, his hand extended in welcome, determined to show his brother that whatever had passed between them should be set aside and it was a time for friendship. But instead of accepting the hand with good grace Matthew thrust it aside to take his usual place at the head of the table.

With a mixture of shame and disappointment Paul followed him. "I see that nothing much has changed, Matt," he said, hiding his anger. "I was hoping that time and marriage had matured you."

"Then you expect too much, especially from marriage." He glared at Grace before fixing his attention on Katerine who had taken hold of John's hand. "And who might you be?"

"This is Katerine, she's a friend of John's," said Grace, also holding back on her own disappointment. "She's here from South Africa."

Matthew gave the girl a cold, sardonic grin. "It seems a long way to come for a meal. Have the Boers taken all the food as well as the mines?"

"Katerine's family were Boers," snapped John defensively. He felt her hand tighten on his. "They were decent people, and she's lost a lot more than a mine."

Matthew gave a derisive snort. "Consorting with the enemy! That wouldn't go down too well with your old army pals."

"Matthew, please," pleaded Grace, "we've got guests, so could you please try not to be so obnoxious, just this once."

"What, and disappoint them all." He swept his hand around the gathering. "Surely my own brothers know me well enough by now, so why need to pretend. And I'm sure our other guest has heard all about me." He stared pointedly at Katerine. "They've always resented me because I was our father's favourite. Mother's boys, that's what he used to call them. He had no time for their childish games, and neither have I." He looked again around the table. "So, let's not pretend anymore and say what we really feel about each other."

"Matthew, that's enough," demanded Grace with an embarrassed glance at Katerine. "I'm sorry about this, what must you think of us."

Katerine was about to dismiss her apology when Paul cut in.

"No, perhaps Matt is right, perhaps it is time we stopped pretending that we can all be friends." He glanced across at his younger brother. "I can't speak for John, but I'm tired of you Matt, your arrogant self-righteousness. All that anger and hatred you inherited from our father is eating away inside you. Yes, you're right, you are like him, but that's nothing to be proud of."

"Please, stop it," begged Grace. "Stop it, the two of you."

"No Grace, I'm sorry, and I apologise to you, Katerine, but it's best you know now all about the family you may be joining." Paul fixed his eyes firmly on Matthew. "You were wrong if you thought I resented you. I always wanted us to be friends, more than you can ever know, but you destroyed any feelings I had for you that night when you …" The words were poised to come out, but they caught in his throat. Even Grace's imploring look could not entice him to continue.

"Why don't you come out and say it?" taunted Matthew, his mouth twisted into a spiteful sneer. "Why don't you tell them all now why you hate me so much?" He glared at Grace who looked away, ashamed. "Do you really want to know why we can't ever be friends? It's because of our mother, because she …"

"Shut your mouth, Matt," shouted Paul, leaping to his feet. "Our mother's dead, for God's sake show her some respect."

"Well, I want to know," said John adamantly, still holding on to Katerine's hand beneath the table. "If all this has anything to do with our mother then I've a right to know, whatever it is."

"No," shouted Paul, thumping the table with his fist. "If you say anything, Matt, it's not just yourself you'll be condemning. You've brought enough shame on this family. Just leave it be."

"Condemn myself!" exclaimed Matthew with no sense of guilt. "It wasn't just father that loved me more, was it?" He glared vengefully at his two brothers, his pale eyes aflame with contempt. "You were jealous of how she felt about me, jealous because it was me who replaced our father, and me who she took into her bed."

Paul's face was florid and his knuckles white as he screamed at his brother. "Damn you, Matt, damn you. That was our secret. For the sake of our mother's memory, I would never have told anyone, never. But now that it's out at least do one decent thing in your life and tell the truth."

"The truth," laughed Matthew. "The truth is she loved me and invited me into her bed."

"That's disgusting, and you're a liar," shouted John, a distraught eye on Katerine. "She would never …"

"Oh, he bedded her all right, I saw them," said Paul with hushed rage, tears of shame clouding his eyes. "But it wasn't by invitation, was it, Matt? You forced yourself on her. She was too ashamed to cry out, too ashamed to risk waking John and me. But I was already awake and I saw what you did to her, I saw it on her face. It was the shame of what you did, of what she did, that killed her. She couldn't live with the shame of that night, and it killed her."

As Grace fell back onto her chair in a faint, Katerine rushed to her side while Paul bent to scoop up Rosemary, clutching the crying child to his chest. John just sat, transfixed with disbelief and disgust. Only now could he begin to understand the hostility between his two brothers, but understanding brought no satisfaction, no promise that everything could be put right. It could never be put right, not while Matthew was still in their lives.

Eventually he got to his feet and limped around the table to where Matthew was still seated. With a strength born out of sheer rage he swung the chair around until the two faced each other. "Is this the truth?" he hissed through clenched teeth. "Is this what you've been hiding all these years?"

"Is there any use denying it?" sneered Matthew. He jerked his head to where Paul was still holding on to his daughter. "Would you ever take my word over his?"

"I would if you gave me some reason to."

"It's the truth, John, I swear it on our mother's grave. Do you think she could ever give herself to him willingly? Only a sick mind could believe that." Paul was at his side and, holding Rosemary in one arm, placed the other around John's shoulder. "Come away from him, there's nothing to be gained from more violence. The damage is done now, and I'm only sorry that you all had to find out."

"I should kill you for what you've done," said John, his eyes red and seething with revenge. He allowed Paul to pull him away. "But perhaps it's best that you're made to live with the guilt, now that we all know." He breathed deeply to retrieve his composure as he turned to Paul. "I'll take Katerine back to Mrs Dobson's tonight, I don't want us spending our first night together under the same roof as him."

"Oh, don't worry yourself on that score, brother," scoffed Matthew defiantly. "I won't be staying here when there's still plenty more that appreciate my company."

He got to his feet and barged past them, storming from the dining room as Grace was recovering from her faint. She sipped from a glass of water that Katerine held for her, her pale distressed features echoing the agony of finally discovering the terrible secret that Paul was so determined to keep from her. Was she any better off from knowing the truth?

"I'm sorry," she said weakly, looking nervously around the room. "Is he …?"

"He's gone," said Paul, "but I've no doubt he'll be back when it suits him." He kissed Rosemary on the forehead and sat her down before taking Grace's hand. "I never wanted you to know any of this, believe me. This was always between me and Matthew, and it should have stayed that way. You had a right to marry him for what you felt for him, not for anything he had done in the past. Everyone has the right to prove themselves, and I thought he would change from knowing you."

"Please, don't blame yourself, Paul. I was deaf to all reason where he was concerned." She turned her eyes to Katerine. "Don't let any of this sour what you and John have, he's a fine man and you are both so very lucky to have found each other."

Katerine smiled as John put a protective arm around her waist. "I know how very lucky I am," she said.

Paul gathered up Rosemary again in a silent apology for what she had been forced to witness on that first day of their life together. He prayed she would remember none of that evening, and he pledged that he would keep her free from all harm. She was his life now and he felt so fortunate to have her.

It was still dark when Matthew returned to Millwood House early the following morning. The scratches on his face and arms were a suitable testimony to the violent passion with which he had tried to exorcise the demons within him. He had shown the bitch who was master, even if it had cost him a few extra shillings to prove it.

The ride over to Daventry and back with little sleep in between had taken its toll, and all he wanted now was to take to his bed. For one day, and possibly much longer, the estate would have to do without his management, and without even bothering to undress he threw himself onto the bed and fell into a deep sleep, unencumbered by guilt or conscience. Such sentiments were the preserve of lesser men, not him.

When Paul came down for breakfast, he found only Jenkins in the dining room. The butler greeted him with a polite, though guarded, 'good morning'. Good sense and the diplomacy required of his calling had kept him at a discreet distance during the previous evening's fracas, although he had heard much of what was said.

"Are the others not up yet?" asked Paul tentatively.

"Not to my knowledge, sir," he replied cordially enough. "The mistress is taking breakfast in her room with the child, and I've not yet seen Mr John or the young lady. Would you like me to enquire if they will be coming down?"

"No, leave them, please. What about Matthew, have you seen anything of him this morning?"

Jenkins raised his eyes in a look if distain. "No, sir, I have not."

Soon after that Paul was joined in the dining room by a sheepish looking John and an anxious Katerine. Although they had spent the night in separate rooms John had gone in to see her earlier that morning and the pair had sat for more than an hour discussing their future. John had spent a fretful night, worried that Matthew's behaviour and the horrifying revelations may have disturbed her enough to send her back to South Africa. But his fears proved unfounded when she was quick to assure him that nothing had altered her feelings for him. That she had been distressed was undeniable and natural, but a good sleep had seen her recover and now she was as eager as John to make up for the time they had been forced apart. What she had discovered of Matthew had sickened her, but she made it clear that John was not his brother, and her love for him was undiminished.

"I want to take Katerine back to Mrs Dobson's this morning," John announced to Paul as they sat down to breakfast. "I think it right that you should stay here because of your daughter, and because Grace will need your support. But there's not much Katerine and me can do, and I think it for the best if I don't see Matt for a while."

Paul nodded his agreement. "Poor Grace, I wonder what she'll do now."

Grace had wondered precisely the same. She had known for some time that her marriage to Matthew existed in name only, but the enormity of his admission had left her devastated. Not only was he a deceitful liar who took his pleasures however he pleased, but what sick mind would drive a man to violate his own mother. She doubted that she could even face him again. She no longer strove to find any redeeming features in his character as she had done in the past, realising now he was beyond redemption. That she had allowed him to take her had left her feeling tarnished and dirty.

Unable to face the others, particularly her husband, she remained in her room for a further hour after breakfast playing with Rosemary before Jenkins interrupted to tell her that the lawyer, Miles Fennymore, had arrived unexpectedly to see her.

"Shall I tell him you are indisposed, madam?" he asked tactfully.

She shook her head, curiosity edging out her distress. "No, it's fine. Put him in the library and say I shall be down shortly."

She checked her face in the mirror to ensure that she displayed nothing of what she felt, and when she was satisfied, she gathered Rosemary up in her arms and went downstairs to see what had brought the lawyer away from his chambers.

In the hallway she handed Rosemary into Jenkins care, promising the child she would be just a few minutes.

"I do apologise for this intrusion, my dear," said Fennymore, bowing his head respectfully as she entered. "But I have some news which I needed to pass on to you as soon as possible."

"And what news is that, Mr Fennymore?" she enquired cautiously, in no mood to be shocked further.

"I wanted to make you aware that we have received an offer for some of the land you have put up for sale."

Grace breathed easier. "Just some?"

Fennymore's mouth twitched apologetically. "These are difficult times, I'm afraid. The buyer is only interested in Hibberd's Farm. I just wanted to ensure you were still committed to its sale."

"No!" The words came not from Grace's mouth but from Matthew's. He was standing in the doorway behind her. His eyes were heavy and bloodshot, and dried blood lined the scratches on his cheeks and neck. "That's my land, you can't sell it."

Startled, Grace spun round, glaring at her husband as he strode threateningly towards her. "This has nothing to do with you anymore," she hissed.

He gripped Grace firmly by the wrist and pulled her close, his breath hot and foul on her face. "It's my land, and it will always be my land."

"I'm afraid not, Mr Pearson, not anymore." Fennymore placed a restraining hand on Matthew's shoulder. "You are well aware of the conditions set out in the agreement you were party to. The majority shareholder reserves the right to sell."

"Then I've been cheated," breathed Matthew, aggressively brushing away the lawyer's hand. "I would never have signed such an agreement if I had known."

"But you did," insisted Grace, trying to free her wrist from his grip. She stared hard at him, her eyes alight with revenge. "You could have had it all Matthew, everything you so desperately wanted, the land, the power, and me, everything. All you had to do in return was to be a good and loving husband, but even that was too high a price for you to pay. You've got no love in you for anything other than your own selfish interests, and for that everyone else has to pay." A cynical smile creased her face. "Well, now you have nothing, and you have only yourself to blame."

The words had barely left her lips when Matthew raised his hand and brought the back of it viciously down across the side of her face. She let out a squeal of shock and pain which brought Fennymore gallantly to her aid. But the lawyer was not a nimble young man, and as he lunged forward Matthew sidestepped, stuck out a foot and sent the older man sprawling heavily to the floor.

Grace rubbed her burning cheek as she tried in vain to free herself. She pointed to the scratches. "Is this how you get everything you want, by force?"

"I only fight for what's mine," he snapped back vehemently, clamping his hand tightly around her throat and forcing her back against the bookshelves. "Perhaps it's time you learnt who you belong to, Mrs Pearson." Grace twisted her head away when he tried to kiss her on the mouth. "You won't get rid of me or my land so easily."

Fennymore dragged himself off the floor and made another valiant attempt to rescue Grace from Matthew's attack. He put an arm around the younger man's neck and heaved backwards. Eventually Matthew released his grip, turning on the lawyer, his rage inflamed further. Taking hold of Fennymore's jacket he launched him violently at the door which he hit with a resounding crash.

"Get back to your miserable little office, this has nothing to do with you now. It's between me and my wife." He clenched his fists and took a few steps forward.

Gasping for breath and clutching at his chest Fennymore looked to Grace for instruction.

"Please go," she cried, frightened for his safety as well as her own. "It's all right, please go."

Reluctantly he reached for the door handle and, as Grace nodded at him, he left.

As soon as they were on their own Matthew returned his attention to his wife who cowered back against the rows of books. "Don't you dare touch me," she warned him as he reached out for her.

Ignoring her he resumed his hold on her throat while his other hand began tearing at her dress. "You're as much mine as my farm, and I'll do with both as I wish." He ripped open the bodice of her dress and the more she resisted the greater the pressure he applied to her delicate neck until she feared for her life. For her own salvation she gave up the struggle and prepared to submit to his will. His teeth bared in an evil grin. "Isn't this what you really want, dear wife."

"That's enough, Matt, leave her alone."

Neither of them had heard the door opening.

"This is none of your business either, brother," barked Matthew without turning. "This is a private matter between husband and wife."

"It's not private any more, Matt, you've forfeited any right to privacy." Paul came slowly towards them. "For once in your life behave like a man and know when you're beaten. Try leaving here with some dignity and honour."

"Honour!" he screamed. "How can you talk to me about honour when all you've done is to try and steal my wife from me, her and the land. You can't bear the thought of her with someone like me, can you? It was the same with our mother, that's why you made up those lies about me. Now I've got it all you just want to take it from me."

Paul stopped a few feet from them. "You're doing that all on your own. You know the truth of it, and now Grace does as well, so there's nothing to be gained from more lies, or fighting. Let Grace go while there's still time to salvage some pride."

With his hand still clamped to Grace's throat Matthew turned on his brother, his face twisted with hatred. "I think it's time for my wife to see which one of us is the best." He pushed her away and the two brothers faced each other. "You're not afraid of losing, are you?"

Paul backed away a little. "This is madness, Matt, you can't win Grace back by beating me. You must know it's gone too far for that. Whatever happens, you will still be the loser."

"Oh, I never lose, Paul, you should know that, and now she'll see just how much of a man you are." With no warning he launched himself at his brother, the two of them falling to the floor, scattering furniture as they went.

"Stop it! Stop it the two of you," screamed Grace, her hands held up to her face as they rolled about on the floor, each trying to get the better of the other. As she tried to part the two of them she got caught up in their fury and was thrown to one side. "Stop it, for God's sake, please stop," she pleaded tearfully.

Matthew was the first to gain the initiative, pinning his brother's shoulders with his knees and both hands around his throat, mercilessly attempting to choke the life from him. Paul fought back, frantically clawing at Matthew's face and forcing his head back with little effect. Matthew was possessed of an evil that could only be assuaged when one of them was dead, and he seemed determined that it should not be him. A dark mist was descending over Paul's vision as he felt his life ebbing away, and in a last desperate effort to save himself he forced back his brother's head so hard he thought his neck would snap. Within the mist were the disembodied faces of John, Grace and Rosemary, all crying at his passing while dominating them all was the laughing features of Matthew.

Paul now had a vision of how death would be, and he accepted it with an uncomfortable resignation. Then, slowly, the mist began to clear and he was able to recognise the sound of a voice. He opened his eyes, and instead of seeing Matthew's distorted face staring down at him he saw Grace bending over him, pleading with him to get up, the broken remains of a vase in her hands.

As he rolled over, he saw his brother next to him on the floor, a patch of dark red blood oozing through his fair hair. Grace took Paul by the arm and helped him to his feet while Matthew moaned as he tried to scramble up onto his knees.

Grace was sobbing hysterically. "I had to do it. I couldn't let him kill you."

She looked as though she was about to crumble and Paul took hold of her, an arm around her waist. He needed to get her from the room. Matthew was now stumbling about, holding his head and knocking into the scattered furniture. Grace watched him, frantic with fear.

"It's all right," gasped Paul, leading her towards the door. "He won't bother us for a while. I'll deal with him when I've got you out of the way."

They had just reached the door when something made Grace glance over her shoulder. "Look out," she screamed.

Matthew was almost upon them and, in his hand, he held a silver letter knife snatched from the desk. The long slim blade flashed as he brandished it in the air above them, ready to plunge it into Paul's back.

Paul spun around to face him, ready to defend himself. But still possessed of a misguided belief she could appeal to her husband Grace pushed him to one side.

"Please, Matthew, you can keep …"

The appeal was lost on her lips as she screamed out in pain. The knife caught her high in the chest, just below her shoulder. She fell back against Paul who caught her and lowered her gently to the floor. In the seconds before she closed her eyes, she thought she caught a glimpse of regret on her husband's face. But that was gone as Matthew stepped over her and fled from the library.

A steady flow of blood ran through the tear in her dress, but she was still conscious as Paul shouted for Jenkins to help, and within a few minutes she was stretched out on a couch in the drawing room. While Jenkins went to fetch bandages and send for Doctor Colley, Paul cradled her head in his arm.

"This is all my fault," she said feebly, forcing open her eyes to look at him. "You would never have fought if it wasn't for me."

"Don't blame yourself, it would have come to this sooner or later," he replied softly, placing a finger against her pale lips. "Don't talk now, save your strength."

Her eyes widened and she looked up at him. "Let him go. For my sake let him go," she pleaded before her eyes closed and she gave in to the effects of her wound.

With Jenkins help Paul bandaged the wound and was able to stem the flow of blood. He remembered what John had told him of Katerine's nursing skills and he wished the two of them had not already left for Mrs Dobson's. He wanted to move Grace up to her room, but Jenkins advised against it, fearing it would cause unnecessary suffering and further bleeding.

"I think it's best she's left where she is until Doctor Colley gets here," he said wisely. "But if you don't mind my saying so I think we should send for the constable. I know he's your brother, sir, but he shouldn't be allowed to get away with this."

"And I don't intend that he should," replied Paul firmly, "but I'd like the chance to go after him myself. Like you said, Jenkins, he is my brother, and I think I know where he can be found."

With Jenkins assurance that he would not leave Grace's side until the doctor arrived, Paul left the house and ran most of the way to the stables. Although it made no sense, he was sure Matthew would turn to their former home for somewhere to hide instead of making good his escape while he had the chance. But Matthew had turned into someone Paul no longer recognised, that all reasoning had been replaced by an obsession. He was sure his brother would seek refuge in the one place he held dear, the place that had been the cause of all their troubles.

As he crossed the river onto Hibberd's Farm, Paul prayed that Matthew had calmed down enough to reflect on the harm he had done, and would be ready to face the consequences of his actions. But even after everything that Matthew had done, Paul was still prepared to swear that the stabbing of Grace was an accident, and he was sure she would support him. He could see no benefit in sending his brother to prison, except to protect him from himself. If he could just talk to his brother perhaps some good could still come from this miserable situation.

After keeping the horse at a steady canter for most of the ride he slowed to a walk as he approached the house. With it being unoccupied for some time the building looked tired and sad, and not at all like their old home. A heavy film of grime covered the windows and the frames rattled in the breeze. Thick tufts of grass grew up between the flagstones of the yard and drifts of dead and rotting leaves had blown up against the back wall, although, close to the door, they had been trodden down. Someone had been there recently.

There was no sign of Matthew, or his horse, but Paul went into the house nevertheless. It felt unnaturally cold and there was the pungent smell of damp and decay as he passed from the kitchen into the parlour. Everywhere he looked conjured up a kaleidoscope of memories, but he pushed these to the back of his mind, the present was what concerned him now, not the past.

Upstairs his search proved no more fruitful. If he expected to find Matthew prostrate of their mother's bed, begging for her forgiveness, he was to be disappointed, both bedrooms were as empty and as dead as the rest of the house.

Outside Paul stared about him, at the land that had formed and split the lives of himself and his two brothers. What had become of them, he thought, as he strode towards the shed that served as a stable. Sally and Roscoe had long gone,

one probably to the knacker's yard, the other absorbed into Haveringham's impressive stables. But there was a horse in one of the stalls, still saddled and sweating from a hard ride.

"Matt, it's me, Paul. I mean you no harm. If you're here show yourself." The horse snorted, but apart from that, an eerie stillness hung over the shed as he searched around for some sign of his brother.

Cautiously he went back into the yard. Matthew was close by. Paul felt that as he looked about him at the various outbuildings, all falling into the same state of decay as the house. It was as though the whole farm had been condemned to a lingering death and only one person cared enough to save it from total destruction. Perhaps there was some purpose in Matthew after all, and as misguided as his methods may be, he had his motives. It was just a passing thought and Paul dismissed it from his mind, no amount of motive could excuse Matthew for what he had done over the past years, and now Paul felt it his duty to make his brother accountable, to make him see the destruction he had caused.

As he approached one of the barns, he thought he heard a noise from inside, a scraping of metal on stone. He pulled open the door, allowing a more light into the gloomy interior. At the far end of the building, he saw Matthew, a pitchfork in his hand, raking together small bundles of straw, the last of the winter feed. For a while Paul stood still, watching, amazed that after everything that had happened that morning his brother could still be distracted by some routine chore.

When he had gathered together five or six piles of the straw Matthew threw the pitchfork down and scooped up one of the piles in his arms. As he turned towards the door Paul stepped out of sight, intrigued as Matthew carried the bundle towards the house.

Waiting until his brother was inside Paul followed, and when he arrived at the kitchen door he was even more confused to see that Matthew had thrown the straw on the floor and was kicking it under the large wooden table.

Unable to contain his curiosity further Paul burst into the kitchen. "What the hell are you doing, Matt? You're sick, you need help."

Slowly Matthew turned to face his brother, his pale eyes appearing devoid of all sentiment. "Sick! Yes, I am sick. Sick of you interfering in my life." He pushed Paul roughly to one side as he strode back out into the yard and crossed to the barn.

Paul went after him, catching him by the arm as Matthew bent to collect another bundle of straw. "Stop this, Matt, it's insane. For God's sake stop and think about what you did this morning."

Matthew shook his arm free from Paul's grasp, gathered up the straw and broke into a trot as he headed back to the house. "I know what happened this morning." He shouted back. "Why do you think I'm here?"

Paul caught up with him outside the kitchen door. "I don't know why you're here, Matt, and I don't understand what you're doing." He shook his head forlornly. "I don't understand anything about you anymore."

"It's all gone, don't you understand that," he said as Paul stood in front of him. There was a hollowness to Matthew's voice, and his face had the blank expression of a man already dead. "It's all gone, the farm, Grace, everything." His thin lips curled into a demented grin. "All I've got to look forward to now is the hangman's noose, and I won't let that happen."

As Matthew barged past him a flash of realisation struck Paul as suddenly and as frightening as a bolt of lightning. "You're going to set fire to the house."

Matthew let out a maniacal laugh. "Not just the house."

"That's not funny, Matt." Paul followed his brother into the house. "If you're thinking about what you did to Grace it's all right, she's not dead. Please, come back with me now and we can sort it out."

Matthew continued to laugh maniacally. "Oh, you'd like that, wouldn't you. I bet the constable's already there, waiting for me. It's a wonder you didn't bring them with you." He threw the straw under the table. "Well, by the time they get here it'll be too late." He stared vacantly around the drear room. "Our father and mother died in this house so it's fitting that I should do the same."

"But you don't have to, Matt. I don't want you too. I swear on our parent's grave that Grace isn't dead. She's badly wounded, but she's not dead. We'll both say it was an accident, you won't even go to prison."

"Why should you care what happens to me, you never cared when you wanted to sell the farm. Well, if it's your conscience that's bothering you now then you can join me." He reached into his pocket and took out a box of matches. He gave an insane chuckle as he struck the match and tossed it into the pile of straw beneath the table. "Now let's see how much you care for me."

For a few seconds Paul was left immobile, traumatised by his brother's madness. It was only when the straw caught alight, crackling and throwing up a shower of sparks that he was jolted into action, and he ran outside to fetch a bucket. But as he came back in Matthew lunged at him, grabbing for the bucket and lashing out with his other hand.

"This is the last time you'll ever interfere in my life," he screamed, as Paul fought to get to the sink. As the fire took hold of the table and the kitchen filled with smoke Matthew dragged Paul backwards, raining blow after blow on his brother with the violence of a madman. "It's your choice, brother, you can clear out now or you can die with me."

"I'm not going, and I'm not going to let either of us die," gasped Paul defiantly, dropping the bucket to defend himself.

Breaking free, he tried to kick the straw away from the table, but the heat drove him back. As he turned away, he came face to face with an even greater threat. In Matthew's hand was the knife that Paul had bought him, the blade flashing with the reflection of the flames that now licked at the ceiling beams. Paul picked up a chair, the smouldering legs held out in front of him.

With the knife held out at arm's length Matthew lunged forward. Paul jabbed back, coughing as the thick smoke caught in his throat. "For God's sake, Matt, stop this before it's too late."

"What a pity Grace can't see you now," sneered Matthew, choking as he spoke. "Do you really think she would want you to save me?"

"She wouldn't want this," coughed Paul, his eyes streaming. He ran forward, forcing Matthew back with the chair towards the door. "She loved you. She still loves you."

Matthew fell to the floor, tripping over a burning chair, his free arm landing in the seat of the fire. He appeared oblivious to any pain as the sleeve of his jacket began to smoulder and burn, but jumping to his feet as Paul threw down the chair to go to his brother's aid. Blind to any reason Matthew mistook his brother's compassion as an act of aggression and savagely lashed out with the blade. It sliced through Paul's coat and shirt, cutting a bloody graze across his chest. Ignoring the searing pain, he seized the opportunity to grab Matthew's wrist with both hands and tried to wrestle the knife from him as smoke and heat engulfed them both. In a few minutes it would be too late for either of them to escape, but Paul was still obsessed with saving his brother, and summoning all his remaining strength he tried to force Matthew closer to the door and fresh air. The smoke was now so dense it was almost impossible to see or breathe, and Paul knew the time was close when he would pass out and they would both perish in the fire.

Fighting against the attempt to save him, Matthew pummelled his brother with his free hand until the smoke had filled his lungs and he began to weaken. Unable to breathe it looked as though he was about to get his wish as he started to lose consciousness. Coughing violently, he slumped forward, bending double over the hand that held the knife. He gave another rasping cough and dropped to the floor.

In a last desperate effort, Paul dragged his brother to the door, kicking it open and falling heavily out into the yard. His eyes and throat burned and he gulped in fresh air to clear his lungs. He was on his knees and it was several seconds before he was able to turn his attention to Matthew's smoke blackened figure, curled up on the flag stones beside him. Rolling him onto his back Paul saw for the first time the knife protruding from Matthew's stomach surrounded by a growing circle of blood.

"Dear God, no," breathed Paul, clutching at his brother as he searched for some sign of life. "Matt! Matt, can you hear me?" He bent over Matthew, his ear close to his brother's face. A faint, ragged breathing mingled with the acrid stench of smoke. "Matt, it's me, Paul. You're going to be all right. I'll go for help."

Somehow Matthew found the strength to reach up, blistered fingers curling around the lapel of Paul's jacket. "You should have left me in there," he gasped in barely more than a whisper. Struggling to speak he pulled his brother closer. "You'll all be better off when I'm dead."

"You're not going to die, Matt, I won't let you," sobbed Paul, running his fingers through Matthew's singed hair.

"You don't have to pretend any more, it doesn't matter, you've won," Matthew gasped.

"You're wrong, Matt, nobody has won here. I so much wanted us to be friends as well as brothers. Just rest now and I'll go for help."

Matthew's fingers tightened on the jacket and his face tensed. "It's too late for everything. There isn't much time, just listen." As he tried to lift his head Paul cradled it the crook of his arm. With laboured breath Matthew spoke slowly and with deliberation. "I was never your brother, father told me you and John weren't his."

As Matthew paused to catch his breath, Paul's eyes widened in disbelief. "That's not true, Matt. You don't know what you're saying. Mother would never …"

Despite his weakening condition Matthew shook his head furiously. "He was my father, not yours. You're not my brother."

"You're wrong. I don't know why father told you that, but it's just not true, I swear it. And even if it was true, it makes no difference to me, you're still my brother and I love you." With tears streaking his blackened face Paul hugged Matthew to him, unable to comprehend why his father should have said such a cruel thing. The thought occurred to him that their father knew only one of his sons would want to continue with the farm. And had he survived their mother perhaps he would have used that to ensure only Matthew inherited. It was a devastating thought, but the only one that made any sense. "You are my brother, Matt, don't ever think any different."

Matthew's eyes slowly glazed over and his breathing slackened. Paul could feel the life slipping from him.

"It's too late now." A thin smile forced its way through Matthew's cracked lips, a smile of contrition. "I'm sorry. Tell Grace I'm sorry. Tell everyone, except mother, I'll tell her myself when I see her." His head fell to one side and a final gasp of air escaped his charred lungs.

"No, Matt, don't go, not now." The words tripped out on a convulsion of sobbing as Paul cradled his brother close to his chest, rocking back and forth in grief.

Gently, he pulled the knife from his brother, dragged him further from the now blazing house and laid him on the ground. He kissed him on the forehead before going for the horses.

With Matthew across the saddle of his horse, Paul led them through the farm and up onto the copse that had been so important to them during their lives. They stayed there for several minutes while Paul cried out all the tears inside him, so that by the time they arrived back at Millwood House he had none left to shed.

After giving instructions that Matthew should be laid out in his room, Paul went to find Grace. She was sitting up in bed, heavily bandaged beneath her nightdress, with Rosemary seated by her side. The expression on Paul's face needed no explanation, and immediately Grace placed a protective arm around the child, cuddling her close.

"I know what you're going to tell me," she said in a hushed voice. "Was it you?"

Paul shook his head. "It was an accident." He sat on the edge of the bed with Rosemary between them. "He didn't suffer."

"I'm pleased for that. I can't cry for him. I want to, but I can't. Is that so wicked?" She breathed deeply to control her emotions in front of the child. "If I hadn't insisted on selling his farm, this would all never have happened. I feel so responsible, but I still can't cry."

Paul put his arm around his daughter and took Grace by the hand. "I'm just as much to blame. I never got the chance to tell him that it was me who made the offer on the farm. I was going to give it to him. He died believing he had lost the two things most precious to him. He may not have shown you any love, but I believe he felt it.

Her hand tightened on his. There were no tears although she was crying inside.

Epilogue

Eighteen months later

On a bright autumn morning, a couple stood before the altar of the small church, having just made their vows. The sun shining through the stained glass window played a kaleidoscope of colours on their backs. Between them was a young girl, proudly looking up at her parents.

In attendance was the groom's brother, and beside him his wife, her hands resting protectively on the new life growing beneath her dress.

On the bride's side of the church were her father, stepmother and aunt, and across the aisle, seated in the pews were two friends of the groom, a big man with a thick black beard, and the other sporting a freshly waxed moustache.

Common to all of them were the broad smiles, reflecting the sheer joy that, at last, everything was as it should be.

As the couple turned away from the altar, the bride bent to kiss the girl on the cheek, and as they walked slowly back down the aisle, the big man squeezed out of the pew and scooped up the child in his massive arms. She giggled and pulled at his beard.

Many of those in the church that day had been touched by so much pain, some of which could never be forgotten, yet the strength of love they had for each other could no longer be threatened by the past. It would now grow with the future.

THE END